STEPHEN JONES lives in London, England. A Hugo Award nominee, he is the winner of four World Fantasy Awards, three International Horror Guild Awards, five Bram Stoker Awards, twenty-one British Fantasy Awards and a Lifetime Achievement Award from the Horror Writers Association. One of Britain's most acclaimed horror and dark fantasy writers and editors, he has more than 155 books to his credit, including *The Art of Pulp Horror: An Illustrated History*; the film books of Neil Gaiman's *Coraline* and *Stardust*; *The Illustrated Monster Movie Guide* and *The Hellraiser Chronicles*; the non-fiction studies *Horror: 100 Best Books* and *Horror: Another 100 Best Books* (both with Kim Newman); the single-author collections *Necronomicon* and *Eldritch Tales* by H.P. Lovecraft; *The Complete Chronicles of Conan* and *Conan's Brethren* by Robert E. Howard, and *Curious Warnings: The Great Ghost Stories of M.R. James*; plus such anthologies as *Horrorology: The Lexicon of Fear, Fearie Tales: Stories of the Grimm and Gruesome, A Book of Horrors, The Mammoth Book of Folk Horror, The Lovecraft Squad* and *Zombie Apocalypse!* series, and thirty-one volumes of *Best New Horror*. You can visit his web site at *www.stephenjoneseditor.com* or follow him on Facebook at *Stephen Jones-Editor*.

## ALSO FROM PS PUBLISHING

Edited by Stephen Jones and Ramsey Campbell

*Best New Horror #1*
*Best New Horror #2*
*Best New Horror #3*


Edited by Stephen Jones

*The Best of Best New Horror Volume One*
*The Best of Best New Horror Volume Two*
*Best New Horror #25*
*Best New Horror #26*
*Best New Horror #27*
*Best New Horror #28*
*Best New Horror #29*
*Best New Horror #30*
*Best New Horror #31*

# BEST NEW HORROR

# BEST NEW HORROR

#31

EDITED AND WITH
AN INTRODUCTION BY
## STEPHEN JONES

DIP

# BEST NEW HORROR
## Volume №31

Front cover illustration by Lee Elias.
Originally published on *Witches Tales* #37, October 1953.
Front flap preliminary sketch by Warren Kremer.
Back cover illustration attributed to Al Avison.
Originally published in *Witches Tales*.

This trade paperback edition published in December 2021
by Drugstore Indian Press, an imprint of PS Publishing Ltd.,
by arrangement with Stephen Jones.

2 4 6 8 10 9 7 5 3 1

ISBN 978-1-78636-823-2

Design and Layout by Michael Smith
Cover design by Smith & Jones

Printed and bound in England by T. J. International

PS PUBLISHING
Grosvenor House, 1 New Road
Hornsea HU18 1PG, England

editor@pspublishing.co.uk
www.pspublishing.co.uk

# Contents

# ACKNOWLEDGEMENTS

THE EDITOR WOULD like to thank Kim Newman, David Barraclough, Mandy Slater, Amanda Foubister, Jo Fletcher, Andrew I. Porter, David A. Sutton, Gordon Van Gelder, Robert Morgan, Rosemary Pardoe, R.B. Russell, Andy Cox, Michael Kelly, David Longhorn, Philip Harbottle, David A. Riley, Ellen Datlow, Jean-Daniel Breque and, especially, Peter and Nicky Crowther, Mike Smith, Marie O'Regan and Michael Marshall Smith for all their help and support. Special thanks are also due to *Locus, Ansible, Classic Images, Entertainment Weekly, ISFDB* and all the other sources that were used for reference in the Introduction and the Necrology.

DEATH IN ALL ITS RIPENESS copyright © Mark Samuels 2019. Originally published for private circulation on Patreon. Reprinted by permission of the author.

SHRAPNEL copyright © Richard Christian Matheson 2019. Originally published in *Brothers in Arms: Stories in Tribute to Richard Matheson's Beardless Warriors*. Reprinted by permission of the author.

PRECIPICE copyright © Dale Bailey 2019. Originally published in *Echoes: The Saga Anthology of Ghost Stories*. Reprinted by permission of the author.

ANTRIPUU copyright © Simon Strantzas 2019. Originally published in *Nightmare Magazine*, Issue 82, July 2019. Reprinted by permission of the author.

A CROWN OF LEAVES copyright © Kristi DeMeester 2019. Originally published in *Black Static #70*, July–August 2019. Reprinted by permission of the author.

A STAY AT THE SHORES copyright © Steve Rasnic Tem 2019. Originally published in *Necronomicon 2019 Memento Book*. Reprinted by permission of the author.

THE OLD MAN OF THE WOODS copyright © Reggie Oliver 2019. Originally published in *The Pale Illuminations*. Reprinted by permission of the author.

IRON CITY copyright © the Estate of Tanith Lee 2019. Originally published in *Strindberg's Ghost Sonata and Other Uncollected Tales*. Reprinted by permission of the author's Estate.

SLOUGH copyright © Glen Hirshberg 2019. Originally published in *Space and Time*, Issue 135, Winter 2019. Reprinted by permission of the author.

*Thank you to everyone who helped us to reach volume #31.
You know who you are.*

# INTRODUCTION

## HORROR IN 2019

B AKER & TAYLOR, one of the two only large book distributors in America, announced that in a "strategic shift" from mid-July it would no longer wholesale books to stores, admitting that, "the retail market has become an increasingly difficult one in which to operate". That left Ingram as the only major national wholesaler of trade books in the US.

The following month it was announced that the largest US book-selling chain, Barnes & Noble, had been acquired in an all-cash transaction (valued at around $683 million) by fund management company Elliott Advisors Ltd., which also acquired the UK chain Waterstones in 2018. James Daunt would be CEO of both companies, although they would continue to be run independently.

According to a NPD BookScan report, overall print book sales in the US dropped by 1.3% in 2019, with the biggest genre drop in science fiction, although sales of horror rose by 16.6%. One Toronto newspaper speculated that this renaissance in horror fiction was possibly being spurred on by the success of *Stranger Things* and *Get Out*, as dedicated horror sections returned to most bookstores across the UK and North America for the first time since the end of the 1980s boom.

Macmillan was widely criticised for trying to limit sales of its titles in e-book format to libraries until eight weeks after publication.

Although CEO John Sargent argued that "the reading of borrowed e-books decreases the perceived economic value of a book", the American Library Association launched a petition to protest against the plan.

Tor Books announced a new horror imprint, Nightfire, scheduled to launch in 2021. The list would publish "across the breadth of the genre—from short story collections to novellas and novels, from standalone works to series, from dark fantasy to the supernatural, from originals to reprints of lost modern classics" in all formats. Fritz Foy was named as publisher and Kelly O'Connor Lonesome joined as senior editor.

The Horror Writers Association partnered with United for Libraries, Book Riot and Library Journal/School Library Journal to launch the Summer Scares Reading Program in 2019. Each year, a special guest author and four librarians would announce a selection of nine recommended horror titles for adult, young adult and middle grade readers. The guest author for the inaugural annual list was Grady Hendrix.

Following the removal of the World Fantasy Award's Lovecraft bust a few years earlier, "call-out culture" or "cancel culture" firmly took hold of the genre in 2019. After the accusation by the previous year's winner, Jeannette Ng, that the person for whom the award was named was a "fascist", the John W. Campbell Award for Best New Writer (founded in 1973 to honour the hugely influential—and admittedly sometimes controversial—American editor of *Astounding Science Fiction*, *Analog Science Fiction* and *Unknown*, who helped shape the direction of modern science fiction and fantasy) was re-named The Astounding Award for Best New Writer by sponsor Dell Magazines.

In an analogous move, The Campbell Conference, held each year since 1978 by The Gunn Center for the Study of Science Fiction at the University of Kansas, renamed the event the Gunn Center Conference. The Conference also announced that it was "discussing" alternative names for its John W. Campbell Memorial Award for Best Science Fiction Novel, which was created in 1973 by Harry Harrison and Brian W. Aldiss.

The "Motherboard" of the James Tiptree, Jr. Literary Award for books "encouraging the exploration and expansion of gender" —which was founded in 1991 and named after the pseudonym of science fiction author Alice Sheldon, who killed her husband and herself in a murder-suicide in 1987—announced in October that it would be changing its name to the Otherwise Award. They also allowed past winners and nominees to decide which title they wanted to retroactively list their achievement under.

In November, the award-winning Canadian independent genre imprint ChiZine Publications was hit with a number of allegations regarding late royalty payments, non-payment of advances, and harassment of authors and staff. As a result of the mounting furore on social media, founders Sandra Kasturi and Brett Savory stepped away from all publishing duties and took out a short-term personal loan in an attempt to cover all outstanding payments owed.

However, this did not appease some people—including the writer who had publicly made the initial allegation—and authors quickly began pulling their books or requesting reversions of rights. Inevitably, ChiZine was soon forced to cease publishing, at least in the short-term.

A decision by Wisconsin's Sauk City Village Board to change the name of August Derleth Park to Sauk City Riverfront Park by a vote of 6–1 resulted in a petition, supported by Derleth fans and family.

Meanwhile, 96-year-old John Richards, a former British journalist who campaigned for almost two decades to outlaw the misuse of apostrophes, finally admitted defeat in December, blaming the "ignorence and laziness present in modern times". Richards, who founded the Apostrophe Protection Society in 2001, added, "The barbarians have won".

Stephen King's *The Institute* was about a gifted twelve-year-old boy who was kidnapped and imprisoned in the titular medical facility in backwoods Maine, where children with paranormal powers were brutally tested and abused until they were dehumanised to the point that they became expendable weapons in a shadowy political war.

King announced in November that he was planning a writers' retreat at the house next door to his in Bangor, Maine, providing housing for up to five writers in residence. His archives, formerly held at the University of Maine, would also be moved there and made accessible to researchers and scholars by appointment only. The Bangor City Council unanimously approved a request by the author and his wife Tabitha to re-zone their home as a non-profit, allowing the plans to move ahead. The couple moved into the red-painted mansion in 1980, and it has long been a tourist attraction thanks to its bat-and-spiderweb wrought-iron gates. The King house is even listed on Tripadvisor.

Meanwhile, when King criticised the *Portland Press Herald* for cutting its local book reviews, his tweet went viral and the Maine-based newspaper received enough new subscriptions to reverse the decision.

Philip Pullman's *The Secret Commonwealth: The Book of Dust Volume Two* was set a decade after the end of the author's *His Dark Materials* trilogy.

Ian McEwan's *Machines Like Me* was set in an alternate London of the early 1980s, where things started to go wrong with a prototype android, and a myserious young woman relived the nightmares of her childhood after stepping in front of a bus in Joyce Carol Oates' *The Pursuit*.

Margaret Atwood's *The Testaments*, the author's long-awaited sequel to *The Handmaid's Tale*, picked up the story fifteen years after her 1985 novel. Unfortuately, despite a worldwide embargo, Amazon mistakenly released 800 copies a week early.

*The Night Window* was the fifth and final volume in Dean Koontz's "Jane Hawk" series, while James Patterson once again "presented" *Capturing the Devil*, Kerri Maniscalco's follow-up to her best-selling *Stalking Jack the Ripper*.

*Anno Dracula 1999: Daikaiju* was the sixth novel in the series by Kim Newman. Set over the millennial New Year's Eve, it included Richard Jeperson and vampire schoolgirl Nezumi of the Diogenes Club, Kate Reed, Geneviève Dieudonné and Penny Churchward of Angels Investigations, plus other familiar characters from the author's increasingly complex alternate vampire world.

A captured Nazi device had the power to change humanity in F. Paul Wilson's supernatural medical thriller *The Void Protocol*, the latest in the author's "Secret History of the World" series.

Archaeologists uncovered the legendary box in *The Pandora Room*, the second in Christopher Golden's "Ben Walker" series, while *A Book of Bones* was the seventeenth volume in John Connolly's "Charlie Parker" series.

In Elizabeth Hand's *Curious Toys*, set in an alternate 1915, a fourteen-year-old girl teamed up with real-life "outsider" artist and writer Henry Darger to hunt for a serial killer preying on victims in Chicago's Riverview Park.

Jeanette Winterson's *Frankissstein: A Love Story* was a transgender re-imagining of Mary Shelley's novel set in 1816 and a soon-to-be post-Brexit Britain.

The prolific yet long-deceased V.C. Andrews* published the psychological thriller *The Silhouette Girl* and started yet another new trilogy about the Dollanganger family with *Beneath the Attic*.


Following the tragic deaths of her husband and son, a woman spent Christmas at a run-down Yorkshire farmhouse that came with its own ghosts in Alison Littlewood's *Mistletoe*.

In *The Saturday Night Ghost Club*, Canadian author Craig Davidson (aka "Nick Cutter"/"Patrick Lestewka") looked back to the summer of 1986, as the titular group of friends investigated the ghosts and urban legends of Niagara Falls, and some of them discovered more than they bargained for.

In Damien Angelica Walters' *The Dead Girls Club*, a member of the eponymous 1990s group discovered that, thirty years later, someone knew her secret, and that the vengeful spirit of a legendary witch might be more real than anybody expected.

Nolan Moore investigated a case of witchcraft for his YouTube show in *The Possession*, the second in the "Anomaly Files" series by "Michael Rutger" (Michael Marshall Smith).

Michelle Paver's Gothic ghost story *Wakenhyrst* was set during the early 20th century, as a scholar discovered that his old manor house was haunted by something with claws.

The ghosts at a Scottish tourist resort turned out to be all too real in Catherine Cavendish's *The Haunting of Henderson Close*, while a woman inherited a Scottish manor that was apparently haunted in Lexie Elliott's *The Missing Years*.

A couple decided to build their dream home on a haunted site in *The Invited* by Jennifer McMahon, and the ghost of a murdered biker set out to revenge himself on the gang members who burned him alive in *Hellrider* by J.G. Faherty.

A woman's ability to see ghosts resulted in her investigating occult secret societies at Yale University in *Ninth House*, the first adult novel by Leigh Bardugo.

A teenage girl on the run from the military authorities took up the position of English teacher at a remote and haunted Argentinian boarding school in Sara Faring's 1970s-set *The Tenth Girl*.

In a twist on the old "three wishes" plot, a young Mexican girl accidentally released an ancient Mayan god of death, who promised to grant whatever she desired in return for her helping him regain his throne from his treacherous brother in Silvia Moreno-Garcia's *Gods of Jade and Shadow*.

A Puritan woman went missing while berry-picking in a Connecticut forest and encountered three mysterious women in Laird Hunt's dark fairy tale *In the House in the Dark of the Woods*, while an author fleeing her past ended up sharing a house in Maine with a ghostly sea captain in Tess Gerritsen's *The Shape of Night*.

An urban legend about a mother and daughter burned at the stake for witchcraft and a former child star trapped in her role in a 1970s slasher movie were part of a true-crime investigation re-told as a ghost story, a movie, a remake and a podcast in Clay McLeod Chapman's *The Remaking*.

A psychiatrist hunted for a serial killer who imitated Jack the Ripper in 1935 Prague in *The Devil Aspect* by Craig Russell; a serial killer known as the "Wraith" returned to an abandoned resort in the Catskills Mountains in Hunter Shea's *Slash*, and the survivor of a campsite massacre claimed a voice warned him to get away in *Those Who Came Before* by J.H. Moncrieff.

A man's dreams of murder appeared to come true in Russell James' *The Playing Card Killer.*

Vincent de Swarte's 1998 novel *Pharricide*, about a new keeper descending into madness in a remote lighthouse (something of a popular theme in 2019), was translated from the French by Nicholas Royle for Cōnfingō Publishing. Patrick McGrath supplied the Foreword and Alison Moore an Afterword.

The boyfriend of a paramedic mysteriously disappeared and left only his phone behind in Jason Arnopp's *Ghoster*, while a ten-year-old girl realised that members of her family were disappearing from their new house in *One by One* by D.W. Gillespie.

A woman discovered a terrifying journal amongst her late grandmother's stack of possessions in *The Twisted Ones* by "T. Kingfisher" (Ursula Vernon); a journalist investigated a supposedly "lost" manuscript by Edgar Allan Poe in Craig Schaefer's *Ghosts of Gotham*, and a former heavy metal guitarist experienced his own personalised terror after reading a mysterious book in *Will Haunt You* by Brian Kirk.

A wannabe writer recalled a book that didn't seem to exist in *All My Colors*, a comic novel by Emmy Award-winning writer David Quantick, while a writers' retreat turned out to be more competitive than expected in Jonathan Janz's *The Dark Game.*

A man's affair with his new neighbour did not go well in *The Devil's Equinox* by John Everson, and two women trapped inside during a snowstorm discovered each others' secrets in Carol Goodman's *The Night Visitors.*

A woman was pursued by four inhuman monsters created by a mystery man to kill her in Tim Waggoner's *They Kill*; patients returned from the dead as different people in P.D. Cacek's *Second Lives*, and Megan Hart's *Black Wings* was about a child genius and her intelligent raven.

C.A. Fletcher's take on a post-apocalyptic future was very different to Harlan Ellison's in the dystopian novel *A Boy and His Dog at the End of the World*, while *The Girl in Red* was a post-apocalyptic re-telling of 'Little Red Riding Hood' by "Christina Henry" (Tina Raffaele).

*The Brink* was the second volume in the "Awakened" series by James S. Murray and Darren Wearmouth, as the creatures released from below New York City spread out across the globe.

Christopher Rice's *Blood Echo* was a sequel to the author's *Bone Music*, and a killer was targeting New York City's mayoral candidates in 1886 in Erin Lindsey's *A Golden Grave*, the second volume in the supernatural series about special Pinkerton agent Rose Gallagher.

*All Roads End Here* and *Chokehold* were the second and third books, respectively, in David Moody's apocalyptic "Final War" zombie series.

*Death Goddess Dance* was the third and final book in the Lovecraftian "Mythos War" trilogy by Levi Black, while *The Edge* was the third and final volume in Tim Lebbon's "Relics" trilogy.

*The Rising: The Newsflesh Trilogy* was an omnibus of the novels *Feed* (2010), *Deadline* (2011) and *Blackout* (2012) by Mira Grant.

*The Summoning*, *The Seekers* and *The Stalking* were the 27th, 28th and 29th titles, respectively, in Heather Graham's alliterative "Krewe of Hunters" paranormal romance series, set in a reputedly haunted property in the American South.

Bram Stoker and Oscar Wilde teamed up to battle the supernatural threat of the Black Bishop in Steven Hopstaken and Melissa Prusi's *Stoker's Wilde*.

In the days before Christmas, Sherlock Holmes and Dr. John Watson investigated the case of a young woman who believed she was being haunted by a demonic Christmas spirit named "Black Thurrick" in *Sherlock Holmes & the Christmas Demon* by James Lovegrove, while *Sherlock Holmes vs. Cthulhu: The Adventure of the Innsmouth Mutations* was the third in the mash-up series by Lois H. Gresh.

Helen Marshall's debut novel, *The Migration*, was set in a near future ravaged by climate change and a pandemic disease that continued to animate its teenage victims after death.

*Last Ones Left Alive* was a YA post-zombie apocalypse debut novel by Irish writer Sarah Davis-Goff, and girls suffering from a disfiguring plague were kept quarantined in Rory Powers' first novel

*Wilder Girls*, which was also available in a "Barnes & Noble YA Book Club" hardcover that included deleted scenes.

A woman found that her town was full of possessed people in Micah Dean Hicks' debut novel, *Break the Bodies, Haunt the Bones*.

Twin sisters had a reunion with their strange family in *A Hawk in the Woods* by new author Carrie Laben, and a mother started having problems with her seven-year-old daughter in Zoje Stage's debut novel *Baby Teeth*.

Teenagers protected their town from a monster trapped in another dimension in Christine Lynn Herman's familiar-sounding first novel, *The Devouring Gray*.

A cynical TV psychic investigator had to prevent the Gates of Hell from opening in stand-up comedian Russ Kane's first novel *The Gatekeeper*, while from Influx Press, *Mothlight* was a first novel by British filmmaker Adam Scovell, about a lepidopterist haunted by a woman from his past.

The debut novel *Death Lives in the Water* was the first in Shoshana Edwards' "Harper's Landing" series, set in that eponymous community.

A woman purchased the possibly haunted house where she survived the murder-suicide of her family in Marie T. Vandelly's first novel, *Theme Music*, and Shaun Hamill's first novel, *A Cosmology of Monsters*, was about a family that operated a haunted house attraction.

Tamsyn Muir's debut novel *Gideon the Ninth*, the first in a trilogy, was a heroic fantasy spoof complete with monsters and lesbian necromancers.

Edited by Lisa Morton and Leslie S. Klinger, *Ghost Stories: Classic Tales of Horror and Suspense* contained seventeen "overlooked" stories and a ballad from the 19th and early 20th centuries by M.R. James, Charles Dickens, Edith Wharton, Mark Twain and others.

Kilinger's *The New Annotated H.P. Lovecraft: Beyond Arkham* collected twenty-five additional annotated stories that were not included in *The New Annotated H.P. Lovecraft* (2014). The volume was introduced by Victor LaValle.

Editor Graeme Davis selected twenty-six early horror stories (1830–1904) from women authors such as Charlotte Perkins Gilman, Edith Wharton, Louisa May Alcott and Mary Shelley for *More Deadly Than the Male: Masterpieces from the Queens of Horror*.

Simon Raven's 1960 vampire novel *Doctors Wear Scarlet* was reissued by Valancourt Books with a new Introduction by Kim Newman, while Russell Kirk's 1961 supernatural novel *Old House of Fear* was reprinted by Encounter/Criterion Books with a new Introduction by James Panero.

Edited by Mike Ashley and containing fifteen reprints, *The Platform Edge: Uncanny Tales of the Railways* was part of the British Library's "Tales of the Weird" series, as was Ashley's *Doorway to Dilemma: Bewildering Tales of Dark Fantasy*, which reprinted nineteen stories by H.G. Wells, Mary E. Wilkins and others.

Ashley's *Menace of the Monster: Classic Tales of Creatures from Beyond* in the British Library's "Science Fiction Classics" series contained fourteen stories by Wells, Idris Seabright, John Christopher and others.

"Edited" with an Introduction by Carmen Maria Machado, Joseph Sheridan Le Fanu's classic 1872 vampire novella *Carmilla* was reissued by Lanternfish Press with illustrations by Robert Kraiza.

Introduced (and probably edited) by Stefan Dziemianowicz, the leatherbound Barnes & Noble anthology *Classic Supernatural Stories* brought together twenty-five tales by H.P. Lovecraft, A. Merritt, Edith Wharton, Edgar Allan Poe and others.

Edited and introduced by Paul Murray, *Japanese Ghost Stories* collected thirty-three tales by Lafcadio Hearn, inspired by Japanese folklore.

*The Last Séance: Tales of the Supernatural* collected twenty stories by Agatha Christie, including one that had not previously been published in America—'The Wife of the Kenite' had originally appeared in Australia's *Home Magazine* in September 1922.

The Folio Society's deluxe, slipcased edition of Neil Gaiman's *Anansi Boys* was illustrated in both black and white and colour by Francis Vallejo and introduced by Nalo Hopkinson.

✑

A twin brother and sister sent to live with their great aunt discovered that her house held many secrets, including a secret friend that lived in the walls and an evil owl, in Irish writer Sarah Maria Griffin's young adult novel *Other Words for Smoke*.

A young girl started having visions after moving into an old hotel in *Remember Me* by Chelsea Bobulski, while "El Cuco", a monstrous bogeyman, preyed upon a group of Puerto Rican teens in Ann Dávila Cardinal's first solo novel, *Five Midnights*.

The lead singer of a high school heavy metal band was pursued by something evil in *Last Things* by Jacqueline West.

The eponymous teenage orphan encountered a ghost in the basement of the New York Public Library in *Trace* by Pay Cummings, and a family's new fixer-upper was rumoured to come with a ghost in *The Haunted* by Danielle Vega.

A cryptozoologist and his teenage daughter travelled to Oklahoma to investigate something inexplicable *In the Woods* in Carrie Jones and Steven E. Wendel's YA supernatural mystery.

*The Cold in Her Bones* by Peternelle van Arsdale was inspired by the myth of "Medusa", while Dawn Kurtagich's *Teeth in the Mist* was a haunted house novel based on the "Faust" legend.

A young girl who could communicate with the dead became a prime suspect after her former best friend was murdered in April Henry's *The Lonely Dead*, and a girl who could sense how and when people will die was contacted by a vengeful ghost in Emma Berquist's *Missing, Presumed Dead*.

Emily A. Duncan's *Wicked Saints* was the first volume in the author's "Something Dark and Holy" series.

Katherine Arden's *Dead Voices* was a sequel to *Small Spaces*, as three teens found themselves trapped with a mysterious ghost-hunter during a snowstorm.

Set in Paris, France, Victoria Schwab's *Tunnel of Bones* followed on from *City of Ghosts* and was the second in the series about a girl who saw ghosts in the world's most haunted cities.

*The Beast* was the second book in the "Darkdeep" series by Ally Condie and Brendan Reichs.

*Return to Fear Street: Drop Dead Gorgeous* was the third in the new series by R.L. Stine, while *Forgotten* was the third in the "House of Night Other Worlds" series by P.C. Cast and Kristin Cast and included a fan Q&A section.

*Tomb of the Ancients* was the final book in Madeleine Roux's Gothic horror trilogy "House of Furies", illustrated by Iris Compiet.

*Carmilla* was a young adult novelisation of J. Sheridan Le Fanu's classic vampire novella by Kim Turrisi.

Edited by Stephen Jones and illustrated by Randy Broecker, *Terrifying Tales to Tell at Night: 10 Scary Stories to Give You Nightmares!* was a YA anthology containing reprints from Neil Gaiman, R. Chetwynd-Hayes, Stephen King, Ramsey Campbell, Manly Wade Wellman, Robert Shearman, Michael Marshall Smith and Charles L. Grant, along with two new stories by Lynda E. Rucker and Lisa Morton.

Edited by Dahlia Adler, *His Hideous Heart* was a young adult anthology containing thirteen updated re-imaginings of the work of Edgar Allan Poe, along with reprints of Poe's original stories and poems.

*Full Throttle: Stories* contained thirteen tales (eleven reprints) by Joe Hill, including two collaborations with Stephen King, and an Introduction by the author (whose biography hid a bonus story). The UK edition was marketed as a tie-in to the Netflix movie *In the Tall Grass*.

The cover of Nathan Ballingrud's *Wounds: Six Stories from the Border of Hell* declared that the title novella (aka 'The Visible Filth') was "Soon to be a major motion picture".

*Growing Things and Other Stories* collected nineteen tales (two original) by Paul Tremblay.

*A Lush and Seething Hell* contained a reprint novella (originally published as an e-book) and new short novel of cosmic horror by John Hornor Jacobs, with a Foreword by Chuck Wendig.

*The Complete Tales of Jules de Grandin Volume Five: Black Moon* was the final volume in the series chronologically reprinting all Seabury Quinn's stories about the French supernatural detective from *Weird Tales*. Stephen Jones' Introduction looked at other markets where the stories apppeared.

∽

At more than 800 pages, and containing thirty stories (three reprints), Ellen Datlow's *Echoes: The Saga Anthology of Ghost Stories* was definitely the bumper anthology of the year. However, despite a line-up that included Paul Tremblay, Alison Littlewood, Pat Cadigan, Joyce Carol Oates, Gemma Files, Terry Dowling, Dale Bailey, Stephen Graham Jones, Garth Nix, Nathan Ballingrud, Jeffrey Ford, John Langan and others, the result was a decidely mixed bag of stories.

Despite the promise of "Brand New Horror Stories" on the back cover, four of the eighteen stories in editor Marie O'Regan's *Phantoms: Haunting Tales from Masters of the Genre* were actually reprints. The impressive line-up of contributors included Angela Slatter, Robert Shearman, Joe Hill, Tim Lebbon, Muriel Gray, John Connolly, M.R. Carey, Kelley Armstrong, Paul Tremblay, Gemma Files and Alison Littlewood, amongst others.

*Three Stories About Ghosts* contained a trio of novellas by Martin Hall, Matthew Marchitto and Ali Nouraei, with an Introduction by David Thomas Moore.

*Hex Life: Wicked New Tales of Witchery* was edited by Christopher Golden and Rachel Autumn and contained eighteen new stories by Kelley Armstrong, Tananarive Due, Amber Benson and others.

*Straight Outta Deadwood* was a weird Western anthology edited with a Foreword by David Boop that featured seventeen new stories by Charlaine Harris, Mike Resnick, Jane Lindskold, Steve Rasnic Tem, Mario Acevedo, Stephen Graham Jones and others.

Reportedly selected "from over 800 submissions", *The Third Corona Book of Horror Stories* featured nineteen of "the best new horror short stories" chosen by publisher Lewis Williams and an uncredited panel of readers. *The Corona Book of Ghost Stories* was a companion volume.

*Voices of the Fall* edited by John Ringo and Gary Poole contained thirteen stories about the zombie apocalypse. It was the second anthology in Ringo's "Black Tide Rising" series.

Published exclusively by Titan Books for the 2019 Dublin World Science Fiction Convention, *Titan Tasters* was a paperback sampler that collected ten short stories and extracts (two reprints) by, amongst others, Charlie Jane Anders, Paul Tremblay, Jennifer McMahon and J.S. Barnes.

*The Best Horror of the Year: Volume Eleven* edited by Ellen Datlow contained twenty-five stories from 2018 by, amongst others, Anne Billson, Michael Marshall Smith, John Langan, Gemma Files, Thana Niveau and Joe Hill, while Paula Guran's *The Year's Best Dark Fantasy & Horror 2019* featured thirty-three stories from Jeffrey Ford, Brian Hodge, Tim Lebbon, Tim Powers, Angela Slatter, D.P. Watt and others.

There were no crossover stories between the two American anthologies, and the only author they shared was Robert Shearman, who was represented in each volume with a different piece of fiction.

Stephen Jones' *Best New Horror #29* covered the year 2017 with twenty-one stories from, amongst others, Helen Marshall, Alison Littlewood, Richard Gavin, William F. Nolan, Angela Slatter, Tim Lebbon, Ramsey Campbell, Felice Picano, Reggie Oliver, Garth Nix and Thana Niveau.

*The Compleat Valentine* was a welcome omnibus volume from UK print-on-demand publisher Black Shuck Books of John Llewellyn Probert's *The Abominable Dr. Phibes*-inspired novellas *The Nine Deaths of Dr. Valentine*, *The Hammer of Dr. Valentine* and *The Last Temptation of Dr. Valentine*.

Kit Power's *The Finite* was published as part of Black Shuck Books' "Signature Novella" series, while *Quiet Houses* was an expanded edition of Simon Kurt Unsworth's 2011 collection.

Edited by publisher Steve J. Shaw, *Great British Horror 4: Dark and Stormy Nights* contained eleven new stories that each began with a variation on that clichéd opening phrase. Featuring ten British authors and one international "guest" contributor, the PoD hardcover included contributions from, amongst others, Phil Sloman, Paul M. Feeney, Alison Littlewood, Catriona Ward, Maura McHugh, M.R. Carey and Priya Sharma.

*Pareidolia*, edited by James Everington and Dan Howarth, contained ten original stories by Sarah Read, Eliza Chan, Tim Major, Charlotte Bond and others about things perceived where nothing apparently exists.

From the same imprint, *Remember the Dead at Halloween & Christmas* was an anthology of reprint stories selected by J.A. Mains with an Introduction by Mike Ashley.

Meanwhile, the excellent Black Shuck Shadows series of micro-collections continued with #9: *Winter Freits* (three original tales of seasonal hauntings) by Andrew David Barker, #10 *The Dead* (three original stories about the undead) by Paul Kane, #11: *The Forest of Dead Children* (five tales of children in peril, one reprint) by Andrew Hook, #12: *At Home in the Shadows* (five haunted house stories, three reprints) by Gary McMahon, #13: *Suffer Little Children* (six stories, five original, about deadly little darlings) by Penny Jones, #14: *Shadowcats* (four stories and a poem of feline fear, two reprints) by Anna Taborska, and #15: *Flowers of War* (four tales set during wartime, one reprint) by Mark Howard Jones.

With an Introduction by Adrian Cole, *Compromising the Truth* was a second collection of eighteen short stories (nine original) and twenty-four poems from The Alchemy Press by veteran British author Bryn Fortey, who also contributed the Afterword. Many of the stories revolved around blues music.

Edited with a Foreword by Dave Brzeski for Shadow Publishing, *Shadmocks & Shivers: New Tales Inspired by the Stories of R. Chetwynd-Hayes* celebrated the centenary of the birth of Britain's "Prince of Chill". It contained thirteen original stories and a poem by, amongst others, Tina Rath, Simon Clark, Adrian Cole, Marion Pitman, John Llewellyn Probert, William Meikle, John Linwood Grant and Stephen Laws, along with an obscure reprint by Chetwynd-Hayes himself and a reminiscence about the *Fontana Book of Great Ghost Stories* by Robert Pohle.

R. Chetwynd-Hayes also had a story reprinted in *Stories to Make You Shudder Book 1*, the first in a new print-on-demand anthology series inspired by the Pan and Fontana volumes of the 1970s, edited and illustrated by Cornelius Clarke. The nine other classic reprints were by the Brothers Grimm, Washington Irving, Amelia B. Edwards, Ambrose Bierce, Sheridan Le Fanu, E.F. Benson, Edgar Allan Poe, H.G. Wells and Charles Dickens.

From Hippocampus Press, *An Imp of the Aether* was a tribute collection of twenty-six stories and verse by Wilum Hopfrog Pugmire (1951–2019), two previously unpublished. Edited and introduced by the author's literary executor S. T. Joshi, it included three collaborations with Maryanne K. Snyder and one with Jessica Amanada Salmonson.

John Langan's *Sefira and Other Betrayals* collected eight stories, including a previously unpublished novella and the short novel of the title, with an Introduction by Paul Tremblay and extensive 'Story Notes' by the author.

Matt Cardin's *To Rouse Leviathan*, also from Hippocampus, collected seventeen stories, including two collaborations with Mark McLaughlin.

*The Boughs Withered When I Told Them My Dreams* was the debut collection from Irish writer Maura McHugh, published by NewCom Press. It contained twenty stories (four original), along with an Introduction by Kim Newman and an Afterword by the author.

Edited by Ian Whates for his NewCom imprint, *Soot and Steel: Dark Tales of London* was an anthology of sixteen stories stories about the city (nine original) by Reggie Oliver, Hume Nisbet, Juliet E. McKenna, Paul Di Filippo, Terry Grimwood, E.F. Benson, Paul StJohn Mackintosh and others.

Fairwood Press' "The Cady Collection" of print-on-demand reprints of the late Jack Cady's work included the novels *The Jonah Watch* (1983) with new bonus material, *The Off Season* (1995) with an Introduction by Gordon van Gelder, *The Hauntings of Hood Canal* (2001) with an Introduction by Nathan Ballingrud and two bonus stories, and the mainstream novel *Street* (1994), which included an excerpt from an unfinished book.

Cady's collection *Phantoms* contained fourteen stories, two essays and an Introduction by Patrick Swenson, while *Fathoms* featured sixteen stories, an essay and an Introduction by Kristine Kathryn Rusch.

Anonymously edited for Death's Head Press, *Dig Two Graves Volume Two: An Anthology of Revenge* contained twenty-two (presumably) original stories by Gary Power, Mark Lumby, Duane Breadley and others.

For his own eponymous publishing imprint (LMP), Len Maynard edited the PoD anthology *Chills*, which was designed to promote new writers. It contained twenty-one stories and a poem, including two reprint tales and an original by the editor.

*The Phantasmagoria Collection Book #1 ... Fantasias of Possibility: The Definitive Edition* was a revised and updated collection of thirteen stories by Trevor Kennedy, issued under the author's own Phantasmagoria Publishing/TK Pulp imprints with a new Introduction by John Gilbert.

Under the same imprints, Kennedy also edited *Gruesome Grotesques Volume 4...In Space!*, an anthology of thirty-seven science fiction horror stories and poems by authors that included David A. Riley, Samantha Lee, David A. Sutton and the editor himself, along with a Foreword by John Gilbert. *Gruesome Grostesques Volume 5... The Outer Zone* featured fifty-six new and reprint horror stories and poems by, amongst others, Ramsey Campbell, Samantha Lee, Adrian Cole, David A. Sutton, David A. Riley and Dean M. Drinkel, illustrated by Jim Pitts.

Funded through Kickstarter by Broken Eye Books, the Lovecraftian anthology *Welcome to Miskatonic University* edited by Scott Gable and C. Dombrowski contained thirteen original stories set around the mythical campus by Kristi DeMeester, Joseph S. Pulver and others, with black-and-white illustrations by various artists.

Edited by C.M. Muller for Minnesota's Chthonic Matter imprint, the fourth volume of *Nightscript* featured twenty-one original "strange and darksome tales" by, amongst others, V.H. Leslie, Steve Rasnic Tem, Daniel Braum, Cate Gardner, Jennifer Loring and Kirsty Logan. Volume Five contained nineteen further tales from Simon Strantzas, Tracy Fahey, N. Lopes da Silva and others.

From the same PoD imprint, *Twice-Told: A Collection of Doubles* was an anthology of twenty-two doppelgänger stories, also edited by Muller. Authors featured included Clint Smith, Jason A. Wyckoff, Steve Rasnic Tem, Tom Johnstone, CC Adams, Tim Major and others.

Billed as "An Anthology of Dark SF", the four quarterly volumes of *Synth* edited by C.M. Muller contained original stories by Jeffrey Thomas, Tim Major, Forrest Aguirre, Jay Caselberg and others.

The forces of Hell had invaded Victorian Britain in editor John Linwood Grant's shared-world anthology *Hell's Empire: Tales of the Incursion* from Ulthar Press. It contained sixteen original stories by Marion Pitman, Phil Breach, Frank Coffman, Charles R. Rutledge and others, with linking text by the editor.

For the same PoD publisher, Farah Rose Smith edited *Machinations and Mesmerism: Tales Inspired by E.T.A. Hoffman*. It contained sixteen stories by, amongst others, Michael Cisco, Sonya Taaffe and Rhys Hughes.

Issued by Luna Press Publishing, *The Controllers* collected seven stories (two original) by Paul Kane and came with a typically succinct Introduction by Richard Christian Matheson and a host of "Bonus Material", including examples of handwritten and corrected manuscripts, and artwork by the author and others.

*The Last Ghost and Other Stories* was a collection of seven stories (one original) by Marie O'Regan that included a short Introduction by Christopher Fowler. It included examples of a handwritten first draft, story notes and a five-page script.

Also from Luna Press, *Murmured in Dreams* contained nineteen stories (two original) by Stephen Bacon with an Introduction by Priya Sharma and story notes by the author, while Tim Major's *And the House Lights Dim* collected fifteen tales (three original), along with a "playlist" of music to listen to while reading a couple of the stories.

Phil Sloman edited *The Woods*, the sixth anthology in Hersham Horror Books' "PentAnth" series. The slim volume contained five original stories about things that lurked down in the woods by Cate Gardner, James Everington, Mark West, Penny Jones and the editor himself.

Edited and introduced by Deanna Knippling and Jamie Ferguson under the Borogrove Press imprint, *Amazing Monster Tales Issue 2: Monster Road Trip* was a PoD paperback anthology of ten stories about monsters on vacation.

Issued under the Pigeon Park Press imprint, *Candy Canes and Buckets of Blood* was a Christmas novel by Heide Goody and Iain Grant, about an invasion of murderous elves.

From Florida's Necro Publications, Alessandro Manzetti's erotic novel *Shanti: The Sadist Heaven* was set in a post-apocalyptic world.

*Tales from the Camp Fire* was a charity anthology, edited by Loren Rhoads and published by Tomes & Coffee Press. It contained twenty-four stories (five original) by Nancy Etchemendy, Gene O'Neill and Clark Ashton Smith, amongst others. All profits went to wildlife relief efforts related to the 2018 Camp Fire in Northern California.

From Wicked Run Press, *Body of Christ* appeared to be a self-published Christian horror novella by Mark Matthews, in which Jesus was resurrected on Halloween.

*Before You Blow Out the Candle…* was a self-published anthology edited by Marc Damian Lawler. It contained eight original stories, along with two reprints by Charles Dickens and Adrian Cole.

After responding to a new medication, a female author decided to start her own cult in *A Sick Gray Laugh* by Nicole Cushing, from Word Horde.

Edited with an Introduction by Scott Dwyer for Plutonian Press, *Pluto in Furs: Tales of Diseased Desires and Seductive Horrors* contained fourteen purportedly erotic horror stories by such writers as Jeffrey Thomas, Kurt Fawver, Richard Gavin, Gemma Files, Thana Niveau, Adam Golaski, Rhys Hughes, Clint Smith and others.

From Black Coat Press, *The Spells of Frankenstein* by Frank Schildiner was the third volume in a series partly inspired by the 1950s French *Frankenstein* novels of "Benoît Becker" (screenwriter Jean-Claude Carrière).

Set in the early 20th century, a young Parisian painter apparently produced supernatural portraits of the dead in Brian Stableford's *The Painter of Spirits*, the first in a trilogy from Black Coat Press that was followed by *The Quiet Dead*.

From the same publisher and busy author, *The Tyranny of the Word* was a historical horror novel set in 1480 France, about a necromantic monk.

Edited by Eric Nash and Peter Sutton, *Tales from the Graveyard* from North Bristol Writers/Iande Press featured sixteen original stories by local Bristol writers, along with an Introduction by Sutton.

Renee S. DeCamillis' debut novella, *The Bone Cutters*, was

published under Eraserhead Press' "New Bizarro Authors Series (NBAS)".

L.S. Johnson's PoD collection *Rare Birds: Stories* from California's Traversing Z Press contained eight reprint tales which came with their own content warnings for more impressionable readers.

*My Dead and Blackened Heart* from the independent UK imprint Sinister Horror Company collected fourteen stories (seven original) by French-born English author Andrew Freudenberg.

Edited by Scott Gable and C. Dombrowski for Broken Eye Books, *Nowhereville: Weird is Other People* was an anthology of nineteen "urban weird" stories from, amongst others, Maura McHugh, S.P. Miskowski, Lynda E. Rucker, Kathe Koja, Ramsey Campbell, Stephen Graham Jones and Cody Goodfellow. Apparently, the stories had all previously appeared on the publisher's Patreon page.

Edited with a Foreword by Craig Spector, *Freedom of Screech* from Crossroad Press' Macabre Ink imprint contained fifteen stories (three reprints) about censorship by Elizabeth Massie, Chet Williamson, Jack Ketchum, Richard Christian Matheson, Robert Guffey, Norman Spinrad, Thomas F. Monteleone and others.

The now-out-of-favour John W. Campbell, Jr.'s *Frozen Hell* was an early draft from the mid-1930s of the novella 'Who Goes There?', which was published under the pseudonym "Don A. Stuart" and filmed three times, most notably as *The Thing from Another World* (1951). Discovered amongst Campbell's papers by Alec Nevala-Lee, the short novel was finally published through Kickstarter by Wildside Press, with historical material by Nevala-Lee and Robert Silverberg (who traced the manuscript's origin).

As part of the same Kickstarter campaign, Wildside also published in trade paperback and limited deluxe hardcover *Short Things: Tales Inspired by Who Goes There? by John W. Campbell, Jr.* Edited by John Gregory Betancourt, the anthology featured thirteen original stories by Alan Dean Foster, Paul Di Filippo, Nina Kiriki Hoffman, Kristine Kathryn Rusch and others, illustrated by Marc Hempel, Allen Koszowski, Raiky Virnicid and Mark Wheatley.

There were not a lot of laughs to be found in *All the Things We Never See* from Canada's Undertow Publications. The PoD volume, published in both trade paperback and hardcover, collected twenty-six stories (two original), three poems and fourteen haikus by publisher Michael Kelly.

From the same imprint, *This House of Wounds* contained sixteen stories (four original) by Georgina Bruce, while Laura Mauro's *Sing Your Sadness Deep* came with fulsome blurbs from Simon Strantzas, Priya Sharma and Robert Shearman. It contained thirteen stories, two of which were previously unpublished.

Owl Goingback's shape-shifter novel *Coyote Rage* was published by Italy's Independent Legions, while Joanna Parypinski's *Dark Carnival* was translated into English by Daniele Bonfanti for the same imprint.

From Australia's IFWG Publishing, *Sherlock Holmes and Doctor Was Not* edited by Christopher Sequeira featured twelve original stories about alternate companions for the consulting detective by, amongst others, Nancy Holder, Dennis O'Neil and Will Murray, along with a Foreword by Leslie S. Klinger.

Published by Australia's P'rea Press, *The Macabre Modern and Other Morbidities* collected reprint and original poetry and artwork by Kyla Lee Ward. Edited by Charles Lovecraft, the attractive hardcover volume came with an Introduction by historian Dr. Gillian Polack and an Afterword by S.T. Joshi.

From PS Publishing, Dan Weatherer's debut *The Tainted Isle* appeared to be a fix-up novel featuring the exploits of Victorian paranormal investigator Solomon Whyte, who explored the origins of Britain's darkest myths through twenty-six encounters with the supernatural.

*The Divide* by acclaimed playwright Alan Ayckbourn was a near-future novel set in a world where contact between men and women was fatal, while Allister Timm's *The Killing Moon* was a fantasy featuring a band of shape-shifting resistance fighters battling the Nazis.

*Something from Below* was a Lovecraftian novella by S.T. Joshi, set in the coal-mining community of northeastern Pennsylvania.

Published by PS in hardcover and paperback, *The Complete Short Stories of Mike Carey* contained eighteen tales (eleven reprints), each introduced by the author.

*Gaslight, Ghosts, & Ghouls: A Centenary Celebration* marked the birth of British author R. Chetwynd-Hayes 100 years earlier. It included fifteen of his best stories plus a previously unpublished vampire novella, an interview with the author by editor Stephen Jones and Jo Fletcher, and the most complete and detailed working bibliography of his publications ever assembled.

Edited and introduced by Steven Savile, *The Best of T.M. Wright* collected thirty-four stories (including one newly discovered original) by the American author, who died in 2015.

Written *and* illustrated by the talented Richard A. Kirk, *Magpie's Ladder* was a debut collection of five stories, while Jeb Burt's debut volume *Lost Americans* contained thirteen literary stories (six reprints).

*Autumn Prose, Winter Verse* collected nineteen pieces of smart short fiction and verse (at least four reprinted) by filmmaker Mark Steensland.

Celebrating sixty years as a published author, *The Companion and Other Phantasmagorical Stories by Ramsey Campbell Volume 1* brought together thirty-four representative stories selected by the author himself, along with a Dennis Wheatley pastiche written when he was just twelve.

Edited with an Introduction for PS by Darrell Schweitzer, *The Mountains of Madness Revealed* contained seventeen original stories and two poems (one reprint) that were not all sequels to H.P. Lovecraft's 1936 novella 'At the Mountains of Madness'. Authors included Adrian Cole, Harry Turtledove, James Van Pelt, Robert M. Price, Don Webb, Paul Di Filippo and the editor himself.

*Ten-Word Tragedies: Nineteen Stories Inspired by One Frank Turner Song* edited by Christopher Golden and Tim Lebbon contained original stories inpired by images on postcards by, amongst others, Michael Marshall Smith, Kelley Armstrong, Stephen Volk, Paul Tremblay, Rio Youers, Alison Littlewood, M.R. Carey and English singer-songwriter Frank Turner.

PS Publishing's series of Midnight Movie Monographs continued with Kit Power's volume on Ken Russell's *Tommy*, while *Coffinmaker's Blues: Collected Writings on Terror* from the same imprint collected

Stephen Volk's non-fiction columns (2004–16) from *The Third Alternative* and *Black Static* magazines, along with two original pieces. David Pirie contributed an Introduction.

Robert McCammon's paranormal thriller *The Listener* from Cemetery Dance was also available in a 600-copy signed, slipcased edition ($125.00) and a traycased, lettered edition of fifty-two copies with added illustrations by Chris Odgers ($500.00).

*Cardinal Black*, from the same author and publisher, was the seventh volume in the "Matthew Corbett" series. It was additionally available in a 474-copy signed, slipcased edition ($125.00) and a traycased, lettered edition of fifty-two copies ($500.00).

*October* was the first print edition of Michael Rowe's ghost novel, first issued by ChiZine in 2017.

*Gwendy's Magic Feather* was Richard Chizmar's solo sequel to *Gwendy's Button Box*, which was co-authored with Stephen King, who provided the Foreword to the Cemetery Dance edition. Illustrated by Keith Minnion, Congresswoman Gwendy Peterson got her button box back just when girls started disappearing in Castle Rock.

*The Long Way Home* collected seventeen stories (one original) by Chizmar, along with a previously unpublished script.

Edited by Peter Enfantino, Robert Morrish and John Scoleri, *The Best of the Scream Factory* collected more than seventy non-fiction pieces, by Kim Newman, Stefan Dziemianowitz, Don D'Amassa and others, from the American small press magazine (1988–97). The book was available from CD in an edition of 450 signed copies, and a leatherbound, traycased lettered edition of fifty-two copies ($350).

Kim Harrison's psychological horror novel *Perfunctory Affection* was available from Subterranean Press in a signed edition of 1,500 copies and a leather-bound, traycased edition of twenty-six copies ($250.00).

A group of teenage paranormal investigators looked into the ownership of a mysterious house in *In the Shadow of Spindrift House* by Mira Grant (Seanan McGuire), with illustrations by Julie Dillon. It was also available in a signed edition limited to 1,500 copies.

C.J. Tudor's *The Taking of Annie Thorne* was reprinted by

Subterranean as *The Hiding Place* with a new Introduction by the author and a previously unpublished alternate ending. It was available in both a signed edition limited to 300 copies and a twenty-six lettered and traycased edition ($300.00).

*Houses Under the Sea* collected thirty revised Lovecraftian tales and an essay by Caitlín R. Kiernan, while *Before I Wake* collected fourteen stories in different genres by David Morrell.

*Legionnaire* was a ghost story novella about the French Foreign Legion by C.E. Ward, while Michael Chislett's *Where Shadows Gather* was a welcome collection of thirteen supernatural stories (five original), both from Sarob Press.

Edited by publisher Robert Morgan, *The Pale Illuminations* from Sarob collected four atmospheric folk horror tales by Peter Bell, Mark Valentine, Reggie Oliver and Derek John. *Their Dark & Secret Alchemy*, also edited by Morgan, contained three novellas by Richard Gavin, Colin Insole and Damian Murphy.

Paul Lowe supplied the dust-jacket art for all Sarob titles.

From Ireland's Swan River Press, *A Flowering Wound* collected ten stories (two original) by John Howard and was limited to 300 hardcover copies.

For the same imprint, Mark Valentine edited and introduced *The Far Tower: Stories for W.B. Yeats*. The beautifully produced anthology featured ten stories inspired by the Irish poet's work from, amongst others, Ron Weighell, D.P. Watt, John Howard, Lynda E. Rucker and Reggie Oliver. It was limited to 400 copies and came with bonus postcards depicting Yeats and the cover of his 1928 book, *The Tower*.

*Ellison Under Glass* collected twenty-nine stories in their pre-edited versions written by the late Harlan Ellison in bookstore windows and other public spaces. It was available in three hardcover states from Charnel House with varying degrees of bonus material at $200, $750 and $1,500 per copy.

*The Night Doctor and Other Tales* from Centipede Press collected twenty-five stories (two original) from the past eight years by Steve Rasnic Tem. Gary Laib supplied the illustrations.

In 2019, Ray Russell and Rosalie Parker's Tartarus Press published two new collections of short stories by contemporary writers, three novels, four non-fiction books, two issues of *Wormwood*, and reprinted two older books as paperbacks.

*The New Inn Hall Deception* by John Gaskin contained the title novella and four other "tales of twilight and borderlands" which explored the threatening and unexplained at the edge of experience and was limited to 380 signed copies, while *Petals and Violins: Fifteen Unsettling Tales* by D.P. Watt contained seven new stories, along with an Introduction by Peter Holman and an Afterword by Helen Marshall. All 300 copies were signed by the author.

Tartarus also published three new novels by contemporary authors: *House of the Flight-Helpers* by Philomena van Rijswijk, *The Way Things End* by Charles David and *The Third Cephalina* by Rebecca Lloyd.

The four non-fiction titles from Tartarus were *Copsford*, Walter J.C. Murray's 1948 account of a young man's life in rural Sussex, and Mark Valentine's further collection of book-ish essays, *A Wild Tumultory Library*; while *Occult Territory: An Arthur Machen Gazetteer* was edited by R.B. Russell, and Machen's own volume of unconventional literary criticism and essays, *Hieroglyphics*, came with an Introduction by D.P. Watt and an Afterword by Nicholas Freeman.

Edited by Mark Valentine, *Wormwood* #32 and #33 included essays on Mark Hansom, Julian Osgood Field, Edogawa Ranpo and 'Arthur Conan Doyle, Dennis Wheatley and the Fiction of Atlantis'.

Tartarus also reprinted as affordable paperbacks two books by John Howard and Mark Valentine, *The Collected Connoisseur* and *Secret Europe*.

Mark Samuels' novel *Witch-Cult Abbey* from Zagava was set at the height of the London Blitz and linked to his story 'The White Hands'. The hardcover edition was limited to just 199 numbered copies, with illustrations by Joseph Dawson, and included head- and tail-bands, a silk ribbon mark and illustrated endpapers. The signed, lettered edition came in a full-leather binding embossed on the cover with the author's signature in gold and endpapers made of hand-marbled paper, custom-made by British artist Jemma Lewis.

And it didn't end there...Five leather-bound "Artist Editions" of

Samuels' novel were offered by Zagava in special sets consisting of the book and a bibliography in a traycase with a Perspex window and an original drawing by Joseph Dawson, while a sixth set was accompanied by the original oil painting used as the cover illustration of the numbered edition.

Zagava also published Rebecca Lloyd's Gothic novel *The Child Cephalina.*

*The Very Best of Caitlín R. Kiernan* from Tachyon Publications collected twenty stories from the previous fourteen years with an Introduction by Richard Kadrey.

*Legends of Cthulhu & Other Nightmares* from Telos Publishing collected six Lovecraftian stories and nine "Other Nightmares" (three original) by Sam Stone, including one collaboration with her husband/publisher David J. Howe.

Editor Paul Finch did his usual fine job putting together *Terror Tales of Northwest England* for Telos, which featured fifteen stories (four reprints) by Cate Gardner, Simon Kurt Unsworth, David A. Riley, Christopher Harman, Stephen Gallagher, Sam Stone, Ramsey Campbell, Anna Taborska and others, including the editor, interspersed with "true" accounts of local legends.

Editor/publisher Dan Coxon issued Volumes 3 and 4 of his paperback anthology series, *Tales from the Shadow Booth.* Containing eleven and fourteen stories, respectively, contributors included Robert Shearman, Tim Major, Lucie McKnight Hardy and Jay Caselberg.

Edited by Christopher Golden, James A. Moore and an "editorial committee", and financed via crowdfunding for Twisted Publishing/ Haverhill House Publishing, *The Twisted Book of Shadows* included nineteen horror stories by Jason A. Wyckoff, P.D. Cacek, John Linwood Grant and Kristi DeMeester, amongst others, along with an Introduction by Linda D. Addison. Inspired by the anthologies of Charles L. Grant, the book was intended to "introduce lesser-known writers to the horror community" and was compiled using a "blind submission" process.

*On the Night Border* from Raw Dog Screaming Press contained fifteen stories (six original) by James Chambers, along with another

Introduction by Linda Addison and an impressive cover painting by Daniele Serra.

Nicole Petit "curated" *Sockhops & Seances,* an original anthology of eleven supernatural stories set in the 1950s, published by 18th Wall. It also included a brief preview of *Gabriel's Trumpet* by Jon Black.

For the same publisher, Peter Rawlik edited and introduced *The Chromatic Court,* an anthology of twelve original stories inspired by Robert W. Chambers' *The King in Yellow* and other colour-linked avatars by such authors as Christine Morgan, Joseph S. Pulver Sr., Paul StJohn Mackintosh, Jon Black, John Linwood Grant and Micah S. Harris.

From JournalStone, *Out of Water* collected eighteen stories by Sarah Read, all originally published from 2014–19, with an Introduction by Gemma Files, while Ross E. Lockhart introduced *Shout Kill Revel Repeat,* a collection of seventeen stories (three original) by Scott R. Jones.

Eric J. Guignard's debut novel from JournalStone, *Doorways to the Deadeye,* was about a hobo who discovered how to change history during America's Great Depression.

For his own Dark Moon Books imprint, Guignard edited and inytroduced *Pop the Clutch: Thrilling Tales of Rockabilly, Monsters, and Hot Rod Horror,* which contained eighteen original tales set in the 1950s by Weston Ochse, Kasey and Joe R. Lansdale, Nancy Holder, David J. Schow, Lisa Morton, Bill Pronzini, Yvonne Navarro, Steve Perry, Jeff Strand, Brian Hodge and others, illustrated by Steve Chanks.

*Exploring Dark Short Fiction #4: A Primer to Jeffrey Ford* from Dark Moon collected six stories (one new) and two essays, plus an Introduction and interview with the author by series editor Guignard, commentary by Michael Arnzen and illustrations by Michelle Prebich.

*Skidding Into Oblivion* from Canada's ChiZine featured eleven recent stories (one original) by Brian Hodge, while Simon Bestwick's *And Cannot Come Again: Tales of Childhood, Regret, and Innocence Lost* contained fifteen tales (two original) with an Introduction by Ramsey Campbell.

*Broken Sun, Broken Moon* collected twelve literary science fiction stories, two original and the others "lightly edited", by Brent Hayward.

New novels from ChiZine included Craig Wolf's *Queen of All the Nightbirds* and *Hollywood North: A Novel in Six Reels* by Michael Libling, while *Summerwood/Winterwood* was a back-to-back omnibus edition of two novels by E.L. Chen, illustrated by the author.

A special 10th Anniversary edition of David Nickle's collection *Monstrous Affections* contained a new Introduction and interior drawings by the author, a new Foreword by John Langan and a new Afterword by Laird Barron, along with the original Introduction by Michael Rowe.

Also out from ChiZine, before the imprint imploded, *Casting Shadows* was a collection of forty-five poems (forty original) by Troy Harkin, while *As Close to the Edge Without Going Over* contained thirty-nine poems by David Silverberg.

Published in trade paperback by Kurodahan Press, *Vampiric Tales of Blood and Roses from Japan* was an anthology of sixteen stories (one reprint) and an article, mostly published in English for the first time, with an Introduction by Raechel Dumas. Compiled by Edward Lipsett, the stunning cover painting was by Kojima Ayami.

Issued by PS Publishing as five "sampler" chapbooks, Robert Shearman's *#25: Petty Vengeance*, *#33: A Short History of Tall Buildings*, *#67: The Touch of Baby Stalin's Skin*, *#75: Taste Me* and *#98: The Curtain Falls* were all taken from the author's forthcoming choose-your-own-adventure collection, *We All Hear Stories in the Dark*.

*Getting Through* by Ramsey Campbell was published as a dual-language chapbook by Italy's Asylum Press.

Available from Black Shuck Books in a plastic DVD case complete with a fake disc signed by the author, Ray Cluley's chapbook *6/6* purported to be a critical examination of a series of short films which had been mysteriously removed from YouTube. It was strictly limited to 66 numbered copies.

Nicholas Royle's Nightjar Press celebrated its tenth anniversary by issuing attractive, signed chapbooks of *Jutland* by Lucie McKnight Hardy and *Broad Moor* by Alison Moore in March, and followed those up with *So This is It* by Paul Griffiths, *Le détective* by H.P. Tinker, *Halloween* by Nicola Freeman and the remarkable '*Doe Lea*' by M. John Harrsion in September. Each booklet was limited to just 200 copies.

Citing a busy family life and health issues, *At the Setting of the Sun* was a collection of two original ghost stories that may have marked the end of M.P.N. Sims' forty-year writing career. The booklet was privately distributed to friends and colleagues.

From Omnium Gatherum, Tom Johnstone's *The Monsters Are Due in Madison Square Garden: A Novella* managed to link together a supernatural serial killer murdering American Bund Nazis during the 1930s and an attempt to interview actor Bela Lugosi in the mid-1950s.

Andy Cox's horror magazine *Black Static* turned out a quintet of square-bound issues, with regular columns by Lynda E. Rucker and Ralph Robert Moore, film reviews by Gary Couzens, and book reviews by diverse hands. There was also original fiction from Stephen Volk, Tim Lees, Tom Johnstone, Erinn L. Kemper, Simon Avery, Mike O'Driscoll, Kristi DeMeester, Steven J. Dines and Cody Goodfellow, along with interviews with Nicholas Royle, Nathan Ballingrud and Paul Tremblay.

*Black Static*'s companion scienice fiction title, *Interzone*, managed to produce a full run of six bi-monthly issues.

Having last published an edition in 2014, the venerable *Weird Tales* returned with "an unthemed issue". With a new publisher, and editorial director Jonathan Maberry joining editor Marvin Kaye, issue #363 benifitted from a square-bound, full-colour format.

Unfortunately, despite original fiction by Victor LaValle, Josh Malerman, Lisa Morton, Sherrilyn Kenyon and Maberry himself, the issue failed to capture the essence of "The Unique Magazine", not helped by a plentiful helping of indifferent flash fiction and poetry, along with undistingushed illustrations and design.

Another long-running magazine under new management was

*Space and Time.* New co-publisher and editor-in-chief Angela Yuriko Smith gave the title a much-needed face-lift with three glossy issues featuring fiction from founder Gordon Linzner, John Linwood Grant, John Palisano, Sarah Avery and Glen Hirshberg, along with poetry by Marge Simon, Weston Ochse, Darrell Schweitzer and Vince A. Liaguno, and an interview with the late Jack Ketchum (translated from the Spanish).

Doug Draa's bumper *Weirdbook* #41 contained twenty-nine stories and five poems by, amongst others, Adrian Cole, Darrell Schweitzer, Steve Dilks and K.A. Opperman. The second *Weirdbook Annual* was titled *Cthulhu* and featured Lovecraftian fiction and poetry from Cole, Schweitzer and Opperman again, along with Robert M. Price, Lucy A. Snyder, the late Paul Dale Anderson, Franklyn Searight, Andrew J. Wilson, Ann K. Schwader, Charles Lovecraft, Frederick J. Mayer and others.

Richard Chizmar's *Cemetery Dance* #77 included stories by Bill Pronzini, Ralph Robert Moore, Gerard Houarner and others, along with interviews with Jack Ketchum, Lucky McKee and Robert Bloch's daughter, Sally Francy. Bev Vincent, Ellen Datlow, Michael Marano, Thomas F. Monteleone and Mark Sieber supplied the usual columns and reviews.

Edited by Charles Coleman Finlay, *The Magazine of Fantasy & Science Fiction* published its quota of six double-issues and celebrated its 70th Anniversary with the September/October issue, which not only included a personal remembrance of the magazine by Robert Silverberg, but also fiction from Kelly Link, Paolo Bacigalupi, Michael Moorcock (his first ever appearance in the magazine), Elizabeth Bear, Esther Friesner, Michael Swanwick, the late Gardner Dozois and others.

Other issues featured the usual eclectic mix of fiction and poetry by Phyllis Eisenstein (a new "Alaric" novella), Andy Duncan, Carrie Vaughn, Adam-Troy Castro, Matthew Hughes, Albert E. Cowdrey, Mary Soon Lee, James Morrow, M. Rickert and Jane Yolen, amongst others.

Charles de Lint, Michelle West, E.G. Neill, Elizabeth Hand, Karin Lowachee, David J. Skal, James Sallis and Paul Di Filippo all contributed book or film reviews to *F&SF*, and Di Filippo was also featured with three 'Curiosities' columns, along with one apiece from Graham Andrews, David Langford and Thomas Kaufsek.

The Christmas issue of the UK's *Radio Times* included a festive ghost story, 'The Quiet House', by Susan Hill. It was connected to the author's novel *The Small Hand*.

Canada's *Rue Morgue* kicked off the year with a "Women in Horror" issue that included an interview with Jen and Sylvia Soska about their remake of *Rabid* and articles looking at female villains of 1980s and '90s cinema.

The monthly newsprint *Classic Images* featured a tribute to the late Julie Adams and a profile of enigmatic *Dracula's Daughter* actress Gloria Holden by Laura Wagner.

Stephen King was interviewed about the new movie version of *Pet Sematary* in the April 5-12 issue of *Entertainment Weekly*.

*Locus* began the year with a special issue that looked at science fiction and fantasy art, featuring interviews with Charles Vess, Kathleen Jennings, Omar Rayyan and others. The June issue included one of the last interviews with author Michael Blumlein (who died four months later), while other interviewees throughout the year included Silvia Moreno-Garcia and Robert McCammon.

The free monthly online publication *Nightmare Magazine*, edited by John Joseph Adams, included reprinted fiction from, amongst others, Paul Tremblay, Kelley Armstrong, Nick Mamatas, Kaaron Warren, Seanan McGuire, Gary McMahon, Cody Goodfellow, Richard Gavin, Nathan Ballingrud and Gemma Files, along with new stories from Adam-Troy Castro, Simon Strantzas and Kurt Fawver. There were non-fiction essays by Christopher Golden, Kaaron Warren, Lisa Morton and Stephen Graham Jones, interviews with Nathan Ballingrud and Lois H. Gresh, and a roundtable discussion about women in horror hosted by Lisa Morton. Each month's e-book contents were serialised throughout the month on the website, along with new material posted on the first four Wednesdays.

Sean Wallace and Silvia Moreno-Garcia's free online periodical *The Dark* appeared monthly and was also available in a digital print edition. It featured original and reprint stories by Angela Slatter, Priya Sharma, Stephen Gallagher, Simon Strantzas, Lynda E. Rucker, Richard Gavin, Alison Littlewood and many others.

Issue #120 of Jason Sizemore's monthly electronic *Apex Magazine* was the final edition before the title went on indefinite hiatus. Maurice Broaddus guest-edited a special issue themed around "Afrofuturism", which featured a collaborative horror story by Steven Barnes and Tananarive Due.

Jeani Rector's monthly electronic publication *The Horror Zine* included fiction and poetry from, amongst others, Piers Anthony, Richard Chizmar, Scott Nicholson, Joe R. Lansdale, Graham Masterton, Jay Caselberg, Lisa Morton, Tim Lebbon, Bryn Fortey, Brent Monahan and Ian McDowell, along with an interview with Ramsey Campbell.

Trevor Kennedy and Alison Weir's print-on-demand and electronic *Phantasmagoria Magazine* went from strength to strength, with some issues exceeding 300 pages. The five bumper editions for 2019 included new and reprint fiction from Peter Crowther, Peter Coleborn, David A. Riley, Johnny Mains, Dave Jeffrey and co-editor Kennedy, along with interviews with Steve Jackson and Ian Livingstone, Les Edwards, Patricia Quinn, Richard O'Brien, Jim Pitts, David A. Riley, David A. Sutton, Dean M. Drinkel, Allen Koszowski, Stephen Jones and Randy Broecker, Peter Coleborn, Jan Edwards, Sam Stone and David J. Howe, Dave Jeffery, Samantha Lee, Jo Fletcher, Adrian Cole, Jeff Strand, Johnny Mains, Mike Chinn, Sophie Aldred and others.

Some of the articles in *Phantasmagoria* covered George R.R. Martin, Neil Gaiman's *Good Omens*, *Buffy the Vampire Slayer*, *The Twilight Zone*, Universal Monsters, *Planet of the Apes*, *The Exorcist*, *Friday the 13th*, *Stranger Things* Series 3, Aurora monster model kits and *The Wicker Man*, while the high quality illustrations were supplied by Les Edwards, Jim Pitts, Allen Koszowski, Randy Broecker and Peter Coleborn.

As if all that was not enough, Trevor Kennedy also launched the *Phantasmagoria Special Edition Series* with a "R. Chetwynd-Hayes

Centenary Collector's Edition". It included fiction by Chetwynd-Hayes, David J. Howe and Marc Damian Lawler, along with reviews and features about Britain's "Prince of Chill".

Following the untimely death of publisher Sam Gafford, *Occult Detective Quarterly* changed its name to *Occult Detective Magazine* under the co-editorship of John Linwood Grant and Dave Brzeski. Along with fiction by Tim Waggoner, Marion Pitman, Loren Rhoads, Ian Hunter and others, the two issues published in 2019 also included an ongoing round-robin serial with contributions from Cliff Biggers, James A. Moore and Charles R. Rutledge, articles on Jules de Grandin and Crimefest 2018, an interview with author Jonathan Raab, plus book reviews.

The two issues of David Longhorn's *Supernatural Tales* contained new stories by Steve Duffy, Tracy Fahey, S.P. Miskowski, Helen Grant, Mark Valentine, David Surface and others, along with the occassional book review.

*Ghosts & Scholars* #35 featured fiction by Christopher Harman and Victoria Day, along with articles from Mark Valentine, Peter Bell and John Howard. Regretably, #36/37 was the final issue of the M.R. James-inspired journal under the editorship of founder Rosemary Pardoe. After forty years, citing family health reasons, Pardoe announced that she was handing the publication over to an informal group of guest editors that included James Doig, Antonio Monteiro, Helen Kemp and John Howard, with Mark and Jo Valentine taking over the publishing and administration of the title. The double-issue of *G&S* featured Jamesian fiction by C.E. Ward and Victoria Day, and a special extra booklet, *The Bishop's Inventory* by Jane Jakeman, along with the usual articles, news, letters and reviews.

Edited by Shona Kinsella, Tim Major and Ian Hunter, all three issues of the British Fantasy Society's *BFS Horizons* contained fiction and poetry by Allen Ashley and Cardinal Cox, amongst other names. Meanwhile, the Society's other publication, *BFS Journal*, added Sean Wilcock as co-editor with Allen Stroud. Unfortunately, despite a welcome return of Mike Barrett to the publication (with a piece on the career of author Michael Coney), it remained the usual dry collection of articles and reviews.

∽

*The PS Book of Fantastic Fictioneers: A History of the Incredible* was a remarkable two-volume set compiled, edited and illustrated in full colour by Pete Von Sholly, which was an A-Z compendium of more than 100 authors, artists and filmmakers who had made a significant impact upon the genre, celebrated in mini-essays by seventy-five esteemed contributors.

The books were also available in a deluxe two-volume illustrated slipcase (limited to fifty numbered copies) that was signed by Von Sholly and included a unique piece of remarqued artwork (£250.00).

Edited by Mark Valentine and Timothy J. Jarvis for Hippocampus Press, *The Secret Ceremonies: Critical Essays on Arthur Machen* contained contributions from, amongst others, S.T. Joshi, Vincent Starrett, Roger Dobson, John Howard, Ron Weighell, Peter Bell, Donald Sidney-Fryer, Aleister Crowley, Mark Valentine and Machen himself.

From the same imprint, *The Tragic Thread in Science Fiction* collected thirteen essays on David Lindsay, Olaf Stapledon, Arthur C. Clarke, Mervyn Peake, William Gibson, Fritz Leiber, James Tiptree Jr. and H.P. Lovecraft.

*Providence After Dark and Other Writings* was a bumper (almost 600-page) collection of essays and reviews by T.E.D. Klein, compiled by S.T. Joshi and David E. Schultz. Amongst the topics covered were H.P. Lovecraft (obviously), Arthur Machen, Robert Aickman, Frank Belknap Long and *Twilight Zone Magazine* (which Klein edited), plus *Twilight Zone: The Movie*, *Star Wars* and Charles Manson. The book also featured a number of interviews with Klein.

Published by The Clive Barker Archive and edited by Phil and Sarah Stokes, *The Painter, the Creature and the Father of Lies* was subtitled *Revised Edition: 35 Years of Non-Fiction Writing* and collected more than 100 essays and introductions by Clive Barker, dating from the early 1980s to 2017. The first 500 copies of the numbered trade paperback were signed by Barker.

*Hidden Wyndham: Life, Love, Letters*, Amy Binns' welcome biography of reclusive British author "John Wyndham" (John Beynon

Harris, 1903–69), explored his relationship with long-term partner/wife of thirty-six years, Grace Wilson. It included numerous letters written during World War II, along with a selection of rare photographs.

*Monster She Wrote: The Women Who Pioneered Horror and Speculative Fiction* by Lisa Kröger and Melanie R. Anderson looked at the careers of forty groundbreaking female authors, including Ann Radcliffe, Mary Shelley, Mary Elizabeth Counselman, Marjorie Bowen, Anne Rice, Everil Worrell, Elizabeth Gaskell, Ann Ward, Dorothy Macardle and Angela Carter, to name just some. It was illustrated by Natalya Bainova.

From McFarland & Company, John C. Tibbett's biography *The Furies of Marjorie Bowen* was the first book-length critical study of the English supernatural writer "Marjorie Bowen" (Gabrielle Margaret Vere Campbell Long, 1885–1952). Michael Dirda supplied the Foreword.

*Perspectives on Stephen King: Conversations with Authors, Experts and Collaborators* from the same imprint featured seventeen interviews conducted by Andrew J. Rausch with authors such as Richard Chizmar and Richard Christian Matheson, along with a Bibliography of King's books and screenplays.

Jason Ray Carney's *Weird Tales of Modernity: The Ephemerality of the Ordinary in the Stories of Robert E. Howard, Clark Ashton Smith and H.P. Lovecraft* looked at how that trio of pulp authors used their fiction to speculate about such philosophical questions as the function of art and the brevity of life.

Although Michael Walton's *The Horror Comic Never Dies: A Grisly History* was issued as a surprisingly thin trade paperback by McFarland (and without any cover reproductions), it was packed with information about horror comics from the 1950s up to the present time.

*Stoker On Stoker: Dracula Revealed* from Telos Publishing offered a selection of notes and observations on the writing and development of *Dracula* by Bram Stoker's great grand-nephew Dacre Stoker.

Published by the University Press of Mississippi, *The Artistry of Neil Gaiman: Finding Light in the Shadows* edited by Joseph Michael

Sommers and Kyle Eveleth collected fourteen critical essays along with short interviews with Gaiman and artist Charles Vess.

Edited by Emily Lauer and Balaka Basu, *The Harry Potter Generation: Essays on Growing Up with the Series* contained twelve essays about the effect of J.K. Rowling's books on popular culture and the people who read them. Meanwhile, *Harry Potter and the Cedarville Censors: Inside the Precedent-Setting Defeat of an Arkansas Book Ban* by attorney Brian Meadors looked at an attempt in 2003 to ban Rowling's series in some US school libraries.

Edited by publisher John Flesk, *Spectrum 26: The Best in Contemporary Fantastic Art* contained over 600 pieces of art from 2018 by more than 300 artists, along with a celebration of Grand Master Award-winner Donato Giancola.

From the same imprint, *Art of Gary Gianni: George R.R. Martin's Seven Kingdoms* featured more than 270 sketches, drawings and paintings (thirty-five of them new) illustrating Martin's "A Song of Ice and Fire" universe. With an Introduction by Cullen Murphy and an Afterword by Martin himself, it was available in both a trade hardcover edition and a 500-copy slipcased edition, signed by Gianni and Martin, that included an additional twenty-two pages ($200.00).

*Clive Barker Imaginer 7: Paintings 1984–2017* was the latest volume of full-colour volumes from The Clive Barker Archive with text by Phil and Sarah Stokes and extensive commentary from Barker himself. The oversized volume was published in a limited edition of 1,000 copies, plus a 100-copy deluxe slipcased edition. James Kay contributed a brief Afterword.

*Harry Potter and the Goblet of Fire: The Illustrated Edition* featured artwork by Jim Kay, while Jody Ravenson's *Harry Potter: Exploring Hogwarts: An Illustrated Guide* and *Harry Potter: Magical Places: A Paper Scene Book* featured illustrations by Studio Muti and Scott Buoncristiano, respectively, along with photos and fun facts.

From IDW Publishing and Yoe Books' "The Chilling Archives of Horrors Comics!" series, *Cry from the Coffin! and Much More* was the seventh volume in the *Haunted Horror* series. It reprinted issues

#19–21 (2015–16) of that magazine, which in turn reprinted pre-code horror comic strips that were in the public domain. IDW founder Ted Adams supplied an excitable Introduction.

Mike Slater and Thomas Roache's *The Necronomnomnom: Recipes and Rites from the Lore of H.P. Lovecraft* was a humorous cookbook illustrated by Kurt Komoda.

Following the shocking death of Rick Grimes in the previous issue, Robert Kirkman and Charlie Adlard's zombie epic *The Walking Dead* from Image Comics/Skybound Entertainment unexpectedly ended with a bumper issue #193.

*The Problem of Susan and Other Stories* from Dark Horse collected two stories and poems by Neil Gaiman, illustrated by P. Craig Russell, Scott Hampton and Paul Chadwick.

Originally published as a series of five comics, *Stephen King's The Dark Tower: The Gunslinger: The Man in Black* was adapted from the fifth book in the sequence by Peter David and Robin Furth, with art by Alex Maleev.

Published by Italy's Independent Legions, *Calcutta Horror* was adapted by Alessandro Manzetti from Poppy Z. Brite's story 'Calcutta: Lord of Nerves' and illustrated in black and white by Stefano Cardoselli.

Movie tie-in novels in 2019 included *Alita: Battle Angel* by Pat Cadigan and *Godzilla: King of the Monsters* by Greg Keyes, while no author wanted to take credit for "the official movie novelization" of *Gemini Man*.

The novelisation of *Men in Black International* by R.S. Belcher included an additional prequel story, and *Happy Death Day & Happy Death Day 2U* by Aaron Hartzler featured two tie-in novellas to the fun Blumhouse movies in a single volume.

*Maleficent: Mistress of Evil* was a young adult novelisation of the Disney movie, adapted by Elizabeth Rudnick.

*Alien: Echo* was a YA tie-in to the movie series by Mira Grant (Seanan McGuire), and Tim Waggoner's *Alien: Prototype* was inspired by the same film series.

Rebecca Roanhorse's *Star Wars* novel, *Resistance Reborn*, filled in some of the gaps between *Star Wars: The Last Jedi* and *Star Wars: The Rise of Skywalker*.

*Scary Stories to Tell in the Dark: The Haunted Notebook of Sarah Bellows* was a collection of six stories based on the screenplay versions which, in turn, were inspired by the series of ghost and urban legend books by Alvin Schwartz. With an Introduction by co-writer and producer Guillermo del Toro, it was illustrated with art and photos from the movie.

*Pan's Labyrinth: The Labyrinth of the Faun* by Guillermo del Toro and Cornelia Funke was a belated YA spin-off to del Toro's 2006 movie, illustrated by Allen Williams.

*William Shakespeare's Get Thee Back to the Future!* was a spoof play, written in the Bard's style by Ian Doescher, based on the 1985 movie *Back to the Future*.

*Stranger Things: Suspicious Minds* was a prequel set in 1969 by Gwenda Bond, while *Stranger Things: Darkness on the Edge of Town* by Adam Christopher and *Stranger Things: Runaway Max* by Brenna Yovanoff were also based on the popular Netflix series.

Sarah Rees Brennan's *The Chilling Adventures of Sabrina: Season of the Witch* and *The Chilling Adventures of Sabrina: Daughter of Chaos* were both based on another Netflix series.

Tim Waggoner's *Supernatural: Children on Anubis* was a tie-in based on the long-running TV series, while Kiersten White's *Slayer* was the first in a new young adult series set in the "Buffyverse" of the 1990s show *Buffy the Vampire Slayer*.

Former "Doctor Who" Tom Baker had a little help from James Goss with the horror-themed tie-in *Doctor Who: Scratchman*, based on a screenplay which the actor had written back in the 1970s.

Meanwhile, *Doctor Who: The Target Storybook* featured fifteen original stories based on the BBC-TV series.

From Telos Publishing, *Daemos Rising – Special Edition* by David J. Howe was an unlicensed *Doctor Who* spin-off that was an expanded version of the author's 2004 fan film and the 1971 BBC serial *The Daemons*, while *Sil and the Devil Seeds of Arodor—Special Edition* by actor Philip Martin was based on a 2019 fan production and elements from the *Doctor Who* episodes *Vengeance on Varos* (1985) and *The Trial of a Time Lord* (1986).

Keith R.A. DeCandido's *Alien: Isolation* was based on a video game, which in turn was based on the movie series, and *Robert Kirkman's The Walking Dead: Typhoon* by Wesley Chu was a tie-in based on the comic series.

Published by Hanover Square Press, *The Lady from the Black Lagoon: Hollywood Monsters and the Lost Legacy of Milicent Patrick* by Mallory O'Meara was a feminist look at the "forgotten" contribution bit-actress and artist Patrick made to the design of Universal's "Gill Man" for the 1954 film.

*Hammer Complete: The Films, the Personnel, the Company* from McFarland & Company was an A-Z guide to the "Studio That Dripped Blood" by Howard Maxford.

In *Dracula as Absolute Other: The Troubling and Distracting Specter of Stoker's Vampire on Screen*, author Simon Bacon examined the Count's role as "the Other" in movies and TV.

Eugenio Ercolani's *Darkening the Italian Screen: Interviews with Genre and Exploitation Directors Who Debuted in the 1950s and 1960s* featured recorded interviews with directors and actors.

In McFarland's *The Haunted House on Film: An Historical Analysis*, Paul Meehan not only covered more than 100 movies featuring spooky settings, but also the real-life haunted house phenomenon and movies based on paranormal case files.

Edited by Amanda Taylor and Susan Nylander, *Death in Supernatural* featured essays about how death was depicted in the long-running TV series on The CW.

*Son of Dracula* by Gary D. Rhodes, Tom Weaver *et al* (with an Introduction from Donnie "Son of Frankenstein" Dunagan) and Scott Gallinghouse's *The Brute Man* were volumes #9 and #10, respectively, in Tom Weaver's "Scripts from the Crypt" series from BearManor Media.

Interestingly, Gallinghouse and his team also produced an "alternative" version of *The Brute Man* that concentrated on the movie's lead actor. *Rondo Hatton: Beauty Within the Brute* featured a cover painting by long-time Rondo fan Drew Friedman.

Meanwhile, Gary Rhodes teamed up with Robert Guffey for *Bela Lugosi and the Monogram 9* for the same publisher. With a Foreword by filmmaker Larry Blamire, the volume was an in-depth look at the nine movies Lugosi made for Monogram between 1941–44.

Philip J. Riley's *Frankenstein Meets the Wolf Man* was the fifth book in BearManor Media's "Universal Filmscripts Series: Classic Horror Films". It was followed by a similar volume covering *The House of Frankenstein*.

From Midnight Marquee Press, Gregory William Mank's *One Man Crazy...! The Life and Death of Colin Clive; Hollywood's Dr. Frankenstein* was a biography of the intense but troubled actor, who died in 1937 as a result of alcoholism. It contained more than 200, often rare, photographs.

From Creature Features, Jeff Bond's exhaustive hardcover *The Fantasy Worlds of Irwin Allen* was illustrated with more than 2,000 images, including concept and production artwork, storyboards, blueprints, design sketches, miniatures and behind-the-scenes photographs, many of them never before published, along with an Introduction by actor Bill Mumy. It was available in a standard edition of 1,000 copies or in a special 250-copy edition autographed by Bond and Mumy.

*The Quite Nice & Fairly Accurate Good Omens Script Book* reprinted the scripts for the Amazon TV series by Neil Gaiman, who also supplied the Introduction. The trade paperback included material that was eventually deleted from the final cut of the show.

Matt Whyman's *The Nice and Accurate Good Omens TV Companion* included an illustrated history of the book-to-screen, along with various cast and crew interviews.

*The Art of Game of Thrones* by Deborah Riley and Jody Revenson included a Foreword by series creators David Benoit and D.B. Weiss and a Preface by the TV show's production designer, Gemma Jackson, while *The Art of Fantastic Beasts: The Crimes of Grindelwald* was a tie-in to the second movie in the series, edited by concept artist Dermot Power and with a Foreword by production designer Stuart Craig.

J.K. Rowling's *Fantastic Beasts: The Crimes of Grindelwald: The*

*Original Screenplay* was illustrated by MinaLima, while Jody Revenson's *Harry Potter and the Cursed Child: The Journey* was a look at the making of the stage play, with a Foreword by Rowling.

Also by Revenson, *Harry Potter: Film Vault Volume 2: Dragon Alley, the Hogwart's Express and the Ministry* was the second in a twelve-volume behind-the-scenes series detailing how the movies were made.

Titan Books celebrated the 40th Anniversary of Ridley Scott's *Alien* with J.W. Rinzler's *The Making of Alien, Alien: The Blueprints* and *Alien: 40 Years 40 Artists*.

John Walsh's *Harryhausen: The Lost Movies* from the same publisher included many never-seen-before photos and artwork from the unrealised films of stop-motion maestro Ray Harryhausen.

Matthew J. Elliott's somewhat obsessive *Lost in Time and Space* from Telos Publishing examined the many "lost" adventures alluded to in *Doctor Who*, chronicling every piece of knowledge the Doctor appeared to have gained off-screen and speculating on where and when he learned that information.

Curated by the pop culture enthusiasts of Printed in Blood, *Stranger Things: Visions from the Upside Down* collected more than 200 pieces of art inspired by the Netflix TV show.

Joe and Anthony Russo's truly epic conclusion to the first Marvel Cinematic Universe (twenty-two movies, eleven franchises!), *Avengers: Endgame*, picked up where 2018's *Infinity War* left off. After the "Snap" wiped out half the universe, surviving superheroes Tony Stark/Iron Man (Robert Downey, Jr. capping off a remarkable run), Captain America (Chris Evans), Thor (Chris Hemsworth), Black Widow (Scarlett Johansson), The Hulk (Mark Ruffalo), Hawkeye (Jeremy Renner) and Captain Marvel (Brie Larson) attempted to move on with their lives until Paul Rudd's Scott Lang/Ant-Man came up with a time-travel twist that could finally defeat Thanos (voiced by Josh Brolin) and recover the Infinity Stones. Not all the heroes made it out alive, although the ending left the door open for some alternate-world stories still to be told.

The movie enjoyed the first worldwide billon-dollar opening

weekend in history, although Marvel was reportedly forced to add actress Danai Gurira (who played "Okoye") to the cast-billing on the *Avengers: Endgame* poster after fans were outraged when it was omitted.

In July, *Avengers: Endgame* also overtook *Avatar* (which had held the title for ten years) to become the highest-grossing movie of all time.

Following a three-year-long bidding war, Disney finally acquired 20th Century Fox for $71.3 billion in March, as Simon Kinberg's delayed *X-Men: Dark Phoenix* supposedly brought Fox's uneven Marvel franchise to an end after almost two decades.

Sophie Turner's Jean Gray acquired apocalyptic powers in a new 1990s-set origin story, while James McAvoy, Michael Fassbender, Jennifer Lawrence and Nicholas Hoult all reprised their series roles and Jessica Chastain turned up as a shape-changing alien. At one point Fox considered releasing the $200 million 3-D movie directly to home video and streaming platforms, which might have been a better idea. It bombed at the summer box-office, losing the studio more than an estimated $130 million.

Tom Holland was back as a likeable Peter Parker/Spider-Man in *Spider Man: Far from Home*. This time he was on a school trip across Europe with his classmates until confronted by Jake Gyllenhaal's underwhelming "Mysterio". At least Samuel L. Jackson's Nick Fury and Jon Favreau's Happy Hogan were around to lend support, and there were cameos from Cobie Smulders, J.K. Simmons and an uncredited Ben Mendelsohn as their Marvel Cinematic Universe characters.

J.J. Abrams' *Star Wars: The Rise of Skywalker* was designed to wrap-up forty-two years of George Lucas' blockbuster franchise. It didn't quite manage to do that, but *Episode IX* featured enough familiar set-pieces to probably please the fans.

Richard E. Grant was a ruthless general of the First Order, and it was nice to see Billy Dee Williams return as Lando Calrissian (for the first time since *Return of the Jedi*); Ian McDiarmid was back as the evil Emperor Palpatine, and the late Carrie Fisher turned up as Leia Organa in previously unseen footage re-purposed from *The Force*

*Awakens*. There were also cameos from Warwick Davis, John Williams, Denis Lawson, Ed Sheeran, Kevin Smith, James Earl Jones as the voice of Darth Vader, and an uncredited Harrison Ford as Han Solo.

Although coming behind the previous two films in the final *Star Wars* trilogy, *The Rise of Skywalker* still managed a first weekend take in North America of $175.5 million, and $198 million in fifty-two international markets. That was a long way behind its predecessors— *The Force Awakens* ($248 million) and *The Last Jedi* ($220 million)—but it was still one of the biggest debuts of 2019, and the third-best December opening behind those earlier two movies.

Michael Dougherty's overblown *Godzilla: King of the Monsters*, the latest entry in Legendary Pictures' "Monsterverse" franchise and a sequel to the 2014 reboot *Godzilla*, threw in Mothra, Rodan and even "Monster Zero" (King Ghidorah, the three-headed monster). Unfortunately, it was the humans (Kyle Chandler, Vera Farmiga, Millie Bobby Brown, Sally Hawkins and Charles Dance's eco-terrorist) who let the side down.

Andy Muschietti's overlong Stephen King sequel, *IT Chapter Two*, was set twenty-seven years after the events in his 2017 movie. Despite the now grown-up members of The Loser's Club being played by Jessica Chastain, James McAvoy, Bill Hader, Isaiah Mustafa, Andy Bean, Jay Ryan and James Ransome, it was the younger cast from the previous film who made the film watchable, as Bill Skarsgård's creepy Pennywise the demonic clown returned to their hometown of Derry, Maine, seeking revenge.

For a week before the movie opened in the UK, a Pennywise pop-up immersive experience appeared in the Vaults at Waterloo in London. The attraction combined nine themed areas built into Waterloo Station's disused railway tunnels.

Mike Flanagan's *Doctor Sleep* was an equally overlong adaptation of Stephen King's belated sequel to *The Shining*. It starred Ewan McGregor as a grown-up Danny Torrance, who was still being haunted by the Overlook Hotel from Stanley Kubrick's 1980 movie as he tried to save Kyliegh Curran's gifted Abra Stone from a group of immortals, led by Rebecca Ferguson's charismatic "Rose the Hat" (who fed on children's "steam"). Carl Lumbly and Henry Thomas were convincing stand-ins for Scatman Crothers and Jack Nicholson, respectively; Carel Struycken turned up as an ancient cult member, and Danny Lloyd (the original "Danny Torrance") had a cameo. There was also a three-hour "director's cut" for those who really felt they needed more.

When rookie agent "M" (Tessa Thompson) was sent to London with Chris Hemsworth's slacker agent "H" to protect visiting alien royalty, things soon started going wrong. It quickly became evident that there was a mole in the agency in F. Gary Gray's lacklustre sequel/reboot *Men in Black: International*.

A babysitter (Madison Iseman) and her friends unwittingly awakened the demonic doll locked away in the occult museum of Ed and Lorraine Warren (a returning Patrick Wilson and Vera Farmiga) in screenwriter Gary Dauberman's directorial debut, *Annabelle Comes Home*, the third entry in the eponymous spin-off series set in "The Conjuring Universe".

Meanwhile, Michael Chaves' *The Curse of Llorona* found Linda Cardellini's social worker trying to save her children from the legendary crying woman of the title. The inclusion of Tony Amendola's Father Perez made this yet another entry in New Line Cinema's linked "Conjuring Universe".

A decade after the smart original, Ruben Fleischer's *Zombieland: Double Tap* reunited original stars Woody Harrelson, Jesse Eisenberg, Emma Stone and Abigail Breslin in a world still overrun by the walking dead. Although not up to the standard of the first movie, fans of Bill Murray who stayed for the end credits would not have been disappointed.

Jessica Rothe returned as likeable sorority sister Tree Gelbman, who found herself sucked into multiple time loops in *Happy Death Day 2U*, director Christopher Landon's enjoyable sequel to his 2017 slasher-comedy.

Tim Miller's *Terminator: Dark Fate* was the sixth movie in the franchise, but only a direct sequel to producer James Cameron's first two entries. Linda Hamilton returned as a grizzled and alcoholic Sarah Connor who, with the help of Arnold Schwarzenegger's original T-800 and an augmented soldier from the future played by Mackenzie Davis, had to protect a young Mexican girl (Natalia Reyes) from Gabriel Luna's liquid REV-9. Lots of stuff blew up.

David Leitch's ridiculously entertaining *Fast & Furious Presents Hobbs & Shaw* (aka *Fast & Furious: Hobbs & Shaw*), the ninth in the fast-cars franchise, was off on its own journey as frenemies—lawman Luke Hobbs (Dwayne Johnson) and rogue secret agent Deckard Shaw (Jason Statham)—were forced to team up to stop a doomsday virus from falling into the hands of Idris Elba's cyber-enhanced super-soldier. Vanessa Kirby, Helen Mirren and Eddie Marsan, along with a surprise Ryan Reynolds and Kevin Hart, were along for the super-charged shenanigans as, once again, lots of things blew up.

Meanwhile, Johnson and Hart were reunited in Jake Kasdan's enjoyable *Jumanji: The Next Level*, a sequel to the same director's *Jumanji: Welcome to the Jungle* (2017), which itself was a sequel to the 1995 original. This time the duo's avatar game-players—along with a returning Jack Black and Karen Gillan—were joined by Danny DeVito and Danny Glover, while Bebe Neuwirth re-created her role from the original.

Kevin Kölsch and Dennis Widmyer's remake of Stephen King's *Pet Sematary* was even darker than the 1989 version, as Jason Clarke and Amy Seimetz's grieving parents attempted to use the mysterious burial ground in the woods to reanimate their dead daughter (Jeté Laurence), despite the evidence of their demonically-possessed cat and John Lithgow's dire warnings.

Having already been remade in 2006, Sophia Takal's woke treatise *Black Christmas* from Blumhouse was the second version of Bob Clark's far superior 1974 slasher, about a group of snowbound sorority girls being stalked by a psychopathic killer. The original 111-minute, R-rated version was edited down to 92 minutes for the PG-13 theatrical cut, which bombed at the box-office.

The Soska Sisters (twins Jen and Sylvia) decided for some reason that they could make a better version of *Rabid* than fellow Canadian director David Cronenberg did back in 1977. Spoiler alert: They couldn't.

Mark Hamill was an inspired choice as the new voice of killer doll "Chucky" in Lars Klevberg's otherwise pointless remake/reboot of the 1988 movie *Child's Play*.

David M. Rosenthal's long-delayed remake of *Jacob's Ladder* also wasn't a patch on Adrian Lyne's 1990 original.

Depressingly, all the Top 10 films released in the UK in 2019 were either sequels, remakes or parts of franchises. The top earner was, of course, *Avengers: Endgame*, taking £88.7 million.

In Alexandre Aja's claustrophobic *Crawl*, the floodwaters from an approaching Category 5 hurricane trapped a number of individuals in a small Florida town with the escaped CGI residents of a local alligator farm. It was produced by Sam Raimi.

Lupita Nyong'o and Winston Duke played middle-class parents whose family was menaced by evil mirror-image doppelgängers in *Us*, writer/director Jordan Peele's meta-take on the pod-people genre. It grossed more than $71 million over its opening weekend in the US, setting a new record for an original horror movie.

Nyong'o was also front and centre of Abe Forsythe's Australian-made zombie comedy *Little Monsters* as a ukulele-playing teacher who took her class on a school trip to a petting zoo, where they were menaced by zombies from a nearby US Army base.

Jim Jarmusch's *The Dead Don't Die* (which stole its title from a Robert Bloch story and TV movie) was a much more understated zombie comedy, as Bill Murray, Adam Driver and Chloë Sevigny's deadpan small-town cops had to deal with a zombie outbreak. The quirky townsfolk included Tom Waits, Steve Buscemi, Danny Glover, RZA, Larry Fessenden, Rosie Perez, Selena Gomez and Tilda Swinton's kick-ass Scottish mortician, while Carol Kane and Iggy Pop turned up amongst the walking dead.

A cosmopolitan London couple (Zoë Tapper and Edward Speleers) tried to save their failing marriage during a zombie apocalypse in the low-budget Scandinavian romantic comedy *Zoo* (aka *Death Do Us Part*), and a group of hopeless stag party friends on a mock zombie-survival weekend encountered the real thing in Ben Kent's comedy *Killer Weekend* (aka *Fubar*).

Following screenings at multiple film festivals around the world Shin'ichirô Ueda's debut comedy *One Cut of the Dead*—about the cast and crew of a low budget zombie movie being menaced by the real thing—finally received a limited cinema release in both the UK and US. It featured an opening thirty-seven-minute single take.

An estranged couple (Florence Pugh and Jack Reynor) attending a Swedish summer-solstice festival found themselves falling foul of a sinister pagan cult in *Midsommar*, Ari Aster's overrated folk-horror homage to *The Wicker Man*.

A pair of 1890s lighthouse keepers (Robert Pattinson and Willem Dafoe) tried to hold on to their sanity on a remote New England island in Robert Eggers' *The Lighthouse*.

Meanwhile, Gerard Butler, Peter Mullin and Connor Swindells starred in Kristoffer Nyholm's *The Vanishing*, which was "inspired" by the real-life case of three keepers who mysteriously vanished from a remote lighthouse off the Scottish coast in 1900. The same incident also loosely inspired the 1977 *Doctor Who* story, 'The Horror of Fang Rock'.

Taylor Schilling's young mother suspected that her super-intelligent son (Jackson Robert Scott) had been possessed by a supernatural force in Nicholas McCarthy's *The Prodigy*, while Seana Kerslake's single mother feared that her young son (James Quinn Markey) had been replaced with a doppelgänger through a mysterious sinkhole in the forest in Lee Cronin's slice of Irish-made folk horror, *The Hole in the Ground*.

William McGregor's feature debut *Gwen*, based on his own short film, was a low-budget folk horror story set in Wales during the industrial revolution.

Octavia Spencer went a little nuts on a bunch of teenagers partying in her basement in Tate Taylor's darkly comic *Ma*, while in Richard Shepard's gruesome *The Perfection*, Allison Williams' troubled cellist eventually had to face the music.

Demi Moore's nightmare CEO took her staff on a team-building trip to New Mexico caves that ended in cannibalism in the horror-comedy *Corporate Animals*, while a group of strangers had to solve the puzzles to survive a series of immersive experiences in Adam Robitel's *Escape Room*, which was basically a PG-13 version of *Saw*.

Bruce Davison and Denise Crosby added an additional touch of class to Micah Gallo's terrific little monster movie, *Itsy Bitsy*. The Kickstarter-funded production found Elizabeth Roberts' damaged single mother and her two children moving into an old house in the country, where they were stalked by a mythological entity that took the form of a giant spider.

Set in the near future, the always-wonderful Udo Kier led a human-hunting safari to the eponymous rural Brazilian village that was cut-off from the outside world by the authorities in Juliano Dornelles and Kleber Mendonça Filho's *Bacurau*. It ended in a bloody battle between the locals and the murderous American tourists.

Samara Weaving's new bride had to first survive her wedding night being hunted by her boyfriend's wealthy but demented family in *Ready or Not*.

A group of college freshmen at an exclusive fraternity signed up for more than they could have imagined in Daniel Robbins' *Pledge*, and a troubled college freshman conjured up the dangerous imaginary friend from his childhood in Adam Egypt Mortimer's *Daniel Isn't Real*.

Kim Da-Mi's amnesiac high school student discovered the darkness of her mysterious past coming back to haunt her in Park Hoon-jung's Korean thriller *The Witch: Part 1—The Subversion*.

London-raised Ronnie (Jaz Deol) returned home to India to discover that his mother's death was part of a series of murders in Neil Biswas' supernatural thriller *Darkness Visible*, while Peter Strickland's *In Fabric* was about a cursed dress that was passed from person to person (does nobody remember Tobe Hooper's 1990 movie *I'm Dangerous Tonight*?).

In David Robert Mitchell's Hitchcockian mystery *Under the Silver Lake*, Andrew Garfield's disenchanted stoner discovered that all trace of the woman next door (Riley Keough) had completely disappeared overnight. When he set off on an occult quest across Los Angeles to find her, he uncovered a conspiracy involving a cult pursuing eternal life in chambers deep beneath the titular body of water.

In Steven Knight's twisty thriller *Serenity*, Matthew McConaughey's laid-back fishing boat captain was approached by his ex-wife (Anne

Hathaway) to murder her current, abusive husband (Jason Clarke). However, nothing was quite as it seemed.

Writer and director Dan Gilroy's *Velvet Buzzsaw*, a satire on the contemporary Los Angeles art scene, boasted an impressive cast that included Jake Gyllenhaal, Rene Russo, Tom Sturridge, Toni Collette and John Malkovich.

A group of children liberated from a Nazi concentration camp in 1945 found their abandoned refuge besiged by the camp's feral Alsatian dogs in the Polish-made *Werewolf*.

Five old friends from University (including Mackenzie Crook, Sophie Thompson and Johnny Vegas) gathered in a remote country lodge to tell each other spooky stories in Abigail Blackmore's comedy-horror portmanteau, *Tales from the Lodge*.

*Nightmare Cinema* was an anthology movie of five stories, directed by Alejandro Brugués, Joe Dante, Mick Garris, Ryûhel Kitamura and David Slade from scripts by Lawrence C. Connolly, Richard Christian Matheson and others. An unlikely Mickey Rourke played the deranged projectionist who brought his audience's worst fears to life on the big screen.

As electrical storms threatened the Earth, Brad Pitt's astronaut had to travel across space to find his long-lost father (Tommy Lee Jones) in James Gray's *Ad Astra*, while Natalie Portman's astronaut returned to a diminished Earth after a transcendent experience in space in Noah Hawley's feature debut *Lucy in the Sky*, which also featured Jon Hamm and Ellen Burstyn.

Robert Pattinson starred in French director Claire Denis' worthy but dull *High Life*, in which a group of death-row convicts on an intergalactic mission became subjects in a creepy human reproduction experiment conducted by Juliette Binoche's crazed scientist.

The passengers of a generational spacecraft knocked off course while on its way to Mars were lost in space in *Aniara*, based on a 1956 poem by Swedish writer Harry Martinson.

Frant Gwo's futuristic epic *The Wandering Earth*, with the jet-powered planet set to crash into Jupiter, became a huge hit in its native China.

Keanu Reeves' grieving scientist attempted to resurrect his dead wife and children in re-grown clones, with predictably disastrous results, in Jeffrey Nachmanoff's bonkers *Replicas*.

Will Smith's ageing hitman was forced to confront a (CGI-created) younger, cloned version of himself in Ang Lee's 3-D *Gemini Man*, which not only appropriated its title from a 1976 TV series, but also had a similar premise to the 2012 Bruce Willis movie *Looper*.

A mysterious serial killer resurfaced every nine years and timed his murders with the lunar cycle in Jim Mickle's twisty thriller *In the Shadow of the Moon*, and Mamie Gummer, Toby Jones and James Caan starred in Carol Morley's metaphyisical murder mystery *Out of the Blue*, based on Martin Amis' novel *The Night Train*.

Robert Rodriguez's 3-D *Alita: Battle Angel* was based on a long-shelved project by producer James Cameron. Adapted from a Japanese *manga* series, Rosa Salazar's digitally-enhanced heroine set out on a quest to discover her mysterious origin.

Although the character originally started in the comics as a male, Brie Larson portrayed Marvel's female version of the intergalactic warrior who turned up in 1990s California with fragmented memories in *Captain Marvel*. Anna Boden and Ryan Fleck's entertaining origin story featured a de-aged Samuel L. Jackson and Clark Gregg as, respectively, S.H.I.E.L.D.'s Nick Fury and Agent Coulson, along with a starry supporting cast that included Ben Mendelsohn, Jude Law, Annette Bening, Djimon Hounsou, the late Stan Lee and uncredited appearances by Don Cheadle, Chris Evans, Scarlett Johansson and Mark Ruffalo as their Avengers characters.

Unfortunately, the movie that *should* have been called *Captain Marvel* was actually titled *Shazam!*. Marvel's first character with the name appeared in 1968 and their movie's female incarnation followed in 1977. However, the moniker originally belonged to Fawcett's Captain Marvel, created in 1939 by C.C. Beck and Bill Parker (and an uncredited Manly Wade Wellman), who starred in his own serial in 1941 and a 1970s live-action TV series also called *Shazam!*.

The rights to the character eventually reverted to DC, and in David Sandberg's irreverent origin story, fourteen-year-old runaway Billy Batson

(Asher Angel) was given the power to transform into the never-named red-clad superhero (played by a likeable Zachary Levi). There was solid support from Mark Strong and Djimon Hounsou (who was also in Marvel's *Captain Marvel*).

While undoubtedly worthy, Todd Phillip's origin story *Joker* was a hard watch. Joaquin Phoenix gave a masterclass in method acting as the mentally troubled comedian who was transformed into Batman's most infamous nemesis by the way society treated him. Robert De Niro and Frances Conroy supplied solid support to the otherwise grim and violent proceedings.

Neil Marshall's smart-alec reboot of *Hellboy* cast David Harbour as Mike Mignola's red-skinned devil, who had to prevent Milla Jovovich's Nimue the Blood Queen from using her witchy powers to destroy the world. At least Ian McShane added a touch of class to the proceedings as "Professor Broom".

M. Night Shyamalan's *Glass* brought together Bruce Willis, Samuel L. Jackson and James McAvoy—the stars of the writer/director's *Unbreakable* (2000) and *Split* (2017)—in a comic book mash-up in which the three gifted individuals from those movies ended up in a high-security ward where Sarah Paulson's psychiatrist tried to convince them that they were all deluded.

A couple (Elizabeth Banks and David Denman) made the mistake of raising a baby they discovered in a crashed UFO in *Brightburn*, David Yarovesky's inversion of the Superman myth which was delayed for six months following the controversy surrounding producer James Gunn's old tweets.

After the 2014 original grossed more than $750 million, Angelina Jolie was back as the titular dark faerie in Disney's delayed sequel *Maleficent: Mistress of Evil*, which found her god-daughter Aurora's (Elle Fanning) marriage to Prince Philip (Harris Dickinson) derailed by a war with her prospective mother-in-law (played by Michelle Pfeiffer). The supporting cast included Chiwetel Ejiofor, Robert Lindsay, Juno Temple, Lesley Manville and Imelda Staunton.

Meanwhile, Disney continued to churn out inferior live-action "re-imaginings" of its classic animated movies with *Aladdin* somewhat improbably directed by Guy Ritchie, in which Will Smith replaced the late Robin Williams as the wisecracking blue genie. At least it was better than Tim Burton's strangely sanitised *Dumbo* and Jon Favreau's CGI-heavy *The Lion King*.

Based on the popular series of urban legend books by writer Alvin Schwartz and illustrator Stephen Gammell, producer and co-writer Guillermo del Toro's *Scary Stories to Tell in the Dark* , directed by André Øvredal, featured three teenage friends (Zoe Colletti, Austin Zajur and Gabriel Rush) who in 1968 accidentally unleashed a number of monsters from a haunted house.

In Joe Cornish's *The Kid Who Would Be King*, Louis Ashbourne Serkis (the son of Andy) played a bullied schoolboy who discovered the legendary sword Excalibur on an abandoned building site with a little help from Patrick Stewart's adult Merlin. Rebecca Ferguson was also around to cause mischief as the evil Morgana.

After being hit by a bus, Himesh Patel's struggling musician woke up in an alternate reality where no one but him had heard of the Beatles in Danny Boyle's *Yesterday*. He soon started passing their music off as his own in this feel-good romcom written by Richard Curtis, which also featured Lily James, Ed Sheeran and James Corden as themselves, plus an uncredited Robert Carlyle as a still-alive John Lennon.

With a cast that included James Corden, Judi Dench, Idris Elba, Jennifer Hudson, Ian McKellen, Taylor Smith, Rebel Wilson and Ray Winstone, Tom Hooper's creepy *Cats*, based on the hit 1981 stage musical by Andrew Lloyd Webber and T.S. Eliot, became the "what were they thinking?" movie of the year. Critics and audiences found it all too weird and the film grossed just $6.6 million during its opening weekend. Despite frantic re-editing and upgraded special effects, it still bombed at the box-office.

Nicholas Hoult portrayed the tweed-wearing young author of *The Lord of the Rings* in Dome Karukoski's worthy biopic *Tolkien*, which also featured Lily Collins, Derek Jacobi, Pam Ferris and Colm Meaney. Unfortunately for the filmmakers, the family and Estate of J.R.R. Tolkien issued a statement saying that they did not endorse the movie "in any way".

Ryan Reynolds voiced the fuzzy yellow star of Rob Letterman's incomprehensible alternate-world mystery *Pokémon Detective Pikachu*.

It was also a mystery why the Canadian makers of *The Addams Family* decided to replace creator Charles Addams' distinctive cartoon style with horribly bland CGI animation. At least the voice casting rose to the occasion, with Oscar Isaac as "Gomez", Charlize Theron as "Morticia", Chloë Grace Moretz as "Wednesday", Bette Midler as "Grandma" and Snoop Dogg as "Cousin It" (*sic*), along with turns by Allison Janney, Martin Short and Catherine O'Hara.

Three children befriended a Yeti and helped him to return to his family in DreamWorks Animation's *Abominable*, featuring the voices of Chloe Bennet, Sarah Paulson, Eddie Izzard, Tsai Chin and James Hong.

Meanwhile, in Laika's *Missing Link*, the titular creature set out to find his long-lost relatives in the hidden valley of Shangri-La. The starry voice cast included Hugh Jackman, David Walliams, Stephen Fry, Matt Lucas, Zach Galifianakis, Timothy Olyphant, Zoe Saldana and Emma Thompson.

*How to Train Your Dragon: The Hidden World* was the third and final movie in DreamWorks Animation's surprisingly successful trilogy (which has taken more than $1 billion worldwide!). Based on Cressida Cowell's series of fantasy books, the concluding instalment featured the voices of America Ferrera, F. Murray Abraham, Cate Blanchett, Gerard Butler, Craig Ferguson, Jonah Hill, Kristen Wig, Kit Harrington and David Tennant.

When a UFO crash-landed near Mossy Bottom Farm, the titular woolly animal (voiced by Justin Fletcher) helped its cute pilot elude the Ministry of Alien Detection in Aardman Animation's *A Shaun the Sheep Movie: Farmageddon*, which included references to numerous other SF movies and TV shows.

Drew Cullingham's low-budget British comedy *Shed of the Dead* found Spencer Brown's unlikely hero and his agoraphobic friend (Ewen MacIntosh) caught up in the zombie apocalypse. Narrated by

Brian Blessed, the surprise supporting cast included Emily Booth and genre veterans Kane Hodder, Bill Moseley and Michael Berryman.

Debuting director Jack McHenry may have been a little too much influenced by *The Evil Dead*, but his 1930s old-dark-house spoof *Here Comes Hell* was still a considerable achievement on a budget of just £20,000.

Elyse DuFour's conniving babysitter unwittngly released a trio of murderous witches known as "The Three Mothers" as she tried to rob the home of a wealthy occultist in *The Night Sitter*.

Kristian A. Söderström's Swedish-made thriller *Videoman* was heavily influenced by the *giallo* genre, as Stefan Sauk's alcoholic VHS collector searched for a stolen tape that could prevent him from being evicted.

From Nunkie Films/ThomThom Productions, the DVD *A Warning to the Curious* featured Robert Lloyd Parry's acclaimed performance as M.R. James reciting the title story, along with a bonus crowdfunded documentary.

Based on the acclaimed graphic novel by writer Jeph Loeb and artist Jim Lee, *Batman: Hush* found the Caped Crusader (voiced by Jason O'Mara) discovering that a mysterious mastermind was using his old enemies—including Riddler, Scarecrow and The Joker— against him. Jerry O'Connell and Rebecca Romijn turned up as the voices of Superman and Lois Lane, respectively.

Alexandre O. Philippe's feature-length documentary *Memory: The Origins of Alien* commemorated the 40th anniversary of Ridley Scott's original by deconstructing the franchise through a feminist perspective with commentary from Tom Skerritt, Veronica Cartwright, Ronald Shusett, Gary Sherman, Roger Christian, Roger Corman and others.

Criterion's *Godzilla: The Showa-Era Films, 1954–1975* not only collected all fifteen Toho films on Blu-ray for the first time, but it came with a wealth of extras, including audio commentaries, archival interviews with cast and crew members, and even a deluxe hardcover book.

Flicker Alley's Blu-ray/DVD combo of Paul Leni's 1928 movie *The Man Who Laughs* included a documentary about the director and a new booklet by Kevin Brownlow, while the same director's *The Last Warning* (1929) came with its own "visual essay" and a gallery of vintage marketing materials and productions stills.

The welcome high-definition restoration Blu-ray release of *Man of a Thousand Faces* (1957) from Arrow Academy included a commentary by Tim Lucas, a featurette with Kim Newman, original sleeve artwork by Graham Humphreys and an illustrated booklet with an essay on the Lon Chaney, Sr. biopic by the British Film Institute's Vic Pratt.

In Netflix's *In the Tall Grass*, based on the novella by Stephen King and Joe Hill, siblings Becky and Cal (Laysla De Oliveira and Avery Whitted) made the mistake of venturing into a Kansas field of tall grass that hid an eldritch black stone with supernatural powers.

Based on the novel by Tim Lebbon, Netflix's *The Silence* starred Stanley Tucci, Kiernan Sparks and Miranda Otto as members of a family trapped in a world where primeval creatures hunted their prey by sound.

Meanwhile, Lebbon's old writing partner, Gavin Williams, scripted *Await Further Instructions*, which also made its way to Netflix. Directed by Johnny Kevorkian, a Christmas homecoming turned nasty when a fractious family found themselves trapped in their own home by yet another mysterious force.

Believing that humanity was extinct, a teenage girl (Clara Rugaared) raised in a high-tech bunker by a robot (voiced by Rose Byrne) received a surprise when Hilary Swank's mysterious stranger came calling in *I Am Mother*, also from Netflix.

A pair of Brooklyn teenagers (Eden Duncan-Smith and Danté Cruchlow) travelled back in time to prevent a killing in Netflix's *See You Tomorrow*. The movie was produced by Spike Lee and featured a nice cameo by Michael J. Fox.

Netflix's festive animated movie *Klaus* featured a voice cast that included Jason Schwartzman, J.K. Simmons, Rashida Jones and Joan Cusack.

It's a mystery why the Syfy channel thought the world needed yet another "Critters" movie after nearly thirty years, but the South

African-shot *Critters Attack!* saw the toothy aliens crash on Earth again and menace a babysitter and her three young charges. At least Dee Wallace, who starred in the 1986 original, turned up in a supporting role.

Meanwhile, a Canadian-shot sequel, *Critters: A New Binge*, was chopped up into eight ten-minute episodes that aired on Shudder.

Despite a last-minute title change and a misguided coda, *Susan Hill's Ghost Story* on Channel 5 (adapted by Barbara Machin from the author and co-executive producer's short novel *The Small Hand*) starred Douglas Henshall as an antiquarian book dealer who bought a dilapidated haunted house and uncovered a forgotten connection to his own past.

Lifetime's "movie series event", *Heaven, Dark Angel, Fallen Hearts, Gates of Paradise* and *Web of Dreams*, was based on the generational "Casteel Series" by "V.C. Andrews" (actually Andrew Neiderman). The cast included Annalise Basso, Julie Benz, Jason Priestley, Kelly Rutherford and Daphne Zuniga.

The BBC's chilly three-part mini-series of Charles Dickens' "ghostly little book", *A Christmas Carol*, was a darker-than-usual re-imagining by Steven Knight. It starred Australian Guy Pearce as Ebenezer Scrooge, Stephen Graham as Jacob Marley and Andy Serkis as the Ghost of Christmas Past. As the Ghost of Christmas Future, Jason Flemyng replaced an ailing Rutger Hauer, who died in July.

More than forty years after Jon Pertwee first portrayed the character on TV, Mackenzie Crook directed, co-scripted and starred as a more creepy-looking version of the eponymous living scarecrow in the BBC's two-part adaptation of *Worzel Gummidge*. Michael Palin portrayed Worzel's creator, the Green Man.

As part of the BBC's apparent attempt to erode support for *Doctor Who*, instead of a traditional Christmas Day special in 2018, they decided to air it on New Year's Day instead. In 'Resolution', Jodie Whittaker's still irritating Thirteenth Doctor and her not-very-interesting companions (Bradley Walsh, Mandip Gill and Tosin Cole) arrived at an archaeological dig in present-day Sheffield (again!), just in time to prevent a newly revived Reconnaissance Dalek from summoning an invasion fleet. Despite receiving an official total of 7.13 million viewers across all UK platforms, the show also set the record for the lowest overnight viewing of any *Doctor Who* special.

In what seemed like a further effort to derail *Doctor Who*, the BBC then delayed Series 12 until January 2020.

Meanwhile, the new BritBox streaming platform that launched in the UK in December added more than 600 surviving episodes of *Doctor Who*, originally broadcast between 1963 and 1996, to its library.

The eagerly anticipated final showdown between heroes, dragons and the Night King (Slovakian actor-stuntman Vladimir Furdik) and his legion of living-dead White Walkers finally arrived in an episode of HBO's *Game of Thrones* entitled 'The Long Night'. Unfortunately, for many viewers, that's just what it seemed like as the epic battle— one of the most expensive in the history of television—was shrouded in darkness. The cinematographer blamed it on people not knowing how to adjust their TV sets properly.

Meanwhile, more than a million fans were so outraged at how the series ended (spoiler: not everybody survived) that they signed an online petition calling on HBO to remake the eighth season, calling creators David Benioff and D.B. Weiss "woefully incompetent writers when they have no source material [i.e. George R.R. Martin's original books] to fall back on".

Still, 13.6 million viewers tuned in to the initial airing of the feature-length sixth and final episode (rising to 19.3 million with other platforms), breaking records for not just *Game of Thrones* but HBO's entire history.

Aired a week after the series finale, Jeanie Finlay's *Game of Thrones: The Last Watch* was a feature-length documentary about the making of the final season.

Set during the summer of 1985, the improved third season of Netflix's *Stranger Things* from The Duffer Brothers found its group of young friends discovering the problems puberty brings, while the town of Hawkins had to deal with exploding rats as it continued to be menaced by the "Mind Flayer" from the Upside Down.

The series' launch on the streaming service on July 4 was viewed by a record-breaking 40.7 million accounts, and that had risen to 64 million views a month later.

The three episodes comprising the fifth season of Netflix's anthology show *Black Mirror* starred Anthony Mackie, Andrew Scott and Miley Cyrus in near-future dystopian tales involving technology-gone-bad.

Writer and director Mark Gatiss' second attempt to revive the BBC's *Ghost Stories for Christmas*, with a half-hour Christmas Eve adaptation of a lesser-known M.R. James story, *Martin's Close*, was another misfire, despite the casting of a wasted Peter Capaldi. Simon Williams played Stanton, the intrusive narrator.

Based on Joe Hill's 2013 novel, AMC's ten-part *NOS4A2* pitted Ashleigh Cumming's motorcycle-riding high school student against Zachary Quinto's immortal Pied Piper, who kidnapped children in his Rolls-Royce and took them back to his imaginary "Christmas-land".

The BBC's delayed three-part adaptation of H.G. Wells' 1898 novel *The War of the Worlds* finally aired in November. It wasn't worth the wait. Although writer Peter Harness retained the original Edwardian setting, a classy cast (Eleanor Tomlinson, Rafe Spall, Robert Carlyle and Rupert Graves) couldn't even make the alien tripods interesting, while the red-tinged dystopian epilogue was simply risible.

Meanwhile, Fox Network's eight-part European co-production, *War of the Worlds*, a loose contemporary take on Wells' novel, was equally as dull, despite starring Gabriel Byrne and Elizabeth McGovern.

More than 20,000 angry Americans organised by the "Return to Order" Christian campaign signed a petition demanding that the six-part mini-series *Good Omens* be cancelled. Based on the irreverent 1990 novel by the late Terry Pratchett and Neil Gaiman (who executive produced and scripted), Michael Sheen and David Tennant starred, respectively, as best frenemies, the angel Aziraphale and the demon Crowley, who attempted to avert the coming Apocalypse.

Amongst the complaints levelled at the show was that it was "another step to make Satanism appear normal, light and acceptable" and that it "mocks God's wisdom". Even worse, apparently, was that

God was voiced by a woman (Frances McDormand)! Unfortunately, it didn't help that the petition was intially addressed to Netflix instead of the show's actual makers, Amazon Studios and the BBC.

The starry cast of *Good Omens* also included John Hamm, Jack Whitehall, Michael McKean, Miranda Richardson, Brian Cox (as "Death"), Bill Paterson, Josie Lawrence, David Morrissey, Reece Shearsmith, Steve Pemberton, Mark Gatiss, Bendict Cumberbatch, Derek Jacobi and Nicholas Parsons, while Gaiman himself made an uncredited cameo appearance.

Gaiman's troubled *American Gods* stumbled into a delayed second season on Starz (without its two main producers and co-star Gillian Anderson), as Shadow Moon (Ricky Whittle) attempted to prevent Mr. World (Crispin Glover) from inciting a great war between the Old Gods and the New Gods. As usual, Ian McShane's enigmatic "Mr. Wednesday" held the whole thing together.

Samantha Morton joined the Season 9 cast of AMC's *The Walking Dead* as the zombie-skin masked Whisperers' leader, Alpha, who was pursued by Carol (Melissa McBride), seeking revenge for the death of her adopted teenage daughter.

The fifth season of AMC's spin-off show, *Fear the Walking Dead*, brought over Austin Amelio's "Dwight" from the original series.

Netflix's eight-part *Black Summer* was set during the early days of the zombie apocalypse, as a mother (Jaime King) searched for her lost daughter amongst the chaos.

Billy Zane, Miranda Richardson, Sean Bean, Robert Glenister, Adrian Lester and Adam Brody were amongst the cast of Sky's *Curfew*, an eight-episode mash-up of *Wacky Races* and the zombie apocalypse, as a group of amateur drivers in a dystopian not-too-distant future raced across Britain trying to avoid the cannibalistic ghouls that only came out at night.

The Australian series *Glitch*, set in a world in which six people returned from the dead with no memory of what happened to them, reached the end of its third and final series with "the Risen" discovering both their true nature and their fate.

In the third and final season of Netflix's savagely funny zom-com *Santa Clarita Diet*, real estate agents Sheila and Joel (Drew Barrymore and Timothy Olyphant) found their secret threatened on all sides, not least by the incompetent agents of the Knights of Serbia (led by Goran Visnjic's "Dobrivoje Poplovic").

ITV's irreverent six-part comedy series *Zomboat!*, created by William Hartley and Adam Miller, found Leah Brotherhead and Cara Theobold's mismatched sisters trying to escape a zombie-ravaged Birmingham on a canal boat with a pair of hapless stowaways (Hamza Jeetooa and Ryan McKen).

Netflix's ten-part *V Wars* was reminiscent of *The Strain*. Based on a series of comics and anthologies created by Jonathan Maberry, physician/scientist Dr. Luther Swann (Ian Somerhalder) and his infected friend Michael Fayne (Adrian Holmes) battled against a viral vampire infection. It was justifiably cancelled after only one season.

Meanwhile, along *very* similar lines, Brad Wolgast's FBI agent helped an orphan girl (Saniyya Sidney) plan her escape from a top-secret military base after a viral vampirism outbreak caused by a secret government experiment in *The Passage*, based on the trilogy of novels by Justin Cronin. Despite paying $1.75 million for the rights, Fox cancelled the show after the first ten-part season.

Kelly Overton's "Vanessa Van Helsing" found herself sidelined for most of the fourth season of Syfy's *Van Helsing*, as the heroes searched for a way of deafeating the "Dark One" in a dystopian world ruled by vampires. Michael Eklund appeared in two episodes as Abraham Van Helsing.

Based on the overrated 2014 New Zealand comedy of the same name, FX's American spin-off series of *What We Do in the Shadows* comprised ten half-hour episodes about a trio of centuries-old vampires (Kayvan Novak, Matt Berry and Natasia Demetriou) who shared a home on Staten Island. It was about as funny as the original film, despite guest-turns by Doug Jones, Taika Waititi, Tilda Swinton, Paul Reubens, Danny Trejo and Wesley Snipes.

Another New Zealand comedy show, *Wellington Paranormal*, followed the exploits of three members of the Wellington police force investigating such paranormal phenomena as aliens, 1970s ghosts, a female werewolf, zombie cops and one of the vampires from the movie version of *What We Do in the Shadows*.

HBO's Spanish-language comedy *Los Espookys* starred creators Julio Torres and Ana Fabrega as a pair of horror enthusiasts who teamed up with another couple to stage creepy and gory scenes for paying customers.

When a college student (Jake Manley) set out to avenge the death of his mother by pledging himself to an ancient secret society, he found himself caught up in an underground war between magicians and werewolves in Netflix's ten-part *The Order*. Guest stars included Matt Frewer, Jewel Staite and James Marsters.

FX's ten-part *American Horror Story: 1984* was inspired by the "slasher" films of that era, as the victims and killers at Camp Redwood discovered that their souls were trapped there forever.

George Takei portrayed a retired fishing captain in AMC's second season of *The Terror*, subtitled *Infamy*. The ten-episode series was set during World War II, where Japanese-American citizens incarcerated in a Californian internment camp were haunted by a ghostly woman (Kiki Sukezane). Unfortunately, she seemed somewhat superfluous to the story the makers actually wanted to tell.

Inspired by the classic novel by Shirley Jackson, Netflix's ten-part series *The Haunting of Hill House* was marred by its annoyingly fragmented narrative structure, some wildly variable acting and, most damaging of all, its underwhelming scare scenes. A good cast—including Michiel Huisman, Carla Gugino, Henry Thomas, Timothy Hutton and Annabeth Gish—struggled to do something with the soap-opera histrionics, but in the end everyone was defeated by creator Mike Flanagan's lacklustre material and the final episode completely subverted the source material. Russ Tamblyn, who co-starred in Robert Wise's infinitely superior 1963 film adaptation, turned up in one episode.

The CW's *Supernatural* celebrated its 300th show in February with the return of Jeffrey Dean Morgan as Sam and Dean's long-missing monster-hunter father, John Winchester. Having discovered in the Season 14 finale that their lives had always been manipulated by Rob Benedict's capricious Chuck (aka God), the long-running show's finale season found the brothers having to live with their decision not to follow his plan any longer.

Katja Herbers' sceptical forensics psychologist was recruited by Mike Colter's flawed priest-in-training to investigate demonic activity for the Catholic Church in CBS' impressive new supernatural vs. science series, *Evil*. They didn't have to look any further than Michael Emerson's creepy chaos-bringer.

Harriet Dyer's psychic used her ability to talk to the dead to help her veteran LAPD detective father (Paul Blackthorne) and his partner (Justin Cornwell) to solve murders in NBC's *The InBetween*. Sean Bolger portrayed the evil spirit trying to stop her. It lasted just ten episodes.

After having been surprisingly cancelled by Fox after three seasons, *Lucifer* was picked up for a ten-episode run by Netflix, as Tom Ellis' fallen angel revealed his darker side when his old flame, Eve (Inbar Lavi), came looking for the bad boy she fell in love with. In the end, Lucifer was forced to make a difficult choice to save everyone he cared about.

A stiff Jordan Peele proved that he was no replacement for Rod Serling (as either presenter or producer) with yet another dull reboot of the classic TV series *The Twilight Zone* on CBS All Access. Not only did four writers manage to make an updated remake of Richard Matheson's seminal episode 'Nightmare at 20,000 Feet' (now '30,000 feet') feel like watching paint dry, but none of the show's other nine episodes were any better.

Over on Shudder, *Creepshow* was a six-part series co-executive produced by Greg Nicotero and inspired by the 1982 George R. Romero/Stephen King movie of the same name. At least some of the two-story episodes were based on the work of such established names as Stephen King, David J. Schow, Joe R. Lansdale, John Skipp and Joe Hill. The cast also included genre veterans Adrienne Barbeau (who was also in the original film), Tobin Bell, Jeffrey Combs, Bruce Davison and David Arquette.

Although co-executive produced by Stephen King and J.J. Abrams, the second season of Hulu's *Castle Rock* still managed to turn King's fictional Maine town into just another horror soap opera, despite all the nods to the author's original stories.

The second season of the Hulu/Blumhouse anthology series *Into the Dark* kicked off with episodes about a haunted board game, a murderous Thanksgiving, a killer Christmas party and a New Year's Eve game that turned deadly.

M. Night Shyamalan directed the opening episode of Tony Basgallop's ten-part series *Servant* on Apple TV+, as a young nanny (Nell Tiger Free) was hired by a wealthy couple (Toby Kebbell and Lauren Ambrose) dealing with the loss of a child. Rupert Grint's brusque relative suspected that all was not as it seemed.

The arrival of more mer-people in Bristol Cove brought its own problems in the second season of Freeform's *Siren*, as mermaid Ryn (Eline Powell) fought to keep control of her pack.

Returning home, Victoire du Bois' successful horror writer confronted her demons, literally, in Netflix's French-made series *Marianne*.

Shades of *Groundhog Day* in Netflix's *Russian Doll*, as Natasha Lyonne's cynical New Yorker kept returning to the birthday party that she repeatedly died coming home from.

Pedro Pascal played the eponymous bounty hunter in *The Mandalorian*, Disney's first live-action TV spin-off from *Star Wars*. Set between the events of *Return of the Jedi* and *The Force Awakens*, following the collapse of the Galactic Empire, the real star of the show turned out to be a cute "Baby Yoda". Guest stars included Werner Herzog, Nick Nolte, Taika Waititi and Clancy Brown, with uncredited voice work by Mark Hamill and creator Jon Favreau.

Commander Michael Burnham (Sonequa Martin-Green) helped Anson Mount's Captain Pike investigate a series of mysterious "red bursts" with a little help from her half-Vulcan step-brother, Spock (Ethan Peck), in the second season of CBS All Access' *Star Trek: Discovery*. Alex Kurtzman was the new showrunner, and he wisely brought Michelle Yeoh's fabulous Georgiou back as a regular crew-member.

The second season of Netflix's dull reboot of *Lost in Space* kicked off seven months after the first was set, as the Robinsons attempted to track down their missing Robot.

The surviving prisoners explored a new planet, while those left on the Mothership had to fight for survival as the mystery of "The Anomaly" deepened in Season 6 of The CW's *The 100*.

Somehow, the Syfy's *Killjoys* reached a fifth season, as its trio of intergalactic bounty hunters faced a final showdown with Alanna Bale's "The Lady".

After the arrival of an alien artefact on Earth, astronaut Niko Breckenridge (Katee Sackhoff) led a mission to the object's home planet, where they discovered a powerful artificial intelligence in Netflix's ten-part *Another Life*.

Twenty years after the original series aired on The WB, The CW reinvented Melinda Metz's series of late 1990s YA books as *Roswell, New Mexico*, as teenagers—both human and alien—worked together to solve several mysterious deaths centred around the titular desert town.

Aidan Gillen and Michael Malarkey played two very contrary investigators into UFO sightings dealing with Cold War paranoia during the early 1950s in the History Channel's fictionalised *Project Blue Book*. Robert Zemeckis executive-produced.

Set in a near-future London, a scientist's brain-implant technology, which allowed people to instantly share thoughts and emotions, fell into the wrong hands in Amazon Prime's ten-part *The Feed*, starring Guy Burnet and David Thewlis.

Based on Daniel O'Malley's supernatural spy novel, *The Rook* on Starz! featured Emma Greenwell as a woman who woke up in a London park with no memory of who she was or where her super-enhanced powers came from. The classy supporting cast included Joely Richardson, Adrian Lester, Olivia Munn and Gina McKee.

The first season of NBC's *Manifest* continued with the passengers uncovering a conspiracy that dated back to when Flight 828 first disappeared, as they tried to understand their increasingly terrifying "callings".

ABC's *Emergence* was cancelled after just one season, as Allison Tolman's Long Island sheriff protected a young girl (Alexa Swinton) with mysterious powers discovered at a crash site. Clancy Brown and Terry O'Quinn also turned up.

Having made the surprise decision to remain behind to rescue her firstborn, Elisabth Moss' increasingly unhinged June matched wits with Bradley Whitford's enigmatic Commander Lawrence as she tried to smuggle fifty-two children out of Gilead in Season 3 of Hulu's ridiculously popular *The Handmaid's Tale*.

The fourth and final season of Amazon Prime's *The Man in the High Castle* had come a long way from Philip K. Dick's source novel set in a dystopian America ruled by Nazi Germany and Imperial Japan, as Juliana (Alexa Davalos) discovered the existence of multiple parallel universes.

Russell T. Davies' six-part social drama *Years and Years* was set in a dystopian 2029, where Emma Thompson's popularist far-right Prime Minister held Britain in the grip of fear and uncertainty, while monkey flu swept across the world.

Set in a post-apocalyptic Glendale, California, a new high-school student from Canada (Colin Ford) set out on a quest with his misfit classmates to travel through a transformed world to find his girlfriend in the Netflix comedy series *Daybreak*, based on Brian Ralph's graphic novel. Matthew Broderick turned up in flashbacks as the school Principal.

Meanwhile, when everybody else mysteriously vanished from the wealthy Connecticut town of West Ham, the remaining teenagers were forced to create their own society—with predictable results—in Netflix's ten-part series *The Society*. It only lasted for one season.

In the second season of the Danish Netflix series *The Rain*, set in a post-apocalyptic world in which a deadly virus wiped out most of the population, the survivors set out to find a cure before one of their number could be used as a weapon to take over the world.

It was a wonder how *The Purge* even got a second and final season on the USA Network, as the show concentrated on the fates of four interconnected characters folowing the annual night of sanctioned violence.

Jason Momoa starred as a sightless warrior in a post-apocalyptic world in which nearly everyone was blind in *See* on Apple TV+, while Ronald D. Moore's *For All Mankind* on the same streaming service was set in an alternate history where the Soviet Union had won the space race.

The third season of the Brazillian show *3%*, set in a dystopian future in which twenty-year-olds underwent a series of challenges so that a small percentage of survivors could live in a utopia called "Offshore", ran for seven episodes on Netflix.

A disparate group of Berlin residents had to face the imminent danger of an approaching asteroid wiping out most of Western Europe in the eight-part German series *8 Days*, while the second season of the German-made *Dark* found the citizens of Winden dealing with uncertain pasts and futures, as the ill-fated town prepared for an apocalyptic event more than thirty years in its future.

After his plan to save the world didn't work, the second season of Hulu's half-hour comedy series *Future Man* found Josh Futturman (Josh Hutcherson) and his companions messing with time travel in their attempts to bring down a secret terrorist organisation called the Pointed Circle. Guest stars included Haley Joel Osment and executive producer Seth Rogan.

The struggling jazz band from South London travelled back to the 1950s in the second and final series of the ITV sitcom *Timewasters*, while Paul Rudd's advertising executive came face-to-face with his better clone in the Netflix comedy *Living with Yourself*.

The second season of creator and star Seth MacFarlane's spot-on *Star Trek* parody *The Orville* on Fox Network featured fan-pleasing guest turns from Kelly Hu, Robert Picardo, Ted Danson, Victor Garber, Tim Russ, F. Murray Abraham and Tony Todd, as the comedy series took on an increasingly more dramatic edge.

David Fincher co-executive produced the eighteen animated shorts that comprised Netflix's *Love, Death + Robots*. Episodes were based on stories by John Scalzi, Joe R. Lansdale, Alastair Reynolds, Peter F. Hamilton, Michael Swanwick and others.

*Weird City* on streaming platform YouTube Premium was a quirky six-part anthology series created by Jordan Peele and Charlie Sanders set in a socially segregated city of the future. The cast included LeVar Burton, Rosario Dawson and Mark Hamill.

Michael B. Jordan, Dakota Fanning, Maisie Williams and David Tennant were amongst the voice cast of streaming service Rooster Teeth's animated SF series *gen:LOCK*, set in the year 2068.

∽

*His Dark Materials*, the BBC/HBO's ambitious eight-part adaptation of the first book in Philip Pullman's fantasy series, starred Dafne Keen as young orphan Lyra, who travelled North to rescue a group of kidnapped children and discovered that she was destined to free her alternate world from the religious-militaristic grip of the Magisterium. The impressive supporting cast included an icy Ruth Wilson (and her evil monkey "dæmon"), a miscast Lin-Manuel Miranda, Ariyon Bakare, Terence Stamp, James McAvoy as "Lord Asriel", and the voices of Helen McCrory and David Suchet.

*His Darker Materials* was a weekly companion podcast, hosted by Dave Corkery and Helen O'Hara, that discussed each week's episode with cast members.

Henry Cavill (sporting a hilariously bad silver-grey wig) starred as the medieval monster-hunter-for-hire "Geralt of Rivia" in Netflix's *The Witcher*, based on the insanely popular series of fantasy books by Andrzej Sapkowski.

In the second season of The CW's *The Outpost*, warrior woman Talon (Jessica Green) attempted to protect her home against the Prime Order while trying to defeat Robin Malcolm's "The Mistress".

*Angel*'s Alexis Denisof turned up as the new headmaster at Mystic Falls' Salvatore Boarding School for the Young and Gifted in Season 2 of The CW's *Vampire Diaries* spin-off, *Legacies*.

The fourth season of Syfy's *The Magicians* found Eliot (Hale Appleman) possessed by an ancient monster and the rest of Brakebills' students transformed into new personalities under a magical witness protection programme. The season concluded with the surprise death of leading character Quentin Coldwater (Jason Ralph).

The CW decided to revive its cult 1990s show *Charmed* for the YA audience with a new trio of racially diverse witchy sisters (Melonie Diaz, Madeleine Mantock and Sarah Jeffery).

After having signed her soul away to the Dark Lord in the show's first season, Kiernan Shipka's teenage witch explored her new powers over nine episodes in Season 2 of Netflix's *Chilling Adventures of Sabrina*.

Orlando Bloom's human detective teamed up with his faerie-warrior lover (Cara Delavigne) to solve a series of murders in the steampunk series *Carnival Row* on Amazon Prime Video Streaming.

The third and final season of Freeform's *Shadowhunters*, based on the YA books by Cassandra Clare, concluded with the Shadowhunters and Downworlders having to team up to stop Jonathan Morganstern (Luke Baines) from wreaking havoc on the Shadow world.

Meanwhile, in Netflix's eight-part *The OA Part II*, Brit Marling's injured "original angel" transported her consciousness into an alternate-universe version of herself. Jason Isaacs, Alice Krige and the late Scott Wilson co-starred.

The second and final overly trippy season of Syfy's *Happy!* found Christopher Meloni's former cop-turned-hitman and his eponymous constant companion, a perky flying blue unicorn voiced by Patton Oswalt, trying to save Hailey Hansen (Bryce Lorenzo) from the clutches of Smoothie (Patrick Fischler). Based on the graphic novel by Grant Morrison and Darick Robertson, screen legend Ann-Margret guest-starred in two episodes, an uncredited Amanda Palmer turned up in the penultimate episode, and Jeff Goldblum was the voice of God in the finale.

Shades of the 1970s series *The Ghosts of Motley Hall*! Charlotte Ritchie and Kiell Smith-Bynoe portrayed a young couple who inherited a dilapidated country house haunted by a group of squabbling spirits (played by the original *Horrible Histories* and *Yonderland* team) in the BBC's half-hour sitcom *Ghosts*. Somehow it became the highest-rated comedy show on British TV in 2019.

After reformed demon Michael (Ted Danson) was given one last chance by Maya Rudolph's Judge Jen to prove his theory that his four humans could be redeemed to save humanity, Eleanor (Kristen Bell) became the neighbourhood architect looking after a new quartet of test subjects in the fourth and final season of NBC's comedy sitcom *The Good Place*. Guest stars included Timothy Olyphant, Lisa Kudrow and Mary Steenburgen.

The third and final season of Netflix's *A Series of Unfortunate Events*, based on the popular "Lemony Snicket" (Daniel Handler) books, found Neil Patrick Harris' dastardly Count Olaf finally put on trial for his plots against the three Baudelaire orphans. The show came to a satisfying ending as the contents of the coveted sugar bowl were finally revealed. Guest stars included Joan Cusack, Richard E. Grant and Peter McNicol.

Based on Jim Henson's 1982 fantasy movie, the prequel puppet series *The Dark Crystal: Age of Resistance* featured the voices of Mark Hamill, Sigourney Weaver, Taron Egerton, Helena Bonham Carter, Natalie Dormer, Toby Jones, Mark Strong, Jason Isaacs, Simon Pegg and Andy Samberg, amongst others. Netflix cancelled the show after just one season.

Netflix's ten-part *Chambers* was yet another twist on the hoary old *Hands of Orlac* premise, as a teenager (Sivan Alyra Rose) discovered herself taking on the personality traits of the donor of her heart transplant. Uma Thurman played the dead girl's grieving mother.

The CW's reboot of *Nancy Drew* found the teenage sleuth (Kennedy McMann) and her friends investigating a supernatural murder mystery that revolved around the legend of a ghostly beauty queen haunting their home town of Horseshoe Bay.

The pupils of Hazelbrook Academy discovered that their mysterious new head (Nicholas Gleaves) was using hypnotism to take control of the school in the BBC's ten-part *The Demon Headmaster*, a remake of the 1996–98 children's series created by Helen Creswell and Gillian Cross.

The third season of ITV's CGI *Thunderbirds Are Go* continued with the voices of Rosamund Pike (as "Lady Penelope"), Sandra Dickinson, Lee Majors (as "Jeff Tracy"), Sylvester McCoy, Jennifer Saunders and Larry Lamb, as International Rescue attempted to avert a series of disasters, both natural and man-made.

Nickelodeon's animated *Rise of the Teenage Mutant Ninja Turtles* resurrected the green superheroes in a shell for a whole new generation. Guest voices included Maurice LaMarche, Lena Headey, John Cena and veteran Frank Welker.

Fox's *The Simpsons* celebrated its 30th year on the air with the Halloween episode 'Treehouse of Horror XXX', which featured a demonic Maggie; a mission to rescue Milhouse from another dimension in a *Stranger Things* parody; a dead Homer's spirit jumping into some new bodies, and Selma finally finding love with Kang the alien in a spoof of *The Shape of Water*. The show also honoured another American holiday with 'Thanksgiving of Horror', a further trilogy of terror tales that featured guest voice Charlie Brooker. It was also the final *Simpsons* credit for Russi Taylor, who died in July.

Meanwhile, *Family Guy* from the same network commemorated twenty years on the air with Stewie making a robot duplicate of Brian, the Griffins finding themselves rebooted as superheroes, and a nice season finale tribute to the late Adam West.

Set three decades after the original 1980s graphic novel, in an alternate universe where a group of outlawed masked vigilantes confronted members of a revived white supremacist group, creator Alan Moore's name was as usual nowhere to be found on Damon Lindelof's nine-part "remix" of *Watchmen* for HBO. The starry cast included Regina King, Louis Gossett Jr., Frances Fisher, Don Johnson, Jean Smart as a wily FBI agent and Jeremy Irons as whacked-out super-villain "Adrian Veidt" (aka Ozymandias, "The Smartest Man in the World").

Released on the on-demand DC Universe channel, the first season of *Doom Patrol* was a smart and funny re-imagining of the characters introduced in the 1960s *My Greatest Adventure* comic and previously seen in an episode of *Titans*. A reluctant group of misfits— Crazy Jane (Diane Guerrero), Elasti-Girl (April Boelby), Negative Man (Matt Bomer) and Robotman (Brendan Fraser)—were brought together by Dr. Niles Caulder aka "The Chief" (Timothy Dalton), who then promptly disappeared into another dimension reached through an albino donkey.

Over on *Titans* itself, the second season introduced a new version of Superboy (Joshua Orpin) and Iain Glen turned up as Bruce Wayne, before the team had to deal with the murder of Aqualad (Drew Van Acker) and prepare for a final showdown with Slade Wilson/ Deathstroke (Esai Morales).

Meanwhile, DC Universe inexplicably cancelled the James Wan-produced *Swamp Thing* series after its first episode, but allowed it to run for a truncated ten-episode season. Crystal Reed starred as "Abby Arcane", who returned home to investigate the mysteries of a Louisiana swamp. The rest of the cast included Virginia Madsen, Will Patton, Jennifer Beals, Ian Ziering and Tim Russ, while there were guest appearances from Adrienne Barbeau (who starred in the 1982 movie version) and Macon Blair, who showed up as "The Phantom Stranger".

The fourth and final series of AMC's *Preacher* moved the action to Australia, as Jesse (Dominic Cooper) and his friends made one final attempt to avert God's Apocalypse.

Over on The CW's *Arrow*, Oliver (Stephen Amell) finally managed to reunite the team one last time as a Crisis on Infinite Earths loomed.

Barry (Grant Gustin) and Iris (Candice Patton) discovered that their daughter from the future (Jessica Parker Kennedy) had unwittingly betrayed them in the fifth season of *The Flash*, before Barry learned in Season 6 that he was destined to die in the forthcoming Crisis.

Having lost the support of the DEO in Season 4, the fifth season of The CW's *Supergirl* found the Girl of Steel and her friends battling a new villain, Leviathan. Meanwhile, Nicole Maines became the first transgender actress to play a transgender superhero ("Dreamer"), and Jon Cryer turned up as "Lex Luthor".

After a promising start, Ruby Rose's caped crusader spent most of her time fretting about her ex-girlfriend (Megan Tandy) and her sociopathic sister (Rachel Skarsten) in The CW's *Batwoman*. Jefferson Pierce (Cress Williams) attempted to protect his superpowered daughters from the meta/human war in Season 3 of the network's *Black Lightning*, and John Constantine (Matt Ryan) had to decide who to save from Hell in the fourth season of the increasingly bonkers *DC's Legends of Tomorrow*.

The CW's much-anticipated annual DC crossover was 'Crisis on Infinite Earths', based on the 1985–86 comic-book serial by Marv Wolfman and George Perez. The five-part mini-series added Williams' Black Lightning and Rose's Batwoman to the mix, as Green

Arrow, The Flash, Supergirl, the Legends and a host of other heroes tried to prevent the evil Anti-Monitor (LaMonica Garrett) from destroying the multiverse.

It might not have been up there with *Avengers: Endgame*, but there was a lot of fun in spotting the cameos from other DC shows and movies—including Brandon Routh's Man of Steel from *Superman Returns*, Tom Welling's Clark Kent and Erica Durance's Lois Lane from *Smallville*, Kevin Conroy's ageing Dark Knight from *Batman: The Animated Series*, Ashley Scott's "Helena Kyle"/"The Huntress" from *Birds of Prey*, Johnathon Schaech's "Jonah Hex", Stephen Lobo's "John Corrigan", John Wesley Shipp and Ezra Miller as the 1990s TV "Flash" and the 2016 movie "Flash" respectively, Tom Ellis' "Lucifer Morningstar", Brec Bassinger's "Stargirl" and Derek Mills' "SwampThing", along with fleeting appeareances from Burt Ward, Robert Wuhl, Wil Wheaton and co-creator Marv Wolfman.

Unlike *Swamp Thing*, Syfy's misconceived *Krypton* was one of those DC shows that really didn't deserve a second (but thankfully final) season. The *Superman* prequel dragged on, as it followed the rebels' rebellion against Colin Salmon's scheming General Zod.

The fifth and final season of Fox's Batman prequel *Gotham*, subtitled *Legend of the Dark Knight*, found Gordon (Ben McKenzie), Bruce (David Mazouz) and their various unlikely allies trying to bring the fragmented city back under control again, before a final episode jumped ten years into the future to reveal the emergence of a new saviour.

Meanwhile, in another Batman prequel over on Epix, Jack Bannon played a young Alfred Pennyworth, a former British special-forces soldier who became the butler for Thomas Wayne, in *Pennyworth*. The supporting cast included singer Paloma Faith and Jason Flemyng, while Felicity Kendal turned up as "Baroness Ortsey" at a debauched party held by Jonjo O'Neill's 1960s version of Aleister Crowley.

The third and final season of Netflix's *Jessica Jones* found Krysten Ritter's reluctant Marvel superhero teaming up with a newly empowered Trish (Rachael Taylor) to stop serial killer Gregory Sallinger (Jeremy Bobb). Carrie-Anne Moss and Rebecca De Mornay were back, while David Tennant's Killgrave left a message and Mike Colter's cancelled Luke Cage dropped by for the series finale.

The shortened sixth and penultimate season of ABC's *Agents of S.H.I.E.L.D.* found the agents scattered across the galaxy and still mourning the loss of Phil Coulson (Clark Gregg, who soon returned in a different role). The two-part finale (aired back-to-back in America) sent the team to Hell before they ended up time travelling back to New York City in 1931.

Jon Bernthal returned for the delayed second and final series of Marvel's *The Punisher* on Netflix, which featured guest turns from Corben Bernsen and Annette O'Toole.

The third and final season of FX's increasingly wearisome *Legion*, a spin-off/prequel of Marvel's *X-Men*, found the super-gifted David (Dan Stevens) running his own hippie cult, as characters jumped around in time trying to deafeat the "Shadow King". Harry Lloyd played a young Charles Xavier.

In the third and apparently final season of Marvel's *Runaways* on Hulu, the group of gifted children battled Elizabeth Hurley's "Morgan le Fey", encountered aliens, travelled to another dimension and went back in time to change the past and prevent a tragedy.

Based on the Dark Horse comic created by singer Gerard Way and Gabriel Bá, Netflix's *The Umbrella Academy* was about an estranged adopted family of former child superheroes who were forced to reunite to avert an impending global apocalypse. Singer Mary J. Blige turned up as a time-travelling assassin.

Created by Eric Kripke and based on the comics series by Garth Ennis and Darick Robertson, Amazon Prime's *The Boys* followed a group of out-of-control superheroes, "The Seven", and the shadowy corporation that funded and marketed them. Guest stars included Elisabeth Shue, Simon Pegg, Goran Visnjic, Jim Beaver, Haley Joel Osment, Billy Zane and Tara Reid, with an uncredited Jimmy Fallon and executive producer Seth Rogen playing versions of themselves.

A widowed mother (Alisha Wainwright) discovered that her seven-year-old son (Ja'Siah Young) had superpowers in Netflix's *Raising Dion*, based on the comics series by Dennis Liu and Jason

Piperberg. The nine-part series co-starred and was executive produced by Michael B. Jordan.

*The Tick* finally got a full ten-part second season on Prime Video before the streaming service cancelled it.

The Turkish series *The Protector* on Netflix featured Çagatay Ulusoy as a young man living in modern Istanbul who acquired superpowers and found himself defending the city from an immortal enemy.

The seventh season of the BBC's *Father Brown* included the M.R. James-inspired episode 'The Whistle in the Dark', in which Mark Williams' sleuthing parson crashed an occult dinner party where a carved bone whistle said to possess supernatural powers—perhaps the inspiration for James' famous story—was being offered for sale to the highest bidder. Despite the double-murderer being revealed as one of the guests, there was a to-be-expected enigmatic ending.

Brendan Gleeson's gruff detective Bill Hodges investigated the death of a local author in the third and final season of AT&T's *Mr. Mercedes*, based on the trilogy by Stephen King. The supporting cast included Kate Mulgrew and Bruce Dern.

DCI John Barnaby (Neil Dudgeon) and DS Jamie Winter (Nick Hendrix) were called in to investigate a murder during a village's local comic book convention in a Season 20 episode of ITV's *Midsomer Murders*. 'The Ghost of Causton Abbey' was a two-part episode about a murder victim found boiled to death in a vat of beer after a new brewery opened on the site of a "cursed" abbey. Guest stars included singers Elaine Paige and Anita Harris.

Co-writer/executive producer John Turturro, Damian Hardung and Rupert Everett starred in the eight-episode *The Name of the Rose*, an Italian/German co-production based on Umberto Eco's medieval murder mystery. The narration was by former "Doctor Who" Peter Davison.

After Season 6 finished on such a perfect note, it was a shame that the seventh and final season of CBS' *Elementary* limped through an additional thirteen episodes that quickly ignored that ending and once again found Holmes (Johnny Lee Miller) and Watson (Lucy Liu) solving crimes back in New York City. James Frain joined the series as tech billionaire villain "Odin Reichenbach" (get it?), while the series finale featured not just one, but two leaps forward in time.

At Easter, BBC2 broadcast *The League of Gentlemen: Live Again!*, a truncated record of the TV series' 20th-anniversary stage show from the year before.

The sixth and final season of Comedy Central's *Drunk History*—which featured historical re-enactments hosted by an inebriated storyteller—debuted in January with a spoof re-telling of Mary Shelley's *Frankenstein*, as Seth Rogen's scientist brought his creation (Will Ferrell) to life. The supporting cast included Elijah Wood as Percy Shelley and Evan Rachel Wood as Mary.

In Netflix's half-hour mockumentary, *Frankenstein's Monster's Monster, Frankenstein*, David Harbour examined his actor father's legacy in a made-for-TV play. Harbour played both himself and his Orson Welles-like father, and the supporting cast included Mary Woronov, Alfred Molina and Michael Lerner.

Shown on Hallowe'en on Sky Arts in the UK, *The Strange Life of Dr. Frankenstein* was a French-made documentary about the literary aspects of the legend that used film clips and talking heads to tell its story. Meanwhile, *Discovering Horror on Film*, broadcast the same night on Sky Arts, relied on pretty much the same technique as four critics discussed some seminal genre titles. Both were as dull at ditchwater.

ITV's five-part reality show *Killer Camp* was inspired by 1980s "slasher" films, as eleven contestants at a lakeside lodge attempted to earn cash and avoid being "killed".

Produced over a decade with its subject's participation, the BBC's documentary *The Worlds of Ursula K. Le Guin* featured Neil Gaiman, Margaret Atwood, David Mitchell and Michael Chabon paying tribute to the American feminist author's life and legacy.

Katie Him's meta-drama *Opening Pandora's Box* on BBC Radio 4 was about a writer (Kate O'Flynn) attempting to turn G.W. Pabst's 1929 silent movie *Pandora's Box* into a radio play.

In Tom Fowler's *Suspicious Minds*, which was originally a stage play at the Edinburgh Festival, a couple (Susannah Fielding and Tom Mothersdale) tried to save their failing marriage by taking a time-travelling holiday to Ancient Rome, 19th-century England, the decks of the *Titanic* and a 1973 Elvis Presley concert.

Toby Stephens returned as James Bond in May in BBC Radio 4's feature-length dramatisation of Ian Fleming's 1954 novel, *Live and Let Die*. As usual directed by Martin Jarvis, the supporting cast included Rutina Wesley as "Solitaire" and John Standing as "M".

Tony Robinson starred in Jon Canter's dystopian comedy *Dangerous Visions: I'm Dying to Help*, in which a future Prime Minister attempted to put a limit on the UK population's growing life expectancy, while *Stillcide* was a series of twelve fifteen-minute readings of Cynan Jones' collection of stories, set in a dystopian near-future where water was a precious commodity.

In September, Jonathan Holloway re-imagined Dostoyevsky's 1846 doppelgänger novella as a steampunk drama in BBC Radio 4's *Dangerous Visions: The Double*.

Writers Daisy Johnson and Mariana Enríquez, biographer and critic Ruth Franklin, and academic Melissa Edmundson Makala discussed how female authors had shaped the ghost story in the half-hour *Haunted Women*, and Simon Hollis investigated how writers and filmmakers had used folk horror in *Fear in the Furrows*.

Toby Jones starred as the titular Danish author in BBC Radio 3's *Dance Til You Bleed: The World According to Hans Christian Anderson*, which in November presented five fifteen-minute dramatisations by Lucy Catherine of Anderson's darker tales ('The Most Incredible Thing', 'The Red Shoes', 'Anne Lisbeth', 'The Ice Maiden' and 'The Wicked Prince').

Lee Ingleby read Michelle Paver's 1930s-set Arctic ghost story *Dark Matter* over ten fifteen-minute episodes in December.

*Ghost Stories from Ambridge*, a spin-off from the popular radio serial *The Archers*, featured Jim Lloyd (John Rowe) reading E.F. Benson's 'The Room in the Tower', M.R. James' 'Lost Hearts' and W.W. Jacobs' 'The Monkey's Paw' to an assembly of residents from the fictional county of Borsetshire.

Neil Gaiman was all over British radio at Christmas. The BBC's *Radio 3 in Concert* on December 23 was a recording from the month before at London's Barbican. Gaiman read from his books, interspersed with music by Gershwin, Wagner, Herrman, Britten and others, while David Tennant and the author's wife, Amanda Palmer, made guest appearances.

Broadcast on Christmas Day on BBC Radio 4, *Neil Gaiman's "Chivalry"* starred Glenda Jackson in a half-hour story about an elderly woman who found the Holy Grail in an Oxfam charity shop and received a visit from a young knight named Galaad (Kit Harrington).

Writer/director Julian Simpson reinterpreted H.P. Lovecraft's original story as a slice of folk horror based around an alleged 1980 UFO sighting in rural Suffolk in *The Whisperer in Darkness* (a follow-up to 2018's *The Case of Charles Dexter Ward*) for the BBC Radio 4's *Sounds* podcast. Simpson's wife, Jana Carpenter, co-starred along with Barnaby Kay as, respectively, occult podcasters Kennedy Fisher and Matthew Heawood.

During the first week of January, the half-hour *Ghost Stories of Walter de la Mare* on BBC Radio 4 Extra featured Richard E. Grant reading 'All Hallows', Toby Jones reading 'Seaton's Aunt', Kenneth Cranham reading 'Crewe', Anthony Head reading 'A Recluse' and Julian Wadham reading 'The Almond Tree'.

Colin Baker starred in Eddie Robson's two-part adventure *Doctor Who—Industrial Evolution*, set in 19th-century Lancashire, while Jonathan Morris' two-part *The Curse of Davros*, featured the Time Lord's arch-enemy.

The fifteen-minute episodes of *Algernon Blackwood's Ghost Stories* featured Matthew Marsh reading 'Keeping His Promise' (1906), 'The Land of Green Ginger' (1927), 'The Transfer' (1911), 'The Man Who Lived Backwards' (1935) and 'The Kit Bag' (1908).

Eric Thompson, Sheila Grant, Judy Bennett and Peter Baldwin starred on BBC Radio 4 Extra in a repeat of John Tydeman's hour-long adaptation of John Wyndham's *Chocky*, from 1968.

Over five episodes in March, Mark Elstob starred as "Number Six" in Nicholas Briggs' second series of *The Prisoner*, based on episodes of the cult 1967 TV series.

First broadcast in 2002, David Soul starred as "Ted" in Harlan Ellison's post-apocalyptic story *I Have No Mouth, and I Must Scream*, with the author himself voicing the psychotic computer "AM".

In March, Matthew Graham and filmmaker Peter Strickland re-imagined Nigel Kneale's 1972 TV film *The Stone Tape* as an hour-long radio broadcast, with a cast that included Romola Garai, Julian Rhind-Tutt, Dean Andrews, Julian Barratt and a cameo by the star of the original version, Jane Asher. A special 3-D binaural mix designed for headphones was also available online and for download from BBC iPlayer Radio.

*Short Works: A Season of Murder, Mystery and Suspense* featured Owen Teale reading fifteen-minute adaptations of Edgar Allan Poe's lesser-known stories 'Morella', 'The Cask of Amontillado', 'Metzengerstein', 'The Man in the Crowd' and 'Ms. Found in a Bottle'.

*Five Tales by Saki* featured fifteen-minute dramatisations of H.H. Munro's 'The Lumber Room', 'The Schartz-Metterklume Method', 'Fur', 'The Toys of Peace' and 'The Open Window', from 2005.

From 1990, David Calcutt's feature-length dramatisation of H.G. Wells' 1896 novel *The Island of Dr. Moreau* featured Kenneth Colley, Neal Foster and Garard Green as "Dr. Moreau".

*A Night with a Vampire* was a five-part series on BBC Radio 4 Extra in which David Tennant read from five Victorian vampire tales by Antonie Calmet, Alexi Tolstoy, Guy de Maupassant, Mary E. Wilkins-Freeman and Théophile Gautier.

Andrew Faulds, David Jacobs and David Kossoff starred in the twenty-episode *Journey Into Space—The Red Planet*, a repeat of the second in Charles Chilton's radio trilogy, from 1954.

Horror veterans Peter Cushing and Vincent Price co-starred in a welcome repeat of Robert Holmes' *Aliens in the Mind*, a six-part science fiction serial from 1977.

Gary Watson, Barbara Shelley and Freda Dowie starred in Giles Cooper's six-part adaptation of John Wyndham's *The Day of the Triffids* from 1968, while Joanna Tope read an abridged version of Wyndham's *Trouble with Lichen* over five episodes.

In August, Tim McInnerny read five, fifteen-minute tales for *Robert Aickman Stories* ('Le Miroir', 'Raising the Wind', 'The Fully-

Conducted Tour', 'The Coffin House' and 'Just a Song at Twilight'), while Michael and Mollie Hardwick's fifteen-minute adaptation of M. Burrage's 1931 story *The Waxwork* was originally broadcast in 1963.

A re-run of the 1984 series *Haunted* at the end of the month on BBC Radio 4 Extra included Patricia Mays' half-hour dramatisations of Agatha Christie's 'The Lamp', R. Chetwynd-Hayes' 'The Liberated Tiger' and 'Which One?', J.B. Priestley's 'The Grey Ones' and the anonymously-written 'The Dead Man of Varley Grange'.

First broadcast in 1978, *Before the Screaming Begins*, in which a wedding anniversary was interrupted by an alien invasion, featured James Laurenson, Jennifer Piercy and Patrick Troughton.

Charles Kay, Gordon Dulieu and Pauline Yates starred in Dan Rebellato's three-part dramatisation of John Wyndham's *The Midwich Cuckoos*, repeated from 1982.

From five years later, Michael Payne's hour-long drama *Lady Faustus* starred Rula Lenska as the mysterious woman of the title.

In October, Peter Meakin starred in a 1996 hour-and-a-half dramatisation of Robert Westall's 1991 novel, *The Stones of Muncaster Cathedral*, while *Spine Chillers* included a forty-five minute adaptation of Peter Redgrove's 'Dracula in White', repeated from 1984.

Colin Baker and Nicola Bryant recreated their roles as the Doctor and companion Peri in Brian and Paul Finch's series of *Doctor Who—The Lost Stories*.

From 1993, Peter Mackie's hour-long dramatisation of *The Mysterious Mansion* was based on the 1832 short story 'La Grande Bretèche' by French writer Honoré de Balzac.

First broadcast in December 1994, Nick Fisher's *Playing with Dracula* starred Nickolas Grace as the mysterious Byron Redgrave, who was ready to get his teeth into an amateur acting group making horror movies. All the other characters were named after those in Bram Stoker's original novel.

Gregory Evans' hour-long play *The Hex* was loosely based on M.R. James' 'Casting the Runes'.

*Ray Bradbury's Tales of the Bizarre* from 1995–96 featured half-hour adaptations of such stories as 'Night Call', 'Have I Got a Chocolate Bar for You!', 'The Jar' and 'The Electric Grandmother'.

From 1991, *The Shape of Things to Come* was a forty-five minute adaptation by Ray Bradbury of his 1948 short story 'The Shape of Things', while H.G. Wells' 1895 novel *The Wonderful Visit* was adapted into an hour-long drama by Stephen Gallagher, from 1988.

Ed Stoppared returned as the British pilot of the future in Simon Guerrier's seven-part *Dan Dare: Reign of the Robots*.

The third and final twenty-episode series of Charles Chilton's *Journey Into Space—The World in Peril* from 1955 found Jet Morgan and his crew returning to Mars to prevent a Martian invasion. It featured the voices of future Member of Parliament Andrew Faulds (as Jet), comedian Alfie Bass, future Hammer director Don Sharp and BBC disc-jockey David Jacobs.

Over Christmas, *Doctor Who: Serpent Crest* starred Tom Baker as the Fourth Doctor, alongside Susan Jameson's Mrs. Wibbsey, in Paul Magrs' two-part radio dramas 'Tsar Wars', 'The Broken Crown', 'Aladdin Time' and 'The Hexford Invasion'.

Jessica Biel played a journalist for American Public Radio investigating the mysterious disappearance of more than 300 people from a secret Tennessee neuroscience research facility in Facebook Watch's ten-part podcast *Limetown*. Stanley Tucci portrayed her missing uncle.

From Bafflegab Productions, a new audio production of M.R. James' *Casting the Runes*, from a script by Stephen Gallagher, featured the voice talents of Anna Maxwell Martin, Tom Burke, and Reece Shearsmith as "Karswell".

In January, The Nunkie Theatre's Robert Lloyd Parry gave a full theatrical performance of James' 'Casting the Runes' at The Old Red Lion in Islington, before taking the show around the country. The following month Parry read 'Pickman's Model' at the same venue as part of the London Lovecraft Festival.

Having premiered at the end of 2017 at London's Almeida Theatre, the stage production of *The Twilight Zone* finally made its West End debut in March at the Ambassadors Theatre. Based on stories by Rod

Serling, Charles Beaumont and Richard Matheson, the show closed on June 1, despite generally positive reviews.

In April, Tim Burton's iconic 1988 movie *Beetle Juice* was adapted by Eddie Perfect, Scott Brown and Anthony King into a Broadway musical starring Alex Brightman as the stripe-suited ghost-with-the-most. Unfortunately, Alex Timbers' stage production repeated the persistent mistake of calling itself *Beetlejuice*.

Matthew Lutton's stage production of Stanislaw Lem's metaphysical 1961 novel *Solaris* (which has been filmed twice) transferred from Edinburgh to London's Lyric Hammersmith Theatre. In a gender-reversed role, Polly Frame played the scientist who was "visited" by a dead loved one (Keegan Joyce), while a videoed Hugo Weaving turned up as a deceased crew member on a space station plagued by delusions and ghostly visitations.

Inspired by the 1951 Ealing movie, Sean Foley's stage version of *The Man in the White Suit* at London's Wyndham Theatre starred Stephen Mangan as the hapless inventor of a fabric that never got dirty or wore out, much to the displeasure of the British textile business.

Tom Scutt's *Berberian Sound Studio* at the Donmar Warehouse was based on Peter Strickland's 2012 cult movie about a British sound engineer working in 1970s Italy on a brutal *giallo* film. Tom Brooke starred in the stage version as the audio expert whose sanity was slowly slipping away.

The Lowry, Salford, was the unlikely venue for the UK premiere of the 2006 Broadway production *Dr. Seuss's How the Grinch Stole Christmas! The Musical*, based on the much-loved children's classic. Griff Rhys Jones was the show's canine narrator, while Edward Baker-Duly portrayed the not-nearly-mean-enough title character.

86-year-old 1960s British pop music icon Petula Clarke turned up as the "Bird Woman" in a revival of *Mary Poppins* at London's Prince Edward Theatre. Scripted by *Downtown Abbey* creator Julian Fellowes, Zizi Strallen played Mary, while Charlie Stemp was Bert.

Jay McGuiness, Wendi Peters, Kimberley Walsh and Matthew Kelly starred in *BIG*—yet another film-to-stage musical—which ran for a nine-week limited season at London's Dominion Theatre.

As part of the Vampfest: The 4th International Vampire Film and Arts Festival (IVFAF) being held in London over July, the Victorian theatre group Don't Go in the Cellar put on *Dracula's Ghost* for one night at Upstairs at the Gatehouse in Highgate Village. The same location also hosted the company's *Sherlock Holmes versus the Sussex Vampire* and magician Jasper Blakeley's one-man show, *Evan Helsing: Welsh Vampire Hunter*.

Iain Bell and Emma Jenkins' opera, *Jack the Ripper: The Women of Whitechapel*, was actually about the impoverished victims rather than the serial killer himself. It had a brief run at the London Coliseum.

The same venue also played host to Luc Plamondon and Richard Cocciante's tasteless musical *Notre Dame De Paris*, with Angelo Del Vecchio as a ginger-wigged "Quasimodo". Originally slated when it played London's West End in 2000, this original French version with subtitles was still panned by the critics.

*Star Trek: The Next Generation*'s Marina Sirtis portrayed a "mature" actress who used to appear in a 1970s British sci-fi show in Michael Dennis' debut comedy *Dark Sublime* at London's Trafalgar Studio 2. Mark Gatiss voiced a highly-strung robot.

Richard Eyre's summer revival of Noël Coward's perennially popular *Blithe Spirit* at the Theatre Royal, Bath, featured Jennifer Saunders as the maniacal medium, Madame Arcati, who managed to materialise the dead first wife of a successful novelist.

First seen at the Leeds Playhouse in 2017, Sally Cookson's stripped-down production of C.S. Lewis' *The Lion, the Witch and the Wardrobe* at the Bridge Theatre, London, featured Will Johnson as "Aslan".

The National Theatre's Dorfman mounted an inventive adaptation by writer Joel Horwood and director Katy Rudd of Neil Gaiman's novel *The Ocean at the End of the Lane* in early December. The author's charming fantasy story about a young boy (played by Samuel Blenkin) who discovered a Narnia-like fantasy world just beyond his bedroom was cleverly brought to life through clever puppetry and dazzling stage effects.

Staged as part of the summer's Toronto Fringe Festival, *Mayhem at Miskatonic: A Burlesque Mystery Game* was a H.P. Lovecraft-inspired choose-your-own-adventure show written by Nick and Ash Cassidy and staged by Pointed Cap Playhouse.

The Immersive Experience of *Jeff Wayne's Musical Version of the War of the Worlds* was billed as "100 minutes of groundbreaking multi-sensory entertainment".

The BBC's *Sherlock* also went interactive with *Sherlock: The Game*, which found Benedict Cumberbatch, Martin Freeman, Andrew Scott and co-creator Mark Gatiss reprising their roles in the 100-minute escape room experience, as players attempted to put an end to Moriarty's evil plans.

Capcom's "remake", *Resident Evil 2*, paid homage to the original 1998 haunted house game while improving upon just about everything else. A rookie cop and a female student had to escape Raccoon City, where a deadly virus had turned everyone into brain-eating zombies.

*The Sinking City* from games developer Frogwares was a mash-up of Sherlock Holmes-like sleuthing and H.P. Lovecraft's Deep Ones, as hard-boiled PI Charles W. Reed arrived in the isolated town of Oakmont seeking answers to his underwater visions.

Twin sisters tried to track down their father, maverick marine BJ Blazkowicz, in a Paris where the Nazis won World War II in MachineGames' futuristic *Wolfenstein: Youngblood*, a follow-up to 2017's *New Colossus*.

Capcom's *Devil May Cry 5* featured series heroes Dante and Nero teaming up with enigmatic newcomer V and his spectral panther to battle an ancient demon that was trying to invade Red Grave City and feed on the blood of its citizens.

With the new PC version of Quantum Dream's *Heavy Rain*, players were multiple characters on the trail of a serial killer, while *Bloodstained: Ritual of the Night* was a new game from the developer of *Castlevania*.

Kojima Productions' *Death Stranding* for PS4 featured a voice cast that included Norman Reedus, Mads Mikkelsen, Lindsay Wagner and Conan O'Brien, and was set in a post-apocalyptic wasteland.

Respawn's multi-platform game *Star Wars Jedi: Fallen Order* filled in the gaps between *Star Wars Episode III: Revenge of the Sith* and *Rogue One*, as Jedi-in-training Cal Kestis (Cameron Monaghan) and his droid BD-1 were hunted by the Empire following Order 66. Forrest Whitaker voiced his character "Saw Gerrera" from *Rogue One*.

*Terminator: Resistance* was a first-person shooter set in the world of the first two movies, in which players got to blast away at an army of T-800s who were hunting humans in the future to extinction.

Nintendo's *Marvel Ultimate Alliance 3: The Black Order* pitted a bewildering number of Marvel superheroes against Thanos and his band of villains in a simplistic "beat 'em up" scenario.

Mario's lesser-known brother, the green-capped Luigi, got a rare starring role in Nintendo's haunted-house game *Mansion 3*, while *Harry Potter: Wizards Unite* was an augmented-reality RPG for smartphones, based on the world created by J.K. Rowling.

Available for £59.99, a replica Harry Potter Invisibility Cloak allowed the wearer to "disappear", thanks to an accompanying app on their smartphone camera. Maenwhile, Samoa's official silver-plated half-dollar Harry Potter Coin, featuring an engraving of Harry and a selectively-coloured image of his owl Hedwig, was available from the Westminster Collection for £29.99 plus postage and packing.

The Bradford Exchange/Hawthorne Village's America's "Most Haunted" Collection of eerily illuminated, hand-crafted sculptures kicked off with "Amityville" for just $59.97. It was followed by "Franklin Castle".

From the same company, *The Nightmare Before Christmas* Tree Collection featured a three-foot "Dark of the Moon" tree, along with additional hand-crafted sculptures, figurines and Jack o' Lantern ornaments inspired by Tim Burton's 1993 movie.

For those who didn't have the patience needed to construct Mattel's Mega Construx *Game of Thrones* Daenerys & Drogon model, there was always Lego's 2,287-piece *Stranger Things* set (£179.99), which came with eight mini-figures.

Frank Frazetta's painting *Egyptian Queen*, which originally appeared on the cover of Warren's *Eerie* magazine in 1969, sold in

May for $5.4 million, which was reportedly the highest price ever paid for a piece of original comics art sold at auction.

A near-mint copy of *Marvel Comics* No.1 (1939), featuring the Human Torch, Sub-Mariner and Ka-Zar, sold at auction in November for $1.26 million.

The late Bernie Wrightson's original cover art for Marvel Comics' 1983 adaptation of *Frankenstein* sold at auction by Profiles in History in December for $1.2 million. It was part of a private collection of original comic book art that also included work by Jack Kirby, Steve Ditko and John Byrne. The auction achieved a total of more than $3 million.

A rare 1941 insert poster for Universal's *The Wolf Man* sold for $96,000 in March, well beyond the pre-auction estimate. It was almost rivalled by an insert for the same studio's *Bride of Frankenstein*, which was bought for $90,000 at the sale, while a window card for the same movie went for $38,400. A German magazine promotional advert for F.W. Murnau's *Nosferatu* (1921) also exceeded its estimate, eventually selling for $52,800, as did a half-sheet poster for *The Wizard of Oz* (1939), which sold for $108,000.

Meanwhile, a rare and unopened Kenner's *Star Wars* toy found in a loft sold for £2,100, which was ten times its pre-auction estimate. The die-cast "Tie Bomber" spacecraft belonged to a worker at Coalville's Palitoy factory, which made *Star Wars* models and figures in the UK, and had lain undiscovered in its unopened original box, in Leicestershire, for around forty years.

Many other *Star Wars* toys, dating back to the early 1980s, went under the hammer at the auction in Derbyshire, which realised around £24,000 in total—more than double the expected sum. Amongst the toys was a "Boba Fett" figure made by Palitoy, still in its plastic bubble and attached to a card. It sold for £2,300, several times its estimate of between £300 and £500, while a toy based on the character of "Greedo" sold for £1,000, having only expected to make between £80 and £100.

A first edition of Rowling's *Harry Potter and the Philosopher's Stone*, bought twenty years earlier at a library table-top sale for £1.00

and stamped "withdrawn from stock", sold at auction on July 31 for £34,200 (including buyer's premium and VAT). The book was one of only 500 copies published by Bloomsbury in 1997, complete with two typos.

In December, Julien's Auctions in Beverly Hills held an Icons & Idols: Hollywood auction that included one of Christopher Reeve's capes from *Superman* (1978), which sold for $193,750. Patrick Stewart's Starfleet dress uniform as "Captain Jean-Luc Picard" in *Star Trek: The Next Generation* went for $28,800, but Bilbo Baggins' tobacco pipe from *The Lord of the Rings: The Fellowship of the Ring* (2001), which was estimated to fetch more than $100,000, was not sold.

Stanley Kubrick: The Exhibition featured costumes and props from *2001: A Space Odyssey*, *A Clockwork Orange*, *The Shining* and the director's other work. It ran from April until September at the Design Museum, London.

Running from July until the following January, Toronto's Royal Ontario Museum (ROM) hosted It's Alive! Classic Horror and Sci-Fi Art, an exhibition of the collection belonging to Metallica's Kirk Hammett. It apparently allowed attendees to "explore the connection between artistry, emotion, and the dark side of popular culture."

Margaret Atwood was named a member of the Order of the Companions of Honour in Queen Elizabeth II's New Year's Honours list for her "major contributions to the arts over a long period of time". Author Philip Pullman was knighted, while artist Chris Riddell and actress Thandie Newton were each awarded an OBE.

The 91st Academy Awards were held without a host (for the first time since 1989) on February 24. Marvel Studios' much-lauded *Black Panther* won in three of its seven nomination catagories (which included Best Picture) for Best Original Score, Best Costume Design and Best Production Design, while *Spider-Man: Into the Spider-Verse* picked up the Oscar for Best Animated Feature.

StokerCon 2019 was held over May 9–13 at the Amway Grand Plaza Hotel in Grand Rapids, Michigan. Guests of Honour were Josh Boone (who couldn't attend), Kathe Koja, Josh Malerman, Robert R.

McCammon, Kaaron Warren and Stephanie M. Wytovich. The Horror Writers Association announced the winners of the 2018 Bram Stoker Awards for superiority, voted for by the HWA membership, at a gala presentation on the Saturday night.

Superior Achievement in a Novel was awarded to Paul Tremblay's *The Cabin at the End of the World*, *The Rust Maidens* by Gwendolyn Kiste won Superior Achievement in a First Novel, and the award for Superior Achievement in a Young Adult Novel went to *The Dark Descent of Elizabeth Frankenstein* by Kiersten White.

Rena Mason's 'The Devil's Throat' (from *Hellhole: An Anthology of Subterranean Terror*) won Superior Achievement in Long Fiction, and James Landry's 'Mutter' (from *Fantastic Tales of Terror: History's Darkest Secrets*) received the award for Superior Achievement in Short Fiction.

*That Which Grows Wild* by Eric J. Guignard received Superior Achievement in a Fiction Collection, while editor Ellen Datlow's *The Devil and the Deep* won the same award in the Anthology category.

*It's Alive: Bringing Your Nightmares to Life* edited by Joe Mynhardt and Eugene Johnson was given the award for Superior Achievement in Non-Fiction, *The Devil's Dreamland* by Sara Tantlinger won in the Poetry Collection category, and the Graphic Novel award went to *Victor LaValle's Destroyer* by Victor LaValle, Dietrich Smith and Joana Lafuente. 'The Bent-Neck Lady' episode of Netflix's *The Haunting of Hill House* picked up Superior Achievement in a Screenplay.

Raw Dog Screaming Press won the Specialty Press Award, Graham Masterson was announced as the recipient of the HWA Lifetime Achievement Award, and there were other HWA awards handed out to J.G. Faherty, Jess Landry and Brad Hodson.

The British Fantasy Society announced the winners for the 2019 British Fantasy Awards on October 20, during FantasyCon 2019 at the Golden Jubilee Conference Hotel in Glasgow, Scotland. Guests of Honour were Jen Williams (who couldn't attend), Paul Tremblay and TV tie-in writer Dr. Una McCormack.

The Robert Holdstock Award for Best Fantasy Novel was won by *The Bitter Twins* by Jen Williams, and the August Derleth Award for Best Horror Novel went to *Little Eve* by Catriona Ward.

*The Tea Master and the Detective* by Aliette de Bodard was considered Best Novella, and G.V. Anderson's 'Down Where Sound Comes Blunt' (from *The Magazine of Fantasy & Science Fiction*) was awarded Best Short Story. Best Collection went to *All the Fabulous Beasts* by Priya Sharma, and Best Anthology was won by *Year's Best Weird Fiction Volume Five* edited by Robert Shearman and Michael Kelly. Both volumes were published by Canada's Undertow Publications.

Unsung Stories was voted Best Independent Press, Ruth E.J. Booth's column 'Noise and Sparks' from the online magazine *Shoreline of Infinity* received the award for Best Non-Fiction, and another online publication, *Uncanny*, was the winner of Best Magazine/Periodical. The Best Artist award went to Vince Haig.

The self-published *Widdershins Vol. 7: Curtain Call* by Kate Ashwin won Best Comic/Graphic Novel, and *Breaking the Glass Slipper Podcast* was given Best Audio. The Best Film/Television Production award went to *Spider-Man: Into the Spider-Verse*, and the Sydney J. Bounds Award for Best Newcomer went to Tasha Suri for her debut novel *Empire of Sand*.

All the winners were chosen by juries, except for the Karl Edward Wagner Special Award, which was presented to Ian Whates of NewCon Press by the BFS Committee.

The 45th World Fantasy Convention was held over October 31–November 3 at the Marriott Los Angeles Airport Hotel, California. Guests of Honour were Margo Lanagan, Beth Meacham, Reiko Murakami, Sheree Renée Thomas and Tad Williams, with Robert Silverberg as Toastmaster.

As usual, the juried World Fantasy Awards were presented at a Banquet on the Sunday afternoon.

*Witchmark* by C.L. Polk won the Novel award, Kij Johnson's 'The Privilege of the Happy Ending' (from *Clarkesworld*) won Novella, and the Short Fiction award was a tie between 'Ten Deals with the Indigo Snake' by Mel Kassel (from *Lightspeed*) and 'Like a River Loves the Sky' by Emma Törzs (from *Uncanny Magazine*).

*Worlds Seen in Passing: Ten Years of Tor.com Short Fiction* edited by Irene Gallo received the award for Anthology, while the Collection award went to *The Tangled Lands* by Paolo Bacigalupi and Tobias S. Buckell.

Rovina Cai won for Artist, the Special Award–Professional went to Huw Lewis-Jones for *The Writer's Map: An Atlas of Imaginary Lands*, and the Special Award–Non Professional was given to Scott H. Andrews for *Beneath Ceaseless Skies: Literary Adventure Fantasy*.

Lifetime Achievement Awards were announced for Japanese *manga* filmmaker Hayao Miyazaki and literary academic Jack Zipes.

With publishing picking up again, Hollywood churning out mega-blockbusters based on our kind of material, and countless genre-related TV shows streaming across multiple platforms, 2020 looked set to be a banner year for horror and its related fields.

What could possibly go wrong...?

Welcome to the final volume (at least in this format) of *Best New Horror*.

This shouldn't come as a surprise to anyone—I publicly announced nearly two years ago that the series would be ending, and there have been clues on the covers of the previous two volumes for those who were paying attention.

Everything has to come to an end eventually and, after more than three decades, I have decided to close this series while it is still relevant. And make no mistake—this is *my* decision, not the publisher's.

There is also a nice synergy to the fact that the first volume, co-edited by Ramsey Campbell and myself for Robinson Publishing and Carroll & Graf, looked back at the year 1989, and this present volume ends with the year 2019. Obviously, today's round-ups are a lot longer than they were in that inaugural volume!

It was always my plan that when—or more likely, *if!*—*Best New Horror* ever reached volume #31 (one more volume than the world's longest-running horror anthology series, *The Pan Book of Horror Stories*) then I would retire it.

Today's market is flooded with "Year's Best" anthologies devoted to every sub-genre of fiction imaginable, plus *Best New Horror* has grown over the years to become an annual anthology that now takes nearly two years to compile. That kind of workload is just not sustainable any longer.

It remains my hope that *Best New Horror* will set the record for many years to come as the longest-running annual horror anthology series from the same editor.

I *could* have kept going and tried to beat the record for longest-running anthology series set by the late Gardner Dozois with thirty-five volumes of *The Year's Best Science Fiction* (our companion series at Robinson for many years), but out of respect for Gardner and all that he achieved, I am more than happy to let that monumental record continue to stand.

And so, finally, before I sign off, a few thanks are in order: To Nick Robinson, Kent Carroll and Herman Graf, who had faith in the series from the beginning. To all the in-house editors who worked on the book (and its omnibus editions) over the years. To Pete and Nicky Crowther, Mike Smith, Marie O'Regan and the whole team at PS Publishing for keeping it going. To Ramsey Campbell, who was my invaluable editorial collaborator on the first five volumes and has been a staunch supporter of the series ever since. To Michael Marshall Smith, who has been my creative collaborator on the cover designs for more than fifteen years. To all the authors and artists whose work we have showcased over the past thirty-one volumes and, most importantly, thanks to *you*—the readers—who kept us going for all those years.

I couldn't have done it without any of you.

The Editor
September, 2021

# SCOTT BRADFIELD

## ZOMBIE-ISH

S COTT BRADFIELD is a novelist, short story writer and critic, and former Professor of American Literature and Creative Writing at the University of Connecticut. His books include *The History of Luminous Motion*, *Dazzle Resplendent: Adventures of a Misanthropic Dog*, *The People Who Watched Her Pass By*, *The Millennial's Guide to Death: Stories* and *Reading Great Books in the Bathtub: The Home Edition*.

Bradfield's stories, essays and reviews have appeared in *The Magazine of Fantasy & Science Fiction*, *The New York Times Book Review*, *The Los Angeles Review of Books*, *The New Statesman*, *The Baffler*, *Albedo One*, *The New Republic*, *The Weird Fiction Review*, *Flash Fiction Magazine* and numerous "Best of" anthologies.

He lives in California and London.

"As the gestation of this story might attest, my creative 'process' is a mess," admits the author.

"Every five or six years or so I happily run into Stephen Jones somewhere in London, and about ten or twelve years ago he told me he was editing an anthology of original zombie stories. I have never had an idea for a zombie story in my life, but for some reason I had one now. I spent a few years writing this story and revising it, and then several more years getting it right (especially those pesky opening and closing paragraphs.) By the time I sent the story to Steve two or three years ago, he informed me the zombie anthology had been closed for ages, and already long published. I went back to revising 'Zombie-ish' until the good folks at Centipede, and S.T. Joshi, included it in their lovely *Weird Fiction Review*.

"Being a Californian, apocalypses start to feel pretty run-of-the-mill, and I always figured that the zombie one would not be any less mundane, inconvenient or uncomfortable. I also figured we would adjust to it pretty quickly. (By the way—we have.) At least until the next apocalypse came along."

**M**ARILYN JANSEN HATED Fridays. There were always too many people moving up and down the thinly-carpeted corridors of her Co-Op on Fairfax Boulevard, knocking on doors, dragging their tools and pushing their trolleys, and it was impossible to tell the normal residents apart from stray Airbnbers, mail-order delivery people, and the general circulation of building contractors, plumbers, and electricians. Every time a window slammed, or a power drill revved, Marilyn's heart jumped. Fridays were supposed to be her study-at-home days, but she never did much studying. Instead, she sat at the balcony window and kept one eye on the streets below while browsing absently through her thickly bound textbook: *Media Relations—Communications or Spin: 5th Edition*. She found it impossible to focus on the world *inside* her apartment for more than a few seconds at a time; it all seemed too fragile and unconvincing. *Outside* was where real-life happened—clamorous, self-determined, and motivated by secret forces that were never properly explained by the six o'clock news.

Then, one Friday morning, as if signalling the delivery of a parcel, the front doorknob rattled. Low, muffled voices reverberated in the corridor, and large clumsy shapes thudded dimly against one another, like whispering kids lining up to ring the doorbell at Halloween.

"Hello?" Marilyn said.

Something pressed against the door like an exertion of physics.

"Can I please come in?" A woman's voice, rough and moist. "I'm really thirsty. Do you have a telephone? Can I make a phone call?"

Sick people rarely made it this far into the building.

"Go away, please," Marilyn said softly. She switched off the television with the remote. "I've called Guard Squad. You have two minutes. Tops."

Guard Squad "surveillance" consisted of urgently-lettered *Intruder Watch* phone numbers taped above the elevator call-buttons on each floor. Marilyn couldn't remember the last time she had seen an actual guard.

"I need a bathroom," the woman said. "I'm thirsty. I don't have anyone with me. I've had my shots. We need to use a phone."

Several heavy footsteps clomped randomly in a small circle like shoes coming to a stop in the revolving drum of a dryer.

Marilyn went to the open-plan kitchen. The knife drawer was empty; the knives in the dishwasher were soiled with last night's roast beef and gravy. She couldn't bear the idea of using a dirty knife on anybody. Not even a sick person.

Outside, the woman's voice changed. "Please let us in. We aren't like the others. We're thirsty. It isn't fair. You have this nice apartment and all we're asking for is a glass of water. Think about your own children. Would you want somebody to treat *them* this way?"

Marilyn considered rinsing off the chopping knife, but was afraid to turn on the tap. The sound of running water might draw more attention to her side of the door.

Finally, she took a large, freshly-dishwashed frying pan from the stove. It felt heavy and permanent, just the way Marilyn wanted.

They were trying the doorknob more forcefully now. Their whispering agreed about something. Their thirst, their needs, their momentary eruption into Marilyn's world. It was always the same. Sick people thought about nobody but themselves.

"Guard Squad's on the way!" Marilyn shouted. She couldn't prevent her voice from sounding loud and urgent. "You better leave!"

The rattling doorknob subsided. The bodies stopped moving.

Then, down the long hallway, the elevator pinged.

And suddenly, like a crack of thunder, the unseen bodies went shuffling and thudding in a mad scramble towards the only thing that made sense to them anymore.

Later that night, when Mac got home, Marilyn was boiling water for instant chicken-flavoured ramen noodles on the stove.

"Why's Mrs. Watanabe all over the elevator? And who's the other one—is that Mr. Watanabe?"

Marilyn had been trying to interpret the minuscule, multi-lingual cooking instructions on the back of the crinkly green package. Didn't anybody write in English anymore? Everything seemed to be written in Arabic, Serbo-Croatian, Swedish or Chinese.

"I don't know, honey, and I don't want to know. Did you pick up bottled water like I asked?"

"Forgot." Mac double-bolted the door and latched the latch. "But I'm meeting the guys for a drink later. I'll swing by Target on the way home."

After Mac left for the second time that day, Marilyn re-bolted the front door, and stood listening for sounds from the hallway. Occasionally, a door opened or closed; the elevator pinged; individuals strolled past, speaking into their cells.

"No, I'll take a cab... Everything's fine, don't worry. That was Mrs. *Watanabe*. She was like a hundred years old..."

At one point, Marilyn thought she heard gunfire from the basement garage. But it turned out only to be a gangster film playing on a neighbour's Home Cinema system.

She didn't know what to do with herself; it felt like being left in cold storage. She channel-surfed, checked out the medicine cabinet and, every few minutes or so, gravitated back towards the front door, where she resumed listening. Eventually, the only distinct voices she could hear were coming from the street, so she took her glass of Chardonnay out to the concrete balcony and gazed down at the illuminated traffic.

You could identify sick people from far away. They comprised weird diversities, like gang-member extras in a 1970s-era made-for-TV movie. In the front shuffled an elderly black woman in a sun hat, followed by a skinny white barefoot man in a cheap greyish suit, a Mexican boy wearing a plastic red fire-hat, and a teenage Asian boy with a crew-cut and a large hairy mole on his cheek. You never saw demographics like this wandering the streets in a healthy neighbourhood, Marilyn thought. It wouldn't make sense.

A few yards from Marilyn's balcony, they staggered to a stop and looked up at her.

"Do you have anything to drink?" the elderly black woman asked. "We're so thirsty. Are there any stores around here? Could you give us some water?"

The Mexican boy was chewing on something black and oblong that resembled one of those deep-fried turkey legs sold at a county fair.

Across the street, an elderly white woman in a pink velour tracksuit was walking her manicured white poodle on a jewelled pink leash. The poodle started to bark.

"That lady's got a dog," Marilyn told the black woman. "Why don't you run along?"

"We're not looking for trouble," the skinny man said. He seemed to be addressing the dog. "Can we come inside? I need to call my wife. The last time I saw her, she didn't look very well."

"Hey!" It was the old lady across the street. "I'll sic Lucy on you! Get!"

The little boy in the red fire-hat looked up from his turkey leg. His mouth was stained by something red and coagulant that resembled barbecue sauce.

"I don't like dogs," the little boy said.

At Target, still buzzing from beer and bourbon chasers, Mac pushed his large plastic shopping cart down the aisles of gloaming merchandise. He loved Target after midnight. Everything you could think of buying was available at half the cost of anywhere else.

"Could you help me open this?" the woman said softly, emerging from the cosmetics aisle with a neon-yellow bottle of Lucozade. She wore dirty Lycra bicycle pants and a baggy, multiply-stained Sonics T-shirt. "I have a fever and can't find my way home." Her teeth and lips were sticky with a brown, purplish substance.

Mac struck her firmly in the belly with the front of his shopping cart and she staggered backwards.

"Get!" he said.

She took three slow gliding steps backwards, one two three, as if counting them in her head. She seemed amazed by Mac's presence. He liked that look on the face of a person he didn't know.

"Don't make me angry," she whispered abstractly. She seemed confused by dimensions and distances. "When I'm angry, I'm not very nice."

*Who is?* Mac thought.

One of the blue-uniformed security guards trotted over from the front door, carrying a short-stock shotgun with simulated wood-grain finish. His unholstered walkie-talkie crackled.

"You're in a lot of trouble, lady," Mac said. "Get out of here while you can."

She showed him her teeth. They were cracked and stumpy, as if she'd been chewing rocks.

"I just need a little help with this bottle. I have friends outside. Everybody's so thirsty. We need a sip of Lucozade and we'll be okay."

The guard waved the shotgun as if it were a lost jacket someone had left behind at the counter.

"Hey!" the guard shouted. "You aren't welcome around here!"

Other customers appeared at the mouths of aisles. Or at least they looked like customers. Mac was never sure about anybody after a few bourbon chasers.

The lady reached towards Mac. Her fingernails were broken, with little flecks of rose-pink nail polish, like the fingers of a vintage doll in an antique store.

"It's too late now, lady," Mac said. "You had your chance."

Then he pulled back his shopping cart like the spring of a slingshot and gave it to her one more time.

"I don't see the point in moving to Colorado, Mom," Marilyn was saying on the phone when Mac came back through the front door with two large Target carry-bags. "They have sick people in Colorado, too. They just don't talk about them on the national news... I don't know why, Mom, maybe because nobody's interested in Colorado. But whenever something goes wrong in California, it's a big deal…Of course I'm safe. Mac's here. We've got Guard Squad… Everything'll be fine. At least that's what they keep saying in the newspaper."

*Marilyn and her mom,* Mac thought. *They drive each other crazy, but they can't stand to be out of contact for more than a few hours.*

He left the bags of bottled water on the kitchen counter, removed his shoes, and examined his wavy reflection in the burnished metallic-grey surface of the refrigerator-freezer. It felt like witnessing the secret emergence of somebody he used to be.

"It's like everything else, Mom," Marilyn said. "Earthquakes, tornadoes, terrorists at travel resorts, and what about all this global warming they keep talking about? The world isn't a safe place; we have to accept that. Now, I've really got to go, Mom. Mac's home and I haven't seen him all day. Give Dad my love. And when you get a chance, come visit real soon."

By the time Marilyn showered and got into bed, Mac was rolled over on his side facing the window.

Outside, cars raced their engines. Occasionally there was a loud screech of tyres and a low, hard thump, like the sound of a tennis racquet striking a feather pillow.

"Kids and their cars," Mac said.

Marilyn sat up in the darkness and looked at the open window.

"If they're so harmless," she said finally, "what about Mrs. Watanabe?"

Outside, male voices hooted and laughed.

"Mrs. Watanabe could hardly carry her cane to the elevator. Anybody could dismember an old bat like Mrs. Watanabe."

Marilyn thought about this for a while.

"What about when *we* get too weak to carry our canes to the elevator? Or what if one of us gets the flu? What if they get stronger, or remember how to use weapons, or operate machinery? We can't be complacent. What if someday there's more of them than there are of us?"

It was Mac's turn to think for a while. Outside, the voices diminished, and traffic subsided to a low, susurrant hum.

Finally, Mac said, "Look, babe. We've had our shots and we're taking the supplements. These things are like waves. Eventually they go away and the next wave comes along. Like that monsoon in Thailand a few years ago. Or that nuclear reactor breaking down in Japan."

The next morning, Marilyn drove to her part-time job at the Buzzy Bee Day Care Centre on Seventh Avenue. In the tanbark-strewn playground, several of the older children were huddled in a circle.

"One got in the yard," Sarah, the assistant manager, said. "Steve and Johnny hit it with a Whiffle bat and it went down like a wet bag of laundry."

Marilyn could hardly see them through the smudged, mesh-layered window.

"Are you sure they should be playing with it?"

Sarah shrugged. "It empowers them to accept the reality of social-illness, or something like that. Anyway, if they haven't had their shots, that's not our responsibility. It says so in the parent-teacher contract."

At the first Co-Op Residents Meeting of the spring, an LAPD patrolman named Officer Ramirez presented a talk on public health and safety.

"You gotta remember," he said, leaning one elbow against the wooden podium, "that these characters haven't got any upper body strength. No muscle density. They're like cardboard cut-outs of people with basic autonomic functions. Light, hunger, heat, maybe some minimal hearing. All they understand is eat and drink, eat and drink. They're like those battery-powered robots that run in circles until they lose power; then they plug themselves into a power source, recharge, and start running in circles again. They're self-sustaining biological programs that look like people, and talk like people, but they'll never actually *be* people ever again."

Marilyn didn't recognise many of her fellow residents at the meeting. There was Mrs. Buckland, who sat behind the podium with her husband, wearing a lapel card that told everybody she was *Co-Op Director*. There was a fifty-ish black couple that lived across the hall. And finally, an old Japanese-looking man with a wooden cane and a hearing aid who, Marilyn decided, was probably Mr. Watanabe.

"If they're so helpless," said a bulky, well-exercised man in cargo pants and a Gold's gym T-shirt, "what about my Range Rover? Or that antenna they tore off Sue's car in the basement?"

Everybody nodded sombrely, as if agreeing with some vaguely-worded axiom in church, such as "do unto others", or "turn the other cheek".

Officer Ramirez shrugged. His various attachments—gun, mace canister, billy club and walkie-talkie—rattled like a set of clumsy wind-chimes.

"How do I put it? Bad things happen to good people. But if there's only two or three of them, and you're in reasonably decent health, you should be okay. And as for that car antenna, these characters will chew through anything that gets in their way. Just make sure it isn't you."

It got to the point where Marilyn couldn't focus on anything but sick people. When she was driving down the street, she only noticed human figures that shambled, or lurched, or lay face down on the pavement, quivering like stroke-victims. When she was teaching or being taught, she routinely kept one eye on the primary exit; and at home, she habitually sat facing her front door, like a bouncer guarding the entrance to her own life. She didn't even know what she was waiting for anymore. She only hoped it would get here soon.

Every knock on the door felt significant, like a phone call from an almost-forgotten relative.

"Good afternoon, Ma'am. We're with the Church of Latter Day Saints. Could we please come in? We can't talk very easily through this door."

"We don't open our door to strangers," she said. It was a point of pride. "Why don't you go back to Utah where you came from?"

"We're from South Alameda, Ma'am. Could we please come inside? You seem to have some misconceptions about our faith."

"Faith" was one of those words that always made Marilyn anxious, like "race" or "underarms".

"I don't have any misconceptions. I just want to be left alone."

The voices conferred. It made Marilyn recall the way sick people banged against one another when moving through a small corridor.

"We don't all marry lots of women, Ma'am. Or perform blood atonement ceremonies in our back yards. We're just normal Americans who believe in God. We want to help you understand who we are, so you don't go around suffering misconceptions that make the world more confusing than it already is."

But that was one thing Marilyn definitely *didn't* want. She didn't want to *understand* the world. She didn't want the world to understand *her*. She just wanted to live her life without the world getting in her way. She just wanted to be left alone.

Then, just as the sickness had arrived in Marilyn's world, it went away again. The awkward bands of shuffling and mismanaged pedestrians disappeared from streets and parking lots. The local evening news went back to running stories about office fires and gas refinery explosions. And even Marilyn's HMO stopped sending her discount coupons for booster-inoculations and sickness-prevention clinics. Now, when Marilyn's mother called, the subject of sick people didn't even come up. They spent all their time talking about the latest shooting incidents in pre-schools and movie theatres, El Nino, tornadoes in the Midwest, and the Republican and Democratic National Conventions.

"I just don't understand anything anymore," Marilyn's mother said, her voice partially drowned out by her revving juicer. "All I know is that you better take care of yourself in this world, honey, because nobody's going to take care of you. It's not the world I was born into, but it's definitely the world I'm going to die in, whether I like it or not."

Sometimes, there was a brief retrospective documentary on PBS, in which relatives of sick people spoke about the random brutalities they had witnessed.

"It was like watching something horrible through the wrong end of a telescope," recalled a middle-aged woman with a scar running slantwise across her right eyebrow. "It was like none of these things were happening to me. Some of the sick people used to attend the same PTA meetings I did; one of them babysat my kids. Then, all of a sudden, they turned into people I couldn't talk to. They kept coming at me, without any sense of anger or remission, like they were half-asleep. They wanted something from me that I couldn't give them. I was just somebody who got in their way."

Later that night, after Mac went to bed, Marilyn filled a Tupperware bowl with the remaining lasagna, and left it outside Mr. Watanabe's front door. It felt like delivering a secret message to the world that nobody would ever read except her.

# MAURA McHUGH

## WAKE THE DEAD

MAURA McHUGH lives in Galway, Ireland, and writes across all media. She has published two collections of re-imagined stories—*Twisted Fairy Tales* and *Twisted Myths*—and a collection of original fiction, *The Boughs Withered (When I Told Them My Dreams)*, which was nominated for a British Fantasy Award for Best Collection. She's also written for radio, theatre and computer games, as well as writing comic books for Dark Horse and *2000 AD*.

Her look at David Lynch's 1992 film *Twin Peaks: Fire Walk with Me* (from PS Publishing's Midnight Movie Monographs imprint) was nominated for a British Fantasy Award for Best Non-Fiction.

She walks and dreams in the woods every day.

"'Wake the Dead' features the eerie Irish tradition of the Straw Boys," explains McHugh, "a mummers' ritual where people dress in outfits constructed from straw and call to homes to perform songs for a few coins. This traditionally happened at *Samhain* (Ireland's Hallowe'en) on St. Stephen's Day, but Straw Boys also used to visit a house the night before a wedding to bring good luck. I might write a story based on that aspect one day.

"This tale caused me problems during its first draft, as half-way through it started to go askew. I rested it until I could encourage it to return to its intended trajectory. The delay resulted in it missing a submission deadline for an anthology, but that meant I was free to include it as one of the original stories for my collection, *The Boughs Withered (When I Told Them My Dreams)*. 'Wake the Dead' was also selected for *The Best of British Fantasy 2019*, edited by Jared Shurin, so it has rewarded me for my long dance to its insistent tune."

"I F YOU'RE RUNNING from yourself you'll always come in second."

Donnacha hadn't understood this cryptic statement when he'd heard it as a kid, impatient and bored, in his gran's kitchen. She'd been counselling his father about his restless job-hopping. Yet a haunting vision lodged in his mind, despite his desire to return to his mam's house and his unfinished Zelda game. He imagined his dad being pursued by a better, fitter version of himself in a long race, but dream-like, his father's faster self outpaced him, and drew away until he disappeared into a hazy horizon. Uncatchable.

Red-faced and panting, his father slogged on, alone. Too proud to admit defeat.

In the car ride home, Donnacha puzzled over it, and concluded Gran was implying his dad was a loser; and looking at him, compulsively wringing the steering wheel, crumpled, unshaven, and permanently broke, Donnacha reckoned she was right.

Now, after a month of driving around rural Ireland, trying to evade his cracked adult life choices, Donnacha had a grudging new insight to her meaning, and unexpected empathy for his dad.

But he wasn't ready to admit he couldn't dodge his demons.

"I'll run them ragged first."

He glanced guiltily around his car. Talking out loud wasn't a good sign.

He signalled, and drove into another small town that existed half in the past and half in the present. A shabby, boarded-up hardware shop cringed next to a shiny Thai street food restaurant. A statue of the Virgin Mother and Child cast a shadow over the town square that pointed at the lingerie store opposite. Teens loitered together on a street corner with their individual faces illuminated by their mobile phones, while a tractor motored past them and the *auld fellah* in a cap driving it waved at the older locals.

"He even has the sheepdog on the passenger seat," Donnacha marvelled. The collie lolled his tongue at him, as Donnacha pulled his car around the slowpoke driver.

This was typical of his impromptu tour of the cultural blind-spots of his homeland. Ireland had emerged from its colonial chrysalis, but its new form was not yet set. It was malleable and shifting. Underneath the wet flesh some of the old bones were resistant to change. They could establish the new form from their obstinacy.

Perhaps there were even more ancient shapes that might re-emerge. From when people chanted to stone and paid respect to trees. When blood was spilled for nature's tribute. And primordial forces responded to such offerings...

Donnacha blinked rapidly, surprised at the strange direction of his thoughts. Luckily he spotted the B&B he had booked for the night, and made a sharp turn into its driveway. This owner had a quixotic array of statues and potted plants in the small garden. A gnome wearing sunglasses held court with a duck dressed in a raincoat. A hedgehog in a Hawaiian shirt lounged beside a dancing, piping satyr.

It was another in a series of cheap, unassuming B&Bs he had picked for his wandering. He avoided hospitable homes with cheery fireplaces, chatty guests, and reminders to review the premises kindly online. He preferred the old-fashioned, reserved host, who took money without questions and offered a spartan experience.

Donnacha craved their cell-like rooms. He read books, anything abandoned in the lodgings he occupied briefly, and never turned on the TV. Perversely, the world continued to turn without his attention. He heard snatches of news via the radio in his car, but he thought of them as stories. Fantastical yarns of tyrants, villains and beasts, wrangling in distant kingdoms.

Each day he got up and drove, over drenched rolling hills, past indistinct villages, through tangled, black-boughed woods, and over swollen rivers. Dependable Ireland rolled out a sepulchral chill as

October deepened, and around him every dark rock and huddled glade was damp and glistening.

His funds had ebbed. What remained from his share of the house—Mairead had done well out of that showdown between solicitors—had paid for petrol and a frugal month of roving around a landscape he had never explored.

He could get work as a barman. That well-honed skill was ever needed. He wasn't the best at feigning interest in customers, but his supply of sardonic commentary was limitless, and there was nothing his countrymen liked better than banter, especially if it skewed bleak.

That evening Donnacha fired up an antique computer in the beige living room of his current residence. He browsed through job ads on local towns' forums, and noted some likely contenders. It meant he had to log into his e-mail account, and endure the few concerned messages from old friends. The ones that knew him from his happier days in Boston, before he and Mairead returned home, or those childhood mates who stubbornly believed there was some spark of that original kid left within his chest. The most difficult was the patient reminder from his younger brother Fintan that a room was available at his home. He responded with a one-line thanks, but he knew that Juanita wouldn't welcome him. She and Mairead had always been tight.

He scrawled a couple of addresses and numbers on the complimentary notepad by the asthmatic PC. His pay-as-you-go phone was a primitive plastic savage. His address book was slips of paper in his wallet.

Donnacha didn't notice the lady of the house enter the room until her shadow obscured his writing. He startled and turned.

She could have been in her twenties or her fifties: a tall, thin grey woman with big plastic spectacles, and a smile that hung on her long face like a titled picture. She wore some orthodontic contraption that gave her a slight lisp and added to her indeterminate age.

"Buster Mahon needs a hand."

He blinked at her, a variety of interpretations crossing his mind, including a joke about prosthetics.

She pointed at his scrawl. "You're looking for work?"

"Depends on the job."

"Pub. Town's so small if you sneezed while passing through you'd miss it." She snorted a laugh. 'It's the pub, and the grocery shop, *and* the funeral parlour. They used to do petrol too, but gave that up when the big companies took over. Traditional place. Old men in wellies and caps. Young people go elsewhere."

"And I'm not young?"

"You'd fit right in there. They want pints pulled while they read papers and complain about the weather or the price of sheep."

"Is the pay as attractive as the company?"

She shrugged. "Buster has a room above the place. It could be right for someone minding his own business."

Donnacha stood up. She was half a head taller. "You've come to some conclusions about me."

She met his direct look without any caginess. "I know people." She held out a piece of paper with an address.

His bitterness rose like addictive bile. "That's impossible. We're all pretending."

But he reached for the paper anyway. She held onto it for a moment longer than necessary, and he met her gaze again.

"I see you Donnacha Sweeney."

Her knowing stare pierced his bravado. A shiver rippled down his back, and his hand jerked back involuntarily with the paper.

She smiled, and the row of metal bands covered her teeth so completely it was as if they were fashioned from iron. "I'm away early tomorrow. Busy day. I'll leave a cold breakfast for you, and you can let yourself out."

He watched her leave the room as soundlessly as she had entered.

It was one of the occasions he cursed not having a smart phone. The town wasn't on the map, which lay in a crumpled mess on the passenger seat. He had been circling through a series of winding *boreens* at a crawl because of the silvery rain shroud. The car clock said it was 1:00 p.m., but he had set out at 11:00 a.m., and the place should only have been thirty minutes away. Through the haze he spotted the smudged shape of the apex of a stone church he was sure he had passed twice before.

"Fuck's sake!" he shouted, and gripped the steering wheel to knuckle-white tightness.

He pulled the car into a scrap of earth by the barred gateposts, beyond which lay the outline of a church after a long, gravelled path. Listing headstones and ivy-strangled vaults studded the mist.

He hoped some farmer's son in a souped-up Honda Civic wouldn't bash into him while he consulted his map. His finger traced along the creased page for a telltale cross that would indicate the church, but there was only a squiggle of lines. They met in a crossroads where he suspected the town was located.

A bell tolled, oddly muffled. He glanced up. A shape moved down the path towards him.

Donnacha reached over to roll down his passenger window, and plastered on a bewildered smile. It appeared to be a man in a dark suit, who walked steadily but didn't get any closer.

He squinted. The mist had already seeped into the car, and a fine film of water beads clung to his face, obscuring his vision. He wiped at his eyes, trying to focus properly on the approaching figure.

It walked, but it gained no ground.

Warmth leeched out of him, along with his enthusiasm to meet the person. The bell clanged again, dully.

At this, the figure *blipped* forward on the path. Donnacha could make out a translucent face with black voids for eyes that radiated malevolent triumph. Long-figured hands hung loosely from the sleeves, as if the suit was badly fitted. A costume for an intruder.

There was no other sound. No crunch of gravel, or the complaint of crows.

Again, the bell rang out strangely.

The man-shape was almost at the gatepost. His pretend mouth was a vicious slash, curved up in the delight of the predator. His arm reached up as if to hail Donnacha—

He put the car into gear and slammed his foot down on to the accelerator.

The car caught on the mud and the back swerved slightly, to scrape against the stone post. The grind of metal merged with the bell. Donnacha refused to look at the path, despite the freezing gust that swept through the window causing his rapid breaths to materialise before him.

With an anguished shriek his car surged onto the road and sped forward quickly, but he had to slow immediately because of the mist.

Donnacha glanced in the rear-view mirror for any sign of his pursuer, but all that was evident was the concealing rain.

His heartbeat slowed down again, and he broke into a stuttering laugh, mocking and congratulatory.

Then, he spotted the signpost, at a drunken angle, pointing to an obscured road, and the name of the hamlet: RATHDEARG.

He turned the car, and heard the protest from the back wheel, relieved he was only a couple of miles from his destination.

Rathdearg was a collection of houses, rather than a village, yet the road widened to accommodate a small green area with benches and a saint's statue. Everything was tidy, with walled gardens up front. The pub/shop was called The Haunt. Next door, what looked like a home also had the green flash that indicated it doubled as a post office. A bus-stop pole punctuated either side of the street.

He parked the car in a small concrete space at the side of the building and got out. He wilfully ignored examining the damage. What did it matter when he couldn't afford to fix it?

At the entrance to the pub sat a collection of turnips, carved with deranged faces, and with a light flickering inside each one. The hanging sign depicted a revenant dressed in a 19th-century black suit, sitting inside the pub and holding up a pint of porter in a perpetual toast. A skeleton in an apron grinned from behind the counter.

He pushed open the door, which had wavy glass inset, and it squealed loudly as if griping about its use. Inside, the dimly-lit room was narrow due to an ancient counter running along the left-hand side. It was composed of glass and wood, and displayed a variety of canned goods, including baked beans, peas and Spam. Behind it were shelves with toilet paper, washing powder and giant boxes of tea. A small fridge containing juice and milk hummed. An old-fashioned register sat unattended. A rack of newspapers, containing national and regional publications as well as *The Farmer's Journal* and *Ireland's Own*, finished off the row.

After the shop, a swinging half-door opened into the pub itself.

*It's the Wild West*, Donnacha thought as he entered.

This space was roomy, with a smoke-stained counter at the back, which looked like it had been worn smooth by generations of elbows. The array of tall stools didn't have padding or cushions. *The townsfolk have hardy backsides.* The usual pumps for the dominant breweries were on display, but he was surprised to see a craft beer from a nearby town given a prominent spot. Glass shelves behind the bar displayed the selection of spirits, and rows of glasses. He noted the lack of dust on the bottles of Babycham—someone had professional pride. A turf fire blazed in the large stone fireplace on the right. In front of the hearth lay a grey, grizzled hound. It raised its head at Donnacha's appearance, and watched him with wise, brown eyes.

A faded, hand-written sign pasted on the back of the bar proclaimed NO CAPPUCCINOS!, but underneath that it offered a Wi-Fi password.

He crossed the tiled floor towards the counter. The dog stood up, revealing its height. It was a cross, but with a strong wolfhound pedigree.

"Hello," he said, and cautiously extended his downturned hand.

The dog sniffed at it from a distance. A tag dangled from his collar, and Donnacha sank down on his hunkers to read it.

"Joxer," he read out loud. The dog's ears twitched.

"I'm Donnacha."

Joxer walked right up to his face, licked it once, and returned to his post by the fire.

Donnacha straightened, and looked around, but no one appeared. He walked to the counter, leaned on it, then coughed politely. An old clock hanging amongst black and white photographs ticked loudly.

After another minute crawled by, he noticed the black door at the back of the room. No doubt it led to the toilets and some quiet room where people retired for the lock-in.

He walked to it and placed his hand on the old-fashioned metal handle, but before he opened it he glanced back at Joxer. The dog regarded him placidly. He clicked the door open.

The short corridor beyond was icy cold, and he was glad again for his parka. A fragrance of lilies and beeswax lingered. He cautiously opened another black door, and formed his mouth into a "Hello?" as he entered.

The word died in his mouth when he took in the tableau before him.

It was the funeral parlour, and it was in session.

The first thing he saw in the rectangular room was a huge, ornately-framed picture of the Madonna hanging from the wall facing him. It was painted in a modern—or primitive—style. Her radiating halo—perhaps gold leaf—glowed in the subdued candlelight cast from four huge wrought-iron standing candelabras positioned in the corners of the room. Her skin was blue, and her raiment red, but her yellow eyes contained compassion despite their eerie, direct gaze.

A plain, wooden coffin, painted black, sat in the centre of the room on top of a plinth covered in maroon velvet. Donnacha could not tell what was in the open coffin from this distance, but a skin-creeping horror of dead people shivered through him. He could still remember the waxy, lifeless features of his grandmother when she had been waked, in the old way, in her home. Donnacha had been eleven, and his father insisted he kiss her goodbye. He had practically dragged Donnacha to the coffin in her old living room, where the gathered neighbours drank cups of tea and glasses of whiskey. His lips only grazed her forehead, but he'd had to choke back a retch.

The old revulsion, and the shock at intruding on such a private ceremony, paralysed him.

The room was lined on all sides by seats, and they were occupied by people wearing traditional black. Their faces, grey with grief he supposed, turned to stare at him.

A wide man in a coal-black suit emerged from a darker part of the room and walked up to him.

"I'm so sorry," Donnacha began in a whisper, "I was looking for Buster Mahon. I had no idea—"

"I'm him," the other said in a quiet tone, and held out a square hand.

Donnacha took it, and Buster gave him the shake that implied with one extra pulse of pressure he could crush his hand. Buster had the gait and carriage of someone who used to be a rugby player, or a soldier. Someone not afraid to apply force if provoked.

"You're Donnacha Sweeney I'm guessing?"

Donnacha nodded to cover his surprise.

"Connie warned me you might be dropping by."

"Ah..."

"Constance Harte. You stayed in her B&B last night."

"Yes, of course!" He never remembered the names of any of the people he stayed with. "Tall lady," he added, idiotically.

Buster smiled in a neutral way, and titled his head back slightly as if appraising him. "Yes, she is. Good judge of character."

Donnacha looked about, unsure what to do. The people in the room were standing now, but remained fixed on him and Buster. He could not tell who the lead mourners were. They all seemed equally... morbid.

"You're looking for work?"

"Yes, but I don't have a CV—"

Buster waved him into silence. "Paper doesn't tell the tale of a man. Work does. Anyway, you got past the dog."

"I'll have to thank him."

This time Buster's eyes crinkled along with his smile. "He likes avocado."

Buster gestured to the door back to the pub. "Let's see how you handle yourself. After that we'll know what you can deal with."

"Now?"

"There's an apron behind the counter. A tradition of my father's. He always liked us neat."

"Okay."

Buster nodded at the door. "We'll be coming through in a minute, and you can begin."

"Connie said something about a room."

"No matter how it goes tonight, you can stay in the flat upstairs. Tomorrow we can assess."

Donnacha inclined his head, glad he'd thought to wear his black jeans and shirt, which he considered his uniform for bar work. He turned his back on the room and felt an unnerving vulnerability. A sibilant drone began, but Donnacha could not make out the words or even the language. He imagined it was a decade of the rosary or some other chanted prayer. He was relieved to depart and return to the vacant pub. Joxer didn't even raise his head from his paws when he entered.

A black apron hung from a peg behind the bar. He swapped it for his coat, and tied the apron around his waist. It hung to mid-shin, and he felt more like a European waiter than a barman. He spotted a dishcloth by the sink and began a wipedown of the counter even though it looked perfectly clean. It was his ritual for getting into the right mindset for the job: clean down the space and prepare for the array of mad ones and saints: always in proportion of ten to one.

Joxer got to his feet and gazed at the door. Buster walked in, and the dog gave him a tail-wag before he sat down, looking like a regal stone statue.

Buster noted Donnacha's final polish of the counter.

"Good habits," he said with approval.

The sea of mourners washed in behind him, and soon Donnacha had no time to think. It was a pints-of-stout and balls-of-malt crowd, with a sprinkling of shandies and white wines. A tab was established—no one's hand was allowed near a wallet. All the seats were full, and people milled around the bar—none obstructing orders. A buzz of conversation built up, but even illuminated by the cheery fire, which Buster kept feeding, the customers' faces retained a greyish cast.

After an hour, a sturdy woman in an old-style housecoat and a crocheted cap knocked through the swing doors with a big tray of sandwiches in her muscled arms.

"Delores! Just in time," declared Buster. A muted cheer rang out from the assembly. He relieved her of the tray, and set it down on the nearest table. Hands grabbed the offerings in moments.

"Two more trays, and cake coming," she told him, before she swung out again.

Within minutes most of the bar were chewing contentedly. Buster snagged a few for himself and for Donnacha. He deposited a plate bulging with ham and cheese sandwiches and moist teacake behind the counter for Donnacha.

"Get these in you boyo, quick. They'll call for another round once they've scarfed that lot."

At the same time, Delores returned with two china plates covered in tin foil, and left them on the corner of the counter. Nobody touched them.

"Delores, my beauty", Buster began, and curled his arm around her shoulders affectionately. She beamed at him. "Meet Donnacha Sweeney. Tonight's attendant. Connie sent him to us."

She eyeballed Donnacha the way a farmer appraises livestock.

"You seem competent."

Buster laughed. "Steady on, Delores! Such praise. It'll be offers of matrimony next."

She raised her eyes in an exaggerated eye-roll. Clearly they were old friends.

"Delores is our hamlet's post-mistress, professor of all the town's legends and gossip, and our establishment's provider of pub grub when required."

Buster was opening his mouth to say something else when a disturbance from outside the pub slipped in between the mumble of conversation.

*Drumming; whistles; chimes.*

The pub hushed, and the cacophony drew closer.

Nobody moved, or took their eyes from their drinks.

Joxer stood up.

Donnacha glanced at Buster, ready to ask a question, but the expression on the man silenced him. Buster looked like someone with a sombre duty. Next to him, Delores had her hands stuffed in the pockets of her housecoat, and her lips tightly held, as if holding back an alarm.

Three knocks hammered the front door.

"You!" Buster said with quiet urgency to Donnacha. "Come with me."

A path through the bodies opened, and the two men pushed through the swing-doors.

Through the wavy glass of the front door Donnacha could make out three figures.

"What—?" Donnacha started, but Buster clamped a big hand on his wrist and the pressure quietened him.

Buster opened the door.

Outside waited three capering characters, resplendent in suits of gleaming straw, wearing rough animal-masks of straw: a goat, a hare and a bull.

The goat played a battered tin whistle in an eerie melody that stuck to the minor keys, while the hare shook an old-fashioned tambourine, and the bull banged an ancient, stained *bodhran* drum.

They danced in the glow cast through The Haunt's windows, and the flickering candle-light from the carved turnips in front of the door. Behind them, darkness and fog. It was as if the town had melted away, and nothing existed except for these players and Buster and Donnacha.

The trio became stock-till, then struck up a folk tune that sounded familiar in a warped way. They sang a chant:

"Hungry we stand before your door
No food nor drink since the year before
Give us whiskey, give us bread
Open the door, *let's wake the dead!*"

They performed it three times, increasing their volume after each turn, until their last version was a shouted demand.

Silence again, except for their excited breaths through the masks. There was only darkness behind the eyeholes.

"Welcome to our hearth Mummers," Buster said. He carefully handed each one a coin.

He jerked his head at Donnacha to indicate he should open the door. Donnacha stood aside and held it open. The three Mummers swept past him, bringing with them the smell of a field of barley bending to a wild wind under starry skies.

When Donnacha pushed through the swing-doors after the entourage, he froze.

They had brought the coffin into the pub. It stood on six stools, parallel to the hearth, but not close to the fire. Joxer had vanished. The three Mummers stood in a half-circle around the head of the coffin.

Everybody was standing. Delores was stationed to the left of the coffin with a plate of cake, and Buster was at the counter collecting the other plate. He waved in an underhand manner to Donnacha to urge him to his side. Donnacha had to swerve by the coffin and Delores. This was his first chance to see what lay within. He darted a glance, and could only make out a dark shape. Something glinted into his eyes when he tried to see the face. Further unnerved, he almost hopped forwards to reach Buster.

The big man picked up a china plate filled with thinly-sliced pieces of meat, cheese, fruit and soda bread. He pointed at a small silver salver, on which sat three glasses of whiskey. He pointed back at the coffin.

Donnacha picked up the tray, and followed his boss, who took up a position opposite Delores. Buster tilted his head to indicate that Donnacha should stop at the foot of the coffin.

Donnacha kept his attention firmly on the glasses, concentrating on keeping the tray level, and halted where indicated. Immediately, the Mummers stuck up another tune, the weirdest disharmony so far, accompanied by occasional cries, squawks and yelps that were more animal than human.

The sound bounced off the walls in the room which magnified it. Donnacha felt like he was *inside* the song. An updraft caught the flames in the hearth and they roared and leaped, pumping out tremendous heat. The din began to reach intolerable levels, and at some unknown signal the crowd joined in, stamping, clapping and crying out encouragement.

The clamour became a great beast whipping around the room, seeking a prize.

Donnacha squeezed his eyes shut against the fear and the overwhelming sensory overload. A chilly breeze wafted past his neck and he nearly dropped the tray in shock.

He opened his eyes. The glasses were empty, the food taken from the plates.

Silence fell like an anvil dropped from a great height.

The Mummers spoke in unison:

"Look now, don't wait,
Learn your New Year's Fate.
One heartbeat: past
Two heartbeats: truth
Three heartbeats: dare
Four heartbeats: death."

Delores lowered her plate, and leaned forwards slightly to stare into the coffin. Donnacha found himself counting a slow beat, and it seemed to him that she pulled back after a couple of seconds. A line of people formed behind her, and they repeated her action.

Most only attempted a moment or two. One man slumped after three, and staggered away, helped by a friend in the crowd.

Donnacha remained motionless, the tray of glasses balanced in his hands. His mind stalled; the black eyeholes of the goat, hare and bull remained fixed on him, unwavering throughout the parade of questers.

Finally, Buster stood in front of him, his solid face serious. He removed the tray from Donnacha's hands and gestured to the coffin.

Everyone else had looked. They waited on him.

He moved forwards stiffly, and his trembling right hand clamped on the side of the coffin. He could almost smell his grandmother's perfume, and feel his lips brush her lifeless forehead.

The shape of a body, wrapped in a black shroud, lay in the coffin lined with black silk. An aged oval mirror covered the face. Its surface was dully reflective, and splattered with ink-blots of tarnish.

Donnacha leaned forwards so a dim version of his face appeared in the mirror.

One heartbeat: *he was with Mairead, dancing and laughing at the Irish Cultural Centre in Boston.*

Two heartbeats: *he staggered, blindfolded, after a version of himself dressed in gleaming white who walked arm-in-arm with an ethereally happy Mairead.*

Three heartbeats: *he stood behind the counter in The Haunt, Joxer by the fire, with a small group of contented customers; but once a year the Mummers would call…*

He tried to pull his gaze away from the mirror, and he sensed the moment stretching into what came next. A memory of the grinning spectre in the graveyard reaching out to him rose in his mind. A cool mist settled against his face, numbing it and blinding his sight. A dreadful bone-deep understanding of the constant proximity of death settled into him. During this night, as the tissue between worlds became as soft as dandelion down, the illusions of life were easily rent, and the reality of time's quick passage revealed.

The race existed to be run, not won.

He tried to say something, a gasp, a grateful cry for the unbearable beauty and doleful duty of living, but his body was locked as if bracing for an anticipated blow… until a sudden pain at his ankle yanked him out of that vision, and he fell, clutching his leg.

"I've got you lad," he heard Buster say, and his hands held Donnacha's shoulders, offering support and comfort.

Under the coffin Joxer watched him alertly.

"It's over," Buster said, and he drew Donnacha up.

The Mummers were gone. Delores and the crowd had departed.

The coffin lay empty.

Donnacha heaved in a ragged breath.

By the counter, Connie saluted him with a glass of whiskey. "Happy Hallowe'en," she said with a solemn expression.

Donnacha turned to look at Buster.

"I want time-and-a-half for that."

Buster slapped him on the back. "Let's talk terms and conditions. But first, how about a drink?"

Donnacha shook his head. "I need to get that dog some avocado."

Both Buster and Connie laughed, and Donnacha lurched forwards, his feet awkward and unsteady. He could not sprint yet, but he could shuffle to the counter.

Around him reflections abounded: in a copper coal scuttle, the mirror over the fireplace, in the glass case of the clock, and the glint in the eyes of his patrons.

And in each one a hazy hand stretched to seize him.

# CAITLÍN R. KIERNAN

## MERCY BROWN

C AITLÍN R. KIERNAN has been heralded by *The New York Times* as "one of our essential writers of dark fiction". Their novels include *Silk*, *Threshold*, *Low Red Moon*, *Daughter of Hounds*, *The Red Tree* (nominated for the Shirley Jackson and World Fantasy awards) and *The Drowning Girl: A Memoir* (winner of the James Tiptree, Jr. and Bram Stoker awards, and nominated for the Nebula, World Fantasy, British Fantasy, Mythopoeic, Locus and Shirley Jackson awards).

To date, their short fiction has been collected in fifteen volumes, including *Tales of Pain and Wonder*, *From Weird and Distant Shores*, *Alabaster*, *A is for Alien*, *The Ammonite Violin & Others*, *Confessions of a Five-Chambered Heart*, *Two Worlds and In Between: The Best of Caitlín R. Kiernan (Volume One)*, *Beneath an Oil-Dark Sea: The Best of Caitlín R. Kiernan (Volume Two)*, the World Fantasy Award-winning *The Ape's Wife and Other Stories*, *Dear Sweet Filthy World*, *Houses Under the Sea: Mythos Tales*, *The Very Best of Caitlín R. Kiernan*, *The Dinosaur Tourist* and *Comes a Pale Rider*.

Between 2017–20, Tor.com released Kiernan's Lovecraftian spy-noir "Tinfoil Dossier" novellas—*Black Helicopters*, *Agents of Dreamland* and *The Tindalos Asset*.

They have also won a World Fantasy Award for Best Short Fiction for 'The Prayer of Ninety Cats'. During the 1990s, they wrote *The Dreaming* for DC Comics' Vertigo imprint and, more recently, scripted the three-volume *Alabaster* series for Dark Horse Comics. The first third, *Alabaster: Wolves*, received a Bram Stoker Award.

In 2017, Brown University's John Hay Library established the Caitlín R. Kiernan Papers, archiving juvenilia, manuscripts, artwork and other material related to their work.

They live with two cats, Selwyn and Lydia, and their partner, Kathryn A. Pollnac.

"I try not to write vampire stories," explains Kiernan, "because, as I have publicly stated since the 1990s, I feel rather strongly that the world does not *need* new vampire stories, that all has been said that needs saying, and it has been said repeatedly. However, while that may very well be true, some imp of the perverse keeps spurring me to write new vampire stories.

"Case in point, 'Mercy Brown', a story written in late November 2019 whose title is taken from an infamous Rhode Island 'vampire' incident, even though the story does not actually concern Mercy Brown. The title just seemed right. Also, I will note that this story began as a sort of joke (a hair vampire) and proceeded to one of my speculative biological fascinations (Why can't elephants evolve wheels? Is ammonia biochemistry possible? How much blood could be sucked through a head full of human hair, if the hairs were hollow and functioned like a mosquito's proboscis?), which led to a full-blown story. *Another* vampire story.

"I'd like to think it's the last one I'll ever write. I know better."

## 1

"**A** *HAIR* VAMPIRE?" she says, looking back at me from the mirror on the medicine cabinet door, raising one eyebrow sceptically, her eyes blue as ice. "Are you serious? What does that even mean, a 'hair vampire'?"

"I'm still working on that part," I reply, and I light a cigarette, then look around for something in the bathroom that I can use as an ashtray, not finding anything and deciding my left hand will have to suffice.

"Jesus, that's one of those ideas that's so bad it might be brilliant," she says, then rinses her toothbrush beneath the tap before she sets it back into its appointed hole in the white ceramic toothbrush holder mounted on the wall. There are four holes in the ceramic fixture, but only one toothbrush.

"That or one of those ideas I should bury in a deep hole in a vacant lot."

"You ever heard of the *rokurokubi*?"

I say that I never have, and I take a long drag on my cigarette, then exhale towards the open window, but at least as much of the smoke stays in the bathroom with us as finds its way outside.

"I thought you'd quit," she says.

"I thought I had, too," I reply, and then she frowns and asks me to light one for her, so I do.

"When I die of cancer, they're sending you the bill," she says.

"So, what's the *rokurokubi*?" I ask, and she leans closer to the mirrored door of the medicine cabinet and stares at a blemish on her neck.

"Evil Japanese spirits" she tells me. "Women whose heads come loose from their bodies at night and fly around drinking people's blood. I read about them somewhere, but I can't remember where it was. Or when. I might still have been in college. Anyway, You have to admit, that's at least as silly as a hair vampire."

"You're going to be late for work," I say, glancing at the clock.

"I honestly don't think they much care anymore. I'm waiting to be fired and put out of my misery. Dad would be pissed, though."

I tap ash into my hand, and she taps ash into the sink. Her skin is only almost as pale as the white porcelain. She goes back to staring at the spot on her throat.

"Heads will roll," I say, and she smiles but doesn't laugh.

Outside, down on the sidewalk, a man's shouting at a barking dog.

"It's just a mole," I say, because it's starting to make me anxious the way she's still staring at that spot on her neck, and she takes the cigarette from between her pale lips and says, "That's what everyone thinks, until it's *not* just a mole."

"So, these *rokurokubi*," I say, "how do you kill them? What's their weakness?"

"Their weakness?"

"You know, like Count Dracula and cloves of garlic."

"Oh," she says, "her weakness. Hell if I know. Maybe she doesn't have one. Maybe the flying heads of Japan are impervious."

"You could destroy the body while the head's away," I suggest, and she laughs, probably because she's starting to suspect that I've taken the whole business too seriously, that I'm actually sitting there on her toilet seat trying to work out how you'd kill the *rokurokubi*, because she suspects I take everything too seriously. Like being late for work. Like losing a job, even when I know perfectly goddamn well how her daddy will be there to pay the bills.

"Sure," she says, "that might work. Then again, it might not. It might just piss her off, and then your goose would be cooked, wouldn't it?"

Down on the sidewalk, the man's stopped shouting and the dog's stopped barking.

"It's kind of messed up when you think about it," she says, and the smoke curls over her head like a ghostly question mark.

"When you think about what? What's kind of 'messed up?'"

"How just about every culture in the world, probably every culture going back to the fucking Neanderthals, has some sort of vampire. How human beings are so obsessed with something sidling up next to them in the dark and drinking their blood."

"Did I ever tell you about the time I got a leech on my leg?" I ask, and she stops staring at the blemish and makes a disgusted face.

"No," she says, "and I would prefer if you did not. Some of us didn't grow up in the sticks, and we were spared such grotesque indignities as leeches and rabid possum attacks and what the hell ever else."

"I'm not even sure possums can get rabies," I say.

"Now you're just being pedantic."

"Serves you right, not wanting to hear about my leech. I was wading in a creek, and before I noticed it was on me—there's some sort of natural anaesthetic in their saliva, I think, so you don't feel when they bite—"

"I said I don't want to hear this."

"—and before I noticed, the thing was swollen about as big as my thumb."

Then she says that if I won't shut the hell up about leeches, I can find some other fuck-buddy, because, after all, she's not that hard up, and, by the way, did I at least leave enough milk that she'll have some for her coffee? I tell her sure, I left enough milk, and I don't say anything else about leeches. Or ticks. Or fleas. Or hair vampires.

"Well, don't just mope around the apartment all day," she says. "If you can't write, go somewhere. Take a walk or go to a movie or something. You're getting morbid again."

I say I'll look at the paper and see what's playing, that a movie might be a good idea. If I can't write, that is, and lately there have been more days when I can't than there have been days when I can. I want to point out that, morbid or not, I wasn't the one who brought up flying, detachable, blood-sucking lady heads. I'm just a horny freelance between cheques. I know which side my bread's buttered on. You betcha.

## 2

It rains on Monday, and I lie here in bed listening to the raindrops spattering across the roof and windows, and it sounds so much to me like bacon frying that I would almost say the two sounds are indistinguishable. Every now and then there's thunder, but no lightning, just the storm dry-heaving over the city, and me listening, and the apartment as still as it ever gets. You're at work. I'm not. I should be at the typewriter on the desk, here in this spare bedroom you're letting me use until I'm on my feet again, but I'm lying here in bed, instead. The rain sounds like cooking meat, but I've said that already. And I'm thinking about the last time I was in Philadelphia, one of those cities I find myself in, from time to time, even though I have no particular fondness for it. But, that last time, one thing or another had taken me to Philadelphia, it doesn't really matter what, and I looked up a friend there, someone I'd known in college but hadn't seen for years, and she asked had I ever been to the Mütter Museum at the College of Physicians, and I told her no, I never had. I told her that, in fact, I'd never even heard of the Mütter Museum, and she said I'd love it. She said it was right up my alley, unless I'd changed an awful lot in the decade and a half since college, and I said no, I didn't suppose that I had changed very much at all. Not really. I don't think any of us do, she told me, and I didn't argue. I know that, after a fashion, it's my job to understand people, not the same way it's the job of a psychiatrist or a psychologist, but it's part of my job, all the same. But knowing people is one of those parts of my job that I'm not very good at. Anyway, she said we should have lunch first, and later I'd understand why, so we met at a sandwich shop on Market Street, just a couple of blocks from the museum, and we ate and drank coffee and caught up, the way that friends who have become only close acquaintances do. She talked about her children and her husband, and we reminisced about school, and I talked about writing and the books and the things I did to pay the bills whenever the books weren't enough. I told her that it was a point of pride that I'd not yet resorted to prostitution or selling illegal drugs, and she laughed as if I were joking. I told myself I was. She picked up the check, and then I put more change in the parking meter, and we walked hand in hand to the Mütter, as though *this* were still *then* and she were still playing at and trying on a life and a sexuality that she'd shed shortly after graduation, easy as a snake sheds its skin. I don't hold that against her. I never have. Truthfully, at times I have been jealous that I was unable to do the same, but that's nothing I have ever told her. It's nothing that I would ever tell anyone. It doesn't take long to reach the black iron gates and the white marble columns and pediments of the museum, COLLEGE OF PHYSICIANS etched into the stone, a façade of sturdy Federal architecture to conceal the menagerie of horrors tucked inside. I won't go into all those particulars. I'm not in the mood. But it would be difficult to conceive of an affliction of the human body, whether congenital or inflicted by disease or injury, that was not represented among those jars of formaldehyde, the plaster casts and skeletons, the wax models and teratologies and row after row after row of human skulls, all of it kept safe behind glass, framed in garish Victorian splendour. It wasn't right up my alley, or if it was, I'm now pretending that it wasn't. But she led me from case to case, and I followed, dutiful as a hound, and I feigned interest (and not revulsion) while she talked enthusiastically about this or that or some other malformation. Siamese twins. A paper-thin bit of Albert Einstein's brain. A human embryo with two perfectly developed heads. Examples of hydrocephalus and microcephaly. And then we came to a case with odd bits of gold jewellery, and she explained to me how the stones set into the rings and pendants were actually bezoars, hardened masses of food and other substances that sometime form within the human intestinal tract, believed by some to have magical or medicinal properties. Beside the jewellery, a jar preserving a trichobezoar, an ugly tangle of half-digested hair taken from the gut of a young woman who suffered from "Rapunzel syndrome", trichophagia, and as if the trichobezoar weren't awful enough, there was a larger jar inside the same display case, a jar with something else inside, something larger and much more awful than the trichobezoar. That time I almost looked away, while she read the printed label aloud to me and said how she didn't recall this from any of her other trips to the Mütter. Occasionally they swap things out, she said. The thing in the jar was mostly hair, but there was also the lump of flesh that the hair was attached to. It made me think of a heart, even though it really didn't actually *look* much like a heart. It almost looked like a sea urchin, I thought, but still it reminded me of a heart. Unidentified growth removed from the base of the skull of a man in Timișoara, Romania in 1972, she read, and I stared at it, thinking of a pumping heart, sending oxygenated blood one way and deoxygenated blood another, but also thinking of something clinging to a rock at the bottom of the sea, all that hair drifting to and fro in the current, poisonous tendrils cast about to ensnare plankton and tiny, unsuspecting fish. Then we moved along to the next exhibit, the next assemblage of monstrosities, and look at that, she said, and isn't that remarkable, and isn't that just the most hideous thing ever?

## 3

And *this* night, this night here that I am putting onto paper and rendering only sterile words by the *clack, clack, clack* of the antique keys of my sturdy German-made Olympia, *this* night *right* here I have left the window partway open, because on summer nights this apartment would become an oven. I have left the window open, and if my sorry, broken life is only a ghost story, told so many times the truth of things has been forgotten, if that's the truth, then this night is what I sometimes think of as the fulcrum in the void. Three apartments ago now, because I move around a lot, which is what happens when you neglect, on a regular basis, to bother paying the rent.

"I have a big box-fan I'll bring over," she said, and I said sure, if you're really not using it. And then she said, "It must be a sauna in there. It must be a kiln."

Something like that, I replied.

"You could get a window unit," she said, "maybe something second-hand. I can't imagine that would set you back very much."

No, I said, but the electric bill might.

So, it's this night in August, this August 12th, to be precise, and I am lying on sweaty sheets, unable to sleep for the heat. I've just switched off the light, because it was also too hot to read and I kept dripping sweat on the pages. Don't ask what I was reading; I honestly do not remember. But I remember switching off the lamp beside the bed and having a cigarette and listening to the traffic down on Highland, and I remember hearing a train. I remember the *smell* of my sweat and thinking that I needed to make a trip to the laundry soon. I stubbed out the cigarette, only half-smoked, and I shut my eyes, and I tried to sleep. I can hear a night bird, but nothing that I recognise, and I'm thinking how when I was a kid, when I was a boy, I could name just about every bird-call there was, at least the calls of the birds that live around here. And so I am lying there sweating and stinking of sweat and thinking about bird-songs I don't recognise, and the bedroom window is partway open, and—even though there's a screen on that window—something gets in, flowing not-quite silently over the sill. It made a sound like velvet drawn across bare skin, a soft sort of a sound that is almost not any sort of sound at all. And I remember turning my face towards the window, not startled, only curious and expecting some utterly prosaic explanation for whatever I'd heard. I am not by nature a superstitious person. I never have been. I have never been afraid of the dark. I have never jumped at shadows.

"Well," she said, "I'll bring the fan over tomorrow. I doubt it uses as much electricity as a window unit would."

I told her I didn't know whether it would or not.

"Maybe it'll be cooler tomorrow," she said, but then I say no, not if the weathermen are to be believed. If anything, it's going to be worse.

"I had an apartment like that," she said. "A few years back. I'd take long cold baths before bed, just about every night in the summer."

And what I almost said then, I barely manage to keep it to myself.

*So what happened next, after the bird and after you heard that sound?*

*I really don't think the bird was a part of it, a part of whatever did or didn't happen that night. I think the bird was only a bird.*

*Was it an owl?*

*No, it wasn't an owl.*

*Well, the Greeks and the Romans, they believed in something called strixes, and the strixes were birds, or something like birds, like owls, They would attack babies in their cribs and drink their blood. They would disembowel infants.*

*That's fucking awful.*

*Ovid wrote about strixes attacking a baby. Petronius wrote about strixes, too.*

Jesus, how do you know all this shit? Anyway, it wasn't an owl. It didn't sound anything like an owl. It was something else, not an owl.

"Well, I'll bring the fan over tomorrow evening, after work. I'll get some take-out, because Lord knows it's too hot to cook, and we'll drink beer and watch old movies. I think TCM is having some sort of *film noir* festival. You'll be done writing by the time I get off work, won't you? I don't want to interrupt. Just tell me what time, because I don't want to interrupt.

I tell her sure, I'll be done writing by the time she gets off work.

I'm not stalling. Somehow, it all fits together, if you look at the haunting from just the right angle. Somehow, it's all of a piece.

Or maybe I'm not *only* stalling.

*And I'm a goddamn coward, but, then again, so are you.*

... something gets in, flowing not-quite silently over the sill. It was a sound like velvet drawn slowly across bare skin. It was that sort of sound that is almost not any sort of sound at all. And I remember turning my face towards the window, not startled, only curious, and someone is standing there beside the window. In the room with me. I cannot see her clearly. The only light is the glow of the streetlight getting in through the window, and mostly I can only see her in silhouette. She is tall and thin and obviously female, or at least something that's doing a very good job of passing itself off as female. She isn't wearing any clothes, and her hair is so long that it comes all the way down to her ass. She stands there staring at me, still as stone, and I realise that I'm not the least bit afraid, and for a moment that seems more remarkable than whatever has slipped over the window-sill and into my stifling hot bedroom. My heart isn't racing. My mouth hasn't gone dry. The hairs on my arms and the back of my neck are not standing on end.

She takes one step towards the bed, and I start to sit up, but she tells me to be still.

Her voice is like the voice of a night bird.

Her voice is like broken glass.

And thunder.

"Are you death?" I ask, and as soon as the words have left my lips, I wish I'd kept them to myself.

"I don't have to be," she says, and then she says, "Why don't you wait and see?"

Her skin is as pale as milk, and her hair is as black as coal dust.

When her eyes catch the streetlight, they flash back a blue-green iridescence.

"Do you even have a name?" I ask.

"Why don't you wait and see?"

When did I start shifting tense. That's never a good sign. I mean, when I do it by accident like that. It always makes me think of Billy Pilgrim coming unstuck in time. But my memories of that night, they are both past and immediate and, in some sense, they seem almost like a presentiment, all at once.

"Why don't you wait and see?"

*What scares you most of all? What scares you more than dying the most horrible death you can imagine, that's the sort of fear I mean. I don't mean what merely frightens you, the way that people are afraid of spiders or germs or failure. I mean something that absolutely fucking terrifies you, like Moses must have felt looking at that burning bush, like that. Maybe I mean awe. Maybe I mean wonder as much as terror, and maybe there really isn't any difference between those things.*

*What scares me most of all? I won't tell you that . . .*

4

Only a few days ago, after breakfast, and she's washing up, rinsing the frying pan and plates and placing them inside the dishwasher. I'm sitting at the table by the window (and there is so much to this about windows, I know), smoking and watching her. She made eggs and bacon and toast. She made me eat breakfast, because she knows how often I skip breakfast and lunch. She says I'm losing weight. She says I'm looking thin in the skin. I blow smoke at the ceiling and wonder if there's enough coffee for another cup. She rinses her hands, then shuts off the tap. The air smells like food and cigarettes and dishwashing detergent.

"I've read about the Mütter," she says. "I've never been there, but I've read about it. I've seen pictures. I don't think I'd enjoy the experience."

I balance my cigarette on the edge of a souvenir ashtray shaped like the state of Florida. There's a tiny ceramic alligator perched right about where Jacksonville would be.

"I can't say I did, but I didn't tell her that. I made like I was having a blast, ogling the dead and the maimed, the diseased and the stillborn. Anyway, it's where this whole business started. The hair vampire, I mean."

"You still haven't finished the story."

"No, and I'm starting to think that I won't. It might be one of those I stick in the filing cabinet and leave stuck in the filing cabinet. It's probably one of those I never should have started."

"I can't do that," she says.

"You can't do what?" I ask her.

"I can't start something and not finish it. Even if I know I shouldn't have begun it to begin with. I wonder if psychiatrists have invented a phobia for that, for people with a morbid dread of not finishing things?"

"They've invented one for just about everything else."

"So," she says, shutting the door to the dishwasher, "that's the inspiration, the thing in the jar from Romania?" She turns a dial and the machine clatters and makes a loud, wet hissing sound, and she says how one day it's gonna blow up and take the whole damn kitchen with it.

"Have you told your landlord about it?" I ask.

"Only fifty or sixty times," she says. "I don't think fixing my dishwasher is high on his list of priorities."

"Then fuck him," I say, and she laughs and sits down and lights a cigarette of her own. And I say, "Yeah, it was the thing in the jar. And I started in wondering about hair and blood and mosquitoes—"

"Mosquitoes?"

"Think about it," I say. "The diameter of human hair varies from seventeen to one hundred and eighty-one micrometers in diameter. The proboscis of a mosquito, specifically the part called the internal tubular labrum, the part that draws blood when you get bitten, it's about forty to one hundred micrometers in diameter. And the diameter of a human red blood cell is only six-point-two to eight-point-two micrometers, with a maximum thickness of maybe one micrometer. If human hairs were hollow—"

"Which they're not."

"But if they *were*," I say, "if they *were* . . . well, the average human head has about a hundred thousand hair follicles. Now, hungry mosquitoes can hold about three millionths of a litre of blood, which isn't very impressive, given our bodies hold about five litres. At the rate a mosquito drinks, speaking hypothetically, it would take about two thousand of them a day and a half to completely drain a human body dry. But the hairs on your head, well, that's like *ten* thousand mosquitoes worth of hair, *if* those hairs functioned as hollow proboscides—"

"I think you might be right about the file cabinet. Also, I think it's proboscises, *not* proboscides."

"Look it up," I say, and I tap grey ash at the alligator's feet. "But do you see what I'm getting at, whether it's a dumb idea or not?"

"Oh, it's a dumb idea," she says. "It's most definitely a dumb idea."

"I've sold dumber."

"I'm not sure that's something I'd go around bragging about, dear."

## 5

"It was a dream," you tell me, and I say no, it wasn't a dream, that I was wide awake, that I'm very sure I was awake, as sure as I'm awake right now and having this conversation, and you say, "Fine, so maybe it was sleep paralysis. Maybe you were waking up, but you couldn't move, because that's what happens during sleep paralysis," and then you start in talking about hallucinations, how people who suffer from sleep paralysis often imagine there's someone in the room with them who isn't, an intruder, someone who isn't supposed to be there. You say how, once upon a time, long ago, people probably would have thought of the intruder as an incubus and a succubus, but now we tend to imagine we're being abducted by little grey aliens from Zeta Reticuli. "I wasn't asleep," I say. "I wasn't even partway asleep, and I could move just fine. I was even able to talk just fine. So, it wasn't sleep paralysis." I realise that I'm starting to sound annoyed. From the look on your face, I might even be starting to sound a little angry, and you say, "Okay, have it your way. There was a woman in your room. She climbed in through the window, like in that Joe Cocker song." I say that in the Joe Cocker song it was a bathroom window, not a bedroom window, then add, "And, anyway, it was a Beatles song. Joe Cocker only covered it." You shrug and tell me you've never heard the Beatles version and that I'm being pedantic, just arguing to hear my own voice, and I say that doesn't change the facts, Ma'am.

*What scares you most of all?*

*I used to think it was dying in a fire, being burned alive. Or being dead but still fully conscious and having to be aware while I was being embalmed and buried and everything.*

*But now it's something else? Now it's something even worse?*

*Isn't there always something worse?*

*Isn't there always?*

And you say, "So I used this wire coat hanger that I'd straightened out, which now they say you're not ever supposed to do, because these days all the pipes are shitty PVC and not copper or iron or whatever pipes used to be made from before we started making everything out of fucking plastic. I stuck the wire down the drain and sorta fished about with it for maybe—I don't know—five minutes or so until I finally hooked the clog and could starting pulling it out. Jesus, *that* was nasty. Some of that hair had probably been stuck in there for years, catching toothpaste and little bits of food and dead skin and whatever, right? And turns out, the worst of it wasn't the stench of all that rotting hair. But the worst of it was how the damn sink still wouldn't drain, even after I got all the hair out. Well, all of it I could reach. I could only get the coat hanger in just so far, because of the S-bend or the P-trap or whatever plumbers call it. I think I washed my hands about a hundred times afterwards. I was a regular goddamn Lady Macbeth for the rest of the day."

## 6

Silhouetted against the window, silhouetted by the streetlights, her pale skin seems almost luminescent. It reminds me of the moon. *Maybe it's supposed to,* I think. *Maybe that's exactly what it's supposed to do. Maybe she's something the moon sends down whenever it's hungry.*

The woman, the thing that might be a woman, takes a step nearer the bed, and I start to sit up, but then she tells me to be still, to lie there just exactly as I am, and I do as I'm told. I do as she's *told* me to do.

Her voice is like the voice of a night bird.

Her voice is like broken glass.

And thunder rolling across the face of the world.

I've said all these things before. I have spent night after night after night, day after day, saying these things, never coming any nearer to the truth of it, knowing that I never, ever will.

"What if I'm not afraid of you?" I ask her. "What if I'm not afraid of you at all."

"What if you're not?" she asks me, not quite an echo.

"Isn't that what you're for?"

"I don't have to be," she says.

"Then why are you here?"

"Why don't you wait and see?"

I smell flowers then. I think that I smell morning glories, but I can't be sure. The last time I smelled them was when I was a child, and there were morning glories in my mother's garden. The seeds of morning glories can be as potent a hallucinogen as LSD, if you eat enough of them. My mother only warned me they were poisonous.

The air smells like flowers, and I imagine that I can hear thunder.

"I want to know what you are," I say.

"Why do you assume that I would know?"

"Don't you?"

"Why don't you wait and see?"

She's very close to the bed now, very close to the foot of the bed, and she reaches out with her left hand and gently touches my belly, but that's impossible, unless her arms are much, much longer than they seem. Her hand is cold, but not yet *ice* cold. On these hot nights, I sleep above the covers because it's too hot to sleep beneath them, so all she had to do was reach out farther than she should have been able to reach and touch my bare skin. All she had to do is touch me, only she's still too far away. Her fingers trace a circle around my navel.

"Why, my dear, you're burning up," she says. "I always forget that part. I always forget that there's so much heat. Sometimes, I have even forgotten what warmth is."

"If I told you to leave, would you have to go?" I ask, and my voice doesn't sound even the least bit afraid.

"Is that what you want? For me to leave?"

I don't answer the question, because I honestly don't know the answer. Maybe that's exactly what I wanted when I first saw her standing by the open window, but it seems like that must have been hours and hours ago now. Her index finger draws a line through the sweat on my abdomen, all the way up to my breasts, and I can't help but suspect that she's looking for something. And I wonder if it's my heart, and I wonder if it's my soul, and I wonder if it's only the memory of something she's lost. Her cool finger is as good as any plough, splitting open the rough sod of me, digging invisible furrows in fallow meat, not like anyone was using it for anything, anyway, not like I haven't been sleepwalking through the years leading up to this sweltering August night. *Maybe she knows what I'm for*, I think. *Maybe she'll tell me, and so maybe, finally, I'll know, too.* It occurs to me that she can hear every word I'm thinking, and I'm surprised that I really don't care. After all, doesn't that make it all so much easier, that at last there's no need to talk or to type or to worry over correct syntax?

*Maybe she knows what I'm for.*

*Why don't you wait and see?*

Her hands are colder now.

I ought to shiver, but I don't. I only close my eyes.

She climbs on top of me, and the cold that wears her like a mask becomes a living presence, not a part of her, a being unto itself, and I can hear the whisper of snowfall and the splitting apart of ice on a frozen river and the almost imperceptible bone-deep rumble of a glacier grinding its slow path between mountains and down to the sea. I wonder what will be left of me when she's done, if there will be any more than the dust that a glacier makes of the hardest granite.

In the heart of a blizzard, a woman is lost and wandering alone.

*Is that you?*

*I don't know anymore. It might have been almost anyone. It's an old and evil memory, and you shouldn't dwell on it. You shouldn't have even seen it.*

The woman in the blizzard has long black hair, hair as black as coal, and the wind whips it into fantastical, impossible shapes.

*Once, I saw something awful in a museum.*

*I know*, she whispers somewhere deep inside my head, between the secret convolutions of my brain. I open my eyes again, and I gaze up at her face and all that hair, hair blown about her face by a wind that brings winter wherever she goes, a wind that is a dying woman's remembrance of the storm that lured her out into the snow, that got her so turned about she could never find her way home again. The storm that took her life. She leans down to kiss my lips, and I still smell morning glories. She leans down to kiss me, and I wonder how long it will take, and if there will be anything at all left when she's finished. I think these thoughts as black hair flows over and into me, searching and probing and piercing my skin like the needle-mouths of hundreds and thousands of starving mosquitoes, seeking warmth, and—lost and alone and drifting through the cold, howling heart of a blizzard—any warmth at all will do.

# JONATHAN CARROLL

## MAMA BRUISE

J ONATHAN CARROLL has published twenty novels, the latest
being *Mr. Breakfast*. He has won the World Fantasy Award, the
Bram Stoker Award, the British Fantasy Award, and France's Apollo
and Grand Prix de l'imaginaire awards.

"No matter how much we say we love them, too often dogs are
only bit-players in our daily lives," Carroll observes. "Worth a few
minutes of belly scratches or pets, maybe a short wrestle if they like
that, for some an occasional napping partner. But not a whole lot
more. Great companions because, face it, they make few demands
and love to do anything you're doing because well, they love you.

"But what happens if one day they suddenly demanded centre
stage in your life? What happens when they somehow take control
of your life and you have no idea how or why? What do we do when
Man's Best Friend suddenly holds your fate in its paw?"

S HE WAS THE first to fall. As she walked the dog one night, it
saw something off to the side and bolted. The strength of the big
animal's lunge on the leash spun her violently around and she lost her
balance. Falling into that awful moment we've all known, the "I can't
stop this" moment, her only thought was: *Not my head. Not my*

*head*— But the drop was brutal and when she went down her head hit the kerbstone. Luckily she wore a thick woollen cap, so the blow was softened. But her body took a full hit. She stayed down on the pavement long moments—breathless, shaken, and heart-poundingly disoriented. The dog stood calm nearby, staring at her.

When she got back to the apartment her stricken face said it all. Doing the dishes at the kitchen sink he looked up, saw her, and hurried over. "What's wrong? What happened?" He made her sit down and drink a cup of tea. Unsteadily, she recounted the trauma. Talking it over with him helped a little to lessen the aftershocks but not enough. A fall like that always reminds us how, in a second, life can skid off the road straight into our very own black hole. Down deep we know sooner or later it will, God forbid. A trip, a bad stumble, stagger, and fall shouts the ugly fact we're never *really* in charge or control of our steps, our days, our lives. No, not really.

As soon as she woke the next morning, she walked naked into the bathroom to look at her body in the full-length mirror there.

He stayed in bed as long as he could stand it, waiting for her to come out and tell him what she saw. But the anticipation was too great and he had to get up and go see.

She stood in front of the mirror, twisting from side to side, hands on her hips. The livid black bruise on her thigh was about ten inches long and spelled out in perfectly shaped block letters: MAMA BRUISE.

He winced when he saw it. "Jesus!"

"Where is he?" she asked quietly, still looking in the mirror.

"I guess in the kitchen in his bed."

She looked at him. "Are you sure?"

"No. Do you know what you did? What might have caused it?"

She shook her head. "No, nothing—I did everything as I always do. Gave him the same amount of food, took him out when he likes to go... but then this. It's getting worse. You know that—it's getting worse."

"What can we do? We've tried everything but nothing works. He just seems to get angrier. It's almost every day there's something that bothers him."

It had begun weeks before, on the night they went to the opera. In the excitement of preparing for the special night out, they'd forgotten to feed the dog. During intermission, the man went to the refreshment stand to buy two glasses of champagne. Taking his wallet out of his pocket, he saw written in what looked like thick, purple magic marker on the back of his right hand the word LADDIE. He stood there, scowling. When and why the hell did he write *that* there? He had absolutely no idea. It was just weird. Wetting his left thumb, he tried to wipe the word off but to no avail. Days later, it was still there, although it had just recently slowly begun to fade.

That night, after they returned home late from the opera, the man was opening a can of the dog's food and half-consciously noticed the name on the label: LADDIE.


A week later it was the cookies. For his birthday, she baked a dozen of his favourite chocolate chip cookies and left a plate of them fresh out of the oven on a corner of the kitchen table to surprise him when he came in from work.

When he entered the living room she raised her eyebrows in anticipation. "Did you go in the kitchen?"

"Yes. Why?"

"Didn't you see what was on the table in there?"

He looked puzzled. "No—there was nothing."

"*What?*" She got up from the couch and crossed the room to enter the kitchen. The table was empty. No cookies, no green plate. She looked quickly around, then down at the ground just in case. For a moment she questioned whether or not... Damn it, of course she did! She'd baked the cookies half an hour ago and put a plate of them out on the table for him when he got home. Happy birthday. The room even still smelled of baking. So where the hell were they? The dog lay on its bed at the far end of the room, watching them. She looked its way, wondering for a second if maybe it had eaten them. But if that were so, where was the plate?

"This is nuts! Where did they go?"

He stood behind her. "Where did *what* go?"

"Cookies! I made cookies for your birthday and— Wait a minute."

She went to a cabinet over the sink and opened it. Inside on a shelf was a plate with the rest of the cookies. That didn't calm her. She pointed to them and made a face. "There you go—that's the *rest*. But where are the damned ones I put on the table?"

He had to fight to keep from smiling. She was getting pretty wrought up over...uh...cookies.

"Oh, anyway..." She moved over to the broom closet and, opening the door, took out a big, grey, nondescript box with a red bow tied around it. "Happy birthday, sweetheart. I hope you like it."

But she already knew he would because he'd been talking about getting a really good cowboy hat for months. She thought they looked dorky on anybody except cowboys a hundred years ago. But he loved them so she kept her opinion to herself and bought him a genuine, top-of-the-line Stetson Silverbelly 10X Shasta Fur Felt Hat—the gold standard of cowboy hats.

Taking the box over to the table, he put it there and sat down in front of it, placing his hands on the red bow. He grinned and she was really excited to see how he would react when he saw what it was, although she kept thinking about those stupid cookies.

"What is it?"

"See for yourself, birthday boy."

"You always give great presents."

"Open it." She stood a few feet away from him, so at that angle she couldn't quite see into the box.

He pulled slowly on the red ribbon and it slid off. He took off the top of the box and looked inside, his expression all happy anticipation—for a few seconds. Then it changed. It torqued into a sort of quizzical smile, an "am I being tricked?" smile. An "I don't get it" smile.

She read the confusion immediately and came over to look. Inside the box was a green plate with five chocolate chip cookies on it.

The couple looked at each other sceptically, wondering if a trick was being played. Had he discovered her present and slipped the cookies into the box to give her a nasty little freak-out? From his perspective—was she playing some kind of not terribly funny prank on him on his *birthday*?

They'd been going through a rocky period lately, and at one point had only just brought their boat into shore before their emotional storms grew fierce enough to capsize them. Sometimes they still looked at each other warily, sadly, worriedly, both wondering if their marriage was strong enough to survive. In happier times they would have taken this moment to look slyly but delightedly at each other and assumed the best kind of joke was being played on them by their partner. But now, if this "what's in the box?" was a joke, their gut reactions were mixed.

"There's only five."

"What?"

She pointed at the cookies. "There's only five there. One is missing. I put six cookies on that plate."

They looked around the kitchen, as if the missing cookie might have escaped the plate while it was being put inside the box.

"Did you do this? Did you know about the hat?"

"*What* hat?" he asked.

She needed a long silent moment to look at him, at his expression, to make sure he was telling the truth. In the old days, in their solid love days, she would never have needed that moment.

"The hat I bought for your birthday; the Stetson."

His face opened like a child's in wonder. "*What?* You bought me a *Stetson*? Really? That's crazy!"

Instantly she took what he'd said the wrong way. "Why crazy?"

"Because it's great; because they're expensive and you didn't have to do that. What an amazing present!"

He could be so open, so full of joy and appreciation sometimes. It was one of his most loveable qualities. She didn't see it so often these days, but knew that was partly her fault.

Still grinning, he asked, "So where is it?"

"Where's what?"

"The hat, the Stetson—I can't wait to see it."

"It was in the box. *This* box—the one which is now filled with chocolate chip cookies. Abracadabra. What is going on?"

He held up a hand to slow her down. He knew when she got really wound up it was time to run for the hills. "Take it easy—"

"I don't *want* to take it easy—I want to find your hat and know why the stupid cookies are in there and not on the table where I put them."

"It's no big deal—we'll figure it out." He didn't know what else to say, and could tell from the rising tone of her voice that she was about to blow.

She stopped checking the kitchen for evidence and slid her eyes back to him. They were cold as Antarctica. "I *know* it's not a big deal, but the whole thing is very strange; no—actually, it's *creepy*, and I don't like creepy. Know what I mean? I had everything planned out for tonight: The cookies, the hat, a nice dinner with you on your birthday—"

"We can still do that! Where would you like to go?" But now *his* voice started to rise. Not a good sign. Not good at all.

Maybe it was the tone of their voices. Dogs seem to know when the human voice goes grim, and what that often portends. Whatever the reason, it got up from its bed in a corner, stretched, and walked over to them. Standing next to the man, it wagged its tail slowly. It looked from one human to the other. The man felt its presence and looked down at his old friend. He knew the dog didn't like it when they raised their voices. Recently, when that happened, the animal had taken to slowly skulking out of the room as if it were to blame for their unhappiness with each other.

The man patted it twice lightly on the head, forgetting for a moment the article he'd read the other day that said dogs don't like to be patted on the head.

"I just want to find your damned hat right now."

The dog looked up at the man to see if he was going to answer. When he didn't, it walked out of the kitchen, across the living room, and into the bedroom. There it started to bark. And bark and bark. In the kitchen, the couple looked at each other quizzically, because it never barked.

"What the hell—" They left the kitchen to see what was going on. Following the barking to the bedroom, they saw the dog sitting by the side of the bed, facing the door, as if it were waiting for them to come in.

Placed on the middle of the man's pillow was a beige cowboy hat. On her pillow was a fat chocolate chip cookie.

She gasped.

He loved it. Turning to her, he said gleefully, "That is so *brilliant*, honey. Really! This whole set-up—you had me so fooled."

"I didn't."

"Didn't what?"

"I didn't do this."

"Come on." Smirking at what she said, he walked to the bed, plucked the hat off the pillow, and plopped it on his head. He stepped to the wall mirror to check his reflection. "*Damn!*" Turning to face her, he pointed to the hat with both hands. "Come on—tell me I do not look *gooood* in this."

She thought he looked ridiculous. But he was so happy, so proud and pleased with himself. How could she say no? She gave a wan smile, a tilt of her head to the side she hoped would tell him, *You're right—you're the man!* without her actually having to say anything.

"But really—I didn't do this. I didn't switch these things."

"I heard you."

"No, but you've got to believe me—somebody else or *something* did."

He took the hat off his head and held it tightly in two hands in front of him. She wasn't joking—that much was clear by the tone of her voice. But what was he supposed to say, or ask? Half-sarcastically, he asked, "Well, who do you think did it, *him*?"

Standing a little off to one side, the dog watched and listened as the man pointed at it.

They didn't put the strange incident behind them, but were able to shift it to a corner of their lives—for a while. Secretly, she continued to wonder if *he* had moved the cookies and the hat as a dumb joke. But if he did, why keep denying it? There was nothing funny about it, and he knew things like that kind of unexplained chaos, however small, disturbed her.

In college she had been diagnosed with a mild case of obsessive-compulsive disorder, and no one knew better than he how it affected her. How many times had they returned to their apartment just one more time for her to check *again* to see if she had turned off the stove? It was imperative to her that certain matters and details be arranged just so—silverware in specific drawers, daily schedules, clothes lined up just so in the closet, the order in which she ate her food, the way she thought the world *should* work. It didn't, of course, so she fretted about too many unknowns and unlikely possibilities, most of which never happened. Time and again, her husband told her she was too full of what-ifs, and more times than he liked to admit, they screwed up the balance of their relationship. It was certainly part of the reason why they'd been so at odds with each other recently. Our quirks may define us, but they're not always endearing or attractive to those who love us, no matter how much they care.

She understood that and could sympathise with how her eccentricities (she preferred that term) burdened him. On the other hand, wasn't the wedding vow "for better or worse" what it was all about: Empathy, understanding, forgiveness?

And didn't she put up with his shortcomings? The soul-withering tight-fistedness with money, and his loutish, sometimes truly embarrassing behaviour when they were with friends or at social gatherings (the crude jokes and comments told to absolutely the wrong people who more than once looked at her with pitying eyes). But the worst of all were his dreadful parents, who from day one had made it very clear they didn't like her and would be happy if she disappeared from their son's life altogether. How they openly mocked her, but her man never said anything to them in her defence. When she brought it up, and she did often, he dismissed their gibes, derision, and personal insults as if they were nothing, or his parents didn't really mean them, or they'd had too much to drink, or perhaps she was being a little oversensitive, thin-skinned . . . She'd even gotten right up from meals on two occasions and walked out the door after his father said something so cruel and hurtful that momentarily she could not believe what she'd just heard. Both times, she'd turned to her husband and asked if he was going to say anything. But he only looked away from her volcanic glare, embarrassed but not about to stick up for her against "Pop". Well, bullshit on that.

The last time her father-in-law said awful, unnecessary things to her, thinly frosting the remarks with his brand of "humour," she told the old man to go to hell. He was a seventy-two-year-old asshole, and she'd had enough of him. Then she marched like a majorette out of the restaurant. Later, she told her husband that was the last straw. He could visit them whenever he wanted, but she was done with both his parents. "Pop" had finally crossed the line. No, he'd crossed it a long time ago, but tonight was the end.

"What do you mean, *crossed the line*? What line?"

She patted her chest over her heart. "*This* one—this line. Remember it? For years, your father has said terrible things to me that hurt my heart, and you were there every time to hear him. But you never, *ever* told him to stop, or at least shut up. Fair enough—that was your right, because he's your dad. But he isn't *mine*, so I don't have to put up with him like you and your mom obviously do."

His mouth tightened. "What's the matter with my mother?" His voice was a growl.

She growled right back at him, "Besides the hundred mean things *she's* said to me, only in a quieter voice? She *enables* him; in her own slinky way, she eggs him on. You've said it yourself. But I'm done with both of them now, and you know why. Please don't pretend you don't. Go see them whenever you want—I'll stay home with the dog."

The first time he did go for dinner alone with his parents, she ate hers standing up in the kitchen. As usual, the dog sat on its haunches, watching. She thought it wanted a piece of the large chicken leg she held, but no, there was something else there, some sort of different look in the hound's eyes that night as it stared at her.

"*What?* Do you want some of this?" She often spoke to the animal as if it were a person, and felt no shame or embarrassment doing it in private or when there were others around. She'd had dogs all her life and always considered them just another member of the family.

She was leaning with her back against the sink as she spoke, the dog directly in front of her. As soon as she finished speaking, there was a loud explosive *shishhhh* noise behind her. Shocked, she staggered forwards then turned around to see what it was. The faucet was shooting water into the sink full-blast, as if some invisible hands had turned on both hot and cold handles all the way.

"What the hell?" She knew she hadn't touched them, and water doesn't turn on by itself. The first surprise of the sound and discovering what it was receded, but she was still a little shaken up when she went back to the sink and turned off both spigots. Firmly. She stood there and looked down at them, trying to figure out how it had happened.

Then she remembered the chicken leg she had been eating. "Damn it!" She must have dropped it when the water started gushing. Looking down at the floor around her feet, it wasn't there. For a moment she thought had she already finished it? No. It was definitely in her hand when the water started flowing, She was sure of it. But so where was it now?

"First the water goes crazy, then my dinner disappears. What's next?"

What came next was the usual—when things got agitated in her life she almost always had to pee. Even the smallest things could set her off and start her bladder screaming *NOW OR ELSE*. Her husband thought it was cute and she knew he kind of secretly enjoyed her discomfort sometimes because normally she was such a control freak. But when it came to her bladder, she was its slave.

Stupid as it sounds, crazy water in the sink and a disappearing chicken leg set off the alarm this time, and she headed for the toilet. The dog watched her leave the room and padded after her. When she got to the bathroom, she opened the door and slid her hand up and down on the wall just inside, searching for the light switch. When she found it she flipped it on. The first thing she saw was the chicken leg placed on top of the lowered toilet seat.

After that, things got crazier in a hurry. They went from whimsical to worrisome and *whaaaat?* to dangerous and destructive. They kept coming and coming. But never once did either of them think any of it was because of the dog until finally, finally the writing appeared again on both of their bodies.

SPILKE changed everything.

One bright November morning, that name was inexplicably spelled out in clear black letters down the length of her right index finger. She did not notice it until she was brushing her teeth and saw it out of the corner of her eye.

Her hand froze and then slowly she lay the toothbrush down on the edge of the sink. Raising her hand to eye level, she stared at the finger, incredulous at what was written there: SPILKE.

Dennis Spilke. My God, how long had it been since she thought of *that* name, or him? He was her first boy-crush when she was eleven years old. Because she loved and trusted her father much more than her mother and considered him her best friend in the world, he was the only person she told about her love for Dennis. Her father was such a good guy back then. Back before the drinking and later the drugs hollowed him out and shrunk him into someone unrecognisable, then crazy as a fly banging against a window, then dead at fifty-one. Even her girlfriends at school didn't know about her short-lived swoon for Dennis. Even Dennis Spilke didn't know. Only her dad, and when it was over weeks later, he was the one who comforted her. He said: *Somewhere out there in the world right this minute is the man you will one day marry. Can you believe it? He's out there doing stuff, living a life like you. But all the time that's happening, he's moving slowly, slowly towards you. Think about that for a minute: He's coming—that boy is coming just for you. And when you two meet, you'll be so crazy about him that all the Dennis Spilkes you've known till then will seem like* cockroaches *compared to this new guy.* Just the word "cockroaches" got her laughing and, as always, her father's words made the hurt of her small world less.

But now here it was again, SPILKE, a zillion years later written in black on the inside of her finger. That odd name, all the forgotten memories of a boy and that time in her life suddenly came back *zap* into her head like an electric shock. A moment later she happened to look in the mirror above the sink. In the reflection she saw the dog sitting in the bathroom doorway behind her. Very humanly, it nodded at her as if to say, *Yes, it was me—I did that to you.*

Days later, when she finally told her husband the whole story, he exploded. "What do you mean it *nodded*?" Despite the loud scepticism in his voice, he threw a quick mistrustful glance at the dog lying near them on its bed. Its body was relaxed but the eyes were watching. When it saw the man look, its tail thumped once on the floor.

"Just what I said—it nodded, and then when I directly asked if it had written on my finger, it nodded again."

"Bullshit! That's completely bullshit!" He threw up his hands in exasperation. His wife could be nutty sometimes, especially about her obsessions, but this was way beyond that. This was stone-cold crazy.

She blew a strand of hair off her face. "Bullshit? Really? Then watch this."

He glared at her.

"No don't look at me—look at him." She pointed to the dog.

He looked and the dog nodded to him.

He looked back at his wife. "It nodded. Great. Nice trick. So what? Dogs do stuff like that."

"Now look at your fingers."

He was right-handed. He saw nothing there. He looked at his left hand. Down the fat pad to the base of his thumb were black letters spelling TURLEY. Jennifer Turley was the name of his first girlfriend.

"*What the fu*— What is this?"

"I think it's my father."

After that it took almost a full hour for her to explain to him what she thought was going on. She used example after example, some of which he had experienced, to prove her point. At the end, he told her about the night at the opera when the word LADDIE mysteriously appeared on his hand.

She wasn't surprised. "My dad died and came back as a dog. It explains why we chose him over all the others at the animal shelter that day. What made him so special? Just look at him—he's completely plain, nondescript—just a dog-dog. Why would we choose him over all the other sweet ones we saw there?"

"*You* chose him. I just said okay."

"Exactly—I chose him and now I know why, but I didn't then. I just thought he was cute."

While she spoke he kept glancing over at the dog. "How much does he know? I mean, does he know everything; can he understand everything we say?"

"I don't think so, and that's part of what's so frustrating. He knows little bits and pieces, which come and go like fireflies. I think his mind or his soul is caught between three places—human, dog, and death, or back from the dead. When his head is clear he can do all kinds of magical things, but a minute later he's like an old, old man with very bad Alzheimer's disease. Absolute blank, or just absolute *dog* and only dog. He can't remember or express anything; he doesn't understand anything you say. No, he *does*, but only in the way a dog understands human commands. He knows and can do amazing things but it's all broken up and scattered. Like, how did he know the name of your old girlfriend? And then the things he *does* know, he keeps forgetting. But he also can do these wild things, like making those words appear on our fingers, or turning on faucets, or..." She stopped and looked at him, her face almost guilty.

He sat up in his chair, sensing something. "*What?* Come on, what?"

She nodded slowly, as if telling herself it was okay to continue. "I told you about my father at the end of his life, remember? How he stole all of my mother's savings to buy drugs. He even took fourteen dollars I'd saved for a skateboard and spent it, too. He was completely out of control by then—mean and scary and desperate. God, he was so desperate. He probably would have sold our house, too, if the deed hadn't been in my mother's name." She made to say more, but instead got up and went to a desk nearby. She opened a drawer, took something out, and walked back with a bankbook in her hand. She opened it, leafed through some pages, found what she was looking for, and handed it to him. "Look at the balance."

It was their joint savings account. Because he was a tightwad, he knew exactly how much was in there, or *did* until that moment. When he saw the new, hefty balance his eyes widened. His mouth opened and closed like a fish out of water.

Watching his reaction, she put a hand over her mouth and then flapped it away. "I didn't tell you about it until I checked with the bank to make sure the money was real. It is. I believe he's paying me back for all the money he stole from us when he was alive."

He snorted. "Paying you back with interest! This is amazing. You're sure it's real?"

"It is real. And it fits a pattern—I think he came back to make amends."

But their wonder and delight was short-lived because, like a person with severe dementia, whatever the dog knew or whatever powers it had brought back from death rapidly began to blur, fade, and slip away like a human mind sucked down into the quicksand of the disease. And with that fade came the frustration and fury of the sufferer.

For a while, a short while, there were fascinating glimpses of what the dog had experienced after it died as a human, what death was like and how reincarnation worked. But only in mysterious, tantalising fragments—three words written in sugar across the coffee table in the living room. Or a paragraph on Tibetan *bardos* in a book about after-death experiences magically highlighted right before the woman's eyes in vivid yellow as the woman was reading the words for the first time. When the highlighting stopped, three exclamation points appeared beside the paragraph and then, in black, the word *this!*

No more money was put into their account, but a beautiful new ornate gravestone for her mother was in the cemetery the next time they went there to lay flowers on her plot.

One night, his awful parents appeared at the door and invited themselves in on the excuse Mama had baked his favourite chocolate chip cookies and just knew he'd want to eat them fresh out of the oven. The real reason they came was for one of their periodic snoops around the house to find things to fault and be nasty about. But first the old bitch had to show off and there had to be a cookie unveiling followed by the son's required yumming over how delicious they were.

The cookies were in the large red tin she always used and, for the umpteenth time, said she needed it back when it was empty. Why would the harridan think anyone would want to keep her old dented box?

The four of them sat down on the couch and Mama leaned forwards to present the goodies. As she did, a loud sound—a sort of *burp-urup-urup* came from inside the box. When she pulled the top off there were no cookies inside but an enormous, slimy, brown African goliath frog as big and wide as a Frisbee; it must have been ten inches by ten inches. The giant thing fit perfectly inside the tin. Before any of them could react, it hopped out of the box, across the coffee table, and onto the floor. The dog took one look at it, leapt forward, grabbed the huge frog in its mouth, shook it violently from side to side, and ran out of the room with his catch going *urup-urup* all the way.

The old woman squealed, her husband squawked like a parrot, and the two of them fled.

The younger couple sat on the couch, staring straight ahead. The woman fought back a smile but it didn't work. The smile turned into a giggle and then a howl of laughter. Her husband, his parents having just jetted out of his house in abject horror, cracked up, too. Neither of them felt the need to go find the dog.

When it reappeared later, its muzzle was covered with cookie crumbs.

Soon after that things got darker. The dog, that until then had slept peacefully, began having what sounded like terrible nightmares every time it slept. It twitched and shook, growled and barked. Several times, they tried to wake it, but that was dangerous because it came out of sleep in a rage, snapping and snarling, as if fighting off its dream enemies in real life.

The few messages it conveyed became more and more incoherent, most of the words misspelled; toward the end, strung together, they made no sense at all. The dog grew surly, sullen, and aloof—a complete change from the loveable goofy, friendly, warm guy who in the past liked nothing more than to cuddle up next to you on the couch and snooze.

After it pulled the woman to the ground, things got even worse. MAMA BRUISE was the last coherent message it communicated until right before the end. Twice after that it knocked the man down from behind when he was walking to answer the front door after the bell had rung.

"It's like he doesn't want me to answer it—like he's expecting someone bad."

And by its behaviour in other ways, it did seem like that. For hours it sat on the couch looking out the picture window onto the street, just watching. When they took it outside for a walk, it moved its head from side to side like a searchlight, its body so tense that it shook much of the time when it stood still.

The day it bit her, it ran away. She was walking it around the block when they saw another person coming towards them with a large white poodle on a leash. As soon as the two dogs saw each other, they stopped. Then the poodle flew into a barking, growling, snapping fit. It started jerking wildly on the leash, as if to get off and attack her dog however it could.

She'd never seen an aggressive poodle before, so she was surprised and caught up in watching it act out. Then she felt a terrible pain in her right hand—the one holding the leash. Looking down, she saw her dog biting her for the first time in its life. Yelping, she dropped the leash and the dog ran off as fast as it could, the leash trailing behind.

She just stood there watching it, helpless, her hand exploding with pain from the bite.

Although the dog had all of its rabies and distemper shots, her husband insisted she go to the hospital to be checked.

Driving home, he asked quietly, "Do you think we should try to find him?"

"No."

He nodded and said nothing more.

Hours later, in the middle of the night, he awoke and found she was not in bed. He got up and padded around searching for her. She was sitting in the dark in the living room on the couch, in the same place where the dog had stationed itself in the past days, staring out the window there.

Her husband sat down next to her. She turned to him and held up her bandaged hand. "*This* was a message. He didn't bite me because he was angry or trying to get away. He was telling me why, and that was the only way he could convey it at this point." She stopped and swallowed. "This was the only way he could tell me."

"Tell you what?"

"It came to me before when I was sleeping. It might've been the bite. Somehow it connected us in a way we hadn't been before. What came through was when you die and are reincarnated, you're not supposed to bring anything from your past life into the new. But for some reason he did, somehow he stayed part human—my father—part dog, and God knows what else. I think that combination should never have happened. But it gave him those special powers like some kind of weird alchemy. After a while, though, it all started to mix together in bad ways and then implode. Like a medicine gone bad, or that stops working. At the end, everything was slipping away from him. But whatever he was by then, he still knew one thing—they were coming to get him."

Her husband frowned. "*Who* was?"

"Other dogs and whatever else didn't want him alive. It's why he sat at the window all the time watching. He knew something was coming for him. That's why the poodle went crazy tonight when it saw him. They *know*. They all know that, with his mixed knowledge, no matter how debased it is, he's a threat, and they're out to get him."

"Get him? Why? What did he do?"

"Nothing. He didn't do anything—somehow it was done to him or it happened by mistake. He's like a calf born with two heads. A freak, but a dangerous one, because he knows things he's not supposed to. We're not supposed to communicate with animals, or know what happens to us after we die. But he does, so as long as he's alive he might tell us—" She stopped, cocked her head to one side, and held up a finger for him not to speak.

In the midnight quiet that followed, after a few moments they both heard it—a faint scratching. A faint scratching on their front door.

Then loud sniffing—scratching and sniffing. Then, their ears attuned to the sounds, they heard more of them, many more just outside the house, all of them near, all of them growing louder. Scratching, hard scratching now, frantic sniffing and whining. Louder, all those familiar sounds times ten, louder and more every minute, everywhere out there in the night. Very close.

# ALISON LITTLEWOOD

## THE SAME AS THE AIR

A LISON LITTLEWOOD's novel *Mistletoe* is a seasonal ghost story with glimpses into the Victorian era, as well as the early mid-winter festivals that lurk, phantom-like, behind our Christmas celebrations. Her other books include *A Cold Season*, *Path of Needles*, *The Unquiet House*, *Zombie Apocalypse!: Acapulcalypse Now*, *The Hidden People* and *The Crow Garden*. She also wrote *The Cottingley Cuckoo*, under the name "A.J. Elwood".

She has won the Shirley Jackson Award for Short Fiction, and Littlewood's short stories have been selected for a number of "Year's Best" anthologies and published in her collections *Quieter Paths* and *Five Feathered Tales*.

The author lives with her partner Fergus in Yorkshire, in a house of creaking doors and crooked walls. She loves exploring the hills and dales with her two hugely enthusiastic Dalmatians and has a penchant for books on folklore and weird history, Earl Grey tea, fountain pens and semicolons.

"This story is rooted in Tim Lebbon and Christopher Golden's idea for their anthology, *Ten Word Tragedies*. Inspired by a Frank Turner song, which spoke of him buying postcards by the yard in thrift shops, they contacted Frank and had him provide some of those postcards to inspire new stories.

"I was given one of those postcards, and as part of my delving into the possible meanings it could yield, I looked up the sender's name. 'Edda' turned out to be of Scandinavian origin, meaning 'great-grandmother'. That struck me as perfect for a storyteller, and so the connection between the postcard and a Swedish fairy tale began: one of my favourites, whereby a maiden loses herself in the forest, forever staring into a pool. The nature of her bewitchment is hinted at but never fully explained, and I always found that compelling and magical.

"Weirdly, way back when I was a student, I bought a poster of an image by John Bauer and hung it on my wall. I didn't know it illustrated a story, not then; I simply liked the picture. It showed a young girl with golden hair, sitting amongst the trees, staring down into a pool. That picture hung on my wall for years, long before I knew it was inspired by the very story that would so captivate me later. Another little postcard from the past, perhaps..."

THREE DAYS AGO, when I went to the Ebersole house, I didn't peek through the window or call out or try the door handle before I turned the key in the lock and walked in. I just watered the aspidistra, sprayed the orchid and sprinkled fish-food into the bowl, where Goldie rose to the surface, opening and closing his—or her—mouth.

This time, I peek through a window into the empty snug and then through another, from which I can see that the hallway is still clean and bare, before I take out Edda's fluffy owl key-ring and open up.

I call out when I'm standing inside, and I wait for the answer, but it's already clear that the house is empty. It still has that closed-up, gone-away feel. Their shoes aren't on the rug; their jackets aren't thrown over the newel post. It's absolutely quiet and still and I don't even want to move, though I call for them a second time when I go into the kitchen to check that Goldie's still swimming, and again when I tiptoe upstairs to their bedroom, where the bedspread doesn't have a crease in it.

I stare at the door across the landing, but I don't go in.

A little later I'm walking through my own front door, trying to release the stiffness in my shoulders, or maybe shake off the dust that's settling in the Ebersole house.

"Marni?" I glance into my own kitchen, at the postcards on the pin-board, the trail of Edda and Dick's travels mapped out in pictures. I don't like the silence that comes back and I hurry up the stairs, throw open the door to my daughter's room—but that's quiet too. She's left the Everly Brothers on the turntable but it's switched off.

Through the window, I see the corner of the pool; two feet, close together in the water.

"Marni!" I run down the stairs again, almost falling down the last few, then rush to the back-door, and stand there while my pulse thrums in my ears.

She's drifting in the pool, only that. She's on her back, her arms crossed behind her head as if on an inflatable, but she's simply floating; her eyes gaze up into the sky, which is story-book blue and scattered with fluffy clouds.

It takes her a moment to stir, as if her name had to pass through layers of deep water to reach her, and she suddenly flails as if my voice has robbed her of the ability to float. Splashes darken the Mexican tile.

"Mom! You startled me."

"I see that." I try to smile, hiding how she startled me too, though it's not easy with our friends so present in my mind, and the thing they'd written: *Say hello to Ada.*

"So, are they back?" she asks, and my smile fades.

Dick and Edda were supposed to be back two days ago. That's when their vacation ended; when Edda should have dropped in to collect her keys, when Dick should have gone back to the cider mill that fills one side of Maplewood with the scent of fermenting apples.

I shake my head, thinking of that empty house, and I have no idea what to tell her.

What's really weird is, the next day, when the police arrive, I already have the postcard in my hand.

I've been looking at it more closely, examining the postmark, the picture they selected, their every word; and of course, that extra line—the one that gave me a chill even when I first saw it. But I had told myself then that everything was fine; the cold trickle that ran down my back was only the air-conditioning fighting back the humidity a little too hard.

It had begun with my name, written neatly over our address: Margret. I had put the misspelling of Margaret down to the Florida heat, but then Edda had gone back and carefully written *Miss* over the top of it, rather than *Mrs.*—as if she'd forgotten my husband, Paul, altogether. Was that a joke, or something else? Was it because the postcard held some message meant only for me?

When I had read the block of text, nothing else was strange, not really:

*Dick and I having a wonderful time. Weather is beautiful. Today we went swimming for a couple of hours. The water is wonderful warm, 84 degrees the same as the air. On Thursday we leaving for the East Coast. Love Dick + Edda.*

*PS. Hi Marni! Next card we send is going to be for you again.*

I had put that grammatical lapse, *we leaving*, down to her rushing; that, and the way she'd crossed out the word *water* and scribbled another word over the top. It still gave me a strange feeling though, mainly because I couldn't read the word she'd added—what else could they have been swimming in?—but then I realised it said *gulf*. Of course it did, and that was perfectly normal too, except that the idea of Dick and Edda going swimming was just so odd; not something they'd do at all. Why had the word *water* not been enough? And why was her description so entirely different from the image they'd chosen—the Ringling Residence, a mock Venetian-Gothic mansion with its marble fireplace and arches and balconies and chandeliers? That was more their kind of thing, the sort of place Dick would admire while smoking a cigarette, without having to dirty his neat leather shoes.

It had all just seemed a little off, though it was nothing more than that—until I saw the line she must have appended last of all, written in a space at the very top of the card but upside down, as if floating there.

*Say hello to Ada.*

I had stared at that for a long time, as a darker feeling took hold somewhere inside me: dread, perhaps. The first inkling that something was very deeply wrong.

I had tried to put the postcard out of sight, but Marni had seen it. She snatched it from my hand, read quickly then stuck it on the pin-board and left. I had no idea if she'd noticed that extra line and I didn't point it out to her. I figured if she hadn't, it was best hidden right where it was, in plain view: the picture outward, revealing nothing but that opulent, mannered, but *normal* red and gold interior.

*Say hello to Ada.*

Ada had been their daughter, not mine. And she had been dead for two years.

I show the line to the policeman, though, when he calls to see if I know where the Ebersole family have gone. He frowns and gives it back to me. "So you think their state of mind was disturbed?"

"I have no idea." Do I think that? *Having a wonderful time.* They were on vacation. They had seemed fine when they drove off, Edda waving out of the window of their Studebaker until they passed out of sight. I look down at the tightly slanting letters she had written. It pains me to think of her forming the words and not being able to ask her why.

He tilts his head and takes the postcard back, peers at it. "Says here they're going to the East Coast." He glares over the top of it. "And you really have no idea where they went?"

"No. I'd have told you. I supposed Fort Lauderdale or Cocoa Beach or one of those places."

"You've heard nothing from them since?"

"Like I said."

He yields up the postcard again, a last communication from—where? An absence, now. A mystery. I have a sudden image of Dick and Edda floating in deep water—or perhaps it's the sky, or perhaps it's all one: *84 degrees the same as the air.*

"It's just strange," he says, "because that's not where they went."

I think of that picture of the Ringling Residence, combined with the information that they'd been swimming in the gulf.

He goes on. "Their last known location was only a few miles inland from Sarasota. They were at a cabin at Myakka River, at the state park."

If he has any suspicion I know more than I'm saying, it must be allayed by the expression on my face. A state park—Dick and Edda? It seems as likely as them going swimming. Less likely, even. I have an image of Dick tiptoeing through a swamp in his smart shoes, grimacing up at the wild birds.

"Well, Ma'am, you'll keep us informed if you hear anything."

I agree that of course I will and close the door after him, only then realising that Marni has been listening from the top of the stairs. I hear the bang as she shuts herself in her room and a moment later 'All I Have to Do is Dream' floats into the air.

Marni doesn't come down, not even when I call her for dinner. I walk up the stairs again, wondering when she stopped playing her records. I hadn't noticed the silence creeping back into the house.

When I go into her room she has the same sightless expression in her eyes as when she was floating in the pool, but instead she's gazing down at a book held in her lap. It's illustrated, meant for a younger child, and my misgivings don't subside when I see that it's *her* book— the one Edda gave to her when Ada died. The girls used to love it when they were small, and it was always Marni's favourite.

It's a book of Swedish fairy tales. Edda was of Scandinavian origin, her family having travelled the ocean to settle in New Sweden, further north on the Delaware. Dick was Pennsylvania Swiss; my husband was of English extraction, and I was born in the old country. Maplewood always had been a melting-pot.

Edda told us once that her name, in ancient Scandinavian, meant "great-grandmother". It was the perfect name for a storyteller, and she'd spread her book of fairy tales before her and read them aloud, enchanting us all.

I knew which story Marni would be reading before I looked at the page. There was the picture they used to love—a little princess sitting at the edge of a dark pool, staring down into the water.

Her name was Cottongrass, and she lived contentedly at her castle until she saw an elk, a thing of the wild, and begged him to take her to see the world. He warned her there was danger in it, but of course she wouldn't listen. She flung herself onto his back and off she went, encountering wicked elves and the witch of the forest with tangled hair and reaching arms. Eventually they found a dark pool amid the trees. Cottongrass leaned over the water and saw there another forest, one she couldn't reach; and the golden heart she wore about her neck slipped into its depths.

She stared after it, caught in some spell, until no one could tell she had ever been a princess. There was only a tall plant tipped with cotton leaning over the water, and there she remained, always looking after her lost heart.

The way Marni was staring at that picture now discomfited me, and I called her name, hearing the echo of another voice, another time:

"Marni comes from the word Marina," Edda had once said. "It means 'of the sea'." And then, "Margaret is from the Greek Margarites. It means 'pearl'. A secret and underwater thing."

I reach out and take the book from Marni's hands, closing it against that image of the dark pool. It is only then that she shifts, only then that she seems to realise I'm standing in front of her. There are tears in her eyes, salt water, and I want to brush them away, but her smile is so confused that I don't touch her.

"What did they mean?" she asks.

"Who, sweetie?"

"They said the next postcard they sent was going to be for me."

An unpleasant jolt passes through me. "Nothing. Only that they'd address it to you, like they used to—remember?" Even as I speak, I wonder if there was more to it. Had it been another way of saying that this card was meant just for me?

She frowns, as if she doesn't understand. "Yes," she says, "but what did they *mean*?"

I just look at her. And all I can think is, *why doesn't she ask about the other line—the one about Ada?* If she hadn't seen it before, she must have heard the policeman talking about it. Why isn't she wondering about that?

But we don't mention it. We remain quiet and a little dull all through dinner, although her father is home early. Paul keeps looking from one of us to the other as if to puzzle us out, but he doesn't say much either. He tries to start a conversation about where we should go this summer, what we should do, but he soon gives up.

After she helps clear the dishes, Marni goes outside into a golden evening full of the hum of insects. Somewhere close by, some boys are shooting baskets; the noise they make doesn't seem to trouble her. She's quite motionless, sitting by the side of the pool, staring down into the clear and lovely water.

We hadn't used to vacation apart. We used to go with the Ebersoles every year, having met through the girls, who were the same age. We'd grown close—had barbecues together at their peach-painted colonial, pool picnics at our place, hung out together at the block parties which were a regular feature of life in Maplewood. So when it came to the summer it seemed natural to choose a rental together too, to decide between us where to go and what to see.

On the last trip we took together, Dick had wanted to visit some old country house. It had sounded dull even to us adults but we said we'd go too, and so did Marni; only Ada hadn't. She'd just turned thirteen, though she was sensible, we all said so, and when she insisted she was old enough to take care of herself for a couple of hours, we'd agreed. And we hadn't worried, not really; not until we got back and walked through the empty rooms, hearing no reply when we called her name.

I can still remember, with absolute clarity, looking out of the French doors and seeing two feet floating in the pool, though I hadn't recognised what they were, not all at once; not with the toes pointing downward.

She was just as she had been in that line on the postcard: at the top and upside down, though she would never say hello to anybody ever again.

I look out of the window now at Marni's downturned face. Her hair is hanging over her eyes so that I can't see her expression, and something about the scene makes me shudder—the similarity, perhaps, to an illustration in a book. Is it the water itself that so draws her attention, or something else? It almost seems as if the word *water* should be crossed out and replaced by something more mysterious: not a thing, but an empty space; an absence; a gulf.

I jump when Paul comes and puts his head on my shoulder, wraps his arms around my waist. "About the summer," he murmurs.

"Myakka," I hear myself say. "The state park, Paul. I want to go to Myakka River."

We're gone later that same week—school is out, Paul is due the time off, and there's no point in waiting. I only go to the Ebersole house once more, to retrieve Goldie—I leave him with a neighbour, likewise the orchid. The aspidistra's too heavy; it will have to fend for itself.

I called ahead, managed to reserve the same palm-log cabin that Edda and Dick last stayed in, but when we walk in the door I can't sense anything of them. Of course, there's no sign they've ever been here, which is to be expected. The park ranger told me they'd left their luggage behind, still unpacked in the various drawers and closets, but it's all been cleared away. The police came by and looked at it, he said, but haven't been back since.

The cabin was built in the 1930s by the Civilian Conservation Corps, along with the picnic pavilions and visitor centre. It's pretty comfortable, but too big; it was designed to sleep six and I can't help thinking that's how many we would once have been.

The park, too, is huge. It hadn't occurred to me before how very extensive it is—how impossible to follow where they have gone. Myakka River flows for mile upon mile through wetland, prairie and pineland. We saw the prairie from the road, dry and empty with treacherous sugar sand interspersed with grasses and palmetto, and I don't feel drawn to it at all. But there are two lakes as well as the river, and thousands of wetland areas scattered across the park.

We don't go far on our first day. It's getting late and we pause only to watch the sun spreading itself over the Myakka, Venus shining low in the sky. Marni scowls and slaps at the mosquitoes biting her arms. The banks of the river are hidden in reeds, and it takes me a while to see the night-heron standing at the edge, staring fixedly into the water until its head darts down. It straightens, its catch lost, and takes to wing.

It was the Seminoles who called the river *Myakka*. If there was ever a translation, it has long since been lost.

*The water is wonderful warm, 84 degrees the same as the air.*

It's so humid that night I don't think I'll be able to sleep. Paul's a twitching weight next to me and it's too hot to bear touching his skin. I must sleep, however, because I wake at some unknown time of the night, thrashing the single sheet away from me, feeling like I'm drowning in its folds. *Wonderful warm*, I think, and open my eyes to see shifting veils of cloth and think of Dick and Edda immersed in some liquid too warm to be the sea; viscous and dark, like amniotic fluid. They're waving their arms, though not to me. Their eyes don't see me and I wonder what it is they're focused upon. Have they found a pool they can stare into forever? Or is it the faces of the dead they see all around them—have they found Ada at last?

I lie there listening to the lonely cries of shorebirds coming out of the night until I sleep again. When I wake, Paul and Marni are making pancakes, and the smell is of home and Maplewood, somewhere safe and known, and I smile.

We eat at the table in one corner of the big empty room. The sun is low, but it's already warm, and I sense the heat of deep green water coming from somewhere beyond the window.

"I want to go swimming," Marni says, but that's not what we do. It had come as an indefinable relief to me to know that she couldn't, not here—the water isn't fit for swimming. The river is wide and deep and wild. It's a nature reserve. There are rare birds: roseate spoonbills as pink as flamingos, bald eagles, caracaras, sandhill cranes, black vultures. There are raccoons and opossums and whitetail deer, and there are alligators too, hidden in the reeds at the edge of the wetlands.

And yet I know why my daughter longs for the water—the heat

will be unbearable by midday. Is that why Dick and Edda had overcome their aversion and gone swimming, wherever they were? Had they simply wanted to cool off—something as ordinary as that?

We spend the morning following the park drive, then trying to spot wildlife from the boardwalk by Upper Myakka Lake. We don't see much; a couple of noisy families keep the birds at bay. Marni says little and I can see she's bored already, unless it's her innermost thoughts that are keeping her lips pursed. And suddenly I know what will happen. We'll spend a day or so here, then the two of them will want to leave. They'll want the cooler breezes of the coast; they'll crave the sea. We'll head west rather than east, having learned nothing. We'll go home and eventually the Ebersole house will be sold and Ada and Edda and Dick will be nothing but a memory that occasionally surfaces, like a fish in a lake, there and then gone.

When Marni clamours to go on the airboat lake tour, I plead a headache. Someone has to look for our friends; they can't be altogether forgotten.

I go back to the cabin first, searching the place as if Edda could have left some clue for me—a postcard perhaps, stuck to a pinboard—but there's nothing, only plain log walls, not even a picture hanging there. I rummage through the field guides and nature books and information about the park, but they're all printed glossy pictures; there's no way to reach beneath the surface. But it's not in here that I'll find them, I know that. They're gone—vanished into water that feels like air, or perhaps into the soupy air that feels like water.

I step outside again, not sure where I'm going to go. No one else is around—we're surrounded by trees, though I can see other cabins through the trunks. The place seems empty. Any other guests must be out sightseeing, and there's no reason for anyone else to wander here. A narrow track leads back to the road and a dirt path, narrower still, winds into the woods. I imagine Edda and Dick walking away between the trees, her blonde head next to his dark one, until they pass out of sight. But in that direction they'd only reach the lake—it's where everyone goes, all the families with matching shirts and hats and sunburned noses.

Instead, on a whim, I walk into the trees. There's no trail here, no wooden signs to point the way. A straight line is impossible and I wind around their trunks, duck beneath low branches. Hard-packed dirt soon gives way to softer earth that stifles the sound of my steps. The wind turns the leaves this way and that, sighing like waves on the seashore. It feels almost as if they're talking to me and I keep going, wandering until my feet begin to sink. Patches of reeds are showing beyond the trees; the purple of wild iris marks the edge of a marsh.

I take another step and my sneaker is soaked. I draw back as a bird starts up from the reeds—black body, long legs, some kind of wader. I watch it go, then I'm startled again by the fleeting brilliance of a monarch butterfly.

It's beautiful, but I can't continue, not this way. This is real wilderness. Surely no one could have come here. There's no path and it's half-flooded, and I suddenly realise I've wandered at random—how will I find my way back with no markers, no map, no compass? But a leap of hope comes: the ground's so soft I can surely follow my own footprints, and I turn and see a deer standing in front of me.

It's a whitetail, delicately boned, its hide softly dappled. Its nostrils are flared, twitching after my scent; its eyes are wide and fixed and looking straight at me. For a moment we regard each other. I wonder if there's knowledge in its eyes, but all I can see is fear; it must be reflected in my own.

The deer bounds off, crossing my path in one huge leap, and away. Where it pushes the undergrowth aside I glimpse a new trail, hollowed into the earth and overgrown, canopied with twisting branches dripping with moss. Even the light is green.

When the twigs spring back over it, it's like the closing of a door. The energy drains from me. I could wander here for days. There are miles and miles of trees and swamp, all of it appearing exactly the same.

I hurry to retrace my steps, but everything looks different. How could I have been so stupid? I picture Paul's face when he realises I'm lost, his annoyance passing into disbelief. I imagine what he'd say to me if he could: *But it was you who wanted to come*, as if that should have protected me from this—the wilderness around me, the miles and miles of nothing.

But there's a twisted oak I recognise, and I duck under it, and then there's a footprint after all. I keep walking, winding around the trunks, and eventually I catch a glimpse of hewn logs: the side of a cabin. It's only then that my pulse ratchets, as if I hadn't dared to admit the possibility of truly being lost until I was safe.

I don't want to return to the cabin though, not yet—I'll only sit there, dwelling on the empty spaces and my own futility. Instead, I go to meet Marni and Paul from the boat. I arrive just as it's coming in to dock and I see Marni leaning over the side, her hair stretching down towards the water. When she lifts her head and waves, she doesn't look entranced; she only looks like what she is—a girl on vacation, saying something to her father and laughing, not thinking about anything else. Then she points—I'm just in time to catch the smooth slide of an alligator entering the lake.

They're all exclamations and laughter. Paul bought some gator jerky on board and we share it, though I grimace at the salty taste. Marni doesn't. She pulls a piece of it away with her back teeth then tells me they've done a deal; Paul is taking her kayaking tomorrow, if she'll try some freshwater fishing. But she'd rather go fish in the sea.

That evening the dark drops over the land before I even notice it's there, and we settle down to read our various books. There's no television in the cabin, but we can hear birds calling to each other, their eerie cries coming out of the tangle of trees that quickly fade out of sight. We close the curtains against them and I take out the volume I borrowed from Marni before we came away. It's her book of fairy tales, and I read again about the girl's encounter with the wilderness.

The similarity with another tale strikes me—one that my mother had passed onto me, about Narcissus of Greek myth. He hunted stags in the forest, where he was followed by the nymph, Echo, who tried to embrace him with her reaching arms. When he rejected her, she faded away amid the lonely glens until only her voice remained. Narcissus, though, was punished by Nemesis. He discovered a deep pool hidden in the trees, and when he glimpsed his own reflection he fell in love. He gazed down at it until he died, when a flower grew in his stead.

I suppose Edda too had been cursed with a love that could not be returned, that would always now be out of reach.

Of course, it was not a stag I saw in the forest, or an elk; but the image returns to me of a deer's fathomless eyes, its twitching ears, its wide nostrils; the strength in its slender legs as it left me in a few brisk leaps. It had no name, the thing I saw. I wonder what it sensed when it looked at me. Was it fleeing from the scent of something other? Or was it running towards something—had it caught the scent of the wild itself, and heeded its call, going ever deeper without looking back?

I go to the window and peer through the curtains. I wonder if Edda had once stood in this very spot, doing the same thing. What had she heard, calling to her from out of the wilderness?

I try to reach out to her with my senses, but I see only the reflected light from the room behind me. She isn't altogether gone, though. I can almost hear the echo of her words as she said my name, giving to me its meaning like some kind of gift: *Pearl. A secret and underwater thing.*

The next morning, when Marni and Paul prepare to set out for the boat ramp, I tell them I'll join them later. They don't seem especially surprised. I hug and kiss them and tell Marni to be careful around the water and she rolls her eyes. When they're gone, I pull on my hiking boots and a hat to keep the sun off—though when I think of those canopied trees stretching to meet each other, I don't suppose I'll need it.

I'm going off the trail again. That is where Edda and Dick must have gone—I feel sure of it, though I don't know why; it could be nothing but a story I'm telling myself, in the absence of anything else. I have no reason to be certain, but then, I don't think reason will help me now. I can almost scent the wilderness in my nostrils; I mean to heed its call. I think that's what they must have done. They went into the forest, immersing themselves in its warm humidity, the water and the air like a single element.

I think of the deer that paused to look at me under the trees. Was she trying to warn me that there is danger in it? But I turned back once; I won't again.

I try to follow the same route I took yesterday. Almost at once I feel a presence tracking my footsteps, though when I look around, there's nothing to see; only moss hanging from the trees like tangled hair, branches reaching towards me like pale arms. I imagine a witch, or perhaps it's only an echo; my own thoughts, maybe. The words that come to me are *great-grandmother*.

After a time I realise I'm standing in the same place I saw the deer. She isn't here now, but I think I catch a trace of her scent, musky and vibrantly alive. I lean under the trees and push the undergrowth aside and see that narrow path, barely wide enough for a deer or a human to pass. The thick canopy makes it appear almost like a tunnel. Sunlight filters through the leaves; the air is redolent of green and living things.

I duck under a trailing strand of Spanish moss and sink into the path to my ankles—I'm not sure if it's made of earth or water. The liquid is warm, making me think of leeches, of black and wriggling and slimy things.

Marni's face flashes before me, and I suddenly have no idea what I'm doing here. The certainty I felt earlier evaporates. I know nothing about this place, or about my old friends, not really. I don't know where they went or what happened to them. How could I? Possibly they're still lost in some corner of the Ringling Residence, surrounded by its red and gold opulence. If I looked hard at their postcard, I might even see their faces peering from behind an archway or between the pillars of the balcony. I might see their eyes reflected in the crystals of the chandelier or a golden statue.

I look up, with that civilised, normal, *safe* interior filling my mind, and am fixed by the sight of a hawk perched on a branch not far above my head. It challenges me with its yellow eyes. A snake dangles from its talons.

Something inside me goes still. *Here*, I think.

I don't call out for Dick and Edda. What would be the use? But I step forwards, brushing hair-like moss away from my face, ducking beneath the branches, stepping from root to root. I know I'm growing close when I see little clouds floating past me: the cotton-like seed of a water-loving plant. There is something ahead of me—not yet seen, but I feel its presence anyway. It's shadowy under the trees and difficult to make out, but it appears to be black water. I hear the sudden loud buzzing of flies.

With another step comes the trace of something on the air—a terrible sweetness. There is knowledge in that sound, that scent.

It surprises me not at all when I see the pool beneath the trees. I knew it would be there, waiting for me. I peer between the branches, trying to see its surface; to look beneath. The water isn't black after all. It is every colour—brown and blue and darkly green, flecked with shining gold. And I see another forest growing within its depths. I wonder if I will be able to reach it—to learn the secrets it has kept all these long days.

The buzzing grows louder. I brush a fly away from my face—it has grown fat on whatever bounty it discovered here. I take another step. I want to look into the pool. What will I see—something beautiful? Will I find a nymph—a great-grandmother—a witch? Or only my own reflection: a secret and underwater thing?

Whatever it is, it will be like a story that has already been told. I will never again be able to discover its ending—or forget what it is that I have learned.

I take a deep breath and walk towards the pool.

# RAMSEY CAMPBELL

## GETTING THROUGH

R AMSEY CAMPBELL is described by *The Oxford Companion to English Literature* as "Britain's most respected living horror writer". He has been given more awards than any other writer in the field, including the Grand Master Award of the World Horror Convention, the Lifetime Achievement Award of the Horror Writers Association, the Living Legend Award of the International Horror Guild and the World Fantasy Lifetime Achievement Award. In 2015 he was made an Honorary Fellow of Liverpool John Moores University for outstanding services to literature.

Among his novels are *The Face That Must Die, Incarnate, Midnight Sun, The Count of Eleven, Silent Children, The Darkest Part of the Woods, The Overnight, Secret Story, The Grin of the Dark, Thieving Fear, Creatures of the Pool, The Seven Days of Cain, Ghosts Know, The Kind Folk, Think Yourself Lucky, Thirteen Days by Sunset Beach, The Wise Friend, Somebody's Voice* and *Fellstones*. He recently brought out his "Brichester Mythos" trilogy, consisting of *The Searching Dead, Born to the Dark* and *The Way of the Worm*.

*Needing Ghosts, The Last Revelation of Gla'aki, The Pretence, The Booking* and *The Enigma of the Flat Policeman* are novellas. His collections include *Waking Nightmares, Alone with the Horrors, Ghosts and Grisly Things, Told by the Dead, Just Behind You, Holes for Faces, By the Light of My Skull* and a two-volume retrospective round-up (*Phantasmagorical Stories*) as well as *The Village Killings and Other Novellas.*

His non-fiction is collected as *Ramsey Campbell, Probably* and *Ramsey Campbell, Certainly,* while *Ramsey's Rambles* consists of his video reviews, and he is working on a book-length study of the Three Stooges, *Six Stooges and Counting. Limericks of the Alarming and Phantasmal* is a history of horror fiction in the form of fifty limericks.

His novels *The Nameless, Pact of the Fathers* and *The Influence* have been filmed in Spain, where a television series based on *The Nameless* is in development. He is the President of the Society of Fantastic Films.

Ramsey Campbell lives on Merseyside with his wife Jenny. His pleasures include classical music, good food and wine, and whatever's in that pipe.

"I can't write science fiction unless I persuade myself I'm not doing so," the author reveals. "My few attempts back in the early 1970s are clumsy and sluggish, though the later story 'Slow' seems to work for folk.

"I liked the idea behind 'Getting Through'—the notion of retreating, mentally or actually, into a better world at moments of stress—well enough to risk writing it. Perhaps at the back of my mind I had a story that has haunted me since childhood, James Blish's 'Testament of Andros', which may be science fiction or a study of psychosis or both."

"**W**E NEED TO get him out of his room, Bob."

"He'll be reading his magazines if he isn't putting them in order."

"It can't be healthy for him to be stuck up there all day."

"I'm agreeing with you, Jean. Reading all that rot isn't healthy either, time machines and spaceships as if real life isn't good enough for us."

"He's got a better mind than that, and we don't want him ending up a hermit when we're gone."

"Almighty God grant us a long time yet, but he can't make friends while he's shutting himself in."

"Then we need to do something, Bob, because I don't think he will on his own."

"If we get rid of all that stuff he reads he won't have anything to stay up there for."

"Is that going a bit far, do you think? Suppose we just tell him how long he can spend in there?"

"I've had enough of never seeing him all day. It's worse than having a lodger. I'm sorting this out right now and for good. Those magazines are going out the window if that's what it takes."

As Desmond heard a door open downstairs he leapt off the bed, clutching the magazine he'd been reading. Even if he found somewhere to hide it from his father, his bedroom shelves were full of more than he could hide. A bright shard of panic had lodged in his brain, and the rest of him felt brittle as a reflection in a mirror. His father was tramping up the stairs, and the relentless sound made Desmond feel suffocated, even worse than being in a crowd affected him. He wasn't far from crumpling the magazine, because he thought he might never learn the end of the story he'd begun. He was backing into a corner, where he could crouch and hug his treasure so hard that nobody would take it from him, when he saw that the shelves and their contents had taken refuge in the dressing-table mirror.

Why did it remind him of a window? He had to go close to be sure that none of the spines of the magazines, which were arranged by title and then by date, were reversed. He could read every word and every digit with an ease that felt like passing through the glass. He didn't know whether he was stooping towards it or straightening up when it showed his father entering the room. "Finished reading, have you, son?" his father said.

Although his glasses enlarged his eyes, they showed none of the determination Desmond had tried to prepare for. "Not yet," Desmond said.

"When you do we were wondering if you'd like to go out for a walk."

Desmond thought this must be designed to lure him away from his room. "What about my magazines?"

"You can leave those till we're home, can't you? Come and get some fresh air."

Desmond could only conclude that his father had experienced a change of heart on his way upstairs. He watched his father leave the room and listened while he rejoined Desmond's mother. Were they having a discussion Desmond couldn't hear? Surely his mother had to question why his father had gone back on his decision. Its retraction left Desmond's head feeling eagerly capacious, and he lay on the bed, where a quilt not quite as teenage as himself bore a map of the stars, to finish reading his tale. Once the narrator had stopped migrating to his bodies in alternate universes, Desmond went downstairs. "Ready to be sociable?" his mother said.

To test her attitude he said "I was making space for next month's magazines."

"That's right, you keep everything tidy like you always do."

Presumably his father had persuaded her in favour of Desmond's reading. There weren't many people in the park, which let Desmond's mind feel as wide as the sky. The bright stud of the sun held the blue expanse in place and lent leaves on the trees the energy to unfurl while discovering more colour, so many greens that he couldn't even think of counting them. The only problem was how tense his parents grew whenever they saw a dog. "Don't let it come near him," his mother used to call out, "he doesn't like them," and his father wouldn't merely shoo but stamp. "Dodge the dog," Desmond had taken to muttering like a charm, low enough that he could hope his parents didn't hear. He knew he embarrassed them, and their dogged attempts to hide their feelings simply made it worse. It left him anxious to qualify for university, however many years that took, and leave home.

All this came back to him on the day of the English Literature examination. As he opened the folder and read all the topics he found himself wishing he could flee back to a time when the examination had represented hope. Now he saw that he'd been so bound up in the magazines the intervening years had brought him that he'd revised nothing like enough. There wasn't a single question he could even start to answer. The examination hall seemed to have grown oppressively dim, and the sky beyond the long windows was as dull as his mind. The nearest window displayed his face, and as he watched it twist with panic he recalled the mirror in his bedroom.

Had it come to his aid that day? Could his reflection help now? He'd begun to feel no more substantial than it looked. He glanced at the invigilator, who was leafing through papers on her desk. Before she could notice what he was doing and disqualify him on suspicion of cheating, he picked up the folder and turned it to the window. The print on the cover was big enough to be legible in the reflection, especially since it wasn't reversed. Before he finished taking a breath he felt his body regain its substance while a sensation like a splinter that was lodged between his eyes subsided into his head.

He wasn't sure what to expect on reopening the folder. Though none of the questions had changed, they no longer daunted him. Once he took time to ponder them he found he knew more than enough. He was completing his final answer when the invigilator announced the last five minutes of the session. "Needn't have worried," he told his parents, knowing they had.

He could have fancied they'd saved up their muffled concern for the day his father drove him and a vanload of magazines to the university they'd helped him choose. Desmond failed to see why his parents should worry, since he had a room to himself and space for every magazine. At first he was happy to learn of a society for people like him, despite his reservations about its name—Sci Fine. It met in a pub, in a small crowded noisy room further shrunken by a pall of smoke from ragged amateur cigarettes. At least there were almost no girls in the group, though Desmond supposed he would have to cope with some of those eventually, never having managed at school. The girls in the society had to be more like him if they liked science fiction. He did his best to stay in the room and make himself heard, but felt as if the heat and noise and the closeness of so much flesh had merged into a solitary intolerable medium that was gathering on him. Retreating outside, he waited under a lamp that made his shadow imitate his slightest twitch and magnified every movement of his hands. When the group emerged he accosted the secretary, a longhaired student half Desmond's width. "I think you should change your name."

The secretary's mouth shrank towards imitating an exclamation mark in collaboration with his beaky nose. "What's your problem with my name?"

"Not yours, the Sci Fine one." Was the secretary making what some people called a joke? "Just the fine bit," Desmond said. "It sounds like you want to fine people."

"Not to me." A glance at his friends let the secretary add "Not to anyone."

"Don't you like Sci File? It could be with a pee aitch like scientists use."

Without bothering to glance at the others the secretary said "We don't, no."

As he and his entourage sauntered away a girl murmured "I do."

She was as blonde as Desmond had ever seen the sun, with a small pert lightly highlighted face and a figure that would have graced the cover of any of his magazines. He imagined her in a space helmet and bikini—he'd lingered over similar pictures—and decided he might like some girls in the flesh after all. Just the same, he felt provoked to ask "Why?"

"I thought it was quite witty, your joke."

He hadn't been aware of making one or even that he could. The revelation left him feeling there was more to him that he had yet to discover. He was wondering if he should thank her when she said "Are you new?"

"No, I'm nineteen."

This time she seemed uncertain whether he was joking. "What's your name?"

"Desmond. What's yours?"

"I'll have a lager and lime."

"That's a peculiar name."

Her frown was faint enough to let her face stay pretty. "It's Dianne with two ens and an e."

"That's more like one." To demonstrate maturity, which might involve overcoming his aversion to crowds, he said "I'm going for a drink."

"Is that an invitation, Desmond?"

"It can be if you want."

Apparently she did. At least there were empty booths in the main bar. "You sit down," he said in a bid to ensure they had one to themselves. "Do you still want a lager and lime?"

"That was rather the idea."

The price of this and a pint of beer took him aback. As he carried them to the booth the barman put on a tape of the latest Beatles album, and Desmond had to fight an urge to tell the man to turn it down as he would have told his parents. He centred his tankard on a beermat while he gave Dianne the bad news. "That was twenty pence."

"You're saying you'd like me to pay."

"Weren't you going to?"

She appeared to take this as an accusation. Opening her bag, a scaly item reminiscent of the body of a lizard flattened by a mangle, she produced a purse that might have been its offspring, which she unclasped as well. Once Desmond pocketed the coin, having waited for Dianne to place it on the table, a Beatles song about the universe took the place of conversation. When it was over Dianne said "You like science fiction, then."

"Of course I do." Perhaps this sounded too harsh, although only because he was having to talk over the next song, which was all about I and me and mine, though not Desmond himself. "Which magazines do you like?" he said.

"*Galaxy*'s my favourite."

"That's the worst one. The name doesn't mean anything. Even the way they print it is wrong."

Dianne laughed before appearing to decide she shouldn't have. "Wrong how?"

"The letters all feel spiky in your head."

"Not in mine, and the name means plenty. You know what a galaxy is."

"That magazine's not one. You can't just stick a word on things and say that's what they are." Since it was plain she was as unable to grasp his reasoning as he ought to have expected any girl to be, Desmond said "*Amazing* is amazing, and *Astounding* is astounding, and *Authentic* is authentic..."

Her face began to lose expression before he came to the fantastic, but he carried on to the end, by which time she'd halved her drink. "Which is your favourite?" she said.

"All of them except yours."

He thought she was inclined to smile or even grin, but she did neither. "We'll agree to differ, then," she said.

"You can't just say that. You have to ask me if I do, and I don't."

Dianne reached for her handbag and stood up. "Excuse me, please," she said, though he wasn't in her path.

Several manly gulps of beer left his mouth tasting increasingly metallic, unless panic did. Had he driven her away? When the Beatles began exhorting someone to get back he knew Dianne wouldn't do so. Had she even bothered to pretend she was heading for the Ladies? She wasn't to be seen as he made for the Gents.

Though he'd touched nothing but himself, he spent more than a minute at a sink. Since the roller towel would have been recycled, he wiped his hands with toilet paper. In the extended mirror above the sinks he saw his forehead glistening with sweat, which it presumably had been while he was talking to Dianne. As he raised a hand to rub away the shameful evidence of tension he caught sight of his wristwatch in the mirror.

It wasn't reversed, unless his perceptions were, and what would that have to mean? That he was the reflection, confronted by himself beyond the glass? When he reached his other hand towards the mirror he had no idea what he was expecting to feel. He remembered feeling nothing as he straightened up. As soon as he emerged into the bar he saw Dianne in the booth. "Sorry I was such a time," she said. "It's my round."

He might have asked where she'd been, but he was nervous of breaking some kind of spell. She waved away his move to help her carry the drinks to the booth. "Have you brought any magazines with you?" she said.

He liked how she was continuing the conversation as if they hadn't disagreed. This kind of agreement he could take. "All of them except for your one," he said.

"Then we could be a team."

"We could be our own group and have the name they didn't want." Since she seemed open to the notion Desmond said "Would you like to see my magazines?"

"I'd love to, but let's not waste our drinks."

Presumably she'd sensed his impatience, which had him digging his fingertips into his thighs while she lingered over her lager. As she took the final sip he headed for his room so fast that he almost forgot to look back to confirm she was following. He switched on his light and retreated to the window, leaving her more space to admire his achievement. "You're fearfully tidy," she said.

"A tidy home means a tidy mind."

"I could learn from you. I should be tidier."

"Learn all you like." When she ventured to the shelves he said "You can borrow one if you take care of it."

"I'll treat it like one of my own."

"Does that mean taking care?"

As though forgiving an insult Dianne said "Of course."

Desmond eased his oldest issue of *Amazing* off the shelf. "You'd better start with this one."

When she returned it two days later it looked as unread as it always had, so that he wasn't sure she'd even opened it until he questioned her about the contents. He was happy to lend her the next issue, and able to concentrate on lectures now that he needn't worry about her doing any damage. She was taking science while he took modern literature, and so he could put her out of his mind except whenever they met. This was increasingly often even when she wasn't bringing back a magazine, and the first time his parents came to check how Desmond was progressing she met them as well. She was still meeting them a year later, a date Desmond celebrated as fantastic, since that was the magazine she was borrowing now. "I hope you two aren't getting up to mischief," his mother said like a line she'd rehearsed.

"Some of us believe in waiting till we're married," Dianne told her.

"More power to you and anybody like you," Desmond's father said. "His mother and I did."

The three of them seemed more embarrassed than Desmond found any need to feel. He'd discovered that he quite liked not just kissing Dianne but poking his tongue in and running his hands over her, but beyond this lay territory he felt nervous of exploring. When his parents left for home he suspected he and Dianne were meant to overhear his father murmuring "I think she's going to be ideal for him."

"For each other," Desmond's mother said quite like a rebuke.

Not only Dianne stayed ideal throughout Desmond's university years, which felt nowhere near as long as that. It seemed appropriate that his magazine she was reading when their studentship ended was *Venture*, since they would be setting out on one. His thesis on alternate universes as fictional searches for an ideal world earned him a degree, and Dianne gained its equal in science. As they each took the stage at the graduation ceremony both of them had already been accepted for a job, and their wedding followed shortly after.

When Dianne said "I do" Desmond thought she was repeating the first words she'd addressed to him. He had the odd impression that his life contained echoes of events or even consisted of them. He was disconcerted by how many guests at the reception he didn't know—friends of his parents and Dianne—and relieved when they dispersed. He was on the way to relaxing until his father said as a farewell "You two be good, now."

"We'll be listening for tiny feet soon," his mother said.

Apparently champagne had swept away their worries, but Desmond's only multiplied once he grasped that his mother hadn't meant there were mice in the bridal suite. Even the bedroom threatened to overwhelm him, especially the four-poster that looked crystallised with dazzling linen. The bathroom with its fat white towels and puffy toilet seat offered no refuge. He stared at the mirror until his eyes stung as though they'd been soaped, which failed to turn the image of his watch around. As he bruised his fingertips against the glass Dianne called "I'm ready, Desmond."

"Turn the light off," he shouted in case not seeing helped.

A pale glow from floodlights in the hotel car park turned the bed into a shrouded ghost of itself. The canopy squatted four-legged over the area of action. Dianne's head was sprouting over the quilt, which was blank as an unwritten page. Perhaps he should think of it as a cover on which he could imagine a picture, Dianne's body attired like a cute spacewoman, but the image dwindled into a shard of pain when he climbed into bed and discovered how naked she was. He rubbed her and poked at her mouth and wished his penis was as manageable as his tongue. The unresponsive protrusion continued to flap as he climbed aboard Dianne, and as soon as it touched her it shrivelled. He had to struggle not to close his hand over it, to protect it from the spiky nest it had encountered. At least he couldn't see his pitiable toil in the dressing-table mirror, though the edges of the glass were visible. He was staring at the nuptial cards Dianne had arranged in front of the mirror—he was striving to feel they could encourage him somehow—when he read a manufacturer's name on the back of a card.

Though it was in the mirror, it was the right way around. He almost sprawled off the bed in his haste to make sure, driven by an instinct to see himself. As he craned around the headboard for a sight of his blurred face Dianne protested "What are you doing, Desmond?"

He couldn't reach the mirror, but he felt his penis try, which proved to be enough. At once he felt as substantial as it had grown. "It's all right now," he said, gagging her with his tongue as he boarded her once more. This time his penis found a hospitable entrance in the spiky place. "Oh," Dianne started to declare, and before long so did he.

Very little time seemed to have passed—certainly less than three months—when she phoned him from the industrial laboratory, where he imagined her mixing the contents of phials in the manner of a scientist dressed like a model on a cover. "Are you sitting down?" she said.

He was preparing new books to be shelved, one of the library tasks he found most satisfying. "That's one thing I'm doing," he said.

"Soon there'll be more of us, Desmond."

He felt nervous of learning "Where?"

"Right here at the moment." Before he could urge her to be clear Dianne said "We've made a bit of the future."

This sounded as if it belonged in a magazine, though he couldn't think how. "Which bit?"

"We won't know for a little while yet. Either a boy or a girl."

His bewilderment must have been visible, since one of the library assistants was blinking at him like a query in code. "My wife's saying either a boy or a girl," Desmond said.

Her eyes widened with delight, and she informed her colleagues "Desmond's having a baby."

"I'm not. I can't. You mean my wife is." As this caught up with him he told Dianne "Well done."

"You're responsible as well, Desmond."

Although he didn't think this was an accusation, it left him feeling hemmed in. What might be expected of him? He was glad to return to the books, and later to the magazines at home, where he'd persuaded Dianne to file hers among his even though the spiky type on the spines felt invasive. Despite her condition she looked no different at first, but presumably her state led her to suggest he should learn to cook. He set about it while her shape grew so unfamiliar that he thought she could no longer appear on a magazine except as some species of alien. At least this meant that bedtime required him just to drape an arm around her increasing circumference until she fell asleep. Sometimes he found himself gazing across the bedroom at the mirror while he waited to follow her into unconsciousness. Dreaming made him feel he was in someone else's dream or was the dream itself, and he did his utmost to waken.

Perhaps his interrupted sleep was to blame for a persistent sense that he wasn't entirely awake in the daytime, not to mention in danger of dreaming. Every dinner he made for Dianne and presumably for her parasite felt like a version of an earlier meal, since he hadn't many recipes at his disposal. The sight of himself in the kitchen window only reminded him how limited he was, in some areas at any rate. Whenever his parents came to the apartment for dinner his mother helped him at his task, and she was peppering a casserole on his behalf when Dianne raised her voice in the main room, louder than Desmond liked. "I think I need to go to hospital."

As he hurried after his mother he called "Why, what's wrong?"

"I can't believe you said that," his mother said. "Sometimes I feel I don't know my son at all. Nothing's wrong, is it, Dianne? Everything is as it should be."

Desmond hardly thought so. Why couldn't babies be produced the way they were in several of his magazines—generated in a phial and developed in a laboratory like Dianne's? His father gave him a look that summarised agreement with Desmond's mother, and Desmond felt excluded, wishing he were someone else or a better model of himself. "I'll drive us," his father said.

He helped Dianne to clamber onto the back seat of the car, since aiding her hadn't immediately occurred to Desmond. Gripping Dianne's hand, his mother said "Go as fast as you dare, Bob."

On the motorway he drove faster than Desmond had ever seen him drive. Desmond felt useless and desperate to take control of events somehow. He might as well have reverted to his childhood self for all the benefit he was to anyone—all the use he'd failed to be for too much of his life. He gazed at Dianne in the mirror while his father overtook lorry after elongated lorry, but she didn't meet his eyes. If her reflection looked at him, what might that do? A lorry with a logo the length of a terrace of houses—FUTURE SOLUTIONS—drifted backwards past her window, and he was about to draw her attention to the words when her face contorted in a grimace. He sensed she was keeping in a cry so as not to distract his father, and the insight made him feel as if he'd discovered at last that there was more to him. He twisted around, reaching for her hand. "I'm here if—"

His elbow thumped his father in the face and knocked his glasses off. Perhaps lurching to retrieve them robbed his father of control, though in any case he must have been left little better than blind, or perhaps he meant to head for sanctuary on the hard shoulder. The car slewed into the path of the Future Solutions lorry, and the oncoming cab filled the side windows. In a moment the world shattered like a mirror.

Some of the high sounds were human, some were screeches of

metal. Desmond hardly realised he'd squeezed his eyes tight shut until he opened them. The car was full of glass and silence and an increasing amount of bright red, well on the way to blotting out its sources. Desmond risked a glance in the mirror, though the movement sent a dull pain through his neck and downwards, and was about to look away in haste when his attention fastened on the sight beyond the contents of the back seat. He could read the maker's name on the front of the lorry, because the letters weren't reversed.

He lowered his head until he could see nothing worse in the mirror than the name. When he stretched out a hand to the glass, expanding the pain that had occupied his spine, he saw the hand was spattered red, though not from him. He almost snatched it back so as not to see it, but he had to do whatever he could do—whatever the mirror could. He needed to be somewhere the last few minutes had never happened to his family or him. As he touched the glass he found he couldn't feel it, but he seemed to hear his mother speak. "We need to get him out," he thought she said.

# STEPHEN BACON

## THE CHILDREN OF MEDEA

S TEPHEN BACON lives near Sheffield, South Yorkshire, with his wife and two sons. His short fiction has appeared in publications on both sides of the Atlantic, including *Black Static, Shadows & Tall Trees, Postscripts, Nightmare, Cemetery Dance* and *Crimewave*, and has been collected in *Peel Back the Sky* (Gray Friar Press) and *Murmured in Dreams* (Luna Press Publishing).

He is also the author of the novellas *Lantern Rock* (Pendragon Press) and *Laudanum Nights* (Hersham Horror Books).

"'The Children of Medea' marries together two of my favourite aspects of fiction," he explains, "stories based on the very brutal Greek myths, and the uncanniness of the 'fish out of water' trope which forms the basis of many great stories in the horror genre.

"When Luna Press agreed to publish my latest collection, I wanted to write two new pieces to be included in the book. 'The Children of Medea' was an idea that had been bouncing around in my brain for several years, probably inspired by family holidays to Greece and my love of such films as *The Wicker Man* and *Don't Look Now*.

"It seems to me that horror writers must have some sadistic aspect of their brain that compels them to conjure darkness to such tranquil locations as an island paradise."

⚭

SAXTON STOOD ON the quayside, squinting against the shimmering sea. He could just make out the island across the flat expanse of water. It looked fragile and insignificant. He closed his eyes for a minute, enjoying the sunshine that prickled his face. Birds wheeled overhead, occasionally cawing as they squabbled for food. The gentle lapping of water against the harbour-side was hypnotic. He opened one eye to glance at his watch. The ferry was due any minute.

Three young boys sat cross-legged on the quay, chattering amongst themselves. Saxton watched them for a while, trying to pick out the odd word. They were leaning over something. One of them laughed, tossed his head back, and Saxton saw their attention was fixed on an object moving on the cobblestones. He stepped closer for a better view. A grey fish flapped languidly between them, opening and closing its mouth, eyes bulging. One of the boys was carefully stabbing a penknife into the creature's side. They laughed, examining the bloodstained scales that adhered to the blade. One of them caught sight of Saxton watching but continued to pierce the fish, unmindful of Saxton's withering glare.

A rattling noise rang out from behind and Saxton turned. The ferry was approaching. His heart sank at the vessel's crude construction—it was little more than a raft, barely able to hold a handful of passengers. This didn't bode well for the island's appeal. He walked back to the quayside and watched as it glided into dock. The driver tied a length of rope to the jetty and stepped onto the wooden platform. Saxton called, "Kyriabos?"

The man nodded sullenly. He was bare-chested, wearing a pair of white three-quarter length jeans and sandals. Saxton stepped over the chain and walked along the platform until he reached the ferry. The driver unclipped his gate and allowed Saxton to board. A transistor radio dangled from a hook, playing what sounded like Greek pop music. The driver grabbed a bottle of water and took a swig, surveying the harbour with heavily-lidded eyes. He didn't seem surprised that Saxton was the only passenger. The air was thick with the greasy stench of diesel. Saxton felt the throbbing engine shudder through his legs, accentuating the nausea.

Presently the driver fastened the gate across the entryway. He moved assuredly, almost casually. He flicked a switch on the wheel's console and the engine roared. Saxton gripped the railing as the ferry backed away from the jetty in a churn of frothy waves. In no time at all they were juddering across the bay towards the island.

Saxton shielded his eyes as he studied their destination. It looked to be barely more than a rock, with several houses crowding the western edge and a series of larger buildings further up the slope. Sporadic patches of green appeared stark against the otherwise grey shale. A couple of boats bobbed about in what served as the island's harbour.

Kyriabos was further away than it looked. By the time they had reached it, Saxton felt sick to his stomach. It took the driver an extremely long time to dock the ferry and secure the gateway. Saxton wasted no time in crossing the jetty and hurrying up the quayside, which consisted of a rectangle of decking stretching the short length of the harbour. A middle-aged man sat on a bench at the corner, a folded newspaper resting on his lap. He stood as Saxton approached, tucking the paper beneath his arm.

"Mr Saxton?" He offered his hand. "I'm Kiron Laskaris, the school's principal." His English was precise. He wore a thick beard.

Saxton suppressed a wince at the man's iron grip. His skin was rough and tanned. Keen eyes peered out from beneath a pair of bushy eyebrows. His hair was a mass of grey coils.

"Nice to meet you," said Saxton, relieved there was someone there to meet him.

Laskaris glanced down at Saxton's empty hands. "No bags?"

Saxton tutted loudly. "Delayed at Athens. Apparently en-route to Latvia by now." He shook his head. "The airline company have assured me they'll get them here within forty-eight hours."

Laskaris shrugged. "Nevertheless—welcome to Kyriabos. We're extremely grateful to you for stepping in at such short notice."

"Not at all."

They walked up the incline. A row of clay-built single-storey houses stood to the left, their brilliant whiteness accentuated by sunlight and the azure sky beyond. Saxton could hear crickets in the scrub grass.

"I'll take you to your apartment," Laskaris said. "No doubt you'll want to freshen up."

There was an asphalt track at the top, which meandered along the length of the coast like a black ribbon. Two bicycles were leaning against the low wall. A bored-looking teenager glanced up from the saddle of his own bicycle, attached to which was a rickety metal trolley.

"It's fine—go, go," Laskaris said to the boy, waving his hands in a shooing motion. "Mr Saxton's bags haven't arrived yet."

The boy shrugged and slowly pedalled away.

"The school is on the north side of the island, down by the waterfront." Laskaris pointed. "You can't see from here but it's just past that hill. Your apartment's only a few hundred yards from it." He tucked the newspaper into his back pocket and mounted one of the bikes. "Please make use of the bicycle—the island's too small to accommodate cars, so we find these are the best method of transportation."

Saxton awkwardly picked up his bike. It had been many years since he'd ridden one. There was a part of him that felt ridiculous. Nevertheless, he pushed with his toe and set off. Laskaris led the way.

The track took a rather wandering route along the elevated shoreline. They didn't go fast, but Saxton felt a thrill of exhilaration as the breeze combed through his hair. Every so often he caught a glimpse of rocks protruding through the waterline to his right. Black stone and white sand created an alternately patterned backdrop. The narrow track was pot-holed and random, and Saxton had to concentrate in an effort to avoid serious injury. A grove of fruit trees stretched further up the slope to the left; the citrus smell was engaging. Saxton experienced a brief flash from his old life—a memory of being in Body Shop with Joanne; her spraying some overpriced tester onto her neck whilst he did his best to look enthusiastic... Saxton pushed the thought away and concentrated on his pedalling.

There were several cottages on the incline, and an ivy-smothered structure built from crumbling stone perched on the lip of a craggy ledge. Outside one of the residences—a decrepit cottage by the water's edge—a barnacled fishing boat lay upside down in its dry-dock. A bare-chested man was working on the hull, and he glanced up in surprise as they passed.

Eventually Laskaris drew to a halt and climbed off the bike, resting it against the stump of a felled Mimosa tree. "We're on foot from here." He led the way down a narrow track that descended steeply across the incline in a jagged path. Just visible was a small white-stone building nestling in a hollow, almost as if it was taking shelter. Sunlight glinted off the roof's skylight, blinding Saxton momentarily.

Saxton parked his bike next to the other and carefully made his way down the uneven path. He could feel the sting of sea-spray on his face. The building was a double-storey cottage with ocean-facing windows and a tired, weather-eroded façade. Laskaris unlocked the peeling door and pushed it open, handing the key to Saxton. "The school's just up there on the ridge."

Saxton nodded. "*That's* a commute I can handle." He stepped inside the cottage, wrinkling his nose at the unfamiliar smell—something distinctly feminine, with a rather pleasant allure, mixed with polish and disinfectant.

Laskaris gave him a brief tour. The cottage consisted of just a ground-floor living section and kitchen, with a single bedroom and bathroom upstairs. At least there was a flush toilet. They'd even installed a boiler so hot showers shouldn't be a problem. The bedroom's skylight allowed a rectangle of sunshine to bathe the floor. Saxton noticed some of the corners cluttered with filled boxes and a stack of bulging cases.

"I'm afraid they're Miss Hemsworth's things," explained Laskaris. "They'll need to be stored here until her family can make arrangements to have them shipped back to England."

Saxton nodded. "Still no news?"

"I'm afraid not." Laskaris shrugged gravely. "The police think she just took off. There were no signs of anything...*untoward*."

"Why would she do that?"

Laskaris shrugged again. "Who knows? She seemed a little... preoccupied just before she disappeared." He blinked soberly and tipped his head. "It can get a little lonely out here sometimes. You know—claustrophobic."

Saxton glanced around the room, nodding. "I'll be fine." He puffed out his cheeks. "To be honest I think the change of scenery will do me good."

Laskaris' eyes clouded. "They did mention your...*tragedy*. I'm very sorry."

Saxton waved his hand dismissively, his head angled away as he peered around the cottage. He remained like that for a few moments. When he turned back, he swallowed, making firm eye-contact with the other man. "Thanks." He shook Laskaris' hand, breaking the moment of discomfort. "I needed to get away, to be honest—leave the ghosts back in England."

Laskaris nodded again. He pursed his lips, as if unsure how to continue. Then he blinked and shrugged. "Well, I'm sure the children will keep you busy, keep your mind occupied." He wrote something on a piece of paper. "This is my number. I live on the south side of the island. If you need anything, just give me a ring." He thought for a second. "There's a little shop down by the beach where you can get milk and bread and stuff."

"I'll find it."

Laskaris shook his hand again. "I hope you'll be very happy here, Mr. Saxton." And with that he was gone.

Saxton stood alone in the cottage, suddenly aware of the abrupt silence that had descended.

The next few days felt never-ending. Saxton did his best to settle into the cottage but, with the airline still failing to deliver his luggage, it just felt like he was an interloper, a listless holidaymaker. He visited the island's only general store and managed to stock up on provisions. From time to time he stared at his mobile phone's display.

The absence of a signal seemed to increase his desire to call Anya, but he knew it was not a temptation he could ever act on; too much had been said, too many tears had been shed; too much time had passed.

He explored the island. There looked to be about several hundred people living on Kyriabos. The majority of the men-folk seemed to be fishermen. He'd hear the boats setting off in the early hours of the morning, listening to their owners' shouts from the harbour as he huddled beneath the starched sheets of his bed. Then in the afternoon he'd watch them streaming back into the quay, their nets laden with shimmering fish. Most of the island's women seemed to attend constantly to their laundry; nearly everywhere you looked, clotheslines billowed with garments. They resembled restless ghosts.

The bicycle was useful for traversing the island. There was, ostensibly, just one main road, which skirted the coastline around Kyriabos, managing to link the houses that were clustered together in sporadic communities. But thin tracks criss-crossed the landmass like veins, rising up into the hills and weaving through the scrub. The highest point of Kyriabos was its geographic centre, a narrow plateau of rock marked by several Date-plum trees. One afternoon Saxton biked up there and sat in the shade, breathing in the scent of persimmon while he caught his breath and rested his aching legs. This vantage-point afforded him a perfect view of the entire island. He took out his binoculars and surveyed his new home.

The primary school stood prominently down by the water's edge, adjacent to a hamlet of adobe cottages. Its windows reflected the sunlight like the faceted eyes of an insect. Further around the shoreline he could make out the home of a local artist; clay pots and vases stood drying on a plinth. The island's only taverna, Cristo's, lay close to the harbour, conspicuous by its colourful display of garden parasols. Saxton angled his view to the west and it was then, as he turned the focus-wheel in an effort to make out some detail, that he caught sight of the ruined building barely visible through an overgrown canopy of olive trees. Its crumbling dome was adorned with gilt-edged depictions of the sun, although it looked to be in a rather poor state of repair. Several arched windows had been smashed. Curious, Saxton stood and peered with renewed interest.

"So, how are you settling in?"

Saxton took a sip of his juice and nodded. "Very well, Mr. Laskaris. It's a beautiful island, and very peaceful—just what I'd imagined." He smiled and added, as if it wasn't at all an afterthought, "and I'm looking forward to meeting the children."

Laskaris smiled across the desk from him. They were in the principal's office. It was a poorly-ventilated room, filled with shelves weighed down with box-files and textbooks. There was an overflowing ashtray on the desk, next to a manila folder. Laskaris took out some papers and glanced at them for a moment. "All the children speak English, so language shouldn't be a problem. I believe they discussed the syllabus requirements at your interview in Athens?" Saxton nodded and the principal continued. "These papers will give you an insight. I don't think the remaining term will be too difficult. Once we break for the summer, the education authority will be able to recruit someone permanent. We're very grateful for you coming at such short notice."

"It'll be good to get back to work," said Saxton. "To move on."

"Precisely." Laskaris put the papers back into the manila folder. Saxton noticed how large his knuckles were, how much hair there was on his forearms and the backs of his hands.

"Any news on Miss Hemsworth?"

Laskaris looked confused for a second, then understanding seemed to dawn. He shook his head. "Still nothing, I'm afraid. Like I said, her personal effects shouldn't be in your way for too much longer; her next of kin are arranging to move them."

Saxton made conciliatory noises, suddenly feeling awkward for implying her belongings were troublesome. To change the subject he said, "I notice the gravestones share just a few names." He added quickly, "I took a stroll through the cemetery the other day."

Laskaris shrugged. "Kyriabos is a close-knit community. Most of the residents have family stretching back several generations, myself included. We like to bury our dead close by. As a child, I attended this very school before moving to the secondary one on the mainland."

"Really?"

"Yes, it's a real honour for me to work here." Laskaris stood and offered his hand. "Well, good luck with everything, Mr. Saxton."

The first few days were less taxing than Saxton had anticipated. His class of nine-year-olds—all seventeen of them—appeared rather more attentive than the group he'd previously taught back in England. They seemed more studious and mature than any nine-year-olds he had previously come into contact with. He put this down to nerves; after all, their usual teacher had disappeared partway through the academic year, and it was only natural they might appear reticent. There also seemed to be very little interaction between them. Each child sat at their own desk, staring ahead with wide expressionless faces. Saxton was reminded of that old film about a village of blonde-haired, glowing-eyed children, but did his best to suppress such inappropriate humour. He tried hard to engage them, telling of his experiences in teaching back home, describing the cultural differences between their two countries. At one point he had to leave them unattended whilst he went to fetch a new pack of paper, fully expecting, upon his return, for mayhem to have broken out. But as he re-entered the classroom, he was surprised to find them just how he'd left them. Uncannily identical, almost as if they'd frozen, the minute he'd departed the room.

There was one pupil that was rather more curious that the others. Her name was Taryn. She sat on the second row and spoke very little English, preferring to murmur occasionally in Greek. When Saxton addressed her directly, she responded in a polite, if rather taciturn, manner. Her eye-contact was never maintained for more than a second.

By the end of the first week, Saxton was feeling positive about his current employment. He sat on a wicker chair on the paved area outside his cottage, sipping wine as he watched the sun descend. The ceaseless crashing of the tide was relaxing. Nearby, insects chirruped in the grass. He could smell food cooking as it wafted across from the taverna; luscious garlic- and wood-smoked chicken. Saxton felt his stomach growl. He watched gulls wheeling overhead, buffeted by the warm breeze. He closed his eyes and tried not to think of Joanne.

The airline had delivered his luggage several days ago. He'd unpacked it with a degree of guilt, feeling like he was erasing all trace of his predecessor. But time moved on. Things progressed. It was impossible to halt the inevitable.

Feeling mildly drunk, he took out his phone and reread the texts from Anya. It felt unreal, as if the whole thing had happened to someone else. The signal drifted in and out intermittently. At the present time there was one bar indicating network coverage. His fingers hesitated over Anya's speed-dial number. His mind wrestled with uncertainty. *What good would calling her do? The past was the past.*

Instead, he scrolled through the photos. There were several of Anya, mostly taken in busy pubs or swanky cocktail bars. His heart lurched as he stared at her image. That vivacious smile, those limitless eyes. He blinked and began flicking through his stored pictures, finally coming across one of Joanne taken several years before. They'd gone out to celebrate her birthday. He'd ended up getting drunk and they'd argued. Another night spent on the sofa. The ones of Charlie were stored in a different folder, but he still felt too raw to view them.

He powered off the phone, tossed it into his lap. Then he downed the rest of the wine and watched the final vestiges of sunlight disappear.

On the Sunday he rode his bike up the trail to the summit of Kyriabos again. He'd been thinking about that ruined building. There was something about the derelict nature of the place that had intrigued him: that copper-dome, the gilt-edged icons, the ornate windows— it had resembled a church, yet the air of neglect suggested it might be worth exploring.

Saxton caught his breath on the wooded slope, enjoying the sense of isolation. The birdsong reminded him of his childhood back in England. He leaned his bike against a tussock and stood for a few minutes, taking advantage of the respite from the blazing sun. Up ahead, the dome of the church protruded through a canopy of trees.

He walked up the incline, feeling dry leaves crunch underfoot. As he approached, he caught a view of the ruined church through the branches. A stone path had been constructed in front of the building. The church's doorway lay in deep shadow. There was a smashed window to the right. Lichen and moss coated the exterior walls.

The wooden door was ajar. He pushed it wide, and there was a squeal of hinges and a sudden aroma of brackish soil, earthy and organic. Saxton wrinkled his nose and stepped inside.

The dimness blinded him for a second. He paused until his vision returned. Discarded cans and food wrappers littered the dusty floor. Several rows of chairs stood in angled lines along the length of the church. The stone walls were decorated by a series of etchings, now rendered faint by mildew and age. Saxton approached the illustrations and peered at them through their patina of grime.

In the first one a robed woman with a knife stood over a pair of cowering infants. Blood flowed freely from their wounds. The next one depicted the woman riding in a chariot. Her face was grotesque, insane. The third illustration showed a man standing by a graveside, drowning in his own tears. The final image was of the robed woman ascending skyward in the chariot. Despite the aged state of the pictures, there was a chilling aspect to them: a bold fluency to the artwork that unnerved Saxton.

He turned abruptly. Something had startled him. The interior of the church was dim, shadows motionless. Yet there was a low hum, like the murmur of voices, too indistinct to hear. Barely audible. Just beyond reach. Saxton felt the hairs on his forearms bristle.

A ruined altar lay at the end of the aisle. Rotting wood protruded through its ancient structure, like the ribcage of a dead animal. Airborn dust tickled his nose. He suddenly had the feeling that he was being watched. He backed out of the church and escaped into the sunlight. There was no fear in his movement. The murmuring had been not at all threatening; if anything, there was a compelling aspect to the tone. Almost welcoming.

A few days later he quizzed the children about the island's history. He knew very little of it personally, so it was as much for his own curiosity as it was for the benefit of the class. A pale-faced boy in the back row raised his hand. "Sir, our families have lived on Kyriabos for years. My great-grandparents are buried in the cemetery." He glanced around the class. "All our grandparents are."

Saxton had tried countless times to get them to address him as *Mr. Saxton*, so he ignored the overtly formal version the boy had used. "I see. So your families have lived on the island for many generations?"

A series of nodding heads. The original boy continued, "Even during the war we were left alone. The Nazis didn't bother us."

Saxton pursed his lips and frowned. "But I thought Greece was occupied by the Germans in World War II, so surely—"

"They were afraid of the island," said a girl sitting closer. "Of what the island was."

"*What the island was?*" Saxton struggled to comprehend the words. Maybe the meaning had been lost in translation.

Taryn caught his eye, a strange smile playing around her thin lips. "Kyriabos is *tainted* island—bad history." Her voice was guttural and sharp.

"Tainted?"

There was silence for a moment. Then the boy in the back row spoke up again. "It is diseased island. A colony. For hundreds of years the people here suffer from bad disease—disease of Hansen? It make skin go scaly and . . . *deformities?*"

Saxton scratched his head. "Hansen? You mean leprosy, don't you? Hansen's disease is leprosy."

"*Leprosy*, yes."

"The soldiers are afraid of us." Taryn smiled serenely. "They leave us alone. Just send food to us."

Saxton was still puzzled. "But if leprosy was still here in the 1940s, there would be signs today, surely?"

Someone shrugged. "It is gone. We pray. Our God stops the suffering."

At that moment the bell rang, signalling the end of the lesson. Saxton, distracted, stood and gathered together some textbooks. The children filed out of the room, eager to escape into the playground. But an air of disquiet lingered in the room afterwards.

At night, the island seemed different. Brooding. Vigilant. Gone was the birdsong and the restless surf and the daytime sounds of everyday life, replaced by an eerie silence, broken only by the occasional returning fishing-boat. Even the tide sounded different at night, the darkness lending it an unnaturally hesitant quality, a suggestion of activity that existed just beyond Saxton's perception. Like whispers in an empty room.

He had become used to the cottage's air of unreality. The sudden aroma of perfume, sometimes a sense of being watched, occasionally the sound of faint breathing in the bedroom at night. The skylight created a silvered, moonlit square that crept imperceptibly around the tiled floor. Something scratched and scampered behind the walls. Water gurgled through subterranean pipes. Distant, yet close-by.

Sometimes at night, the urge to call Anya became an obsession. He imagined her cuddled up with her husband back in England. He wondered if she had deleted his number, and the photos, from her phone. Always he resisted the temptation to call. That wound was healing over, the last thing he wanted to do was pick the scab and expose it again.

His dead son's face swirled in the darkness, so he stared at the skylight instead. Yet Charlie's voice broke the silence within his head. Saxton tried to busy his mind with life instead of death.

He thought about his job. These past few months had seen little progress in his relationship with the children. They remained impassive, unreachable almost. He'd finally begun to question his own teaching skills.

One night he woke in a fever, tangled in the damp sheets. A dull ache throbbed at the back of his head. He tried to mop his brow. As he turned, he noticed a silhouette at the skylight, limned by the moon, peering in at him through the glass. It was a face, too dark to discern any features, yet somehow he knew it was watching him. For several minutes he remained frozen, holding his breath as he stared back at the shape. There was a shimmering quality to the image, as if he were viewing it through a heat-haze. It undulated and wavered. Like its mass and the surrounding shadows were merging. Then, sickeningly, it lurched in a solid gathering movement, as if it had poured through the glass and reformed itself inside the room. Saxton felt his throat click as he struggled to speak. The black shape crept slowly across the angle of the ceiling. He could make out rail-thin limbs, a slender torso, clutching child-like hands. He watched in horror as it made its way to the corner, where it paused in the shadows, waiting.

A rushing noise in Saxton's ears made him swallow. He was still in bed, too frightened to move, yet conversely the sound was comforting. Harmonious. There was a rhythm to the noise that quelled Saxton's terror. It rose in volume and he recognised it as the murmuring he'd heard in the church. The layers separated until he could identify individual voices for a second, then they harmonised again to become one. Although what he was staring at was horrific, the sense of acceptance he took from the voices overrode any feelings of disquiet. It was angelic and sweet. *Joyous.* He closed his eyes and lay back on the pillow, allowing himself to be embraced by the choir.


Saxton gave the signal and the children began peeling back the foil from the lids of their milk cartons. They were usually eager to drink their milk, an event that occurred daily at 10:30 a.m. It was a quaint habit. Saxton enjoyed it, the sight of their milk-moustaches reminding him of his own childhood back in England, years before the government ended the practice.

Once they had finished, he walked around the room with the bin-bag and collected the empty cartons. The class began to take out their books. Saxton returned to his desk. "Does anyone know anything about the old building up on the slope?"

A boy in the front row raised his hand and waited for Saxton to point to him. "Yes, sir—it's the church."

"I took a trip up there. It hasn't been used in years."

The boy shared a glance with his classmate to the left. "Our church is no longer needed. The Lady's presence is everywhere."

"The lady?"

Saxton felt troubled by the profound silence. The kids looked cagey. He pressed again. "What do you mean—*the lady*?"

"It is the church of Medea, our mother." The boy stared at Saxton. Challenging. Defiant. "We are *all* her children."

Saxton could feel a tic twitching at his left eye. He blinked. There was something familiar about the kid's words. His memory struggled with the English literature he'd studied at Uni. "Medea? Wasn't that a play?"

The pale boy in the back row chipped in. "The church is in honour of Medea, who murdered her own children to hurt her adulterous husband, Jason."

Saxton frowned. There was a sour taste in his mouth. "Why would you worship someone like *that*?" He could hear how unsteady his voice was.

A girl spoke from the second row. Saxton felt his heart lurch as he realised it was Taryn.

"Jason rejects Medea for another woman called Glauce." Taryn's voice was emotionless. "Medea cannot contain his love. So she kills Glauce. Then, when this revenge does not hurt Jason enough, she murders their children with a knife."

Saxton was furious. "Who taught you such things?"

"It is our culture," said the boy from the back row. He shrugged. "Euripides wrote of the poor children—Mermerus and Pheres—and their innocence in a cruel world. Kyriabos for centuries has been an island of disease. We are all children, living in a cruel world. Sometimes innocence is punished."

"What did Miss Hemsworth make of it?" Saxton rubbed his forehead. The room was stifling.

A few of the children giggled. "She did not like it."

"I really must talk to Mr. Laskaris about this. I mean, it's not as if you're old enough—"

"Your wife killed *your* children, did she not?"

Saxton stared at Taryn. The question was stark. Unreal. He couldn't believe he'd heard correctly. "*What did you say?*"

She met his glare and returned it with equal measure. "Your wife—Joanne. She murdered your children. She was vengeance herself."

His vision felt like it might lurch at any moment. He began to stammer. "My—my wife died in a car crash. She didn't—she didn't kill anyone. I mean, well, she was killed in the crash with my young son." He could barely swallow. Stars were blooming behind his vision. "It was just a horrible accident..."

"She knew about you and the other woman." Taryn's voice had taken on a dream-like quality, as if she was talking in her sleep. "She did it to punish you."

"Shut up!" He was close to hysteria now. The entire class was watching him. "Shut up!"

"Your other son was growing inside her. She murdered him, too."

His eyelids flickered uncontrollably. He reached to the desk to steady himself. He could taste bile in his mouth, and slowly, in such a way that at first he couldn't be sure he was hearing it, he became aware of the susurration in his head. That serene murmur of harmonies. A chorus that spoke a language he couldn't understand. It rose in volume until it overwhelmed the sound of Taryn's voice.

"I'm sorry, Mr. Laskaris, I really don't know what happened." Saxton shrugged. "I admit—I've been struggling lately."

The principal scratched his beard and rearranged some papers in front of him. "Mr. Saxton, I'll be entirely honest with you—the education authority has arranged a permanent teacher for next term. Your contract won't be renewed."

They were in the principal's office. The air was thick with cigarette smoke. The overflowing ashtray exuded a stale aroma. Somewhere close by, someone was practising chords on a piano.

Saxton sighed. "Listen—I think they just got under my skin. There's no need to go and—"

"I don't need to remind you of your behaviour these past few weeks? It's been observed that you've been under increased pressure." As he spoke, spittle flew from the principal's mouth. "The children seem rather disturbed by your erratic conduct."

Saxton hesitated, licking his lips. His hands shook. He closed his eyes. "They're not like the children I'm used to dealing with." He could hear the disappointment in his own voice. "What I mean is... they're cruel. Callous, actually."

"Mr. Saxton, children are very selfish by nature. It's down to us as adults to teach them the right way to—"

"They talk about wartime atrocities. They speak about things that children shouldn't know. I've even seen them torturing insects in the yard."

Laskaris wrote something on the notepad. He looked up. "How's your health been lately? Sleeping okay?"

"What?"

"The owner of the grocery store mentioned that you were troubled by rats." Laskaris raised an eyebrow. "He said you'd ordered a canister of rat poison. He had to get it from the mainland especially."

Saxton nodded. "I can hear them at night, running around the cottage. It keeps me awake."

"Kyriabos has never had a rat problem before. It's strange that it should happen now."

Saxton blinked. He felt confused. Detached by the events of the past few weeks. "It's eerie at night." He laced his hands together, as if in supplication. "I've seen things. Heard things."

Laskaris blew out his cheeks. "It's been a very difficult eighteen months for you—the loss of your wife and son, the upheaval in relocating here. We're very appreciative of your help, of course, but you're only human—it's understandable that things might catch up with you."

"They knew about the child," Saxton said quietly, staring at the desk.

"The child?"

"They knew... that my wife was pregnant when she died."

Laskaris tutted and shook his head. "I've recommended that you take some time off. You've been through hell this past year."

"They mentioned names." He stared at Laskaris. "I never mentioned names to them, yet they knew..."

An awkward silence. Laskaris cleared his throat, unsure of what to say.

Saxton ran his hands through his hair. "There's an old church. Horrible paintings. They said it was in honour of a woman who killed her sons to avenge her husband's infidelity."

"Medea? The church was built in the 18th century to celebrate a wonderful piece of Greek culture—Europides' ancient tragedy. We're proud of the play. It's performed annually in the open-air theatre on the mainland."

Saxton closed his eyes tight. "I can hear singing wherever I go on the island..."

"It *can* get claustrophobic—I think I said that when you arrived. Island life's not for everyone, unfortunately." The principal smiled a sad smile. He waited a few beats. "I'll need you to put together a report, I'm afraid. So I can brief your replacement for next term." He cocked his head. "I'm sure you understand."

Saxton nodded, feeling resigned.

"I'm sorry things didn't work out." Laskaris stood and offered his hand. "Good luck with everything."

It is the final day of term. An unusually overcast morning. Clouds steal away shadows, usually ever-present. A warm breeze shivers the trees in the playground, rolls footballs into corners. The grey sea is flat and subdued. Saxton has spent his final day on Kyriabos with a strong sense of purpose.

The children appear sad to be saying goodbye. There is an air of finality about the classroom. Saxton waits while they file in from the playground and take their seats. He watches them examining the cartons on their desks, some of them sharing quizzical glances because for the first time the foil has already been removed from the lids of their milk cartons. Saxton nods at them. *It's okay, it's okay—I took it off this time.* Reassured, they begin to drink their milk. He watches their faces carefully, but none of the children seem to detect a difference in the taste.

Saxton studies the handmade good-luck cards the children have presented him with. They cover his entire desk. Declarations of affection, wishes of good fortune. The children drink their milk in typically quiet fashion. He waits until they have all finished. During this time, he thinks about those he has lost. He remembers Joanne's anger when she discovered his affair. Maybe there is a small part of him that can understand Medea's desire for revenge. He adjusts the position of his feet under the desk, careful not to knock over the empty canister.

Now the children have finished their milk. He looks up at those innocent, expressionless faces, and waits for things to start happening.

# DON WEBB

## THE WATER OF DHU'L NUN

**D**ON WEBB has been writing Lovecraftian fiction for thirty-eight years—while Lovecraft himself only did so for two decades. He teaches Horror Writing for UCLA (online) and has been one of their highest-rated instructors since 2002. His work has appeared in *Amazing, Analog, Asimov's, Back Brain Recluse, Fear, Interzone, The Magazine of Fantasy &Science Fiction, Weird Tales* and more than fifty anthologies. As a Texan, he has a better secret chili recipe than you do.

"In 1976," he recalls, "the Amarillo Public Library got a copy of Edward P. Berglund's anthology *The Disciples of Cthulhu*, and I was thrilled. I had discovered Lovecraft a few years earlier, but here were *other* people playing the game.

"My favourite story was 'Where Yidhra Walks' by Walter C. DeBill, Jr. Later I was able to co-write a story with him and create two sequels (of which this is one). My local librarian was keen on Lovecraft and also the 'New Wave'. My brothers had given me their Edgar Rice Burroughs paperbacks, and I found their collection of Beat writers—spin all that in your blender, and you get me."

**S**USAN HATED MLANDOTH, TX. The name, she supposed, came from some bad white mispronunciation of some American Indian word for "No the fuck where". She was driving Jose to the tiny local airport. Jose was going back home to Indianapolis, where he made middling bucks in an advertising firm. At least he was going back to twenty inches of snow, whereas she was facing an eighty-degree afternoon since she was stuck in Texas in a town where you couldn't drink the water. After Flint, Michigan; Crystal City, Texas, and St. Bernard Parish, Louisiana toxic water didn't even make the news anymore. She assumed that her oil company's big-ass refinery was to blame. It was the major employer in these parts. Everything else serviced its employees—the tiny bank, the two liquor stores and the Catfish Parlour. She marvelled at how ugly, how pulp-fiction monster ugly the big catfish on the pole that advertised the place was. It was *ginormous*, and at night its blue neon outline wiggled as though some even more giant creature had hooked it. Even on this overcast day it looked too alien.

At least Exxon was buying bottled water for the town. Which she supposed was a tacit admission of guilt.

It was awkwardly silent in the car. She and Jose were supposed to have a fun weekend, but it devolved into the same old fight. No, she did not know how long this assignment was going to last. No, she didn't think she could tell Mr. Walters that he either had to bring her home or she would walk. She made more money than Jose, which bugged him. Not much more, but more. He was threatening to go all Erin Brockovich on Exxon. He would rat out the company, unless she returned home. She tried to explain that taking on big oil would end both of their careers, but the real story was she was fairly sure that if she just hung on for six months, she would be up for promotion to a Regional Manager. That meant serious money, and that would either make their marriage better or give her enough to live pretty well on her own. Depending on the phase of the moon, Susan was happy with either. Her green car sped by the Tikki House, a quasi-Polynesian BBQ place with its own ugly advertising. It featured this tall wooden figure that was a cross between Groot and an Easter Island head. Again ugly and creepy. The first night she had been in Mlandoth she thought some barbecue pork with pineapple sounded good. She'd driven here from the Best Western. A group of drunks were standing around the wooden man singing or chanting to it. She was creeped out, running every bad movie scenario of some strange BBQ cult that served long pig, and drove away. She bought damp plastic-wrapped turkey and Swiss cheese sandwiches at the 7-11, drove back to the hotel and put the chain on the door.

If only Jose could be supportive of what she was trying to do.

Or maybe he was, but was confused by some blend of machismo and not knowing how to deal with ambiguity. Part of him might be proud, part of him missed her, part wanted to protect her. And there was something about Mlandoth that just seemed some unsafe. Some vibration in the air, some strangeness in the proportions of the architecture, maybe the sound the soda machine made before it dropped your bottle—there was something, some recurrent datum or data that just told your brain that things were strange. Of course, the smell of the refinery and the inbred look of the locals probably didn't help. Or that they seemed to worship ugly advertising icons.

Susan knew that after the cold and stiff scene at the airport there would be tentative happy texts full of heart icons and then, hours later after she had turned off the lights in her hotel room, he would call and there would be apologies and promises to never "be that way" again.

Susan went to a McDonald's for dinner. She didn't like to be out at night. Things would catch her eye. One night, when she first arrived in December, she found herself looking at the methane flame that shot out of the vertical flare-stack over the refinery. She was walking from her car to the hotel and looked to the west, and there it was. It didn't scare her, or give her ecstasy, she just found herself staring at it. Another night, it was a fountain in a little park downtown. Nothing very elaborate, just a fountain that alternately illuminated its water spumes with red, yellow and green. Yet she had watched for fifteen minutes without a thought in her head. Maybe there was something else besides the water that was contaminated. Maybe it was a sound, maybe a quality of light.

Not a town to read Stephen King in at night. Techno-thrillers were okay. She had been jonesing for dope. Now she hadn't smoked weed since college, but alcohol didn't take the edge off. Of course she wasn't going to ask/hint to the employees at the plant—mainly Baptist whites and Catholic Hispanics that were scared of her powers to audit. She couldn't have asked Jose to bring anything—he was pretty straight-edge. She couldn't meet anyone else. She didn't do bars—and didn't have the nerve to walk into the one head shop in town, Yidhra's Cauldron. As she ate her oatmeal, two sausage burritos and drank her large diet coke, she listened to the four teenage boys in the booth behind her with some jealousy. There was a tall, thin half-Hispanic boy (probably what her kids with Jose would look like if they ever got to that place in their careers where they could have kids)—his dark blue jeans had worn threads where the knees were. Next to him was a pudgy, slug-like kid with black nerd glasses and ginger hair. Across the table was a smaller, younger Hispanic, much darker with a slightly idiotic grin, and a muscular Anglo guy with bad acne and a much faded DON'T MESS WITH TEXAS! T-shirt.

Half-Hispanic: "The town is dry, there is no weed."

Glasses: "Well, it's not like we can't get high."

Half-Hispanic: "I tried that once, and I didn't like it."

Muscles: "Because you're a pussy."

Half-Hispanic: "You did it? You reals did it?"

Muscles: "My sister's boyfriend did and said it was ggucchi. All flowers and shit."

Half-Hispanic: "Well it fuckin' aint. At least not for me."

Glasses: "Were you purposeful? Did you plan it out?"

Half-Hispanic: "Who would plan that shit? I cleaned out the garage for my old man. It was hot. I forgot and took a drink from the hose. Dad was working a double-shift. I lay down in the hammock and sort of vegged. I fell asleep. I woke up at twilight and the tree was trying to eat me and my pit-bull had those octopus things. Testicles."

Glasses: "Tentacles. *You* have testicles."

Muscles: "No he don't, 'cause he's a pussy."

Glasses: "My point is, you could have known it was going to happen. You could've had some bottled water on hand to drink if it got scary. You could've had friends to tell you to watch out for the testicles."

Idiot giggled.

"So," asked Half-Hispanic, "How *should* we do it?"

Glasses sighed.

Susan thought, *that kid is going to have a rough go of it, when they read* Lord of the Flies *in senior year.*

Glasses said, "First we do the phone drill. You tell your mama you're at Rodrigo's, you tell your dad you're staying with me at my grandmother's house, etc. Then we bike to the Dairy Queen on 193. We each buy a bottle of Nestlé's. We bike to that place, that creek." He looked at Idiot.

Idiot said, "Arroyo Secca. We go to Indio rock."

"Yeah," Glasses continued, "we go to Indian Rock. I'll bring a big canteen full of town water. We each take a big slug. Then when it comes on, we watch the petroglyphs dance. If it gets scary, or when we get bored, we drink the bottled water, wait fifteen minutes and bike back to my grandmother's. We sleep in the storm cellar. I'll convince her the next day she knew all about it."

Muscles: "Petroglyphs?"

Glasses said, "Pictures, dummy. The pictures they painted on the rock."

That night Jose called and they had make-up phone sex. As Susan lay snuggled in the blankets, he talked about his "research". Jose liked to look things up on the Internet, it made him feel smart. "It seems that Mlandoth had some sort of hippy eco-cult in the 1960s and '70s. The FBI shut them down with the usual subtlety they showed in Waco and elsewhere. The abandoned houses had been bought up cheap by Exxon. A few of the cultists remained, but Exxon used the really cheap land (maybe even not exactly purchased, if you know what I mean), to put in its refinery. The water problem started in 2001. Exxon claimed that they had nothing to do with it—maybe it was a parasite. Certainly there were no petroleum by-products in the town's water. There was a federal investigation. Two of the investigators died suspiciously, and, get this, the Federal government pays for the bottled water. Not Exxon. Your fucking tax dollars at work, right?"

Susan applauded his brilliance, and then asked if he had found out what the name meant.

"I couldn't find it. There's the exact same name in Tibeto-Burmese languages, but that couldn't be the same source. It means 'Hungry

Ghost'—apparently some sect believes that you and I don't have souls. But instead of us all being part of some friendly group soul, all life in this solar system is possessed by a parasite. We're like its legs and arms. Our self-consciousness in an unintended side-effect. Of course, maybe the hippies had picked up on this. Didn't Timothy Leary have people reading the *Tibetan Book of the Dead*?"

Jose kept talking while Susan fell asleep.

She got the bad news the next day. She had been expecting good news. Her audit showed that four mid-level managers were skimming off some expenses by buying from a company that their wives owned in no-bid contracts. She assumed this would be a promotion and her ticket out of Mlandoth. Instead, it was her job to fix it. She would be here at least another six months. Screw it. She took the afternoon off and went to Yidhra's Cauldron. She figured her good (well at least, better than average) looks, lean body and blonde hair might give her more purchasing ability than a foursome of teenage losers.

It was a nondescript head shop in a tiny strip mall that also hosted a tattoo parlour, a pawnshop and a martial arts studio. It was rows and rows of shiny glass pipes; legal herbal pills to give you energy, clean up your urine or make you last longer in bed, and graphic novels. There was a used books area big on sci-fi and old paranormal paperbacks with gee-whiz titles like *UFOs on Colonial America*. Behind the counter were nudie mags and bumper-stickers—mainly supporting legalisation. KEEP ON THE GRASS MAN! I'VE GOT A HIGH IQ! (made of stylised marijuana leaves). YOU CAN'T BEAT A WASTED LIFE.

It was deadsville. Only the grey-haired bear of a man in a denim jacket that manned the counter (and probably owned the joint) was there. An enormous black dog, probably half-lab and half-Godzilla snored and farted on the dirty grey linoleum floor. She dropped a few hints about being new in town, looking for people to party with, etc. but no help from the owner. She leaned over the counter a few times so he could ogle her firm breasts. He ogled, but gave out no useful info. She saw he was wearing a turquoise bolo with a rather deformed thunderbird motif.

"What's that?" Susan asked, "Something Indian?"

"Older than the Indians. It's the mother goddess, Yidrha."

"Oh," said Susan, thinking this might be the ticket. "Are you one of the town's original inhabitants?"

He smiled, "You know your history?"

His tone told her that was *not* the question to have asked.

He continued, "I came after the FBI raids. I came in 2001. The EPA was trying to nail Exxon. I was one of the investigators. Who would have thought a doctorate in chemistry would've enabled me to run the best little head shop in Texas?"

Susan asked, "So what's the deal about the water?"

"Nothing," he said. "It's perhaps the purest water in the world, certainly the purest drinking water in North America."

He stepped back from the counter and opened the door to the employee rest room. With exaggerated motions, so Susan could watch clearly, he drew himself a drink in a Scooby-Doo glass from the bathroom tap. He put the water to his lips and chugged it down, making an exaggerated sigh of relief when he had finished it. He looked at her with hatred.

"See?" he asked.

"What happened to your fellow investigators?" Susan asked.

"They couldn't handle the purity. The FBI said it was murder-suicide."

Susan was betting on murder. She had a clear shot at the door. She decided to ask one more question.

"If you weren't part of the cult, how come you wear the amulet?"

"Just figured out a lot of it. Mainly by living here. Some by reading poetry, myth. I'm a regular Joseph-fucking-Campbell, I am. Found the amulet one day when I was walking along I93 picking up cans. Won at the lotto after that, bought this place. The American Dream if you ask me."

"Did the amulet make you win the lottery?"

He shrugged, "Who fucking knows?"

"So it wouldn't hurt me to drink the water?"

"Didn't say it wouldn't hurt you." He handed her a bumper sticker. THE TRUTH WILL MAKE YOU FLEE. "On the house."

"Thanks." She turned to leave.

As she walked out, he said, "It's Mlandoth's Curse. Everywhere, everywhere *but* here. Duh'l Nun. Google it."

She resolved to tell Jose her bad news that night that her stay in Mlandoth would be longer. But he was grumpy, and so she told a less scary version of her encounter with the head shop guy. She didn't say that he was one of the EPA scientists, just that he was kooky and told her to Google "Dual Noon".

Man, could she use some relief besides beer and fast food. The water couldn't be that bad, could it? She had seen the head-shop guy chug it. She could drink some town water and, like the kids, have her bottle of water as relief. So she tried a little from her motel-room faucet. Nothing. A little more, still nothing. A fucking gallon. Nada.

She asked the waiter at the breakfast bar next morning.

"How much of the bad water do you need to drink to have the hallucinations?"

"I hear not too much. Of course the hotel has treated water, so anything you drink here is safe."

At work she took two gallon jugs of bottled water from the employee supply. After work she drove to Yidhra's Cauldron. She said, "I'd like to buy some of your very pure water. Please empty this bottle and fill it from your sink."

The owner nodded and said nothing.

When he handed her the recently refilled bottle, he said, "I know the temptation is strong. I know you think it doesn't really matter. We all thought that. You know, when my friends killed themselves they didn't have guns. All they had was a steak knife from Western Sizzling. Not even a sharp steak knife. It took a while. If you open the doors of perception, remember you *can* close them again."

"Yeah? Then why didn't you do so?"

"I'm a scientist—or at least I was. I valued objective truth. It's kind of overrated."

"But you're not going to stop me?"

"You could've filled up your bottle at the Shell store on Bowie St. I know you passed it between here and your hotel. You wanted to see me. You needed to see me. I don't know why, but I can guess. I was a loner here once. The one pretty honest guy with a good education. People are weird here, some try the water—others get a little bit on themselves while watering the lawn or washing their cars. Mainly, it makes them mean or crooked or just a little dumb. If I was younger, or if you came on more desperate, I would make a pass at you."

She marked the refilled bottle "TW" and the unopened bottle "PW", for "pure water".

The first night she wasn't brave enough.

The second night she wasn't brave enough.

The third night Jose mentioned that he had had dinner with his ex-wife. She was brave enough.

She decided she would trip out between 8:00 p.m. and midnight. She locked and chained the door of her motel room and pushed a chair in front of it. She sat in the room in another chair near the bed, facing the window. The window faced the west and looked out over most of the city of Mlandoth. There would pretty lights as eighteen-wheelers sped north from Mexico towards Dallas/Fort Worth. She put the Town Water to her left, the Pure Water to her right. She reused her large Styrofoam cup from McDonald's. She lay her iPad on the bed, so she could watch the time or play games if the mood struck her. She drank half a cup of Mlandoth water. It did taste sweet and pure. She distracted herself with Facebook.

After thirty minutes it seemed her fingers were sinking into the iPad. It was becoming warm and liquidy—but also velvet. It became a puddle on the bed. Outside, a cop car chased a truck. The flashing lights became eyes, and the car grew great bat wings, while the truck turned into some kind of rhino/slug-looking thing. The windows became jelly that breathed. This was becoming a little much, Susan thought, but it was also fascinating. She could see the Catfish Parlour sign. It really was a giant, living fish impaled on a pole, twisting in agony. Its blue neon was glowing blood and, as drops were being flung in the air, glowing insect-bats were sucking it up. The tall god of the Tikki House was looking up at her, and she knew its *name*, which hurt her mind to think it, and she wanted to give it small warm gifts. She turned from the window, and she saw her pale scabby face in the mirror with its extra line of vestigial eyes. And she opened her mouth with its three rows of teeth and screamed a sound like the strings a cello might make if you struck them with a file. Her longer arm swirled up and covered her eyes (all of them) by circling her head several times. She dropped to the floor, which was covered in soft mushrooms that released clouds of minty-smelling spores. She scuttled back around the bed and stuck her proboscis into the Pure Water and sucked it in—feeling it make millions of tiny bites as it came into her. She cried oily green tears and convulsed.

And slowly...

And slowly...

And slowly the world she knew came back to her, as she lay next to the bed and sobbed.

She didn't go to work the next morning, and stayed inside until her hangover drove her from the room. She took the two bottles with her.

At work she visited the plant chemist and got two specimen bottles. She had a friend at the Exxon offices in Houston, a chemist with not one but two PhDs. An old college fling. She sent the bottles to her with a letter saying that one was from land she was thinking of buying, and one was bottled water as a control. Could she do a full analysis of each—they tasted the same, she just wanted to know if the water from her well was okay. She poured the rest of the TW water into a toilet.

She didn't know what she was looking for—a strange army drug? A parasite that re-wrote the mind? Something she could sell the CIA? Something she could denounce her own company with? She just wanted to know something. Some solid ground to set her jelly-quivering mind upon.

The next three days went by slowly. She drew her drapes in her hotel room. She threw herself into work—getting done what would have normally taken a week. She had twelve panic attacks. Anything could cause them: hearing loud music from a low rider's candy red car, seeing a cockroach scuttle across the asphalt in the hotel's parking lot, the murmuration of a flock of birds at sunset, a funny-looking raisin in her oatmeal. She thought of driving out to Yidhra's Cauldron, but what would she say? The guy had warned her. Maybe the chest-pounding fear would lessen with time. Maybe.

Jose said she sounded distant on the phone.

The results came back. One sample had an amoeba-like parasite that had a cellular membrane that gave it great affinity to human neural tissue. The other sample killed the parasite. The bad water was the bottled water. The good water was from the wells of Mlandoth.

Maybe she had mislabelled the bottles? But she knew she had not.

That night Jose called. It wasn't "Dual Noon". It was Dhu'l Nun, a Sufi saint. Jose read to her from a website: "Dhu'l Nun is known for a famous teaching parable. The Khidir, the teacher of Magi, came to Moses and warned him that Allah was pissed off at mankind, and was going to punish them by driving them mad. Allah was going to do this by poisoning the waters. So the wise could hoard up water now, and thus remain sane. Many did so. They sealed the water away in special jugs marked with the six-pointed star of stasis. They were sure they could remain sane. But as they went forth into the world, they noticed that men now spoke in strange ways, and they could not understand the actions of men. They noticed that men now acted in strange ways, and they could not understand what men did. And men hearing the wise either grew angry, or full of compassion for these madmen. So one-by-one, due to loneliness, and to economic reasons, and to fear of the madmen, the wise gave up drinking pure water and drank the waters of the Earth. They forgot all about their special store of water, and slowly they became like the rest. The rest of mankind welcomed them with open arms—seeing them as madmen who had regained their sanity."

Jose asked, "Does that make any sense?"

Susan said, "I just think he was some old hippy. Too much acid."

Then she told him tales from the office, the usual banter of their couple-hood, and Jose was happy.

The next day she drove to Yidhra's Cauldron.

The owner was in the same denim jacket over (she guessed) the same yellowed T-shirt. His medallion seemed alive, moving. She tried not to look at it. He looked sad.

He said, "So you drank the water. And you want to know why it caused such terrible hallucinations."

"No. Like you I have access to science, not to mention the lovely little parable you told me. I realise that the water *stops* hallucinations. I realise *that* was the real world. I just want to know why and when. When did the world become that?

"Don't know for sure. There are a lot of strange forces that game and gambol on this haunted planet. Yidhra gave a Gift to her Children that they could see the real world. The consensus world is ruled by much more terrible gods and goddesses than her. Some of it slops through—the death of bees and butterflies, the global heat wave, the extinction of the mega-fauna, violence. Since you seem pretty sane, I'm guessing you didn't watch TV news when you could *See.*"

"Which is better?" Susan asked. "Knowing or not knowing?"

The old man was silent. His medallion grew an eye and *winked.*

*For Walt DeBill and Forry Ackerman.*

# RON WEIGHELL

## UNDER THE FRENZY
## OF THE FOURTEENTH MOON

RON WEIGHELL's stories first started appearing in the late 1980s in such small press magazines as *Ghosts & Scholars, Nocturne, Dark Dreams* and *All Hallows*, and he had stories reprinted in Karl Edward Wagner's *The Year's Best Horror Stories: XX* and *Best New Horror #26* and *#27*.

His short fiction is collected in *The White Road: The Collected Supernatural Stories of Ron Weighell, Tarshishim, Summonings, The Irregular Casebook of Sherlock Holmes* and the chapbook *The Greater Arcana*. Weighell also contributed novellas to Sarob Press' *Pagan Triptych, Romances of the White Day* and *From Ancient Ravens*, along with John Howard and Mark Valentine.

In November 2020 he suffered a major stroke and died on Christmas Eve, aged 70. 'Under the Frenzy of the Fourteenth Moon' was his last story.

"—for the Sidhe are dextrous fishers, and they fish for men with dreams upon the hook."
—*The Only Jealousy of Emer*

I HAD ALWAYS been fascinated by the poetry and occultism of W.B. Yeats, and written a few critical pieces on both subjects, so when I caught a rumour of unpublished material in the possession of the only surviving member of the Powers family, who were related to the Pollexfens of Sligo, I was understandably keen to pursue the matter. I had Irish family connections in Adrigole, on Bantry Bay, and by chance my Uncle Brandan was on good terms with the near-recluse in question. He and Thias Powers had apparently "supped deep, and chased the colleens together all over Cork" in their youth. Powers had himself written on Yeats in a modest way, having published accounts of his father's recollections of conversations with the great poet, particularly on the subject of "dee-ah-bolism" and faery lore, which had evidently interested Yeats greatly. What interested me most, of course, was that cache of unpublished papers. The family connection enabled me to get permission to see them.

So after a pleasant stay with my relatives in Adrigole, I visited Thias Powers at his home, which proved to be a beautiful little Palladian manse hidden amid picturesque, if discreetly dwindling, acreage. The Gardens of Ilnacullin were close enough to make me suspect that Harold Peto might at some point have added a few features of his own to the formal gardens. The interior was decidedly run-down, but still magnificent, boasting a fair number of marbles, bronzes and paintings that had survived from the days of the Grand Tour. Thias Powers lived alone there amongst his books, an undeniable echo of Yeats's high, lonely tower where Milton's Platonist sat late.

If I was beguiled by the house, I was overwhelmed by the library. The financial straits that had necessitated the selling off of parcels of land had spared the artworks, and had clearly not prompted the equally deplorable wholesale culling of books. Here were no outdated encyclopaedias and Reader's Digest anthologies bound in plastic, bought by the yard to fill gaps left by painful extraction; but everywhere the kind of books that had to be tied along the fore-edge with cords to stop the vellum boards bowing, or held closed with metal clasps of intricate design, as though to contain all the beauty within. Fore-edge decoration of the most exquisite kind was common. If the collection was ever sold, the great auction houses would have been spilling each other's blood to be first through the front door.

Thias was elderly, and not apparently in the best of health, but still a dapper dresser, with a full head of gunmetal grey hair greased into a style I have always associated with the "Brylcreem Boys" of the 1940s, and retained some shadow of the looks that had charmed the ladies of his youth. With his well-stocked cellar, his incunabula and private press treasures, there was much to admire, but any temptation to allow envy to raise its head was somewhat mitigated by a single unfortunate feature. If Thias had once been irresistible to women, there must surely have been a time when his teeth were still on good terms with his toothbrush. But at some point in the remote past the two had parted company, and the result was a mouth full of rotten fangs of a shade of green that once seen could never be forgotten. I spent most of the visit struggling to keep my eyes from this source of horrid fascination. Even a Palladian mansion and the library of my dreams, I concluded, wouldn't compensate for facing every day with those in your mouth.

In all fairness, Thias was in every other respect a charming individual, and a quite mesmerising talker, subscribing enthusiastically to Yeats' belief that every modern nation was like a tower half-dead at the top. His view of the Master's mysticism was just as positive, quoting with approval the injunction:

> But seek alone to hear strange things said
> By God to the bright hearts of those long dead,
> And learn to chaunt a tongue men do not know.

He also quoted, with even greater relish, the dictum that all dreams of the soul end in a beautiful woman's body, which I took then to be a mere reference to the roistering ways of his youth.

So he had spent his latter days dreaming in this impossibly beautiful old house, lost in huge folios of alchemical engravings, surrounded by his paintings and drawings, icons, antique gods and goddesses, and those towering shelves of books bound in rich colours and intricately ornamented. He was in no hurry to talk about the subject I had come for, but took me on a tour of his more arcane bibliographic treasures, introducing me to rare works by Morienus, whose epistle to Khalid was the first alchemical work to be translated from Arabic to Latin; Avicenna, who believed all life proceeded from corruption; Alfarah, who could invoke joy or trance by the power of his lute; Raymond Lully, and Nicolas and Pernelle Flamel, who, he said, had lived for centuries, and lived still among Dervishes of Arabia. Producing alchemical texts like the *Splendor Solis*, and magnificent folios of works illustrated by William Blake, he invited me to consider how, to the uninitiated, it was difficult to distinguish where the painted images of alchemy ended and those of Blake began.

Then he revealed his greatest treasure. The *Liber inducens in Evangelium aeternum* in a silver box Benvenuto Cellini himself had decorated with gods and demons. The volume itself was of leather with filigree decorations of tarnished silver. I was allowed to glimpse many exquisitely coloured and gilded pages. It had passed, he said, from Cellini to Giulio Clovio, then to the Roman engraver Raimondo, and thence to Aretino, student of Pico della Mirandola.

Eventually he got round to the matter of Yeats.

I had recognised his easy charm immediately, but had underestimated his knowledge. When he began at last to speak of Yeats' *A Vision*, of Pernes and Gyres, and the Hindu parallels with his Great Year, I was quickly lost. He knew it was those unpublished papers I wanted most to see, but he was in no hurry to get round to the subject. Not that his conversation was boring. His forebears had evidently been members of every occult group from George Russell's Hermetic Order to one of the main branches of the Golden Dawn, so the insights were fascinating.

"A.E. thought any pursuit of magic was dangerous because its strength was drawn from 'a sinister fountain,'" he observed. "But even he admitted that it could inspire in art a strange new beauty. No doubt Yeats would have called it a truth summoned out of that darkness where lay the crowns of Nineveh and Tyre."

There was a quaint charm akin to Yeats' own in the way he talked of faeries as if they were real. "Don't seek to know too much about them. They can appear beautiful beyond dream, but remember, they will deceive you if they can."

Eventually a chance presented itself to push him gently on the matter of the Yeats papers. To my exasperation he had made no attempt to prepare them for me in the days before my arrival; indeed wasn't even sure where they were. He suggested I take a walk while he sought them out. I would have been happier to browse the library, but I suppose the thought of a stranger thumbing through those treasured tomes without supervision was hardly appealing. Besides, he seemed insistent that I walk up to a hill he pointed out from the window, to see "The Faery Thorn" that stood in the field beyond. No one came without visiting it. I did not argue. It was a pleasant day, so it involved no discomfort to humour him.

The Faery Thorn proved to be a remarkable sight.

The whole field in which it stood was farmland, showing all the signs of having been ploughed and sown over many a year. Every other square inch had been cultivated, and removing the tree would have made the work much more straightforward, but the lines left by ploughing divided at the tree like currents breaking around an island and re-forming on the other side. Hung with offerings, mainly in the form of strips and rags of cloth, its gnarled joints were contorted by the prevailing wind into a distinctly sinister crouching form worthy, I thought, of Arthur Rackham.

The offerings, it seemed, were not restricted to the boughs of the tree. About its roots a multitude of stones and other small objects lay scattered. Glancing around, I saw a stone in the form of a shallow black disc no bigger than the flat of my hand. It was smooth, as if polished, and I liked the way it fitted into my palm. It must have lain there for a long time, washed smooth by the rains. I took it away with me for a lucky stone.

Thias had found the papers and spread them out on his desk by the time I got back. He made it clear that he did not wish them to be published, but had no objection to me taking notes and quoting from them "for the purposes of criticism". With that, he took a thick leather quarto down from the shelves and left the room.

Even the first, cursory glance was fascinating. Yeats and Georgie, as I well knew, had produced over fifty Vision Papers recording their psychic experiments, of which only thirty-six had been identified. Thias had not actually said that some of the others might be amongst his cache, but the tantalising possibility was there. The bulk seemed to be made up of automatic writings—produced by Georgie under trance invoked by ritual magic—as well as fragments of verse and gnomic exclamations.

*Awaking the silent twin.*
*Fallen they may be, but to us they are as gods.*
*Rules for Discovering True and False Masks.*
*—hear the new-dropped lambs of Faery crying in November snows.*
*Riding the wrack of endless skies*
*each moon is born again only for you,*
*for you each waning moon's demise—*
*Unlock not the gates of Pluto. The people of Dream wait within.*

This proved an encouragement to some unproductive meditations. Just what would the crying of the new-dropped lambs of Faery sound like?

When I took a break and scanned the shelves, I was further distracted by another kind of treasure, a solid quarto entitled *Rosa Alchemica*, which I had hitherto thought to be a work of Yeats' imagination. It did indeed seem to match his description of "a little work on the Alchemists in the manner of Sir Thomas Browne". Slipped into it like bookmarks were two small drawings on stiff, heavy, brown-tinted paper: one a spirited depiction of a rearing unicorn, the other a square with scrolls at the corners which showed the alchemical signs of the elements. Inside this was a double circle enclosing images of the four phases of the moon, astrological signs and the numbers one to twenty-eight. Within that was a heraldic looking device with a rose, a chalice, an apple and a wand gripped in a fist.

I recognised them immediately as early versions of Edmund Dulac's drawings of the Great Wheel and the Unicorn for Yeats' *Speculum Angelorum et Hominem*. Both were overlaid with faint pencil grids. Perhaps no one had recognised them as original Dulac drawings, or thought them too small and workmanlike to be extracted and framed. I thought them charming.

In retrospect I credit my unfamiliarity with Yeats' deeper mysteries, and the resulting leap to the simplest conclusion, for the discovery that followed. Rotation in Yeats' work was usually assumed to refer to gyres of cosmic time or to cycles of reincarnation. I simply noticed that the two images were drawn on unnecessarily heavy paper, and that there was a pinhole at the centre of each drawing. I remembered, too, that Dulac had once produced an alternate version of the Great Wheel with the Unicorn at the centre. This was usually seen as a minor aesthetic design issue between the two men, but I wondered if it referred to something more than the final printed form of the Great Wheel?

What I needed was a drawing pin. My search through the first few desk drawers produced little more than old bills (an alarming number of them unpaid) and a small bundle of erotic postcards that might have been considered risqué in their day, but had assumed with time the status of amusingly quaint collector's items. At last I found one loose drawing pin rattling around a lower drawer, and pinned the Unicorn to the Wheel.

When the Unicorn was rotated, the horn pointed in turn to the numbers on the rim of the circle. I had apparently discovered some sort of code-wheel which a great poet and a famous artist had constructed together. There might just be a modest place for me yet, I thought, in the august halls of Yeats studies. The question of which numbers to choose, and what that signified was of course another matter beyond conjecture, which took a little edge off the discovery.

I returned my attention to the psychic papers, and later in the day came upon instructions in the hand of Georgie Yeats for some kind of arcane ritual progression or dance.

*Take five steps through the waxing crescent in balance. The Twins take four towards the full. The Ram takes but two paces waning. Let the Goat take three strides in the direction of the New Moon.*

The reference to a goat and a ram suggested ritual masks, common to Golden Dawn rites and Yeats' dramas. I thought no more of it.

Not all the papers were psychic utterances or ritual instructions.

The full extent of Georgie's magical knowledge was at that time just emerging, so I was not entirely surprised to find a sheaf of notes in her hand on Kabbalah and Notarikon with drawings of the Tree of Life and the Path of the Serpent. Included was a list of twenty-eight numbers alongside twenty-six letters and two indecipherable symbols, headed *Nemo Sciat*, her motto in the Golden Dawn, which translated as "Let Nobody Know". I was puzzled to see that the numbers and letters did not correspond in the usual way. Even I knew that in all alphabets where letters were related to numbers, "a" or *aleph* should have equalled one, "b" or *beth* two, and so on. These numbers and letters were paired randomly, or by some arcane method that eluded me.

But both this list and the Great Wheel had twenty-eight numbers!

There were four phases of the moon and astrological signs on the Wheel. Georgie's instruction to take "five steps through the waxing crescent" or "four towards the full" took on a new meaning. Rotating the horn as requested, and relating each resulting number to its indicated letter, I soon produced the hidden text.

*Imgratz oombaava mayermeekra ooshtalaa makooshakamak shaada.*

It was disappointing to say the least. I supposed there must be a further key to produce a readable text. I went on looking through the papers, somewhat crestfallen, before I stopped and pondered, gazing down at the smooth lucky stone I had been rubbing between my finger and thumb.

What was it that Thias had quoted from Yeats about hearing strange things said, and learning "to chaunt a tongue men do not know"? They were apparently gobbledegook, those strings of letters, but what if they were just that—a tongue men do not know?

I recited them aloud.

*Imgratz oombaava mayermeekra ooshtalaa makooshakamak shaada.*

The sound they made was certainly resonant. I repeated them.

I found I was staring at the smooth surface of the stone in my hand. Letters formed on its surface, glowing like slots in a smouldering grate. I glimpsed a face in it, mouth moving to the words as I spoke. I stopped and closed my eyes. The dizziness took some minutes to pass.

I decided not to tell Thias of all this.

When we parted, he shook my hand and looked searchingly into my eyes.

"I hope you have found something to make your journey worthwhile, young man. *Beannachd lerbh.*"

My discoveries were not, it seemed, to be obtained without a price. I became prey to disturbing dreams. At first they were unconnected glimpses of standing stones and old trees and kindly looking men indicating passages in old books, but they soon intensified. I would find myself restrained in a room where pale, horribly emaciated figures examined me, even inflicted wounds on me. Most horrifying were the battles between ferocious warriors of massive size and strength, bloody and dreadful conflicts of unspeakable cruelty fought with brutal weapons of ingenious design. At other times I was among refugees, or survivors, fleeing these conflicts. Some of the faces around me showed terror, but others were ecstatic with a mad enthusiasm.

Most often, though, I was in some kind of ceremonial parade without end, sometimes on a high, windy plateau, sometimes marching through the doorways of an endless succession of immense rooms, an enfilade for giants. Or we were processing through some vast, echoing space. The nature of the light suggested a tunnel or cavern of immense dimensions, through which I was being jostled and pushed by the flow of the crowd. All my senses were assailed. Drums and flutes and unhuman howling; odours sweet and nauseating; they were a wildly disparate horde, some human but with horns, or with stunted wings, as well as goats, donkeys and dogs of unnatural sizes and colours. Some of the people were in period costume, some in relatively modern attire. A few were naked. Some, though bipedal, were not human at all. Ragged and musty banners flapped at the head of the column, bearing fiery figures and letters strange to me, but curiously reminiscent of heraldry, or devices of alchemy. We were always led by a group of alarmingly large and very beautiful men and women resembling the visions of Gustave Moreau, god-like creatures glittering with barbaric ornament and a Byzantine splendour.

In such dreams I was always utterly exhausted. It seemed we had been marching for days without end. Some amongst the crowd carried great baskets of fruit, trays of cooked meats and ornate wine carafes, but no one ever ate or drank. The hunger and thirst were a torment. Some of the faces I glimpsed in the throng have haunted me. There was one old man with as much flesh on him as the claw of a bird, crying heartbrokenly as he shambled along. I would, though, catch fleeting glimpses of a young woman—normal size, in modest dress—of an exotic beauty that stunned me. Her features suggested a mingling of Asian and Latin elements, overlaid with a melancholy that somehow completed her perfection. Occasionally in the jostling throng our eyes met, and a look passed between us that twisted my heart.

One morning I rose from such a troubled night and dressed, stepped through a doorway and found myself parading the echoing space and strange light of those endless caverns. I had not been awake at all.

From then on even my days took on the character of nightmare. I could never be sure which world I was in; if my awakenings were real. The confusion was not helped by the fact that even when I was awake, and on the streets of what I hoped was the real world, I would occasionally hear strange music, and see someone I had walked with through those endless nights. They all looked tired and stressed. Some were vagrants, even the kind of troubled souls who should not have been loose on the streets at all. Others were not poor and were obviously employed. They only had one other thing in common. Not one ever seemed to recognise me.

And that is how I might have remained, locked in a perpetual struggle to maintain my sanity, snatched away at will, as it were, by the Tribes of Danu, when something happened that shifted my whole world on its axis. I caught a waft of wonderful dream perfume on the air, and saw in the passing crowd the exotic woman I had occasionally glimpsed in those endless dream parades. Half-fearing I was still asleep, I struggled to think of what I could say to her: "I've seen you in my dreams"? It sounded like a cheap pick-up line, the recycled lyric of a sentimental song. Then she glanced in my direction, and it was obvious that *she* recognised *me*. She approached me without hesitation, and we were soon deep in conversation.

That was how I met Leanan Foley. I learned the correct spelling of her first name only later, because she pronounced it "Lenorn". The charming similarity to the name of a Poe heroine prompted me to subtly misquote "a rare and radiant maiden whom the angels name Leanan". I was a little deflated when it became clear that the quotation meant absolutely nothing to her, but it caused no awkwardness between us. She took the rather trite compliment with good grace. We spent the rest of that day together, and we got on well. She knew of Yeats, but strangely not as a poet. She revered him as a man wise in Celtic lore.

When I talk of the love that developed for her, I am talking of something sacred, a form of worship. So you must understand that I accepted the strangeness of what followed without demur. We must never discuss the nature of those dreams. We must meet at a pre-arranged spot on the edge of a forest outside the city. She was always waiting for me there, standing by the crumbling base and stump that were all that remained of an ancient pillar. Taking my hand, she would pick her way swiftly, treading a path well known, and bring us at last to a building so embowered and creeper-covered that only an arched door and one small window was visible. That was all I ever glimpsed of the exterior.

The inside was dimly-lit and womb-like, hung with rich fabrics and heavy with sweet odours. A fire burned in a wrought-metal grate of intricate design. There was always wine of some kind, potent and dark, and she fed me fruit I did not recognise: soft and succulent with delicious juice. Then she introduced me to a level of passion I had never known, and with it fantastic visions.

Sometimes we seemed to be loving in a glittering chapel of Byzantine richness, or on some dream Island of Statues ruled over by an all wondrous serpent clothed in gems and rich array. And always there were words, portentous incantatory words, which I could never forget, and would never reveal, as we lay entwined together like some living caduceus.

From the first it was nothing less than a magical rite, an ecstasy in which it was impossible to tell whether the loving inspired the visions and the utterances, or the visions and utterances were inspiring our love. Somehow she made of each moment a sacrament. Everything was so richly intensified, exalted to a new and wonderful level. It seemed that we fed a hunger in each other's hearts. These moments were the most intense of my young life. I was bewitched, and even found myself inspired to write verse.

When we first parted at the shattered pillar, she revealed there must be a wait before our next meeting. She asked me to be patient, and to trust her without question. That wait proved to be a whole month, during which I was sure I had lost her. Then she summoned me again, and all was as before. That became the pattern. Brief ecstasies between long periods of torture.

I tolerated these strange conditions because our love was all I had ever longed for. We would be like Nicolas Flamel and Pernelle, I thought, like Thomas Vaughan and Rebecca, William Blake and Catherine, or, yes, like Willie Yeats and Georgie. I hoped that eventually she would abandon the strange regime and let us be together all the time. I pictured us joyfully performing our passionate magic together every day of our lives.

Then the foundations of my hopes were pulled away, bringing the glittering edifice of my dreams down upon my head. Leanan disappeared from my life as abruptly as she had appeared. The invitations stopped, and my attempts to take the initiative by making my way to the house proved futile. Finding the ruined pillar was easy, but from there the path was beset with ragweed and wildly overgrown, an impenetrable wall. I searched until nightfall, and on, under the silence of the moon. The only life I found was a bat that rose up and circled me with its squeaky cry.

I was tortured with a quite unjustified guilt. What could I have done or said to drive her away? The borders of my life closed in, became a tumult of broken dreams. Quietly, without attracting much notice, I died into the labyrinth of myself. About this time the dreams ceased, too. Life fell back into its previous dull pattern. My new-found flair for verse deserted me.

Then, browsing abstractedly over a volume of Yeats, I found the poem 'On a Picture of a Black Centaur by Edmund Dulac' and read there the words "your hooves have stamped at the black margin of the wood" and "my works are stamped down into the sultry mud". I turned from the page, and by some literary Sortes, found "Magical Unicorns bear ladies on their backs. The ladies close their musing eyes". Considering my own experiences, was it any wonder that the words came like a message from Yeats to me?

Synchronicities continued. I came across a portrait of Georgie Yeats by Dulac that featured a unicorn, and her bookplate, designed by T. Sturge Moore, with the same beast leaping from a shattered tower. The latter was obviously based on the tarot card representing destruction leading to profound change. It could have been an image of my fate.

I resorted again to the black polished scrying stone and the incantation, but the power had been taken from me. Then, at about the time of the month that Leanan and I had experienced our most passionate and productive unions, I adapted a method I found in Paracelsus, by placing the stone beneath my pillow when I slept, and was granted a vision. It was night, under a gibbous moon, and I walked over the hill to the field with the Faery Thorn. The ragged offerings that draped its branches were flapping in a bitter wind, and little creatures, vaguely human, but with something about their limbs and movements of the stick-insect or the spider, were crawling through them. Crouched against the trunk of the tree was Leanan, and I could see that she was heavy with child. That was all I was *permitted* to see. The stone beneath the pillow never worked again.

As I tried to take in the full implications of the vision, some words of Thias Power, which had seemed melodramatic at the time, came back to me. That the Sidhe could "fill the sleeping blood with unquiet dreams, and use ungoverned feelings for their own ends. They will deceive you if they can."

For a while I even entertained the idea that Thias himself had been party to some intricate plot to lure me into the trap. Had he not displayed a deep knowledge of the ways of Faery? Had he not been insistent that I visit the thorn tree where I had found the stone? His words of apparent warning could as easily have been subtly-dangled bait. But it was unlikely. I concluded that he was what he seemed; an old scholar dreaming amongst his books. His utterance about all dreams of the soul ending in a beautiful woman's body now seemed wiser than I had thought. Was it all a betrayal, a cunning manipulation of my affections for her own ends? Or are the fay simply incapable of more than the fleeting passions of the moment?

I still recognise people from those "dreams". One, a heavy-set man with receding red hair, made it plain that he thought me mad. How I knew about his strange dreams he didn't know (perhaps his friends had put me up to it?), but to him they were just that; he wanted nothing to do with me. A grey-haired woman I had once glimpsed struggling to keep up with the mad procession merely shook her head fearfully on sight of me and scurried off, calling over her shoulder, "The fret is on you!"

Although the betrayal is still raw, I have come to think of Leanan as I might one of those mythic daughters of ocean who haunt certain misty western isles, assuming forms of great allure only to ensnare the souls of men. I don't say that I have stopped living. I eat and drink, and even love. But food and drink have lost much of their savour, and love brings with it an incurable sadness.

Yeats would have wondered why I expected anything else. Did I not understand the function of the alchemist's Esh M'saref, the Refiner's Fire? That in Blake's alchemy the furnaces of Los are fierce and unrelenting for the purposes of our transformation? So, too, it seems, are the gates of Faery. I walk outwardly unscathed, but forever scorched by the golden smithies of a realm unguessed. And it is not just Leanan that I miss. Against all reason I find myself yearning always for that other, hidden country with its cruel, unfathomable laws and mad ceremonials; yes, even those endless processions under the darkly radiant banners of the Sidhe.

# ANGELA SLATTER

## THE PROMISE OF SAINTS

A NGELA SLATTER is the author of the Gothic fantasy novel *All the Murmuring Bones* (Titan Books), and the supernatural crime novels *Vigil*, *Corpselight* and *Restoration* (Jo Fletcher Books). She has also written eleven short story collections, including *Sourdough and Other Stories* and *The Bitterwood Bible and Other Recountings*, as well as the novellas *Of Sorrow and Such* and *Ripper*.

The winner of a World Fantasy Award, a British Fantasy Award, a Ditmar, two Australian Shadows Awards and seven Aurealis Awards, her work has been translated into Bulgarian, Chinese, Russian, Italian, Spanish, Japanese, Polish, Hungarian, Czechoslovakian, Turkish, French and Romanian.

Forthcoming is a novel, *The Path of Thorns* (Titan), and a novella, *The Bone Lantern* (Absinthe), both set in the Sourdough world.

"I wrote this story for Mark Beach's very beautiful *A Miscellany of Death and Folly* (Egaeus Press)," recalls the author, "and I didn't know where it came from. I do love the idea of bejewelled saints—I first discovered their existence in *Heavenly Bodies: Cult Treasures & Spectacular Saints from the Catacombs* by Paul Koundounaris—and I've used the image before in 'No Good Deed' (in Mark Morris' *New Fears* anthology).

"It was only after I finished that I realised it was really a

Sourdough-world story and belonged at the beginning of my recent collection *The Tallow-Wife and Other Tales*—because my mind is always half in that place. So, here it is again, slightly re-jigged from its original appearance."

I N THE CHURCH of Mary's Mercy, which sits upon a hill overlooking the sea, there lies a bejewelled saint, attended by nuns of various vintages. Girls and women come to her to pray or beg (some would say there's little difference) for one thing or another. Sometimes she hears, sometimes she does not. Or perhaps life simply takes its path without her attention or otherwise.

Back when she died and was laid here—so very long ago—her attendants, the sisters-that-were, dressed her in the richest of robes, a cloak with an ermine collar as if to keep the chill from her bones. There's no flesh on her, merely a fragile canvas of thin-thin skin, so she's also been wrapped in fine netting to keep all her component parts together and in roughly the right order and shape. Her organs were purportedly removed by her first curators and kept in jars, but no one's found them in many a year, so possibly they were carried off by someone with strange tastes, or simply thrown out by a careless sacristan.

Her teeth are fitted with braces made of rubies set in a gold framework; sapphires that might or might not echo the missing eyes sit in the sockets; and her skull is covered in a bonnet that looks like a constellation of diamond daisies. Epaulets made up of a rainbow of gems sit on the shoulders of her cloak, and beneath is a cloth-of-gold vest over her dress that helps keep her ribcage intact. The bony hands protruding from the bottom of the sleeves are encased in items that are a combination of rings and bracelets. Her legs are covered, and if anyone's ever lifted her red woollen skirt (the hem worked with silver embroidery) to see if there's any adornment there, no one is admitting to it; indeed, no nun has any memory of her being moved for several lifetimes. The skeletal feet have been hung with silver chains dangled with tiny engraved foxes and bells.

She's been here a long time, the Sainted Maiden, lying on a bier in the tiny alcove to the left of the altar.

Tales are told, as they often are when the truth is lost, and they say she moves around at night. They say she dances across the green and purple marble squares of the nave as if at a wedding. Some say her dance is one of exultation, some say of defiance. But the fact is that no one knows anything about her, what her name was, who her people were (for no one in the town claims kinship), or even how she came to be venerated so.

Unprotected by barriers of any kind, the dust settles freely upon her, but no one's game to touch her—everyone's aware that disturbing the holy dead with anything more than entreaties is never a good idea—not even the Sisters who tend to her as the years of their lives march away. Certainly none of the supplicants, and there are many, can bring themselves to offer her the slightest contact. All they bring are demands, generally marital in nature.

The Hallowed Girl, it's said, was once a bride herself—although no one knows if the marriage was completed and consummated, or aborted, so her titles are varied and perhaps contradictory—and that's why these others come to beg what she may or may not have had.

Adalene first brought Elspeth to see the Saint when she was five. The child had shown no interest, no gratitude nor enthusiasm for her mother's hopes, but kept her eyes downcast, stepping deliberately on the cracks in the floor for all she was worth, little bitch. Adalene's grip on her daughter's hand was desperate and hard, even to her, as she pulled Elspeth along. Finally, they halted and Elspeth still didn't look up.

Not until Adalene said, "That'll be you, one day."

The girl raised her eyes then, took in the skeleton caught in its cocoon of tulle and wool and fur and gold. The gems encrusting it sucked in the light of the torches but threw out less than they ate, it seemed. Elspeth looked at the skull with its jaw slightly askew, slightly ajar, no eyes except those gleaming sapphires hard as hearts, and she screamed.

Elspeth thought her mother meant she'd be dead. That someone would stick her with shiny pins and make her into an exhibit, as pretty and useless as a butterfly under glass. She took it for a threat, and it was a long while before she calmed. A long time before her mother could get her to listen that they were there to ask for a blessing: that Elspeth was to beg the Sainted Maiden for a good husband.

Elspeth had no such desire and couldn't imagine ever wanting a husband. At that very moment all she truly wished and wanted was to never lay eyes on the hallowed, hollowed girl ever again.

It was then that one of the nuns—the youngest of them, but already nearing fifty—drawn by Elspeth's screech, came over from whatever task she'd been attending to in the shadows to place a broad palm against the girl's cheek. The woman was terribly tall, her face gentle and her smile absent-minded, but there was something about her touch that leeched away much of Elspeth's fear, or at least enough that she could ask a question.

"What's her name?"

"She has none, only titles."

"Everyone should have a name," said Elspeth.

The nun looked at the girl properly this time, actually focused on her, and the smile was different, not simply something she aimed at everyone. "And yet she has none."

It made Elspeth terribly sad, and she wished aloud for the Bride to be named and loved; she wished with the same strength as her mother had wished for her to be well-married. Such very different things, one propelled by a kind of greed, the other by a sort of kindness. And that latter desire removed whatever vestiges of fear might have remained, so that Elspeth did something no one had done in untold years: she touched the Hallowed Girl.

Small fingers to skeletal digits, the most glancing of contacts—soft flesh against dusty bones, a small shudder of shock—but it was a touch nonetheless. The first in so very, very long. Whether it was that or the sort of magic stirred up by wishes, no one will ever know. Whatever the cause, something was woken.

That night, the Maiden visited Elspeth for the first time.

It would not be the last.

Perhaps it was in her sleeping or perhaps her late waking—it was so difficult to tell, but Elspeth could have sworn she felt the tender touch of bony hands, felt the shifting of her bedclothes and mattress beneath a weightless weight, felt the breath that was not breath flowing across her face as the Maiden whispered to her. The Hallowed Girl, the Sainted Maiden, the Immaculate Bride told Elspeth that she would be her one and only. That Elspeth was her truest love and would tend to the Saint as lovingly as any wife. Elspeth would require no husband for, in return, all of her needs would be met in the Church of Mary's Mercy. And that the Saint would, on their wedding day, offer her the highest of bride prices.

In the moonlight that flooded the room, the Hallowed Girl touched a finger to Elspeth's, the one that leads straight to the heart, and in her dream or waking she saw a silver ring—tiny foxes chasing each other, nose to tail—form on that finger and glint. It soon sank into her flesh, but the following morning she could still feel it there beneath the skin. A promise and a chain.

Adalene took her daughter to the Saint all those years ago, and hasn't she had reason to regret it ever since?

What she'd hoped would result in a profitable match had seemed to simply have developed into a religious mania. From that time forwards, Elspeth had spent part of her days (and some of her nights, if Adalene did but know it) in the Church, tending the shrine of the Hallowed Girl.

Frankly, Adalene had despaired. It's tremendously hard to match-make if one of the parties has a tendency to not appear when they are meant to. Numberless days was Adalene left clutching a damp scone and rapidly cooling cup of tea in the sitting room of some other mother-on-the-make, while Elspeth failed to arrive for a meeting with a potential suitor and his dam. Nothing Adalene said or did made a whit of difference.

But then, ridiculously, one of those potential suitors found her daughter's lack of interest appealing. Fascinating, apparently. He pursued her in spite of his own mother's warnings—oh, Adalene knew there'd been warnings, she'd seen the woman's expression as her son's questioning about Elspeth became positively fervid.

"Can she weave?"

"Yes." *Barely.*

"Can she manage a household?"

"Of course." *An outright lie that would only be discovered too late.*

He'd nodded. "She carries herself well, I have seen her around town and her posture is notable. She will wear finery beautifully, that is an important thing for a rich man's wife."

"Yes." *A truth at last.*

Elspeth's husband-to-be is prosperous, precisely the sort Adalene would have wished for herself if she'd got another chance, but her combination of ill-temper—which renders discontent as her constant companion—and plain face closed that avenue. Had she been sweeter of one or the other, she might well have had suitors lining up at her cottage door. As a widow, she was regarded with pity by the young women of the town; the older ones, knowing better, called her blessed. She views them all with contempt, though she smiles politely at them in the market square and when she takes in their mending, or whenever she'd offered her daughter to wife.

But this oncoming son-in-law pleases her for the moment—he will no doubt disappoint in time, but for now he is sufficiently unknown a quantity to furnish a sort of contentment for Adalene. He'll furnish some financial stability too, and that will smooth over a multitude of sins.

Adalene only knows she'll be as close to happy as she's likely to get when Elspeth is wed, and that day cannot come too soon, before the girl ruins even that.

The Saint had promised so many things.

In the silent space between the shadows of the Church, and in the dim twilight of her visits to Elspeth's bedroom, words had come like covenants on a breath that smelled like nothing from the living. *Freedom. Love. Eternity.*

Some days, when sunlight brings clarity, Elspeth wonders if she is mad. If that moment all those years ago when fear burned through her like wildfire hadn't consumed her sanity. Her mother certainly thinks so, what with her refusals to marry, her defiance. Though Adalene can be unpleasant, Elspeth loves her mother. She believes her mother loves her, despite the terrible things she says. The girl knows her mother wants to provide for both their futures, but Elspeth's was mapped out sixteen years ago, wasn't it? And through Adalene's own actions, did she but know it.

Her mother's despair was what caused Elspeth's silence when the suitor appeared at the door, avid and ardent and determined. That and the promises her Saint had made, that there'd be no wedding, no matter what Adalene coaxed or cajoled or threatened. That and the knowledge that skeletal saints are notoriously bad at providing a dowry or portion for a widowed mother's old age. That and the suspicion that perhaps she was addled, holding onto the promise of a fever-dream long stale. So she'd remained silent when the proposal was made and accepted; she behaved like a girl about to be wed to the man who sought her.

But she clung, too, to a thin thread of hope. To the fact that the Saint on one of those long-ago nights of shadows and breaths and caresses, also promised the one thing that no one else has ever had, or at least not in the longest time, so long ago it wasn't recorded or remembered.

Ultimately Elspeth knew that the vow she'd held most dear was the promise of the Saint's very own name.

Jasque is a wool merchant, or rather the son of a recently deceased one. His mother still holds the reins of enterprise, but Jasque is free to act as though he makes important decisions. He's quite happy to live with a heavy purse and light responsibilities.

He could have chosen a better-bred, but less beautiful bride—indeed his mother, Ernestine, had urged him in the direction of a girl whose left eye turned but a little, and whose family owned many flocks of sheep. But he decided the lovely Elspeth was for him, precisely because it seemed he could not have her.

Ernestine knows how troublesome beautiful girls can be (she was one herself), what with wills of their own and everyone falling over themselves to please in hope of their favours, or even just a glance, kind or indifferent it matters not. But her son's a fool for a pretty face and all she can do is love him anyway and shrug. Oh, and tie up whatever parts of the business she can in legal machinations, and hide profits, so it's hard for her boy to fritter them away on expensive offerings, and harder still for a girl to extract gold from the spinning of wool like some voracious fairytale princess.

But this girl, this Elspeth, doesn't seem to want anything; she makes neither demand nor request; she's nothing like that grasping parent of hers. She's polite when given a gift, but there's seemingly no greed in her; and she's pious, too, spends part of every day at the Church, helping the last ageing nun to tend the shrine. This makes Ernestine, quite naturally, suspicious. She's never known a girl to look at her very fine son with his very fine robes and very fine face (which, admittedly, will go to fat soon enough just like his father, so she'd best get him married off quickly), and the heavy coin purse at his belt and not want *something*. Therefore there must be, she reasons, something that rides beneath the surface, some need or desire that cannot be seen by daylight.

She doesn't say this to her son, for her mother's heart is soft, no matter that her mind is practical and wary. Besides, fewer things drive a man into another woman's arms than a mother's displeasure and, though her son's already made his decision, there's a tiny hope in her breast that something will happen to make the machinery of this match fall apart. Tomorrow her boy will marry and that will be the end of it, and Ernestine will have plenty of time to discover her daughter-in-law's faults and flaws.

Jasque, however, has his own concerns, though he'd never voice them to his mother.

Tomorrow his bride is to walk barefoot along the path from her home to the Church of Mary's Mercy. She'll be attired in a dress heavy with seed pearls and silver thread (paid for from Jasque's pocket). Then they'll stand in front of the altar and say their vows before the priest. Jasque knows that the source of his disquiet will be lying not so many feet away, just out of sight, but there all the same, like some mote in his eye that cannot be removed.

Another thing he's never mentioned to Ernestine: Elspeth's

acceptance of his proposal was made by *her* mother. He'd had to propose in front of Adalene, for the woman protected her daughter's virtue like a dragon on a mound of gold, and Jasque has no good reason to claim she was wrong to do so. But when he'd offered his suit, it was the older woman who'd said *yes*. The girl had looked over his shoulder, as if there was someone standing behind him, someone else to whom she might answer.

She'd smiled, batted her lashes, and seemed to acquiesce.

But she has ever refused to meet him at night, no matter how he's pressed her, and she's also refused to stop her devotions at the Church. She did so gently and politely, as she does everything, but her refusal was no less adamant. The last of the Sisters would soon be gone, she'd said, and someone must be there to take her place.

He had been displeased, but was smart enough not to press. Yet, spoiled only child of too-indulgent parents as he was, Jasque was not one to take "no" for an answer.

And Jasque was certain that Elspeth could not serve what no longer existed.

Elspeth wears her wedding dress to church the next day, although the Hallowed Girl has promised there is to be no wedding, at least not to Jasque. The gown is beautiful, and it seems perfect for the occasion. When will she get a chance to wear it again? Besides, it seems only right to come to the Bride in such finery.

As she walks, barefoot, she notices that there's no one by the side of the road, and a weight lifts from her shoulders. This is good: she takes it to mean the Saint's promise is true—otherwise there would be crowds, waiting and watching, throwing flower petals and wishes for happiness, fertility and long life. Her steps become much lighter, swifter. But when Elspeth turns into the last windy street, the one that runs up to the hill upon which Mary's Mercy sits, it is *there* that she sees a crowd, and the breath in her stops for long seconds.

She continues on, however; she cannot turn tail and run, not now. And as she approaches the congregation, she realises there's no sense of revelry and no one looks happy; this gives her courage. Townsfolk cluster in the churchyard, gossiping in groups.

Elspeth keeps walking. At the great double doors, with their bands of silver engraved with a series of skeletal figures dressed in funereal finery, are Adalene and Ernestine, both wailing in the arms of the remaining nun—the one whose touch first brought Elspeth's heart to the Bride. Ernestine's howls are renewed as she sees the daughter-in-law-to-be, but the energy is mostly spent, the emotion behind them is broken. Adalene echoes her much as a cat does another, trying to outdo a rival. Elspeth wonders how long they have been here.

The elderly nun, expression serene, makes no effort to stop Elspeth as she enters the church. Whatever lies inside is meant for her gaze. Around her finger, she feels the ghostly ring shifting, moving up through her flesh, strangely painless.

Light comes in through the coloured glass of the windows, painting the aisle and pews in a rainbow, yet the Maiden's bier remains in shadow, so it takes some moments for Elspeth to make out the details of the scene.

On the floor are some gems that have fallen off the corpse, and a thick wooden cudgel too, as if dropped by a careless hand. The Hallowed Girl still reclines in her place, skeletal head on the red velvet pillow, jewels catching the light and eating it.

But Elspeth's Bride does not lie alone.

Jasque is in her arms, held tight as a lover, his head tilted to rest on her shoulder as if he sleeps, though his eyes stare. There is blood, quite a lot of it, dripping down and pooling and seeping through the cracks between the purple and green tiles; some of the spatters look like flowers blooming. As Elspeth draws nearer, she can see that the Bride's ribs have broken through her fine netting and have entwined with Jasque's, just as lovers' fingers might.

Elspeth's first duty as a wife will be to unlock them.

The promise of saints is expensively bought.

But soon she will know her beloved's true name.

# RICHARD GAVIN

## CRAWLSPACE ORACLE

RICHARD GAVIN lives in Ontario, Canada. He describes his work as "exploring the realm where horror and the numinous converge". He has authored six volumes of short fiction (the most recent being *Grotesquerie*), as well as several works of esotericism and meditations on the horror genre. 'Crawlspace Oracle' marks his fifth appearance in *Best New Horror*.

"Waxwork figures, mannequins and other forms of simulacra have always fascinated me," he explains, "because of their ability to evoke the Freudian uncanny. Equally interesting to me is the concept of apophenia—humanity's innate tendency to find supposedly meaningful patterns in sheer randomness.

"While pattern-making may be an evolutionary tool to help us feel more in control of our lives, I believe that human beings are capable of endless self-deception. Therefore, those who believe themselves to be most attuned to reality may in fact be mired in subconscious delusion.

"'Crawlspace Oracle' afforded me the opportunity to explore both these concepts through a horror narrative."

⦰

A FEW MOMENTS under the strange red lamps of the restaurant was all that was required to cause Rhiannon to wonder if she was dreaming. The long bus ride through the rainy afternoon certainly hadn't helped matters, nor did the reason behind her trip: a reunion with a woman she'd considered, at best, an acquaintance in the office where she'd worked before Iain and marriage and the birth of the twins. It had been a long time since she'd ventured out on her own. She now regretted that her first outing was to this anaemic town that was notorious for being a haven for dismal weather and washed-up entertainers.

For reasons Rhiannon could never unearth, these entertainers seemed to migrate to this colourless burg to collect their meagre pensions while waiting to die.

Today, Rhiannon had seen plenty of bleak weather, but only one example of the latter feature; when she'd de-boarded at the bus depot she'd witnessed a scarecrow-like man on crutches attempting to juggle a trio of shining spheres. He'd watched Rhiannon hopefully as fluid (rain, perspiration, or tears, she could not tell) streamed down his cheeks. He'd made a pitiful sound as she'd walked by, clinging firmly to her purse. His whimper had been like a baleful note blown on an old wooden flute.

Rhiannon had no intention of ever coming to this town, or of seeking out Hyacinth again. The very thought of Hyacinth provided Rhiannon with pangs of guilt, pangs that worsened when her memory trawled up specific details, such as the lavish gift Hyacinth had given her for the baby shower. But seven years had passed since that time, and there'd not been so much as a single call or Christmas card between them.

But once Rhiannon had arrived at the curious eatery and was able to see Hyacinth in the flesh, she wondered if they'd both been living on different calendars. If she were to use Hyacinth's face as a gauge, it looked as though decades had passed since their last encounter, for Hyacinth appeared old and drawn and brittle.

Rhiannon wondered if this was partly due to the strange macrobiotic diet that Hyacinth had spent the first part of their evening explaining in detail. She'd ordered queer, tiny delicacies from the menu and had requested a small pot of boiling water and an empty mug, in which she steeped some pungent herbs that she'd bundled in a small piece of cheesecloth.

"I can't thank you enough for inviting me to dinner!" Hyacinth said. "But I can't allow you to pay the tab."

"Please," answered Rhiannon with a casual wave of her hand, "it's my pleasure. I only wish we'd done this sooner."

"Time is a startled bird flitting away from us, as my father used to say. Well, since you insist on buying dinner, if there is ever anything I can do to repay you, you may consider it done."

Rhiannon grew cagey once she recognised this opportunity to state her true motivation for this reunion. The opportunity was too perfect, both in timing and tone. It thrilled and unnerved her at once.

"Funny you should say that…" she began, anxiously. The words were swirling about her head, just out of reach.

Hyacinth flared her sallow eyes with interest. "Oh?" she said.

"Yes. I was hoping to pick your brain about money." Rhiannon flinched at her poor choice of words. Hyacinth's expression darkened.

"No, no, not like that! I'm not asking for a loan or anything of that sort!" sputtered Rhiannon. "I'm just looking for some advice."

"Oh."

The cord of tension that Rhiannon had felt tightening between the two of them began to slacken, to her immense relief.

"You see, Iain's had quite a good year at the agency: four quarterly bonuses on top of his annual salary increase. We're looking to invest this extra money, put it towards something sound. It's not a huge amount, but Iain's pretty convinced we can make a respectable profit if we play our cards right."

Hyacinth shaped her sapped expression into something vaguely happy. "First off, I am truly thrilled for you; all snug with a husband and those little darlings you made. I'm tickled to hear that you have money besides. But when it comes to investing, I'm afraid I wouldn't know one market from another."

"But those stories in the *Gazette*..."

"Those..." Hyacinth said dismissively, "...those articles were inflated."

"They referred to you as Queen Midas," Rhiannon said. She felt a peculiar pride when her comment caused her guest to visibly blush. "But you never gave those reporters the secret of your success, did you?"

"I'm only as good as my guide," Hyacinth confessed.

"Your guide? So, you do have some sort of an advisor?"

"Some sort, yes."

A fine balance was required for Rhiannon to probe her guest further without seeming rude.

"Do you have a card for this person?" she asked. "Some way I can reach them?"

Hyacinth stared past her dinner companion, towards the restaurant's front window and through it. Rhiannon wondered what, if anything, the gaunt woman might have been looking for on those miserable streets.

Whatever she was scanning the soggy night for, Hyacinth suddenly appeared to have found. Her eyes brightened with fresh inspiration.

"I like you, Rhiannon. I always have. More than that, I trust you. And so, yes, I will show you. I will let you in."

With that, Hyacinth rose and tugged her long coat from the pole by their booth.

"You mean now?" Rhiannon asked, suddenly flustered by her own lack of preparation. The world suddenly seemed to be spinning too quickly.

"Of course!" Hyacinth gushed. "Come along. My car is just around the corner."

"I...it's just that...I mean, surely their business will be closed by now."

Hyacinth was already halfway to the door.

The car Rhiannon was led to was far humbler than what she'd envisioned a woman of Hyacinth's standing would drive. She squeezed into the littered cab and endured the deafening rumble of an unmuffled engine. Her head was aching by the time Hyacinth chauffeured them off the main roads and down a maze of bleak-looking side-streets.

When she noted the house before which Hyacinth stopped her car, Rhiannon was bewildered. Could the woman be playing some type of joke? She'd never known Hyacinth to have a sense of humour.

This confusion cooled into apprehension once Rhiannon closed the car door and watched her guide scaling the cement steps that connected the ugly lawn to a residence that was not much larger than a storage locker, and every bit as tasteless. It was a frame house, stunted and misshapen. It was as if an unskilled carver had whittled this stingy dwelling from a greater house, then tucked their shameful creation on a poorly lit back-street in hopes of concealing it. The roof bowed where it should not, and the walls stood in a manner they could not, and the patina was the grey of curdled mushroom soup.

Hyacinth unlocked the narrow front door and held it open for her guest.

With that, as if on cue, Rhiannon's surroundings conspired against her. A pair of men rounded the corner and began shambling in her direction (their voices deep, their laughter at some imperceptible joke scary), the lone street-lamp on the block began to flicker, the rain resumed falling.

She crossed the lawn and scaled the steep concrete steps as quickly as she could.

The realisation that this entire adventure had been a grave mistake, which had been nagging faintly at the corners of Rhiannon's attention from the moment she boarded the bus to come here, fully erupted the instant she crossed the threshold of Hyacinth's house. What she was feeling was not the threat of immediate danger, but something vague, something dizzying in its menace. The nearest Rhiannon had ever felt to this sensation was déjà vu. She wondered if she had perhaps dreamed this reunion with Hyacinth years ago and was just now discovering that her dream had been an omen, a warning to avoid this detour on her life path. But it was too late now to heed.

"Just throw your coat anywhere," Hyacinth said as she shut and bolted the door. "Would you like something? Water or tea?"

"No, thank you." She kept her coat on.

Hyacinth moved down the little hallway and snapped on the kitchen light, revealing a countertop piled with unwashed dishes and rows of hanging cupboards with their doors open, flaunting their vacancy. Queen Midas was evidently nearer to Old Mother Hubbard.

Glancing discreetly through the archway to her right, Rhiannon saw a living room that was empty except for a folding lawn chair whose seat held a stack of rumpled magazines. The kitchen was as lacking in furniture and appliances as it was in foodstuffs. Rhiannon noted a small hotplate and a barstool stationed before the warped countertop. And that was all.

"I apologise for the state of the house. Don't think I'm not aware of the fact that it has seen better days."

"Oh... I..." stammered Rhiannon. "Are you in the process of flipping it?" she asked, her voice soaked in hope.

"No," Hyacinth replied. "I've been living here for some time now."

"What about your money?" Rhiannon immediately regretted her choice of words and scrambled to re-frame her panicked interrogation. "What I mean is, surely you can afford to live a bit more comfortably than this?"

"I have before. I hope to again. But the money's gone."

Rhiannon wished that the woman's tone wasn't so cheerful.

"I'm confused. I thought you had this excellent advisor, that the advice he'd been giving you was sound."

"Oh, it is. It's very sound indeed. The fault lies with me, not my advisor."

"How so? Did you not take their advice?"

"For a long time, I did. As my father did before me, and his father before him. But it's all about correctly interpreting the messages. That's the key. I've not been interpreting the messages properly, obviously. Or maybe it's that the nature of the messages has changed."

"I don't follow."

Hyacinth stood leaning against the cluttered counter, studying her guest, scrutinising her.

Rhiannon looked away and loudly cleared her throat. "Um... did you happen to have that advisor's phone number?"

Hyacinth shook her head. "No need."

She crossed the tiny kitchen and pulled down the gingham towels that hung from a mounted rack. The removal of the towels revealed a door of whitewashed wood.

Hyacinth pulled this back from its jamb, unto a black void, or so it seemed to Rhiannon, whose legs were losing their strength. Fear had rendered her helpless. She stood mutely, watching as her host clawed at the debris on top of the stained refrigerator until she found a large black flashlight.

Though she appeared to merely be testing the batteries, Hyacinth had the light upturned so that its beam shone against her chin, a sight that stirred in Rhiannon frightening memories of ghost stories around bonfires during those awful weeks when she'd been left to fend for herself at summer camp. She recalled how immersive those tales had been for her, the horrible impact they'd had, tainting the strange world around her as something seething with hidden peril.

Standing here now, in this dingy kitchen, Rhiannon came to appreciate how true those impressions had been.

Without a word, Hyacinth turned the flashlight to the open door and began her noisy descent of the basement steps.

Recognising this opportunity, Rhiannon turned to charge for the front door, but a chanced view through the living-room window crushed her plan of escape.

The straggling figures she'd seen moving down the unfamiliar street when she'd arrived were now loitering by Hyacinth's rusted car. Or were these the same figures? No, for where there had been but a pair, there was now a group. Forlorn-looking women now stood alongside the imposing men. They looked to be huddling under the sputtering street-lamp like moths.

Rhiannon reached into her purse for her phone to call a cab, or perhaps call Iain. She stole another look. The figures were ordering themselves. They were lining up single-file along the sidewalk.

"Everything is ready," announced Hyacinth.

The sound of her voice made Rhiannon squeal. She spun and looked into a flash-lit grin.

"You look frightened."

"I am!"

"But there's no reason to be. I'm coming with you, it's fine."

Hyacinth began down the basement stairs first, which made Rhiannon feel just secure enough to move to the doorway and look down at those ruddy steps; anything to keep her focus off the strange congregation outside.

The basement was no longer a wall of blackness. In addition to the gleaming finger from Hyacinth's torch, it now hosted an intriguing sheet of prismatic light; something festive, carnivalesque.

It was to this cloistered aurora that Rhiannon moved, one hesitant stair at a time, until eventually she found herself standing amidst the cluttered cellar.

The room was reminiscent of an army bunker, with its stifling confines and its drab cinderblock walls. It also looked as though it hadn't been properly cleaned since the analogue age.

Hyacinth was standing in wait between two towers of stacked plastic bins, an unnerving smile staining her face. She turned and wriggled herself down the tiny row, then crouched down, her shadow now stretching amongst those flickering trails of multicoloured light.

Rhiannon manoeuvred through the maze of detritus to find her hostess squatting before a tiny hatch door that was set into the wall, just above floor-level.

"Come see," cooed Hyacinth. Politeness (and, if she was being honest, the curiosity of the unknown) moved Rhiannon towards the open doorway, but as soon as she was able to see the room and what it contained, this curiosity instantly twisted into fear.

The illumination guttered from a lanky strand of Christmas lights, which had been wound about the beams that served as the thick bones of the house itself. Insulation bulged between the wooden beams; pink as lung tissue, fluffy as candyfloss. The floor of the crawlspace was but a single board that stretched from the doorway to the far end of the hatch like a ship's fatal plank.

And it was there, upon that long runner of un-sanded pine, that Rhiannon saw the body. It was as large as life and its presence amongst the festive bulbs was confusing, uncanny, terrible, and yet, irrefutably, shockingly, just . . . there.

The figure was slumped at the back of the room. Its head was swollen, and its eyes were shimmering, bulbous things. The mouth was gaping but expressionless. It was dressed in a dingy leotard that lent its body the lumpy, colourless appearance of bagged flour.

Hyacinth pulled herself through the crawlspace opening and proceeded to slither across the long plank, towards the crumpled form.

"My grandfather built him," she explained. "He helped my family flourish during the Great Depression. We've looked to him ever since." Hyacinth fussed with the figure while she talked, adjusting its posture like a fretting mother would her child, pushing the cobwebs from its head using the heel of her longish hand. "I'd be lying if I told you that we've always benefited from his words, but really, it's a matter of interpretation. That's the art of it. Are you familiar with *Sortes Sanctorum*? It's divining one's fortune through a seemingly random flip of the Bible page. Great-grandfather was a believer, and he taught my grandfather. But grandfather took it beyond the gospels. He felt that the great pattern was everywhere, in all things at all times. So he devised this."

Rhiannon watched as Hyacinth reached around to the back of the figure's plaster head. Its mouth began to glow with faint amber light, which revealed the too-wide grin of the dummy to be a fabric-covered speaker, the kind that might bring one feelings of nostalgia if one had memories of wartime gatherings around a cathedral radio to listen to melodramatic plays. Rhiannon had no such memories and therefore the mouth was horrible.

Static gushed from the dummy's speaker/mouth. Underneath this incessant whirr, Rhiannon could hear faint strains of music and distant voices all struggling to be heard, to emerge from the static like fish breaking the surface of deep water.

The great lidless eyes began to spin. They were twin plastic discs, each bearing a spiral pattern. They glowed as they spun around and around and again. Was Hyacinth attempting to hypnotise her?

No, this effigy was a radio receiver, its dial-eyes prowled the bandwidths in search of transmissions.

Hyacinth nestled close to the thing and whispered something into where its ear should be.

Rhiannon had already begun backing away from the colourful crawlspace, but when she heard the doll speak as if in response to Hyacinth's question, Rhiannon turned and ran.

On hands and knees she scaled the wooden steps, dragging herself towards the landing.

Her hands had managed to slap down on the linoleum of the kitchen floor when Rhiannon felt something grip her ankles. She screamed and tried to kick, but Hyacinth was unnaturally strong for so slight a person. She scrabbled upon Rhiannon's prostrate form, looped her wiry arms around Rhiannon's waist and heaved her clean off the stairs.

"Shhh," she cooed, "shhh...shhh. It's fate, darling. It's not about you or me."

Swiftly and inexorably, Rhiannon was being pulled back towards the hatch in the wall.

"All we ask is that you listen, just listen."

Rhiannon was thrust through the square aperture. The wooden lane was filthy and rough. The blinking lights made her nauseous. And the sight of the horrible mannequin reduced her backbone to putty.

Closer to it now, closer than she would have ever wanted to be to such a thing, Rhiannon could see that the effigy's body was nothing more than a hollow frame of chicken wire wrapped in a cheap white leotard. The pattern of the wire mesh was pushed firmly into the fabric, creating the illusion of reticulated flesh. And yet the gardener's gloves that capped the hands betrayed the thing's true nature: it was nothing but a pathetic scarecrow, without so much as a post to perch upon.

But scarecrows with their heads of straw and sackcloth cannot speak as this thing spoke. Its voice was as ugly as its shell. The spiral eyes spun around and again, pulling in random fragments from countless broadcasts. Hyacinth's advisor was a child of Babel.

Time seemed to halt for Rhiannon as she faced the thing and planned her escape. The angled beams forced her to crawl like a slug. She tried to push herself back towards the hatch.

She felt the draft and heard the slam of the hatch door as Hyacinth sealed her in. There was the recognisable *clunk* of a lock being fastened, followed by the roar of heavy things being dragged, both of which rendered the crawlspace door immovable.

She kicked at it, hammered at it until the heels of her hands began to swell. All the while the cheery lights continued to flash, and the endless babble of Hyacinth's advisor mounted.

Rhiannon's joyous moment of inspiration that came when she thought of using her cell phone to call 911 turned black and came crashing down around her when she realised that her purse had slipped off her shoulder during her struggle on the stairs.

Her screams shredded her throat, but roused not so much as a sound from beyond the door.

Some time later, the Christmas lights went out and the only illumination that remained was the mannequin's endlessly spinning eyes and the amber glow of its fabric mouth.

Three days and three nights passed before Hyacinth finally deemed to unlatch the crawlspace door. But by then Rhiannon had shed all conceptions of time and lost every ounce of will, strength, resistance. Like Lazarus, she slinked, broken but alive, out of the open hatch door, a living creature from a stifling crypt. Some Logos, some obscure alchemy of sound and isolation, had altered her world. It was powerful enough to transform Rhiannon's tomb to womb, potent enough to spore her back amongst the living, her head brimming with messages. She felt as though her skull was on the verge of cracking, erupting like a volcano, so gigantic was this fresh knowledge.

Hyacinth had been keeping vigil. Her tiny form was propped upon a scuffed wooden stool and she held a burning white taper in her hands. The melted wax ran down in rivulets, splattering upon the already waxy skin of Hyacinth's unsteady hands. Rhiannon looked at her face, so ghastly in the candlelight.

Hyacinth looked past Rhiannon. The sight of the effigy lying broken and silent inside the crawlspace did not faze her. She returned her gaze to Rhiannon.

"*Yes?*" she whispered. "*Yes, please... speak.*"

Speaking just might relieve some of the unbearable pressure in her head. Rhiannon opened her mouth, but for what purpose? Was she going to scream? To beg for pity?

She heard a voice resounding in her skull, could feel words shaking over her palate, but the statements she was making bore no resemblance to the ones she was trying to make. Many of the words were from languages of which Rhiannon had no knowledge. Some of the sounds were not even words but were, instead, almost musical: the blurt of a trumpet, the pluck of a cello string.

Hyacinth's face became a mask of delight. She puffed out the candle and sat it smoking upon a stack of old books. She advanced to Rhiannon, wrapped a switch-thin arm around her back and guided her towards the basement steps.

The climb was almost impossible for Rhiannon, whose ankles buckled with each footfall. By the time they reached the kitchen she had lost all feeling in her legs.

She was frightened to discover that the main floor of the house was not appreciably brighter than the crawlspace, for the windows had been sheathed in tarpaper and every lamp she passed had its light bulb purposely smashed.

With care, Hyacinth guided her form, which grew weaker with each tick of the clock, into the living room and sat her in the folding chair Rhiannon had spotted on the way in.

"This is only temporary," Hyacinth purred, her tone maternal and assuring. "We'll get you a chair befitting a woman of your stature as soon as we're able to understand your message. Can you hear what I've been saying to you? No, no, don't try to speak. Just blink your eyes once for yes and twice for no. That's it. Good. And can you understand what I've been saying to you? Very good. Do you know what it is that has happened to you? No. Well, that's to be expected, my dear. Don't let it alarm you. It will take time."

Hyacinth moved around to the front of the chair, hunched slightly to level her eyes with Rhiannon's.

"There are some people outside, some really lovely people. They've been waiting a long time to see you. May I send them in?"

Rhiannon's arms felt like concrete. Unable to lift them, she closed her eyes to press away the tears that were welling up and blurring her vision. Hyacinth took this to be an affirmative answer and squealed with delight before rushing to the front door.

The first pair to make the hesitant entry into the living room were the men Rhiannon had seen laughing on the street the night of her arrival, the men who'd loitered in the pooled light of the street-lamp, the men who'd scared her. They held hands as they approached her. They asked about the nature of their father's illness.

Rhiannon's cry for help translated into a staccato message, something in Spanish or perhaps Portuguese.

The men sighed and shed tears and blessed her for this message. Before they exited, they handed a small and crumpled envelope to Hyacinth, who was already greeting the next visitant.

Iain was the sixth or seventh to approach. The sight of him brought Rhiannon a relief that bordered on bliss. She tried in vain to rise. Crying out his name yielded only static. She felt trapped in a nightmare, the kind where she would try to scream but found she had no voice, and all the while the danger—calmly and with notable relish—would close in upon her, mangling her body with a weapon or forcing something thick and fibrous deep inside her mouth, her cleft.

But dear Iain did no such thing. His assault was something far more insidious.

He wrapped his arms around her momentarily, kissed her oily brow.

In her ear he whispered, "Will we be successful?"

Rhiannon's reply was instant, confusing, and delivered wholly without her consent.

Never had her mate appeared so pleased.

This would be the only memory of his face that Rhiannon would have to cling to over the next three years, the first of which was spent solely in that horrid folding chair, meeting with an endless procession of guests.

Hyacinth kept the tarpaper on her windows and succoured her new doll with her choicest teas and macrobiotic delicacies. She cleaned her bucket twice daily without complaint and washed her with a loofah sponge soaked in tepid rosewater.

Iain made good on his promise to Hyacinth. He procured for them a handsome and firm stone cottage in the city's historic district. Gardeners and contractors were hired to see that the house and its humble grounds were kept in good repair. The windows were two-way smoked glass, which assured privacy while not depriving the occupants a view of the elegant street.

Rhiannon was given a chair befitting her at last; a throne-like apparatus of sand-coloured plush and a white lacquered Hepplewhite frame. She was stationed in the bedroom at the top of the stairs (the master bedroom went to Hyacinth). A second chair, comfortable-looking but not as regal, was placed before Rhiannon so that her visitants would feel more at ease during consultations.

A year or so later, Iain finally made his return. Though he still managed the books for this little soothsaying enterprise, this was the first time he'd made a pilgrimage to its source.

Rhiannon's recollection of him was faint, dulled by exhaustion and trauma and time. The young woman who clung to him was wholly unfamiliar to her. The twins who cowered behind Iain had grown immensely during her absence.

"Hello, Rhiannon," Iain said weakly. Then he turned to the young girl at his side. "Sit," he bade her. "Ask." He then instructed the twins to go outside and play.

The young woman was reluctant to obey, and once she found herself facing the glassy-eyed hag with her tea-stained teeth, her marionette-like body, her frumpy floral gown, her black-soled feet with their thick yellow toenails, her voice refused to come. Rhiannon knew the feeling well. Seeing the girl in this familiar helpless state, that of nightmare, that of her very existence since the night in the crawlspace, made Rhiannon pity the girl. She did her best to show empathy through her unfailingly vacant gaze.

"Can you tell us," the girl began, pausing to clear her throat, "will our baby be a healthy one?"

The power inside Rhiannon, over which she had no agency, shared its prophecy.

Iain smiled. His young lover began to cry. He helped her to her feet, and they escaped the room together, like some awkward three-legged hybrid joined at the hip.

Twenty-three weeks after their consultation in the stone cottage, the last of which were filled with punishing nausea, the word was made flesh.

Wriggling, its tiny limbs twitching as though being prodded with an electrical charge, the child's first mewling cry was distorted from the mucus that sealed its mouth like fine stretched fabric. Iain swaddled its body, still greasy with the fluids of the womb, and carefully lifted it from the bed. The cord was still connecting the baby to its host. Iain could feel the lump growing in his throat, could feel himself tearing up, yet he still managed a smile. For and from this child, great things had been predicted.

# MICHAEL CHISLETT

## DOWNRIVER

**M**ICHAEL CHISLETT has had his stories published for more than thirty years in various magazines and books. Two collections have been published by Sarob Press, the award-winning *In the City of Ghosts* and *Where Shadows Gather*, and his short stories have been published in *Ghosts & Scholars*, *Supernatural Tales* and by Oxford University Press. His work has also appeared in translation in Mexico and Japan.

He is currently working on a novel as well as short stories, all of which are inspired by various parts of London.

"My partner, Maria, and I took the Woolwich Ferry over to the north bank of the Thames and walked along the river. I saw that there was a boat moored in the stream, which seemed to be lit from within. It was sunset, and Maria pointed out that the lights were a reflection of the setting sun on the glass windows, which were on all sides of the vessel.

"For a moment I thought that someone stood on the boat watching us, but this was only the changing reflection of the sun and the ripples of Thames water there. Then, as the sun finally set, all went dark on the boat. From this, the idea for the story came.

"Most of my tales are inspired by the London landscape. The 'haunted suburbs', one might call them. Now changing, though the ghosts still remain."

✑

AS THE SHADOWS of the November afternoon lengthened, Scovell and Lily took the ferry across the river. It was later than they had intended to make this expedition and evening was falling early. To the west, London was aflame in the golden autumn light. The Thames water too as they approached the northern bank, was lit by a glow as of some glittery, rippling things that glided beneath and seemingly, guided the boat across the stream.

"Glad to see that there is a part of the old working Thames still in existence Lily," said Scovell to his girl, as they stood together on the ferry's prow.

"Like we are in the movie," she said, adjusting her flowing scarf against the wind on the river, "the *Titanic*."

"Can't see any icebergs," replied Scovell as one of the crew joined them and prepared to open the gate as the ferry pulled into the dock.

A stream of cars poured along the ramp, then the foot-passenger gate was opened and they walked down to the landing. There were few others using the ferry today, it was getting late and was cold. Scovell had told her that if they missed the last boat, then they could walk through the foot-tunnel beneath the river, it being open twenty-four hours a day. They began to stroll along the embankment towards the east, as lights from the Woolwich shore reflected in the water, shimmery and stretching finger-like towards them.

They had already walked part of this Thames path a few months before. Scovell had wanted to venture downriver to the wind farms further along the north bank but, to his annoyance, they had been stopped at the wooden footbridge that crossed the old canal mouth by a police cordon. There had been an incident. The law would not give details, but they were searching further down in the water. For bodies no doubt. So that they had to go back. Scovell knew the area, though not well, and it had been a while ago that he had been here, and where once factories and warehouses had stood were now luxury flats, gated communities, so a detour had to be made from the path before they could return to the river way again. It was then, when they re-joined this, that he saw the boat, moored in midstream and looking sad and abandoned.

The glass-sided vessel looked to have once been a pleasure craft, but there were definite signs of neglect and the ship's bow bore no name. They stood for a while, debating what it might have been and why left in the middle of the river. Then Scovell noticed a movement on the stern, for someone was now there and looking across the water at them. A woman, who raised an arm to wave and beckon, as if urging him to somehow come across the darkly glistening water to her. Scovell returned her wave and was about to call a greeting, but Lily had already turned and walked a little way ahead of him, so he hurried after her.

The boat was still there, but today, instead of being dark, lights shone flaming inside the vessel and there was movement on board. "It is just the sunset, on the glass," said Lily. "A reflection."

"No. I think..." he did not know what, for Scovell was sure that there was a crowd who frolicked in the gaudily-lit interior. Indeed, that someone had come out from there and stood on the boat's stern and looked over to where they stood, watching them, him, in particular. A woman, she whom he had seen there before? Who waved again to him, and he raised a hand to wave back to her.

"Who are you waving to?" Lily asked. Then, when he did not reply but stared in fascination at the bright vessel, said, "You seem to have gone off with the fairies Scove." She looked curiously from him to the boat, then shivered and said, "It is very cold. How much further did you want to go on?"

He was about to reply when the light on the boat began to dim and Scovell realised that she was right; for as the sun fell to the west, very quickly it seemed, the final lurid rays flashed once on the glass and then, abruptly, the ship was dark, its windows grey, like it had been switched off to lay derelict and abandoned on the water. What he had thought to see was just a trick of the evening light.

But on the boat's stern he could still see the woman standing there, as the ship filled with shadow and she became a deeper one amongst them. He then heard a voice, calling. But the words he could not quite make out at first, for there were always strange sounds to be heard on the river, the cries of gulls flocking on the shore revealed by the receding tide.

"Scovell."

It must have been Lily who had spoken his name, her voice echoing over the water and returning to him. She was looking away to where a group of boys and girls were coming, noisily, along the plank-bridge over the canal-head. There was the explosion of a late firework, and the girls began to shriek, so that it was impossible to hear properly.

"We should go," she said nervously, and clung on to Scovell, who could feel her shivering through his long trench coat.

"They won't hurt. It's just kids. I want to continue."

"It's dark in there," said Lily, as she reluctantly let go of Scovell and followed him across the bridge.

She was right, for there was a tunnel of bushes by the river, unlit and already night-black, so that a way through could hardly be made. Scovell, though, was keen to continue, he was not afraid of the dark. But Lily was obviously, despite her overcoat, scarf and red beret, suffering from the chill and nerves, standing there suspiciously peering into the murky lane by the river. She embraced him again, to stop his venturing down into that unknown place.

"I think that we ought to go back, it's getting late. I don't like the look of it down there, and I'm feeling so cold."

"This is the second time that we have come here, and we don't seem to have got any further," Scovell said, studying the path, which did seem to become darker by the second, and he did not know how far it would stretch. Downriver on the north bank was an uncharted region to him, which was why he was keen to explore.

"We can come here earlier, another time." Unusually Lily seemed to be pleading, not like her. She shivered. "It has got dark so quickly."

It had, Scovell noted. There were few lights, and with the overgrowth before them, the empty canal and the darkening river, only the lights from the high buildings on the southern bank told them that they were in London. It was an odd feeling, as though they had walked out of their known world and into another, an older one. Perhaps the primal Thames marshland had taken this part of the city back to a time before man had much walked here?

"Okay then," he agreed. "We don't know how far that path goes, before it comes to somewhere. We will come back another day."

"It might not go anywhere," she said and turned back over the footbridge, taking Scovell by the hand and leading him hurriedly away from there to where buildings, lights and civilisation waited.

There were bushes by the footbridge, overgrown so they had to duck. Scovell tried to push one of these obstructions out of their way, to be rewarded with a thorn stuck into his finger.

The sharp bite made him curse, and he saw in the dim light that it had drawn blood. Bright red beads dripped from his finger and into the water below the footbridge as he said, "Better call the paramedics."

"You will survive, toughie. Shall I suck the poison out?"

She took his hand and placed his fingers to her lips, licking the blood off, then spat that too into the water. "The blood is the life," she said and laughed. Lily had a keen interest in vampires.

As they stood on the footbridge, Scovell looked over at the boat, where it moored as a shadow upon the river. It seemed to have moved closer to the bank. Something made him say, "Vampires are not supposed to be able to cross running water."

Letting go of his hand, Lily produced a paper tissue that she offered to Scovell who, looking at his finger, saw another scarlet berry of blood welling up. His hand felt tingly as he bound the tiny wound as best he could. It was nothing really, just a minor irritation, and something made him look again to the boat. He was certain that someone was there, watching them, and again there was that voice, calling what sounded like his name across the Thames water. Perhaps it had not been Lily at all before?

They began to walk back towards the ferry. The evening was fully fallen now, and lights had come on along on the path. To their right was a park, from where Scovell could see movement in the shadows. Those kids might be about in there, for he could hear voices again, shouts and cries. Someone stood leaning against the railing on the pathway, gazing down at the beach below, for the tide was out. It was a woman, clad in a long dark hooded coat, who turned her head to watch them as they passed. Scovell could not make out any features beneath the hood's shadow. He looked back once at the boat, before the pathway veered to the right and they had to make a detour around a gated block that stood adjacent to the river, but it had vanished in a haze of mist, as though joining the Thames. Then he heard again a voice over the water, and it was laughing, and he realised that the woman they had just passed was now walking slowly behind them.

"But they can," Lily suddenly said, as they waited on the slip road for the ferry. She had hardly spoken as they had walked the embankment, except to complain of the cold.

"What can?" Scovell asked, looking at the lighted glass cupola of the subway and thinking that it might be quicker to walk beneath the river to the southern bank. He noticed that the hooded woman now stood by the subway's entrance, watching those who waited for the ferry. There was a line of cars and a few cold-looking pedestrians. It had turned very chilly and, despite his thick grey coat, now Scovell shivered.

"Vampires. You said that they can't cross running water. They can, Scove. How did Dracula get here from Transylvania, but by boat, over the water?"

"That was in a story, fiction," Scovell spoke as the ferry came into dock and they waited for the ramp to come down and the cars and passengers to discharge. "It's in folklore that they cannot cross running water. I think that's so, anyway. But then, vampires are not real."

"There's vampires and there's vampires," Lily replied enigmatically as they walked up the ramp and onto the ferry. She hurried up towards the prow of the boat, keen to do her Kate Winslet act. He looked back at the north bank and the subway, where he saw the woman still standing there, illuminated by the light from within the cupola for a moment. Then this light was suddenly extinguished, and both she and the tunnel's entrance disappeared in darkness.

There were a few other passengers. A woman with a number of fractious children; a brace of girls, no doubt out for an evening and certainly not dressed for the autumn chill. Lily was calling to him, so he hurried up the stairs to join her at the ferry's prow.

Lily stood there with her arms outstretched as the ferry crossed. Scovell smiled, the woman was a frustrated actress. He then looked downriver to see the misty shadow of the abandoned boat, still upon the grey Thames water, as night enclosed them.

"How's your finger feel?" she asked, as dropping her pose she turned to him as they reached the Woolwich bank.

"Tingly," he said, shaking his hand. The feeling was all up his arm. An irritation rather than a pain. The paper tissue was stained with blood, so Lily handed him another one and, as they walked off the ramp and onto the access road, he tried to put the soiled paper neatly into a rubbish bin. But the wind, which had blown all that day, suddenly rose in a gust to blow it away, as it went skittering along the pavement to stop at the feet of the woman who had just emerged from the shaft of the foot-tunnel.

Lily had begun to wrap the tissue around his damaged finger, as crooning soothingly she went into nursery-mode to tend him. But he saw the woman stoop quickly, as though to pick up something from the ground. Then, equally swiftly, she seemed to drift past them, in a peculiarly fluid way. It was hard to tell, for Scovell's eyes now had begun to water badly from the cold wind, which made all about him a haze.

"There might be a poisonous thorn stuck in it," said Lily, dramatically.

Scovell frowned and shook his head, as though to clear it. For he was certain that somehow the woman's feet were not touching the ground as she passed them, but instead glided along. Then he realised that it was only the long dark coat that she wore, which reached down to her ankles, nothing else.

"I'll survive," said Scovell as his eyes followed the woman, who now stood as if waiting for the lights to change at the crossing. Though when they changed to green she made no movement. He began to have the suspicion that she, for some reason, waited for them.

But that was a stupid thought to have. Why on earth should she?

"You are a tough cookie, Scovell," Lily was saying. "Do you think that the shops will still be open? We need to get some stuff for home."

It was Sunday, early closing, and they had left it late. Lily urged him to get a move on, she could travel fast when it came to shopping. Scovell thought that if it were the same woman that he had seen, on the river side and now standing a little way away and definitely watching them, then she had travelled very fast too, beneath rather than over the water. Strange that he could not get a good look at her. Perhaps it was the cold making his eyes watery that her figure, when looked at directly, seemed to be a blur. Hazy, as though a small cloud shrouded her. But when he looked at her from the corner of his eyes, she appeared sharper, more defined. Her face was still concealed beneath the hood, from out of which a length of long dark hair ran in a braided, snakelike coil down to her breast. He noticed that in the distance, across the water, the light from the glass cupola of the foot-tunnel had now come back on.

It was now almost six and, being Sunday, the shops had closed early. The usually busy town centre was oddly deserted. Those few still about had the air of being stranded there, unable to leave for some reason. Lily, frustrated in the search for an open shop, was complaining. They lacked bread and milk at home and, besides her being cold, the woman felt the pressing need to, as she liked to say, powder her nose.

Scovell too. Handily there was a pub, which they hurried across to. "I'll wait for you outside," he said, and a few minutes later he was standing by the pub's door, looking at the almost empty town centre of Woolwich.

The square opposite, though well lit, had the appearance of a place shunned by humanity. A few folk stood at the bus stops on its fringes. It seemed that Woolwich was, on this Sunday evening, a location that they were anxious to escape from. They would have a long journey back to their flat from here, and Scovell considered the advisability of perhaps having a pint in the pub and something to eat there. They had neglected to shop that weekend, had lain in bed too long that morning.

Then Scovell sensed someone behind him. It must be Lily, who liked to creep up and surprise him when he was unaware of her presence. She had reached out her hands to place them over his eyes, so that he could only see through the web of her fingers.

Wondering what she was about, Scovell shook his head and her hand withdrew. In that moment, as through a veil had been lifted from his eyes, very strangely all about him appeared to have altered: he seemed to be in a somewhat different place than a few moments before, with another companion, or it might be the same one, but changed too.

"What have you done to yourself?"

Scovell regarded her closely. Powdering one's nose could be taken too far. It seemed as if Lily had given herself an extreme makeover. She was darker for one thing; her features rather more, well the lips anyway, rather redder, more sensual. Or was it her at all? For he felt a strange sense of disorientation, as though having stepped out of the mundane world he looked at things in a different way, one rather more intense than usual.

"I was thinking," even her voice sounded different, huskier, "that we should go back, to see that boat again. You were right, there was something going on there. They looked like they were having fun. I am sure that we will be invited on board."

"But," he demurred, feeling a bit confused, "how will we get over to the boat?"

There now seemed to be only the two of them in the street. All others had vanished, and the centre of Woolwich had taken on an almost monochrome, sort of *film noir*-ish look. How had Lily managed to alter herself in such a way? Her light brown hair had become darker and longer beneath the red beret that she wore, falling over one eye to give her a 1940s, Veronica Lake-style appearance. Perhaps it was not her at all, but someone impersonating the girl? But why would anyone want to do that? It was most peculiar.

She had taken his arm, and Scovell found himself being led, there was no other word for it, across the road and back towards the river. The street was now quite deserted, as though they were out of time, and very silent. Then he heard a cry. Someone was calling him. It was Lily's voice, but was he not in her company?

Scovell tried to get a look at this close companion, but her features seemed to shift so that his gaze could not quite focus upon her. There was a sort of protean shape-changing there. After Veronica Lake he thought to see Ida Lupino, then was it Gene Tierney? The full lips trembled and he was with Gloria Grahame.

"Scovell!" It was definitely Lily's voice that was calling him. "Where the bloody hell are you going?"

But was she not here with him? No, it was Gloria Grahame still, who said, insinuatingly, "You would not leave me, would you? Not on my own, in the night, in the dark, down these mean streets?"

Her grip on him grew all the tighter, and Scovell realised that he would not be able to extricate himself from Gloria without a tussle. Best not to make a scene in the street with a woman, especially one as glamorous as *La Grahame*. They were moving very fast now towards the river. The ferry had made its last crossing, but there was still the subway where Scovell was being wafted towards. As they descended the shaft he heard Lily's voice again, close behind them, calling.

"Who is that with you? Scovell, stop, wait!"

"The boat won't wait for you," Gloria urged him on. "We don't want to miss it."

The tunnel stretched out before them, brightly lit. It seemed that after the deserted streets there was much activity there, for shadowy figures moved along its length and there were echoes, hollow-sounding voices, which skittered between the grey-tiled walls. Amongst them, he heard Lily again calling to him.

"Can we wait, just a moment?" he said. "For my…"

"No!" came the emphatic reply. "There's not a lot of time. Time and tide wastes for snowman."

She laughed, as did those others in the tunnel. Who were they, seen as blurred flickers of light? Passers-by, who could not cross running water, but would have no problem in passing *under* that element?

Scovell could not help himself being carried along with her. That with him it seemed to be a fluid thing, her appearance changing. Where was Lily? How had she let this happen to him? Not like her to allow him to wander off with a strange woman. Though he had always been one who was up for such adventures, they had not come his way for a while.

He was whirled up the stairs at the subway's exit, out into the air of the north bank. On the south, Woolwich glittered with light in the cold evening, and Scovell was now feeling very cold indeed as he was led along the deserted riverside. Like a leaf taken by the wind, he found himself to be helpless, for arms of surprising strength held him very tightly.

Behind him a familiar voice called his name. It was very confusing, and he did his best to hold back, but his companion was inexorable and not to be denied.

"If we could...just for a moment...?"

"We don't want to be late for the crossing. It is very important that you don't miss it. Take no notice of her. She wants to spoil your fun."

Fun! Yes, he was always up for that. But it was a bit unfair to Lily, who also liked a merry time too. She would, quite rightly, object to him going on a jolly without her company.

But whose company had he found himself in as they hurried along the embankment, towards the boat glowing invitingly on the dark river? The fluidly changing *film-noir* vamp, the type of woman whom he had always desired? Something was not quite right. Scovell was aware of what tended to happen to the hero in that sort of movie, and he tried to get a proper look at what clung on to him. He saw something, just for a moment, which made him think that it was not a woman whom he was with. Indeed, had not been part of humanity for a long, long while.

His attention was distracted from his companion, for the lighted boat was now moving into the shore. There was a small beach below them, in a slip once used by barges. The vessel slowly drew close, and its prow slid silently into a dock where a concrete ramp gave ease of access, to and from the river.

A crowd was gathered on the vessel, eagerly awaiting Scovell and his companion's coming. The gaily-lighted interior made it difficult to make out any detail of the throng, as he felt a pressure at his back and a voice whispered in his ear.

"You have to jump over, it is only a little way."

There was a gap between the bank and the boat's prow. Scovell looked down, and the glamour that had been cast on him fell from his eyes to reveal below the glistening Thames mud, and he reflected in its dark light with a black, oily companion that wanted to embrace him. And there was a stench, like things that had been rotting for a long time in the water and thrown up by that element to the land.

He cried out and stepped back as it touched him, took the hand that had bled into the water with a slippery but firm grasp, as Scovell found himself pulled towards the gap between the boat and the bank.

"Scovell! What the bloody hell do you think you are doing?"

His right arm was seized, and for a moment Scovell found himself torn, tugged one way then another. Then his left hand slipped from that which held it and the river, and what waited for him on it rose up to greet him.

Lily peered into the darkness. The only light that was streaking the water caught a grey garment, spreading out upon the stream, carried by the current downriver to where the shadowy boat had floated back to its mooring and waited. She saw who climbed aboard to cries of encouragement, as hands reached down to help the new crew member. Then a voice spoke behind her.

"You don't want to miss the party, it's on every night."

She turned to look. What spoke shifted, as if stepping behind something, though there was nothing to step behind except the mist rising from the river. Lily, having briefly seen, decided that Scovell was now a lost cause and turned and ran away towards the foot-tunnel, not stopping until reaching the other bank, where only then did she allow herself the luxury of screaming.

# MARK SAMUELS

## DEATH IN ALL ITS RIPENESS

**M**ARK SAMUELS lives in Kings Langley, England. He is the author of seven short story collections and three novels—the latest being *Witch-Cult Abbey*, which has recently been reprinted in paperback by Hippocampus Press. Zagava Books is now well into its schedule of reprinting all of his earlier published fiction in deluxe limited editions, which project should be completed by the end of 2022.

"There must be many dozens of tales featuring H.P. Lovecraft as a central character now," Samuels observes, "and here is yet another one. I can only plead that I have tried not to make him into a convenient Aunt Sally, which some of the other modern attempts in this line have apparently set out to do, but to pay tribute to a brilliant, hugely-influential, author whose long shadow has reached deep into the 21st century."

"Despite my solitary life, I have found infinite joy in books and writing, and am by far too much interested in the affairs of the world to quit the scene before Nature shall claim me..."

—H.P. Lovecraft, 1916

∼

FROM THE SHADOWS, looking out of one of the windows in his study, he gazed at the first of the fall's russet-coloured leaves as they were scattered by heavy winds across the front lawn of 66 College Street. He had risen at noon, worked for several hours at a single stretch, and then relieved the cramping of his calf muscles by pacing the room before coming to pause at the window. He fixed his gaze across the middle distance. He tried to summon up within himself the old sense of adventurous expectancy at the sight of the rooftop vistas of Providence's colonial architecture but, with this concealed sunset, even all the glories huddled beneath it seemed commonplace in the grey early-autumn twilight. His gaze dropped again to the lawn and he saw a solitary cat, of tortoise-shell colour, padding purposefully through the grass and leaves below. The feline turned backwards and looked up, apparently by chance, at first appearing to acknowledge but then, nevertheless, to dismiss with a haughty resolve of disdain the admiring gaze of its human observer.

He switched on the overhead triple-bulbed electric light, returned to his desk, and settled down in the semi-circular, low-backed Victorian chair. Taking up the Waterman pen again, after shaking it vertically between ink-dotted finger and thumb, he continued making amendments to the manuscript of Mrs. Renshaw's *Well-Bred Speech*. Her last letter, riddled with pleas of the job's supreme urgency, yet not so forward with a date of payment, rested, face down, alongside the lady's impossibly muddled *magnum opus*. He tried to overcome the warning hints of incipient eye-strain, the authoress' egregious errors in style and substance and, most pernicious of all, the ever-present spectre of financial hardship, with the same resolution as was evinced by the feline harbinger.

Wrapping a blanket over his shoulders, he redoubled his efforts on the manuscript of *Well-Bred Speech*.

His fingers had stiffened in the chilliness of the room.

Working through most of the night on that tiresome document now lay in store for Howard Phillips Lovecraft.

It was a few days later, after having finally rid himself of the burden of Mrs. Renshaw's commission, that Lovecraft received the curious package. The brick-sized item was marked PRIVATE AND PERSONAL—and written in a crabbed script that rivalled his own for illegibility.

His aunt had brought it up to him at half-past noon, when it was certain he, a night-person, would have risen from his bed.

He sliced the silver blade of an ivory-handled paper knife—his late grandfather Whipple's—along the top flap and removed the contents of the package. A sheet of paper, written on one side, was wrapped around banknotes. In confusion, he scanned the writing on the sheet rapidly. What began as a fan letter offered the prospect of another commission. To this end, said banknotes were enclosed, two hundred dollars worth, provided solely to secure his undivided services.

Mrs. Renshaw, thought Lovecraft, not without irony, would have been appalled at this method.

The letter ran as follows:

Dear Mr. H.P. Lovecraft,

I read your good work—a lot—in *Weird Tales* and other magazines like that one. I found your home address through my involvement in 'The Eyrie' section of letter writers. I need your help bad with a true occult book like your *Necronomicon* but one based on real country life, not made-up city-folk garbage. This is sure to be a bestseller and will make us both a lot of bucks. I am sending cash to make sure you only work for me. My book is going to be called *The Animal Truth*.

Please reply c/o Shinglemill River General Store, Pennsylvania.

Yours
Ezekiel Nantwich

A low groan escaped Lovecraft's thin lips. On the whole, he welcomed the attention of the admirers of his weird fiction that approached him, but there was always a significant percentage of overly enthusiastic youths full of unrealisable schemes. Only recently he had had to gently explain to another correspondent, Willis Conover, that to attempt to actually write the *Necronomicon* would be doomed to failure, since the reality could not possibly measure up to the suggestive hints and limited partial glimpses that imparted a fictional tome with an aura of absolute terror. Even Bobby Barlow, of late, had occupied huge swathes of his time that he could ill-afford to waste on wildly overambitious and fantastical projects. He looked over the letter again. Still, at least this Ezekiel Nantwich personage seemed to recognise that the *Necronomicon* did not exist, unlike one or two enquiries he had received from youths asking how the volume might be obtained. Moreover, Nantwich indicated that he was actually writing a book and, although it could not conceivably compare to a fictional dread tome, his curiosity was, nevertheless, piqued. Perhaps, he thought, it was his slightly-cracked-in-the-head correspondent William Lumley who had suggested Nantwich should contact him?

He pondered the banknotes for a moment. It would be, he decided, completely unethical for him to consider accepting payment at this stage, from this source. How then, should he proceed so as not to cause offence? Perhaps he might be able to persuade Ezekiel Nantwich to write weird fiction, as a genuine mode of artistic expression, rather than his concentrating on this other scheme. But if he had sight of Nantwich's book, even just one or two chapters, he might have a much clearer idea as to how to proceed. He thought the matter over for a few minutes, took up his Waterman and penned an immediate reply, casting a rueful glance at the small pile of accumulated, unanswered correspondence to which he had yet to attend. Then, putting the banknotes into a package of his own along with the letter he had dashed off, Lovecraft made his way, through the increasingly chilly Providence air, towards the nearest U.S. Mail Office.

Ezekiel Nantwich grinned as he remembered the beating he had given his pa. The old fool had hollered like a mule after discovering

Ezekiel had raided his stash of dollars under the mattress, taking the cash for himself. Pa had said he weren't rightly no son of his anyhow, and that made it robbery, plain and simple. Pa was still laid up, days later, and hadn't said anything else since. He must have learnt his lesson about who was the new boss on their farm; hell, the old critter could scarcely move around much beforehand anyway. Now all he did was lie down and stare. Hard to spot any difference. Hadn't even eaten for days. Well, let him rot there in his bunk.

Ezekiel continued chopping away with his long-handled hay knife at the stack, tied and hauled bundles over to the cattle in the next field. He arranged them just outside the fence and then set them alight. The cattle stared dolefully at the flames and he chuckled to himself. Right funny it was. Then he sat down to rest and think for a while. He pulled out a quart bottle of hooch from the front pocket of his moth-eaten dungarees.

Wouldn't be much longer before slaughtering time. The haystacks were running out, and summer had given way to fall. Cattle need to die. Folk gotta eat them. That was nature's law. Can't be changed for no one.

The neck of the hooch bottle slotted in pretty fine between the front gaps in his dentition where two teeth had fallen out. The rest were reduced to rotten stumps. He swallowed the fiery liquid in great gulps.

Once he'd finished the bottle, Ezekiel tossed it aside, rolled up onto his feet, hitched up his dungarees and set off for town, four miles away. He wanted to get to the General Store to see if that Lovecraft fella had replied yet. Even if he hadn't, Ezekiel thought it prudent to lay in some more hooch.

The countryside around Shinglemill was mostly backwoods and a single dirt-track weaved its way from Nantwich Farm through a domed series of hills sheltered beneath the wilder heights of the Appalachians where brown bears roamed freely and drank from the waters of the west branch of the Susquehanna River.

Folk in those parts avoided Ezekiel if they could help it. Everyone knew he was an ornery cuss, especially when in his cups. So when he finally stumbled into the Shinglemill General Store its proprietor,

Joshua Corwin, cursed under his breath, then corrected himself for taking the Lord's name in vain.

For a longish while, Corwin thought, Ezekiel had had a problem paying back what he owed on the account, though his pa (who'd not been around much lately) had always settled on time. Still, he'd been expecting that Ezekiel would show up soon; a package addressed to him from Providence had arrived just the day before, waiting for him to collect it.

"How ya doing Corwin?" Ezekiel hissed through the gap in his teeth.

"Got a package for ya," Corwin replied, not looking up from the desk.

"Sure, been thinkin' ya would have. Gonna take me a look around first, like," he replied.

Ezekiel made a beeline for the magazine stacks and rifled through the display for a few minutes. He always went away with the same old junk; the latest issue of some heathen trash called *Weird Tales* and any other lurid pulp magazine that captured his attention on the spur of the moment.

After he'd finished selecting half a dozen items of such reading material, he wandered up to the desk and put them on the counter.

Joshua Corwin wrinkled his nose at the offending covers but began to total up the cost.

"Also," said Ezekiel, "four bottles of the usual stuff."

Corwin could smell the same brand lingering on his breath.

"Still owe twenty bucks. Hate to mention it but..."

Ezekiel tossed some crumpled, dirty banknotes that he pulled from his dungarees onto the counter.

"Don't forget my postal delivery," he said as the bottles and magazine were stuffed inside a large brown paper bag.

Corwin got him to sign a form and then handed it over.

It was from Lovecraft all right. It was postmarked *Providence*.

"Got yersel' a pen-pal?" Corwin said, as he slipped the package on top of the other items. "Ain't something ya'd appreciate," Ezekiel said, cradling the bag under his arm and making for the exit, "best stick to your Bible fairy tales. If ya know what I mean and I think ya do."

∽

Pa still hadn't stirred when Ezekiel returned to the farmhouse. He went straight to his room at the back of the dwelling, set down the bag next to his battered typewriter on the card-table and slumped heavily onto the stool in front of it. He was up to a hundred and fifty single-spaced typed pages of *The Animal Truth*, despite having to fill in the letters *s* and *b* by hand.

The room was littered with a multitude of pulp magazines, the walls decorated with torn-off Margaret Brundage covers he'd tacked to the wooden slats. She was a fine artist, his favourite. It was a shame that *Weird Tales* editor Farnsworth Wright stopped answering his letters altogether. Ezekiel had begun accusing him of being badly wrong and biased against him on account of him just speaking his mind, but now he had Lovecraft's services at his command things would be different.

He opened a bottle of hooch, drank a few mouthfuls and then tore open Lovecraft's package.

The banknotes tumbled out.

Must be a mistake.

He read Lovecraft's letter once, then twice, then three times.

The fella was insane.

Someone must have gotten to him in advance and warned him off. Two passages stood out. Not only did he say:

though naturally flattered by your appreciation of my own fictional effusions, I cannot collaborate on the writing of a seriously-intended work of occultism that purports to be factual; indeed, I once embarked upon a debunking of all such claims with the late Harry Houdini, the escapologist and sceptic, and his booking agent and associate of mine, Clifford Martin Eddy, though the work in question, *The Cancer of Superstition*, remains uncomp-leted and thus far has not seen publication.

but he also then suggested:

I should, however, be glad to have sight of your current manuscript and offer non-collaborative and non-remunerative advice and brief suggestions in this regard should you judge this reluctantly-made decline of your proposal not unduly impertinent. By the way, why not try your hand at the creation of weird *fiction*?

Lovecraft was, in a sneeringly polite way, trying to give him the bum's-rush.

*The Cancer of Superstition*!

He couldn't possibly know what he was talking about.

Ezekiel glugged back more of the hooch.

Once Lovecraft had seen a few chapters of the book, he'd be bound to change the tune he was whistling. Ezekiel began to sort out some sample chapters from amongst the carbon copy of his typescript.

A week later Lovecraft received a second package from Ezekiel Nantwich. As well as a half-crazed covering letter it also contained a grubby, liquid-spotted and dog-eared carbon copy of numbered pages, apparently selected at random from his typescript entitled *The Animal Truth*. The offensive smell of liquor still clung to the dozen or so sheets of paper.

Dear H.P.

You don't get it yet do you? I'm telling you this could be big for both of us. It was a bad mistake to return that money. It wasn't easy to get. Now I'm starting to get a little mad at you. The title of your Houdini book stinks. But I'll give you another chance, not that anyone ever gave me one. Read what I've written. It'll change your mind. Then tell me you're sorry and that you're willing to work with me after all.

Ezekiel Nantwich

Lovecraft leaned back in his chair and sighed. He had a personal rule not to ignore correspondence, but it was clear that this was not a person whom he should encourage. This was obviously not just a case of an overenthusiastic youth harbouring unrealisable schemes, but rather one of outright egomania and untrammelled vanity. He had had quite enough experience of such people during the long period of his association with colourful personalities in the hothouse-feud atmosphere of the amateur press. This letter would have to go unanswered: the carbon copies returned without comment. Lovecraft did, however, look over some of the pages of this supposedly-thwarted, yet sure-fire commercial success.

The thing concerned a series of "case studies" of vicious wild animals living out in the woods who gradually began influencing the cattle on a local farm, warning them of the dangers of domestication and encouraging them towards malign actions against their human masters. All of the creatures had been anthro-pomorphised, and talked and debated with one another, apparently vying for the crown of malevolence. It was impossible to determine where Nantwich obtained these "case studies", since he provided no historical sources. The wild animals were supposedly exiled familiars of some sort, left to their own devices, or so Nantwich suggested, after certain historically suppressed witch-trials (and the purging thereof) during the last decade of the 17th century. It was difficult to accurately trace the exact development of this "genuine" out-break, not only because Lovecraft had been supplied solely with sample chapters, but also because the writing was surrealistic in the extreme. Stylistically, it was hopelessly ungrammatical, confused, repetitive and riddled with innumerable—and very basic—spelling errors.

He found it difficult to believe the evidence of his eyes. He suspected an elaborate prank. But eventually he turned the carbon copies face down.

He glanced again at the accompanying letter. Such a communi-cation as that, and sent to a relative stranger, could only be suggestive of serious organic derangement in its author. This Ezekiel Nantwich, whoever he was, required the attention of an alienist. He surely could not be fully aware of his actions. It was an unfortunate combination of chemicals and secretions operating to the detriment of an individual human organism, but it should not be permitted to perturb Lovecraft's own equanimity, and he resolved to forget it. Tomorrow he would return Nantwich's typescript without comment and that, he hoped, would be the end of it.

Ezekiel tramped through the woods all night, letting its essence get under his skin, becoming one with the primal power of hate. He clawed into the dirt with his bare hands, smearing himself with it, scampered around on all fours like a wolf, and hollered and howled until the sound of his own voice lost any trace of humanity. He killed whatever he encountered, leaving a bloody trail of death that confirmed him as the avatar of the motive force behind nature. Not to think, not to pity, not to hesitate in one's actions; only to kill, only to fulfil the innermost purpose of everything. He would pause and survey the trees swaying and sighing in the night and swear that, soon, they, by the will that worked through his hands, would be burnt, blackened and lifeless, a range of charred stumps; monuments to truth. Stars would rage and burn thousands of times more brightly in the sky, reaching out across the void to maim and then destroy one another, whole galaxies, too, and then everything in the rotten cosmos would rend at its own innards and, exhausted, collapse into a great coalescence of mutual terror and ultimate destruction and then finally be as one. The power of the vision bore his spirits up as if on black wings and he grinned madly, his mouth bloodied by his kills, as he watched dawn break in the east and implored the will that generated the power of the sun to accomplish its end-goal; the one that only Ezekiel could grasp, and herald not just another day but the day-of-days; when the blasphemy that was truth would blast and triumph over all the muddleheaded talk of "civilised" men.

He waited, but the birdsong began, the woods began to stir, and the same routine of animate pointlessness carried on as before, as it had for untold millennia.

The great wasp still awaited the right moment to wriggle out in vengeance from the corrupted fruit of its womb. Its emergence could not be put off much longer, of that he was certain.

Ezekiel threaded his way back towards the farm, along tracks with which he had been familiar even as a boy, where he had hunted and tortured every kind of critter, until Pa had caught him once and tried to whip the urge out of him.

He washed himself, clothes and all, in the old creek, and found its dark, sluggish waters still full of thirsty leeches, troublesome as city-folk, but he knew how best to deal with both species: slow suffering, nothing quick and easy.

Though he was tired, the dip had refreshed him. Hunger though, got a hold of his vitals and he plodded up to the house to check up on his pa and put some food inside himself.

The stench hit before he'd even closed the screen-door behind him. Something had turned bad overnight.

The worst of it came from the direction of Pa's room. Cooking seemed a bad idea, Ezekiel thought. Chances were he'd bring anything that had gone down straight back up when he opened that bedroom door. Didn't smell like the old man had fouled the sheets again; more like, well, something finally gone rotten, and something that had been a long while waiting to do so.

Ezekiel laid a hand on the knob, then cautiously pushed open the door, having pinched shut the nostrils of his nose with his other, free hand. He entered. Half a dozen bluebottles buzzed frantically around his head and then settled back on the old man's yellow-tinged, bloodless face. His eyes were open and staring, only the bald, mottled head visible above the sheet that was pulled up to his chin.

"Pa? How ya feeling?"

Ezekiel ventured farther towards the bed. The eyes of the old man still stared, but fixedly, as if at some point directly on the opposite wall, though there was nothing much to look at there as far as Ezekiel could tell; only huge cracks in the sickly-green plaster.

When he took his hand away from his nose he gagged at the disgusting stench permeating the room.

"Pa, ya better not be fooling me," he said, choking out the words. No answer.

Then, in a rage, he leapt forward and tore the thin blanket away from his father's torso and legs. A whole series of bugs had set up home there and were happily milling around in the dirty singlet and underpants covering what little was left of the old man's dignity.

Ezekiel hauled his pa from the bed onto the bare floorboards, causing the bugs to scurry around aimlessly on the stained mattress and the bluebottles to circle impatiently in a circle overhead. He kicked the old man in the ribs a few times, heard stale air whistle from his dead lungs up through his mouth, and then hauled him back into the bed and arranged him in his former position, pulling the blanket up to his chin.

The bugs and the flies settled down again. Pa still stared at the same spot on the wall, apparently unperturbed.

Pa had been useless for years anyhow. Didn't have any friends. Hadn't been in town since '32. No kin left, except Ezekiel himself. He didn't even remember Ma. She was never talked about too. No one else would notice Pa wasn't around. There'd be a whole lot of trouble if folks from town started messing around on the farm asking stupid questions and kicking up a fuss.

Best forget about it.

Something else occurred to Ezekiel.

He closed the door to Pa's room behind him, padded along the short corridor into his own room, and there began to rummage amongst the piles of pulp magazines he'd collected over the years. Finally, after several minutes of rifling through them, he retrieved half-a-dozen old copies of a garish journal called *Home Brew: America's Zippiest Magazine*.

He put them into chronological order so he could reread Lovecraft's serial 'Grewsome Tales' over a bottle of hooch.

There was no work to do around the farm, so he could allow himself some luxury.

After all, he was boss now.

Several days later the telephone started ringing. It was just before one o'clock in the morning. Lovecraft could hear its shrill, insistent summons filtering up the stairs from the hallway where the device was located. His Aunt Annie had retired hours ago. She was a heavy sleeper. Despite her room being on the ground floor, and thus closer to the infernal instrument, he doubted she would be awakened by its noise. The thing, though, was proving ruinous to Lovecraft's concentration. His eye-trouble was taxing enough of late, but to have to suffer such superfluous auditory distractions too; it was as if his own unavoidable physical decline were being hastened by the hustle and bustle of the machine-age. He reluctantly laid down his pen and slid aside the letter he was writing, got to his feet, and made his way in the darkness towards the insistent telephone. He wondered who it could be that would call at such an unsociable hour, though the possibility that some real emergency required his attention seemed fantastically remote. Most of his family were gone and were any of his friends and correspondents to have suffered a calamity (he thought momentarily, with a pang, of the recent loss of Two-Gun Bob and of good old Canevin a few years earlier) he would have been advised of the fact by written communication.

It must, however, be a matter of urgency. Obviously even a telegram would not do in this particular instance. The telephone had been ringing for a period long enough to indicate that the caller had abandoned any scruples about wakening the household or of attempting to make contact again in the morning at a more considerate hour.

He lifted the receiver, placed it to his ear, and spoke into the mouthpiece, feeling a customary distaste with the trappings of modernity.

"This is Plantations 2044, who is speaking please?"

There was a grunting noise, then a long pause, and then some odd clicks on the line. It was rather unnerving, standing there in the dark, in the depths of the witching hour, rather like . . . Lovecraft thought of Harley Warren and of Edward Derby, and then dismissed the absurdity of the sudden mental association.

"Who is speaking please? I can't hear you," Lovecraft said, repeating his plaintive query.

"Got ya number outta the Providence direckty. Tryin' ta fool me calling yurself Mrs. Gamwell, huh?"

The voice was slurred. It seemed clear that whoever was speaking was a victim of that capacity which liquor possessed to hurl men several stages down the evolutionary scale.

"Ya sent ma bits of ma book back, damn ya."

"Who is speaking please?" Lovecraft repeated, for a third time, though he dreaded the answer.

"Ah'm Ezekiel Nantwich, ya know of me well enuff," the voice went on.

Lovecraft was appalled.

He had thought this disturbing affair concluded.

His knuckles went white as he gripped the receiver more tightly in his grasp.

"Callin' from the farm. My pa wants to speak to ya. Says it's *right* ya ain't choosin' to work for me. I'll put him on the line. Ya can straighten him out afore I put him back down..."

"Please don't attempt to contact me again," Lovecraft said.

He replaced the receiver in its cradle.

There were no further telephone calls that night.

Sheriff Barnabas Dudley navigated his beat-up county police car along the four-mile long dirt track that led from Shinglemill up to Nantwich Farm. Joshua Corwin at the General Store had asked him to "look in" on the place a few days ago, but he'd put off doing so. There appeared to him no good reason to go about idly interfering in other people's business, even by way of neighbourliness, if the one doing the interfering, as he would be, carried the authority and weight of a badge and gun. And old Corwin just seemed suspicious of everyone in a twenty-mile radius of Shinglemill who had ever paid a visit to the General Store and had looked at him askance.

There was, however, the matter of that very bad business which had occurred at the farm thirty years ago. Couldn't simply dismiss that. Nothing had been proven against Enoch Nantwich, but Dudley still felt there was something not right about a man like that bringing up a boy—even Ezekiel—alone.

A very bad business indeed.

He jammed a smoke into the corner of his mouth and tried haphazardly to light it as the car rolled over a series of ruts in the dirt track. The steering wheel tried to jerk out of his left hand and he swore loudly before regaining control of the vehicle.

Back in 1906, Enoch had got it into his head that his wife, Bethany, was some kind of witch who talked—and did certain other things—with the wild animals in the woods. He would say so to anyone stupid enough to listen, and some of them got it into their heads too. And it wasn't long after Ezekiel was born that her body was found in the woods five miles north of Nantwich Farm. She was dangling from a tree, hanged by her neck from a noose wrapped round a long, sturdy branch. How she could have got all the way up there "unaided" remained unanswered. Folks said she'd gone mad after the birth, got violent and eyed the child in a furtive way, though Enoch seemed reluctant to confirm the fact.

Nantwich Farm was searched and there was strange stuff found amongst Bethany's possessions. Stuff that some folk thought Enoch had placed there to show she wasn't right in the head, but which others thought had been there all along. There were bundled sticks made up into human shapes, most with hieroglyphic writing etched on them, but some had names.

Not long after Enoch was cleared through lack of evidence, and once Bethany was buried, there started up wild, crazy talk about her still being seen after dark in the woods; scuttling around on all fours with a monstrously crooked neck, clambering up and down trees, and consorting with animals.

Dudley's predecessor as county Sheriff, Job Cooke, drank a lot more after that business, developed the shakes, and finally moved away in the end, taking his family with him. He had told the young Dudley the tale reluctantly, piece by piece, over a period of weeks. For it wasn't the hanging—or even the wild stories—that got to Job Cooke. His nerves were far stronger than most; what really got to him in the end was the other thing that happened twenty miles away.

Someone had paid a visit to the grave over at North Bend Cemetery two months after the interment, dug down six feet, opened the casket and then used kerosene to burn Bethany Nantwich's body to a crisp on the spot, right there and then. Whoever did the deed was interrupted by a patrolling night-watchman and escaped before the soil could be replaced, the plot filled back in and the defilement concealed. The night-watchman said the soil of the same grave had been curiously disturbed on previous occasions after the burial, and he had determined to keep the area under closer observation. The ghoulish outrage was a local sensation and made the papers in most of western Pennsylvania, though the coroner did all he could to keep the most lurid details out of the hands of the press.

These stories, of events from thirty years before, told to him by a drink-sodden Job Cooke, kept turning over in his mind the closer Sheriff Dudley came to Nantwich Farm. Once or twice he even seriously thought about turning back.

But he finally pulled up outside the farmhouse; a two-storied gambrel-roofed structure whose whitewashed paintwork had not been maintained, and which peeled away in large sections from the exterior wooden slats. The windows were dusty; tattered green curtains, little more than grimy rags, hung behind their cracked panes. The whole place had a depressing air of miserable backwoods insularity, slipping, generation after tainted generation, into a deeper, perversely-hermetic, degeneration.

Over in the near distance a herd of sickly-looking cattle, their ribs clearly visible, their legs almost spindly, stood eerily still and watched Dudley with dull, inhuman stares as he made his way from the car and up the steps of the rickety front porch. Some of them began lowing throatily, as if they had not been fed for a long while and were being further tormented by Dudley's not immediately attending to their own needs.

He banged on the entrance. No answer. He tried again.

"Enoch!? Ezekiel!?" Dudley shouted. "You in there?"

Still no answer. And once he'd opened the screen door, the sudden stench that wafted out made him gag involuntarily and he quickly covered his mouth and nose with a handkerchief. The same stomach-churning odour he knew from the time he'd gone over to old Israel Parris' shack, only to discover that its reclusive occupant had been lying there dead for two weeks after a massive heart attack.

The stench of death in all its ripeness.

He found the two corpses in one of the back bedrooms, along with a horde of angry bluebottles, which angrily buzzed Dudley when he entered.

Ezekiel was a ghastly shade of yellow, the blood pooling in his back, his near-toothless mouth bearing the death's-head smile of rictus. His stomach was beginning to bloat with foetid internal gases.

Enoch, however, appeared to have been dead for a longer period; decomposition had already long set in. His sunken, spongy eyes stared lifelessly, his bald pate and face were a mottled tangle-work of sickening corruption.

The room showed evidence of a dramatic struggle having taken place within. Some chairs had been overturned, pictures upon the walls were crazily askew, and various objects lay scattered on the floor.

It seemed to Dudley that the two men had died weeks apart, but that was a matter for a pathologist to determine and upon which the county coroner would pronounce. True, there had been rumours in the papers of a delinquent gang of city youths (doubtless from Allentown, where things were bad) who drove around robbing isolated farmhouses, but those rumours were current more than two years ago. It appeared unlikely such a gang would commit murder in two distinct phases, first Enoch and then returning for Ezekiel, when the latter would have had to have remained silent during the interim.

Amongst the items scattered on the floor were several dozen typewritten pages and Dudley examined them, whilst still keeping his nose and mouth covered with the handkerchief. The pages might also be important evidence.

He couldn't make much sense out of them, but the subject matter made him deeply uneasy; something about talking animals, devil-worship and the rage of nature. Many of the pages had been dappled with bloodstains.

He left Enoch's bedroom and looked over the rest of the farmhouse. Elsewhere, nothing indicated that a gang had raided the place. Though derelict and dirty, the interior showed signs only of terminal neglect, not of having been ransacked for valuables.

It was in Ezekiel's bedroom that Dudley finally decided to torch the entire farmhouse and destroy all traces of what had occurred within. What he saw there made the memory of his talks with a visibly shaking Job Cooke again force themselves to the forefront of his mind.

Dudley found some curiously bundled figures made out of sticks and a huge pentagram scrawled—in what appeared to be blood—on the far wall.

One of the strange human-shaped stick-forms bore a ribbon with the English appellation *Enoch*, and he could not bring himself to handle the thing. Etched into the sticks were indecipherable glyphs written in an archaic language Dudley could not recognise.

There was another such stick figure, bearing a different appellation. Rusty nails had been driven into what constituted its midriff, and he only discerned the English appellation partially (this ribbon being badly torn) as...*craft*, as in—or so he presumed—*witchcraft*.

On an impulse that he obeyed, though which he nevertheless felt to be absurd, Dudley pocketed the grisly item, perhaps as a macabre keepsake or perhaps to prove to himself that all he had seen inside Nantwich Farm was not born of a waking nightmare or the result of some other form of temporary derangement on his part.

Kerosene again did the work of purging. The fire Dudley started began totally consuming the Nantwich Farmhouse and all its vile secrets as the Sheriff drove back towards Shinglemill, a great conflagration of flames and smoke billowing into the early evening sky behind him, mingling with the bloody crimson of the setting sun.

He'd tell Joshua Corwin that the farmhouse had burned down a good hour or more before his arrival there. The place was so remote and so shunned by everyone that his own story, with the authority of his badge behind it, wouldn't be contradicted. The still-lowing cattle were the sole witnesses.

Ezekiel, thought Dudley, had been his mother Bethany's wicked triumph in posterity.

Lovecraft again gazed out of the study window. The russet-coloured leaves were falling in greater numbers; a few weeks more and the trees would be stripped bare. The season had decisively turned. The summer warmth that sustained him had ebbed away, yielding to ever more chillier air, to the firmer grasp of night, and to the virtual hibernation that autumnal existence forced upon him.

He looked once more for the familiar tortoise-shell cat but saw no sign of it, though it had become something of a permanent fixture around the grounds of 66 College Street. Strange independent creature! Lovecraft had prided himself on his ability to strike up a rapport with any feline that chance sent his way, yet this one had remained resolutely hostile, as if no affinity were possible. The thing had probably gone feral long ago. He still bore the scratch-marks on his hand from the single attempt he had made to tickle it under the chin.

He sat down at his desk and again tried to work.

The room felt abominably cold to him, yet the thermometer hung upon the wall insisted upon sixty degrees Fahrenheit.

Suddenly, he felt a pang of grippe seize his lower intestines. The symptoms were familiar, and such attacks had already bedevilled him, on and off, for over a year. The symptoms intensified, ebbing and flowing, alternately, in a tide of nausea and acute stabbing pains. This latest episode was a particularly trying revival of the troublesome ailment.

After half an hour of continued distress, he went into his bed-alcove to lie down and wrap himself in blankets. Removing his carpet-slippers, he noticed the swelling in his feet; here, too, was an unexpected new development in the malady.

He lay on one side, attempting to regain some sense of stoic composure.

Then the cast-iron radiator on the far wall laboriously began its process of interior knocking. At last, it appeared, the central boiler over at Brown University had been fired up and the off-campus residences—such as the domestic satellite he and his Aunt Annie occupied—would receive their promised allocation of heating.

Doubtless an easily distracted janitor had finally noticed the lateness of the season.

# RICHARD CHRISTIAN MATHESON

## SHRAPNEL

RICHARD CHRISTIAN MATHESON is a best-selling author
and screenwriter/producer who *The New York Times* has
described as "...a great horror writer". He has worked with Steven
Spielberg, Tobe Hooper, Nicholas Pileggi, Joe Dante, Roger Corman,
Richard Donner, Mel Brooks and many others.

Matheson has created, written and produced acclaimed TV series,
mini-series and films, including cult favourite *Three O'Clock High*
and Stephen King's *Battleground*, which won two Emmy Awards. He
has adapted novels for film by Dean Koontz, Whitley Strieber, Roger
Zelazny, Stephen King, H.G. Wells and George R. R. Martin.

His short stories have been collected in *Scars And Other
Distinguishing Marks*, *Zoopraxis* and *Dystopia*, and been published in
more than 130 anthologies, including many 'Year's Best' volumes.
Matheson's other books include the novel *Created By* and the novella
*The Ritual of Illusion*.

A professional drummer (he studied privately with Cream's
Ginger Baker), he is currently working on several feature films and
TV series.

"War's traumas to flesh and psyche can remain captive in the
body," Matheson observes, "...like haunted POWs. The wages of
anguish.

"This story, about their dire inflictions, first appeared in *Brothers in Arms*, the anthology I edited, honouring my father Richard Matheson's iconic 1960 war novel, *The Beardless Warriors*. As an eighteen-year-old, in the 87th Division in Europe, he came to despise war.

"In his moving dedication, he hoped the reading of the book was the closest I'd ever come to it."

T HE WAR WOULD come soon; slip into bed with him.
*Flashlight beams. Platoon searching. Moonlight on gutted street. Village asleep.*

He felt skin go cold. Stared into blackness.

*The Sergeant. Eyes dead. Despising. Half-mad.*

Why didn't they refuse?

*Village faces smiling betrayal. Kids with cell phones rigged to blow. Platoon tired. Scared.*

He felt sick. Room spinning.

*The sweet girl with the smile who made the cake. American flag frosting. Hands locked in prayer; gratitude for them saving her town and family. Giggling, running off before they could examine it.*

It would come soon now.

He stumbled into bathroom. Splashed face with water. Looked into mirror.

*When he saw her he should have slit her throat like the Sergeant ordered. Like the little boy, in the other village, the Sergeant killed. Like his mother, who ran to them, pleading with the Sergeant.*

He felt dizzy. Fell to knees. It was almost here.

*Carrying dead babies, bombs hidden in them. Vulnerability and fear; a trick. Sergeant yelling for revenge. Three in the platoon burned alive.*

He contorted on shower floor. Eyes shut. Water scraping scarred body. Saw frantic faces. Mosul streets bloody. Dogs sleeping in hot wind.

*A hundred and twelve degrees. Grandmother screaming. Crippled husband begging as the Sergeant shot them both.*

He began to shake. Felt it tiptoe onto his bones. Wade into his veins.

*South of Kabul. Sergeant sure the boys' giggles hid murder. The way they screamed when shot. The Sergeant's sick smile.*

He stared at drain. Saw their stricken faces swirl.

*The terror when they tried to run, legs torn by rifle. Sergeant sure they lured him to snipers. Five more bullets made them stagger. Sergeant's yelp psychotic.*

His insides shifted; burned. Heart a black spasm.

*The praying woman, shot through head.*

He should have refused. Killed the Sergeant. He pleaded for it to leave him alone. But it was here now.

And it all began.

He felt them hiding under his tongue. Crawling, terrified, in his mouth. Watched in horror as more shapes moved, under his flesh; helpless mouths, surfacing on his palms, screaming without sound.

His chest began to glow dirty orange with explosions under ribs; the smell of cordite burning.

He felt villagers running over his eyes, fleeing, through the smoking fields and gouted alleys of him. Looked at thigh, saw the terrified face of an old woman, dying, trapped under his skin.

*As the Sergeant sliced them, eyes glistening sadism, the villagers begged him to stop.*

He suddenly screamed as his flat belly formed the contours of a knife blade. The shapes of ears and fingers the Sergeant had cut-off; rising like gory islands on his abdomen.

*He laughed, spread their blood on his face; war paint. Ready to slash more when his helmet dented inward, eyes stunned; a sniper. His own men watching him die.*

Explosions and screams deafened, inside his body. Children pleading. He gasped for air. Couldn't breathe.

Froze in shock, seeing the Sergeant's face, surfacing on the back of his hand, grinning hatefully. Slammed hand against cracking shower glass, slicing the face apart. As both bled, he finally passed out.

He awakened, hours later, in bed and wept. The shapes gone; a poison tide fled to sea. Looked at walled photo of his squad; brothers forever. Listened to himself bleed, red guilt draining.

The war inside waiting.

# DALE BAILEY

## PRECIPICE

DALE BAILEY lives in North Carolina with his family. He is the author of eight books, most recently *In the Night Wood, The End of the End of Everything: Stories* and *The Subterranean Season.* Forthcoming is a new short story collection, *This Island Earth: 8 Features from the Drive-In.* His story 'Death and Suffrage' was adapted for Showtime's *Masters of Horror* TV series.

He has won the Shirley Jackson Award and the International Horror Guild Award, and has been a finalist for the World Fantasy, Nebula, Locus and Bram Stoker awards.

"I can trace the origins of 'Precipice' with a clarity and precision that almost always eludes me when I think about how stories happen," Bailey explains. "I was at a beach resort, not unlike the one in the story, with my family a couple of years ago. We had a room on the 15th floor. And on the balcony one day, I was seized with the urge to jump.

"That urge did not go away for the rest of the vacation. It finally got to the point where I could no longer go out on the balcony at all. Even looking out the windows was almost unbearable. Thankfully, this perverse impulse has since diminished, though it still crosses my mind whenever I find myself in a high place..."

∽

STOCKTON HAD HIS first intimation of the fear to come— though he did not then recognise it as such—soon after he checked in at OceanView Plantation and rode the elevator up to the fifteenth floor of the South Tower. The building was hollow. You accessed the suites by long galleries, open to the sky behind a chest-high parapet. Outside the room, Stockton paused to look down. Palm trees grew below. He felt momentarily vertiginous. Some inchoate impulse moved him. He swallowed and stepped back, nearly colliding with the bellhop who was pushing the luggage cart along behind him.

"Sorry," he muttered, and the bellhop said, "My fault, sir," and Judy, who was bringing up the rear, said, "Are you okay, Frank?"

Her voice was tremulous with an anxiety that reflected and exacerbated his own.

"Fine," Stockton said, annoyed. "I'm fine. Why?"

"You look pale," she said.

"I look fine," Stockton said, as if by force of will he could deny the heart attack and all its attendant anxieties. He'd grown thick over the last decade—not fat, but stout, barrel-chested, with the heavy shoulders and arms of a man who'd done years of physical labour. He'd kept in reasonable shape as he aged. But time caught up with you. Six months ago, he'd stopped in to check the progress at one of his building sites. He'd just stepped out of his pick-up when the dizziness struck. "You okay, boss?" Ed, the foreman, had asked. "You look kind of green."

The next thing Stockton knew, he was staring up into the face of a nurse. He had a blurred impression of hazel eyes and high cheekbones. He was just coming out from the anaesthesia. He only half-remembered. "What happened?" he'd whispered through parched lips. "You should be dead," she told him, and then the world had gone dark again.

Stockton shook his head. He waved his keycard in front of the lock. Inside, he directed the disposal of the luggage. He over-tipped and ushered the bellhop out. The suite was roomier than he'd expected: big windows behind the sofa and a balcony that offered a stunning panorama of the resort. Pools glimmered like jewelled teardrops amid scattered stands of palm trees. The sea ran out to a flat line on the horizon. He turned away, wishing he'd booked something on a lower floor.

Heights had never bothered him. He didn't understand.

Judy had wandered into the bedroom. "You should see this whirlpool," she called.

Stockton dropped the keycard on the kitchen counter, stole another glance at the windows, and went to see the bathroom. But the view stuck with him. When they had unpacked, they went out for groceries. Stockton hugged the wall of the gallery coming and going, and later, when Judy invited him to join her on the balcony, he busied himself in the kitchen. But he could not put her off that easily. She asked him to bring her a glass of wine. When he handed it through the door, she pulled him outside.

"It's beautiful, isn't it?" she said, leaning on the railing. "Come over here and look."

Stockton demurred. Dinner was on the stove. He was doing the stir-fry she liked. They were going to be here two weeks. They'd have plenty of time to enjoy the view.

The dizzy spell weighed on him. He could not help thinking of the heart attack.

After dinner, Judy wanted to go for a walk on the beach.

Stockton pleaded a headache. He went to bed early, but his sleep was restless, and fleeting. He opened his eyes deep in the night. He lay still for a long time, listening to Judy breathe. He got out of bed. He found himself at the sliding glass door in the living room. It was like he'd been summoned there. He stared out into the fathomless abyss of sea and sky. Unbidden, an image came to him. He saw himself pushing the door open and stepping onto the balcony. Wind whipped his hair. He could hear the surf on the beach. There was something alluring in the night air.

"Frank," Judy said behind him.

He shuddered. He was holding the railing with both hands.

"What are you doing?" she asked.

"I don't know," he said, bewildered, and then he gasped and opened his eyes.

He was in bed, Judy curled up against him. He wondered in a dull, half-conscious way if he was still asleep, if he hadn't woken from one dream into another. Then he really was awake. He reached for his phone on the nightstand and thumbed it to life. Almost eight o'clock. Pushing back the covers, he stood. The outer room of the suite was dim, the curtains black rectangles framed in light. He was making coffee when Judy came in and threw them open to the morning. The world fell away beneath them in a dazzling burst of radiance. Stockton stepped back, wincing.

"Are you okay?" Judy asked.

"Just tired," he said.

They spent the day lounging on a deck overlooking the pools. Judy was a glutton for the sun. Stockton endured it. He was ill at ease. Towers surrounded them on three sides, like a horseshoe open to the sea. Even when he forced himself to concentrate on his book, he felt their looming presence. He scanned their building, trying to locate the balcony of their suite. What if you fell? Surely someone had. He wondered what they'd thought about on the way down. Nothing, he supposed. Not for long anyway.

"Do you want a drink?" Judy asked him.

"Why not?" he said, heaving himself up.

There was a line at the Tiki Bar. While he waited, Stockton watched a poolside young woman in a pink bikini. The bathing suit was bright against her bronze skin. She stretched languorously and rolled onto her stomach. Their eyes met, or seemed to meet. Stockton was wearing sunglasses, and she wouldn't have noticed him anyway. The woman could not have been more than twenty-five. He was fifty-three—middle-aged, Judy would have said, which lie presumed a life span of 106. He might as well have been wallpaper. Still, he looked away, embarrassed.

"What can I get you, boss?" the bartender asked.

Stockton ordered a gin and tonic for himself, and a concoction involving five different flavours of rum for Judy. A Caribbean Cooler. He carried the cocktails back to their chairs.

Judy sampled her drink. "Wow. How much was this thing?"

"Fourteen dollars."

"We'll go broke."

"We can afford it."

They could. Stockton had worked in construction his entire life, framing houses as a teenager and later subbing out his own crew. He'd been twenty-five by the time he'd saved enough to take on a project of his own, building a spec house in an upscale development. He'd put everything on the line to cobble together the construction loan, a not inconsiderable risk for a young man two years married, with a baby on the way.

He sold the house and reinvested the profits. He had a steady hand in a crisis. He didn't mind taking chances. One thing had led to another. He had his own firm by the time he was thirty. Long after other men his age would have retired to the comforts of an air-conditioned office, Stockton still ran most of his business out of a battered Ford F-150. He wasn't averse to picking up a hammer himself. He took pride in the fact that he had the callused hands of the kid who'd framed houses to keep himself in beer money. He was rich. Two weeks of drinking fourteen-dollar cocktails in an ocean-front resort posed no financial challenge; he could have afforded six.

Stockton sipped his own drink. The bartender had been generous with the tonic. He didn't mind. Moderation in all things the doctor had said. This had not proved as difficult as Stockton had thought it would be. His appetites had waned since the heart attack. Food, drink, sex—he just wasn't as interested. Laurie, his daughter, attributed this to anxiety. She attributed everything to anxiety. The modern condition. Who wasn't anxious? Laurie was a therapist. Stockton didn't have much use for therapy, but he supposed she was right. So he was doing everything the doctor had told him to do. Even exercising. He was walking three miles a day now, increasing his pace and distance every week. He'd done his time on the treadmill that morning in the resort's fitness centre.

"Don't push yourself," Judy was always telling him.

But it was his nature to push himself. He hated the anxiety. What was the point in living if you weren't living? He resolved to moderate his moderation. A steak now and then wouldn't hurt. Or another gin and tonic, for that matter. He went to the Tiki Bar and fetched another round of drinks.

Judy put her hand on this thigh. "I swear this is all rum," she said. "You'll get me drunk."

Stockton forced a smile. "If I'm lucky."

They had another drink before dinner. They ate in the resort restaurant. Judy got the chicken Caesar salad. Stockton ordered the filet. They both had wine. After that, he felt looser, more like his old self. He held Judy's hand on the way back to the suite. Next week they would celebrate their thirtieth anniversary.

The elevator doors opened on the fifteenth floor.

Stockton was suddenly short of breath. His immediate thought was that he was having another heart attack. But that wasn't it. He was afraid. The alcohol seemed to have eroded some internal dike. That obscure impulse was clearer now. He felt himself drawn to the parapet. He clung to the wall of the gallery instead.

Inside the suite, Judy pulled the shades, blocking out the sky and the lights glowing in the neighbouring towers. He felt better then. Judy lifted her face to kiss him. She tasted of wine. He could feel the length of her body against his. He let himself be drawn into the bedroom.

It was no good, though. A disaster.

"Too much booze," he said.

Judy smiled. She pillowed her head on his shoulder. "We have tomorrow night," she said. "It doesn't matter, anyway. As long as we're together."

"Has anybody ever jumped from one of those balconies?" he asked the bartender at the Tiki Bar.

The bartender opened a fresh bottle of tonic water and poured tonic on top of Stockton's gin. He wore shorts and a T-shirt that said GYM, BEACH, REPEAT. He was a big guy, but he had the kind of muscles you got in the weight room. He probably wouldn't last a day pouring footers in the hot sun. It was two o'clock. Judy had driven over to the outlet mall after lunch. The heat was oppressive.

Stockton slid onto a stool.

The bartender dropped a wedge of lime into the drink, a red swizzle stick.

The air smelled of chlorine and salt. A blue-uniformed maintenance man stood nearby, spraying down the decking where someone had spilled a drink.

"What kind of question is that?" the bartender asked.

"Just a question."

The bartender shrugged. "Not in my time," he said. "I've been here for five years. I suppose I would have heard about it."

"I suppose," Stockton said. "Sometimes you wonder about things like that. Has anyone ever died in your room, that kind of thing."

"I don't know of anybody dying, either. Like I said, I would have heard."

"But you wouldn't say even if you had heard, would you?"

The bartender grinned. "Not if I wanted to keep my job, boss."

Which meant what exactly?

Stockton turned away, nodding at the maintenance man as he passed. He sat at a table with an umbrella, nursing his drink. The girl in the pink bikini was sunbathing by the pool below the North Tower. Stockton watched her from behind his sunglasses. She was easy to pick out. The clientele of the resort tended to run older. Most people her age gravitated to the hotels along the boardwalk. Or they were still getting their feet under them and couldn't afford OceanView. She reached into her bag for sunscreen and applied it with lazy efficiency. Stockton tried to generate some prurient interest in her. Maybe he would think of her when he made love to Judy that night. Maybe that would help.

He finished his drink, and thought about having another one.

He went up to the room instead. He had a bad moment on the gallery. As he stood fumbling in his wallet for his keycard, he felt himself drawn once again to the parapet. The impulse was irresistible. He gazed down at the crowns of the palm trees in the garden below.

He saw himself falling. He felt the wind rushing up to meet him. Vertiginous relief seized him, a wild exhilaration. He lurched to the door and let it slam behind him. Inside he drew the curtains and stood panting in the gloom.

He called Laurie and got routed to voicemail, hung up, called again.

This time she answered. "I only have a minute," she said. "Is something wrong?"

Stockton sighed. "Yes," he said. It was the wrong answer, he realised. She would think he'd had another heart attack. He said, "It's nothing, really. Nothing you need to worry about, anyway."

"You're not making any sense," she said.

"I shouldn't have—"

"Dad. Just tell me what it is."

He took a deep breath. He felt unmanned, like their roles had somehow been reversed, parent and child. "It's nothing," he said. "Really. It's just a little thing. I wanted to run it by you."

"Okay."

Another deep breath. "I'm feeling these impulses."

She was silent for a moment. "What kind of impulses?"

"Have you talked to your mother?"

"Dad—"

"Have you?"

"Yes."

"Did she tell you about the room?"

"She told me the view was incredible," Laurie said.

"Sure," Stockton said. "Fifteen stories. But here's the thing. Every time I get close to the balcony, I have this crazy impulse to jump."

To his surprise, Laurie laughed. "That's all?"

"That's a hell of a thing to say."

"It's normal, Dad. Everybody thinks about things like that. You stand in a high place, you think about jumping. You've just gotten fixated on it."

"I'm going to ask for another room," he said.

"Don't do that."

"Why not?"

"Running from it gives it power. It's like fear of flying," she said. "I have a client. I really do have to go. Don't worry about this, okay?"

"Okay," he said. "But listen, Laurie, don't tell your mother, okay?"

"Just between us," she said, ending the call.

Stockton put his phone away, thinking about Laurie's words. He forced himself to the windows and drew back the curtains. The sea ran on forever, glittering in the afternoon light. He touched the handle of the door to the balcony and tugged it open. A DJ had set up shop at the pool below the North Tower. He could hear the throb of the bass. He saw the young woman down there, or thought he did: bronze and pink, infinitely remote. She stood to pack up her stuff as he watched. Shouldering her bag, she looked up towards the South Tower, as though she'd caught him staring. He stood at the edge of the balcony, his hands clenched white-knuckled on the railing, until the girl disappeared in the shadows of the palms below him. He pushed himself away. Inside the suite, he fumbled for the phone on the end table, punched zero, and listened to it ring.

"Front desk. This is Tiffany. How can I help you?"

Stockton said, "I need another room."

"Is there something wrong with your room, sir?" Distant keys tapping. "Mr. Stockton?"

"Yes," he said. He said, "I'm—"

He bit back the word. Afraid. I'm afraid.

"Mr. Stockton?"

"It's nothing," he said.

"If there's a problem, I could send maintenance—"

"It's nothing," he said. "It's okay. Really."

Judy didn't get back until after five.

She called him from the car to ask him to meet her in the lot below the building. "I lost track of time," she said as they fetched her shopping bags upstairs. "Have you eaten?"

He had not.

After Judy showed him her purchases, they went down to the

restaurant. By the time they started back to the room, Stockton was feeling the wine. The elevator door slid back and the young woman from the pool stepped out. Up close, she was even more striking. She had a thick mass of auburn hair and high cheekbones, peppered with freckles. Her hazel eyes were cool and appraising. She wore a sleeveless white dress that fell to her thighs. Stockton let his gaze follow her as she slipped by.

There was something—

"Your tongue's hanging out," Judy whispered, not unkindly, as the doors closed.

"Too young for me," he said, kissing her behind the ear. "I like the vintage model."

She laughed and squeezed his hand.

He watched the floors light up as they went past: 11, 12, 14—

"Hunh," he said as the elevator rocked to a stop on 15. The doors rolled back. "There's no thirteenth floor."

"Nobody wants to stay on thirteen."

"The people on fourteen are screwed, I guess."

"I hope they're not the only ones," Judy said, drawing him out onto the gallery.

The air was clammy with humidity.

Stockton glanced into the void beyond the parapet. "Do you ever think about—"

"Do you have the keycard, Frank?"

Stockton put his back to the parapet. He dug the card out of his wallet and they went inside and closed the door and that dizzying abyss was behind them.

"Would you pour me a glass of wine?" Judy asked. She was pulling the drapes closed, shutting out the night—the lights of the towers and the pools below them and the black, heaving pelt of the sea.

Stockton took two glasses down from the cabinet. He retrieved a half-empty bottle of Chardonnay from the refrigerator, worked the cork lose, and poured. He was putting the bottle away when Judy came around the counter. He leaned against the stove.

"Toast?" she said.

"What are we toasting?"

"Thirty years next week," she said.

They clinked glasses, and drank. The wine was cool and bright, silky on his tongue. Stockton felt something ease inside him. He sighed. "Thirty years," he said, and suddenly Judy was serious. "You scared the hell out of me, Frank," she said.

"I scared you? When?"

"When you were sick," she said.

Stockton didn't want to talk about it. He hadn't been sick. When you were sick they didn't crack your chest open and rewire your heart. They gave you chicken soup and Tylenol and told you to get some rest. He should be dead. If Ed had not been so quick to make the call, if traffic had slowed the ambulance even a minute or two longer, he *would* be dead. You're a lucky man, the doctor had told him. You beat the odds.

"Let's not talk about it."

"We don't have to talk about it. It scared me, that's all. I couldn't stand to lose you."

"Me neither," he said, but the joke fell flat.

They were silent for a moment.

"Come on," Judy said.

Stockton switched off the light and followed her into the living area on the other side of the counter. They sat on the sofa in the dark and drank wine. He tried not to think about the windows at his back, but he couldn't help running the numbers in his head. He'd been in construction too long. It was natural. Say eleven feet per floor and multiply that by fourteen floors, because the builders had omitted lucky thirteen, and what you came up with was—what?—a hundred and fifty feet, give or take. 154. Half a football field. A long way down. He closed his eyes. Laurie had given him some tips to fight the anxiety. Tools, she called them. Use your tools. He deepened his breathing. In through the mouth, out through the nostrils, counting breaths. He felt marginally better.

"You okay?" Judy asked. She was always asking him if he was okay.

"I'm fine."

"What are you thinking about?"

"You," he said.

She elbowed him. "You're thinking about that woman in the elevator. I saw you looking at her the other day at the pool."

"No," Stockton said, but now he *was* thinking of her. Try not to think of something. He saw her exiting the elevator, her filmy dress white against her bronze thighs. So he was thinking of her, then— her high cheekbones, her hazel eyes. And later, as he made love to Judy, he found himself thinking of her again. He was thinking of her when he finished, and afterwards, as he lay sweating in the dark, feeling his heart thunder inside his chest and wondering when something was going to give way in there, some weakened artery, some inadequate repair, he was still thinking of her. Her eyes mainly. Those hazel eyes, taking his measure.

Judy ran her finger up the narrow scar that split his chest. "Frank," she said.

"Yeah?"

"Outside, when we were coming home from dinner. You were going to ask me something. What was it?"

"I don't know," he said. But he did.

He'd said, "Do you ever think about—"

And then she'd interrupted him, looking for the keycard. But now the phrase completed itself in his mind.

*Jumping.*

Do you ever think about jumping?

The question chased him down the rabbit hole into sleep.


Stockton woke from a dream of falling. He sat up abruptly, covers pooling in his lap. He was damp with sweat. He picked up his phone. Three o'clock. Late, then, or early. In either case, sleep was out of the question. He felt jittery in his bones. He supposed he could read for a while, or watch television, but what he really needed was a walk, something to shake out the nerves. He dressed in the darkness and let himself out of the apartment.

He stood at the parapet, helpless to resist. What would it be like to jump? How long before the fatal impact? Three seconds? Four? Not much time to think. And then a single excruciating instant of pain followed by... what? Where had he been after the heart attack? He remembered nothing but Ed telling him he looked a little green, then the nurse—

*—you should be dead—*

—staring down at him in the recovery room. And the interval between? No light, no tunnel, no relatives waiting to receive him. Not even black or void, because black or void implied an awareness to perceive them. These fragmentary thoughts and then he'd blipped out again. The next time he was awake, he was in a private room at the hospital. The face staring down at him had been Judy's.

"You're going to be okay," she said.

"What happened?"

"Your heart," she said. "You're lucky to be alive."

*Lucky.* Stockton wrenched himself back from the parapet. Made his way to the elevator. Downstairs, a briny wind swept in off the ocean. In the moonlight, the maintenance man from the bar was hosing sand off the wooden bridge over the dunes. Stockton nodded as he passed. On the ocean side, he kicked off his sandals and pushed them under the stairs. He crossed the sand and moved out along the edge of the water, the tide washing over his feet. He walked a quarter mile or so beyond the resort before he turned back. A figure stood on the beach, gazing out at the sea.

As he drew closer, Stockton recognised—or thought he recognised—the young woman from the elevator. It was hard to be sure, but the white dress looked familiar. The wind sculpted it to the curves of her body. Was it her?

She turned and started in his direction, striding with purpose.

Stockton angled across the sand to avoid her. The woman, too, changed course. Stockton walked faster. Anxiety pulsed in his chest. It didn't seem like a good idea, a chance encounter with a woman half his age out here on the beach in the middle of the night. Bad enough that he'd been staring at her for the last two days. She probably thought he was stalking her. He retrieved his shoes from their hiding place and climbed the stairs barefooted. On the bridge over the dunes, he glanced back, half-afraid that she would be coming up the steps behind him.

He didn't see her. Not on the steps, not on the beach.

Stockton stood there, puzzled.

"You should be more careful, sir. Nothing good happens on the beach after midnight."

It was the maintenance man—Keyes, according to the nametag pinned on his coveralls. Up close, he was gaunt and stubbled, pale. He'd put aside his hose to stand on the damp slats and stare out at the surf.

"Did you see her?"

Keyes had taken out a cigarette. He lit it and took a long drag. "Sure," he said.

"Where'd she go?"

"She's out there somewhere, I guess."

"What's that supposed to mean?"

"She's always around."

Stockton scanned the desolate beach. "What happened to her? She didn't have time to disappear like that."

Keyes shrugged.

"She didn't go into the water, did she? She could drown out there."

Keyes took a drag off his cigarette and blew out a flag of smoke. "She'll be all right."

"How do you know?" Stockton asked.

Keyes didn't answer.

*She must have gone into the water*, Stockton thought. "Maybe we should call someone."

Keyes grunted. He ground out his cigarette on the wooden railing. He tucked the butt away in a pocket of his coveralls. "Is that what you want to do, Mr. Stockton? A man your age out here in the middle of the night, a young lady like that?"

Stockton thought of Judy, nudging him in the elevator. *Your tongue's hanging out.*

"You go on up to your room," Keyes said. "You get yourself some sleep. That girl can take care of herself."

"But—"

"I got to finish hosing down this deck now."

"Okay, then," Stockton said.

At the base of the stairs he rinsed the sand off his feet, slid on his sandals, and pushed through the gate into the pool area. He rode the elevator up and stuck close to the wall as he traversed the gallery. Inside the apartment, he undressed and slipped into bed. He lay still in the darkness.

"Where've you been?" Judy said.

"Walking on the beach."

"At 3:00 in the morning?"

"Yes."

She didn't say anything for a while. He thought she'd fallen asleep.

"Not a very good idea," she said.

"No, I guess not."

"Something bothering you?"

"I don't think so."

"You don't think so?"

"No."

She waited him out.

He said, "I'm worried, I guess."

"About what?" And when he didn't answer: "The doctor fixed you, Frank. You're as good as new."

"You think?"

"I think. She said so, didn't she? Now go to sleep."

But sleep was a long time coming. Stockton couldn't get comfortable. Something was nagging at him, something odd. He couldn't say what it was.


It came to him the next morning:

Keyes had known his name.

Stockton pondered this over coffee. He'd gotten up late. Judy had long since left for the pool, but she'd thrown open the drapes in the main room before departing. Stockton had closed them, wincing at the shattering sunlight.

Now, he sat at the counter in the shadows, and tried to sort it out.

There was something dreamlike about the whole episode: the moon-washed beach, the young woman striding purposefully toward him. Where had she gone? And the maintenance man, Keyes. How had Keyes known him?

There must be a thousand guests or more at the resort. The odds that a maintenance man would know any one of them by name must be vanishingly small. The problem vexed Stockton. That and the flat certainty in the man's voice.

*She's always around.*

What was that supposed to mean?

Stockton drummed his fingers on the counter. He finished his coffee.

He dressed and went out onto the gallery, averting his eyes from the void beyond the parapet, resolute. That impulse moved within him, stronger now. He could feel it, a dread anticipation in his guts, a kind of longing. He was sweating by the time the elevator doors shut before him. They opened again on the seventh floor to admit a thin woman with two little girls, four or five years old, both of them clutching buckets of plastic beach toys. He realised he'd braced himself against the back wall, half-expecting the woman from the beach to step inside, dreading that as well.

He felt nauseated, dizzy, short of breath.

*Lucky.* He'd been lucky.

"Mommy, what's wrong with the man?"

The woman drew her children close, shushing them. She offered him a weak smile. Kids.

Then the doors slid open and she hurried them off towards the beach.

Stockton stood in the heat, gathering himself. He took air in and let it out through his nose, counting his breaths. He felt easier then, the tide of anxiety retreating.

He walked up between the buildings to the front desk, on the street side of the central tower. "I'm looking for a man who works in maintenance," he told the desk clerk. "Keyes."

"If there's something wrong with your room—"

"My room is fine," Stockton said. "I just need to speak with this one guy."

"And what was his name again?"

"Keyes."

The clerk's face was suddenly immobile, mask-like. "Let me get somebody who can help you," he said, picking up the phone.

Five minutes later, Stockton was being ushered into a private office by the property manager, a tall, blonde woman, maybe a decade his junior, who'd introduced herself as Parker Nelson. The room was luxurious and impersonal. Dark, glossy furniture and plush carpet, innocuous nature prints on the walls. Even the photo on the shelf behind the desk looked like a prop: a handsome man in a golf shirt, and a matching set of kids, male and female, eight or nine years old, as blonde as their mother. Stockton felt sweaty and ill at ease.

Nelson waved him to a chair by the desk. "What can I help you with, Mr. Stockton?" she asked, settling herself on the other side.

"I'd like to talk to one of your employees," he said. "His last name is Keyes. He works in maintenance."

"Is there something in your suite that requires attention?"

"No. It's him I want to talk to. Keyes."

Nelson pursed her lips. She tapped at her computer. "We don't have an employee named Keyes," she said. "Not in any department."

"I saw him. I talked to him. Out on the decking by the South Tower, on the bridge over the dunes."

"When?"

"Last night. It must have been 3:30, maybe 4:00. This morning, I mean."

"Are you sure his name was Keyes?"

"It was on his name tag."

"Maybe you misread it? It was dark."

"No."

She stared at him for a moment. "Is this some kind of joke, Mr. Stockton?"

"I don't understand."

"If it's a joke," she said, "it's in poor taste. If it's not—" She broke off.

It came to Stockton with the force of revelation: "He's dead, isn't he?"

"Is there anything else I can do for you, Mr. Stockton?"

A dismissal. Stockton got to his feet. "Thank you for your time," he said. "I'll see myself out."

He left the office and closed the door. The lobby was busy: a group of kids checking out shuffleboard equipment from the concierge, an ice cream social in the adjoining Seacrest Room. The modest business-centre next door—two desktop PCs and a printer—was empty. Stockton sat down at one of the computers and pulled up Chrome. He Googled *Keyes* and *OceanView Plantation*. Clicked on the *News* icon. It was the third hit down, an article from the local paper dated December 13th, three years ago:

MAINTENANCE MAN KILLED AT OCEANVIEW PLANTATION

Stockton scanned the neat paragraphs of text. The details were simple. An accident, a fatal fall from the roof of the South Tower. Recriminations from the family, carefully worded condolences from OceanView. And further down the page several more hits: a history of depression, a lawsuit, an out-of-court settlement and a non-disclosure clause. Then silence.

Stockton sat there for a long time, staring at the screen.

The ice cream social went on in the Seacrest Room. The concierge was on the phone.

Stockton stood up. The desk clerk busied himself at his computer.

Outside, the heat was breathtaking. Stockton went to find Judy.

But what could he say?

That he'd seen a ghost? Judy would think he was having her on. Frank. Her Frank, the epitome of rationality. He didn't believe in ghosts. He had misread the name tag. It had been late and he'd been strung out from lack of sleep. It was nothing.

He found her on the deck by the Tiki Bar. He sat facing her on the lounge she'd saved for him, and tried to frame the whole thing in his head in a way that made sense: the woman on the beach, his conversation with Keyes, the obscure impulse that he felt move within him. He opened his mouth to speak, closed it. What would Laurie say?

He was anxious, that's all. And no wonder. It had been a close call. He'd been lucky.

"I thought you were never coming down," Judy said.

"I slept late."

"I know. Up walking the beach at three in the morning. What were you thinking?"

Stockton shrugged. "I don't know," he said.

She smiled and patted his knee. "Well, you're here now. Is it too early for a drink?"

"We're on vacation."

"Just what I was thinking."

His muscle-bound friend was at the Tiki Bar. GYM, BEACH, REPEAT. "What can I get you, boss?"

Stockton ordered a Caribbean Cooler and a gin and tonic. He slid a twenty across the bar. "Go a little heavier on the gin, why don't you," he said. The bartender grinned and pocketed the bill. "Why not?" he said.

Stockton signed the slip and turned away.

Back at the lounge chairs, he handed Judy her drink. It was hot, and the cocktails went down easy. Stockton went back to the bar for another round and then another. He got ahead of Judy. The bartender had warmed up to him. He kept the pours generous and made casual conversation. Where was Stockton from and what did he do for a living? Was this his first visit to OceanView? Stockton grew looser. He thought about his encounter with Keyes. The whole thing seemed faintly ridiculous, even embarrassing. Maybe he *had* misread the name.

Stockton looked for the woman in the pink bikini. He finally spotted her down on the far end of the pool below the North Tower. She lay still in the sun, her head angled towards him. She might have been staring at him from behind her dark glasses. She might have been sleeping. More likely, she was entirely oblivious. What was he to her?

Yet she had turned towards him on the beach, as if to intercept him.

He finished his drink and heaved himself out of his lounge chair, unsteady on his feet. He looked at Judy. "You ready for another?"

"I'm fine," Judy said. "Maybe we should go up."

"One more."

At the Tiki Bar, GYM, BEACH, REPEAT said, "Listen, boss, you sure you—"

Stockton slid another twenty across the bar. He watched the bartender mix the drink, signed the slip, turned away. The woman at the far end of the pool was gone. When he got back to the lounge chairs, Judy was packing up. She studied him critically. "Time to get you upstairs," she said. Sipping his drink, he let her lead him to the elevator. The door was sliding closed when the woman in the pink bikini slipped in.

Judy frowned. "What floor?" she asked.

The woman leaned over to punch the button for sixteen. As she stepped back she brushed past Stockton. She pushed her sunglasses up onto her head and glanced over at him. There was something familiar in her hazel eyes. She held his gaze. Stockton looked away. He studied his feet. He thought of the parapet, that impulse moving within him. The elevator lurched higher.

They rode up in silence.

He recalled her on the beach, changing course to intercept him, the way he'd forced himself to walk faster, the anxiety pulsing in his chest.

The elevator stopped at fifteen.

The doors opened.

As he stepped out, Stockton risked another glance at her. She stared back, unblinking.

The doors shut, and it was like a tense line snapping. Stockton drank off the gin. He wanted to keep drinking. He could drink all night. He stood at the parapet and gazed down into the garden far below.

"Come on, Frank," Judy said. "You've had too much gin. You'll fall over if you're not careful."

He stepped back and followed her to the suite.

Inside, he poured a glass of Chardonnay. "Wine?" he asked.

"Not right now. We need to get some food in your stomach."

She opened the curtains and went back into the kitchen. He watched her from the counter. She put in a pork tenderloin to bake and made a salad. Stockton poured himself another glass of wine.

"How much are you planning to drink?" She was cleaning broccoli to steam.

"Have you ever seen a ghost, Judy?"

She looked up. "No, and neither have you."

"I don't remember the heart attack," Stockton said. "One minute I'm getting out of the truck, the next I'm coming out of surgery. I don't remember anything in between."

She sliced the floret off a stalk of broccoli. "You don't remember when you're asleep, either."

"You remember your dreams."

"You were under anaesthesia." She sliced the head off another stalk, the blade snapping hard on the plastic cutting board. Then another stalk. And another.

"Not in the ambulance," he said.

The blade jumped off the cutting board, came down on the next stalk, and took a layer of flesh off her knuckle, thin as the filmy husk of an onion. She threw the knife clattering into the sink. She brought the wounded finger to her mouth. "You're drunk," she said. "I was dead," he told her, and she stormed out of the kitchen. She slammed the bedroom door behind her.

Sighing, Stockton turned off the oven.

He emptied his wine glass and retrieved the bottle from the refrigerator. Holding it by the neck, he walked to the balcony door and stood looking out. Twilight had fallen. The sea was calm. Small rollers broke upon the sand. Someone was flying a kite down by the water. It snapped and turned in the wind before him.

Stockton refilled his glass and placed the sweating bottle on the coffee table.

He sat on the sofa, and looked out over the balcony to the horizon. He didn't know how long he sat there. The sky grew dark. He splashed more wine into his glass. The young woman cut across the sand to meet him. When he dozed off, she followed him down into his dreams.

The nurse leaned over him.

"You should be dead," she told him, and he woke into the silence of deep night.

Stockton clambered to his feet, bewildered. The room tilted, as though the earth had slipped on its axis. Then he was okay. Unsteady, but okay. He drained the wine bottle and set it back on the table. He felt drawn to the balcony. He put his hand on the door handle and pulled, the glass whispering in its track. He stepped outside, into the humid night air. The moon cast a pale streak across the black water. Below him glittered bright pools, garlanded with palm trees. Curling his hands around the railing, he hoisted himself up and over and clung there on the narrow lip of concrete.

The ocean heaved in the dark.

Here it was, then, the crescendo everything had been hurtling towards since he'd opened his eyes in the recovery room. It felt like a circle closing, ineluctable, true, as though he had no choice in the matter, as though he'd been driven to it, or summoned. Now he would unclench his hands, now he would push himself out into the night. He saw the black earth lurching towards him, the pools, the trees—

From the doorway, Judy said, "Frank, baby, please—"

Stockton clutched at the railing. His hand slipped. The building pitched and yawed. Blank terror seized him. And then he had it, he was stable again, and all the world spread out below him. The resort was an island of light in a dark sea that ran out to the horizon, illimitable.

"Frank," Judy said. "Frank, baby, please. Come back to me now. You don't have to do this. Why would you do this? Why would you leave me, baby? Why would you do that?"

She stepped out onto the balcony.

Wind swept in off the ocean. It tugged at him, rippling his clothes, calling out to him, all that dark and void. And Judy. Enjoining him to stay.

Stockton hung there in fine equipoise, balanced on the knife-edge of the moment. There was nothing else and had not ever been or would be, just this fleeting instant of time.

"Frank," Judy said.

And then he was pulling himself up and over, onto the balcony. He went to his knees. Judy knelt to take him into her arms.

"It's okay," she said. "You're okay now."

Stockton was weeping.

They didn't sleep until nearly dawn, and when they woke neither of them spoke of what had happened in the night. They moved carefully around one another and talked quietly about small matters. Stockton's close call on the balcony lay under these surface trivialities like a chasm. To broach it would be to admit how perilous was their position on the brink of the abyss. A time would come when they would have to hash it out, Stockton knew. He supposed he would have to consult someone about it—Judy would insist, and Laurie would be happy, even gratified, to give him a name. But for the present anyway, they acknowledged it no further than in their tacit agreement that it was time to go home.

Judy supervised while the bellman loaded the luggage into the car. Stockton went inside to check out. The same clerk stood behind the desk, professionally courteous. There was something in his voice. He didn't make eye contact, just pushed a sheet of paper across the counter. Sign here, initial this, date that. Stockton didn't bother with the small print, just scrawled his name on the line, dated it, and handed it back.

Done.

Stockton turned away, searching for the men's room.

He found it down the corridor from Parker Nelson's office. Inside, everything was gleaming and clean, the mirror and the countertops, the white towels in their baskets by the sinks. Somewhere an unseen atomiser murmured, releasing into the room a subtle fragrance of oranges. Stockton stepped up to the urinal. Finished, he leaned over the vanity to wash his hands. He was tossing the towel into the bin when someone came in and slipped by at his back. Stockton moved to the door. His hand was on the push plate when—

"Mr. Stockton."

Stockton paused. He took a deep breath.

Somewhere far away the atomiser hissed, releasing another burst of citrus spray.

There was a white roaring in his ears.

You don't have to look back, he told himself. You can push through the door and into the hallway beyond. Walk out through the lobby into the bright afternoon. Judy will have the car idling. It will be cool inside and you can pull away from this place forever, tyres humming on the asphalt. You never have to look back again. This is all behind you now. This is all behind you.

"Mr. Stockton."

Against his will, as if some force compelled him, Stockton turned.

Keyes stood there, so close that a single step would have closed the distance between them. He was gaunt and tall. His eyes were dark wells.

"This is over," Stockton said, "this thing between us. Between the three of us."

"Is it?" Keyes said, and Stockton shouldered through the door, that white roaring in his ears—out through the lobby and past the desk clerk busy at his station, out, out, into the blistering heat.

# SIMON STRANTZAS

## ANTRIPUU

SIMON STRANTZAS lives with his wife in Toronto, Canada. He is the author of five collections of short fiction, including *Nothing is Everything* from Undertow Publications, and editor of a number of anthologies, including *Year's Best Weird Fiction Vol. 3* and the award-winning *Aickman's Heirs*.

Strantzas' fiction has appeared in numerous annual "Best of" anthologies, and in publications such as *Nightmare*, *The Dark* and *Cemetery Dance Magazine*. He has been a finalist for four Shirley Jackson Awards, two British Fantasy Awards and the World Fantasy Award.

"'Antripuu' came together primarily because I wanted to actually tell a horror story," he recalls. "Most of my work is focused on events that are strange or weird or eerie, and not so much on events that are frightening. So I thought perhaps it was about time to change that. Perhaps it was time to scare. And what's scarier than being lost in the woods?

"In the woods we're in touch with nature in a primal way, one that reminds us that we are insignificant and not in control. I wanted to tap into that sense of 'cosmicism without the cosmic' to tell a story that makes people remember that aeons ago our ancestors weren't predators. We were prey."

*✑*

THERE ARE FOUR of us left huddled in the cabin: me, Jerry, Carina and Kyle. And we're terrified the door won't hold. Carina shivers so uncontrollably, her teeth sound like stones rattling down a metal chute. Kyle begs her to quiet down.

But her teeth aren't making enough noise to matter. Not compared to the howling storm. It comes in gusts that build in slow waves, rhythmically increasing in both volume and strength until a gale overtakes the cabin, pelting the windows with hard rain. A cold draught pushes past us while we tremble on the floor, wishing we were any place else.

Still, the draught's not the issue. It sneaks beneath doors and crawls down the chimney, and these are things we may not like, but we expect. It isn't the storm that bothers us, despite its deep-throated howls and the way it screeches around the corners. The problem, instead, is what's beneath the storm, mimicking the howls of the storm, trying to coax us into opening the door and letting it in.

The others are quickly losing hope we're going to survive this.

Not me. I lost hope a long time ago.

Kyle, Jerry and I have travelled up north together, three former workmates who still get along. Kyle, tall and lean, with a confidence born from getting everything he wants without much difficulty; Jerry, his opposite in a way, trying maybe too hard to remain detached from life's upsets. But both are good people, and I need to surround myself with good people. I meet so few of them.

It was Kyle who suggested we hike through Iceteau Forest for a week. Collectively we've spent too many nights in downtown bars and pubs, and he thought time outdoors would do us good. I suspect, though, it was his and Jerry's plan to get me outside my head for a while. Give me something distracting to do, some good stories to focus on for a change. Since all three of us left the socket company, I haven't landed on my feet the way the two of them have, and I know they're worried.

The trip to Iceteau was long, mostly sunny and pleasant. The forecast promised long warm days and short cool nights in that brief window between the rise of the mosquitoes and the fall of the black flies. The perfect time to hike into the woods, Kyle said, and when we left our car at the side of the road I felt buoyed enough to wonder if I'd ever want to return to it. Maybe we'd leave that life behind and start anew, become one with the grass and bushes and trees. But it was clearly a dream; my desire to give up and do nothing resurfaced quickly once we started walking.

The good weather didn't last long. No more than a day; long enough for us to hike too far to make turning back reasonable. As the storm commenced, we rooted through our backpacks for our waterproof shells and trudged through the deepening mud and the increasingly heavy downpour. After a while, the white noise multiplied on itself, becoming as deafening as it was maddening, as though it were trying to prove something to me: that no matter where or how far I went, my misery would always follow.

Maybe that misery was why I didn't notice it. Maybe being unhappy makes it harder to speak. I know the longer we walked through the mud, the less we wanted to talk to one another. Misery loves company, but the miserable just want to be left alone. The wind was hot and drove the rain against the sides of our drawn hoods, creating an impenetrable racket, loud enough to cause hallucinations. Kyle did his best to convince us the storm was abnormal and temporary; that it would be sunny again soon. It sounded like just another story to me.

We hiked single file, picking our way between tall old trees. Kyle led the way, Jerry close behind, but I couldn't keep up with their strides. The mud was too thick, and sucked my boots down no matter how many stones I stepped on. Wet leaves clung to me, their weight slowly building. I heard only my panting breath over the rain, interrupted by the scratching of low hanging branches against my hood, and I saw only the grey of heavy sheets of rain. With each deaf and blind stumble forward I sensed something was wrong, and that sense quickly turned to fear; cold, irrational, debilitating fear.

I kept quiet, told myself the story that everything was fine. That it was only my depression rearing up. But when I peered ahead I saw the shimmer of movement, like some giant thing unfurling. I screamed and Jerry spun, but I knew he saw nothing. Even Kyle asked what was wrong. I was dumb, unable to do anything more than point. The two followed my hand, saw what had until then been camouflaged by old trees.

The thing had to be twenty feet tall, yet couldn't have been more than a hand's breadth wide. Its limbs were thin and elongated as a stick insect, except an insect that towered over us on two narrow legs, and instead of a head there was nothing.

There was nothing.

Just a mouth, too wide, lined with a dozen rows of tiny sharp teeth embedded in undulating flesh. It reached towards us with one of those long creaking arms and only Kyle had the wherewithal to move. He yanked me and Jerry back, breaking the spell of disbelief and terror that had enthralled us.

I chased after Kyle; Jerry behind me where I couldn't see him, but I could hear his boots throwing themselves frantically into the mud. The howling wind grew louder around us, as though the storm were strengthening, yet the rain didn't fall heavier, the sky didn't grow darker: whatever caused that noise was not the wind; it was merely pretending to be the wind.

We scrambled through the downpour, chased by the sound of trees being uprooted and tossed aside. Jerry shouted hysterical gibberish, but I heard nothing from Kyle. Both their reactions were frightening, but I couldn't allow myself to succumb to the fear. I had to concentrate on escape.

Sighting the cabin was more blind luck than anything else. Kyle saw it first, pivoting mid-stride towards the ramshackle structure. I followed without thought, Jerry close behind. I prayed the door would be unlocked.

Kyle stumbled ahead of me, just avoiding the black iron rod driven into the ground. He reached the cabin a few steps before me and wrenched open the door. I dived in, followed close by Jerry and Kyle. They tripped over themselves, tumbling into a heap on the floor, and I scrambled to slam the door shut against that twig creature and its horrifying, undulating teeth. The three of us then froze in place—me curled against the door, Jerry and Kyle tangled in one another's arms—and we stared at the cabin's buckling walls, its trembling windows, waiting for the defences to inevitably fail. But they didn't. Not when the storm howled louder, not when the cabin rattled with anger. I didn't understand why, but I also didn't understand any of what was happening. The swelling of wind and rain against the cabin eventually subsided, and we three instinctively knew that whatever that half-seen thing between the trees was, it had retreated back into the woods to wait for us. Kyle and Jerry hoped, for the moment, we might be out of danger. I didn't share their hope.

The two disentangled themselves from one another and stood. I thought Jerry might be crying but didn't want to ask. I was worried the truth might cause me to do the same. But the whimpering wasn't coming from any of us. It came from behind the closed door of a rear bedroom. It was Kyle who decided to open it despite my protests, and Jerry who stood close with a wooden chair held over his shoulder as a makeshift weapon. I stayed back and waited for whatever they were letting free to kill us.

And Carina and Weston behind the door waited for the same. We found them kneeling on the floor, clutching one another in fear. Carina's eyes were pressed closed as she repeated "*Antripuu*" below her breath. Tears streamed over her quivering lips. She screamed when Kyle touched her shoulder, awakening her from whatever refuge she'd retreated into during the storm's onslaught.

Carina was petite with dark hair that matched her dark, harried eyes, while Weston was tall, blond, with a football player's shoulders. We found out they'd been hiking in the woods as well, and like us they'd become lost in the unexpected storm when their compass failed to steer them out of it. They were in the midst of staking their small tent when the wind took it and lodged it in the trees. Then one of those trees proceeded to eat that tent.

Carina knew what she'd seen even if Weston didn't. And what she was still seeing whenever she closed her eyes. *Antripuu*.

It was the name she'd said earlier, though she denied it. None of us knew what it was, and Carina didn't want to talk about it. She would only say the sight of it sent her and Weston running, their gear left behind in the forest to rust and rot.

The five of us sat in a circle, Carina and Weston on the couch, Jerry on a small stool he dragged over, and Kyle and I on the floor. I had tried to light a fire earlier, but the stove wouldn't open and even if it had, seeping water had already made the pit an ashy swamp. No one said anything for a long time. We just listened to the howling and the rain as it ebbed and flowed. Every so often one of us would startle, certain we saw something at the window, but it turned out to be nothing.

When all that was left was darkness, I thought we should sleep in that rear room, hidden and protected, but Kyle wouldn't entertain it. He did not want us to give in to the fear. I didn't know how to tell him I already had, a long time ago. Nevertheless, I sat in the front with the rest, sharing my sleeping bag with Jerry so Carina and Weston could use his. I was so exhausted from the hike and the subsequent terror that even my anxiety couldn't keep me from sleeping until morning.

When I woke, there was still no sun, but the black had given way to dark, drab grey. I felt the opposite of rested as I struggled out of my shared sleeping bag. Carina was already up, looking out the window at the half-dozen black metal rods planted in the ground and encircling the cabin. Each had a chain leading from the top into the mud. I asked if they were what was left of a fence, to which she shrugged. Then I asked her if they had something to do with *Antripuu*. She shuddered.

An *Antripuu* was a spirit, she whispered. A forest elemental her grandmother had told her about. But it wasn't real, she said. It was just a story from the old country. What did the *Antripuu* want, I asked, but Carina wouldn't answer.

Kyle woke then, but I suspect he'd been pretending to sleep while listening to us because he rose unmoored. We didn't repeat anything and he didn't ask. All he did was sit quietly with his face in his hands. When Jerry woke, he looked at the three of us, and moaned.

Only Weston appeared inured to the storm, emerging from the room chipper and relaxed. He decreed the night before an aberration, a shared delusion that leapt from him and Carina to the rest of us, or vice versa. Despite our arguments he assured us that we hadn't seen anything but the storm playing tricks on us, but now the storm had weakened. It was already getting brighter, he claimed, though it seemed no different to me. He laughed then, maniacally, as though in the grip of depression or delusion. I was understandably concerned.

He suddenly announced he was leaving. We urged him to reconsider, but he was decided, and even Carina's pleas would not deter him. Weston assured us that once he reached a park ranger or some authority in Iceteau Forest, he'd report what happened and insist on our rescue. We told him again it was too dangerous, but he asked about our alternate plan. Was it to stay hidden until we starved to death? None of us knew how to respond. We looked to Kyle and, after a moment, he acquiesced. Weston was right: someone had to go.

With great trepidation we unlocked the door and he stepped out, invigorated by his imminent escape from captivity. Clouds hung overhead, heavy and potent, while mist had risen from the ground to mirror them. Weston kissed Carina, and shook hands with me, Kyle and Jerry, and again told us not to worry, and that he would see us soon. We stood in the doorway and watched him walk off with the pack we'd assembled for him, following the makeshift path towards the trees. He whistled something jaunty as he passed the black iron rods, the sort of tune one might whistle on an invigorating summer's walk. When he was almost at the trees he stopped and turned to wave at us, and from the mist behind him rose the *Antripuu*.

We screamed, but I don't know if there was time to hear us. A roar like howling wind, and Weston was up in the air and gone. Swallowed whole in a single motion.

I came to my senses inside the locked cabin while around me Carina was trembling and Jerry sobbing. That was when I understood how bad things had gone. Once the *Antripuu* appeared, Kyle had dragged us inside before we were noticed, but now he stood at the window stone-faced, watching the day increasingly darken. It was too early for night's approach, so it had to be clouds gathering, blocking the remaining day while lightning flashed and thunder jolted the ground. We looked at one another, then crawled and shuffled towards the middle of the floor and huddled together as a deluge of rain hammered the cabin. When the wind returned, in volume and in force, howling as it had the day and night prior, I was tempted to surrender and follow Weston out the door.

I couldn't take it anymore. I couldn't do it.

That was when Carina slapped me across my face so hard I tasted blood for the next hour. But at least my head was screwed back on right.

We won't escape the forest. That was clear the moment Weston was devoured. Our car is days away, and Carina doesn't know where she and Weston left theirs. Even if she did, he carried the keys. We will not be rescued, we will not get away. Which means there is no consequence to anything we do. Nothing could be worse than what already awaits us.

So we spend the night arguing what we should try and when. Jerry wants to wait the storm out, but I don't think that will stop the *Antripuu*. Carina called it a storm-bringer, and as long as it stays, so will the rain and wind. Like Weston said, there isn't enough food to hold us long. We pile it in the middle of the floor and there's no more than a day's worth. We could ration, but the more we stretch it out the hungrier and weaker we'll be, and we need our strength. It seems so impossibly insurmountable, but Kyle forces us to press on. It takes him until dawn, but he rallies us. Even with the sound of the storm outside, even with the flashes of lightning, and of the *Antripuu* circling, he tells us we can make it, that we can survive. We just need to stick together and stick to the plan.

Once we lose hope, he says, we're dead.

It's a good story. I'm not sure I believe him, but I want to.

We distract ourselves from the howling by sharing bits of ourselves. I learn things about Jerry and Kyle I never knew, like how when Jerry was eight he lost his father in a bar fight, and how Kyle never graduated high school and got his GED much later. And I learn things about Carina. I learn that she and Weston met at a peace rally only a few months ago. I learn that she's struggled with anxiety for most of her life, and her medication was a godsend. I learn she'd wanted to be a poet, but ended up selling pharmaceuticals because of how much more money she makes. And I learn that she is terrified of the *Antripuu* and desperately wants everything to be over. That revelation, if it can be called one, brings a sombre air to our night, and we get down to business planning what we'll do once the day returns.

If it returns.

Our plan is not complicated. It can't be, because we have nothing. There is no fighting back. There is running, and there is dying. The only hope we have is seeing the *Antripuu* before it sees us. We will walk in a cluster, a set of eyes in each direction, and head for our car. Kyle will be our point person, the leader, the one we follow if we have to run. We dress him in all the red clothing we collectively have so he will stand out. Be unmissable in the rain, between the trees. If the *Antripuu* appears, Kyle will run, and we will follow him like a beacon. It's a terrible plan, but it's all we have.

We leave as soon as the sky has turned from black to grey. It's the hardest moment of our escape, when we most question our judgement. For me, the second-guessing is nothing new, but for Kyle, it must be strange to not be sure of something. It takes our cluster some time to find our rhythm, and we worry with each stumble or falter that the *Antripuu* is readying to strike. But it doesn't, and we are in step by the time we reach the black iron rods.

We don't stop long enough to inspect them, but in the morning light I see they are not the remnants of a fallen fence. The chains are not linked together, but instead to metal collars partially sunk into the ground. Poking through the water-logged mud are yellowed bones, and I shift my eyes away, not wanting to think about why the animals were chained. Or if they were animals at all.

I hear only rain pelting my shell and the howling wind. I concentrate on the trees, scanning for the *Antripuu*. There isn't energy left to speak, and if the others do, the din is too great to hear. It doesn't take me long to conclude we're fools, and that we should turn back. Out in the storm, with that thing stalking us from behind the branches, my anxiety coils tight and threatens to explode. I can't imagine how Carina is faring. I feel her trembling beside me. I want to tell her the only way through is to ignore the fear, push it down and forget it exists, but I can't help her. I can't help anyone. I'm on the cusp of losing everything, and I don't know how to stop it.

The four of us move as a unit through the pouring rain. Jerry is surprised the tree canopy doesn't better protect us, but it's clear the trees have given up. Alone in the middle of Iceteau Forest, insignificant and alone, I wonder if they're any different from me.

It's as though my every suspicion about the world has been proven true. There is something out there that wants to destroy me. I haven't been imagining it. No job, no partner, no prospects for either; watching my friends excel while I fail repeatedly. Until now I assured myself I was wrong and things would get better, but now that I'm trapped in this downpour, surrounded by deafening winds and stalked by a creature who craves my destruction, it's become clear I'm right where I belong.

The screaming is sudden, but I don't know from whom or where— the sound is sliced by the savage winds and rain. Kyle is already a red blur bounding ahead through the storm, and I am running before I'm aware I'm doing so. I don't turn to look for the *Antripuu*. I don't turn to look for Jerry or Carina, either. I just pray I'm running fast enough. The mud tries to slow me but I defy it, hurtling over logs and debris. Kyle's red clothing slips in and out of sight as he moves between the trees, looking for the swiftest path to safety. The forest spins, my vision confused and disrupted in a perpetual state of vertiginous mayhem. Then, at some point, I realise I am still running but the red blur ahead of me is gone.

I cannot panic. I will not panic. I keep running straight, hoping to catch another glimpse of Kyle and his red clothing, or of anybody at all. At least anybody real, anybody who is not a mirage of streaming water and shadowy branches, a ghost from my past skittering in the spaces between the trees. Repeatedly, I see an illusion of the *Antripuu* hovering overhead, but I don't stop running as hard as I can. I run until I can't do it anymore, until the adrenaline boost wears off and I find myself staggering through the woods, nearly falling over every root or upturned stone. When I can't go on, I throw myself into the mud behind a tree and wait for whatever is coming.

It's only when I've stopped that my body demands more breath. My limbs rattle and my digits spark as I try to get myself under control. I will not think about the others. I won't. I close my eyes and listen for the howl of the *Antripuu*, but if it's there it's hidden behind the static of rain on the leaves.

I hold no hope I'll see anyone again. Not Jerry, not Carina, not Kyle. I could call out their names, but I don't have enough breath to pretend. The *Antripuu* has found them. I am utterly alone.

We did not plan for this. I have only the vaguest notion of where the car might be, but I start moving nonetheless. Without hope, there is nothing left but the illusion of hope. The treetops above creak and bend, but I do not see the *Antripuu* looming amongst them. I take a hesitant step into the open, then another, and still there is nothing.

As I move through Iceteau Forest, my equipment, food, and friends gone, I question why this happening, what I've done to cause it. The thought consumes me as I watch the trees, hoping I'm still moving towards the road. Towards the car. Towards escape and salvation.

I catch sight of red again between the trunks ahead, the briefest glimpse of Kyle. I yell despite it being impossible for him to hear me through the rain, and he stops. I stop as well. I can make out a red blur through the haze, waiting for me to catch up, and for the first time I feel hope. Kyle has survived. And if he's survived, the others have survived as well.

They have to have. They have to.

I squint, hand on my brow to keep the streaming rivulets out of my eyes, but I can't see any sign of them. They're not behind me, either. But maybe, I hope, they found their way past me when I became lost. Maybe they're up ahead. I turn back, calling out to Kyle to tell him I'm coming, but he's gone; the red blur is gone.

I run forwards, screaming his name despite my breathlessness, each footfall a jarring thud in my ears. The trees ahead cluster tighter, their branches springing lower to the ground, and the mesh of twigs and leaves scrape my skin. I raise my hands to protect my face, sacrificing them to the long scratches and tears. Everything in Iceteau Forest is hungry for my blood.

When the lattice of branches suddenly opens, I'm spit out over an unexpected ravine, and I spin and flail over the edge. I don't remember the fall, only coming to my muddled senses sitting waist-deep in rushing water, staring up at the narrow opening too far above my head to reach. Dazed and bruised, my head buzzing, I raise my aching hand and it's clear my arm is broken. It's much too thin, and flexing it feels like someone slowly pushing a dull knife into my flesh. I cough and everything hurts.

In the gap above there is a glimpse of movement, a momentary red blur. It's Kyle. He's found me. I see his arm stretch over the side for me and I'm elated. I call up through the rain as I reach to take his hand. My ringing head, though, keeps insisting something is wrong, something I'm not seeing, but I can't focus on what, not until my fingers graze Kyle's overlong arm and I jerk my hand away.

The *Antripuu*'s body resolves between the drops of rain, standing astride the chasm's opening, its unhinged mouth grinding against the crevasse's opening—too wide to fit through, but wide enough to show me the row after row of undulating flesh and teeth within. I smell its foetid breath, the odour compounded and worsened by the rain, and I slide my broken body down farther out of reach until all but my head is submerged in the water.

The *Antripuu*, frustrated, struggles against the solid rock, stretching its long spindle arms to snatch at me. I can see the tattered remains of the clothing we'd given poor Kyle tangled around its knotted limbs, and the sight unleashes the anger and frustration I've been carrying much longer than I've been in Iceteau Forest.

I scream at the *Antripuu* to leave me alone, to ask it what I've done that's so horrible, so absolutely vile as to deserve this, any of this. What have I done to deserve having my only friends taken from me? To deserve losing everything I've ever loved? My home? My career? My sense of self? What have I done that's so awful that my dreams should fail, that any promise I ever had should wither away? What have I done to deserve sitting here, alone, deep in water and muck, pounded by rain so heavy it's like rocks, chased by a spirit or a god or figment of my imagination until my body is destroyed and I have no choice left but to curl up and die? What have I done that is so bad that I deserve this life?

The *Antripuu* doesn't have the answer. All it has is a howl like a thunderstorm, and a hunger to consume me.

Hopeless, broken, and alone, I wonder why I even bother to fight.

The voice beneath the howls is a mirage. It must be. Small and pitched barely above the *Antripuu's* roar and the ringing echoing in my head, it can't be ignored, even as I focus my attention on the creature pacing above and wonder how much longer I can hold on. The voice sharpens, grows insistent, and needles into my thoughts, forcing me to turn my head, to take my eyes off the *Antripuu*. On the edge of the ravine's crevasse a short distance away, dishevelled and panicked and skittish, is someone it takes a moment to realise is Carina.

Through the heavy storm and my concussion I see her eyes are wide and fearful as she watches the *Antripuu*. If it sees her, it's too busy grappling with how to best reach me to care. She creeps near enough to ask if I'm able to move. I tell her I'm not sure. She tells me I must.

I wait until the *Antripuu* steps away from the crevasse in search of a solution. First I try to straighten my bent knee stuck in the ravine's muddy bottom. It's painful and exhausting, but I manage to free it, and immediately the rushing water carries me forwards. I use my one good arm and the drag of my legs to slow myself before submerged debris tears me open. Carina races along the bank to keep me in sight while I try to remain as silent and as invisible as possible.

The *Antripuu* returns to the place I was shortly after I've gone—I can see it through the widening opening of the crevasse—circling the spot it last saw me, frustrated and confused, and I almost feel... no, I don't feel anything. I'm numb to everything but my throbbing pain. Carina's harried face appears periodically, peeking over the edge of the ravine, urging me on.

The ravine's banks eventually slope downwards; the eight-foot banks become six foot, then four, then only one, low enough that Carina can wade into the ravine and grab my battered and exhausted body before I float away. She manages to drag me from the water and onto the bank where I lie on my back and let the rain shower my face. Staring into the churning, clouded sky, my body continues to feel as though it's floating, and I wonder if any of this is real, if I'm not actually still in the ravine, swept away by the current. Why else would the rain on my face taper in force, like a storm in its final throes?

Carina says we have to go. The rain may have weakened, but we're not safe. She helps me roll over, then get my knees under me. My joints are swollen and bruised, and even with her help standing seems impossible, but I'm able to move enough that we can get out of the open. I still hear the howling wind, but it sounds further away. Like distant thunder.

We take refuge in the fringes of the tree line, where Carina helps me splint my arm and wrap my wounds. I want to ask her about Jerry, but I know the answer. It's already written on her distraught face. But there's something else there, too, a perseverance that illuminates from beneath the scrapes and dirt and keeps me from losing hope. Once you lose hope, you're dead. I remember Kyle saying that, and it's never seemed truer. Once you lose hope, you're dead.

As soon as I'm able, Carina and I stumble through Iceteau Forest, taking care to study the trees, to listen to the winds, but the rain gently peters out and the wind dies down the farther we walk, which tells me we're moving in the right direction, away from this horrible nightmare. I don't know how far the road is from us. I just know it's somewhere ahead. I hope when we find it the car will be right there, right where Kyle, Jerry and I left it, but it seems impossible. Iceteau Forest is so large, so deep, that the car could be anywhere along the road, or maybe even nowhere. Maybe Jerry and Kyle made it past the *Antripuu* and reached the car first. Maybe they're driving back and forth looking for Carina and me. Or maybe they've left to find help. Or maybe the car will be sitting behind a curve somewhere along the road, somewhere out of our sight, and will remain there until it eventually rusts away.

I don't know what we'll find when we get to the road. It could be anything, or it could be nothing. But the sun is already starting to peek through the drizzling clouds, and my banged-up knees are starting to hurt less. Carina has been telling me stories about the old country and what it was like for her grandmother there. She tells me she loved hearing those stories growing up, and I'm starting to understand why. A good story can make you forget about the bad stories, even if the bad stories are all you want to believe. All you've ever told yourself. And sometimes you have to choose to believe the good stories, even when it feels like there's no choice at all.

I've almost forgotten all the bad stories I know as Carina helps me limp through the trees. I think I hear the sound of a car engine somewhere in the distance. Or maybe it's the roar of wind echoing through the forest. It's difficult for me to be sure.

All I can do is hope.

# KRISTI DeMEESTER

# A CROWN OF LEAVES

**K**RISTI DeMEESTER is the author of the novels *Such a Pretty Smile* (St. Martin's Press) and *Beneath* (Word Horde Publications), and the short fiction collection *Everything That's Underneath* (Apex Books). Her short fiction has appeared in *Best New Horror, The Best Horror of the Year, Year's Best Weird Fiction, Pseudopod, Black Static, The Dark* and other publications.

In her spare time, she alternates between telling people how to pronounce her last name and how to spell her first.

"This story sprang to life because I wanted to write about sisters and perception," recalls the author. "How memory can be clouded and subvert itself, especially in childhood. And witches and trees. Always witches and trees."

**M**ARIBEL HAS THE radio cranked all the way up when we finally turn off the interstate and onto the road that will carry us back to the house where we grew up. Some blues and folk channel filled with low voices and the mournful wails of harmonicas. It's fitting. All of that melancholy wrapped up in melody for this drive back to the place we haven't seen in so many years.

Maribel still insists the things Mama heard were real. Those lovely voices on the wind.

But these are the memories Maribel has fed me like spun sugar. Pretty things meant to distract. What I remember is the taste of raw meat and a howling in the pit of my stomach because there just wasn't enough to fill me up and the sound of Mama's footsteps on the stairs and squeezing my eyes shut so she'd think I was already asleep.

"I can't hear myself think," I say, and Maribel holds her middle finger up before popping in a CD. She sings along with Tori Amos. My music, but somehow she still knows all the words.

"There's nothing to think about, Opal," she says, and I wish I had a drink. Something for my hands to do. Something to dull the too-bright edge of the hollowed-out dark surrounding the car.

She rolls the window down, and the deep smell of rotted Massachusetts pine floods the spaces between us, and I force myself to breathe through my mouth. "Besides," she says. "You were the one who wanted to come here."

"No, I wasn't." The lie is thistle and thorn and rests hot on my tongue. I wonder if the house is even still there. After everything. I barely remember it.

"Consider it an early birthday gift from your big sister. Back to our roots."

There are spaces heavy as lead left in all the things Maribel doesn't say.

She came back here one other time. She'd gone without telling me. Four years after that dark car pulled up to the house and rushed us outside, away from our mother who'd gone into the woods because the voices had threaded their way into her blood, Maribel went back to see all the things we left behind. Our old lives like discarded shells.

Above us, pine trees meld with the darkened rim of sky as if the world and the air have stitched themselves together, clinging tight as lover's skin.

"She used to take us into the woods. Remember? When we were little," Maribel says, and I glance at her but can't see her face. Only the mahogany-tinted swoop of hair she keeps pulled over her eyes.

I twitch my hands against my jeans, my sweater, but it doesn't help. I swallow and open my mouth but don't answer.

"You used to complain that your feet hurt. The rocks were sharp, and she made us stand for such a long time under that old tree. One time you fell asleep right there. She carried you home, and you never woke up. Slept for two days. I thought you were going to die."

Maribel told me about the house after she visited. How the rooms were still like she remembered, only now a thick layer of dust lay over all those old things. She told me about the words left scrawled on the front door or spray-painted across the windows. WHORE. CUNT. WITCH. How she'd gone into the woods looking for the tree she remembered, but couldn't find it.

"There was never any tree, Maribel. We already talked about this."

"Just because you don't remember it doesn't mean it wasn't real, Opal. You were a kid. Fucking Christ," she says, and I fold into myself just a little tighter.

"Put the window up please. It smells like something died out there," I say. Maribel rolls her eyes, but she hits the button, and I wish I hadn't said anything because being in the car with her feels like being stuck with a wounded animal in a tiny, closed-in space. Everything tight and dangerous.

There are gossamer-light memories that I've convinced myself are dreams. They're too strange. Incorporeal. My sister and I standing underneath a pine tree that bleeds into the sky, our hands clasped so tight our blood and the beating of our hearts slowed, as Mama tucked feathers into our hair and stones and twigs into our pockets and filled our open mouths with leaves. The bright green taste of the world broken open on my tongue, and my mother's face tipped up to the sky.

There was never anyone else. Only Mama and Maribel and me. We knew other kids had fathers, but whenever I asked Mama about where he went, she only smiled and pointed into the forest. Eventually, I stopped asking.

I remember thinking Mama wasn't born but just happened. Grew here like the pines.

Maribel flips on the brights and the light paints everything in too-pale tones. Like the trees and earth have been bled out. Somewhere behind the tangle of branches, yellow eyes flash and then a dark shape streaks further into shadow. A deer probably. Something with large eyes and no sharp teeth. That's what I tell myself anyway.

"You were just a kid," Maribel says again, and I don't let myself nod, or say yes, or make any sound at all. Instead, I watch the light race away from us and hope we can find the house and finally bury the girls who used to live there.

"She always said it was in the woods. That it had always been there. The voices. Said it was heavy to bear that crown of leaves. That it was better if she put those pieces inside of her. Inside of us," Maribel says.

"Stop. We're going back. Isn't it enough?" I say, and Maribel flexes her fingers and tightens them against the wheel, but the words are out, and I can't stop myself. "There was something wrong with her, Maribel. When they came to take us away, we were starving. Don't you remember? Catching what we could in the woods and bringing it back, braining it with a rock, and then just eating it raw because there was nothing to cook it in? I might have only been nine, but that much I remember. How Mama would disappear into the trees and come out sometimes weeks later, the centre of her eyes gone white, and I knew then she'd found something she shouldn't have. Something bad. I didn't understand then, but it was probably drugs, Maribel. You know that as well as I do."

Maribel scrubs a hand over her face, but she doesn't say anything else. Right after we left, it was all she could talk about. Mama and her tree and her crown of leaves. The Living Crown. That bitter taste flowing down her throat and filling her up. How Mama would come back for us; how the voices would find us and then we could go back to that little house in the woods and everything would be beautiful.

After a few months, she only talked about it at night as we lay together on the thin mattress, her whispers leaking into the dark. By the time the officer drove out to our fifth foster home in less than two years to tell us our mother had hung herself out in the forest, Maribel hadn't talked about Mama in quite a while.

But lately Maribel has been bringing her up. Countless phone conversations that start with "do you remember" and end with me wondering if my own memory is as thin and transparent as air.

There are things I remember about Mama—how she smelled or how she'd braid my hair at night tight, tight, tight against my scalp— but Maribel's memories are something strange. Terrible, moving things that bend and stretch away from me when I try to take them into myself and absorb them as my own.

"You'll remember soon. The voices," Maribel says and her hand again brushes against the headlight switch and the road goes dark.

"What the fuck," I say and reach for the headlights, but Maribel swats my hand away.

"It's better this way. It's the only way we can find it."

"Find what?"

"The house."

My skin crawls into gooseflesh. "That's insane, Maribel. You're going to kill us."

"Please, Opal. Please. I just need this one thing. Okay? You weren't the one. I just need to go back there. To see if it was real. Any of it. It's been twelve years, and I'm still hunting her in the places where it's darkest. This is the way back. I know it."

The road bumps underneath us, and I know we've drifted onto the shoulder. Maribel keeps her hands locked on the wheel, and even in shadow, I can see the silvered glisten of tears on her cheeks.

I don't say anything, but I reach across the chasm between us and squeeze her arm. Everything inside goes cold; my blood crystallised like ice flowers in my veins.

"Close your eyes, Opal. Let me find the way," Maribel says.

"I can't."

"We've always been coming back here. Our entire lives one endless circle looping right back to the place Mama left for us. Like the Living Crown. The Crown of Leaves. Always breathing. Always linked to each other. To everything beyond."

I close my eyes. Underneath us, the car lurches, the engine whining as it works its way towards wherever we are going.

Maribel whispers, and the sound is a roaring that splits open the darkness behind my lids, the whole world lit up in gold. "Witch. Such a stupid word. It was never *her*. Never. It was this place. The place where she set the crown on her hair and listened to the wind and all that beauty poured itself out of the sky and into her. And now," she stops talking, but I can hear her breath coming hard and fast.

"What if it isn't real? What if it's just a house? What then? All of those years, all of that belief adding up to what?"

"I don't know. Does it matter?"

"I have to move on, Maribel. I can't spend the rest of my life listening to you spin fantasies into memories. I want to finish college. Move somewhere where there are no pine trees. Somewhere with sand and water."

"The leaves on your tongue. The entire world full to bursting. You have to remember, Opal. The three of us. Together. Crowns tangled in our hair and riding on the wind."

I open my eyes. Branches scratch at the windows, pine needles washing over the car, and I sag in my seat. "There was a road to the house. Before. I remember that. The house wasn't in the middle of the goddamn woods."

"I know the way."

I think of throwing the door open, jumping into the tangle of roots and earth and rock, and then running until my breath comes sharp and tasting of blood. Even if I did, I wouldn't find my way out of this forest.

I wonder if I never left.

No one ever called Maribel or me "witch". No childish, gym-class taunts. No whispering behind hands. But Maribel had seen those words painted against the wood. She knew what we were supposed to be. But they were only words. Only words.

I've been telling myself that since the night Maribel came back.

"Can't you hear it?" Maribel's eyes are bright even in the gloom, and the interior of the car smells of sweat and fear and the darker fecundity of rotting leaves. "The voices. So many nights Mama would come into the bedroom. We'd already be asleep, and she'd touch my hair and face until I woke up. Her hands were always sticky, but I never cared. She told me there were other women. So many of us who'd heard the voices. Who bore the crowns and listened. It was our lot to bear, she said."

Ahead of us, the forest clears, the road a deep cut of packed earth instead of the chaos of fallen branches and pine needles. Something flares inside of me. I refuse to call it recognition. I refuse to acknowledge how my mouth has flooded with the taste of something growing.

"How many of us do you think there have been? Over the years? Hundreds of us. *Thousands* of us with our heads tipped to the sky while we listen. And we carry that secret around inside of us. Eventually, it turns us inside out. The hearing of it. They said Jesus cast devils into pigs, and they went mad with it. Threw themselves off a cliff. But I don't think it was like that. I think they knew, after that touch came on them, that anything less wouldn't be worth living."

"I don't want to be here," I whisper, but Maribel is past hearing me. There's another sound inside of her now that's wiped everything else clean. A rainwater baptism.

I claw at the window. "Roll it down. I can't breathe." The air has gone humid, heated like deep summer, but the button doesn't work, and I gag, my face pressed to the glass.

"The Living Crown." My sister's voice pitches low, and she slows the car, her hands lifting away from the wheel and pointing.

I don't turn. I don't want to look.

"Don't you remember?"

When I lift my eyes from the dash, I see the tree first. Tall and pale with leaves gone translucent as glass. From deep within the tree, eyes wink back at us. Hair and bare flesh moving like so many branches in the wind, and I know them for what they are. The women. All the ones who came before us. The ones who knew how to still themselves. The ones who knew how to listen. Their arms and hands reach out for us, their skins pale and dark and their mouths opening and closing as if they could consume the whole world.

On their heads they wear leafed crowns, and their mouths are verdant smears, their teeth like bleached bone.

And then I remember. Mama placing the leaves in my mouth and telling me to bite down. How I listened for the voices she said would come. How they'd never come. Not for me.

I've spent the past twelve years undoing everything Mama tried to give me. Maribel pants beside me, and her voice rises into a high-pitched whine, but she's stopping the car now, her hands fumbling with the keys, her seat belt.

Beyond the tree, is the house. Our house.

Maribel cries out. A single note that's something like keening, and the women creep back to the tree, their crowns dropped in the dirt.

There are no lights on in the house, and this is how I remember it. Those dark rooms that seemed to grow smaller every night when I curled under the thin sheet that was supposed to keep me warm but didn't.

I get out of the car, and Maribel turns to me, her hand extended like when we were girls and she was leading me forward into the forest, her whisper winter-cold in my ear. "Tonight," she'd said. "Tonight you'll hear. And it will change everything. Promise."

I press my palm to hers, and she draws me close. Repeats the old words. The old promise, and together we turn and look at the house.

The tree beyond shifts and glimmers, and then, there is light at the window.

A pale hand presses to the glass and drops away.

When the door finally opens, I can hear everything.

# STEVE RASNIC TEM

## A STAY AT THE SHORES

STEVE RASNIC TEM is a past winner of the Bram Stoker, World Fantasy and British Fantasy Awards. He has published more than 470 short stories, and recent collections include *Thanatrauma: Stories, Figures Unseen, The Night Doctor & Other Tales* and *The Harvest Child and Other Fantasies*.

His novel *Ubo* is a dark science fictional tale about violence and its origins, featuring such viewpoint characters as Jack the Ripper and Stalin, while *Yours to Tell: Dialogues on the Art & Practice of Writing*, written with his late wife Melanie, is available from Apex Books.

"Like many of my stories," explains Tem, "'A Stay at the Shores' came from a random convergence of memory and event: it was the last day of NecronomiCon 2017 in Providence, Rhode Island. I was having lunch in the restaurant before heading to the airport. There was something about the light coming through the window that reminded me of the beach (I hate the beach). That weekend I had toured the city and visited Lovecraft's grave. I was thinking of conferences past and my old friend Ed Bryant who had died earlier that year, almost two years to the day following my Melanie's death in 2015.

"I've always identified with those Jamesian academics, old loners who never seem comfortable in whatever setting they're in. Even though I had a long and happy marriage and am close to my children, years of loneliness had already left their mark. I've never understood exactly how to fit in.

"The outline of the story came quickly, as fast as I could get it into my notebook, there in the Biltmore Hotel, waiting for my cab."

CARSON WAS IN no hurry to return home after the conference. He was single and lived by himself, without even the questionable comfort of pets. He was also between friendships, his last being a widower of similar age who died nine months before this trip. Perhaps his last companion, and perhaps the last person who might remember Carson had ever lived. The man had loved books, and listened to Carson as if he had important things to say. Losing this man's company was a blow whose seriousness he was just now beginning to comprehend. No one would be waiting for him; no one anticipated his return.

Perhaps if he had made more of a splash at the conference someone might recall him in a footnote somewhere. It was the only way he could imagine he might avoid complete oblivion.

It had been a small gathering devoted to transcendentalism. The paper he'd delivered on the sonnets of obscure transcendental poet Jones Very was received with profound indifference, but at least it was another credit for his CV. The college where he lectured was unimportant but his departmental chairman took great stock in such things.

Carson would have liked it if someone had said something nice about his paper. He would have considered it a small victory.

Professor Litton asked him to come for drinks afterward. He was surprised, and worried that perhaps he had unwittingly committed some sort of error. He hadn't thought Litton even knew his name. "Sorry I missed it, Carson." The older man frowned. "That committee meeting always runs long. Was it a triumph?"

Carson shrugged. "At least I didn't stumble."

"Good, good. You're a professional now. How many of these have you been to?"

"This is my twelfth."

"Very good. I'm sure we'll want to draft you into the organising committee eventually."

Litton went on to describe the committee's work, alluding to a long history of mysterious quarrels and ambiguous in-fighting. Although at first he listened for some opportunity for more visibility in the academic community, Carson's attention eventually wandered to the rest of the room, where older men in ill-fitting suits hunched drearily over their small glasses of coloured liquid. These were his fellow transcendentalists, and not one of them displayed even a hint of a smile.

One fellow nearby appeared to be staring at him while clutching his drink white-knuckled. His eyes were brown stains floating on yellow pools.

"Carson? Did you hear my question?" Litton looked cross with him.

"I'm *so* sorry, Professor. My mind wandered but a moment. I've been quite tired lately. I'm never able to sleep at these things."

"Sleep brings clarity, Carson. One cannot investigate the spiritual aspects of nature through a fog of fatigue."

"You're quite right, of course."

"I was simply asking for confirmation that you are unmarried, that there is no one at home waiting for you?"

It unsettled him that the professor should ask about the very thing Carson had been contemplating so much of late. "I am. There's no one . . . at least for now."

"How are you planning to return home?"

"A bus to the airport, then a quick flight. Nothing terribly interesting."

"Quick seldom means interesting." The older man spread his hands. "Are you aware that there exists a rare opportunity to travel by ship from a historic port?"

"Well, no, I've never been on a boat. But we're miles inland here."

"There's a train to the coast. Infrequent, but direct."

"I've never travelled by train either."

"All the more reason! How old are you, if I may ask?"

"Sixty-three in a few months," Carson replied.

"Too old not to have tried. You *must* do this! Although I've never made the journey myself I hear it's a unique experience. Isn't that what we're all about at this conference, exploration?" Litton made an expansive gesture with his arms. Carson again glanced at the men and a handful of women gathered in the bar. No one here looked like explorers. "Survivors" was the word that came more readily to mind. "I'm told that it's the oldest continuously operating port in the nation. And yet so *little* is known about it really. Rumour has it, it was a port not only before the whites, but even before the Indians. I've heard vague stories about religious sects as far back as the Vikings in the area. Currently it goes by *The Shores*, but it has had many, many names. Think of it! All that forgotten history—and boundless opportunities for original research. You could make a *name* for yourself, Carson."

Carson's train would get him into *The Shores* many hours before the ship's departure. Ample opportunity to ask around, find out if there were any threads worth pursuing. That was a blessing. He was a nervous traveller under the best of circumstances, and here he was attempting two unfamiliar forms of travel on the same journey. Carson had been unable to find the place on any Internet maps, but he was able to purchase a train ticket with his cell phone, and reserve a spot on the scheduled vessel. Litton's recommendation had felt like a challenge, perhaps a test, and although Carson disliked the fact that he'd been so easily persuaded, he did feel considerable excitement. He couldn't remember the last time he'd done anything that might be described as *unexpected*.

The train was surprisingly empty. He walked from one end to the other, soaking up the particular nuances of train travel, especially that unsteady passage from car to car as the floor beneath him shook. What if everything uncoupled at the very moment he stood between cars?

In total he counted seven other passengers, unless some were hiding in the bathrooms, and he encountered no staff at all. How could they afford to run such an under-utilised service? And when he examined their faces—those few not obscured by a pillow or blanket or hand—they looked as uncomfortable as he felt.

He would have liked to talk to someone, but with so few people on the train he might appear desperate. He returned to his original car and sat.

After the first few miles of typically urban, then suburban scenes, the view became primarily one of open countryside showing little variation. At first there were the usual traces of civilisation: power lines and telephone lines, roadways with the occasional relatively slow-moving car, the infrequent bridge, and now and then a water tower or prefabricated metal shed.

According to the route map on display in the car, *The Shores* existed at the end of a long appendix-like finger of land descending from the southern-most tip of the peninsula. The land now streaming by was almost featureless, populated by low bushes and the rare stunted tree, with no structures of any kind. Nor was there any evidence of roads, suggesting that rail was the only way to access the area. Except of course by boat, but so far he hadn't seen any boats. He should have been able to catch glimpses of the ocean on either side by now, but had not. Instead, after a hundred yards or so of barren land a thick, low-lying fog appeared which stretched away as far as he could see, eventually joining the low-lying clouds at the horizon to form an ethereal tube through which the train travelled to its unseen destination. The lower edges of this fog were dark and smoky, as if it had picked up some form of contamination.

Carson sat and gazed out the windows, wishing to nap but unable to. He was far too anxious. According to the route diagram the train should have reached their destination long ago, but perhaps the drawing wasn't to scale. He spent over two hours trying to make sense of it. After another hour passed he thought the journey's length defied logic, and outside the windows there was still this streaming sameness, with no indication of sea.

Eventually he detected differences in the low-lying plumes of fog, darker shapes and lighter shapes, forms advancing and receding, menacing approaches and sinister retreats. Eventually he could make out faces among the masses, and appendages that defied all expectation. Were these simply the imaginings of a mind with too little stimulus? Finally he had to look away, his heart thrumming inside his ears.

He'd certainly had these issues at home. Long periods of silent, solitary study sometimes led to waking dreams, illusions of a sort. Sometimes he practically invited them in, thinking them more stimulating, or somehow more truthful than the world of cold fact. Wasn't that what monks attempted to achieve? Breakthroughs into the unconscious? But they had a mission to find such things. Carson simply wanted to find some way to avoid insanity.

Eventually he couldn't just sit there any more, and sprang up and started walking, even though at this point the train's speed made it difficult to do so safely. He staggered back through the cars, avoiding the more threatening faces until he found a young, depressed-looking woman who drew back at his approach. He sat down next to her, even though she looked terrified.

"I'm so sorry. I didn't mean to frighten you," he managed, trying neither to look too dangerous, or too afraid. "But should this trip last so *long*? Look at that route diagram near the ceiling. We really should have arrived in less than half this time!"

She looked surprised, and then said, "I'm *so glad* you said that! I've been thinking the *exact same* thing!"

"Then you've never travelled this route before?"

"I've never travelled by train at all. A casual friend recommended it. I've never done either. A train, then a ship. She thought it might do me some good." He gazed at her, puzzled. "Sorry," she continued. "I lost my husband over a year ago. I'm still . . . adjusting."

Her response relaxed him a bit. But it didn't alter the *wrongness* he felt. They chatted for a few minutes about their lives and where they were from. She asked him what he did, and although she'd never heard of transcendentalism, she claimed to enjoy poetry. Her name was Denise, and she had been married for over ten years when her husband passed away. "This is my first big trip without him," she said. "Well, actually my first trip farther than the grocery store, since he died."

After that he no longer knew what to say, and sat there silently, watching the windows. In only the few minutes they'd been talking the fog had rolled in and completely filled the glass. It felt as if the train was picking up speed in a renewed hurry to find its destination. He jerked his head anxiously from one side's set of windows to the other's. A stretch of windows suddenly darkened, and on another window several black, parallel streaks appeared, followed by a shove that violently rocked the car.

Denise screamed and clutched his arm. Instinctively he placed his other hand on top of hers. He felt embarrassed. He didn't know what he would say if she objected. "Sometimes when I've been by myself for a long time I think I make things up," she said with apparent urgency. "I imagine terrible things are watching me. But even that's better than believing I am completely alone."

They remained like that until the fog began to clear and the train slowed down.

He wasn't sure what he'd expected. A resort atmosphere he supposed, milling crowds and beach umbrellas and lots of people in bathing suits. *The Shores* was none of that. A cluster of heavily weathered buildings—warping grey boards and pitted paint—ran from the small train station down to a larger structure which appeared to be just as weathered, but sported a wraparound deck and windows all around the first floor, and two more stories of darkened windows above. There were a few old deck chairs scattered on the surrounding sand. With not a soul in sight, except those who'd just left the train, *The Shores* appeared to be some sort of abandoned compound.

Still no sign of an actual ocean. The fog had greatly retreated, but still apparently obscured the water.

He noticed that Denise was far ahead of him with the others. He felt a surprising sense of loss. He'd allowed himself to hope, he supposed, but he had no idea what he might have hoped for. He walked faster, trying to catch up.

The sign above the door said THE SHORES—RESTAURANT AND OFFICE. Inside all Carson could see was a restaurant of mostly empty tables. The other passengers sat scattered about. He was suddenly starving, and found a table, walking right past the one containing Denise. He tried to catch her attention but she was too busy studying the menu. He grabbed a table by the window. The menu was a small, typewritten sheet, listing a half dozen or so items, two of which were egg dishes. The rest were seafood, but weren't described specifically, instead using phrases like "Catch of the Day" and "Chef's Seafood Special" and "Mariner's Pot Luck."

"May I take your order?" The woman was in her fifties, perhaps, black hair grey-streaked, with a plain, clearly bored face. She wore a blood-red apron with matching shoes.

"Um. The Chef's Seafood Special I suppose." She turned. "Oh, where do I catch the ship, when it arrives?"

She turned around, looking at him somewhat puzzled. "Well, whenever it happens, it'll happen there at the end of the sand." He glanced out the window. "You can't see the pier because of the fog. But whenever that rolls out, and whenever the tide comes in, well then you'll be able to leave, but not before. Why, are you in a hurry?"

"No, I suppose not. Not really. Oh, is there someone about who could perhaps answer some questions about the history..." But she had already gone.

He was gazing out the window again—the fog appeared to be breaking, but he wasn't sure what was being revealed underneath— when the voice came from behind him. "So, have you been here before?"

Carson twisted in his chair. He thought he recognised the man from his grey and green clothing. He'd been one of those trying to sleep on the train, his face buried in a pillow. "No, first time. I'd like to know more about it—can you tell me something?"

"Not really, my first time too." The man sat down next to him. "Looks like it's seen better days, though. I hear there was some kind of scandal, a religious conflict, a cult, something, a few years back. Maybe that hurt business. I just didn't have anything better to do. A train ride followed by a boat ride." He threw his hands into the air. "Whoopee!"

People were looking. Carson felt embarrassed. "That was it? You didn't hear something that attracted you?"

"I had nothing else to do. I live alone. I've been alone a long time. You?"

"I have ... friends, activities. Too much to choose from, really." Carson looked down at his hands. He owed this stranger nothing. "Maybe one of the other passengers has been here before, or knows some of the history."

The man looked around. "Nope, I've asked. We're *all* first-timers. A couple of people have heard rumours, gossip. I wouldn't put too much stock in that sort of thing. Don't worry about it. Relax. Enjoy your trip. I'm going to try to, at least." He stood up and left.

Carson's food arrived. It was a large plate. A small circular patty of pale flesh lay in the centre. "I ordered fish," he told the waitress.

"And fish you got. A local variety. You've probably never seen it before."

"What kind?"

"Oh, you wouldn't recognise it. Like I said, a local variety. The rest of the world, I think they've forgotten about this little fish." She left.

Carson lifted the meat with his fork. It rose as one solid piece. Underneath there was a pale, flattened fin, and what resembled the remnants of a small leg. He lowered the patty back onto the plate. Then he looked out the window again.

The fog had completely disappeared. But there was no ocean. The shore appeared to drop steeply away at the edge of the sand into a broad and deep basin stained a variety of colours. He might have been mistaken, but he thought he saw movement in the basin. A long pier of black wood projected out over the basin, supported on similarly black, spindly legs.

He stood up to get a better look. Around him the others were noticing this as well, standing up, some of them pressing their faces against the windows. At a nearby table the passenger who had spoken to him earlier was sitting, crying, and digging into the flesh of his palm with a fork. "I knew it. I knew it," he mumbled.

Denise came up beside him. "I really don't understand," she said, "how there could be a ship arriving."

The waitress arrived again, this time with a grubby looking older man in a stained apron. "Can I help you folks?"

"There's no ocean," Denise said, her voice rising. "How could that be? We all paid for passage on a ship!"

"Well, it's the tide, ma'am. You've heard of tides, haven't you?"

"Of course I know what a *tide* is! But there's *no ocean* out there! No way for a ship to come in today, or any other day! What *is* this?"

"You know we used to have brochures that explained all this. I don't know what happened to them. It's an *attraction*! It's what's so unique about *The Shores*! The tide goes out, but sometimes it doesn't come back in for a while. Not for *days* sometimes. Sometimes not for *weeks*. Sometimes it's so long you forget there ever was an ocean here. That's part of the attraction, of course. It's never been explained, or if there was an explanation it's been lost."

Carson walked up to the man in the dirty apron. He didn't mean to be threatening, although he didn't mind if he *looked* threatening. "That's *impossible*. Tides don't *work* that way! There should be a change, what, every twelve hours or so? Besides, we bought tickets for a specific date and time!"

"It should say *approximate* on your tickets. Approximate. It's the best we can do. Uncertainty is part of the *experience*. At one time folks *appreciated* that. We have male and female dorms upstairs. You're welcome to stay as long as necessary. It's included in the price of your ticket. Meals, too. You don't have to pay extra for anything while you're waiting for your ride."

"I want to get back on the train," Denise said. "I feel like I've been lied to. I'll just take the train back to where I got on. I don't care about a refund. I just want to get out of here."

"I'm sorry, ma'am. But that just isn't possible. The train has already left."

The passengers sat quietly, some of them, although a couple laughed nervously. The man he'd spoken to earlier stared out the window at the non-existent ocean. Surely, they weren't giving up this quickly? Carson decided to speak up. "Where did all the water go then, when the tide went out? I'm sorry, but you're not making any sense."

"It's an inexplicable phenomenon, sir," the fellow said, trying to look bold. "A natural wonder we may never understand and can only appreciate. Some say that volcanic action has created caverns beneath the ocean floor where the water stays until forced back into our basin here. Hell, there are even a few who claim a giant creature unlike any the planet has seen before sleeps in one of those caverns. Periodically he swallows the tide and only returns it when he's in the proper mood. Some folks say he's some sort of god, and in times past, he did have his share of worshippers." The man chuckled, but no one was smiling. "I'm not much of a church-goer, myself."

"Why sell tickets to a trip you cannot promise with any precision?"

The man paused and glanced at the waitress. "I don't make those decisions sir. I'm only an employee."

By the time the man in the dirty apron had finished his explanations, or attempted explanations, none of the new arrivals were talking. It was getting late, already much later than the scheduled departure of their theoretical ship. The sun had fallen low in the sky, turning the empty ocean basin an unnervingly red colour. Carson couldn't deal with it anymore and retired upstairs, looking for a place to sleep in the men's dorm.

He was surprised to find the dorm already filled almost to capacity with slumbering forms, with only a few empty cots available. The light was dim—a few small lamps at the corners of the room provided a weak, brownish illumination. Heavy curtains blocked the windows.

Carson walked quietly to a cot and sat down. He slipped off his shoes, one of them falling and making a soft thud. The fellow in the cot next to him sat up suddenly and stared at him. "Has the ship arrived? Has it come?" the man asked groggily.

"No. Sorry. No, I'm new. There's no ship. The tide's still... out. I'm afraid we won't be departing today."

"No ship, no ship at all? You're saying there's no ocean?" The man shook his head, rubbed his eyes.

"No. I'm sorry." Carson stared at the man. His clothes were dirty. His beard was matted, sketchy. He stank terribly. "How long have you been waiting?"

"A few days. Weeks, maybe? Although it could be months? But it's okay—they feed you, they give you a place to sleep. No extra charge. It's free. It's always been free." He looked sharply at Carson, eyes wide open. "You're new, aren't you?"

"Yes I am."

"Well, you'll find out soon enough how it is. You become unsure about what you are seeing, what you are hearing. Every night you listen to the sounds the world makes, and you just aren't sure what they mean anymore. You'll see, or maybe it'll be different for you. Maybe."

The next morning Carson woke up to an almost empty dorm. The restaurant was full, but largely quiet. No one was talking. There must have been a hundred of them or more: men and women, no children.

And outside the restaurant, no ocean. He could see several people aimlessly wandering the beach. He thought he saw a few out in the basin: gesticulating, arguing. But it was too far away. He couldn't tell for sure.

After the meal he took a walk with Denise. They didn't say anything, but it seemed to be taken for granted that they would walk together. They wandered amongst the old buildings leading up to the train station. Most were unfurnished, but a few had the occasional broken table or chair inside. There was water damage everywhere, as if one day when the tide came in it had come much farther in than anticipated.

Carson was looking into the space between two buildings when he thought he saw a familiar figure passing by the other side. He couldn't recall their name at the moment, but it was someone he once knew very well, someone who had been quite important to him. How was it that a person could lose touch like that, that you could lose track of them completely, and even when you find them again you discover you have lost their name? He shouted and ran down the narrow passageway but could find no one. There were still people down on the beach, but no one else walked amongst the buildings.

Later that day Denise swore she had seen a woman she had once known very well. A neighbour or a schoolmate, perhaps even a distant relative. Carson helped her search but they could find no further sign of the woman. Before the evening meal they were sure they could hear the sounds of the ocean. They followed the sound to a narrow, deep hole in the ground. They got down on their knees. When they put their ears near the hole the ocean came through loud and clear.

"That must be the caverns down there," Denise whispered. "Can you imagine? That's where the ocean has gone." Then she reached over and pulled Carson's face to hers and began kissing him. It was wonderful, but then she stopped, and wouldn't talk to him about it again.

That night the dorm wasn't as full as it had been before. Carson wondered where the others had gone. The ship hadn't arrived, and the train had not come that day. He wondered if the others were still out on the beach, or in the basin, arguing.

This continued for several days. He was tired of waiting for the ship, and realised there was no guarantee it would even take you where you wanted to go, assuming you even knew where you wanted to go. He considered the serious possibility that people who took the ship might never be heard from again, and even their names would be lost. Sometimes Carson tried to get on the train when it dropped off new passengers (there were more and more of them each day), but the train doors wouldn't open for him. He watched others try with the same results.

Life settled into a comfortable pattern of the expected. Denise still took walks with him, but she never kissed him again.

Carson had become accustomed to life in the dorm. It wasn't that much different from life at home, except he had many fewer personal possessions, a blessing in some ways. He retreated there every afternoon, sometimes for hours at a time. There were always two or three men sleeping—some seemed never to leave their beds—but no one bothered him.

Just as at home, Carson would lie there and gaze at the ceiling or the walls, and what he saw, he thought, was some reflection of him. Just as at home, he would attempt to identify every sound he heard— some so subtle they were likely no more than a change in ambient air pressure—and he would imagine who, or what, had made them.

It wasn't at all surprising to him when he eventually made contact with that ancient god sleeping in the caverns many miles below, who held the missing ocean somewhere inside its massive form.

What he saw against the dark wall might have been the creature's eye, or whatever the creature itself saw when it gazed into its own mind. The abject solitude and the knowledge that even if they found companionship after all these years, entrance into the final darkness could only be done alone.

He walked out of the dorm, too restless to sleep. He ignored the people who called to him. He ignored even Denise's voice when it rose above the continuous din. He avoided the outstretched hands both of the ones he knew and the ones he'd never met before. He wandered down into the absence of ocean, and found the ones who now made their homes there, who prayed both to the missing sea and to the god who had taken it all away.

And weeks later, when the ocean finally came roaring in, Carson was waiting by the railroad tracks. With his ear to the ground he could hear the train's distant approach, even over the screams of the drowning, and the hoarse enthusiasm of the others as they imagined their salvation was finally at hand.

When the ship did arrive, all sleek and swollen and clamouring with bells, Carson still waited for the train. Even as the ramp was lowered and all those ragged passengers finally boarded, Carson remained, listening to the ground, and anticipating the train.

And at last when it looked as if he'd made a miscalculation, the ship's speakers pleading for any final boarders, the train arrived, and the newcomers began to stream out. He had but a moment to reflect on how arbitrary it was, how unjust, that these late arrivals could simply walk up that ramp into the ship without suffering what so many had been forced to endure.

Maybe this is what they all really wanted. He understood the attraction of letting history swallow you completely and without trace. He supposed it was only his arrogance that kept him from joining them on that voyage to nowhere.

As one of the last passengers left the train, Carson shouldered himself inside, jamming a shovel into the door to keep it open just a little while longer. The passengers looked alarmed, and began to run. "I'd think about staying on the train!" he shouted, even though he didn't really expect any of them to listen. The shovel handle snapped and the door slammed closed.

The inside of the train car was cold, and Carson snuggled into himself to stay warm. Through the train's metal walls he could hear the distant horn of the ship signalling its departure. He didn't know how long he'd have to wait, but he hoped it wasn't too long.

As for the ship, wherever it was headed, Carson knew it could be no place good.

# REGGIE OLIVER

## THE OLD MAN OF THE WOODS

R EGGIE OLIVER is an actor, director, playwright, illustrator and award-winning author of fiction. His published works include six plays, three novels, an illustrated children's book (*The Hauntings at Tankerton Park*), nine collections of short stories (including Children of the Night Award-winner *Mrs Midnight* and *A Maze for the Minotaur*) and the biography of the writer Stella Gibbons (*Out of the Woodshed*).

His stories have appeared in more than 100 anthologies, while three "selected" editions of his stories have been published, the latest being *Stages of Fear* from Black Shuck Books. As well as his own fiction, Oliver has illustrated work by Robert Shearman, Anna Taborska and Susan Hill, amongst others.

"This story is particularly dear to me," he explains, "as it is based on a house in France that my late wife, the actress and artist Joanna Dunham, and I used to own. We had to sell it when Joanna became too ill to get out to it, but the place still has a strong hold over my memory and imagination.

"As in the story, it was a 16th-century farmhouse situated in country which, during the 1939–45 war, was in the borderland between Vichy and Occupied France. From the locals we heard many strange stories about that place and time, quite as strange as the story that they inspired."

✑

BESIDES MYSELF AND M. Chanal, the *notaire*, five people were in his office that morning for the signing of the documents. There were two middle-aged married couples and a rather younger single woman, more *soignée* than they, who stood apart from them smoking a cigarette in a holder, like a vamp in a 1930s film. She intrigued me. The married couples looked like typical French country people, though one pair was better dressed (and presumably richer) than the other. Their figures were thick-set, their skins were tanned and lined; there was something dogged, forbidding, deeply respectable about them. The single woman, on the other hand, had an elegant figure and wore make-up. Her clothes were simple but *chic*, as was her coiffure. Despite this, I got the impression that the four others looked on her with some disdain.

The five of them were, or rather had been, the joint owners of an ancient farm house called Les Bosts on the outskirts of the village of Montpeyroux in the Dordogne. They inherited it from an uncle, M. Gaston Durand, who had died some ten years before; and they had been endeavouring to sell it ever since. That they had hitherto not succeeded was partly due to family disputes and the complexities of the *Code Napoleon* in matters of inheritance, but mainly, I suspect, to the fact that only an eccentric Englishman, such as myself, would want to buy a derelict 16th century building in a small rural village with barely half an acre of land attached to it. Yet this was exactly what I wanted, and could afford; so here I was at the Notaire's in the little nearby town of Villefranche, fearfully, excitedly committing myself to a new life in the Dordogne.

During the course of the lengthy and elaborate process of signing the documents of transfer, M. Chanal was, for some obscure Gallic legal reason, obliged to ask me about my marital status. I replied that I was single, having been divorced some three years previously. The two couples looked away from me and at each other, but the single woman seemed enlivened by the news.

"Ah! *Moi aussi! Je suis divorcée,*" she said. At this the two couples frowned, while *la divorcée* and I exchanged the wry smiles of fellow sufferers.

When the sale was at last completed to the *notaire's* satisfaction, we all shook hands very formally, the two couples without warmth or so much as a smile. The *divorcée*, however, not only shook hands, but kissed me on both cheeks and pressed into my palm, as she did so, a small visiting card.

*Mme. Adeline Pelissier,* it read and there was a telephone number and the address of an apartment in the nearby town of Sainte-Foy-la-Grande. What was I to do with it? Was it some kind of amorous overture? I put it in my wallet and decided to forget it.

A year previously, I had retired from the Civil Service with a handsome pension. I was by that time living alone in a flat in Muswell Hill and there was nothing to hold me in England. I was separated from my wife, and our one child, Beatrice, married with children, was running a successful textile design business in Suffolk. Beatrice had taken her mother's side over the divorce so that our relationship, though not now acrimonious, was distant. I had little to hold me in that country where, despite a not unsuccessful career, I felt something of a failure. I was looking, I suppose, for a new life, and I had always loved France. The friends I had left in England, far from discouraging me from living abroad, seemed enthusiastic about the idea. Perhaps invitations to stay were in their minds, but that is to take too cynical a view. So I made several trips into rural France in search of property, and, by the end of the third, I found Les Bosts.

Though not exactly a ruin, the house showed signs of considerable neglect. It was bare but for a few sticks of worm-eaten furniture, a couple of huge dark armoires, like miniature wooden *mausolea*, and a formidable old *lit bateau*. The stone flags on the ground floor were uneven, and the wooden boards on the upper ones creaked and bowed. Beyond running water and some electricity, whose *puissance* was badly in need of elevation, there were few modern conveniences, not even a bath, but the rooms were large and well-proportioned and the location delightfully rural.

It stood at the foot of the hill of Montpeyroux, on which a picturesque château and a small Romanesque church, a town square and a few dwellings, were situated. The land about my house—hardly to be described as a garden—was dominated by a great oak tree. I could picture myself, even on the hottest days, sitting and reading contentedly beneath its generous shade. Renovating Les Bosts would be, as they say, "a challenge", and might even restore to me a sense of achievement. That is what I told myself.

I will not bother to tell you about my adventures with builders, decorators, electricians and the like over the year following my purchase. If you have an appetite for such things, there are countless books by Britons with titles like *We Bought a House in Gascony*, or *A Little Property on the Gironde*, which will satisfy it. I will only say that I found the process as absorbing, frustrating, and sometimes rewarding, as no doubt did the authors of those books. I will concentrate only on what made my experience differ from theirs.

In the first place my French builders, though perfectly amiable, honest and hard-working, had a habit of fading away from the job after a week or so. No real explanation was given for this, other than that they had commitments elsewhere. Though I was regularly on site to supervise their handiwork, I don't think I was a particularly exacting taskmaster. In the end I had to hire a team of English builders, who lived and worked in the Dordogne, to finish the work. They were no better at the task than their French counterparts, and they were considerably more expensive, but they did at least stay the course; yet even they, by the end, seemed anxious to depart.

I can find no satisfactory explanation for this. The house did not have "an atmosphere", not that I am particularly susceptible to such things. Quite the contrary, for such an ancient building, it appeared to be singularly empty of any mood or tension. It was, you might say, *tabula rasa*—a clean slate onto which I could imprint my own personality and style, and I was glad of that. When, eventually, I allowed my books and pictures from London into it, I believe it did begin to seem like a part of me, though not, perhaps, as much as I had hoped.

A few small events that occurred during the renovation process need to be told.

One morning, a week or so after I had taken possession, there was a letter in my post box, the first to be addressed to me at Les Bosts. *M. Egerton, Proprietaire, Les Bosts* read the envelope. I felt a ridiculous involuntary surge of pride. It was from M. Chanal, the *notaire*, and contained the various deeds and documents relating to my purchase of the house. It was early, and the builders had not arrived, so I took the documents indoors to study at my leisure. On going over them meticulously, I was surprised to see that I was not only the owner of Les Bosts, but also of the little wood that stood opposite my property.

It was situated on the other side of the road that led up to the château, and opposite the front entrance of Les Bosts. It was one of those dense, seemingly accidental, areas of woodland that you find dotted about that part of rural France. The trees were high; the undergrowth appeared impenetrable. It did not look inviting, and it annoyed me that I, all unwittingly, had been saddled with it. I rang up M. Chanal. Why had I not been informed about this wood? I did not want it. Could I not sell it?

M. Chanal, perhaps literally, certainly metaphorically, gave a shrug of the shoulders on the other end of the line. He was *desolé*, but he thought I knew about it. It was a part of the property. No, he did not think I could sell it. No one would want to buy it, because permission to build upon it would almost certainly be denied by the authorities. In any case, would I want a new house directly opposite my front entrance? Besides, he had heard that the little wood was just the place to find cèpes. Did I know cèpes? They were a most delicious wild mushroom, best served simply *à la bordelaise*, fried with chopped parsley, shallots and breadcrumbs. I cut M. Chanal off shortly, but I made a note of the recipe.

At that time I was not actually staying at Les Bosts, but at a small *pension* in Sainte-Foy-la-Grande. The facilities in my future home were still too primitive, and many of the windows had fallen out due to a termite infestation. Most mornings I would drive up to Les Bosts to supervise and sometimes assist any labour that was going forwards. One morning, shortly after I had received the documents from M. Chanal, I had decided to take the morning off in Sainte-Foy-la-Grande. It was market day.

There is something festal about market days in French provincial towns, particularly during the summer months. Fruits and vegetables of every kind and colour on sloping stalls; chickens clucking; rabbits snuffling in cages; Africans selling leather goods; bright garments and chiffon scarves fluttering gently in the breeze; fresh, iridescent fish on little fields of ice: to me it was a delight to the eye, so gloriously distant from Grey Britain.

I had no plans to buy anything because I was taking all my meals out at that time; I merely wanted to wander and gaze. Then I caught sight of a familiar figure in the crowd, dressed, as before, with considerable *chic* in an elegant black and white polka-dotted summer dress and a wide-brimmed black straw hat. It was Madame Pelissier, *la belle divorcée*, and she was haggling very hard with a grocer over some aubergines. Finally the deal was concluded to her satisfaction, and she bore them away triumphantly in her string bag. Even the string bag, black of course, looked *chic*.

I suddenly felt an urgent need for company. I ran after her, but when I caught up, I tried to appear as casual as possible.

"Hello! *C'est Madame Pelissier, n'est ce pas?*"

"*Ah! Monsieur Egerton!*" She seemed pleased to see me. I invited her to take some refreshment with me, and she graciously consented. At that moment we were passing a suitable establishment, so we sat down at an outside table under a striped awning and ordered coffee. For a while we remained in a companionable silence, watching the crowds drifting to and fro along the street in the sun, then Madame Pelissier turned to me and said:

"So, how do you like your new French home?" I had been prepared to converse with her in my very serviceable French, but there was no need. Her English was excellent, almost idiomatic; her accent, which was light, added piquancy to what she said.

"On the whole, very much."

"You know you have chosen a very historical part of France." I nodded. "You are interested in culture?" I indicated that I was very interested in culture. "Very good. Then I suppose you have visited *Le Château de Montaigne?*"

As a matter of fact, this was one of the few expeditions I had made in my time off from renovating my new home. It is only about eight miles away from Montpeyroux.

"The wine of the château is very pleasant, but a little over-priced, but the tower is most interesting. You know the *essais*?"

"I studied them at University."

"Ah good! Michel de Montaigne was *un vrai humaniste*, and in a day when it was even more dangerous than now to be so."

"*Homo sum, humani nihil a me alienum puto.*" I had seen these words carved on a beam in the tower where Montaigne wrote. A quotation from Terence, the African: "I am a man; I count nothing human alien to me."

"Excellent! You know that Michel de Montaigne's brother, Bertrand, lived at the Château of Montpeyroux?"

"I did not."

"Go stand beneath the walls of the Château de Montpeyroux and look across the valley. You can just see the Château de Montaigne from there. Michel and his brother were—how you say?—very close, true brothers. When they were in residence, Bertrand would put a candle in the highest window of his tower, and Michel would do the same in his, so they could be assured of each other's presence, though miles apart. *C'est sympathique, n'est ce pas?*"

"They must have had bloody good eyesight."

"Perhaps it is only a legend. But remember, in those days there would have been no other lights in between to interfere."

"It certainly is a very delightful legend."

"But all history is legend, and all legend history, do you not think?"

I did not want to get into a philosophical discussion, so I broached the subject of the wood.

"Ah! The wood!"

"You knew about the wood?"

"But of course! Why did you not?"

"That's a very good question."

"But what is your complaint? There are good cèpes to be found in that wood."

"So I have already been told," I said irritably. Madame Pelissier seemed amused.

"I have not found any there myself, but..."

"You've been into the wood?"

"Once, I remember, when I was a little girl. My father and his brother, my Uncle Gaston, were not good friends like Michel and Bertrand, but one time we did go to see Uncle Gaston at Les Bosts and had lunch there. After lunch my father and my uncle had business to discuss, so Uncle Gaston told me to go into his wood opposite and look for cèpes. For some reason my mother was not with us, and men are careless about such things, so I went as I was told. It was a bright sunny day like this one, but the wood, it was very—" She searched for a word. "—dense. I was only seven and small for my age. Everything was taller than me, even the grass it seemed. There were no paths, but I pressed on in search of the cèpes, thinking how pleased my papa and uncle would be if I found some. Then all of a sudden I realised I was lost. I looked around me. No path. Nothing! Nothing but trees and grass and bushes in every direction, the sky above very distant, and now it seemed darkening with cloud. The heat oppressed. I became terrified. I ran in all directions; I screamed very loudly. At last my father and uncle heard and came to find me. They took me into the house and gave me some cognac with a little water and told me not to breathe a word to my mother, and my uncle gave me five francs to make sure. Gradually I stopped weeping, but I had been deeply frightened, not simply of being lost: I had been terrified that I might see *Le vieux des bois*."

"'The Old Man of the Woods'? What is that?"

"It is a local legend. A fable perhaps. It had been told to me by the nuns at my first school, not long before my visit to Uncle Gaston, and it was still fresh in my mind. Those nuns, they thought it was a very moral tale, and perhaps they imagined it would frighten us little girls into being better Christians. But if that was so, then they were foolish. You can be frightened into evil but not into goodness, do you not think?"

I had my doubts about her proposition, but I was in no mood to be sidetracked by metaphysical speculation.

"The story?"

"Ah, yes! Well, there is this man. He is young, he is beautiful, he has money, he can do anything. In consequence he does many wild and terrible things, but always he is haunted by the shadow of his conscience. So one evening, when the sun is low and the shadows are long, he enters into a young green wood and he cuts off his own shadow. The shadow dances off and hides itself in one of the trees. Now the young man is free from his conscience and he can do what he likes without remorse. The years roll by, and the man without a shadow becomes very corrupted and old. Then he realises that his pleasures are hollow and he is without feeling. The life he once loved has lost all flavour, and he understands that this is because he has no shadow, no conscience. So he returns to the wood to find it again, but the wood is now dense and overgrown and he cannot recognise the tree into which his shadow fled. And there he remains for ever in that wood, perpetually searching for his lost soul amongst the trees."

"A very pretty story."

"No. Not pretty, I think, but it made a great impression upon my young heart. I was a timid little girl and very pious. You find that hard to believe?"

"Not at all... Tell me more about your Uncle Gaston." Madame Pelissier glanced at her watch.

"Ah, zut! Je suis en retard! I must go. Thank you so much for the coffee, Monsieur Egerton. My apologies but I must fly, as you say."

"Perhaps we could have dinner together one evening?"

"Perhaps! That would be delightful. Au revoir!" And the next minute she had disappeared into the bustling market crowds of Sainte-Foy-la-Grande.

Soon after that, partly for reasons of expense, partly for convenience, I abandoned the pension in Sainte-Foy and hired an old camper-van, which I parked in the grounds of Les Bosts. There was nothing wrong with the camper-van. It was reasonably comfortable, if cramped, but I spent there the most unpleasant and troublesome two weeks of my life.

I could never settle or rest properly in it. I was constantly going over to the house to see if there was something that I could do in it. I suppose I was getting impatient for my new home, but there was more to it than that. At night, when I was trying to sleep in the van,

I was besieged by a whole battery of unaccountable noises. It sounded as if twigs and branches with leaves were scraping and swishing against the sides of the vehicle, and yet I had deliberately placed it out of reach of any vegetation. Often I would hear a bird (or something) walk across the van's roof. The steps it made were slow and deliberate, almost heavy, not very like any bird I knew. Then I would get out of bed and step outside to look, but I never saw anything, except once when I thought I sensed something scuttling away towards the wood. It did not fly, and it was too dark to tell what sort of an animal it was.

I avoided going into the van as much as possible, except to cook and sleep. In the evenings I would sit outside it in the "garden" for as long as possible, but even then I was conscious of disturbance. On the stillest nights some breeze or other would appear to be fumbling with the bushes that surrounded my domain. If I looked over towards the wood, the trouble was even greater there: the trees shuddered in the wind, the undergrowth stirred.

One evening, as dusk was approaching, I walked to the edge of the road to observe this phenomenon. I had still not ventured into the wood; in fact, I chose, whenever possible, to ignore this part of my property altogether. Still, there were times when it could not be overlooked, and on that occasion I was standing on the side of the road staring rather irritably into the wood when I became aware of someone watching me.

I have not said anything about my neighbours in the little hamlet that surrounded me. They were all French country people, pleasant enough, but incurious and not very forthcoming. The exception was the local farmer, M. Bobelet, a squat middle-aged man who had a large cage outside his front door in which he kept an Alsatian that barked and snarled at you as you went by. I must admit I had a slight prejudice against M. Bobelet on account of that dog, which I never saw him let out, though I am sure he must have done. On the wire fence that bordered his land was a notice which read CHIEN MÉCHANT. I did not blame the *chien* for being *méchant*, I blamed M. Bobelet.

He would often come round to my house while the renovation was in progress and sometimes talk to the workmen. I could not make out what he said, because he spoke very rapidly with a thick Southern French twang which was quite impenetrable at a distance. When I approached him, he would always shake hands with me very formally and ask questions, which I would do my best to answer. They were always about what I was proposing to do with the building. He seemed to regard himself as some kind of informal inspector of works, which also did not endear him to me. He had piercing blue eyes.

It was M. Bobelet who stood on the road watching me as I peered into the wood. I had no desire to speak with him, but I thought it only polite to do so, so I greeted him with a wave and a friendly *"Bon soir!"*

This he took as his cue to approach me. I cannot record our conversation exactly, as I only understood half of what he said. He was asking me questions about the wood and what I was proposing to do with it.

*"Rien!"* I said. Nothing! And this appeared to satisfy him. I then asked him if he would like to buy the wood. At this he looked very shocked and shook his head. He glanced at the wood and said *"Non!"* several times, very emphatically. After he had muttered something which I could not understand, he addressed himself to the subject of a large millstone which stood on one corner of my land, half-obscured by a box hedge. What was I proposing to do with *that*? I shrugged. I had not given the object any thought other than to wonder what it was doing there. He told me that the millstone should be respected, as it was a very historical stone. Apparently his father and some friends in the Resistance had, shortly after the Normandy Landings in 1944, rolled that stone into the middle of the road *"pour arrêter les Boches"*—to stop the Germans. But stop them from what? His reply was vague. I became interested. I knew that during the war this part of the country had been a borderland between German-occupied territory and Vichy France, and that strange, wild things had gone on during that period. M. Bobelet seemed disposed to instruct me on the subject, but I could follow little of what he said. Finally I asked him how well he had known M. Gaston Durand, the previous owner of Les Bosts? This stopped his flow. He looked at me,

mumbled something, and shook his head; then, very deliberately, he spat on the ground. After which he quite unexpectedly shook hands with me, wished me *bon soir* and walked off.

Over the next few days the floors were finished, the stairs restored and, most importantly of all, a man came to certify that Les Bosts had been cured of its termite infestation and we were safe to put in new windows. I decided to move into the house as soon as possible, despite the fact that there was still much to be done; but before I could, I had a telephone-call from England.

It was my daughter, Beatrice, informing me that my ex-wife was seriously ill and had not long to live. I said I would come back at once. I think Beatrice was rather surprised by this decision, but she seemed to approve.

On the evening before I left for England, the new windows were finally fixed into the ancient stone walls, making my house at last truly habitable. They gleamed in the sun which, as it set, turned the panes into little plates of gold, flecked and dappled by the branches of intervening trees, making of them dark gilded mirrors of their surroundings. As I was admiring them from a distance, I noticed a strange anomaly: something appeared to be reflected in the glass which was not there in reality.

It was more like a shadow, though it was quite clearly delineated, and it was moving to and fro across the windowpanes and the glass of the French doors. At first I thought it was some trick of the light, brought about by the slight unevenness of the glass panes, or that something was moving about inside the house, but that could not be because I could discern nothing else of the interior. I could see myself mirrored in the glass, and at one point the thing passed between me and my reflection, obscuring my image for a moment.

It moved so quickly and mercurially that it was hard to make out at first, but it looked like the shadow of a man, slightly bent, head thrust forwards, walking to and fro. I watched it for a minute or so, trying to clarify my impression of it, then I began to move towards the house to get a closer, perhaps a clearer view. I think I was hoping that my change of view might dispel the vision altogether and reveal it, after all, as some kind of optical trick.

The figure remained only a shadowy outline, but I thought I could now tell that it was a man, elderly but not completely decrepit. It moved too fast for that.

The reflected shadow changed direction again as I approached, and moved now steadily in one direction towards the entrance to my property and to the wood beyond. Now it was gone, and I could see nothing reflected in the windows except myself, the sunlight and the trees in the garden. It was a relief. Almost unbidden, anxiety had been building up inside me; now it was dispelled. Nevertheless, I was glad that a car was about to pick me up from here and take me to Bordeaux airport. By midnight I would be in England.

I spent longer there than I expected. I visited my wife regularly in the hospice where she spent the last weeks of her life. It would be an exaggeration to say that a reconciliation took place, as she was almost constantly under heavy sedation for the pain and coherent thought was difficult for her, but peace of a kind was established. When she died, I took it upon myself to manage the funeral and all the other arrangements that surround a death. The whole experience had been hard on my daughter, who was finding it difficult to cope. So when the service was done and we were all standing, as one does, rather listlessly outside the church, Beatrice came over and took my arm.

"Thanks for doing all that, Dad, with the funeral and all," she said.

"I only did what I had to."

"Yes, but you *did* it. Are you going back to France now?" I nodded. "Aren't you going to get lonely out there?"

"I don't think so. In the summer, why don't you and the family come out and stay?" I outlined the various attractions that were on offer in that part of the world.

Beatrice said, "Maybe we will."

It was spring when I returned to France, and I was glad to do so. By that time Les Bosts was fully habitable, though I had yet to arrange furniture and pictures to my satisfaction, and unpack all my possessions, in particular my books. This task should have been a pleasant one, and was, occasionally, but I was plagued by restlessness. It was understandable, I suppose, after my emotionally exacting time in England, but there was more to it than that. I would go for long walks in the countryside, mostly along the by-roads, past rolling vineyards and patches of dense woodland like my own. I did it to soothe my anxieties, to tire myself out so that I could sleep at night. I had committed myself to a strange life in a foreign country and I was now beset, all too late, by doubts about it. I did sleep much better at night in my own home than I had in the camper-van, but I was still, if more dimly, conscious of those strange, irrational nocturnal sounds. Then I saw him again.

One afternoon I was in the kitchen, preparing some vegetables at the sink. Above the sink is a window which looks out on a patch of rough ground at the back of the house. Though my head was bent over my task, I caught a glimpse out of the corners of my eyes of a shadow passing across the window. I looked up, but the shadow was gone. I had had the impression of someone walking round the house to the front, yet this was improbable, if not impossible. The back of Les Bosts was an area full of rubble, interspersed with clumps of bamboo and patches of nettles. I had yet to do something about it. No one would want to go walking there.

I left the kitchen and went into the dining room at the front of the house. There, through the window, I saw him again, this time a little more distinctly. It was the same figure that I had seen reflected in the glass of the windows on the evening before I set out for England. The head was thrust forwards, the steps rapid, the figure that of a man not exactly old, but past the prime of life. He was making for the entrance to my property and the wood across the road.

I called to him, but he evidently did not hear me. I ran to the door, opened it and looked out. The figure, now dwindled to a shadow, was disappearing in the direction of the wood. I went to the entrance of Les Bosts and stared after it into the trees. There was a disturbance in the young green undergrowth, a shiver amongst the leaves and leaf-buds. I felt I was being urged to walk into the wood, but the urge was overmastered by reasonable doubt and unreasonable fear. I looked around me, almost hoping to see M. Bobelet. He might give me the requisite courage, or perhaps offer sound advice, but he was not there. His Alsatian, though, was barking violently in its cage.

The following morning I rang Madame Pelissier. She seemed

delighted to hear from me and I invited her to come out to Les Bosts and have lunch with me there. I would fetch her and take her back by car if necessary. The pause on the other end of the line after I had issued this invitation was enough to indicate that it had not met with her approval. Then came a number of excuses and prevarications. I then suggested lunch at a restaurant in Ste-Foy, but no, she had another idea.

"Come to have tea at my apartment tomorrow. I know how you English love your afternoon tea. We French once called it '*le five o'clock*' in your honour."

"When shall I come?"

"At about four, I think."

Madame Pelissier's apartment was smaller than I had expected, and much less lavishly appointed. Her elegant appearance had led me to expect that divorce had left her well provided for. Evidently it was not the case, but there were sufficient indications that she was a woman of taste and culture: the well-stocked bookshelves, the framed posters from art exhibitions on the walls. The tea service was of modern design, very stylish, not mass-produced.

She received me graciously, and listened with sympathy to an account of my recent stay in England. When I started to talk about Les Bosts, I thought I detected a slight lessening of interest, so I switched to more general topics. I tried gently to probe her own circumstances, and gathered that she worked part-time as a receptionist at the local doctor's. She seemed not too keen to go into details about her existence, which I understood. Finally our conversation dwindled and, after a pause, Madame Pelissier looked at me searchingly and said:

"*Monsieur Egerton*, I think you have come to see me not simply for the pleasure of my company. Am I not right?"

I assured her that the pleasure of her company was very considerable, but she was right. I wanted to know about her Uncle Gaston.

She asked why. Was it just curiosity?

No, I said. It was to do with the attitude of my neighbours in the village, and I told her about M. Bobelet.

"That pig!" she said. "But I think it is more than that. No?"

"Perhaps... Yes..." I said nothing more, but she seemed to understand. I saw her gathering strength to fulfil an unpleasant obligation. The story came out hesitantly, prompted by many questions from me. When it was done, she seemed relieved but drained.

Gaston Durand had been the brightest of the four sons of a prosperous Dordogne farmer. Before the war, Gaston ran several businesses in the Bordeaux area and they all prospered. He married a beautiful girl called Francine, who had been a *mannequin* in one of the dress shops that he owned. The relationship was passionate but troubled from the beginning. Then came the war, Francine formed a *liaison* with an S.S. Colonel in Bordeaux, which was just over the border in German-Occupied France. Gaston was at first devastated by this, but he and Francine somehow managed to maintain cordial relations. Gradually Gaston began to take advantage of her liaison with the Colonel. His business ventures were favoured by the Nazis. It was said that he managed to acquire several houses in Bordeaux which had belonged to a deported Jewish family, and sold them again at a considerable profit. Soon after the Normandy landings, however, his fortunes suffered a reverse. His wife Francine disappeared; some said she had fled with the S.S. Colonel, others that she was killed. No one was sure, and if Gaston knew he kept silent. After the war various accusations were made against Gaston for collaboration, but none stuck and he managed to hold on to his businesses. Increasingly, though, he became reclusive and began to neglect his work. He retreated to Les Bosts and spent most of his time there, in spite of the fact that the local inhabitants shunned him because of his wartime associations. Eventually he sold his businesses and lived off a dwindling capital. When he died, his relatives were shocked to find that he was practically destitute. He could be seen occasionally taking long solitary walks in the district of Montpeyroux. In particular, he was frequently observed wandering into his wood, where he would spend hours shooting small birds and animals, or looking for cèpes. It became his only pastime.

"It is my belief that my Uncle Gaston imagined he had lost something during the war," said Madame Pelissier, "—apart, of course, from his wife. Maybe he had. His soul perhaps? If you believe in such things. Are you a *philosophe, Monsieur Egerton?*"

"I suppose I try to be."

"Ah! *Moi aussi!* That is good!" She leant over and patted my knee. It was a gesture of affection, but more maternal than amorous. Just then I heard the front door of her apartment being opened. Madame looked momentarily disconcerted. The door of the sitting room opened and a young man in blue overalls came in.

He must have been in his twenties, with the body of a fully-grown man but the soft-featured face of a teenager. He had black curly hair and large brown eyes like those of a young calf. His features were even, if a little lacking in definition, but he was decidedly good-looking. You might say pretty. Could this be her son? If he was, why had she not mentioned him before?

Madame and I rose from our seats together, and she introduced the young man to me as Fabrice. We shook hands formally, Fabrice eyeing me with a blatantly sulky and suspicious expression on his face. Madame Pelissier observed this, and immediately engulfed him in a flood of talk of which I could only gather fragments. Still talking volubly, she hastened Fabrice out of the room as if she were packing a recalcitrant child off to bed. I heard the conversation continuing in another part of the flat, Fabrice replying to her mostly in resentful monosyllables. After a few minutes, Madame Pelissier returned smiling.

"I have told Fabrice to take a shower. He is *mécanicien* at the garage by the bridge, and he always comes home smelling of oil." I looked at her interrogatively, as I thought it would offend if I asked her outright if Fabrice was her son, but she understood.

"Non! Fabrice, he lives with me," she said. "My—how do you say now?—'partner'. A good boy: he has no culture, but he is a superb lover." She looked for my reaction, and I must have given one, for she laughed. It was a charming laugh, if a little studied.

"Ah! You English! Always the respectability!" I laughed too; it seemed only polite.

"I think I should go," I said, and thanked her profusely for my 'five o'clock'. She escorted me to the door. I could hear Fabrice singing a pop song in the shower.

"But you must come again," she said, smiling.

"Really?" I said, glancing in the direction of the singer.

"Nothing in this life is permanent, *mon ami*. We should know." Fabrice in his shower hit a wrong note and Madame Pelissier winced, then laughed.

"One more question, *Madame*."

"Yes?"

"How did your Uncle Gaston die?"

There was a pause.

"He shot himself."

"In the wood?"

"But of course."

During the next few days, I spent most of the time arranging my books in all the shelves that had been made for them. It was a deeply satisfying activity, and I even began to devise a scheme of reading for myself in the future. I would start by re-reading and finally finishing Proust—that, I was sure about. And then? One shouldn't think ahead too far. Nothing in this life, as Madame Pelissier said, is permanent. *Tout passe, tout casse, tout lasse.*

Knowledge, they say, is power. That is not always the case, but it does invariably change things. The information I had been given about Uncle Gaston never left me. I found myself at odd moments looking out for him passing the window—or rather the apparition that I had supposed to be him. I reflected on his life, and began to experience a fellow feeling with a man who, like me, had become a kind of exile in his own country. No doubt he had done terrible things during the war, but we were beyond that now.

One lovely evening in June, when the longest day of the year was almost upon us, I sat reading in my salon with the French windows open. The air was warm, the sky cloudless. Birds were singing, and the nightly chorus of frogs was just starting up from behind the hill of Montpeyroux. I was utterly absorbed in my book when, quite suddenly, all these pleasant little noises stopped. I looked up, startled, shocked. It was so unnatural. In the garden was the man, head bowed, walking across my line of sight in the direction of the wood. He seemed darker than his surroundings, as if he existed in a different light from the rest of us, dimmer and more crepuscular.

It was instinct more than reason which made me put down my book and get up to follow him. Reason and caution told me to go back to my reading and ignore this psychic interruption, but instinct prevailed. Without looking to left or right, he crossed the road and entered the wood. Though he was perfectly solid in appearance, he made no sound and the undergrowth did not move as he passed through it.

I was directly behind him and about twenty feet away, as I too entered the wood. It was my first time in there, and I noted that the feeling of enclosure and oppression was strong. I was perfectly aware of the strangeness of what I was doing, but I felt detached from it. I registered dread, bewilderment, extreme anxiety, but almost as if these emotions were being felt by someone else, albeit close to me.

The figure—I suppose I should call him Gaston—walked on further into the wood, I following until I had no sense of where we were. We inhabited a pathless jungle of thick undergrowth, waist-high ferns and myrtles, lush grasses, dense stands of beeches whose leaf canopy almost shut out the sky above. Green was everywhere; the scents of warm earth and vegetation were overpowering.

Gaston stopped and so did I. We were now little more than a dozen feet apart. This, I knew, was the moment. He began to turn around to face me. It was a slow turn, timelessly, all but infinitely slow. I heard my heart thumping and recognised that I had a choice of whether to run or stay. It was a very pure decision, the forces on both sides being strong, perhaps in some ways stronger on the side of flight, but balanced. I chose to stay.

Now he was fully facing me. I saw a ragged hole where his head and the upper part of his chest should have been, as if blown away by a shotgun blast. Yet within the hole there was no tangled confusion of blood and sinew and bone, as there should have been, just a blackness. A tunnel into the void had been drilled through his body. The fear I felt was not that of physical danger, but of something far greater and more perilous, yet still I held my ground.

I sensed something reach out to me from Gaston's darkness, as if hoping to engulf me in its misery and despair. It wanted me to share its fate and become a companion. I felt it pulling at my thoughts and twisting them, as sleep sometimes does before you submit to it, but I held on. I would not receive it, but at the same time I would not reject it. Words from my late wife's burial service about rest and peace came to me; and, without exactly believing in them, I said them to myself, as if they were a mantra, or a magic spell.

The figure of Gaston began to change. He became more indistinct, and at the same time the blackness of his upper body was beginning to heal. I started to see features on his face, grey and smoky, yet recognisably those of a person. He was no longer trying to envelop me; there was more of a sense of communication. The grief and anguish were still intense, but they had assumed human proportions. I waited while he became whole, if insubstantial, then while he dissolved quietly into the night air like smoke from a dying fire. It was almost dark when the process was complete, but there was just light enough for me to see my way out of the wood, following the tracks that I had made on entering. Slowly the birdsong and the frog choruses were restored to my ears.

It was a clear but moonless night when I emerged from the wood. I felt I needed a walk before returning to Les Bosts, so I took the road that leads up to the main village of Montpeyroux, to the church and to the château which had once, according to local legend, belonged to Montaigne's brother. It was, like the rest of the village, silent and dark, but not quite! Far up in the topmost window of the château's main turret there gleamed a small steady golden light, like that of a candle flame.

# TANITH LEE

## IRON CITY

TANITH LEE is the author of more than 100 books and several hundred short stories. A discovery of Donald A. Wollheim, her novels include *The Birthgrave, Death's Master, The Silver Metal Lover* and *Red as Blood*, while some of her short fiction is collected in the Arkham House volume *Dreams of Dark and Light* and NewCon Press' tribute volume *Tanith by Choice*, the contents of which were selected by those who knew her best. She also scripted two episodes of the BBC series *Blakes 7*, and her story 'Nunc Dimittis' was adapted as an episode of the TV series *The Hunger*.

The first woman to win the British Fantasy Award, she followed it with two World Fantasy Awards and Life Achievement Awards from the World Horror Convention, the World Fantasy Convention and the Horror Writers Association.

Tanith Lee died in 2015 at the age of 67. The newly-discovered story which follows dates back to 1987 and first appeared in *Strindberg's Ghost Sonata and Other Uncollected Tales* (2019), the first of three anthologies to be published by Immanion Press intended to showcase a wide selection of the author's lesser-known works.

∽

I RON CITY
So says the green neon ten yards high, and under the legs of the tower, the lime-green girls plying their wares, stop one and buy me . . .

Raining, knives of water in the old gutters. The sky is made of cables, steel, the tops of buildings and the smog, city-breath, shut down like a lid.

Wet night to be out.

Better come in.

The girl with the long green tresses which, out of the neon, will be blonde, sees a client.

Rags of hair, pelt of rain, two glass eyes of a toy rat.

*The girls of Iron City*
*Are cruel and seldom pretty*

"Like me?" says the girl to the rain rat.

"You? Like?" The rat blinks his rainy eyes. He smiles, and takes her hand.

"Thirty," she says, "to you."

"Thirty blackbirds," he says," baked in a pie."

Arm-in-arm, they. She doesn't understand the quotation, or that he has altered it.

Under the iron stalks of the bridge, up a stair of wooden bones, to an apartment. Below, the river runs. The walls are red.

When blood splashes up the walls, it doesn't show.

She has no time to deny him. Never argue. The customer is always right.

Right, right, left, right the rain knife goes.

Under the slope-roof of his garret, the poet writes. Fingers cramped from keying at the antique word processor.

Words of the city, the lost of its streets moving like rain along a window, empty hearts and open mouths longing to swallow everything. Shadow citizens singing songs of blood. He writes of night's dark perfume and tastes so strong they cut the tongue.

The poet sips his black gin.

Down on the street, a bottle breaks, shouts and the scraping of razors. Screeching. Feet which race, without haste, away, and one pair not.

The city kills. The metal jaws of its industry chew up carcass after carcass. Bodies fall from high sills like autumn leaves. That day saw twenty or so accidents leaving a trail of maimed and dead. A train, mounting the rail of sky, fell from the elevated bridge through the glass roof of a pleasure dome. A thousand pieces of overtime for the undertaker.

The poet taps out another line—

*Something is out there.* Bright-eyed, lips parted, *Waiting.*

Morticians, whores, engineers. Lovers. Others. The City's saliva creeps.

The teeth of night shut together, spitting out the body of the half-boy into the river's icy gloom.

3:00 a.m. sees his machine-mangled remains raked up on to the riverbed. An industrial accident, some might say. At the factory, the straws of his bones and overalls are picked from the steel jaws of a well-oiled mechanism. Metal racks hosed down, the gory rags of another nightshift sluiced away. Mark off one more time card. No overtime invoiced.

What is left of the trainee is shovelled, dripping, into a labelled body bag. Removed. Off to a freezer to escape the chill.

A thousand crows perched upon the bridge, watch and wait.

Something is out there.

Something clicks and skips along the pavements, under the busted neons. Glimmer on wet teeth, wet eyes, knife. Not troubling to conceal anything, the face of the rat-catcher is only business-like. He has completed one transaction. There is time for another before the solstice of the winter dawn. Light comes late, goes quick from Iron City, snagged on girders and put out, loathe to make the morning struggle back up from the slimes and soots, the chemical sloughs; not liking its reflection in last night's sick, bloody street spillage.

Later.

A girl is on the waterfront. Against the low wall, where the walls of higher ships push out the sky. Light streaks the river. Orange rind and little bags of death, condoms by the million, armour against disease, filled, tied and floating with dead children strung out like mists into the water.

The girl is not touting for custom. She has lost her way from the upper levels. White face above water-proof garment. Low heels. Not a whore. Yet here she is, a twilight Madonna. She qualifies.

"Got a light?" clichés the rat-catcher.

The girl looks blankly at him. Does anyone smoke any more? Or does he only want a match to set the world on fire. In places, they have done that too.

"Sorry."

"What you doing, here?" asks he.

"Walking."

"You never moved," he accuses her. Already condemned, but not for a lie. Contempt of caught.

"I—" she says.

"Want see?" says the rat. He shows her the knife.

She nods. She came here for this.

Did she come here for this?

He holds her and delicately slips the knife through the black layer of her waterproof, the white crystal layer of her skin. Red petals, as from a broken rose, shower on the dirty wharf. It's a pity to waste them. He sips. She hangs over the arm of her death as he portions her. Her eyes are still open wide. They look at the stars, as if there were any. There are no stars. It was all a con trick. One night someone pinned shards of cut-out glass to the black lid laughingly referred to as the sky. The moon was more difficult. When too many questions were asked, they invented pollution, and they made smog. That hid everything.

"No moon. No stars. You can close your eyes now."

∞

The City kills.

The train, crumpled, still. Beached in pleasure-dome ceiling glass. A man's body, roasted on the train's aerial. Audible static, next crackling snatches of voice . . . Jingle advertising something sweet. Terrible tunes playing on some new receiver.

The train:

Dead.

Silver, grey, blue-lined. Streaked with red now, nose down, this metal engine. The train. Only a machine, not fitted for the thinking or the doing of things, except carrying the living, sometimes the dead, not able of such things as love, hate. Any emotion.

Only a train. A thing on wheels, never, no *never* capable of suicide.

So why is it glad? Why do the bloodied struts of steel turn upwards, smiling, see?

Why is the train happy now it lies there. Iron of the iron city, smouldering, with only the *faux* sky for shroud.

Silver. Grey. A machine insane.

*The girls of Iron City*
*Are cruel and seldom pretty.*
*They make you cum to the beat of a drum*
*And rob you without pity.*

The sailor off the ship clutches madly at the girl in the jade-green corset and stockings the colour of canaries. Her red hair catches the dull light behind her as she rides him down. He sees the flash of her red nails too. Something sets him off, some twist of her practised loins. Or the slick of light on her bare breasts, the feeling of her heavy pumping thighs in his grip. He groans and gasps and arches into her, giving his seed, the generations of his body, not to her sterile inner core, but to the little bag provided.

No natural exits here. Leave in a body bag.

Farewell my sons, my daughters. Out on the river with you. Go float down the Styx with all the others. Massacre of the innocents. Farewell my lovelies.

Released, the girl dismounts, leaves him. She goes to her cubicle, sluices her internal parts. She towels, and rubs off his musk. She walks through into another place, a chapel of sisters of the night.

"Gotta light?" Yes, someone still does smoke. Lean little tabs, cancer-free (but who can be sure?), all filter. Flavour: Wild Mint, choc-ice cigarette.

"Jesus, he took a time."

"Didn't know you had Jesus in there tonight, Luly."

"That sailor. Reckon his cock was constipated."

Luly, foul-mouthed but fair, stretches her body to the raw crimson light. Oh, her hair is like unto a fabled garden of peonies, poppies. Red, so very red. Her eyes are cool green, paler than her strident corset. She wears laced boots, purple and black, striped over wasp-like yellow where the stockings peep through. Don't get stung.

"Did you hear, Luly, two more tonight."

Luly shakes her blood-red hair.

"A girl by the river. That was the other. He unseamed her like a dress."

Luly doesn't care. Death is always out there. But she is here in the warmth, in the air made of aerosol scent and little trails of non-cancerous smoke. She drinks down a whisky laced with cream. She eats a piece of chicken. Nearly a whole half-hour before her next client will be shown up. (Would have been three-quarters if that clown hadn't been so lazy. What did he think he was doing, giving her a good time? Making her cum? Stupid. Only Death really cums. Death cums every time. Every time he takes. Multiple orgasm.)

She works to keep her little brother. Another cliché. Luly knows she is a cliché. Isn't everything? Her little brother has no arms. Such a pity. Beautiful, all the rest. Even his shoulders, like polished Adonis marble, ending in smooth round finalities. His breath is sweeter than any aerosol. His eyes greener than any choc-ice cigarette and bright as the real stars that maybe once there were. His long hair, dark as river, flows. Luly loves her brother. When she goes home she bathes and scrubs, wipes off all her make-up, ties back her wet flame of hair, embraces him. Kisses. Makes him meals. Feeds him chocolate. He eats so couthly. She would like to eat *him*, too. Not in the sexual way, in the Bacchic way. Yet she would protect him against all the world. He never speaks. He can never touch her. Such a relief.

A thousand crows and more—The night.

The little boy wanders from shop front to gaudy shop front, not looking in at each and every delectable behind the glass, but looking for his mother. His tiny feet carrying him here and there, there and over there, but he still cannot find her.

Watching, the crows shiver.

Rat, rain, man, eater of sweet fleshes, lurks in a doorway, slurping down entrails, the noodle "life". Wipes whiskers clean on grey cuff, twitches, sniffs, ignores now the self-service body at his feet and sees them, two of them. Close. He and she, swaggering Nu-Forms with pretend lobotomy scars and stick-on misfortunes. Down from upper levels, must be slumming it here. Closer. And then they see him and the bloody bundle in which he stands. No more swaggers, or bravado. Just terror.

Run, run, run!

*To the beat of my drum . . .*

The She's heel breaks, she topples, does not fall. The He has left her behind. Running past a blur of crows perched upon a blur of bridge, running for the rusted stairs leading up. Scream and scream the He and She.

Rat sniffs twice, two times, shuffles off.

Feathers, so many feathers, blue-black, fall, spiralling to the river. Oily shimmer ripples.

The little lost boy cannot see or smell the rancid gathering plumage, automatically takes for granted that the ends of his vision will finish in waters, dark and deep.

No waters. Only feathers.

The river swarms with countless crow feathers. The carrion birds have shed their winter coats.

Boy's eyes full of tears, cannot see straight, will fall down through cracks in the broken bridge, fall in to drown in the black heaven of a sea of crows. He loses footing, tumbles—

But no.

Rain in a raincoat with eyes and nose, catches the boy, holds him, holds him close.

"Want Mam, my Mam."

"Course ya's do."

Tight incisor smile now. Rat-paw reaches into manky pocket. Pulls out small, white. Thing.

*Watching.*

Pain in a raincoat takes the boy's hand.

"Shut eyes, and them to be kept shut, hear?"

Nodding, obedient the lost one, shut, bolted.

"There."

*Only feathers.*

Just the boy now, no rat, no raincoat, no footsteps scampering off, just the lost boy by the broken bridge.

One eye opens, nothing, nobody. Two eyes. Looks down. In his hand, a present. A bone. A perfect finger bone.

Still lost, motherless, uncaring of such things now. The boy plays happy with a new toy.

Lifting limply from the bridge, one by one, myriad featherless crows fly off, following the rain rat, following their shepherd. One by one, flying off, making morning.

Factory sirens scream. Clocking-off time for all the nightshifts.

Home they go, some pausing to piss in gutters, to augment the filth there, the rinds and blades, the blood and grief, the weeping of the city's wounds.

The poet, too, is venturing home. Back to his unmade shabby bed with the horrid patch where once the black gin spilled—or he wet himself at a vile dream of a rat in a raincoat, wiping his knife upon a woman's hair. "Stop dreaming me, stop *writing* me, you cunt," had said the rat.

The young man had recently been brought in. Another accident. Just half of him now. The mortician takes her time, stroking her fingers through his dead blond hair. Tracing a slow, painted nail along the lips of his blue-crow feather-black open mouth.

Smeared with dirty tears, the dawn is in the east. Luly walks home in the part-light of day, and sees the clot of vehicles around the upstairs room near the bridge, where a blonde blushed red last night from her pelvis to her eyes. Luly stares, looks off. Notes the shards of glass and squinnied metal from the train that fell into the Palace Hotel. (A stately pleasure dome decreed.)

Luly reaches her street.

Steps inches thick in unmentionable stuffs. The hallway grows rare algae. The lift is stuck between floors. A drunk, or corpse, hangs out of it.

Luly extinguishes her cigarette and climbs up slow to her one true love.

He is lying in his bed asleep, like an angel. The sheet reaches to his perfect shoulders. He looks normal. Only too clean, too pure to be any of that. Luly creeps to the shower and scours herself of all the night, before she will come back. She plants, with naked washed lips, a kiss on either temple, on the eyelids, the long lashes, either cheek, the space between upper lip and nostril, the chin, one shoulder, the other shoulder. Then as he sleepily awakes and smiles at her, Luly whips off the sheet and climbs in. She lies along him, as if neither of them has any sex, and she is able to forget it. Luly sleeps her one-hour sleep of morning, her lips pressed to her brother's side where the arm should be and isn't, and if it were, would he not be out there in the muck and shit of Iron City, besmirching his soul with all the rest of the rotten world?

The rat-catcher rat sleeps in darkness. Curled up. Where he is quite invisible.

Does it even exist, this city of rust? Some forgotten undreamt dream, some concocted hole; the anus of the world which may also be another imaginary poet's unwritten, shameful fiction.

The cats are running from the intersections up the rails and posts and broken-glass-topped cliffs of the city. Black masks, dominoes;

white masks as if the eyes had been drawn round with chalk. Morsels of dead rats between their teeth. Good hunting.

A big black wagon stops outside a brick tenement.

It is full grey-brown day, eleven o'clock if anyone knew or cared.

A nasty great box is being uncrated from the van, and borne slowly down into the road. Someone has knocked on a door. A young girl stands there. She looks frightened, as if being scared would do any good.

"He was your brother?" says the man in black overalls.

"I ain't got no money," says the girl.

"No charge," says the man. His face a wedge of stone.

Already the girl is crying, as if it could help.

"Got in the way of the big one. Can't turn that one off. Against orders. Dangerous machine. Very quick, you see."

Nailed down in the past. The water of life dripped away.

Drip, the tears and running nose of the girl who won't dare say a word.

"Can't have felt it. Never do. Always happening. Not even time to cry out. He's in that box. Where do you want it?"

"Just put it in the hall."

"Sign here. Nice and tidy. The Collector will be by later, unless you want to make funeral arrangements."

"Thank you," says the girl. White as the dawn, tear-stained.

The wagon goes.

She looks at the box in the hall which is her brother.


Luly makes breakfast at three in the afternoon, or fifteen by the old clocks. Eggs in an omelette with a pinch of flour, spices and black pepper, cream and cheese for filling. Black market bacon. Real food, not synth or fake, not dubious. Nothing if not the best. Wheat toast. Oranges and maple syrup. A green apple—green as his eyes. He eats with economy and neatness as she gently fork-feeds him.

When he was three, Mumma tried to poison him. With petrol. Luly remembers this like an evil story told at bedtime. Mumma's dead anyhow. Mumma went under the wheels of the one shiny car Luly never saw.

Luly reads to her little brother, a foot taller than she is. She reads during the afternoon old tattered books (rat-gnawn) got off book-seller patrons, when they finished kicking against her body, biting her basque. Often the books miss pages, have neither start nor end. Just like life really. But life did have an end, if you could believe *that*. Or she reads him newspapers. She expurgates these. No news of crashes, accidents, rippings.

She doesn't know if he understands any of it. He likes the sound of her voice she thinks, the only one who does. "You're the only one what loves me, you are, an' you do, don't you?" His dreamy smile. So beautiful. If their old whore-mother knew—Christ, what a thought.

Sometimes she just sits. Looks at him. It's enough. Ain't it?

D Section. North West. Level 88. Bars and brothels heaving with factory overspills. Sweaty blue-collars, shoulder to shoulder loud with excitement and bad ale. They've come to watch the hanging. Vast screens taped to exterior bar walls. Public execution as entertain-ment. Keep the workers happy. Top brass have even sent a camera-crew down, nosing in at drunken oafish faces, missing teeth and industrial facial scars worn with pride.

Rat slides through the scene, liquid.

The crowd stamps its feet, punches fists to air, chants, calling for the Drop. Epic screen music distorts through dodgy overhead speaker drones. A "4-D Family Extravaganza". Apparently.

Eyes in a raincoat, blades of vision peer through the bodies, lunches? No. No women. Just laborious male flesh. No tenderness, no succulence.

A hooded figure fills the huge screens. The hood is pointed, a dull red fluffy clown's nose stitched beneath the two torn slits of eyes. The mob roar. It's the WireMan. The jovial executor with his arm draped casual-like 'round the shoulder of the tied, gagged, squirming accused; a thin metal noose collars his neck.

"Drop! Drop! Drop!" they bellow, not knowing why.

Drones spit out the accused name, *Brian E*. A disgraced employee of the month. A fatherless son and guilty of failed youth theft.

"'Ang 'im! Fuckin' 'ang 'im!"

Brian E has pissed himself. His crime—to have wound-back watches, to be a pre-dater of calendars, to polish his hair and whiten his crumbs of teeth. Condemned for wanting to recapture his prime years, the long-gone heyday of his life. So selfish. No one memory is sacred. We are all in this together. We must all work, grow old and die. That is the way it has always been. (Or so they were told.) No slackers needed. All he's fit for is the Drop.

"Drop!"

WireMan pulls the lever. The crowd holds its breath. Brian E slips in slow-motion, his feet fall down through the trapdoor, his body follows. The metal rope around his neck tightens, sinks into his flesh, severs bone as his head with eyes stretched wide, sliced clean off, topples to the studio floor in a fountain of blood. There is a close-up to show the eyelids flashing their last. Cheesy music plays as the WireMan cavorts about the televised stage as if on an imaginary horse.

Crowd is wild. Throwing its arms around itself, hugging, jumping up and down, singing violent nonsense words. Vindicated. Just, in its belief of born, toil, die. Not chancing to think of younger days, however rotten they were, or of a clock's second-hand pushed sly back. Not knowing that time is a forgery.

There is a fear in knowing.

An extendable fish-eye camera lens is pushed into rat's pinched face. He backhands it out of the way and exits through gaps in the jubilant heat of strong, scared bodies.

The rain-rat-man with a blade in each pocket and one upon his tongue, would have made a commendable WireMan, but for his deformities.

Ah, such a pity to be perfect.

*Four and twenty blackbirds,*
*Ripped in a pie . . .*

There are dead men under the bridges. As the light begins to go—get out quick—they settle in the mud like a warm bed. On the tall buildings the lights start to come back on. An electric confession. All is forgiven. Not.

That was day. Short. But the night is so big, outside. Limitless. It was always this way, from the first cave-mouth with its lick of flame with endless sabre-toothed darkness beyond, to the cave-pocked buildings one-sixty storeys high, putting on their diamanté lights as if it mattered, as if it could do any good.

Old sun, crust crimson, sinking down behind the docks, where sooty birds dine out on dead men.

The poet is wrapped in the amber glow of the word-processor screen. Hasn't written a word all day. Still thinking of a title for an unfinished poem. He looks at his notes, cuttings from pale papers, smudged newsprint. Witness testimonies. Is it true? Could it be? Did he really kill a nun? Slice her up, breakfast upon her? Some say he did. Others that this is impossible. Eating her body would be like consuming the Holy Ghost in reverse. They say he cooks some of them on a little stove. Crisped white flesh tanned in the oven. Choicest cuts. But it's the street-walkers he takes, or girls he thinks are prostitutes, out alone in the night-place, the woods of the world. Fair game.

All the city must be a market for him. Just imagine how the street looks to him, shelves and cupboards. There a pastry on legs, there a girl in gingerbread with angelica feet. That one a delicate chicken, in a rich cream sauce. Offal isn't awful.

But up there, off sidewalks, levels so high, they're out of the danger zone. Prey which has climbed trees.

In the glass towers, on the concrete balconies, level 1, they are safe . . . as houses.

Straw houses.

*I shall huff and puff and . . .*

Sweet dreams, little candy Juliets.

And it is only from that safe height that the unspoken past can sometimes still be viewed. Over there, faraway off, beyond the Tannhauser perimeter, shifting, searching, the tall, lumbering silhouettes in the marshlands and swamps. Steam-and-clockwork relics left over from the Cola Wars.

Luly puts on her purple corset and green stockings, and sits painting her nails (scoured for her brother). She feels pleasantly dirty now, garnished with powder, lipstick, gloss, mascara. Quite a dish. Only waiting. She tries not to think of kissing him goodbye. It had been so poignant, it always almost makes her cry. Even now. Daren't let him see. He cries easily if she does. Can't bear to see those silk-strand tears slip down the smooth planes of his face. But here, where she is not allowed to think of her brother, Luly scratches herself under the arm, drinks urine-coloured gin. By midnight her piss too will reek of alcohol.

Too easy. The third girl of that early night (still a wisp of rose-red in the west) slips down amongst the garbage. Her exquisite entrails taper out, coils of jewellery. The heart still gives a tiny tremble, an aftershock.

The rat carries his knife sadly through a sluggish rain, which washes it, wiping off the badge of his red courage. Sighing, he nibbles only one thin rice-paper of young skin.

It was untrue about the nun. There are no such things any more, more myths like the stars. Moon, stars and nuns extinct.

"One extra," she says. "An' you're to do it, Tipper," she says.

"Long as he's quick."

"Can barely hold himself. Probably do it in his pants."

Luly opens the door and lets in her unexpected guest. He is small and thin, slick black rainy hair, rain eyes like those of a toy animal. Had brought the night in with him, stinks of it.

"You take a wash," says Luly. "The things are in the dispenser. I'll put it on for you. Full protection guaranteed."

He goes into the bathroom. Does not wash. Comes out without the condom and stands and looks at her. Jesus. A fool. But he may be easy then. Not even need one.

"Nothing to worry at," says Luly.

As she walks over to him, she has a feeling she is on a midnight pier. Strings of light are all out, hanging in dead clusters, like amputated eyes. The river feathers by. She is suddenly afraid.

"No," she says. "You got it wrong. I ain't wanting it. I've *got* someone—I have things I wanta *do*—"

She feels the knife go in softer than a petal brushing her skin. When she looks down, through a mist, her breast is in his hand. She stares. No longer *her* breast, as no longer attached to her. She feels the pain only as terror, and screams. There are frequent screams here. How often she has screamed in simulation for clients. No one cares. (As if they would.) The rat-catcher, catcher of rats, son of rat-catchers, father to none, observes the whore with her white and purple and red, and red and red. He shakes his head, and slits her in half.

*Sing a song of sixpences*
*Covering your eyes.*

Easy then, this time, only a success. Slip down the stairs, head bowed. Fate accomplished. Before they send her the next punter, he is away. How many brothels he can visit like this. Why did he never try before. So simple. So perfect. He carries beauty in a carrier bag. The nicest take-away.

He trots along, clicking, skipping beneath the poet's window. The processor suddenly clacking noisily out. The ratty-rat pays no heed, who cares who immortalises him? He can do the job himself, will never be caught. Not even stopped, though the rain streaks him with white along his mask of blood. She splashed him. (Sip.) He, too, flushed with pride. The gutters swill with blood and horrors. What's one more. There are no nuns, or stars. No Moon. No gods and no policemen.

The poet reads aloud what he typed moments earlier:
"*The beast the beast*
"*The feast the feast*
"*At least at least*
"*There's plenty to eat*
"*On the iron plates of the city.*
"Doggerel," says the poet, disgusted.

He deletes all of the files. Wiped clean. He wrenches the plug from its socket, heaves the word processor up, kicks open his room door and exits, carrying the weighty machine down to the riverside where he hefts it into the watery muck. Bubbling, gobbled down. Swallowed.

Iron City eats everybody alive. Merely to live is to be devoured, years, inches and yards at a time. The jaws of steel will have everything. A cream tea, sudden and sodden, sucked in without a murmur.

Gone.

At Luly's funeral (the brothel staff had insisted there be one) everyone cries.

They throw roses on her grave, a compacted two feet (anyone buried must be put in folded-up, the graveyards yawn not only, but overflow. Easier with Luly, partly depleted.) After the ceremony, at which the Madam reads the lesson, drunk, there is a booze-up, knees-up, throw-up ultimately.

Luly will not be forgotten.

They never knew, she did not want to stain him with their knowledge, about her little brother.

The poet escapes. Gone over high walls, picked his way through the dried-up barbed wire canals, negotiated the forest of ashes and wild boar to find himself in the everglade. There he will find the inspiration to write (with a found crow-feather cut to quill) of a dynasty of blind herons and their eternal battle against the Messiah-Toads.

She is standing on the corner in her old ragged coat, skirt and cardigan. Some cheap beads at her throat, perhaps an ancient rosary re-painted. Her eyes are black with shadow, and her lips crayoned red. She tried to dye her hair. It has turned three colours, all of them wrong. Scarecrow. But here on the corner of night, available, and not so far from the neon of green welcome—the other whores moved her off a ways—the stalks of the bridge where tonight the smog is thick as rancid butter.

She shakes. Chicken. She didn't want to.

She stands there, thinking of her brother in the metal mouth of the big machine they wouldn't turn off, let it chew him, and gave her back the pieces in the box. Three days it was in the hall, waiting for collection. The second night she opened it, and ran to spew her heart into the dark. Her brother. Who kept her. Who worked and saved her and was eaten by a steel machine and left her here alone with nothing to do but this.

"It ain't me," she says to him and the night. "And when I have to—*then*, it won't be me neither."

But it will, she knows it, and he will see, her brother gone to Jesus meek and mild, who will love him, and both Jesus and her brother will watch when she—when she lies back on the wall and lifts one leg and lets—

Someone stands there, even though she pulled the smog closer around herself, trying to hide from what be done.

"Like me?" she asks, coy, the way she has heard them say, under the stalks of the bridge.

But she senses he has only paused out of a kind of courtesy, on his way to somewhere more urgent and important, seeing her standing here alone in the murk.

"You? Like?"

A rat-like man with rainy eyes. Romeo in a raincoat.

She leans forwards, unbuttons herself. She is full of dreadful aching agony. Don't let God see. Hate him, the man, the bastard, it's the only answer.

"Ten," she says, knowing what she's not worth.

"Room?" he says.

"Oh—no. Here."

Juliet down on the ground. Oh, bid me leap—

He too leans forwards.

Suddenly she sees he is offering her a knife. She takes it from his hand and pushes it home into his gullet. He makes a gurgling noise. The right one. She has heard it before, outside. She is glad. Glad when he slides down into the mush of foulness underfoot. Jesus saw. Jim saw, too. She runs away crying, but not sorry.

Only later does she wonder if he truly was offering her the blade, or if he was offering to kill her. Did she make the right decision? Incision?

*The feast*
*The feast.*

*At least*
*At least.*

Where he sits, the light gets in, through the broken window. At first he waited here for Luly to come back. Then he only waited. At first he cried, too. Then crying gave way to other things, some sublime introspection of nothing.

He is thick in filth now. Without her to help him, he is all the dirt and foulness, the ordure and puke of the streets. He *is* the Iron City, once fine, now architectured over in decay and dung, in bad and bitter things.

But his eyes have stayed the way they were. Calm and beautiful. No iota of filth has reached them, or inside them. Windows of the soul, their lights go on burning against the coming night of death.

And when he topples over, any day now, gives up the ghost as they say, pegs out, *leaves*, his eyes will stay open until the flies and mice and microbes have eaten them. His eyes will remain focussed on stars. Perhaps upon the moon.

And when all the flesh of him has been picked clean, his skeleton will lie couthly on the floor, its white and peerless bones in a pearly alignment.

You can't ruin everything. No, you *can't*. See?

# GLEN HIRSHBERG

## SLOUGH

G LEN HIRSHBERG lives with his family and cats in the Pacific
Northwest. His novels include *The Snowman's Children*, *The
Book of Bunk, Infinity Dreams* and the "Motherless Children" trilogy.
He is also the author of four short story collections: *The Two Sams*
(a *Publishers Weekly* "Best Book of 2003"), *American Morons*, *The
Janus Tree* and *The Ones Who Are Waving*.

Hirshberg is a three-time winner of the International Horror
Guild Award and he won the Shirley Jackson Award for his novelette
'The Janus Tree'. With Peter Atkins and the late Dennis Etchison, he
co-founded the Rolling Darkness Revue, an annual reading/live
music/performance event that toured the west coast of the United
States every fall between 2004 and 2015. He is also the owner/
proprietor of Drones Club West, through which he offers online and
in-person creative writing classes, as well as manuscript editing and
consulting.

"One of my best friends from college kept disappearing from
school," recalls the author. "Often, he didn't tell anyone he was going.
He'd be gone overnight, or for a month. Once, he was gone for a year
and a half. Another time, another friend ran into him in Central
Park, where he was somehow now working as a ranger.

"Years later, I drove down to see my friend in an old, old enclave
of crumbling houses at the bottom of Rhode Island. The drive took

longer than seems possible given the size of the state, and the whole way, I was followed by this dripping, misting rain that blurred pretty much everything outside my windows. When I finally found my friend's place, we went swimming in the ocean, in the misting rain, in the twilight, amid those beautiful, collapsing dwellings which felt like they'd been there since the violent birth of the country. Out of all that, and the stories on the radio that night about riots in Missouri and Oakland and elsewhere, came 'Slough'.

"The pronunciation of the title, by the way, rhymes with "you"…"


"WAIT 'TIL YOU hear why," I said into my phone. I had it wedged between my shoulder and ear so I could repack my cameras.

"Why?" said Daniel in that tone he's perfected: interested in spite of himself. It's partly an act, he knows I know it, and it doesn't matter; it's sexy to me.

"The rain."

"What?" The laugh is not an act, and the actual key to the sexiness. Daniel *is* interested. It's the in-spite-of he plays at.

"You heard me. Actually, not the rain. The storm."

"It's storming?"

"Did I say it was storming?"

"Gabby, just—"

"Don't you read the weather? There could be thunder. This is a family organisation, remember."

"Oh God, that's so good. All white supremacists must wait at least thirty minutes after lightning strikes before re-donning jackboots."

I set down my bag and leaned against the bridge railing, watching the grey-green, relocated Woonasquatucket pool docilely below. The bridges didn't really make Providence look like Venice, I decided. But they heightened my awareness of the decay I could almost smell beneath all these swanky, restored façades, or lurking just out of sight down the surrounding blocks. That block, there, say, past the first

Baptist church in America, where Roger Williams set up shop after the Puritans kicked him out for learning Native languages and railing against slavery.

Ironies.

"Ooh, but I forgot. The trip wasn't a total waste. Daniel...they've found a third F."

"A...okay, what?"

"...of the Fox, Daniel. They're now the Faith Families of the Fox. They have a banner. It has a fox on it."

"You're fucking kidding."

"That would be four Fs."

"Yeah, and then they'd be...medically excused?"

"Hah." I was laughing for real, though. Daniel, too. Sometimes, we really do feel like lovers. Talk like lovers. Usually not when we're trying to be lovers, though. Overhead, clouds scudded, grey and grimy, like smokestack smoke but pumped from up there, in some decrepit factory of the air.

I didn't want to go back to the Bronx yet. Not to the tiny basement office from which Daniel and I ran the photos-for-commercial-reuse business we'd kept solvent for more than seven years. Not to Daniel's nearby one-room, half-bath apartment we sometimes shared. Certainly not to the Staten Island studio efficiency I'd inherited from a wastrel uncle, paid rent control for, and had last seen weeks ago because it just took too long to get there. Right then, none of those places felt like mine. I wondered when I'd last had a place that felt like mine. College, maybe. At the school I'd named NW NoPlace.

But that wasn't the moment I decided to call Julian. Why would I even have thought of him then?

"Did you get a shot of her at least? Gab?"

I hate *Gab*. He knows it. Maybe he sensed I wasn't coming back and was annoyed.

"Of Mrs.—sorry, *Dr.* Tilley? I did indeed. That hair, Daniel. It's *huge*. It really is like waterfall spray. You've never seen old lady hair that wild. She stood on this bridge like Grandma Moses—"

"Probably not so much like Grandma Moses. Who didn't have wild hair, I don't think."

"More like her than you'd think. More than you'd want to believe. Okay, Dr. Tilley has more hair. But she's little, full of sparkle, big violet eyes, keeps a pug-nosed, pasty grandkid on each arm. 'We are not *like* the fox that roams these hills,' she said. Have you heard her speak? There's nothing little about that voice. Like a fucking hanging judge. 'We are not *like* the fox. We *are* the fox.'"

"Just one?" Daniel laughed again.

"'For this land and of it. It is us. We are it.' The woman is magnetic, Daniel. Scary as shit."

He heard the anxiousness in my voice, or disgust, or whatever it was. He stopped laughing, but too late.

"I'm staying here today. I need to . . . I'll be home tomorrow."

Some, rare times—when I'm tired, drinking, aware of being thirty-eight and still not sure I actually don't want children, or when I decide out of nowhere I'm not coming back and he doesn't protest—I still think I could marry Daniel. If he still wants me to or ever really did.

Bugs clouded the surface of the water, hummed in the grass at either end of the bridge. But none came for me. The sticky morning heat slicked my skin but hadn't suffocated me. The protesters and counter-protesters, such as they had been, had dispersed, and hours would pass before business lunchers streamed into the park. Dr. Tilley had called for bonfires all along the redirected bank, fox flags and white pride in the streets, smoke in the air. Even without all of that, Providence felt far from the city or country I imagined I lived in. Which consisted mostly, honestly, of New York now.

"The FFF," Daniel murmured.

"Got it in one, as our former overlords across the pond put it."

"But . . . Ku Klux Klan. Isn't that supposed to be the sound of a rifle being cocked? What's FFF, then?"

"A fart when it's tired?"

We both laughed.

"You sure you don't want to come home, Gabby?"

That was what actually caused it: the word *home* in my ear in his voice, at once over-familiar and detached. A euphemism. In the weirdly airless gusts of breeze, the gaps of grey between greyer clouds massing, on the matte-flat surface of water that reflected nothing, certainly not me, I could feel—could actually see—myself floating. Drifting in that liminal space between lives where most people I know live.

*Julian lives here*, I suddenly remembered. In Rhode Island, somewhere.

"See you tomorrow, Daniel," I said, disconnected from him, and swiped to my contact screen.

Even there, Julian showed up out of order and adrift, the only person filed by nickname: *Boom*. I had no idea if the number was current. For an address, what I had was SOUTH COUNTY? I'd added his wife's name, but apparently hadn't been sure of that either, because LORI had a question mark, too. When had I last even heard from him?

In R.I., I texted, heart hammering for no good reason. R u?

His answer pinged before I got my phone back in my pocket.

COME. Please?

Not "Hi." Not "Who is this?" or "Gabby. Wow."

COME. Please?

It was an archetypal electronic communication, so denuded of meaning that it could have meant anything I feared or wanted. I've learned the dangers of interpreting texts like that the same painful way most people do.

But Julian apparently wanted me to come to wherever he was. *Really* did. How often does that happen with other adults, if we're honest? An invitation without any suggestion of whatever they're swamped with and will have to put aside, audible grinding of gears as days get recalibrated and to-do lists assessed, hesitation over the room that's thank God clean-ish or isn't? How much more peaceful and comfortable our friends look in the glowing little fish-tanks of our phones. They hardly even need feeding.

Come where? I responded.

Within an hour, I was headed south down the 1A in a tiny rented Civic. The tininess proved crucial, as I almost grazed three parked cars manoeuvring free of the jammed lot onto a packed downtown street better suited to bike messengers than drivers. Admittedly, the problem might have been that I hadn't driven in five years.

Once out of the city, the road opened up. Traffic didn't exactly evaporate, but it loosened, chaperoning me down-country, over bridges, past bays glimpsed through trees. So many trees. Maples, oaks, American beech, all bursting with bright summer green under threatening grey sky. I passed signs for harbours, bridges, a light-house, a pond. How small does your state have to be before you start signing ponds? Every now and then, I'd get a glimpse of grey water, red brick buildings huddled on some hilltop rise, picnic tables in clearings. Mostly, though, the trees hemmed me in, decorous and stately and weirdly intimidating as Buckingham Palace guards. *Welcome to look*, I imagined them saying, in some invented accent that was probably more Down East—not even the right state—than Rhode Island. *Beautiful, yes? Keep moving.*

Once, trapped behind a seafood truck with painted crabs scuttling over it, and with rain clouds still blanketing the landscape, I glanced left and thought I saw faces in the branches of a maple across the freeway. Pasty, grinning, long-nosed. Dr. Tilley's grandkids in their centuries-old tree-blinds. Fox-kids who could climb. To absolutely no one, and for reasons having mostly to do with being afloat in a day I hadn't planned, I waved. The faces dissolved into the branches and leaves and the patches of blank sky between them.

The drive took longer than it should have. Rhode Island is forty-some miles long, and traffic stayed light. The freeway, such as it was, ended but the road kept going. There were turnoffs for the 1, the 2. Directional signs for Jamestown. Jerusalem. Trees got scruffier, hunkered back. Towns appeared: low clapboard gas stations, red-cedar main streets with taverns at one end and ice cream shops at the other. Still, Julian-land did not appear.

Finally, having caught red at all three stoplights in a town comprised of a Check Cashing Laundromat, a hardware store, and an incongruous Luxury Living Real Estate office, I pulled into a sandy parking lot. There was ocean ahead, now, or water, anyway. It seemed I was pointed straight off the end of the island.

I'd taken the place I stopped for a gas station, possibly abandoned. But when I got out of the car, I heard voices pouring through the screen door of the squat, square hut at the back of the lot. "Shut up,

Cindy," some kid said. Then came a clank, a mechanical gurgle, some sloshing. Slushie or Soft-serv sounds, from faltering machines.

*Like coming home,* I thought, though nothing about that made sense. I hadn't been "home", meaning Iowa, since my mom died, and Slushie sounds gurgled somewhere in the strip-malls around every American's "home", and I'd never been to Rhode Island in my life.

Think I missed you, I thumbed into my phone. Pretty sure that last sign said South Carolina.

Julian's answer, again, came back instantaneously.

Keep going.

Don't you want to ask where I am? I threw in a smiley-face emoji for good measure. I do that when I'm unsure of myself. Julian, I remembered, had always made me feel this way, which was kind of funny, given Julian.

I stood there a long time but got no additional response.

The restaurant—quick-stop, lemonade stand, whatever—did have a sign, I saw now. It was hand-painted, leaning out of the dirt by the screen door, staked like a tomato plant to keep it upright. But instead of a name, the sign boasted two declarations, both hand-inked: WHERE TUNA COMES TO LIFE and, under that, SMALL STATE. BIG FLAVOUR.

Reaching back into the Civic, I grabbed a camera, headed inside. There were only three people in there, two freckle-faced brothers and Cindy, I presumed. Cindy was taller than either boy, spindle-armed, long-legged, pointy as a shark fin. None of them looked older than sixteen. I snapped some shots before they even processed my entrance: three kids; serving counter full of cardboard vats behind cooled glass that should have held ice cream but instead contained tuna salad variants; chopping counter, scratched-all-over silver, shiny-clean.

"Okay, kids," I said. "Bring tuna to life."

Which, I had to admit, back in my car and another twenty minutes down the endless spit between bays and tiny towns, they absolutely had. It wasn't even whatever they'd spiced it with, which wasn't much, honestly. It was the freshness, still tingling on my lips, my tongue, way down my throat. So fresh I half-thought I could feel it flipping around, reconstituting. A bracing taste, not entirely pleasant.

"New York?" Cindy had asked, dead flat, folding my sandwich perfectly into its wrapper.

*Iowa*, I'd wanted to say and almost did. *Why? As an expression of solidarity? I'm you, not me? For you and of you?* I'd snapped her picture again and offered to send it to her. She'd just shrugged.

I still wonder how long that drive actually lasted. There's only one road, and it's the one I drove. But I'm convinced that if I ever went back, took Daniel—I've considered it, he's asked—that road would empty into water a good hour before we actually got to Slough. We'd maybe see Slough floating on the horizon, a place the country once connected to. But we wouldn't be able to drive or walk there.

The first, fat raindrops spattered on my roof and hood, as though a horse had galloped past overhead. *One if by land,* I remember thinking. Humming, even. To my right, inland, a curve of water lay tucked into the land, serene and waveless. The scatter of moored sailboats there twitched in the spits of drizzle like the ears of sleeping cats. To my left, down weed-pocked streets, the ocean roiled.

*Boom,* I thought, and with a surprised snort, remembered why we'd called Julian that. All this time, I thought *I'd* coined it, a trademark Gabby-ism referring ironically to his elusiveness, his ability to be in a room without so much as rippling the air let alone tilting a conversation, unless he was playing guitar. But that wasn't it at all.

All through our heads-down, two-jobs-plus-classes, finish-fast-before-the-money's gone lives at NW NoPlace—a particularly rank Gabby-ism for our not-little, undistinguished Midwest university, our Directional School for those without direction planted squat in the middle of a dying college town (meaning a dead town with a college in it), somewhere I'd actually genuinely loved and still missed—Julian kept disappearing. Sometimes he'd do it right in the middle of a term, sometimes two days into one. He'd be gone two weeks, a month. The last time, he stayed away three years, and Daniel and I had long since decamped for my inherited Staten Island studio by the time he returned. He never said where he went, not even when he came back. But he always wrote from his home—from Slough—right before he reappeared.

Daniel had given him the name, not me. *Boom,* as in *boomerang.*

There weren't many signs of any kind along my road by that point. Certainly none that said SLOUGH 4 MI. or anything. All drive long, the clouds had been congealing into a single, miles-long, fathoms-deep thunderhead. But now, when I stopped staring around for markers long enough to glance up, I saw only wispy grey which was no longer congealing or even moving. The rain thinned and steadied. Instead of beating, it beaded on my windshield and hood, draping me in itself. It was like going through the world's longest mechanical car wash, except instead of scrubbing off road-grit, it was coating me in it.

Then I was there. I'm not even sure how I realised it; there was no fancy Narragansett Towers landmark, no banner announcing an upcoming Crafts and Crabs Fair. I know I saw the words SLOUGH LIBERTY-GUARDIAN on a dirt-caked newspaper box, the kind you put a quarter in and then pray the lid actually lifts so you can get your paper out. The words were white, fading into metal that was rusted, pocked with holes.

There wasn't a kerb. The street, which I guess counted as paved—more sprinkled with paving crumbles, but there was paving involved—seemed to pool between buildings, flowing like shore-water up to and underneath the weedy grass and dirt paths that abutted the scatter of storefronts. Most of the structures were clapboard, single-storied, the windows filthy. Along the bases, especially, the remaining paint was coated in a yellow-brown rime which could have been street-muck or salt decay or markings from the coyote packs I suddenly imagined roaming this street after dark. Assuming there were coyotes in Rhode Island.

Mostly, Slough looked past its use, the buildings soft, somehow, permeable, vulnerable, like covered wagons ossified in place. Feeling sneaky even with no one around, I rolled down my window and snapped surreptitious photos. Then I grabbed my phone off the passenger seat.

The first thing I typed was **Wow. Can see why you always came** back. Then, annoyed with myself, I deleted that and just asked for directions.

Those proved surprisingly elaborate, and ended with When in doubt, go left.

I went left. Paving crumbled away, became dirt or maybe sand. It didn't so much grind under my wheels as suck at them. Trees sprang up on either side of the road, all different kinds. Oaks, beeches, elms, maples, a cherry or two, broken-branched or stripped of bark all the way up their trunks or just pocked and pecked all over. They were all still alive, though. It was like driving through some pre- or maybe post-industrial train yard, but for decommissioned trees instead of engines.

Between trees, set back from the road on irregular lots, I glimpsed houses with fences, some two-storey, some ranch, clapboard or stone, hunkered against the rain. Once—and only once—I caught sight of two kids way back in a marshy clearing with a couple of tipped-over bikes in the long grass between them. As I watched—but not because they noticed me watching—they launched into side-by-side sprints and then threw themselves into the reeds, which swallowed them.

*Like eagles after shrews*, I thought as I drove, bore left some more, wondering how much more *left* there could possibly be.

*Or kids with a Slip-n-Slide.* I smirked at myself in the rear-view mirror.

One more left, and suddenly I was back on pavement, gliding down some sort of frontage road between, on one side, slumped houses with leaning verandas and neatly mowed lawns, and on the other sand dunes. Every now and then, the dunes dropped and paths opened between them. Down those paths, I saw ocean, grey in the drizzle.

The strangest thing about those houses was the way they angled into their lots, turned at least partway towards each other instead of the street. Settle onto those tilting porch-swings or cheap wicker chairs, and you'd be staring not at passing cars or the dunes but into your neighbours' front windows. Again, I thought of frontier wagons circled for safety or company or both. The street ended in a cul-de-sac, and on the veranda of the white two-storey at the very back of that—just maybe the literal last house on land—I spotted Julian with his guitar.

*His guitar!*

I hadn't thought about that in so long. To call Julian's flamenco playing his trademark at NW NoPlace would have been overstating. *Vanishing* was his trademark. But a couple times a quarter, he got on the bill at the folk pub under the dining hall and did a set that wowed the thirty or so of us in attendance, if only because it seemed so out of place and character, for him, the school, the whole state. The country as we knew it. Stocky, paste-skinned, flop-blond Julian in his New England Patriots hat, strum-stuttering through Spanish rhythms as though born to them.

*Was he even good?*, I wondered now as I rolled gently to a stop in the curve of the cul-de-sac? Rain ticked over the roof and windshield, blearing the lawn. Stepping out, I expected breeze but felt none. In the open air, the rain made almost no sound at all, barely even moved the leaves on the trees. Julian raised a hand with a pick in it and waved. Then he stutter-strummed. It was impossible not to move across the grass to that rhythm. So I did that, shyly. I swayed a bit, dragged a foot, then flung it in front of me. Julian smiled and kept playing.

One thing I knew: he'd seemed awfully good at 12:30 on a Saturday night in the pub under NW NoPlace. He sounded good still.

He'd balded on top since I'd seen him last, the hair just as messy but sparser, like beach grass. His cheeks had maybe spread a bit, but he'd always had wide cheeks, a little snowman's nose, flat blue eyes that got bluer towards the centre, as though whatever was behind them dropped off at the pupil, got deeper. He had one of those not quite definable faces, handsome when you thought about it except you wouldn't. Didn't. It was a running joke with Daniel and me, had stayed one all these years. We'd see an actor in some movie or show, and one of us would say, "Hey. He looks like Julian." It was always true. The joke was that none of those actors looked like each other.

"Hi!" he said, smiling wide, then blushing. "Gabby. You're here."

"Hey, Boom." I would have hugged him except for the guitar. "What's it been, fifteen years?"

He turned towards the screen door of his house. "Girls, hurry up," he called. "Don't forget towels."

I'd heard he was a parent, probably from him. Years ago. But watching him be one caused a twinge of ache or else just surprise. As in college, Julian wore a faded, no-colour T-shirt at least three sizes too big that draped him like a little kid's cape, and yet I got the sense that he'd taken on weight. His exact shape seemed even harder to define than I remembered.

"Hmm," he said. "You look…"

I caught myself leaning in, weirdly anxious. *Busy? Older? Energised? Harder?* All things I knew I was. Feared I was. Celebrated about myself.

But this was Boom, practical in his human interactions if nowhere else in his life. "…Yep. I think one of one Lori's would fit you. Want to swim?"

From inside, I heard clattering, scrambling. A girl's shriek, then laughter. The *pop* of plastic food container lids pried open or snapped shut. Kitchen drawers rattling open. Already, before he confirmed it—*did he ever actually do that?*—I knew this was the same house Julian had always vanished to.

Glancing over my shoulder, I remembered the rain. "Swim? At a pool?"

"In the ocean."

"It's…" Even as I said it, I felt the absurdity. Looking back now, from the Bronx, and my life, and land that's actually on land attached to the world, I know what I meant. But at the time, I felt ridiculous. "…wet," I finished anyway.

Julian raised an eyebrow. Then he said, "I'm so happy you're here. You have no idea." He rolled a Spanish chord before opening the screen and leaning the guitar against a wall inside. "Come in."

I was moving through the door he held open as I asked, "What if Lori wants to swim?" So I didn't actually see him flinch. It's possible that the pause I remember is one I inserted.

"Lori's…" Instead of finishing, he gave a wave of his hand in the direction of the yard, the rain, the road. He could have meant she was at the cleaners or visiting her mother or doing Taekwondo for all I know. He didn't, though.

She was gone. Whether that meant dead or just away from Julian, I wasn't sure then and am not now.

The whole house ticked. I only saw the one grandfather clock opposite the front entryway, wedged under the staircase. It must have been gorgeous once, a century old at least, the finish on the beech wood casing glossless now, faded and speckled all over with what could have been bug-smear, salt decay from the air, or even sand, the wood itself not so much warped as softened, sickly-looking, like liver-spotted skin, the panes of glass across the face and workings bleared by layers of fingerprints that had been wiped at but not away. Despite its condition, that clock didn't so much tick as thump, steady and fierce as a heartbeat.

There had to have been more clocks, though. Ticking and tick-echoes poured from overhead and through the walls on either side of the surprisingly close, low-ceilinged entryway. I felt it through my shoes, in the floor.

"Doesn't it bother you?" I asked Julian's back as he hurried down the hall into a bedroom. Air moved the moisture on my bare arms. In the breaths between ticks, I thought I heard a fan somewhere. Fans.

Because of the rain, I was having trouble processing how hot it was. Smothering, midsummer-Atlantic Coast awful. In the kitchen, giggling erupted like birdsong. Instinctively, my lips pursed to *shush* it, but I stopped myself. *Why did* that *sound seem too loud for the house, which already shuddered all over with sounds? And who was I to decide?*

Julian reappeared with towel and bathing suit draped over his arm, saying, "Doesn't what?"

If I tried, I don't think I could design a one-piece black bathing suit as ugly as the one he handed me. I can't even tell you what made it so hideous, or how I could tell even before he held it out. The blackness had leached from the Lycra, for one thing, leaving a sort of husk-black, like sun-bleached beetle shell. The straps were bulky, blocky, like links of chain.

It felt like a bathing suit, though. Idiotically, what passed through my head was, *It'll keep off the rain.*

"The ticking," I said. "I mean, it's amazing, but how do you sleep?"

Julian glanced past me towards the kitchen. "Girls," he said.

Meaning, *shush*? Or, *Come meet the guest*? The word had no impact as far as I could see.

He grinned again. "Inherited. The clocks. Family heirlooms. One of my great-great-greats made them, I think. Or, um." He stopped grinning, watched me, gave a little shrug. "I mean, his slaves did. On my mom's side."

"Slaves? In Rhode Island?"

"Biggest percentage of any northern colony."

Somehow, that information just made the sounds more insistent. "And . . . you sleep to this? This doesn't bother you?"

"Only when one's out of step."

My knees twitched just at the thought. "Oh my God. That would drive me screaming batshit. Wait. Boom, when that happens, how do you go about—"

"Don't you live in the Bronx?"

"The Bronx doesn't tick."

"It makes every other sound known to mankind, pretty much all the time. Right? Are those sounds ever in unison or alignment?"

Again—from here and now—those questions only tangentially relate to mine. But at the time, in that ticking house, with girls giggling and rain rilling down the windows, Julian's argument made perfect sense.

"Point," I answered.

He showed me a bathroom so I could change.

In total, I spent maybe ten minutes in that house. Even so, I should have clearer memories. I know there was a strip of tan or grey floor-covering that ran the length of the hall. It crackled when I walked on it and felt stringy on my bare feet, like beach matting. Something about the expanse of wall suggested generations of family pictures that should have blanketed it. But I saw only a few photographs, mostly of two tow-headed girls at various ages, shot from behind or far away, splashing in water, tumbling down dunes, bundled in scarves and stacked on top of each other on a toboggan as they sailed down a slope as white as these walls must once have been. The photographs weren't in rows and had been hung crookedly in cheap frames that glinted in the low light like half-buried shells.

I lingered a few moments in that ticking hall, stealing glances— that's what it felt like—up the stairs into the house's hidden upstairs heart. I imagined skylights, beds with white duvets tucked into eaves. The carpeting on the stairs was the same dull blue as the entryway walls. Julian had returned to the front door or never left it. In that light, he looked blue, too.

The girls were already outside, trundling towels and flippers and sand tools down the drive in a wagon. I don't know why I expected them to be younger, frail and bedraggled Julian-kids. These were gawky, long-legged tweens, trotting out of their yard towards their ocean, giggling and shoving, bending abruptly to birds or animals in the bushes, thwacking each other with towels. White-yellow hair bounced on their bare backs, which were New England-pale despite the time they clearly spent in the sun.

Or rain.

"Sorry," Julian said. "Can only keep 'em penned so long."

"No reason to pen them for me. They don't know me." *And won't,* I thought. That was true, but why think it?

"I'm *so* glad you're here," Julian murmured, pulling the screen shut behind us without locking it.

"You don't have to be *that* glad. I just came to make fun of you. Mr. Escape-Artist Flamenco Man, holed up from the world in the land of Living Tuna."

"There's still world out there?" He said it lightly. The inflection I hear now is one I put there.

The walk proved short, maybe a quarter mile back down that frontage road, past those shady houses turned towards each other. The rain didn't so much tap the trees and tarmac as breathe over it. I got wet without feeling it, or without feeling different than when I was dry. Branches and bushes twitched all around. I'd probably glimpsed or sensed more living things on this walk, I remember thinking, than I did on my average workday sprint down crowded sidewalk to catch the 2 or 3. The houses, though, stayed motionless and silent, but not in any sort of peopleless way. They just seemed nestled in place, rooted as tree-trunks.

"Big dunes," I said, my gaze having slipped towards the water I couldn't yet see. The sand flowed so easily, almost liquidly out of the grass and neighbourhood that I hadn't processed its height. These dunes were taller than me, high enough to obscure everything beyond them.

For some reason, Julian laughed. Ahead, the girls abandoned their wagon at the foot of a dune and vanished. I glanced at their dad, my old friend I hadn't seen in fifteen years, the man who'd brought flamenco to NW Noplace, disappeared, come back, disappeared, come back. Boom. He was still in the same shorts he'd had on when I drove up, same shapeless shirt. Rain slicked his skin without beading or running anywhere on him. *As though sinking into sand*, I thought, and finally, after all these years, realised what Julian's skin-tone was: literally, sand. This sand. Dune-colour. *He's even dune-shaped*, I decided, in that way of dunes not quite having shape. Not the same shape, anyway, from one instant to the next.

Only when we came abreast of the wagon did I see where the girls had gone. A sandy path cut between two dunes fully twice my height, demarcated by ramshackle, red wooden fencing on either side. The path led to beach, wide and not quite white and empty. Beyond that lay ocean, slapping in white-tipped crosscurrents against the shore.

"Should we bring the wagon?" I asked Julian's back as he moved purposefully, almost eagerly down the path.

He turned, raising an eyebrow again as though just remembering I was there. "What for?"

From way off to the right, further than seemed safe or even possible, one of Julian's girls shrieked. I hurried forward, realising even as I did that Julian hadn't reacted. I caught up, and we cleared the dunes just in time to see both girls maybe hurtling down the strand, arms outstretched and heads thrown back, sailing over the surface of the water like seabirds before plunging into it.

They'd dropped their towels in a heap near more red fencing that jutted a surprising way out onto the beach, almost to the water's edge.

Beyond it, I was surprised to see a curve of green hillside ringing the edge of the bay—I decided it was a bay—wreathed in mist. It was hard to tell how far that hillside stretched. Far, though; another full-on peninsula, and in the mist, I saw houses, white and palatial, like docked ocean liners.

*Not rooted*, I thought, with no context or source for the thought. "Who lives there?" I heard myself ask.

Again, Julian's answer was to some other question. "They have their own beach."

"What beach is this?"

"Slough. What's left."

Unless he meant *What's Left*. It could have been the beach's nickname. Or full name. What's Left Beach. Unless it was a self-abnegating joke, or a comment on land erosion. Julian was proving as tough to pin down as he'd ever been, even in conversation. Asking him questions was like talking to rain.

I almost tripped over the old woman.

I hadn't seen her, or anyone. Suddenly my foot caught in sand or discarded sandal, and I almost toppled into the laps of a white-haired couple I swear must have crawled out of the earth like crabs. There'd been no one there, then there was, and they almost had me. Hands out, stumbling and apologising and swearing, I staggered sideways and somehow kept my feet.

"Sorry," I breathed, got steady, glanced down. Instinctively, my hands flew to my chest where at least one of my cameras generally hung.

*How the fuck did* she *get here*, I thought, and only when Julian greeted her, said some name other than "Dr. Tilley" did I realise it wasn't her. This woman didn't even look like her once I got a clearer view: too rumpled, stick-thin. Same shock of hair, same startling sparkle in the eyes, I guess, but that was it. Just another old woman who'd sucked something juicy out of life and retained it, somehow. There was no other resemblance.

Her husband—brother, manservant, how do I know?—looked surprisingly burly, broad-shouldered, his pectorals heavy, only slightly saggy, like folded sails. But the sand had sunk a little more underneath him, or he'd settled more deeply into it. That, more than anything else, is what suggested the Tilleys to me: his strength, subservient to her regal, straight back. Sand dotted them all over, coating their legs and abdomens, as though they really had been buried in it. The thought should have been funny, and was, but only momentarily.

*Not crabs clawing out of the beach at all.*

*Foxes by their burrow.*

"Wet one today," Julian said, eyes on the bobbing blonde heads of his girls in the water.

"Might go all week," the old man answered.

The woman sighed. I've never heard a more serene sigh. "Suits me," she said.

It wasn't her voice that jolted me. It sure as hell wasn't that sigh. It may have been the way she kept her hands buried to the wrists in What's Left Beach, never once glancing at the hillside houses or Julian or me. Or it may not have been anything to do with her. But what I heard in those two words was, *Fuck you all.*

"Friends of yours?" I muttered as we moved away.

"Known them my whole life," Julian said. Not quite answering. Again.

That's where I'd got *Fuck you all*, I realised. She'd known Julian his whole life, never once seen me. Hadn't asked. Wasn't interested.

Closer to the water, the clouds lowered still more over the bay like the lid of an aquarium. I wasn't actually considering swimming. I hadn't swum in years, probably since Daniel and I moved to New York. As a kid, during summers, I'd jumped off a low, disused railroad bridge with a few other girls into a way-too-shallow river. Our very own poor-kid, What's Left river. Swimming had never drawn me much.

But now I experienced an unexpected moment of dread. Mostly because it had been a seriously long time since I'd seen Julian's girls.

Grabbing at his hand, I raked the surface of the bay with my gaze. I saw nothing for what felt like a full minute, and that's counting from *after* I'd noticed.

"Julian, fuck, where...?"

Girl One, the elder, popped up way out to sea, half-turned towards us, like a sleek blonde whale breaching. She vanished again just as Girl Two surfaced much closer to shore, rose halfway into the air, and sank.

"Coming?" Julian said, kicking off his flip-flops and moving fast, seemingly keeping himself from running only by force of will.

"I think I'll just—"

"You're already wet. Keep me company." He grinned wide and guileless. "I never have company."

Dropping my towel, not quite shaking my dread or managing to stop my eyes from darting around for another reassuring glimpse of girl, I followed. Inanely, I remembered some lifeguard admonition from the one summer of sleepaway camp my parents had managed to afford: *Never, ever swim alone.* Of course, I wasn't alone. I wished for my phone so I could text Daniel anyway.

By the time my toes touched water, Julian was waist-deep, sinking fast. Rain slid down him. Girl Two popped up startlingly close, splashed him, and kicked away and under. Glancing back, I saw dunes, the fenced stretch of all but empty beach, the old couple wavering in the drizzle. The second old couple—white-haired woman, this one in some kind of bonnet, guy in a Panama hat with a cigar drooping so far out of his mouth it looked like an icicle—just spreading towels and joining them.

Without meaning to, I edged further from shore. The bay climbed over my knees, splashed at my thighs. Except when looking straight down at my waist, I couldn't even tell where my submersion point was. Not only was everything wet, everything was the same clammy warm: air, bay, skin, rain, Lori's black bathing suit, which hung heavy and surprisingly hard like a turtle shell. Something closing over or growing out of me.

I didn't like it. I turned to wade out.

She hit me—Julian's daughter, one of them—just hard enough to knock me off-balance. I swore as I fell, submerged momentarily, felt bottom and stood. I couldn't have been under for more than a second. Just long enough for sensations to slam me.

The *sound*: shells rolling, water slapping and popping, Girl Two's laughter, which I couldn't really have heard and did, streaming around her, filling the bay.

The *scratching*, as if Girl Two had raked me as she knocked me over. But there were no marks. What I'd felt was just her skin. Scaly sandpaper. Like a shark's.

The single glimpse: blonde hair, long body wriggling effortlessly away. Vanishing. The way sharks do.

Scrabbling to get my feet under me, I stood, swayed there streaming in the rain. I couldn't see Julian or his children, just grey water and sky knitting together. *A more perfect union* scrolled nonsensically through my head. If I turned, I thought—I *knew*—the beach would be gone. The fence, the dunes, the old couple. Couples. I was Noplace, but for real, this time. I'd grown up somewhere that had never really been its own place, a half-suburb of a not-quite-urb. *This* had been somewhere, though. A region.

Colony.

Country.

It wasn't now. Was barely an appendage.

Julian popped up straight ahead, smiling wide. My feckless flamenco-friend, streaming. Melting. He beckoned. I didn't want to come, stepped forward anyway. I felt myself sinking. Mirroring him as he lowered towards the water. I went under when he did. That's how I finally saw them.

*Or did I?*

*What did I see? How could I have?*

They were fifteen feet away, maybe more, far enough that I shouldn't—couldn't—have seen anything.

And yet I was scrabbling, half-screaming as my feet flailed for sand to stand on. I vaulted up, gasping for breath as though I'd been held under, near-drowned. Turning, I kept jerking my head down, tensing to leap if one of those girls suddenly eeled around me, bumped me again. I was watching the water, not the beach, so I didn't see everyone else until I was already back on land.

I never stopped moving. I'm sure of that. Mostly, I'm sure of that because I'm still here. Still me. I don't know what that means. I never have. I just know it's true.

Questions bombarded me, poured down like rainwater.

*Where had they all come from? When? How long* had *I been under?*

They were in a sort of semi-circle, not really a formation. All on their beach towels, and not all of them old. Spread across the sand like an extended family to watch fireworks. One spindle-armed, pointy-shaped girl—not Cindy from the Land of Living Tuna, it didn't even look like Cindy, any more than any of these people looked like Dr. Tilley, except in the way they all *did*—even had a bag of marsh-mallows. Or something squishy. She kept sticking in her fist, squeezing, then lifting and licking the goo from between her fingers. Laughing.

The old couple I'd seen first still sat on their blankets. Instinctively, I lurched to the right to skirt them. Which meant having to dart between the towels of two other families. At the time, I was just praying, clenching my hands, silently begging them not to lunge for me, to let me go.

But in retrospect, I'd almost rather they *had* lunged. What they did instead was ignore me. As though I wasn't there. As though I never had been.

Nevertheless, I almost leapt as I crossed the barrier they hadn't exactly created, then fled between the dunes back to the road.

Running back to Julian's took too long. Impossibly long. Like the drive from Providence, and that whole, insane day. Houses seemingly lurched closer to the street, leaning over their own leaning fences. But no tenants stepped from doorways. Rain shadows moved in curtained windows, but no curtains stirred. Maybe everyone was on the beach, I thought. Still, I kept my eyes on those porches. It was better than blinking, which would have meant seeing the bay. Seeing beneath it.

I almost didn't go back into Julian's house. I'd already wrenched open the car door when I remembered my clothes and keys.

I didn't hesitate, just threw myself through the unlatched screen. *Move*, I was snarling in my head. But for one second, I stopped. I had no idea where to go. I whirled, half-expecting to find Julian and his girls floating in mid-air, snaking up the drive. But they weren't out there.

*They're already in you*, I thought, ripping abruptly at the leaden straps of Lori's bathing suit, which had gone on solidifying and gaining weight like lava hardening, land forming. It took agonising seconds to shed it, and when I kicked into motion, I did so in intentionally jerky lunges and hops because I didn't want to fall into rhythm with the ticking. Those clocks. *How many fucking clocks were there?* I still only saw the one, but felt and heard the rest, on the other sides of walls in rooms I never went. Forming a fairy ring, like redwood trees make around the dead space where something mighty and towering and old had spawned them and died.

I was almost sobbing by the time I found my clothes neatly folded together, keys and phone on top. I considered just grabbing them and fleeing naked into the rain. But I got myself calm enough to dress. Staring the whole time out the open door.

At some point during that mad, hours-long drive back, I stopped to text Daniel. Two points, actually, or else I texted while driving. Daniel showed me when I got home. I have no memory of sending either.

The first reads, One if by land.

The second, For the land, and of it.

*For it and of it.*

Daniel still pulls up those texts sometimes, whenever he catches me feeling competent. He still wants me to explain.

Sometimes, I try. I tell him they're about the way Dr. Tilley made me feel. The thing I almost understood, for that one day, about the nature of her hate.

Sometimes I tell him they're about why Julian always went home.

Mostly, I say I don't know. That's closest to true. That whole day hangs in my mind like a memory from early childhood, something assembled out of a series of days over a period of years and embellished with elements that weren't there, bits of things I was told, other people's memories. It's not real, or it's not reachable.

Except for what I saw under water. That memory stays imprinted. That single moment when I opened my eyes to the bay and saw them, Julian and his girls, half-concealed half-disclosed, shining in the swirl and streaming grey light. Disintegrating like sand sculptures.

Breaking up into the billion particles and old bits of dead things that made them up, the intrinsic impulses and old hatreds that would ground and sustain them for as long as they *were* them, then lay down with them in the gloom of their graves. I watched them wave in the deep like flags.

I will never know if it was one silver fish or a school that they had trapped between them. I will never know if they were playing or bare-hand fishing or hunting. Toying with prey like a pod of orcas as they swirled around, darted in, swirled back.

If they had hands, they were holding them. If they had eyes, they were watching what they'd trapped, not me. The only thing I'm certain they all still had—the only thing that had stayed on their faces—was mouths. Their desperate, hungry, wide-open mouths.

Julian and his girls, from What's Left Beach. From that land and of it, whether they wanted to be or not—whether we want them to be or not—forever drawn back to their beginnings. To their house full of clocks their slaves made them.

I will never even know if they were laughing or screaming.

# D.P. WATT

## A Species of the Dead

D.P. WATT taught drama, literature and philosophy in UK universities for twenty years before focusing on writing. His stories have appeared in various anthologies published by such presses as Mount Abraxas, Zagava, Side Real, Egaeus, Sarob, Swan River and Tartarus.

He has six collections of short stories to his credit, and *Almost Insentient, Almost Divine*, published by Undertow Publications, was nominated for a Shirley Jackson Award, as was his story 'Blood and Smoke, Vinegar and Ashes'.

His most recent collection, *Beatific Vermin*, appeared in Egaeus Press' "Keynote Series" in 2020, while four volumes of *Collected Stories* will be published by Zagava Press over the coming years.

"'A Species of the Dead' grew from an interest in taxidermy," Watt reveals, "and its unusual way to preserve the dead; and how the glassy eyes of these animal specimens seemed somehow accusatory... as though revealing some curious, malevolent animation."

S HE RAN THE blade down the back, to the base of the tail. Her knife was old, thin and worn from many years of sharpening. She slid the tail-bone out carefully and made another incision along the length of the tail. She continued with the little legs, and feet, making sure the claws were still attached to the hide. She folded the skin back out and moved on to the head, carefully peeling over the skull with gentle prods of the knife to loosen stubborn, clinging threads of flesh. She set the skull aside in water for later cleaning and lit a cigarette.

The squirrel's hide lay on the table, half-inside-out, tufts of grey fur poking from a wallet of skin, flecked with bloody clumps. The carcass itself looked sadly foetal; a marvel of sinews and purple veins, the majestic skeleton beneath holding the entire masterpiece together. She folded it carefully inside newspaper and wrapped it in bright red crêpe paper, tying the whole together with a strand of purple ribbon and carried it through to the garden with solemnity and ritual. The open fire pit was already lit. As she knelt by the flames, she whispered words of thanks and words of love and placed the package upon its pyre.

Back in her workshop she sewed the mouth together and cleaned the skin of the last flecks of flesh. She rinsed it well and then placed it into methylated spirits to soak for a couple of hours. She also prepared the skull to bleach and went back through to the main house for some lunch and to watch the news. She also flicked through that morning's post as a further procrastination—that afternoon required her to finish two mounts for a client and she was not looking forward to them; an awkward pair of pigeons dancing together, a quirky gift for a wedding.

There was a rare thing—a hand-written letter—in amongst the colourful marketing leaflets and super-fast broadband offers. She opened it eagerly.

*Folding Gallery*
*13 The Mount*
*Shrewsbury*

*9th August, 2018*

*Dear Alison,*

*I hope all is well with you. I was so sad to hear of Michael's passing.*

*He was a great artist and he will be sorely missed. Claire and I still walk past his 'Horse in Winter' every morning on our way to the gallery. Do come over to Shrewsbury any time you'd like, we'd be very happy to see you.*

*I am writing to ask the schedule for your piece, 'Flight from the Divine', and whether it might be possible to get its manoeuvres to coincide with an exhibition on* The Animated Object *we are hoping to arrange around February 2020. Might this be possible at all? I believe it is currently in Warsaw but am not sure what other destinations are planned between there and when we are thinking. If it was back in the UK by then that would be a great help with our budget, but let me know what you think, and if it's a possibility then send me a cost breakdown for it (I know it is difficult to install, but fingers crossed we have the funding for it!).*

*I know you don't like e-mail so am happy to do things through letter if you'd prefer. If you've started to get on with the computer better now obviously that would make things easier at our end—we have two good interns at the moment who'll do a "social media blast" on it, or something!*

*Take care,*
*Benjamin*

It was from Benjamin Meyer, who ran a gallery on the outskirts of Shrewsbury, with his mother. He only contacted Alison when he needed something and was usually unreliable on the financial side of things. Whatever they might agree would probably end up being halved due to "unforeseen expenses" and other excuses. Still, it was important that 'Flight from the Divine' continue doing the rounds— it was one of her few almost-permanently exhibited pieces, and now with her husband gone she needed to maintain a decent income from gigs like this. It was a very complicated piece and she really doubted that Benjamin had the resources to display it properly. It consisted of over four hundred birds erupting from a darkened space, through a stained glass window that hung in over fifty shards. It was a beautiful piece, and she'd been approached to sell it a number of times; no doubt the time would come when she would have to. She'd get the costs together and then hear nothing from him for months, no doubt.

Mention of her husband's sculpture, 'The Horse in Winter', upset her though, and a wave of grief came over her. It had only been six months since he had died, quite suddenly, and each day something would bring him back to her and force her to sit down and remember, in tears or laughter. The relentless extremes of emotion were shattering. The sculpture had been dedicated to her and was the first he had completed after they married. It consisted of four great vertical timbers, blackened by fire, with a metallic cage above, from which shards of iron came down, like cracks of lightning. It was commissioned by Shrewsbury council to celebrate some civic event that she had entirely forgotten the purpose of now. She was one of the few that knew that under its base there was a plaque that read, *I dedicate this beast to my darling Ali, may he charge through the years carrying our love forever, Michael.*

Thinking of it now brought back how lonely she was and how uncertain she was about the future. She'd had a number of exhibitions back in the late '90s, with some unusual works; five eagles carrying a musket between them, rats at a conference on poison resistance, two dogs doing a drug exchange, a Siamese cat in a shop doorway with a sign that read, HOMELESS AND HUNGRY, PLEASE HELP! They were well-produced pieces, with a facile social critique. Looking back on that period of her work she was embarrassed by them. The few interviews she now had focused on them to the exclusion of the more recent work, which was more mature, she thought. The works were tragic and grand now, with a kind of sympathy; she had managed to combine the materials with a proper response to the world. But few were interested in the subtlety it had taken her twenty-five years to perfect. It hadn't helped that she'd had to also maintain a more commercial aspect to the work, so alongside the more artistic pieces she'd also had to churn out the carol-singing mice, the toads on surfboards, and those damned wedding pigeons. And now that Michael was gone she wasn't sure she wanted to do any of it anymore.

They had met at university. He was a tutor and she was his student—twenty years had separated them. They had lived for many years beneath the shadow of others' assumptions about the origins of their relationship. Even those they considered good friends would make occasional remarks—good-hearted enough, but painful nonetheless. Michael's colleagues were the worst, some of whom had taught her. It was, if their assumptions had been true, a betrayal of the ethical relationship between a teacher and their student. But none of their innuendo and fantasy was true. Ali had courted him; rather than the predatory man in power, grooming her and bending her mind to his desires, she had pursued him. Once she had her mind set on something, little could stop her. He had been married before, but they were estranged. His work fascinated her; he sculpted animal figures, but his style was more to capture the essence of the creature in stylised movement—a hare became a jagged zig-zag of brass and dried grasses; an owl was a swathe of dark cloth swooping between two poles of grey driftwood; a badger a round stone that rolled gently through a circular groove in a slab of granite. That stone came to her regularly in dreams since he had died, just rolling and rolling and rolling, on and on through the tormented synapses of her sleeping brain.

She was introduced to Dr. Jozsef Szarka at her lowest ebb. It was a conspiracy of well-meaning friends that had arranged for them to meet, at an exhibition launch party she'd been nagged into attending. He was a nutritionist and lived up in Yorkshire, but he seemed to work most of the time in Somerset, for various health centres and spas. He was charming, witty, kind and quaintly gentlemanly. He invited her out to the races and for dinner. They went to the theatre a couple of times together. She felt awkward and guilty being out with another man so soon, it seemed to her, after Michael's death. Her friends assured her that it was not unreasonable to start thinking of another relationship by now, and she really did need some company. It seemed that there could be more between them, but he never pressed the matter and Alison was reticent.

As she struggled on through her sorrow, he suggested pills to help her sleep. He recommended vitamins and supplements that gave her energy and helped her focus. Everything about him exuded vitality and confidence. She even met his mother and father when they came over from Hungary. They spoke excellent English, but seemed quiet and withdrawn. They commented on what a lovely woman she was and hoped she would be happy again soon after her loss. Jozsef stayed at her house frequently, talking long into the night about politics, books and philosophy. He reminded her so much of Michael; the passion of his earlier years, and the creative energy. He offered her pills and powders to improve her mood, to help her move on. At first he simply gave them to her but, after a few months, he said he couldn't afford to keep providing them to her free—it was a reasonable demand, they must be costly, after all; and they really seemed to be working. She felt quite elated now, most of the time. Occasionally though, when she was running low on her medication, and had to start to ration it, she began to dwell on darker things.

She thought of Michael rotting in the ground; the crawling, sliding creatures that would have penetrated his cardboard eco-coffin, devouring him, transforming him back to soil and sludge. What a waste of a fine carcass; his skin pale and rotten, his soft hair matted and patchy. Then she thought how fine he would have looked, mounted—the kind of insane idea that comes to one in the depths of grief. She laughed, imagining him stuffed in his workshop, a couple of tools in his hand; at work on another sculpture, frozen like it forever. The arts they had practised were not so different really, both attempting to lock the world into a permanent record—hers was more literal, no doubt; the preservation of things that had existed. His was more abstract—a reflection upon the thing, rather than its actual representation. And, if the preservation of people's pets was considered morally acceptable, why not the preservation of one's loved ones? Why was it that Gunther von Hagens could exhibit his anatomical bodies around the world, yet it was illegal to keep the ones most precious to you? There were societies that had made the veneration, and preservation, of ancestors and family the foundation of their civilisation. Not everyone was as squeamish about skin and bone as modern, supposedly civilised, humanity—it was the barbarity of a sterilising social amnesia. Such things were considered primitive. In an evolved world of shiny metal and garish plastic, who wanted great-aunt Maud's skull looking down on them from a shelf in the corner of the room—everything is life, life, life; forget the dead. The dead called to be remembered.

Jozsef arrived, with light and laughter, with flowers and prescriptions. The days were illuminated with walks and conversation, with wine and forgetting. He was full of the energy of enthusiasm; a new business venture, his sister's new daughter, a recent film he had watched—everything was flow and force. He needed a little more money to get him through it all. She sold some older works, and one of Michael's lesser pieces. They visited Venice. She had always wanted to visit Venice.

She was living again. Michael would have wanted her to be like this. He'd have wanted her to be happy—he'd probably have wanted her to begin a proper relationship with Jozsef and start a new life. Or would he? Perhaps that is our greatest misunderstanding, she thought. Maybe the dead lay there in permanent envy of the living, craving that they join them, sooner rather than later. Six feet under, across the planet, lay tonnes of putrid flesh festering with resentment and hatred. Why us? Why do you still live? Your time is coming, we will see you eventually! But she did not believe that consciousness of any kind continued beyond death. She had seen too many dead things; she had worked with their remains and knew the empty eyes; the nothing that lay within. But human beings might be different; she might glimpse a soul.

She called Jozsef. She was low on pills. He came, late one night and briefly. He gave her a package. She gave him some money. He would call soon; he promised he would call her soon. They would go out— she needed to go out.

Months of morbid meditation took her thoughts to the darkest of places. What were bodies, after all, but intricate contraptions forged through others' flesh and chemicals, atoms upon atoms that were all once other things? Everything she touched might once have been a being, or would become one at some point in time. Her house fizzed with fecundity—even the most basic of household chores set her pondering the bacteria in the plug-hole of the sink; the microbes multiplying in the washing machine; and behind them all that growing mound of what once was, reforming itself for another time. What did they say? Two-thirds of a human body is water, and each body supports millions of life forms, from the mouth to the anus— all exchanging substances, all busy with the exigency of existence. She stared at her fingers, at her toes. She wriggled them and imagined they were different creatures. The musculature of her arms, her thighs—tight sinews that belonged to some other entity that flexed and contorted itself around a being made of bone; and somewhere within their struggling forms there resided her—a pair of eyes peering from the darkness, hovering on the edges of non-being.

Joszef sent her a package; she paid into his account.

The question was not what the secrets were beyond death, but what differentiated anything from anything else. If, in time, all became everything else, then who was anyone? The quest was not what lay beyond, but what lay within. She was resolved. It would take some considerable effort, if it were achievable at all. It would take much planning. She began her research immediately.

Jozsef would be able to acquire what she needed—what could see her through her task.

When he was led through the house he knew it was going to be a tough one. He'd already had the outline of what had happened from his colleague and that was bad enough, but the house itself gave him the shivers. Everywhere there were stuffed animals and birds, reptiles and insects in cases. The high walls were crammed with shelves supporting glass cases and domes with endless rows of glassy eyes that watched as he made his way carefully between the clutter of books and drawings, sketches and notepads that were strewn everywhere about the place. It hadn't been ransacked or vandalised, but rather than a home it had been transformed into a site of urgent endeavour—all leading to what he was about to witness.

He vomited three times before he was able to stay in the room for any length of time. He'd worked for many years on gang crime and thought he had seen most things. He believed he had become immune to the sight of a tortured, ruined body, but this was different. He'd seen a flaying once before; a dealer who hadn't paid up and ended up without the skin of his upper body. But, from the report he'd had, she had done this to *herself*.

The skin was hanging on a large wooden hanger that was suspended from the ceiling light. The face hung limply over the right shoulder, no features were discernible. It looked like a thin hood on an old coat. Sitting in a white plastic garden chair opposite the horrific skin was something worse. A flayed corpse, but one that had clearly lived for some time beyond the flaying; all about it were dozens of used syringes, pills and white powder, blue disposable gloves, scalpels and thin blades of varying lengths. There was a lot of blood, but not as much as he might have expected. And strangely, there was a glass of red wine, half-drunk, and an ashtray with three cigarette ends in it.

A voice beside him said, "Yes, she seems to have had a drink while she was doing it, and a few fags too. She left a note, for what it's worth. Do you want to see it, sir?"

He nodded.

He was handed a sheet of thin blue airmail paper with a few shakily written words, smeared with dried blood:

*I have seen the place where I once was. I have looked into those endless mirrors and my empty eyes; on through eternity into the space where I became an illusion. All of this world's varied garments—leaves, feathers, shells or skin—are thin shrouds draped over reality; everything is anything.*

# MICHAEL MARSHALL SMITH

## THE BURNING WOODS

MICHAEL MARSHALL SMITH lives in Santa Cruz, California, with his wife, son, and cats. He is a novelist and screenwriter. Under this name he has published nearly 100 short stories and five novels—*Only Forward, Spares, One of Us* and *The Servants* and *Hannah Green and Her Unfeasibly Mundane Existence*—while a retrospective collection, *The Best of Michael Marshall Smith*, appeared from Subterranean Press in 2020.

Writing as "Michael Marshall", he has published seven *New York Times* and *Sunday Times* best-seller conspiracy thrillers, including "The Straw Men" series, *The Intruders* (adapted by BBC America into a TV series starring John Simm and Mira Sorvino) and *Killer Move*. In 2018, under the name "Michael Rutger", he published the adventure thriller *The Anomaly* (now in development as a podcast series), while a sequel, *The Possession*, appeared the following year.

Smith is currently co-writing and executive-producing development of *The Straw Men* for television. He is also Creative Consultant to The Blank Corporation, Neil Gaiman's production company in Los Angeles.

He has won the Philip K. Dick, International Horror Guild and August Derleth awards, along with the Prix Bob Morane in France. He is also the only author to have won the British Fantasy Award for Best Short Fiction four times.

"'The Burning Woods' started as I love stories to start: a few mental images, a strong idea of location, and a mood. The location was the kind of place I love in real life—wooden cabins in dark forests, chill lakes, unfriendly mountains—and also the kind of place that often seems to occur in my fiction.

"I had a sense of a man turning up one night, and a feeling that there was a story behind this event that perhaps even he didn't understand. Not much else, apart from the title, which arrived right way but with no indication of what it was supposed to mean.

"Working out how and why all these pieces fitted together was the journey of the writing process, and I hope a satisfying one for the reader too."

# 1

I'D BEEN THERE a couple weeks before he mentioned the island, which I guess would make it the third or fourth time we'd talked. For the few days he left me alone. I checked into the resort (a designation accurate only in the old-fashioned sense, of a collection of old, mossy cabins somewhere mountainous and remote) late one cold, dark afternoon, smelling of wood smoke and with one small suitcase and a demeanour that said company and conversation were nowhere on my list of priorities. It's possible Ralph had encountered people like me before. It's equally likely he was glad of anybody's money out of season and didn't give a damn.

He led me to the cabin furthest from his own, which stood in the middle of the compound and also served as the office. Mine had a sitting area with kitchenette, bedroom, basic bathroom, and a narrow deck along the front. It smelled damp, but he showed me where the wood lay in a neat pile around the side and lit a starter fire in the grate while he explained what there was to explain. He told me the nearest store was a mile back down the road but I knew this already, having bought beer and cigarettes half an hour before. I'd kept the brim of my cap low while I gathered my goods and paid. Ralph further informed me that the nearest bar was three miles in the other direction, and they served food from midday until eight most days, but it wasn't great. Nearest actual town was another twenty miles beyond that.

Then he left me to it, wandering back in the direction of his cabin. A couple minutes later I heard his door shut.

I put my bag in the closet, not sufficiently confident of the duration of my stay to make it worth the five minutes of unpacking. I opened a beer instead and took it onto the deck, where I sat in one of the battered chairs and smoked.

The cabin was sparsely surrounded by trees on all sides and backed up against where the forest started in earnest. About fifty yards below, at the bottom of a gentle slope, was the shore of the lake.

I could see four other cabins from where I sat, not including Ralph's. I'd seen nine hooks on the wall behind his desk, so presumably there were additional ones not in line of sight. A thin hook of smoke spiralled out of the office chimney but from none of the others, and it was already cold and would get a lot colder when the light faded. That suggested Ralph had been telling the truth when he said I had the place to myself. I'd no reason to disbelieve him, but I don't trust most things until I've established them for myself.

It was very quiet.

Twilight came seeping towards me from between the trees and off the surface of the frigid lake. He'd told me its name, but it was a long adaptation of some Native American original and I forgot it immediately. It was very large, surrounded by thousands of acres of forest, and dotted with small islands. It was right there in front of me.

I didn't need to know its name.

Over the next few days I settled in. I walked back down to the ramshackle general store and gathered further supplies from its few shelves. It dealt mainly in tinned goods and alcohol, basic provisions for small groups of men on their way into the woods for annual re-bonding exercises. As these trips usually involve the attempted destruction of wildlife, the store also sold ammunition. I did not buy any. I did however allow the clerk to see my face this time. He was entirely uncurious.

I came back with a couple bags of things that could be turned into basic meals, and when I'd put them on the shelf in the kitchen area decided I may as well unpack my suitcase too. I had just finished when I heard a knock on the cabin door.

I opened it find Ralph standing diffidently on the porch. Tall, angular, a face of big planes, deep creases in his forehead, sharp in the lamplight. Late fifties. "Just checking everything's working out for you."

I'd seen him a couple times during the week, from afar, when setting off or returning from my excursions in the woods. These were not taken out of a desire to experience nature, which I can take or leave, but to maintain a basic level of fitness. I would walk for an hour, run for thirty minutes, repeat, until it was time to head back to the cabin. I set off at a different angle each day. I did not try to find a path because there aren't any. I had seen a lot of trees.

I had also stood on the shore of the lake, looking at the small islands in the distance. If you wanted, you could presumably drag a boat or kayak to the water and spend a day navigating between them. In summer, people likely did just that.

"Fine," I told him. "Need more wood soon, though."

He pointed into the trees. "Main pile is over there. You got enough for tonight?"

"Yes."

"I'll bring some by in the morning."

"I can do it, now I know where it's at."

"It's what I'm here for. Anything else?"

I shook my head. He walked away. I stood a few minutes longer looking up at the sky. It was grey and frosted. Snow was coming.

It didn't fall that night, however, so I walked down to the store the next morning and this time bought some ammunition. Not much. Just enough.

## 2

A few evenings later the first snows came, enough to put a couple inches on the ground and the roof of the cabin. I sat on my deck and watched it slowly fall. After a while I saw Ralph trudging from cabin to cabin in the half-light, making sure they were mothballed against the heavier falls to come. As he passed he looked up at me.

"Shipshape?"

"As it's gonna be." He stood looking around into a gloom flecked with falling white. "We're closed now," he said. "For the winter."

"But I'm good?"

"From what I seen, you being here is no more trouble than you not being here."

I had a six-pack on the deck next to the chair. I lifted one out, held it up. He thought a moment, came up and sat in the other chair.

We each drank one, in silence, and he left.

Next morning I made a few trips to the woodpile, making sure I had plenty for the days ahead. I took another walk to the store in the late afternoon, laying-in supplies in advance of the first inevitable heavy snowfall. On my way back, on a whim, I kept going past the turn-off to the cabins.

The bar up the road was a featureless oblong with a door and a sign. The parking lot was empty. Inside was a deserted pool table of considerable age, a non-functioning jukebox and three people drinking in silence. I stood at the counter for ten minutes. Nobody appeared, and none of the patrons offered an explanation. I left.

That night I dreamed of a house. I was inside and it was long and low and it was humid and dark and I was running. I passed a wall covered in a spray of blood. As I turned the corner I realised I had a gun in my hand, its muzzle pressed into my own temple. I ran faster.

When I woke, the world was white.

I went out into the woods, but only for half a day. Impossible to run in the snow, hard to even walk any distance. The edge of the lake was turning opaque, icing up. I stepped a couple of feet out onto it, heard it cracking.

That evening I sat on the deck again. It was so quiet that I heard the click of Ralph's cabin door opening. I turned my head and watched, curious as to why he'd come out. He didn't seem clear on the subject either. He lurched a few yards and then came to a standstill, visible at the edge of the glow from the lamp above his door. Stood, as if listening for something. Then glanced in the direction of my cabin.

I lifted the hand in which I was holding a bottle of beer. He seemed to take this as an invitation. Perhaps it was.

He stayed longer this time, and we talked a little. I learned he'd inherited the place from his father and spent the last thirty years running it. That it got busy in the summer, people come to fish and kayak around the lake, grilling up a storm in the evenings. That the reason I hadn't been able to get served at the bar was the proprietor was a drinker and spent a portion of every off-season day passed out on a pile of sacking in the back. Regulars knew to serve themselves and leave payment on the bar, even adding a tip, because the owner was basically a decent guy, and if the place shut down there'd be nowhere to go to escape their lives for a while; and being trapped in your home with your beloved family for weeks at a time can be a heavy burden for all concerned.

I learned also that Ralph read a lot, armfuls of second-hand paperbacks from a thrift store twenty miles up the road in Renton, where he drove once a month for supplies. That his wife died ten years ago of cancer. No children.

I learned all this while we drank three beers, in no special hurry. He didn't learn anything about me.

<br>

### 3

More days passed. It snowed, twice heavily. Walking in the woods became an exercise in frustration. I did it anyway, though I stuck mainly to the shore of the lake. The ice gradually spread further over the water. I stood for a time one afternoon looking down through its frosting at the pebbles and rocks beneath, before squatting and using my knuckles to break the thin coating of ice. I picked up a stone and turned it over in my cold fingers. An anonymous piece of rock, rounded by millions of years of history, none of which mattered or would ever be known. Countless small events over a span twenty times longer than the tenancy of humankind on the Earth. Now lying there, on the edge of a frigid lake in the back of nowhere, its past and future amounting to nothing because it was on the way nowhere. No path, no trajectory, nothing to wait for except the waiting itself. I would in all probability be the only person to ever pay it attention. To weigh it, examine it. To whom it would be real. There were countless others like it around this lake—cold, muddy pebbles of no importance—and unless they happened to scrape the underside of your boat, you'd never know or care.

I considered keeping the pebble, raising it above its peers, making it something, instead of just a thing, but I had no need for it and dropped it back onto the ice a yard from where I'd found it, another random step along its stoic progress through time.

I walked away feeling as if it was watching me go, but knowing I hadn't even been a blink in its life. I wondered if God felt the same about me.

Or if he thought about any of us, at all.

That night I had to call Ralph over to the cabin because the stove wasn't functioning properly. Normally I like to fix things myself, but propane is something I fundamentally distrust.

He fiddled around until he had it working again. When he re-opened his bag to put his tools back I saw a six-pack in there. He didn't hurry to close the bag. He'd drunk my beer. I knew he'd feel this should be returned in kind, if not tonight then soon. It might as well be now.

"I could help lessen the load you got there."

"Hoped that might be the case," he said.

It was too cold to sit out on the deck. I had a fire going. We sat in chairs on opposite sides.

"Snow getting in the way of your hiking, huh."

"I'll be out again tomorrow, though."

"Looking for something?"

"Like what?"

"I don't know," he said. "Just until the last few days you've been out there eight hours at a stretch. That's a lot of walking. Wondered if you were looking for something."

"Nothing in particular," I said.

"Find much?"

"Trees."

He nodded, took a sip. "Used to walk a lot too, back in the day. When my wife was alive. Felt like I needed time to myself then. Now she's gone and it's all I've got."

"A person needs space."

"I guess. Though now I think maybe I could have survived with less of it. And I never found anything either."

"Except trees."

He smiled. "Plenty of those. I did use to go looking for something, though, sometimes."

"What?"

"The burning woods."

"The what?"

He shook his head ruefully. "My dad told me about them one time. Like a bedtime story. He said there was part of the forest that was on fire, always had been."

"How would that work?"

He shrugged. "Special trees, he said—that grew and then burned up and grew again from the ashes. He said you could get there and back in a day, if you went in the right direction and it was the right time for you to find it. I fell asleep while he was telling me, and maybe that's why it stuck. Got into my mind by the back route. I used to go looking, anyway, and maybe I even half-believed in them. Started again when I took to walking later in life. Didn't believe then, of course. Though maybe I wanted to."

"Like how older kids go along with the idea of Santa," I said. "Because it'd be nicer if it was true. And there are times when you need something to look for. Whether it's real or not."

"True, both. But I didn't find it."

"Sometimes that's better."

"Maybe. And could be the whole thing was just his way of getting me out of the house for the day, too. Dads are cunning with that crap. Mine was, anyway."

We drank and looked at the fire. I thought about my own father, but found it difficult to bring anything to mind.

"Pretty sure I saw the island once, though," he said.

"The island?"

I could see him wondering whether he should have mentioned this, whatever it was. I didn't press. But I opened a couple more beers. He sat looking into the flames. I waited. Eventually he spoke again.

"That one, it was Granddad told me. I don't know if he even told my dad. Dad never mentioned it."

"Your grandfather owned this place before?"

"He built it. He was the most anti-social human being I ever met. People were just not his thing. Yet he built this camp around their homestead—that fell apart years ago, but it used to be where my cabin is now—and so he wound up spending most of the year having to deal with people. A lot of them, pretty dumb people."

"No other way to earn a living, maybe."

"No, he could of. He was uncanny good at trapping. Had lines going out into the woods in all directions. Could catch anything, skin it after, make it look like it never died."

"Enough to support a family?"

Ralph shrugged. "Maybe not. But I asked him about the resort one time, why he built it. He told me that when you lived in a place like this, it was a good idea to have people around. I pushed him on it, a few weeks later, one night when the place was full and everybody was partying loud. How could he like having all these people up in his face, when he was such a solitary soul that even the company of his own family seemed to try his patience a lot of the time? He said 'Didn't say I liked it. Said it was a good idea.'"

"What'd he mean by that?"

"I have no idea. He'd already answered two questions in a row. I didn't push my luck. You knew my grandfather, you wouldn't either. He was okay some of the time, but others it'd be like he was hanging around for something he knew was never going to come, and had gotten tired of the process."

I stayed quiet, assuming Ralph would get back to the island he'd mentioned. We'd finished his six-pack and started on one of mine, though, and his mind had begun to go in slow circles.

"I talked with my dad about the Burning Woods one other time, which is what made me wonder if maybe it wasn't just a story. Though he was dying of cancer then and cruising high on pain drugs, so maybe it didn't mean anything. There's a lot of waiting when someone's leaving that way. You can run out of things to say. One afternoon I told him I'd gone looking for the burning woods when I was a kid. I was twenty-five by then. Guess I was trying to signal that the guy he was handing over to wasn't a child any more. That I understood it had been a joke, and I was older now. Man enough to take his place. My dad nodded, and I figured that was that, maybe he'd got my point, maybe not, and probably he was going to sleep now. But then he said 'I think I nearly found them.'"

"Huh."

"Well, right. So I told him—I thought you were just kidding. He shook his head. His father told him about them, and just like me— he knew I'd gone out looking, day after day, I don't know how he knew, but he knew—he'd tried to find them. One afternoon it was cold, bitter cold, but the sky was frosting over. He knew snow would be coming soon, so he walked harder and faster than usual, and instead of stopping and turning around at midday—my granddad had told him it was a half-day hike, like he'd told me—he kept going. Meanwhile the sky's getting heavier and darker and lower. It's coming on for three o'clock and he knows he's got himself in a pickle and it's time to turn round now because he's got the same hike back plus his legs are a lot more tired than they were. But then . . . he saw some-thing."

"What?"

"A glow. Up ahead, through the trees. You've spent time in these woods now. You know what you're going to see."

"Silvers, dark green, greys, black."

"Right. Ain't nothing that glows. A kind of yellow with some orange in it, he said. Way up ahead. So now he doesn't know what to do. He really wants to go on. His father never found the burning woods. So he wants to. He wants to be the one. But it's late already. And finally it starts to snow. For a while it's just a light fall, like how it started here last week. But then it comes on stronger and stronger. He's got his work cut out getting home already. With this kind of snow? He's grown up in these woods and he knows he's putting himself in danger with every minute he dicks around."

"So what did he do?"

"He turned back. And good call, say I. Otherwise I wouldn't be here right now. And still he barely made it. There was a record fall that year, and a lot of it came down that first day and night. He didn't get home until two in the morning, half-dead, probably three-*quarters* dead by the time his mother finished bawling him out for scaring her to death. My grandmother was a small woman, but I wouldn't have bet against her in a bar fight."

"Did your dad try to get back there?"

"Of course. Wasn't able to for a few days, though, until he'd got his strength back. And guess what?"

"He couldn't remember where he'd seen the glow."

"Not a clue. He'd tried to mark it on the way back, but gave up and focused on staying alive, and anything he'd left was buried with snow for weeks, and gone by the time it thawed. He never saw the glow again."

"So maybe it's true after all."

"Or maybe not. He died a couple hours after he told me that story. Could be he was confused and it wasn't a memory of anything that happened, and instead he was talking about some other kind of light. A light he could see in the distance that afternoon, as he lay dying."

I waited to see if Ralph would say anything more about the island, but he just finished his beer and left.

### 4

Next afternoon I found myself standing on the edge of the lake again. This time I did not look down at the pebbles, but at the water itself. It was grey-blue. The nearest of the islands was a couple hundred feet away. It was small, home to six trees, tall and straight and meaningless in the context of the hundreds of thousands in the forest.

There's something about an island, though. The fact that it's set apart from the land, and from the water, even from other islands—

no matter how similar they may be, or how close—confers a singularity upon it. Every island is different to every other island, because it is an island.

And John Donne was wrong. Not every man is a piece of the continent, or a part of the main. Some men are just islands. We know that. It's why we're drawn to islands in the first place. To the idea of being an island on an island.

Never having to listen to any bell tolling but your own, and you never hear that one until it's too late to do anything but sing along.

Ralph didn't seem surprised when I said I was thinking about going out on the lake. He'd evidently been expecting it.

"The islands are there," he said. "Limit to how long a man's going to be able to resist setting foot on one."

He asked if I'd used a kayak before and I said yes. He took me to the shed where they were stored for the winter and handed me a life-jacket. We both knew I wasn't going to wear it. He asked if I wanted help moving the craft to where I could get it in the water and I said no.

"Beer, later?"

"Sure," I said.

I dragged the kayak down across the snow using the rope loop at the front provided for the purpose. I had to keep dragging it for a while, as the lake had iced up twenty yards from the shore, and was barely deep enough to navigate for another twenty after that.

The gloves I had were not thick, and my hands were very cold before I even got in the kayak. My weight pushed it down onto pebbles and I was reminded of the one I'd looked at a few days ago. I had to shove at the lake bottom for several minutes with the paddle before the kayak started to move more freely.

But then suddenly it was floating, carrying me out into the silence. The sky was low and white. The water was silver-grey. Except for when my paddle touched the water, everything was utterly without sound, the quietest place I had ever been.

There were no birds.

I'd been on the lake for an hour before I decided to head towards an island. It took that long for me to get over the initial rush of moving freely, after days of trudging through snow and weeks tramping through forest undergrowth. I felt as though I could paddle forever, but knew this was an illusion. I'd already done enough that I was going to feel it in my arms and shoulders the next day. And it's as well to remember—when you do anything in life—that you're not just going outward. You have to conserve the energy to get back to where you started. And you've got to remember where it was.

The nearest island was a hundred yards away. It was thirty yards long, twenty across, dropping steeply into the lake without a shore. I paddled round until I found an accessible tree root and tied up to it. Knowing there was a good chance I was about to wind up in the freezing water, I steadied the kayak as best I could and grabbed the root. I wondered whether I should go find an easier island instead, but that would have felt like a defeat.

So I pulled hard and pushed up with my legs. The kayak tried to fly out backward, but the knot held.

I kept pulling, reaching out and grabbing another root with my other hand and jamming one foot into the mud. I didn't fall. My gloved hands weren't secure on the slippery roots, however, so I went straight to scrabbling up the slope, keeping my movements steady and even so I didn't slip.

One end of the island held a few trees, the same green-black pines that filled the forest around the lake. The other was just mossy rock. I walked around it. As a quantity of space it felt constrained—because it was surrounded by water—but not oppressively so. It was about the same area that most of us live out the bulk of our lives in, after all: the size of a house with a small yard. The amount of space we're used to. The size of the average human cage.

It wasn't clear what I'd achieved, but returning to the kayak was going to be even harder than getting out of it, so I hung around a while, smoking and looking out across the lake. I stood on the side I'd come from, then went and stood on the other. The difference still felt clear, and I wondered how far from your starting point you had to go before that ceased to be the case, before you'd truly left the place you were before. The point where you became committed. There's probably no kind of math that will work that out. It depends how much you're leaving behind, and what kind of person you are, and what—if anything—you hope to find in the other direction. How far you're prepared to keep walking without looking back.

I managed to get back in the kayak without incident. I paddled back to the resort and spent the afternoon in front of the fire, looking into the flames. Ralph came over in the evening and we drank a few beers but didn't talk much.

I thought I would sleep well, but I did not. Smoke from the dying fire seemed to permeate the cabin, lying over me like a shroud. In the middle of the night I was woken by something like the sound of a gunshot, very close by, almost as though it was in the room. It must have been a branch outside breaking under the weight of snow.

But the echo seemed to go on for a long time.

## 5

When I got up next morning the sky was low and heavy. My arms and shoulders felt tight. On the back of these facts it made sense to walk in the woods instead of going out on the water again. Or to simply stay indoors.

Ralph was standing by his cabin smoking as I dragged the kayak down towards the shore. He'd told me his wife didn't like the smell, and so smoking had always been something he did outdoors. Even after ten years of living alone it seemed this was still true. The dead get their way more often than the living, it seems.

He glanced up at the sky. I didn't say anything.

I took it easy at first. One of the advantages of having no destination is that slow will get you there as quick as fast will.

Wasn't long before I was past the island I'd visited the previous day. As soon as you've been a certain distance, it becomes near, and you can't help but wonder what's beyond it. I kept going..

The next few islands were small, including one barely a couple of yards across and home to a single tree. It was the most solitary thing

I'd ever seen, and I wondered what John Donne would have had to say about it.

There was a patch of open water after that, but I didn't feel done. As I paddled out into it the first flakes started to come down. It was quite something to be moving near-silently across the water, while snow dropped all around.

The fall was light. I figured it would stay that way for a while.

It started to come down in earnest when I was on another island. I'd been there only a few minutes and had already decided to leave—the sole reason I'd visited was it had a conveniently gentle slope on one side, and a few feet of rocky shoreline, making it an easier proposition than the one I'd been on the day before. But there was nothing to see. Just a piece of rock, without even the distinction of being the first I'd stood upon. I ate half the sandwich I'd brought with me and decided I was done being there.

As I walked back to the kayak the snow increased in volume, suddenly, all at once, as if someone had turned a knob. Nothing like a blizzard—six on the dial at most, not all the way up to ten—but pretty hard all the same.

I got in the kayak and pushed back, knowing now was the time to head home. It was beautiful, though. Within a couple of minutes I couldn't see the island I'd just left—it, or anything else. A shifting curtain of falling white, appearing as if by magic out of a steel-grey sky, now hung so low it felt like I could reach up and touch it.

I let my reversing strokes carry me around in a half-circle and then started forwards again. Slow, measured back and forths, until I hit a rhythm that felt eternal, forging out into the white, squinting to stop it going in my eyes.

I had no idea what direction I was going, and it didn't matter. There was no destination. My mind blanked out but my muscles kept moving, as if grateful to have stillness in which to do their work for once. It is a blessed relief when you stop trying to think, when you commit to a course and keep going. It was certainly the closest I had felt to peace in a long time, and after a while I stopped having any sense of where I was or what I was doing.

## 6

I don't know how long it was before I came back into myself.

The process was sudden. I had been somewhere else, deep in my head, and then I was back in reality—warm under my coat, but very cold at the extremities, unable to feel my fingers, my ears hurting, aware that the snow falling around me was even thicker than before. The front of the kayak had over an inch lying on it.

I stopped paddling, let the craft keep moving under its own momentum. Looked around.

I couldn't see a damned thing.

The day before, the whole time I'd been out on the lake, either the shore or an island had been in view, however distantly and however small. Now there was nothing to be seen in any direction, and of course that was partly due to snow reducing visibility to thirty feet, but for all I knew I'd got myself out into a portion of the lake where there weren't any islands. And so nothing to navigate by.

As soon as I'd had this thought, I realised it was dumb. For an unknown period (I don't wear a watch, but some internal clock said at least half an hour, maybe longer) I'd been driving myself out into nothingness. In a straight line, theoretically, but I'm not a good enough kayaker that it would have been absolutely straight, and so there was actually no telling where I was now, and any fixed point I found would tell me nothing other than that I was . . . here.

The snow was now up to around eight on the dial with no sign of slackening, and I accepted the fact that I'd got myself into something of a situation.

When you're young there's an unspoken assumption that everything can be put right, pulled back on track. You feel this partly because most of your mis-steps are in truth pretty small, within the parameters of common human error, and you have other people— usually your parents—with the experience and compassion to reach out, lift you up, and put you back on the rails.

Then you get older, and experience shows there are actions for which there is no undo button. With most of these you just reconcile yourself to taking the hit, sometimes a big one, and steer cautiously forwards into an altered future.

But there are some dark days and nights where you realise you've gone ahead and rowed yourself right off the edge of the world. Where you do something that feels as natural and right as continuing to paddle, but find you've gone the wrong way and there's no road back, that you were burning the path behind you with every step you took—and are now in free fall.

I didn't think I was in trouble that serious. Yet. I was cold, but continuing to row would keep my core temperature elevated. The kayak was made of very thick plastic, and had evidently been bashed around plenty in the past without springing a leak. I had a little food left. It could be worse.

I basically had two options. Stay where I was, hoping the snow dropped and visibility increased. There was no reason to believe this would happen any time soon, and I was mindful of tales Ralph had told about years where it had dropped steadily for two days straight. The alternative was to head back to base, as best I could.

I let the kayak cruise to a halt while I considered the question, but really I'd decided as soon as the choice was articulated in my mind. I made sure the paddle was secure across my lap and got out the rest of the sandwich. I ate every scrap and then used the wrapping as a half-assed shovel to get some snow up to my mouth. I'd sweated a lot already and dehydration would do more harm than hunger, ironic though that would be, given where I was. The chances were the lake water was drinkable, but I'd put myself sufficiently at risk.

Then I took the paddle and cautiously turned round a hundred-and-eighty degrees, or as near as I could judge it.

The view looked exactly the same in that direction. The snow was still coming down relentlessly. I felt a twist of panic in the pit of my stomach, and waited it out. Setting off fast would be a dumb idea. The feeling faded.

I dipped the right tip of the paddle into the water and pulled it back, then did the same on the other side.

It seemed to take longer than it should for the kayak to come up to speed, as if the water was thickening, freezing up. That made no sense, though. Or at least I hoped it didn't. More likely it was my tired, cold arms protesting against being put back to work. I was going to be hurting in bed tonight.

*Assuming I made it back there.*

Within a few minutes I started to warm, the kayak moving smoothly in what I hoped was the right direction. Slow and steady should get me to the general area of where I'd been.

*Wherever that was.*

I told the doubting parts of my mind to shut up, and settled to sustained work. But a few minutes later I stopped again, staring into the snow ahead.

At first I wondered if it was merely an especially thick patch of snowfall. Wind was starting to pick up, making the snow chaotically variable in both strength and direction.

The kayak kept moving forwards, however, and soon it was clear that it was something else.

An island.

Visibility was too bad to get a sense of how big it was, but the curve of the craggy rock face ahead and the size of the trees on top suggested it was notably larger than any previous ones I'd seen.

On my current course I was going to run right into it. And that wasn't good. It meant I couldn't have turned the kayak around accurately, because I would have had to have come right *through* this island to get to where I'd been when I stopped. Evidently I hadn't judged the hundred-and-eighty degree turn perfectly. But logic said that I must have at least come *past* this island, sufficiently to the side that I hadn't been able to see it in the snow. So what I had to do now was angle to the left and head in that direction.

Maybe this was even good news. Without the island to demonstrate my turning error, I could have continued paddling in a direction that must be at least twenty degrees wrong.

I made the manoeuvre and started off.

I watched the side of the island as I paddled alongside, realising another option would be to hole up on it instead. I didn't know how long it was going to take for the snow to slacken, however, and while there might be shelter up among the trees, it would remain a very cold way of spending a number of hours, more likely the night. It must be getting towards mid-afternoon, which meant only an hour or two of light remained, at best. If trying to paddle back to the resort in a snowstorm was dumb, it'd be dumb squared to attempt it in the dark. Better stick with the lesser of two dumbs, not least as the island was continuing to present a steep, rocky aspect straight up from the water to a height of maybe fifty-feet. Nowhere to moor the kayak, and no way to get up to the top.

After a few minutes the island started to curve away. I realised it would soon stop providing an indication of the direction I should take, and tried to figure a way of ensuring I maintained a consistent bearing after I left it behind. I couldn't, and decided to hope instead that so long as I failed to zone out, I'd be able to keep paddling in a straight line without a marker.

I found myself reluctant to leave the island behind, however, and allowed my course to bend to the right, keeping a consistent distance from it while it was still there.

Then I found myself braking.

I was thirty yards away, the falling snow between it and me turning most of it into nothing more than blocky masses in shades of grey. But I realised that the island looked different on top—and then I understood why.

There was a house on it.

A long structure, multi-level, predominantly of grey wood. This was no mere cabin, either, some rudimentary structure thrown up a hundred years ago. It had the look of something that had weathered both time and storms, but whoever put it there did so either with the help of an architect or natural talent.

It was the kind of thing Frank Lloyd Wright might have come up with on a limited budget and if challenged to build only with what was available on the island, which made sense. Getting materials out here would have been time-consuming and expensive. As I stared up at it, letting my momentum carry me along the remaining stretch, I saw chunks of rock had also been incorporated into the structure. At the end there was a deck sticking ten feet out over the water.

There was someone standing on it.

The deck was sixty feet above my head and the snow made it look like something glimpsed in old black-and-white footage, fractured with jittering vertical lines. A woman was standing there. She had dark hair, curly, not long. I couldn't make out what she was wearing. She was up against the railing, arms folded, looking out into the snow.

"Hey."

She didn't hear, or at least gave no indication of having heard. I tried again, louder, with the same result, although by then I was almost directly in front of her.

She stood, arms tightly crossed, staring out into the falling white, as though either not seeing what lay in front or looking so intently for one thing in particular that anything else—like me—simply failed to register.

I stopped paddling. The house and the woman proved there had to be some way onto the island. There was shelter up there. There would be warmth and maybe food.

I shouted again, but still she did not hear. I turned and paddled back to where I was a few yards from its rocky face. I pulled around the end and set off up the other side, knowing there must be a landing somewhere.

Except there wasn't.

I kept close, because the snow was now falling so heavily it seemed continuous. It was three inches deep on the front of the kayak, and I had to stay within ten feet of the island to even be able to see it.

I paddled right the way around, down the long side, past the other end, and then, baffled, back along the side I'd already paddled past. There was no beach, no dock. Just the same wall of slippery, jagged rock all around the island.

And when I got back to where the deck stuck out over the lake, there was no one on it any more.

I couldn't land. I couldn't stay where I was.

I turned the kayak and set off into the white.

## 7

I have no idea how long I was out there. Hours. Long enough to go through alternating stages of dogged effort and mounting panic. Long enough for exhaustion to set in. I stopped being able to feel my hands, much less my fingers. My toes and feet were also lost to me, and patches of my face. For long periods I kept my eyes shut against the constant jabs of snowflakes flying into them. My ears sung with sharp, deep pain.

The water felt like frozen treacle. I fought it in one direction for a long time, then in desperation altered my course more or less at random and fought in another direction instead. After a while this came to seem like the stupidest decision on a long day of stupid decisions, and I tried to right myself back to my original course, but naturally I could not—especially as what little light there had been had started to fade. The falling snow stopped seeming dimly-lit from within and began to turn grey instead: at first faintly, then darker and darker by shades—until I was paddling in pitch darkness, nothing but the cold sting of flake after flake against my face to tell me it was still coming down.

All I could hear was the jagged rhythm of my strokes, each a self-contained little noise, like a sound effect on repeat. I considered turning and heading back to the island, trying to shout up at the house once again, but by then I had absolutely no idea of what direction it would be in. For all I knew I was back there already, only yards away, paddling round and round it in the swaddling, deadening blackness, gripped in its gravitational field and unable to escape.

My body told me to give up and die, but the mind would not. Then my mind told me the same, but found the body had re-evaluated and now would not listen. The cold settled deeper until my ears ached so badly that for a while I thought I could hear singing, the absent-minded song of a child brushing her hair after a shower, wrapped in a towel too big for her, happy in a home she assumed would be eternal, warmed by adults she'd thought would be there forever.

I kept going, stroke after stroke, my eyes sparkling against the cold and the undifferentiated darkness, until I realised there was something in the distance, that instead of retinal flashes I was perceiving something real, something that lay ahead.

The island. It had to be.

Suddenly I knew that I'd been right, that I'd somehow managed to do nothing more than go round and around it, sometimes close, sometimes far, held within its orbit by my soul yearning for somewhere to be, somewhere safe to go. Yearning for landfall of some kind. Any kind.

I headed for the light, knowing that the woman had come back out onto the deck, perhaps hearing the sound of my paddling. I headed for the light, knowing that she would shout down this time, explaining that I'd missed an easy way onto the island, telling me where to go and how to climb out of the kayak and onto the land where I could rest. I paddled with what remained of my strength, my face a frozen mask, grunting with exertion, knowing that it was her, guiding me home.

But then I saw it wasn't.

It was Ralph, standing on the edge of the shore at the resort, holding up a lantern.

## 8

I came back to consciousness to find myself in one of the chairs in my cabin. The fire was burning. There was a thick blanket over me. The entire surface of my skin was tingling. There was a soft glow around everything.

I blinked, slowly. Turned my head, which felt like it was splitting in two. Ralph was in the other chair. He had a beer in his hand. There was another on the table between us, already open, next to a couple of empties.

"Be dumbass to drink that," he said. "But it was a dumbass idea to go out today in the first place."

It was a while before I felt able to bring my arm from under the blanket. The bottle felt like it weighed twenty pounds. It nearly slipped from my hand on the way to my mouth. I drank half of it slowly, before trying to speak.

"Cigarettes."

Ralph nodded towards the arm of my chair. I hadn't even noticed they were there. I eventually got one lit with fingers that felt swollen and dead. "How'd I get here?"

"Carried you from the shore. Well, dragged. You got the kayak to within a couple yards and then tried to get out. I got to you just before you fell over."

"Thanks. And for coming to look for me."

He didn't respond. It felt strange being in the cabin, like a dream. Now it was over, part of me was acknowledging I hadn't been at all sure I was going to make it back. That I'd been very scared. To be somewhere warm, where it wasn't relentlessly snowing, and where I knew where I actually was . . . the little things you take for granted can seem magical when you get them back. But consequently fragile, and undependable.

"Is it still coming down out there?"

"Yeah."

"Christ."

"It's the big one. Why'd you stay on the lake so long?"

"I got lost. Got out too far, didn't have anything to take my bearings by. Couldn't see a damned thing."

"You're lucky you made it back."

"I guess."

"Someone vanishing on the lake—it doesn't look good."

"Has it happened before?"

He looked pre-occupied, like he had something else on his mind. "Of course."

"How often?"

"Couple times. While back."

"Together?"

"Separate." He said this as though it had been a dumb question.

"What happened?"

"Same as you. Went out when they shouldn't of."

"Did anybody miss them?"

He shook his head.

"You think anybody would have missed me?"

He looked me straight in the eye. "I'm assuming not."

Fuzzy-headed though I was, it was obvious Ralph's manner was different tonight. Perhaps out of concern for me, or out of time spent worrying. Perhaps not. "Are we okay?"

"Do you want another beer?"

"Sure."

We drank in silence for a while.


"So what happened? Out there?"

I'd gone into a daze. My skin wasn't hurting so much, settling into the dull sparkle you get after a bad dose of pins and needles. The pain in my ears was receding, too, though it still sounded a little as though someone was singing, a very long distance away.

"Snow started coming hard, and I lost visibility. Tried to turn around and thought I'd judged it, but obviously not."

"How did you know, if you didn't know where you were?"

"I saw something I hadn't before."

He looked into the fire, as if to avoid my eye. "What did you think you saw?"

"An island."

"Lots of those out there."

"Not like this. It was bigger. And it had a house on it."

He shook his head. "No inhabited islands on that lake."

"This one was."

"Maybe back in the day."

"No. There was a deck. I saw someone on it."

"Who did you think you saw?"

"A woman. Late thirties, early forties. Mid-length hair, curly. I didn't see her clearly."

"You didn't see anything at all."

"Excuse me?"

"Nobody lives out there. There's no island with a house on it. You didn't see it. You just thought you did."

"Are you serious?"

"You were cold, exhausted, lost. In a snowstorm. The eyes will play tricks. The mind, too. That's all."

"Bullshit."

"It's the truth."

"I don't get it. I don't understand why you're even saying this."

"Because it's true."

"You can't have any idea of what I saw."

"Yeah, I do. And you didn't see it."

We finished our drinks in silence, and then Ralph stood.

"You're welcome to stay to the end of the week," he said. "After that, I think we're done."

9

I woke up next morning in the same place, in the chair. The world outside the window was white. The fire had died to a few embers and the end of my nose was cold. I tried to pull the blanket up over my face, but every part of my body ached. Arms, shoulders and back worst of all, and my stomach, but there wasn't a bit of me that didn't feel badly-used, strained, leaden. I stayed where I was until I felt strong enough, then gingerly levered up out of the chair. I laboriously put a few pieces of wood on the fire and made a cup of coffee and took it with me into the cabin's tiny shower and ran warm water over my body until it felt more like it belonged to me.

I spent the rest of the morning in the chair, drinking cup after cup of warm water, waiting to feel better.

By the afternoon I had moved to the bench near the window. It was still snowing, though not as heavily.

Yesterday felt as if it had happened a year ago. The hours I'd spent lost and flailing, though intensely real at the time, now seemed insubstantial. The few parts where something specific and different happened began to swell, like islands of substance in a cloud of white.

Foremost amongst these, of course, was the house. And the deck, and the person on it. If I closed my eyes I could see her clearly, or as much as I'd been able to see her at the time. The description I'd given Ralph wasn't great, but it was enough. Couldn't be too many full-time residents in this area. The woman must have to visit the store, perhaps even the bar up the road. Ralph had been here all his life. There was a good chance he knew who she was. So how come he'd denied not only this, but that she'd been there at all?

Come to think of it, hadn't he been laying the way for denial before I even mentioned her—asking what I'd *thought* I'd seen out on the lake, rather than what I *saw*? My memories of the conversation were not sharp, but that sounded right.

I didn't know how seriously to take his suggestion that I be on my way. I hadn't done anything wrong, except unnerve him by nearly coming to grief out on the lake. Sure, the place was closed for the season and had been for a couple weeks. He'd be within his rights. But up until last night he'd seemed content for me to be there.

As I sat mulling this over, I saw movement down towards the lake. The door to Ralph's cabin opened and he came out. He was dressed in a coat, on his way somewhere.

He glanced towards my cabin, as if wondering whether he should come check on me. But then he stomped off into the snow in the direction of where he parked his truck.

A couple minutes later I heard the engine start, and the sound of him driving away.

I wound up back in the other chair in front of the fire, where I dozed for a while. When I woke up I felt better. Well enough that I took a coffee and cigarette out onto the deck. The snow was light, sparkles drifting through muted light.

The question of Ralph's change in manner had evidently been picking at me while I slept, because it was front and centre in my head now I was back up on my feet. And it suddenly occurred to me that it might have nothing to do with me being out on the lake at all.

I went back indoors. I didn't know how long I'd been passed out in the chair after he got me back in the cabin, but I'd bet it was a half-hour or more. There'd been two empty bottles on the table.

I walked to the kitchenette and opened the cupboard. My meagre groceries were there, cans and a couple boxes and jars. But there used to be a small paper bag stashed behind them.

It was gone.

## 10

I stewed on it for a while. There didn't seem to be much else I could do right away.

Maybe there was even a rule about it, though it seemed unlikely. In hunting season there had to be a bunch of guys who'd come up here to go hunting, and came prepared. I doubt Ralph made them store their bullets in his shed or a safe.

Either way, he could have talked to me about it instead of doing what he'd done, and he shouldn't have been looking in the first place. Poking around a guy's stuff when he's unconscious, and taking his ammunition, is not okay.

After a while the snow started to grow heavy again.

And I got tired of waiting.

I hadn't heard his truck coming back, but that didn't mean he hadn't returned. Snow will play tricks with sound. If he wasn't home then I'd slip the note I'd written under his door. I'd kept it short and polite, only saying I'd like my ammunition back. As I tramped from my cabin to his, my fingers and toes started to complain, immediately. They'd had a narrow escape the day before and didn't want me fucking with their welfare again.

Ralph's truck wasn't there. I trudged up to his door and was about to bend down to shove the note under it when a thought struck me. I reached for the door-handle and gave it a twist. Sure enough, it was unlocked.

There was a different way of handling this, and the fact it came so swiftly to mind showed me how pissed I was at what he'd done. Instead of leaving the note, I could go in there. Take a look around. I wouldn't ransack the place or open cupboards or drawers, but if he'd set the bag down on a counter when he got back last night, then I would pick it up and leave. To get angry about my doing this would involve him opening the box of what he'd done in the first place.

I knew the moral math on this was shaky—and there were arguments that he owned the place and could set whatever rules he wanted, and he was only in my cabin last night because he'd helped me out of a tight spot—but I knew I was going to do it anyway, so I might as well get on with it.

The cabin was warmer than outside, but not by much—he hadn't lit a fire yet, and the smell of smoke from yesterday was thin and weak. The floor plan was similar to my own cabin, though a little larger, with a real kitchen and a small second bedroom. I guess people who live alone decide either it doesn't matter how the place looks, or go the other way. He'd gone the other way. It was very tidy, everywhere, which made scanning around for a small paper bag very easy.

I found it in the kitchen, on the counter.

I headed back out through the sitting room, feeling a dull, childish triumph at getting back something that belonged to me. I remembered when I must have been about eleven, and another boy at the school had taken one of my marbles, to which I had been attached. I eventually got it back, and had felt much the same as I did now. This recollection diminished my achievement, making it even smaller than I'd already understood it to be.

Was this all there was? Did forty years of life take you nowhere but a return to "that's mine, give it back"? So I had my bullets. Big deal. I didn't even have a gun.

I was a couple of steps from the door when something caught my eye. It was on the mantle, above a fireplace from which yesterday's ashes had already been tidily removed.

I stared at it, understanding that Ralph's change in manner was nothing to do with the bag of shells after all.

## 11

The knock came a little before eight. I already knew he was back. I'd been watching out of my window late afternoon, thinking things through, and saw his truck return. He went in his cabin without looking at mine. A while later I saw smoke curl up out of the chimney.

I opened the door to find him there holding a six-pack. Amongst men, there are few better ways of indicating that conflict is not intended, at least not immediately.

"Where'd you go today?" I asked, when we sat in front of the fire.

"To a funeral."

"Who?"

"Don. Guy who owns the bar up the road."

"What happened to him?"

"He died."

"So what happens to the bar?"

"It'll be closed tonight."

"And then?"

"It will open again."

"Who'll run it?"

He looked at me, as if to judge whether the inquiry was rhetorical. It was not, though a dim understanding was perhaps beginning to form. He shook his head. This was evidently a question I had to be able to answer for myself.

"You knew I'd come looking for my shells, didn't you?"

He nodded.

"And that I'd see what I saw."

Nodded again.

"Why couldn't you have just told me?"

"You wouldn't have believed. The things people tell you, they never amount to much. People have to see stuff for themselves. Haven't you found that?"

"That doesn't mean I understand what I saw."

"I've told you things. You've listened, but not said much back. I don't know anything about you."

"I don't tell people much."

"I get that. But it's why I mentioned the island in the first place."

"And then let it drop," I said, realising that Ralph's method of dealing with me over the last weeks had been more subtle than I'd given him credit for.

"Right."

"To let it work at me."

"Which it did."

"And you didn't do much to stop me going out yesterday either, did you, now I think about it."

"It was going to happen. When it happened was your choice. I wasn't going to stand in the way."

"You wanted to know what I'd see."

"Yes."

"Because that would tell you something that I had not."

"Smart, aren't you."

"Smart, but slow."

"Slow gets you there eventually. And you're more likely to understand what you find, than if you get there fast."

"And so what *did* I see?"

"You tell me."

"Your wife," I said. "The woman on the island was your wife."

"Sounds that way."

"I know it was. I saw the picture in your cabin. The woman standing on the deck in the snow was your wife."

"Okay."

"But you said she was dead."

He sat looking into the fire. "She is."

We drank a while. It became clear that the next person to speak was going to have to be me.

"Is she the only thing to see on the island?"

"No."

"What else could it have been?"

"I didn't know," he said. "That's why it had to happen the way it did. I was pretty sure already. I've been in your cabin before, couple weeks ago, when you were out walking."

"Why?"

"To see what I could find."

"And what did you find?"

"Shells, but no gun."

"How do you know I don't have one stashed out in the woods somewhere?"

"Because you don't."

"How do you know?"

"You're done with guns now."

"Why do you even care?"

"I don't have much else to do. And if you had a gun here, it could have changed things, a little."

"I don't."

"I believed that. But the island made me sure."

"What happened? Why is she there?"

He didn't speak for a long time.

I got more beers from the fridge. Then went outside for a cigarette. I smoked it on the deck, watching the snow come down, little drifting ghosts against a sea of black.

"It's hard watching someone die," he said, when I sat back down in front of the fire.

"I imagine it must be."

"I'd done it with my pa. Some with Grandpa, too. But mainly I was kept away from that. My dad took a long time. And like I said, it was long, slow afternoons. There's a lot of waiting in any part of life. I get that. But most of it's going somewhere. Waiting for something new or better or at least not as bad. You wait for the girl to notice you. You wait for work to get easier. You wait for the spring. You wait for grief to fade."

"Dying is different."

He nodded. "Dying is different. It's not going anywhere. It's time *itself* dying, minute by minute, hour by hour. My dad, he didn't mind too much. He'd always been a slow, tidal guy. Don't get me wrong— he did stuff. A lot of stuff. Never met a guy who could work so hard, for so long. But he had his own pace and it was timely and gracious and he was accustomed to things that took a while. She wasn't like that."

"Your wife?"

"Always in motion. Doing this or that, moving something here or there, thinking about the next thing. But then all that was lost to her and she was just lying there day after day, nothing to do, nothing to move. And there *was* no next thing. Wasn't going to be. *Ever.* And she knew it."

I knew what he meant. I had seen this. I had seen it in the mirror, for weeks and months and years.

"How did you do it?"

"A pillow. She was weak by then, but not as weak as I'd thought. She woke up."

"Did she fight?"

He shrugged. "I don't think so. But it took longer than I thought it would." He looked wretched. "We spoke before she went to sleep. We said nice things. I'd stopped trying to tell her she was going to get better, and that made it easier, because she'd known for a while already and you don't want to be sitting there lying to someone day after day, or to be the person listening to those lies. If you have loved and been loved for a long time, you do not want the last days between you to be nothing but untruths, however kind. I told her I loved her, just before she drifted off, and I told her again after she was asleep. I told her many times. So I thought it would be okay. I didn't do it for any bad reason. I didn't *want* her to go. I just didn't want either of us to have to keep waiting. Especially her. She was not a patient person. The waiting was killing her worse than the cancer. We'd talked, and I thought it might as well happen now. That it would be the best thing. The *kind* thing, for both of us. And maybe that made it okay."

He lit a cigarette and smoked it right down before continuing.

"That next winter I was out on the lake. It hadn't snowed heavy yet, and so it was bitter cold. There was icy drizzle coming down. Like being sandblasted."

"So why did you go out?"

"I was beating myself up. I need to explain that?"

He did not.

"And after a couple hours I got lost out there, like you did, and a while later I saw the island too."

"The same one?"

"I don't know. It didn't have a house on it. But the sides were steep, like you said, and one end jutted out over the water, looked kind of like a deck, so, I don't know. Maybe, maybe not."

"And you saw her?"

He nodded.

"What did you do?"

"Tried to get to her, of course. Went round the island, twice, though by then my arms were dead. Couldn't find any place to land. Tried to tie up but the rope kept slipping off the rocks. Tried to throw myself onto the rock face, thought maybe I'd be able to climb it. But it didn't happen, and that's for the best, because the boat would have drifted away and my bones would be on that island right now."

"Would they?"

"You know what I mean. Anyway, in the end I gave up and paddled around the end and she was still there, looking out, and not at me. So I set for home."

"You ever been back?"

"Nothing will have changed."

"The other guys you mentioned. The ones you said disappeared out there on the lake."

"They wouldn't have seen her," he said. "I can't know for sure, because I didn't get a chance to ask, but I know they didn't. They saw their own people. I figured that might happen to you, too, yesterday—if my guess about you was wrong. But I was right. You haven't killed nobody."

I remained silent. He was correct, but he wasn't right. He knew some things, but he didn't understand.

Or maybe he did, because then he looked up at me and smiled, sadly. "On the other hand, here you are."

## 12

Next afternoon I walked the three miles up the road. It took a while. The snow was deep and there were no tracks in it, suggesting Ralph hadn't done more yesterday than leave the resort and park up for a few hours, long enough to give me a chance to go look in his cabin.

Eventually I trudged up to the bar. From the outside it looked like it had been shut for several months, but it had looked that way the other time too. There was nobody at any of the tables, but a man came from out back and stood behind the counter. His hair was white and his face blotchy, but his eyes were clear and sharp. I ordered a beer and he set it down in front of me. I asked to see a menu.

"No food today."

"How come?"

"It's made the night before."

"And you were unavailable."

He just looked at me.

"You're Don, right?"

He nodded. "What's your name?"

"I don't know. Do you?"

He shook his head. "We never met."

I took the beer to a table in the corner, near the small fire he had going. After a while I got another. When I went up again he wasn't there and didn't come out. I left some money on the counter and poured myself a beer and drank it, and did that a couple more times and then left.

It was snowing again and getting dark, and after a while I fell over and found it hard to get back up, and in all honesty couldn't think of a particularly good reason for doing so.

After an indeterminate period of time, I opened my eyes to see Ralph standing over me, his head a shadow against the falling snow.

I was still in no hurry to move. The snow was cold but comfortable. "Got to stop meeting like this."

He looked down at me with something like compassion, and helped me up and led me back to the resort.

### 13

I was awake before the dawn. Packing my case did not take long. I left the couple remaining tins and boxes on the shelf in the kitchenette. There had been a few things there when I arrived. You pass it on.

As soon as it was light I left the cabin. It was bright and crisp outside, but I knew that would not last long. I did not stop by Ralph's cabin to tell him I was leaving. Once he'd got me back to mine the night before, he said goodnight and left. He did not come by later. He was done with me, and waiting for me to go.

Or so I thought, but then I found a note he'd left on the table. *I'll be round tomorrow night*, it said. *And you're going to tell me what you did.*

But I could not, and so I left.

I wish I'd known him better. I wish we had not lost touch. I know he did what he did for the right reasons. I knew that at the time, I think, or sensed it at least. I should not have let it come between us. Things might have turned out differently. I should not have allowed it to work at me until I came to wonder whether it was something you could do for yourself, like turning a broken machine off and on again.

But that's not his fault. Nobody lives your life but you, even if for much of the time you're just quoting the lives of others, walking tracks they cleared for you.

I didn't know what direction to go, but as I'd lain in bed in the small hours in the dark, listening to echoes and wreathed again in the smell of burned timber, I'd come to suspect that was the point. That there are things you'll never find if you have a goal in mind. Any goal, however small. There are paths that only fall under the feet of those who are going nowhere, merely waiting. Staring into mirrors late at night, and seeing a stranger. Paddling, snow-blind, with no direction home. That's why Ralph had never found it. He'd been looking too hard.

I walked a little way along the edge of the lake. I realised I'd been wrong about islands. You look at them and they seem separate. But *they do not float*. Every island drops beneath the surface, stretching down to the lake bottom. This continues in all directions, meeting the lower portions of other islands, joining them. It is all connected, beneath the surface. If you stand on one, you stand on them all. If you are one, you are all.

I looked back towards the resort, recognising it now. It was a happy place, perhaps the last such recollection I carried of my childhood. The last vacation we took, the three of us, when my dad still laughed and my mother was still forever doing something, always planning the next thing, forever on the move. I was eight years old. We walked in the woods every day and kayaked and grilled up a storm.

Two weeks later we found out my mother had cancer. Nine months after that, my dad did what he did.

I didn't know about it at the time, of course. I just knew she had gone. And it's so long ago now that all I can get back of her with any clarity is that single image of her standing by the fence in front of our old house, arms folded, waiting for something she'd been expecting in the mail. Not waiting for me, nor my father. Nothing of substance. I don't remember her smiling at me or hugging me or making me a sandwich or singing me to sleep.

Just her standing at the fence, waiting for some dumb thing that was coming in the mail.

I walked. The snow was thick on the ground, and it was cold, and the sky frosted over and got lower and lower. At first I didn't notice because of the trees, but finally the snow started to come down, and I looked up and knew it had settled in for the afternoon. I'd been going four or five hours then, half a day. I had changed directions several times, altering my course by a few degrees, one way or another, randomly.

Some are born with a destination. Some find one later in life, or else elect to designate some place or person to perform that function. Others merely wait the whole thing out, because that's what you do, one way or another.

But there are those who don't. Who can't.

Some drink themselves to death, like Don—my grandfather, who I never even met. He had his own method of making the waiting stop, by following the endless circular path of being drunk, hung-over, getting drunk again, and it may have been witnessing this slow, sip-by-sip drowning that made my father do what he did to help my mother. The last time I saw my dad, twenty years ago, I think he tried to explain it to me. But I was pretty drunk myself at the time, and angry at him, or the world, or something, and I didn't hear.

I thought I was better than that. Better than him, better than his father. I thought I was the guy who'd find what we'd all been looking for, the path they'd both missed. I thought I had it all figured out. Or some of it, at least. I hadn't realised that the three of us were islands in the same water, our feet planted in the same lakebed, connected and surrounded by the same currents. Or maybe I never even got to be an island, never grew up that much.

Perhaps I was just a lost boy in a kayak, trying to find a route between those men who had come before me, but always in the dark, and forever running into them.

I kept walking, paying no attention to where I was going. Wherever there was a gap between trees was good enough. There is only a road to follow because one day someone put it there, and once it's there it looks like a path and so we assume it must go from one meaningful place to another. But it's not like that. Nowhere in the woods is more a place than any other, just as each of the moments that fall are going nowhere other than to rest upon all the others, to melt into what was, a cold mass of that-happened-but-now-is-gone.

I kept walking, a man trudging through deep forest in the snow, carrying a small suitcase.

Eventually I began to see a glow in the distance. It was pretty dark by then, and so it was hard to tell how far it was. It didn't matter. I wasn't going back.

It took maybe another hour to get to where I could hear the crackling of the flames. The trees around me looked the same as they had all day. My father had been wrong about that, and his father before him. They weren't any special kind of trees, just more of the same.

They were on fire, though. I'll give them that.

I walked into the flames, deep into the burning woods. I walked until all around me was yellow-orange and searing, and then I sat down on the forest floor, looking up at glowing embers as they tumbled out of the black sky.

The trees are on fire in the way it feels when a bullet carves into your brain. There are no pain receptors in there, and so the fire is not that kind of pain. It is not physical. It is the righteous fire of the end of it all. It is the burning of permanent and irrevocable mistakes, of sailing off the edge of the world. It is the percussive echo of that last sound, the gunshot with which I ended it all.

And that's why I always leave before Ralph and I have that last beer together. How can I tell my father that's what I did? That the boy he used to kiss on the head, and lift up into the air, waited until his family was out of the house and then took his own life by blowing that same head to pieces? Even if it's maybe partly his fault, and his father's fault too, and so on back to the dawn of time.

Because it's not. I didn't know that then but I know it now. They didn't buy the gun or the shells. They didn't tell themselves that by ending the waiting by their own hand they were finally understanding and forgiving their father for what he'd done to help his wife, my mother, along; or that by doing it drunk—as I did—I felt I was honouring my grandfather's path too. It made sense at the time. Or seemed like it did.

I'm not sure I regret it, even now. And it's possible the wife and daughter I left behind don't regret it either. I have no idea how long it's been. Though I do not believe it was a conscious factor in the timing of my action, my daughter was eight years old when I left her life. I accept that is a curious coincidence. And I'm aware what shape an eight makes when turned on its side. I wonder if she still sings when she combs her hair after a shower. I hope so. I hope I didn't take that from her. I hope her mother found someone else.

Some men are destined to find the burning woods. I am one of them. I think my wife knew that by the end. It's better this way. Or if it's not, it doesn't matter. What's done is done.

And yes, of course I know I'm dead, and I am fine with it. Being alive was worse. Alive is just an expression we use for those parts of being dead where it feels like you might be able to change something. You can't.

You're just waiting for the waiting to stop.

In a while, I will stand and pick up my case and walk out the other side of the burning woods and keep on walking. I will eventually find a road on which it has not yet snowed, and head up it. I will buy beer and cigarettes at the store and continue on to the resort, and my father will check me in and affect not to notice that I smell strongly of wood smoke.

This has not happened before. It's *always* happening, and it's only the fact every moment lasts for infinity that makes it feel like you're going around in circles. All paths seem straight while you're following them. It's only when you look back you see the curved line. You circle yourself and those who made you. You revolve around your point in time. You happen, and you will keep happening.

I will get up eventually, and happen again, or still.

But for now I will sit here and watch my woods burn.

# STEPHEN JONES & KIM NEWMAN

## NECROLOGY: 2019

FOR THE PAST thirty-one years we have commemorated in these pages the passing of writers, artists, performers and technicians who, during their lifetimes, made significant contributions to the horror, science fiction and fantasy genres (or left their mark on popular culture and music in other, often fascinating, ways). In this final column, we pay tribute to one of America's finest short story writers, one of Britain's most important anthology editors, three pioneering women writers of SF, a pair of memorable supporting actors and the Philippines' most famous horror star...

### AUTHORS/ARTISTS/COMPOSERS

British children's book illustrator and author **John Burningham**, who supplied the artwork for the original publication of Ian Fleming's *Chitty-Chitty-Bang-Bang: The Magical Car*, died on January 4, aged 82. He also worked on illustrated volumes of *Around the World in Eighty Days* and *The Wind in the Willows*. Burningham twice won the Kate Greenaway Medal for British children's book illustration.

British author "**Solomon Strange**" (Anthony Livingstone) died of pancreatic cancer the same day. His ghost novel *The Haunting of*

*Gospall* was published by Telos in 2018, and he had a story in *Terror Tales of Northwest England*, edited by Paul Finch for the same imprint.

American TV scriptwriter **Henry Sharp** died on January 9, aged 106. He worked on such shows as *The Man from U.N.C.L.E.*, *The Addams Family*, *The Wild Wild West* (he was also story consultant), *Bewitched*, *The New Addams Family* and the animated series *The Amazing Chan and the Chan Clan*, *Super Friends*, *Valley of the Dinosaurs* and *Korg: 70,000 B.C.*

**Robert S. Friedman**, the publisher of The Donning Company, died the same day, aged 76. During the 1980s, Donning published the original editions of Robert Lynn Asprin's "Myth" novels under the Starblaze imprint, along with titles by Algis Budrys, Marion Zimmer Bradley, Robert Adams, Robert Silverberg, S.P. Somtow and many others.

American comic-strip writer and artist **"Batton Lash"** (Vito Marangi) who, in 1979, created the humorous "Wolff and Byrd, Counselors of the Macabre" (aka *Supernatural Law*) series, died of brain cancer on January 12, aged 65. He also wrote the one-shot crossover *Archie Meets the Punisher* and eight issues of the Eisner Award-winning *Radioactive Man* for Bongo Comics.

**Bettina F. Bradbury**, the daughter of author Ray Bradbury, died on January 13, aged 63. She was a Daytime Emmy Award-winning TV soap opera writer whose credits include episodes of *Santa Barbara*, *All My Children*, *As the World Turns* and *Days of Our Lives*.

British comics artist **Ron Smith** (Ronald George Smith), who drew 'Judge Dredd' for *2000 AD* and the *Daily Star* newspaper, died on January 19, aged 90. He had been suffering from Parkinson's disease. Smith also worked for such comics as *Knockout*, *Eagle*, *The Wizard* and *Hotspur* (illustrating the time-travelling 'Nick Jolly' and the superhero 'King Cobra' strips). He retired in 1990.

American short story writer and journalist **Michaelene Pendleton** died on January 21, aged 72. From the late 1980s and through the '90s she had fiction published in *Omni*, *Amazing Stories*, *Isaac Asimov's Science Fiction Magazine*, *The Magazine of Fantasy & Science Fiction* and *Dragon Magazine*.

Oscar-winning French music composer and jazz musician **Michel** [Jean] **Legrand** died of septicemia on January 26, aged 86. He scored such films as *Castle Keep*, *Donkey Skin*, *Wuthering Heights* (1970), *The Smurfs and the Magic Flute*, *Gulliver's Travels* (1977), *Les fabuleuses aventures du légendaire Baron de Munchausen* (1979), *Slapstick of Another Kind* and Sean Connery's "alternate" Bond outing *Never Say Never Again*. Legrand also created the Academy Award-winning song 'The Windmills of Your Mind' (with lyricists Alan and Marilyn Bergman) for *The Thomas Crown Affair* (1968).

Bookseller **Cary Heater**, who worked at San Francisco bookstore Borderlands Books since 2002, died on January 31 of complications from a severe head injury sustained in a fall two weeks earlier. She was 57.

British editor, writer, bibliographer, publisher and bookseller **George** [Walter] **Locke** died on February 1, two days before his 83rd birthday. Starting in the late 1950s, he had a number of short stories (mostly credited to "Gordon Walters") published in such magazines as *Authentic Science Fiction*, *New Worlds Science Fiction*, *Fantastic Stories of Imagination* and *Amazing Stories*, and he self-published the novel *Pattern of Terror* under the pseudonym "Ayresome Johns". Locke edited the anthologies *Worlds Apart: An Anthology of Interplanetary Fiction* and *The Edge of Space* and, under his Ferret Fantasy imprint, *At the Mountains of Murkiness and Other Parodies* and *The Land of the Unseen: Lost Supernatural Stories 1828–1902*. He also self-published many important non-fiction studies, including *Ferret Fantasy's Christmas Annual for 1972*, *From an Ultimate Dim Thule: A Review of the Early Works of Sidney H. Sime*, *Ferret Fantasy's Christmas Annual for 1973*, *The Land of Dreams: A Review of the Work of Sidney H. Sime 1905 to 1916*, *Voyages in Space: A Bibliography of Interplanetary Fiction 1801–1914*, *Science Fiction First Editions: A Select Bibliography and Notes for the Collector* and *A Spectrum of Fantasy: The Bibliography and Biography of a Collection of Fantastic Literature*, along with various chapbooks. Ferret Fantasy also published *The Raid of "Le Vengeur" and Other Stories* by George Griffith, *From a Surgeon's Diary* by "Clifford Ashdown" (R. Austin Freeman and John J. Pitcairn), *The Year of the Sex Olympics and Other*

*TV Plays* by Nigel Kneale and *Poems of the Sea* by William Hope Hodgson. For many years Locke ran a mail-order business out of his south London home, before eventually moving to one and then another retail location in the city's West End.

**Carol Emshwiller** (Agnes Carolyn Fries), Nebula Award-winning feminist SF author and the widow of artist and experimental film-maker Ed ("Emsh") Emshwiller, died on February 2, aged 97. She began publishing stories in the mid-1950s in magazines such as *Smashing Detective Stories, Future Science Fiction, Science Fiction Quarterly, Science Fiction Stories* and *The Magazine of Fantasy and Science Fiction*, and her short fiction is collected in *Joy in Our Cause, Verging on the Pertinent*, the World Fantasy Award-winning *The Start of the End of It All and Other Stories, Report to the Men's Club and Other Stories, I Live with You* and *In the Time of the War and Other Stories of Conflict/Master of the Road to Nowhere and Other Tales on the Fantastic*. Her novels include *Carmen Dog*, the Philip K. Dick Award-winning *The Mount, Mister Boots* and *The Secret City*. Carol Emshwiller received the World Fantasy Award for Life Achievement in 2005.

American author and book dealer **Carrie Richerson** died after years of poor health in a Texas rehabilitation centre the same day, aged 66. She began publishing fiction in the early 1990s in such magazines and anthologies as *Pulphouse, Amazing Stories, Realms of Fantasy, The Magazine of Fantasy & Science Fiction, Asimov's Science Fiction, More Phobias: Stories of Unparalleled Paranoia, Gothic Ghosts* and *The Year's Best Horror Stories XXI*, and some of her stories are collected in *Something Rich and Strange* (2001). In both 1993 and '94 she was a finalist for the John W.Campbell Award for Best New Writer.

American screenwriter and director **Larry Brand** died of heart failure on February 9, aged 69. Having got his start in the film industry as a driver and production assistant to Orson Welles, Brand went on to co-write and direct the 1989 remake of *Masque of the Red Death* and *Paranoia* (1998), and he also worked on the script for *Halloween: Resurrection*.

Swedish-born SF writer **F. Alexander Brejcha** died in a

Pennsylvania hospital on February 11, aged 61. Starting in the late 1980s, his short stories appeared mostly in *Analog Science Fiction and Fact*, along with *Science Fiction Age*, *Dark Planet* and *Absolute Magnitude*. In 2004 Brejcha self-published two collections, *No World Warranty* and *People First!*.

American scriptwriter and producer **Stephen Hattman** died the same day, aged 73. On TV, his writing credits include episodes of the 1990s *The Flash* (which he also produced), *Mortal Kombat: Conquest* (also executive produced) and *Flatland*.

American scriptwriter **Christopher** [Edwin] **Knopf** died of heart failure on February 13, aged 91. He co-wrote *20 Million Miles to Earth* and scripted the 1973 TV movie *A Cold Night's Death*.

**Dave Smith**, the founder and chief archivist of the Walt Disney Archives, died on February 15, aged 78. He joined the company in 1970 and was the author of *Disney A to Z*, *Disney: The First 100 Years* and four volumes of *The Ultimate Disney Trivia Books*. Smith received the Disney Legends Award in 2007.

**Glen D. Johnson**, who edited the influential news fanzine *The Comic Reader* from issue #26 to #40 (1964–65), died on February 16.

American writer and musician **Clark Dimond** died on February 19, aged 78. He wrote comic scripts (with Terry Bisson) for Warren Publishing's *Creepy* and *Eerie*, along with *Web of Horror* (which Bisson edited), as well as contributing to *Castle of Frankenstein*. Dimond also contributed an essay about comics artist Wally Wood and an interview with John Severin to Bhob Stewart's 2003 volume *Against the Grain: Mad Artist Wallace Wood*.

Pulitzer Prize-winning American opera composer **Dominick Argento** died on February 20, aged 91. His work includes *The Voyage of Edgar Allan Poe* (1976), with a libretto by Charles M. Nolte.

Colonial India-born pioneering American editor and publisher **Betty Ballantine** (Elizabeth Norah Jones) died on February 22, aged 99. She began her publishing career in the 1930s, but it was with her husband Ian (who died in 1995) that she helped shape the mass-market paperback market from the mid-1940s onwards, most notably through American Penguin, Armed Services Editions and Bantam Books and, in the early 1950s, the creation of Ballantine

Books. They soon became the world's premier SF paperback publisher, and were instrumental in sparking the fantasy fiction revival in the late 1960s with the first authorised editions of J.R.R. Tolkien's books and the influential "Adult Fantasy" series (curated by Lin Carter). They also spearheaded the publication of fantasy art books, with projects such as *Gnomes*, *Fairies* and *Dinotopia*. Betty Ballantine was awarded a World Fantasy Life Achievement Award in 2007.

American paperback author **Victor J.** (Jerome) **Banis**, known as "the godfather of modern popular gay fiction", died the same day, aged 81. As "Don Holliday" he created "The Man from C.A.M.P." series for Earl Kemp's Greenleaf Classics imprint in 1966. He also wrote the science fiction novel *Man Into Boy* as "Jay Vickery", the supernatural novel *The Gay Hunt* as "Victor Jay", and the heterosexual Gothic romances *Shadows*, *The Wolves of Craywood*, *House of Fools*, *The Second House: A Novel of Terror*, *White Jade*, *The Devil's Dance*, *House at Rose Point*, *The Girl Who Never Was*, *The Glass House*, *The Glass Painting*, *Moon Garden*, *The Bishop's Palace*, *Darkwater*, *The Haunting of Helen Wren*, *Blood Ruby*, *The Lion's Gate*, *Green Willows* and *Blood Moon* as "Jan Alexander". Banis' autobiography, *Spine Intact, Some Creases: Remembrances of a Paperback Writer*, appeared in 2007.

American psychiatrist, psychoanalyst and author **Janet Asimov** (Janet Opal Jeppson), the widow of science fiction legend Isaac Asimov (who died in 1992), died on February 25, aged 92. With her husband, who she married in 1973, she co-wrote ten volumes of the children's SF series about "Norby, the Mixed-Up Robot" (1983–91), co-edited the anthology *Laughing Space*, and co-authored the non-fiction title *How to Enjoy Writing: A Book of Aid and Comfort*. Her own books include the novels *The Second Experiment*, *The Last Immortal*, *Mind Transfer* and *Murder at the Galactic Writer's Society*, while her short fiction is collected in *The Mysterious Cure and Other Stories of Pshrinks Anonymous*. She also edited a collection of her late husband's letters, *It's Been a Good Life: Isaac Asimov* and wrote *Notes for a Memoir: On Isaac Asimov, Life, and Writing*.

British scriptwriter **Graeme Curry**, who wrote the three-part

*Doctor Who* serial 'The Happiness Patrol' (1988), died the same day, aged 54.

German-born music composer and jazz musician **André Previn** (Andreas Ludwig Priwin) died in New York City on February 28, aged 89. A four-time Oscar winner, he joined MGM in 1946 at the age of seventeen, where he worked as a conductor on such movies as *The Secret Garden* (1949). He composed the score for *Dead Ringer* (1964) and conducted the music for *Rollerball* (1975). The third of Previn's five wives was actress Mia Farrow (1970–79).

Pioneering British anthology editor **Hugh Lamb** died on March 2, aged 73. Beginning with *A Tide of Terror* in 1972, he published many important anthologies of supernatural fiction, not only bringing "lost" stories and authors back into print, but also showcasing the work of contemporary horror authors. His books include *A Wave of Fear*, *Victorian Tales of Terror*, *Star Book of Horror No.1*, *Terror by Gaslight*, *The Thrill of Horror: 22 Terrifying Tales* (which included the "lost" M.R. James story 'The Experiment'), *Return from the Grave*, *The Star Book of Horror No.2*, *The Taste of Fear*, *Victorian Nightmares* (aka *A Bottomless Grave and Other Victorian Tales of Terror*), *Cold Fear*, *Forgotten Tales of Terror*, *The Man-Wolf and Other Horrors*, *Tales from a Gas-Lit Graveyard*, *New Tales of Terror*, *Gaslit Nightmares* (1988), *Gaslit Nightmares 2*, *Terror by Gaslight: An Anthology of Rare Tales of Terror*, *Gaslit Nightmares* (2006) and *Gaslit Horror*. He also compiled a number of important collections, such as *E. Nesbit's Tales of Terror* and *In the Dark: Tales of Terror* by the same author, *The Black Reaper: Tales of Terror* by Bernard Capes, *Stories in the Dark: Tales of Terror* by Jerome K. Jerome, Robert Barr and Barry Pain, *Ghosts in the House* by A.C. Benson and R.H. Benson, *Out of the Dark Volume One: Origins* and *Out of the Dark Volume Two: Diversions* by Robert W. Chambers, *The Night Wind Howls: Complete Supernatural Stories* by Frederick Cowles, and *The Invisible Eye* by Erckmann-Chatrian. During the late 1990s and early 2000s, Lamb was a regular contributor to the small press magazine *Enigmatic Tales* with his 'Tales from the Grave' series of rediscoveries.

American author **Frances Yerxa** [Hamling] (Frances Deegan Ferris) died on March 3, aged 101. During the 1940s she had four short stories published in the pulp magazines *Amazing Stories Quarterly*, *Amazing Stories* and *Fantastic Adventures*. Following the death of her first husband, SF writer Leroy Yerxa, in 1946, she married publisher and editor William Hamling the following year and became the managing editor for some of his magazines, including *Imagination*, *Imaginative Tales* and *Rogue*. Hamling predeceased her in 2017.

Italian-born American artist **David Palladini**, who created the cover for the second edition (1987) of Stephen King's *The Eyes of the Dragon*, died on March 13, aged 72. He also illustrated children's books, including *The Girl Who Cried Flowers and Other Tales* by Jane Yolen and *Beauty: A Retelling of the Story of Beauty and the Beast* by Robin McKinley, and created two covers for *The Magazine of Fantasy and Science Fiction* in the late 1970s. Palladini created the Aquarian Tarot deck (1970, aka the New Palladini Tarot), and his artistic memoir, *The Journal of an Artist*, appeared in 2011.

British anthologist and author **"Charles Black"** (Michael Duggan) died of stomach cancer on March 15, aged 51. In 2007—as a homage to *The Pan Book of Horror Stories*—he launched *The Black Book of Horror* through his own Mortbury Press imprint, and the original anthology series ran for eleven volumes until 2015. Black's own short fiction appeared in such small press publications as *Eldritch Blue: Love & Sex in the Cthulhu Mythos*, *H.P. Lovecraft's Magazine of Horror*, *Horror Carousel*, *Best New Zombie Tales Volume One*, *Kitchen Sink Gothic* and *Lovecraft's Disciples*, and was collected in *Black Ceremonies* (2015).

American TV writer **Lawrence G. DiTillo** died on March 16, aged 79. He scripted episodes of such animated shows as *He-Man and the Masters of the Universe* (both the 1983–85 and 2002–04 series) and *She-Ra: Princess of Power* (along with the spin-off movie *He-Man and She-Ra: The Secret of the Sword*), *Galaxy High School*, *Captain Power and the Soldiers of the Future*, *The Real Ghostbusters*, *Conan: The Adventurer*, *Beast Wars: Transformers* and *Kong the Animated Series*. DiTillo's other credits include episodes of the live-action series *Swamp Thing* (1990), *The Hitchhiker*, *The Hidden Room* and *Babylon 5* (for which he was also executive story editor from 1994–95).

Veteran American comics illustrator **Ken Bald** (Kenneth Bruce Bald) died on March 17, aged 98. Some of his fan art was published in *More Fun Comics* in 1936 before he joined comic book "packager" Jack Binder's studio. During the Golden Age of Comics Bald illustrated such characters as Captain America, the Sub-Mariner, the Blonde Phantom, Miss America and Sun Girl (which he co-created). During the 1950s his work also appeared in the ACG horror titles *Adventures Into the Unknown*, *The Clutching Hand*, *Forbidden Worlds* and *Out of the Night*. In 1971, Bald (credited as "K. Bruce" for contractual reasons) created the *Dark Shadows* newspaper strip, which ran for two years. He retired in 1984.

British author **Paul** [William] **Hugli** died the same day, aged 67. He had been suffering from multiple health problems for some time. He contributed eight short stories to anthologies edited by J.M. Lofficier and Randy Lofficier for their Black Coat Press imprint.

Transylvanian-born author, editor and poet **Leonard Wolf** (Leonard Ludovic) died in Oregon on March 20, aged 96. Best known for his popular non-fiction studies *A Dream of Dracula: In Search of the Living Dead*, *Horror: A Connoisseur's Guide to Literature and Film* and *Dracula: The Connoisseur's Guide*, he also edited *The Annotated Frankenstein*, *The Essential Dracula*, *The Essential Frankenstein*, *Carmilla and 12 Other Classic Tales of Mystery* by J. Sheridan Le Fanu and the anthologies *Wolf's Complete Book of Terror*, *Doubles Dummies and Dolls: 21 Terror Tales of Replication* and *Blood Thirst: 100 Years of Vampire Fiction*. Wolf's novel *The Glass Mountain* appeared in 1993, and during the 1950s he had a number of poems published in *The Magazine of Fantasy and Science Fiction*.

Distinctive American author of Lovecraftian fiction and poetry **W.** (Wilum) **H.** (Hopfrog) **Pugmire** (Wiliam Harry Pugmire) died of heart failure while in hospice care on March 26, aged 67. The self-described "Queen of Eldritch Horror", he began publishing stories in the 1970s in such small press magazines as *Space and Time*, *The Diversifier* and *Astral Dimensions*, and edited the 1980s magazine *Tales of Lovecraftian Horror*. Pugmire's baroque fiction is collected in *Tales of Sesqua Valley*, *Dreams of Lovecraftian Horror*, *Tales of Love and Death*, *Sesqua Valley and Other Dreams*, *Weird Inhabitants of*

*Sesqua Valley, The Tangled Muse, Gathered Dust and Others, Some Unknown Gulf of Night, Uncommon Places: A Collection of Exquisities, The Strange Dark One: Tales of Nyarlathotep, Encounters with Enoch Coffin* (with Jeffrey Thomas), *Monstrous Aftermath: Stories in the Lovecraftian Tradition* and *An Imp of the Aether*. His only novel, *Witches in Dreamland* (with David H. Barker), was published in 2018.

American underground comix artist **Leslie Sternbergh Alexander** died of multiple system atrophy on March 27, aged 58. Her work appeared in *The Comics Journal, MAD* magazine and DC's *Wonder Woman Annual #2*. Alexander's comic-book artwork was also included in the 1989 movie *Alien Space Avenger*, in which she appeared in a supporting role.

American music composer and arranger **Maury Laws** died on March 28, aged 95. Best known for his work with animation studio Rankin/Bass, his credits include *Return to Oz* (1964), *The Daydreamer, Mad Monster Party?, Frosty the Snowman, Santa Claus is Comin' to Town, The Mad Mad Monsters, 20,000 Leagues Under the Sea* (1972), *Jack O'Lantern, Around the World in 80 Days* (1972), *Alice in Wonderland* (1973), *The Hobbit* (1977), *Jack Frost, The Return of the King* (1980), *Pinocchio's Christmas, The Flight of Dragons, The Wind in the Willows* (1987) and the 1966 TV series *King Kong*, along with the live-action movies *The Last Dinosaur* and *The Bermuda Depths*.

American fantasy and science fiction author and TV scriptwriter **Allan Cole**, died of cancer on March 29, aged 75. With Chris Bunch he created the best-selling "Sten" (1982–2018) and "Far Kingdoms" (1993–96) series, and his other novels include the "Timura Trilogy" (*When the Gods Slept, Wolves of the Gods* and *The Gods Awaken*) and *Lords of Terror* (with Nick Perumov). Cole was also story editor on the 1980 TV series *Galactica 1980*, and he scripted an episode of that show along with *Buck Rogers in the 25th Century, The Incredible Hulk, Defenders of the Earth, Werewolf* and *Shades of LA*.

Hugo and Nebula Award-winning American SF author **Vonda N. (Neel) McIntyre** died on April 1, aged 70. She had been diagnosed with metastatic pancreatic cancer less than two months earlier. Her early stories appeared in *Venture Science Fiction Magazine, The*

*Magazine of Fantasy and Science Fiction* and various anthologies, including Damon Knight's *Orbit* series, before her debut novel, *The Exile Waiting*, appeared in 1975. Her other novels include *Dreamsnake, Superluminal, Starfarers* (and its three sequels) and *The Moon and the Sun* (filmed as *The King's Daughter*), while some of her short fiction is collected in *Fireflood and Other Stories*. She edited the anthologies *Aurora: Beyond Equality* (with Susan J. Anderson) and *Nebula Awards Showcase 2004*, and during the 1980s and early '90s McIntyre wrote a number of *Star Trek* tie-ins (including *Star Trek: The Wrath of Khan, Star Trek III: The Search for Spock* and *Star Trek IV: The Voyage Home*) and one *Star Wars* novel.

British children's author **Antonia Barber**, whose 1969 novel *The Ghosts* was filmed three years later as *The Amazing Mr. Blunden*, died on April 4, aged 86.

**David Farrant**, Wiccan High Priest, self-styled psychic investigator and the founder (in 1967) and president of the British Psychic and Occult Society (BPOS), died after a long illness on April 8, aged 73. He explored his somewhat obsessive interest in the supposed "Highgate Vampire" myth in such books as *Beyond the Highgate Vampire: A True Case of Supernatural Occurrences and Vampirism That Centred Around London's Highgate Cemetery, The Vampyre Syndrome: The Truth Behind the Highgate Vampire Legend* (with Dave Milner), *The Highgate Vampire Casebook: 1* (with Patsy Langley) and *Don Ecker's Final Report on the Highgate Vampire* (with Ecker). Farrant also published *Dark Journey: True Cases of Ghostly Phenomena from the Files of the British Psychic and Occult Society* (with Chrissie Demant) and *Pact with the Devil*, along with two self-published autobiographies: *David Farrant: In the Shadow of the Highgate Vampire* and *Out of the Shadows*. In 1974 he was charged with vandalising and desecrating tombs in Highgate Cemetery and jailed for three years.

Nebula, British Fantasy and World Fantasy Award-winning American author **Gene** [Rodman] **Wolfe** died after a long battle with heart disease on April 14, aged 87. He began publishing stories in *If, New Worlds, The Magazine of Fantasy and Science Fiction* and Damon Knight's series of *Orbit* anthologies before his first novel, *Operation*

*Ares,* appeared in 1970. However, Wolfe was best known for his ambitious fantasy sequence "The Book of the New Sun" (1980–82), which began with *The Shadow of the Torturer, The Claw of the Conciliator, The Sword of the Lictor* and *The Citadel of the Autarch* before he expanded it into a further eight volumes. His other novels include *The Fifth Head of Cerberus, Peace, The Devil in a Forest, Soldier of the Mist* and its two sequels, *Free Live Free, There Are Doors, Castleview, Pandora by Holly Hollander, The Knight* and *The Wizard, The Evil Guest, The Land Across* and *A Borrowed Man.* Wolfe's short fiction was collected in, amongst other titles, *The Island of Doctor Death and Other Stories and Other Stories, Storeys from the Old Hotel, Endangered Species, Strange Travelers, Innocents Aboard* and *The Best of Gene Wolfe.* He was married to Rosemary Frances Dietsch from 1956 until her death in 2013. Gene Wolfe received a World Fantasy Life Achievement Award in 1996 and was named the 29th SFWA Grand Master in 2012. He had stories in *Best New Horror #2, #11, #14* and *#18.*

American comic book and movie memorabilia collector **Malcolm Willits** died on April 15, aged 85. With Leonard Brown he opened the Collectors Book Store in Hollywood in 1965. Between 1950–54 Willits co-edited the SF fanzine *Destiny,* for the first two years with Jim Bradley and the second two with Earl Kemp.

American psychic investigator **Lorraine Warren** (Lorraine Rita Moran), who investigated haunted houses with her late husband, Ed Warren, died on April 18, aged 92. Best known for their investigations into George Lutz's house in Amityville, Long Island, in 1975, the Warrens are portrayed by Patrick Wilson and Vera Farmiga in The *Conjuring* Universe movies. The Warrens founded the New England Society for Psychic Research in 1952, and their many books on the paranormal include *The Haunted: The True Story of One Family's Nightmare* (filmed in 1991), *Ghost Hunters: True Stories from the World's Most Famous Demonologists, Satan's Harvest* and *Ghost Tracks.*

British India-born author and scriptwriter **John** [Griffith] **Bowen** died the same day, aged 94. In 1957 he had a short story published in *Science Fantasy,* and his apocalyptic novel *After the Rain* appeared the following year. Bowen then virtually abandoned his career as a novelist in the 1960s to write for TV, including the influential "folk horror" episode of the BBC's *Play for Today*, 'Robin Redbreast' (1970), and its semi-sequel 'A Photograph' (1977). He also dramatised M.R. James' *The Treasure of Abbott Thomas* (1974) and scripted the 1978 TV movie *The Ice House*, while his other credits include episodes of *Mystery and Imagination* (J. Sheridan Le Fanu's 'The Flying Dragon'), *The Guardians*, *Dead of Night* and *Bedtime Stories*. In 1966, *After the Rain* was adapted into a stage play and first performed at the Hampstead Theatre Club in London, while 'Robin Redbreast' was turned into a play for the Yvonne Arnaud Theatre, Guildford, in 1974.

American artist and illustrator **Greg Theakston** (aka "Earl P. Wooten") died on April 22, aged 65. He not only worked for Marvel Comics, DC Comics, Warren Publishing, Archie Comics, *Worlds of If*, *MAD*, *National Lampoon*, *The New York Times*, *Playboy*, *TV Guide* and *Rolling Stone*, but Theakston also created the poster for the 1986 remake of *Invaders from Mars* and did book covers for such authors as Gordon R. Dickson, Michael Moorcock, Bram Stoker, A.E. van Vogt, Philip José Farmer, Poul Anderson and many others. In addition to his work as an artist, he also developed a bleaching process (dubbed "Theakstonizing") for restoring old comics for reprinting.

British SF fan **H. Stanley** ("Stan") **Nuttall** died on April 26, aged 92. A member and former chairman of the Liverpool Science Fiction Society and a member of the British Interplanetary Society, in 1957 he was made a "Knight of Saint Fantony" at Cytricon III. With John Owen he wrote fanfiction about "Sir William Makepeace Harrison" for the Liverpool Group's club fanzine, *Space Diversions*.

American book collector and dealer The Reverend **Allen L. Lewis** (aka "The Padre") died on April 29, aged 77. He was a regular dealer at World Fantasy and World Science Fiction Conventions on both sides of the Atlantic. Over the course of several decades, Lewis amassed one of the largest private collections of science fiction, fantasy and horror first edition hardcovers in the world. The bulk of his collection was donated to the University of Iowa in 2015.

British reproductive biologist and SF fan Dr. **Jack Cohen** died on May 6, aged 85. He worked as a science consultant on TV shows and with other authors, and collaborated with mathematican Ian Stewart and Terry Pratchett on the four-volume *The Science of Discworld* series. Cohen and Stewart also teamed up for the SF novels *Wheelers* and *Heaven*, along with the non-fiction study *What Does a Martian Look Like? The Science of Extraterrestrial Life.*

Oscar-winningAmerican screenwriter **Alvin Sargent** (Alvin Supowitz) died on May 9, aged 92. He began his career in TV in the late 1950s, and his credits include *Bogus*, *Spider-Man 2*, *Spider-Man 3* and *The Amazing Spider-Man* (2012), along with an episode of *The Alfred Hitchcock Hour*. He once said, "When I die, I'm going to have written on my tombstone: 'Finally, a plot.'"

British author and poet **Walter Harris**, who is credited with writing the 1977 Universal monster novelisations *Creature from the Black Lagoon* and *The Werewolf of London* under the "Carl Dreadstone" or "E.K. Leyton" house names, died the same day, aged 93. A broadcaster with the CBC and BBC, his other books include *The Day I Died*, *The Fifth Horseman*, *Saliva*, *Godhead* and *The New Avengers* tie-in, *To Catch a Rat*. Harris also had a short story in Richard Davis' 1968 anthology *Tandem Horror 2*.

British *Doctor Who* fan **Paul Condon** died after a short illness on May 10, aged 49. He organised a number of conventions and curated online content for various BBC television shows. Condon edited *1001 TV Shows You Must Watch Before You Die* and the anthology *Doctor Who Short Trips: A Christmas Treasury*, and with Jimmy Sangster he wrote the reference books *The Complete Hitchcock* and *TV Heaven*. His other books include *The Matrix: Unlocked*.

British actor, teacher and prolific children's author **Tommy Donbavand** died of throat cancer on May 14, aged 53. He wrote a number of novels in the "Too Ghoul for School" (as "B. Strange"), "Scream Street", "The Creeper Files" (as "Hacker Murphy") and "Fangs Vampire Spy" series, along with the "Shadow Vanguard" SF series (as "Tom Dublin"), *Zombie!* and the *Doctor Who* tie-in, *Shroud of Sorrow*. Donvanand also scripted comic strips for the *Beano*. *Scream Street* was turned into a stop-motion animated TV series on

CBBC, while his *Doctor Who* audio play, *What Lurks Down Under*, was released posthumously by Big Finish Productions.

German-born British author and illustrator **Judith Kerr** OBE (Anna Judith Gertrud Helene Kerr) died after a short illness on May 22, aged 95. Her classic 1968 picture book, *The Tiger Who Came to Tea*, has sold more than five million copies worldwide. Her other books include the "Mog the Cat" series and the autobiographical *When Hitler Stole Pink Rabbit*. Kerr was married to author Nigel Kneale from 1954 until his death in 2006, and she helped him build and operate the special effects for the BBC-TV serial *The Quatermass Experiment* (1953).

American pulp and comics artist **Everett Raymond Kinstler** died of heart failure on May 26, aged 92. Best known for his Western and romance work, he also contributed to such pre-code horror titles as Avon's *Witchcraft, Eerie, Space Detective* and *Phantom Witch Doctor*, Ziff-Davis/St. John's *Nightmare*, Standard's *Mystery Comics* and Atlas' *Strange Worlds*. Kinstler contributed interior artwork to the *Avon Science Fiction and Fantasy Reader* and *Startling Stories*. In the 1950s he moved into portrait painting, producing official portraits of eight American presidents, including Gerald Ford and Ronald Reagan.

One of America's finest writers of short horror fiction, **Dennis [William] Etchison**, died of cancer on May 29, aged 76. His early stories were published in the 1960s and '70s in such markets as *The Magazine of Fantasy, Cavalier and Science Fiction* and John Carnell's series of *New Writings in SF* anthologies before he established himself as a master of Californian dark fantasy. His fiction is collected in *The Dark Country, Red Dreams, The Blood Kiss, The Death Artist, Talking in the Dark, Fine Cuts, Got to Kill Them All & Other Stories, A Long Time Til Morning* and *It Only Comes Out at Night*. Etchison's original novels are *Darkside, Shadowman, California Gothic* and *Double Edge*, along with movie novelisations of *The Fog, Halloween II, Halloween III: Season of the Witch* and *Videodrome* (the last three as "Jack Martin"). He edited the three-volume *Masters of Darkness* anthologies (1986–91), as well as an omnibus edition, and his other anthologies include *Cutting Edge, Lord John Ten: A Celebration, MetaHorror, The Museum of Horrors* and *Gathering the Bones* (with

Ramsey Campbell and Jack Dann). He was a consultant for Stephen King's non-fiction study *Danse Macabre* (1981), revising subsequent editions, and served as a staff writer on the HBO TV series *The Hitchhiker* in 1985. A multiple winner of the British Fantasy Award and the World Fantasy Award, he received the Bram Stoker Award for Lifetime Achievement in 2017 and was a former president of the Horror Writers Association (1992–94). Etchison had stories reprinted in multiple editions of *Best New Horror*, starting with volume #3.

British surgeon, botanist, film director and author **Andrew [Annandale] Sinclair** died on May 30, aged 84. His novels include *The Project, The Facts in the Case of E.A. Poe* and the "Albion Triptych" (*Gog, Magog* and *King Ludd*). In 1966, Sinclair and Peter Whitehead founded Lorrimer Publishing to publish film scripts of classic films (including *Alphaville, Clockwork Orange, If...*, Fritz Lang's *M* and *Metropolis, Pandora's Box, The Cabinet of Dr. Caligari* and *The Seventh Seal*). He also directed the 1973 horror movie *Blue Blood*, starring Oliver Reed, Fiona Lewis and Derek Jacobi, and scripted an episode of *TV's Hammer House of Mystery and Suspense* ('Tennis Court').

American artist **Dennis Neal Smith**, who contributed interior artwork to the 1983 Arkham House collections *The Wind from a Burning Woman* by Greg Bear and *The Zanzibar Cat* by Joanna Russ, died of cancer in May. He also chaired Westercon in San Diego in 1966 and created the art for the first progress report for the inaugural San Diego Comic-Con.

American screenwriter **Brian Taggert** died of a heart attack on June 1, aged 81. He scripted *The Spell* (1977), *Night Cries, Visiting Hours, Of Unknown Origin, Poltergeist III*, the 1991 TV movie remake of *What Happened to Baby Jane?* (which he also co-produced), *Child of Darkness Child of Light, Omen IV: The Awakening* and *Trucks* (based on the story by Stephen King). Taggert co-scripted the TV mini-series *V: The Final Battle* and was an executive script consultant on the 1984–85 *V* series. He also taught a script-writing course at UCLA's film school entitled 'Things That Go Bump in the Night: Writing the Thriller/Horror/Sci-Fi Picture'.

Polish author, artist and editor **Maciej Parowski**, who edited the SF magazine *Nowa Fantastyka* from 1992–2003, died on June 2, aged 72. In 2007, he was awarded the silver medal for cultural achievement.

59-year-old American Muscogee Creek-Cherokee artist **Keith Birdsong** died on June 4 from injuries sustained in a car wreck. Following a hemorrhagic stroke in 2018, he was told that he would never speak, walk or paint again, before recovering the ability to do all three. Birdsong's photo-realistic art began appearing on book covers in 1989. He was best known for his work on tie-ins to *Star Trek* and the cyberpunk role-playing game *Shadowrun*.

Japanese editor, translator and fan **Yoshio Kobayashi** (aka "Takashi Ogawa") died of an ischemic heart attack on June 13, aged 67. He founded the awad-winning fanzine *Palantir* in 1981.

American-born British publisher and editor **Tom Boardman** (Thomas Volney Boardman, Jr.) died on June 15, aged 86. He joined the family publishing company, T.V. Boardman, in 1949, and remained on as managing director when the company changed ownership in 1954. Boardman also became a SF adviser to such UK imprints as Gollancz, Four Square, Macdonald and New English Library. He was the business manager for Brian Aldiss and Harry Harrison's short-lived critical journal *SF Horizons* (1964–65) and edited five reprint anthologies: *Connoisseur's Science Fiction*, *The Unfriendly Future*, *An ABC of Science Fiction*, *Science Fiction Horizons 1* and the juvenile *Science Fiction Stories*.

Chinese-American animator and bit-actor **Milton Quon** died on June 18, aged 105. He worked on Disney's *Fantasia* and *Dumbo* and, after World War II, returned to the studio to run its publicity/promotions department. He also turned up in a 1996 episode of TV's *Mighty Morphin Power Rangers*.

American TV writer **Peter Allan Fields** died on June 19, aged 84. He wrote for such shows as *The Man from U.N.C.L.E.*, *The Six Million Dollar Man*, *Man from Atlantis*, *Darkroom*, *Knight Rider*, *Star Trek: The Next Generation*, *Xena: Warrior Princess* and *Star Trek: Deep Space Nine* (also producing the first two seasons).

American author, poet and editor **Edward P.** (Paul) **Berglund** died in late June, aged 76. Beginning in 1970, his Lovecraftian short fiction appeared in such fanzines as *Etchings & Odysseys, Space and Time, Dark Messenger Reader, The Arkham Sampler* (1984) and *Eldritch Tales*, and much of his short fiction was collected in *Shards of Darkness* (2000). He edited the fanzine *From Beyond the Dark Gateway* (1972–77), along with *Readers' Guide to the Cthulhu Mythos* (with Robert E. Weinberg), the anthologies *The Disciples of Cthulhu* and *The Disciples of Cthulhu II: Blasphemous Tales of the Followers*, and a collection of the late James Wade's work, *Such Things May Be: Collected Writings*, for Shadow Publishing.

American hardcore horror writer **Charlee Jacob** (Neil Rain Jacob) died after a long illness on July 14, aged 67. The Texas native had suffered from fibromyalgia, Parkinson's disease and narcolepsy for years. She published around 150 stories and more than 200 poems, and was nominated for thirteen Bram Stoker Awards, winning for her novel *Dread in the Beast* and the poetry volumes *Sineater, Vectors: A Week in the Death of a Planet* (with Marge Simon) and *Four Elements* (with Simon, Rain Graves and Linda Addison). Jacob's other novels were *The Symbiotic Fascination, Haunter, Vestal, Dark Moods, Soma, The Myth of Falling, Season of the Witch* and *Containment: The Death of Earth*, while her short stories are collected in *Dread in the Beast, Up Out of the Cities That Blow Hot and Cold, Flowers from a Dark Star, Taunting the Minotaur, Skins of Youth* (with Mehitobel Wilson), *Guises, Cardinal Sins, The Desert, Heresy* and *The Indigo People: A Vampire Collection*.

British role-playing and video game designer and writer **Mike Brunton** died on July 18. He worked at TSR UK and Games Workshop, and edited the magazine *White Dwarf* in the late 1980s.

**Greg** [Charles] **Shoemaker**, the founder and editor of the influential Godzilla fanzine *The Japanese Fantasy Film Journal* (JFFJ, 1968–84), died of a heart attack on July 19, aged 72. He has been described as "The father of Western *kaiju* fandom".

American author, editor and publisher **Sam Gafford** died on July 20, after suffering a massive heart attack three weeks earlier. He was 56 and never regained consciousness. A scholar of William Hope Hodgson and H.P. Lovecraft, he wrote the non-fiction studies *William Hope Hodgson: Master of the Sea, Hodgson: A Collection of*

*Essays*, the Bram Stoker Award-nominated *William Hope Hodgson: Voices from the Borderland* (with Massimo Berruit and S.T. Joshi) and the graphic novel *Some Notes on a Non-Entity: The Life of H.P. Lovecraft*, illustrated by Jason C. Eckhardt. Gafford began writing short stories in the early 1980s, and some of his fiction is collected in *The Dreamer in the Fire and Other Stories*. He also published the novels *Whitechapel* and *The House of Nodens*. Gafford was was also the publisher of Ulthar Press. He edited the anthologies *Carnacki: The New Adventures* and *Carnacki: The Lost Cases* and, with John Linwood Grant and Dave Brzeski, co-founded the magazine *Occult Detective Quarterly* in 2016.

American composer **Ben Johnston** (Benjamin Burwell Johnston, Jr.), regarded as "one of the foremost composers of microtonal music", died of complications from Parkinson's disease on July 21, aged 93. In 1970 he composed the tonal score for the hour-long chamber opera *Carmilla: A Vampire Tale* (based on the novella by J. Sheridan Le Fanu), staged at the La MaMa Experimental Theatre Club in Manhattan's East Village, New York City.

Welsh-born British software developer and SF fan **Martin Hoare** died from a septic infection following emergency surgery on July 26, aged 67. He co-chaired two Eastercons, Seacon '84 and Helicon 2, and worked on many more convention committees, including acting as Division Head at ConFiction, the 1990 Worldcon in The Hague, Netherlands. Hoare received the Doc Weir Award in 2015. He was probably best known for accepting David Langford's numerous Hugo Awards at various overseas World Science Fiction Conventions.

American singer and songwriter **Richard Gillis** died of complications from a fall on July 31, aged 80. He composed the music scores for *The Bees* (1978) and *Demonoid* (1981), and the song 'When the World Was New' for *A Boy and His Dog* (1975), based on the novella by Harlan Ellison. Gillis also turned up as a police officer in John Landis' *Schlock* (1973).

Australian composer and conductor **Barrington** [Somers] **Pheloung**, best known for his themes for the TV series *Inspector Morse*, *Inspector Lewis* and *Endeavour*, died on August 1, aged 65. He also composed the music for such films as *Friendship's Death*, *Truly*

*Madly Deeply*, *Nostradamus* (1994) and Tobe Hooper's *The Mangler* (based on the short story by Stephen King), along with the BBC's 1987 *Bookmark* documentary 'The Vampire's Life', about author Anne Rice.

World Fantasy Award-winning American author **Barry Hughart** died the same day, aged 85. His "Master Li" series of Oriental fantasies comprised the novels *Bridge of Birds*, *The Story of the Stone*, *Eight Skilled Gentlemen* and the omnibus *The Chronicles of Master Li and Number Ten Oxen*.

Puerto Rico-born American comics artist **Ernie Colon** (Ernesto Colón Sierra) died of colorectal cancer on August 8, aged 88. He began his career in the mid-1950s at Harvey Comics, going on to work on such titles as *Casper the Friendly Ghost* and *Richie Rich*. Colon later worked for Warren's *Creepy*, *Eerie* and *Vampirella* titles, as well as Skywald's *Psycho* (under the pen name "Jack Purcell"). Colon became an editor at DC Comics (1982–85), where he co-created such characters as Arak, Son of Thunder and Amethyst, Princess of Gemworld, while for Marvel he illustrated such titles as *Battlestar Galactica*, *John Carter Warlord of Mars*, *Red Sonja* and *Savage Sword of Conan*. Colon also worked for such companies as Atlas/Seaboard (*Grim Ghost*, *Thrilling Adventure Stories*, *Weird Tales of the Macabre*), Gold Key Comics (*Doctor Solar Man of the Atom*) and Valiant Comics (*Magnus Robot Fighter*).

American children's author and editor **Lee Bennett Hopkins** died the same day, aged 81. He edited the 1970s anthologies *A-Haunting We Will Go*, *Monsters Ghoulies and Creepy Creatures* and *Witching Time*.

American libertarian SF writer **J.** (Joseph) **Neil Schulman** died on August 10, aged 66. He had suffered a pulmonary embolism three days earlier and never regained consciousness. His novels include *Alongside Night* (filmed by the author in 2014), *The Rainbow Cadenza: A Novel in Logosata Form*, *Escape from Heaven* and *The Fractual Man*, while his short fiction was collected in *Nasty Brutish and Short Stories*. Schulman also published *The Robert Heinlein Interview and Other Heinleiniana*, and scripted a 1986 episode of TV's *The Twilight Zone* ('Profile in Silver').

American children's book illustrator **Charles** [Joseph] **Santore** died on August 11, aged 84. Possibly best known for his more than forty covers for *TV Guide*, he also illustrated such classic books as *The Velveteen Rabbit*, *The Wizard of Oz*, *The Night Before Christmas*, *Alice's Adventures Under Ground* and *Jabberwocky*. Santore, who usually spent two or three years illustrating a project, also did the cover for *J.R.R. Tolkien: Architect of Middle Earth* (1976).

Australian editor, publisher and author **Robert N. Stephenson** committed suicide on August 14, aged 57. He had long battled with seratonin deficiency, depression and bipolar disorder. Stephenson edited the SF magazine *Altair* (1998–2000), published the novels *Life Light* and *Vanishing Light*, and his short fiction is collected in *We Would Be Heroes*, *The Clever Nature of Wool*, *The Mess in My Head*, *To an Untrained Mind* and *Blue Reasoning and Other Lesser Tales*. He also edited the anthologies *Zombies* (2007) and *The Worlds of Science Fiction, Fantasy, and Horror* series from 2016–19.

American comedy writer **Larry Siegel** (Lawrence H. Siegel), who had two stories published in *The Magazine of Fantasy and Science Fiction* in the early 1950s, died of Parkinson's disease on August 20, aged 93. He became a TV scriptwriter, and his credits include co-writing the four-minute pilot *Wonder Woman: Who's Afraid of Diana Prince?* (1967). Siegal also contributed many movie satires to *MAD* magazine and scripted Harvey Kurtzman's 'Little Annie Fanny" comic strip in *Playboy* from 1965–69.

British author **A. (Anthony) A. (Arthur) Glynn** died of pneumonia on August 22, aged 89. His first short story was published in *Futuristic Science Stories* in 1952, and he had several other tales published in that magazine in the early 1950s, along with *Worlds of Fantasy*, *Wonders of the Spaceways* and *Supernatural Stories*. Following the publication of two SF novels with Badger Books, *Search the Dark Skies* (1960, as "John E. Muller") and *Plan for Conquest* (1963), Glynn didn't return to writing until the early 2000s, when new short stories appeared (under the byline "Tony Glynn") in Philip Harbottle's *Fantasy Adventures* magazine and were collected in *Mystery in Moon Lane: Supernatural Mystery Stories* (2013). His final SF novel was *Storm Over Utopia* (2016).

British comic book artist **Nigel Dobbyn** died of a heart attack on

August 24, aged 56. He worked for *2000 AD* on such strips as 'Future Shocks', 'Medivac 318', 'Trash', 'Red Razors' and 'Strontium Dogs'. In the 1990s he moved to *Sonic the Comic*, based on the Sonic the Hedgehog video game character, and also worked on Dark Horse's *Digimon*, Classical Comics' Shakespeare adaptations, Panini's *Spiderman and Friends* and a graphic novel adaptation of *Nightrise* by Anthony Horowitz.

American film researcher and writer **Billy H. Doyle** died from a series of strokes the same day, aged 86. He was the author of three seminal reference books from Scarecrow Press in the 1990s: *The Ultimate Directory of Silent Screen Performers: A Necrology of Births and Deaths and Essays on 50 Lost Players*, *The Ultimate Directory of Silent and Sound Era Performers: A Necrology of Actors and Actresses* and *The Ultimate Directory of Film Technicians: A Necrology of Dates and Places of Births and Deaths of More Than 9,000 Producers, Screenwriters, Composers, Cinematographers, Art Directors, Costume Designers, Choreographers, Executives, and Publicists*.

American book editor **Charles M.** (Michael) **Collins** [Jr.] died on August 26, aged 83. During the 1960s he edited the horror anthologies *Fright* (aka *Harvest of Fear*), *A Feast of Blood* and *A Walk with the Beast*. In 1969, Collins co-founded the Centaur Press (later Books) imprint with Donald M. Grant, reprinting works by Robert E. Howard, H. Warner Munn, Talbot Mundy, J. Allan Dunn, William Hope Hodgson, E. Charles Vivian and others in the "Time-Lost Series" before it closed in 1981. A former publishing rep, Collins was also associate editor of *Castle of Frankenstein* magazine.

British scriptwriter, script editor, producer and novelist **Terrance** [William] **Dicks** died after a short illness on August 29, aged 84. Best known for his various contributions to the BBC's *Doctor Who* (1968–83), other TV shows he worked on include *The Avengers*, *Moonbase 3*, *Space: 1999*, *The Hound of the Baskervilles* (1982), *Jane Eyre* (1983), *The Invisible Man* (1984) and *Alice in Wonderland* (1986). Dicks wrote numerous *Doctor Who* tie-in books and novelisations, starting with *Doctor Who and the Auton Invasion* (1974), and his other books include the *Star Quest* and *The Unexplained* series, along with his "Monsters" quartet (*Cry Vampire!*, *Marvin's Monster*, *Wereboy!* and

*The Ghosts of Gallows Cross*). He contributed *Aries: Blood Storm* to the *Horrorscopes* series and two volumes to the *Doctor Who* spin-off series, *The Sarah Jane Adventures*, while *Jonathan's Ghost* collected three of his novellas. Dicks also wrote two *Doctor Who* stage plays: *Doctor Who and the Daleks in Seven Keys to Doomsday* (1974) and *Doctor Who—The Ultimate Adventure* (1989).

American libertarian author, scriptwriter, producer and actor **Brad Linaweaver** (Bradford Swain Linaweaver) died of cancer the same day, aged 66. His first story appeared in *Fantastic* in 1980, and some of his short fiction is collected in *Clownface*. Linaweaver's novels include *Moon of Ice*, *The Land Beyond Summer*, *Anarquia* (with J. Kent Hastings) and novelisations of *Doom* (with Dafydd ab Hugh), *Sliders* and *Battlestar Galactica* (with Richard Hatch). He edited the anthology *Free Space* with Edward E. Kramer and the magazine *Mondo Cult*, and co-authored the non-fiction study *Worlds of Tomorrow: The Amazing Universe of Science Fiction Art* with Forrest J Ackerman. He worked on the original stories for Fred Olen Ray's *The Brain Leeches*, *Jack-O*, *The Low Budget Time Machine* and *Her Morbid Desires*, and co-scripted Kramer's *Terror at Tate Manor*, *Dead Reckoning* (2013) and the online series *The Silicon Assassin Project*. Linaweaver also executive produced such low-budget movies as *Crustacean* (starring Peter Atkins), *Super Shark* and *A House is Not a Home*, and he had acting roles and cameo appearances in a number of movies.

American author and artist **Melisa** [Corrina] **Michaels** died of pneumonia and complications from lung cancer on August 30, aged 73. She began publishing short fiction in 1979, and her novels include the "Skyrider" sequence (*Skirmish*, *First Battle*, *Last War*, *Pirate Prince* and *Floater Factor*), the "Rosie Lavine" series (*Cold Iron* and *Sister to the Rain*), *Far Harbor* and *World-Walker*. Michaels' artwork appeared on the covers of *The Darkover Concordance: A Reader's Guide* by Walter Breen, *Bones of the World: Tales from Time's End* edited by Bruce Holland Rogers and William Sander's *The Ballad of Billy Badass and the Rose of Turkestan*.

American scriptwriter **Gordon** [Joseph] **Bressack** died the same day, aged 68. He wrote for such TV cartoon series as *Bionic Six*, *The*

*Smurfs, The Real Ghostbusters, Tiny Toon Adventures, Teenage Mutant Ninja Turtles, Captain Simian & The Space Monkeys, Animaniacs* and *Pinky & the Brain*. Bressack also co-directed/co-scripted the live-action movies *Dark Tales* ('The Keeper' segment) and *Virus of the Dead*, and had bit-parts in *Blood Lake: Attack of the Killer Lampreys, Virus of the Dead* and *Blood Craft* (directed by his son, James Cullen Bressack).

Nebula Award-winning American SF writer **Katherine** [Anne] **MacLean** died on September 1, aged 94. Her first short story was published in *Astounding* in 1949, and she went on to contribute to *Galaxy Science Fiction, Worlds Beyond, Super Science Stories, Science Fiction Quarterly, Planet Stories, Thrilling Wonder Stories, Science Fiction Stories* and numerous other periodicals and anthologies. Her short fiction is collected in *The Diploids, The Trouble with You Earth People* and *Science Fiction Collection*. MacLean's novels include *Cosmic Checkmate* (aka *Second Game*, with Charles V. De Vet), *The Man in the Bird Cage, Missing Man* and *Dark Wing* (with her third husband, Carl West). MacLean was named a SFWA Author Emeritus in 2003, and received the Cordwainer Smith Rediscovery Award in 2011.

Prolific American author **David Hagberg** died on September 8, aged 76. Although best known for his techno-thrillers featuring super-spy "Kirk McGarvey", he also wrote six uncredited *Flash Gordon* novels for Tempo Books in the early 1980s, along with *Croc* (as "David James"), *The Trinity Factor* (as "Sean Flannery"), *Last Come the Children* and the 2013 tie-in *Terminator 3: Rise of the Machines*. Hagberg's short story 'Genesis' was included in the 2009 anthology *Twilight Zone: 19 Original Stories on the 50th Anniversary*.

Australian author **Hal** [Gibson Pateshall] **Colebatch** died on September 10, aged 73. He contributed to Larry Niven's "Man-Kzin Wars" shared-world series with the collection *Man-Kzin Wars X: The Wunder War* and stories in *Man-Kzin Wars XII, Man-Kzin Wars XIII* and other related anthologies (sometimes in collaboration with Matthew Joseph Harrington or Jessica Q. Fox). Colebatch also published *Return of the Heroes*, a study of heroic fantasy, and contributed to the *J.R.R. Tolkien Encyclopedia*.

Best-selling American author **Anne Rivers Siddons** (Sybil Anne Rivers) died on September 11, aged 83. Best known for her Southern novels, her 1978 book *The House Next Door* includes supernatural elements. It was filmed as a TV movie in 2006. Siddons also contributed an Introduction to a 1994 edition of Stephen King's *The Dead Zone*.

67-year-old American comics historian and artist **William Carl** ("Bill") **Schelly** died on September 12 of a blood clot in the lungs during chemotherapy for his recently diagnosed multiple myeloma. He edited and published the fanzine *Sense of Wonder* (1967–72) and in 1998 became associate editor of the comics magazine *Alter Ego*. Schelly's books include the Eisner Awad-winning *The Golden Age of Comic Fandom, Comic Fandom Reader, Harvey Kurtzman: The Man Who Created Mad and Revolutionized Humor in America, Man of Rock: The Biography of Joe Kubert, Founders of Comic Fandom, American Comic Book Chronicles: The 1950s, Otto Binder: The Life and Work of a Comic Book and Science Fiction Visionary* and *James Warren, Empire of Monsters: The Man Behind Creepy, Vampirella, and Famous Monsters*, while his autobiography, also entitled *Sense of Wonder*, appeared in 2001.

American SF fan, collector and bibliographer **Norm Metcalf** (Norman Clarke Metcalf) died on September 21, aged 81. His *Index of Science Fiction Magazines 1951–1965* appeared in 1968, he edited the fanzine *New Frontiers* (1959–64), which only had four issues, and was the anonymous editor of the 1960 anthology *The Science-Fictional Sherlock Holmes*. Metcalf also wrote for the sword & sorcery semiprozine *Amra*, and he had an article (written with Chuck Hansen) reprinted in *The Conan Swordbook: 27 Examinations of Heroic Fantasy* edited by L. Sprague de Camp and George H. Scithers.

**Les Cole** (Lester Hines Cole), who co-chaired SFCon, the 1954 World Science Fiction Convention in San Francisco, died on September 26, aged 93. He published the fanzine *Orgasm* (aka *The Big O*) in 1951 with his wife, Esther, and Clarence Jacobs, and his short stories appeared (usually under the psuedonyms "Es Cole", "Les Collins", "T.H. Mathieu", "Roy Carroll" and, in collaboration with Melvin Sturgis, "Colin Sturgis") in *Science Fantasy, Future Science*

*Fiction, Science Fiction Stories, Venture Science Fiction, The Magazine of Fantasy and Science Fiction* and *Amazing Science Fiction Stories* during the late 1950s. Cole's essay, 'How to Write Science Fiction' was published in the December 1959 issue of *Astounding Science Fiction*. Along with his wife, Esther, Cole was inducted into the First Fandom Hall of Fame in 2017.

American movie historian **Rudy Behlmer** (Rudolph Herman Behlmer) died on September 27, aged 92. He wrote a number of books about the Golden Age of Hollywood, including the definitive volume on producer David O. Selznick. Behlmer also contributed audio commentaries to DVD releases of such films as *Frankenstein, The Invisible Man* and Disney's *20,000 Leagues Under the Sea.*

British illustrator **Paul Birkbeck** died in early October, aged 80. He illustrated Salman Rushdie's 1990 children's fairy tale *Haroun and the Sea of Stories* and did the cover for Rushdie's follow-up, *Luka and the Fire of Life* (2010).

American author **J.** (John) **A.** (Alvin) **Pitts** died from amyloidosis (a rare disease that occurs when an abnormal protein, called amyloid, builds up in the organs) on October 3, aged 54. He is best known for the "Sarah Beauhall" urban fantasy series: *Black Blade Blues, Honeyed Worlds, Forged in Fire, Night Terrors* and *Rainbow Bridge.* Some of his short fiction is collected in *Bravado's House of Blues.*

American graphic designer and advertising executive **Philip** [Sheldon] **Gips** died of complications from chronic obstructive pulmonary disease and pneumonia the same day, aged 88. Amongst the movies he created iconic posters for are *Rosemary's Baby* (1968), *Catch 22, Tommy, Alien* (with the tag line "In space no one can hear you scream", which was written by Gips' wife, Barbara), *All That Jazz* and *Superman* (1978).

American children's book author and illustrator **Berthe Amoss** (Berthe Lathrop Marks) died on October 6, aged 94. Her books include *Lost Magic, The Great Sea Monster* and *The Loup Garou.*

American small press horror author and poet **Lisa Lepovetsky** (Alice E. Harvey) died on October 11, aged 68. Some of her short fiction appeared in *Twisted, Not One of Us, Grue Magazine, Cemetery Dance, The Tome, After Hours* and *Palace Corbie*, along with the anthologies *100 Wicked Little Witch Stories, 100 Vicious Little Vampire Stories, Blood Muse* and *Horrors! 365 Scary Stories: Get Your Daily Dose of Terror*. Her poetry is collected in the Bram Stoker Award-nominated *Voices from Empty Rooms*.

Soviet cosmonaut **Alexei Leonov** (Aleksey Arkhipovich Leonov), who in 1965 became the first human to "walk" in space as part of the Voskhod 2 mission, died the same day, aged 85. He co-scripted the 1980 SF film *The Orion Loop* (*Petlya Oriona*), while Arthur C. Clarke's novel *2010: Odyssey Two* featured an interplanetary spacecraft named in honour of Leonov. In collaboration with science fiction artist Andrey Sokolov, he also created a series of USSR postage stamps based on the theme of space.

American TV scriptwriter and producer, Edgar Award-winning playwright and songwriter **Sam Bobrick** died from a stroke on October 11, aged 87. He scripted episodes of *The Flintstones, Get Smart* and *Bewitched*.

American academic **Edgar L.** (Leon) **Chapman** also died the same day, aged 83. Professor Emeritus in the English Department at Bradley University, Peoria, Illinois, where he taught writing and literature from 1963–2002, he also authored the non-fiction studies *The Magic Labyrinth of Philip Jose Farmer, The Road to Castle Mount: The Science Fiction of Robert Silverberg* and *Classic and Iconoclastic Alternate History Science Fiction* (with Carl B. Yoke).

British children's author **Alison** [Mary] **Prince** died on October 12, aged 88. She wrote the novels *The Others* and *Bird Boy*, and the non-fiction study *Kenneth Grahame: An Innocent in the Wild Wood*. Mary Danby published Prince's stories in her anthology series *The Armada Ghost Book, The Fontana Book of Great Horror Stories* and *Nightmares*, and her short fiction is collected in *Haunted Children, The Ghost Within* and *A Haunting Refrain*.

One of America's most famous and controversial literary critics, **Harold Bloom**, died on October 14, aged 89. His one novel was *The Flight to Lucifer: A Gnostic Fantasy* (1979), but he is best known for his non-fiction studies of such authors as Mary Shelley, Edgar Allan Poe, Doris Lessing, Ursula K. Le Guin, George Orwell, Stephen King and Ray Bradbury, along with the critical volumes *Classic Horror*

*Writers, Modern Horror Writers, Frankenstein* and *The Lord of the Rings*. In 1985 he received a "genius grant" from the MacArthur Foundation.

West German-born American romance novelist **Johanna** [Helen] **Lindsey** died of lung cancer on October 27, aged 67. Her books sold more than sixty million copies around the world. Lindsey's best-selling titles include the futuristic "LySan Ter" trilogy (*Warrior's Woman, Keeper of the Heart* and *Heart of a Warrior*), along with the romantic fantasy *Until Forever*.

British poet and critic **Glen** [Tilburn] **Cavaliero** died on October 28, aged 92. Tartarus Press published his poetry collections *Steeple on a Hill* (1997) and *The Justice of the Night* (2007).

American writer and medical doctor **Michael** [John] **Blumlein** died of a heart attack on October 29, aged 71. He had been diagnosed with lung cancer seven years earlier. Blumlein made his fiction debut in 1984 in *Interzone*. His story 'The Brains of Rats' was nominated for a World Fantasy Award, while 'Bestseller' was a Bram Stoker Award finalist, and his transgressive short fiction is collected in *The Brains of Rats* (also nominated for World Fantasy and Bram Stoker awards), *What the Doctor Ordered, All I Ever Dreamed* and *Thoreau's Microscope*. Blumlein's novels are *The Movement of Mountains, X, Y* (filmed in 2004), *The Healer* and *Longer*.

Canadian-born scriptwriter **Bernard Slade** [Newbound], who created the ABC-TV series *The Flying Nun* (1967–70) and NBC's *The Girl with Something Extra* (1973–74), both starring Sally Field, died of Lewy Body Dementia in Beverly Hills on October 30. He was 89. Slade also wrote episodes of *Bewitched, My Living Doll* and *Good Heavens*, while his 1974 unsold pilot *Everything Money Can't Buy* starred José Ferrer as a wish-granting angel.

American small press author and publisher **Tom Johnson** (Thomas E. Johnson) died on November 5, aged 79. With his wife, Virginia, he founded the pulp fiction imprint Fading Shadows, Inc., and together they edited and published such magazines as *Weird Stories, Classic Pulp Fiction Stories, Action Adventure Stories, Starling Science Stories* and *Alien Worlds*. Johnson also wrote the series of novels *Jur: A Story of Predawn Earth* (with James Reasoner), *Savage*

*Land of Jur, Lost Land of Jur* and *Queen of Jur*, along with *Tunnel Through Space* and *Three Go Back*. His non-fiction books include *Secret Agent-X: A History* (with Will Murray), *From Shadow to Superman, The Green Ghost, The Mummy in Fact, Fiction and Film* (with Susan D. Cowie) and *The Christopher Lee Filmography: All Theatrical Releases, 1948–2003* (with Mark A. Miller).

Scottish-born publisher [Francis] **Ian Chapman** CBE died on November 7, aged 94. The former chairman and CEO of William Collins is credited with discovering author Alistair MacLean. In 1989 he set up Chapman Publishers with his wife Marjory, which was later purchased by Orion.

British author **Andrea Newman** died of breast cancer on November 9, aged 81. Best remembered for her groundbreaking 1970s TV series *Bouquet of Barbed Wire*, based on her own novel, she also scripted episodes of *Tales of Unease, The Frighteners* and *Rod Serling's Night Gallery*. John Burke published her short stories in his anthologies *Tales of Unease* and *More Tales of Unease*. "Andrea Newman" was a pseudonym adopted for her first novel in 1964, and her original names remain a secret.

**Tom Spurgeon** (Thomas Martin Spurgeon), who edited the comics trade magazine *The Comics Journal* from 1994–99, died on November 13, aged 50. With site designer Jordan Raphael, he launched the Eisner Award-winning blog site *The Comics Reporter* in 2004, and Spurgeon and Raphael co-wrote *Stan Lee and the Rise and Fall of the American Comic Book*. His other books include *The Romita Legacy* and *Comics As Art: We Told You So*, a history of his former employer, Fantagraphics, co-authored with Jacob Covey. However, publication of the latter title was delayed when Harlan Ellison launched a lawsuit, claiming that the authors had defamed him in the book. It was finally released in 2017, with the references to Ellison omitted.

American publisher **Walter J.** (Joseph) **Minton** died on November 19, aged 96. As president of G.P. Putnam's Sons from 1955–78, he challenged the then-current guardians of decency by publishing the first American edition of Vladimir Nabokov's *Lolita* in 1958, the bawdy 18th-century novel *Fanny Hill* as *Memoirs of a Woman of Pleasure* in

1963 (which led to a landmark decision by the United States Supreme Court three years later), and Terry Southern and Mason Hoffenberg's *Candy* in 1964. Amongst many other titles he also published at Putnam's was William Golding's *Lord of the Flies* (1962). Minton acquired the paperback imprint Berkley Books in 1965.

American comic-book artist and writer **Tom Lyle** (Thomas Stanford Lyle) died the same day, aged 66. He worked for Eclipse Comics (*Airboy, Airwolf*), DC Comics (*Starman, Robin, Detective Comics*), Marvel Comics (*Spider-Man, Punisher, Mutant X*) and Dark Horse Comics (*Star Wars*).

Legendary American cartoonist and author **Gahan** [Allen] **Wilson** died of complications from dementia on November 21, aged 89. Although his art originally appeared in such digest magazines as *Fantastic, Amazing Stories* and *Weird Tales* in the 1950s, Wilson is best known for his often dark, grotesque and macabre cartoons in *Colliers, National Lampoon, The NewYorker* and, especially, *Playboy.* Starting in 1964, he also became a regular contributor to *The Magazine of Fantasy and Science Fiction.* His art has been widely collected in such volumes as *Gahan Wilson's Graveside Manner, Still Weird, Even Weirder, The Best of Gahan Wilson* and *Gahan Wilson's Out There.* He reviewed for *F&SF, The Twilight Zone* and *Realms of Fantasy*, and some of his short fiction is collected in *The Cleft and Other Odd Tales* and *A Little Purple Book of Phantasies.* Wilson designed the original bust of H.P. Lovecraft World Fantasy Award in 1975, contributed cover art to books from Arkham House, Fedogan & Bremer and other publishers, and he edited the anthologies *Gahan Wilson's Favorite Tales of Horror, First World Fantasy Awards* and *Gahan Wilson's The Ultimate Haunted House* (with Nancy A. Collins). He won the World Fantasy Award twice, along with the Bram Stoker Lifetime Achievement Award in 1992, the World Fantasy Lifetime Achievement Award in 2004 and the International Horror Guild Living Legend Award in 2005. His stories appeared in *Best New Horror* #2, #5 and #17.

American children's author **Andrew Clements**, who wrote the "Things" trilogy about a boy who can become invisible, died on November 28, aged 70.

Pioneering American TV scriptwriter **D.** (Dorothy) **C.** (Catherine) **Fontana** died after a short illness on December 2, aged 80. She worked as a script consultant on the first two seasons of the original *Star Trek* (1967–68), and as story editor on such shows as *The Sixth Sense*, *Star Trek: The Animated Series*, *The Fantastic Journey* and *Logan's Run*. Fontana wrote scripts for episodes of *The Wild Wild West* (as "Michael Edwards"), *Star Trek*, *Circle of Fear* (Harlan Ellison's 'Earth, Air, Fire and Water'), *Star Trek: The Animated Series* (which she also associate-produced), *The Six Million Dollar Man*, *Land of the Lost*, *The Fantastic Journey*, *Logan's Run*, *Buck Rogers in the 25th Century* (as "Michael Richards"), *He-Man and the Masters of the Universe*, *Star Trek: The Next Generation* (she was also associate producer on the first season), *War of the Worlds* (1989), *The Legend of Prince Valiant*, *Star Trek: Deep Space Nine*, *Babylon 5*, *Hypernauts*, *Captain Simian & the Space Monkeys*, *ReBoot*, *Earth: Final Conflict*, *Silver Surfer* and *Beast Wars: Transformers*. She also wrote the novelisation of the Gene Roddenberry pilot *The Questor Tapes* and the *Star Trek* novel *Vulcan's Glory*. Since 1981, Fontana was married to Oscar-winning special effects designer Dennis Skotak.

British-born writer, music journalist and critic **Andrew** [Simon] **Weiner** died after a short illness in Toronto, Canada, on December 3, aged 70. His first fiction sale was to Harlan Ellison's *Again, Dangerous Visions* (1972), and he published more than forty stories in such periodicals as *Asimov's*, *The Magazine of Fantasy and Science Fiction* and *Interzone*, some of which were collected in *Distant Signals and Other Stories*, *This is the Year Zero* and the French-language *Envahisseurs!* and *Signaux lointains*. He also published the SF novels *Station Gehenna*, *Getting Near the End* (aka *En approchant de la fin*) and *Boulevard des disparus*. Two of Weiner's stories were adapted for TV's *Tales from the Darkside* in the 1980s.

American literary agent **Charles Schlessiger**, who represented such authors as Joan Aiken and Kate Wilhelm at Brandt & Hochman, died the same day, aged 86.

British-born American bookseller **Terry Davies** died on December 6, aged 85. From 1974–98 he co-owned The Earthling Bookshops in Santa Barbara and San Luis Obispo, California, with his wife Penny, where they hosted signings by such authors as Ray Bradbury, Charles Schultz and Ann Rice.

American-born British illustrator **Tom Adams** (Thomas Charles Renwick Adams) died on December 9, aged 93. Best known for producing the distinctive covers on Fontana's paperback series of Agatha Christie novels for eighteen years (1962–80), his other credits include covers for such authors as Robert Silverberg, Peter Straub, John Fowles, William Rotsler and Brian N. Ball. *Tom Adams' Agatha Christie Cover Story* (aka *Agatha Christie: The Art of Her Crimes*) and *Tom Adams Uncovered* collected some of his artwork. Adams also worked on the movies *2001: A Space Odyssey*, *Flash Gordon* (1980) and *Lifeforce*, while his design for the Fontana edition of Christie's *Death in the Clouds* (featuring a giant wasp) inspired the monster in the 2008 *Doctor Who* episode 'The Unicorn and the Wasp'.

British SF fan and bibliophile **Ian Covell** died of a stroke on December 11, aged 66. He compiled the non-fiction chapbooks *J.T. McIntosh: Memoir & Bibliography*, *An Index to DAW Books* and *A.E. van Vogt: Master of Null-A* (with Phil Stephensen-Payne), and from 1994 produced the monthly 'British Books Received' column in *Locus* for twenty-five years. Covell also co-edited the 1990s fanzine *The Time Centre Times* with John Davey, Maureen Davey and D.J. Rowe, and contributed essays, reviews and interviews to various publications.

American fan artist **Joseph A. West** ("JAW") died the same day, aged 97. His illustrations appeared in such publications as *Etchings & Odysseys*, *The Diversifier*, *Fantasy & Terror*, *From Beyond the Dark Gateway*, *The Arkham Sampler* (1984) and *The Hannes Bok Memorial Showcase of Fantasy Art*, while West's poetry, prose and artwork was collected in the 2012 volume *Aim High*.

American screenwriter **John** [Richard] **Briley**, who won an Academy Award for *Gandhi* (1982), died of a blood disorder on December 14, aged 94. He also scripted the 1964 sequel *Children of the Damned*, inspired by the novel by John Wyndham, and *The Medusa Touch*.

Film historian, professor at the University of Southern California and cinematographic archivist at the Library of Congress since 1990,

**Brian Taves** died on December 17, aged 60. He was Vice-President of the North American Jules Verne Society, publishing *The Jules Verne Encyclopedia* (with Stephen Michaluk, Jr.) and *Hollywood Presents Jules Verne: The Father of Science Fiction on Screen*. Taves also translated a number of little-known works by Verne, including 'Le Mariage de M. Anselme des Tilleuls' and the play *Monsieur de Chimpanzé* (both 2011).

**Jean Yeaworth**, who worked on her husband Irvin S. Yeaworth, Jr.'s movies *The Blob* (1958) and *4D Man* as music supervisor and co-scripted *Dinosaurus!*, died on December 24, aged 93.

Scottish author, poet, playwright and painter **Alasdair Gray** died on December 29, the day after his 85th birthday. Best known for his 1981 debut novel, *Lanark: A Life in Four Books*, many of his books and plays also contain fantastic elements. His short fiction was collected in *Unlikely Stories* and *Every Short Story 1951–2012*, while his autobiography, *A Life in Pictures*, was published in 2010.

**Sonny Mehta** (Ajai Singh Mehta), Chairman of the Knopf Doubleday Publishing Group, died of complications from pneumonia on December 30, aged 77. He began his publishing career in Britain at Rupert-Hart Davis and Granada, co-founding Paladin Books before becoming publisher of Pan Books, where he re-launched the Picador imprint. He moved to New York in 1987 after Alfred A. Knopf's president and editor in chief Robert A. Gottlieb handpicked him as his successor. By 2015—Knopf's centennial—the publisher was releasing 550 titles a year, contributing to a major share of Penguin Random House's $3.5 billion in revenues.

American artist and self-proclaimed "visual futurist" **Syd Mead** (Sydney Jay Mead) died of lymphoma cancer the same day, aged 86. He was the conceptual designer for such movies as *Star Trek: The Motion Picture*, *Blade Runner*, *TRON*, *2010*, *Aliens*, *Short Circuit*, *Solar Crisis*, *Journey to the Centre of the Earth* (1993), *Timecop*, *Strange Days*, *Mission to Mars*, *Elysium*, *Tomorrowland*, *Blade Runner 2049* and the TV mini-series *The Fire Next Time*. Mead also published a number of art books, including *Sentinel*, *Oblagon*, *Sentury* and *The Movie Art of Syd Mead: Visual Futurist*. He was made a Spectrum Awards Grandmaster in 2007, and had recently been named as the recipient of the William Cameron Menzies Award from the Art Directors Guild, for his innovative neo-futuristic concept artwork on numerous legendary movies.

## PERFORMERS/PERSONALITIES

Cuban-born American character actress **Louisa Moritz** (Luisa Cira Castro Netto), perhaps best remembered as Sylvester Stallone's buxom blonde navigator "Myra" in *Death Race 2000* (1975), died of complications from a fall on January 4, aged 71. She was also in *The Man from O.R.G.Y.*, *New Year's Evil*, *Galaxis*, *The Independent* and an episode of TV's *The Incredible Hulk*. In 2014, Moritz was one of the first women to accuse comedian Bill Cosby of sexual abuse and rape.

American-born British singer and actress **Diana Decker** (Isabella C.D. Decker), whose final film appearance was in *Devils of Darkness* (1964), died the same day in London, aged 93.

Busy British-born character actor **W. (William) Morgan Sheppard** died in Los Angeles on January 6, aged 86. He began his screen career in the early 1960s, and his film credits include *Marat/Sade*, *The Elephant Man*, *Hawk the Slayer*, *The Keep* (based on the novel by F. Paul Wilson), *The Doctor and the Devils*, *Elvira Mistress of the Dark*, *Lucky Stiff*, *Star Trek VI: The Undiscovered Country*, *Seduction: Three Tales from the 'Inner Sanctum'*, *Needful Things*, *Sometimes They Come Back... Again*, *The Lottery* (based on the story by Shirley Jackson), *The Prestige*, *Transformers*, *Over Her Dead Body*, *Star Trek*, *Mysterious Island* (2010, as "Captain Nemo"), *The Devil's Dozen* and *April Apocalypse*. On TV, Sheppard was a holographic regular on *SeaQuest 2031* (1993–94) and appeared in episodes of *The New Avengers* ('Gnaws'), the Polish-made *Sherlock Holmes and Doctor Watson*, *Hammer House of Horror* ('Carpathian Eagle'), *The Day of the Triffids* (1981), *Hammer House of Mystery and Suspense*, *Max Headroom*, *Werewolf*, *Star Trek: The Next Generation*, *Quantum Leap*, *Dead at 21*, *Babylon 5*, *Poltergeist: The Legacy*, *American Gothic*, *Timecop*, *Star Trek: Voyager*, *Charmed*, *Doctor Who* (2011), *Dexter* and *The Librarians*. He also voiced numerous cartoons and video games, and often appeared on screen with his son, Mark Sheppard (the demon "Crowley" in *Supernatural*).

American actress **Verna [Frances] Bloom**, who starred opposite Clint Eastwood in the supernatural Western *High Plains Drifter* (1973), died of complications from denmetia on January 9, aged 80.

American actor **Don [Kay] Reynolds** (aka "Little Brown Jug") died the same day, aged 81. A former child actor, in Westerns since the mid-1940s onwards, he became a horse-trainer and wrangler on such movies as *Santa Claus: The Movie*, *Big Top Pee-wee*, *The Lord of the Rings: The Fellowship of the Ring*, *Kate & Leopold*, *The Lord of the Rings: The Two Towers* and *The Lord of the Rings: The Return of the King*.

German-born, Canadian-raised character actor **Paul Koslo** (Manfred Koslowski) died of pancreatic cancer in California on January 9, aged 74. Often cast as villains, he was in *The Ωmega Man*, *Robot Jox*, *Xtro II: The Second Encounter*, *Solar Crisis* and *Shadowchaser*, along with episodes of TV's *Buck Rogers in the 25th Century*, *Galactica 1980*, *The Incredible Hulk*, *The Greatest American Hero*, *Blue Thunder*, *Knight Rider* (1984), *The Hitchhiker*, *Misfits of Science*, *Highway to Heaven*, *The Highwayman*, *The Flash* (1990) and *Stargate SG-1*.

American-born actress **Lucretia Love** (Lucretia Hickerson) died in the Seychelles the same day, aged 77. She appeared in Michael Reeves' *The She Beast* (with Barbara Steele), *Fenomenal e il tesoro di Tutankamen*, *When Men Carried Clubs and Women Played Ding-Dong*, *L'assassino ha riservato nove poltrone*, *A Black Ribbon for Deborah*, *Enter the Devil*, *A Whisper in the Dark* and 1980's *Dr. Heckyl and Mr. Hype*, which was her final screen credit.

59-year-old Greek-born American free-fighter and actor **Stefanos Miltsakakis** also died on January 9. He portrayed "Frankenstein's Monster" in *Waxwork II: Lost in Time* (1992), and his other credits include *Weekend at Bernie's*, *Cyborg*, *Legion of Iron*, *T-Force*, *Daredevil* (2003) and an episode of TV's *Eerie, Indiana*. Miltsakakis made five action movies with Jean-Claude Van Damme.

Swiss-born character actor **Paolo [Arturo] Paolini** died in Rome the same day, aged 89. He was in *Dr. Jekyll Likes Them Hot*, Dario

Argento's *Inferno, Cannibal Holocaust,* Lucio Fulci's *The House of Clocks* and *Voices from Beyond,* and *The Haunting of Helena.*

Colombia-born Mexican leading man **Fernando** [Ciangherotti] **Luján** died of respiratory failure on January 11, aged 79. A former child actor, he appeared in the vampire Western *El pueblo fantasma, Neutron Battles the Karate Assassins* and *The Wind of Fear.*

American leading lady of the 1950s **Sally Fraser** died after a long illness on January 13, aged 86. Her credits include Roger Corman's *It Conquered the World, Giant from the Unknown* and Bert I. Gordon's *War of the Colossal Beast* and *Earth vs. the Spider,* along with episodes of TV's *Space Patrol, Captain Midnight, A Christmas Carol* (with Basil Rathbone, 1954), *Men Into Space* and *One Step Beyond.* She retired from the screen in the early 1960s.

Tony Award-winning Broadway actress **Carol** [Elaine] **Channing** died on January 15, aged 97. On screen, she appeared in the musical comedy *Svengali and the Blonde* (1955, loosely based on the novel by George L. Du Maurier), *Sgt. Pepper's Lonely Hearts Club Band, Alice in Wonderland* (1985) and an episode of TV's *Touched by an Angel.* Channing contributed voice work to many cartoons, including the 1992–93 TV series *The Addams Family* (as "Grandmama Addams") and *The Brave Little Toaster Goes to Mars* (based on the book by Thomas M. Disch).

British character actor **Windsor Davies** died on January 17, aged 88. Although known as the star of such TV sit-coms as *It Ain't Half Hot Mum* (1974–81) and *Never the Twain* (1981–91), he was often cast as policemen and also appeared in Hammer's *Frankenstein Must Be Destroyed* (with Peter Cushing), *Endless Night* and *Alice in Wonderland* (1985), along with a couple of *Carry On* movies and a *Confessions* film. On TV, Davies was in episodes of *Adam Adamant Lives!, Doctor Who* ('The Evil of the Daleks'), *UFO, The Guardians, The Donati Conspiracy* and *Gormenghast.* He also voiced "Sergeant Major Zero" on the Gerry Anderson "Supermacromation" puppet series *Terrahawks* (1983–86). Davies had a surprise #1 hit record in the UK in 1975 with 'Whispering Grass', a duet with his *It Ain't Half Hot Mum* co-star Don Estelle.

British TV actress **Sylvia** [Margaret] **Kay** died on January 18, aged 82. She appeared in episodes of *Tales of Mystery* ('The Woman's Ghost

Story' by Algernon Blackwood), *The Avengers*, *Dead of Night* ('The Exorcism') and *Woof!*. Kay retired from the screen in the late 1990s. Her first husband (1962–72) was director Ted Kotcheff.

American supporting actor **William** ("Bill") **Swan** died on January 20, aged 90. He had an uncredited role in *The Monster That Challenged the World* (1957), and his other film credits include *Lady in a Cage*. On TV, Swan appeared in episodes of *One Step Beyond* and *The Twilight Zone* (1964).

American singer and comedienne **Kaye Ballard** (Catherine Gloria Ballota) died of kidney cancer on January 21, aged 93. Her credits include *Cinderella* (1957), Disney's *Freaky Friday* (1976), *Pandemonium* and *Alice in Wonderland* (1983). She was a regular on the sit-com *What a Dummy* (1990–91) and appeared in episodes of TV's *Fantasy Island*, *Monsters* and *The Munsters Today*.

American character actor **Merwin Goldsmith** died the same day, aged 81. He co-starred in Arnold Schwarzenegger's first movie *Hercules in New York* (1970), and his other credits include *Making Mr. Right* and *Unholy* (2007). Goldsmith was also the voice of "General Rieekan" on National Public Radio's 1983 audio serial of *Star Wars: The Empire Stikes Back*.

52-year-old Canadian stunt performer **Dean** [Ilia] **Copkov** was one of two men fatally shot by a homeowner while participating in a home invasion with two other masked assailants on January 22. He was due to be sentenced in Montreal soon for drug offences. Copkov's many credits include *Gothika*, *Dawn of the Dead* (2004), *Resident Evil: Apocalypse*, *Silent Hill*, *The Incredible Hulk* (2008), *Outlander*, *Cyborg Soldier*, *Orphan*, *Survival of the Dead*, *Resident Evil: Afterlife*, *Saw: The Final Chapter*, *Pacific Rim*, *Carrie* (2013), *RoboCop* (2014) and TV's *American Gods*. He made headlines in 1993 when he was one of four men who escaped from a minimum-security prison, where he was serving time for shooting a man in the leg.

American character actress **Erica Yohn** (Adella Fishman) died on January 27, aged 90. She appeared in *Song of the Succubus*, *Good Against Evil*, *Pee-Wee's Big Adventure* and *Amazon Women on the Moon*. On TV, Yohn was in episodes of *Fantasy Island*, *The Incredible Hulk*, *Shadow Chasers*, *Quantum Leap* and *Picket Fences*.

Australian-born British actress **Diana** [Vida Jean] **Fairfax**, who co-starred in a 1948 TV production of Arnold Ridley's *The Ghost Train* with the writer himself, died in London on January 28, aged 91. Fairfax also appeared in an episode of the 1970s TV series *Dead of Night*. She was married to actor Derek Godfrey until his death in 1983.

Prolific genre icon **Dick Miller** (Richard Miller) died on January 30, aged 90. Roger Corman gave him a rare starring role as homicidal beatnik sculptor "Walter Paisley" in the cult classic *A Bucket of Blood* (1959), but he was more at home in supporting roles in *It Conquered the World*, *Not of This Earth* (1957), *The Undead*, *War of the Satellites*, *The Little Shop of Horrors* (1960), *Atlas*, *Premature Burial*, *The Terror* (with Boris Karloff), *X: The Man with X-Ray Eyes* and *Death Race 2000* (1975). In the mid-1970s Miller was "rediscovered" by a new generation of directors (including Joe Dante, Jim Wynorski, Fred Olen Ray and Larry Blamire) who cast him in such movies as *Hollywood Boulevard* (as "Walter Paisley"), *Piranha* (1978), *Dr. Heckyl and Mr. Hype*, *The Howling* ("Walter Paisley" again), *Heartbeeps*, *Twilight Zone: The Movie* ("Walter Paisley"), *Space Raiders*, *Gremlins*, *The Terminator*, *Explorers*, *Chopping Mall* ("Walter Paisley"), *Night of the Creeps* ("Walt"), *Project X*, *Innerspace*, *Amazon Women on the Moon*, *The 'Burbs*, *Ghost Writer*, *Gremlins 2: The New Batch* (with Christopher Lee), *Evil Toons*, *Amityville 1992: It's About Time*, *Matinee*, *Tales from the Crypt: Demon Knight*, *The Warlord: Battle for the Galaxy* (aka *The Osiris Chronicles*), *Small Soldiers*, *Route 666*, *Looney Tunes: Back in Action*, *Trapped Ashes*, *Trail of the Screaming Forehead*, *The Hole*, *Burying the Ex* and *Hanukkah* (as "Rabbi Walter Paisley"). On TV, Miller was a semi-regular in *The Flash* (1990–91) and he also turned up in episodes of *V: The Final Battle*, *Tales from the Darkside*, *Amazing Stories*, *Star Trek: The Next Generation*, *Freddy's Nightmares*, *Eerie Indiana*, *Lois & Clark: The New Adventures of Superman*, *Star Trek: Deep Space Nine* and *Weird Science*.

British character actor **Clive** [Walter] **Swift** died after a short illness on February 1, aged 82. Although perhaps better known for his light comedy roles, he also appeared in *A Midsummer Night's*

*Dream* (1968), Alfred Hitchcock's *Frenzy*, *Death Line* (aka *Raw Meat*), *Dr. Jekyll and Mr. Hyde* (1980) and *Excalibur*. On TV Swift was in *The Stalls of Barchester* (1971) and *A Warning to the Curious* (1972), both based on stories by M.R. James, along with episodes of *Dead of Night* ('The Exorcism'), *The Frighteners*, Nigel Kneale's *Beasts*, *1990*, *Shadows*, *Tales of the Unexpected*, *Doctor Who* ('Revelation of the Daleks', 1985), *The Ray Bradbury Theatre* ('The Coffin'), *Woof!* and the 2007 *Doctor Who* Christmas special. He was married to author Margaret Drabble from 1960–75.

American actress **Lisa Seagram** (Ruth Browser) died in an assisted care facility the same day, following a nine-year battle with dementia. She was 82. During the 1960s Seagram appeared in episodes of TV's *Bewitched*, *My Favorite Martian*, *My Brother the Angel*, *The Girl from U.N.C.L.E.* and *Batman*, and was in the movie *2000 Years Later*. She retired from the screen in 1976 and later worked as an acting teacher in Hawaii.

Canadian character actress **Sheila Paterson** (Sheila Joan Lane) died on February 2, aged 92. She only started acting late in life and her credits include *The Stepfather* (1987), *Quarantine* (1989), *Omen IV: The Awakening*, *The Man Who Wouldn't Die* and *Convergence*. On TV, Paterson's credits include episodes of *Highlander*, *The X Files*, *The Outer Limits* (1989), *The Lone Gunmen*, *So Weird*, *The Dead Zone*, Stephen King's *Kingdom Hospital*, *The 4400* and the 2000 mini-series of Dean R. Koontz's *Sole Survivor*.

73-year-old American actress and writer **Catherine Burns** died the same day of injuries from a fall in her home and cirrhosis of the liver. The Oscar-nominated actress appeared in the TV movies *The Crucible* (1967) and *A Christmas Carol* (1982), along with episodes of *The Bionic Woman* and *Seeing Things*.

American leading lady **Julie Adams** (Betty May Adams, aka "Julia Adams"), who co-starred in Uiversal's iconic *Creature from the Black Lagoon* (1954), died on February 3, aged 92. She began her screen career in 1949, and her other credits include *Francis Joins the WACS*, *The Underwater City*, *Psychic Killer* and *Black Roses*. On TV, Adams was a semi-regular on *Murder, She Wrote* (including 'The Witch's Curse') and appeared in episodes of *One Step Beyond*, *Alfred*

*Hitchcock Presents, The Girl from U.N.C.L.E., Rod Serling's Night Gallery, Search, Kolchak: The Night Stalker, The Incredible Hulk, Sliders, Lost* and *CSI: NY* ('Boo'). In the early 1950s, Universal Pictures insured her legs for $125,000 with Lloyds of London. Adams was married to scriptwriter Leonard Stern (1951–53) and actor Ray Danton (1955–78), and her autobiography *The Lucky Southern Star: Reflections from the Black Lagoon* (co-written with her son, Mitchell Danton) was published in 2011.

British actor **Albert Finney** died from a chest infection on February 7, aged 82. His credits include *A Midsummer Night's Dream* (1959), *Night Must Fall* (1964), the musical version of *Scrooge* (1970, in the title role), *Wolfen* (based on the novel by Whitley Strieber), *Looker, Delivering Milo* and Tim Burton's *Big Fish*. He also supplied the voice of "Finis Everglot" in Burton's *The Corpse Bride*. On TV, Finney starred in the BBC's three-part adaptation of Kingsley Amis' *The Green Man* and the four-part BBC/Channel 4 adaptation of Dennis Potter's *Cold Lazarus*. The second of his three wives was actress Anouk Aimée.

American leading man **Jan-Michael Vincent**, who starred in the TV series *Airwolf* (1984–86), died of cardiac arrest on February 10, aged 73. He was an alcoholic for many years and, following a car crash in 1996 that resulted in a broken neck, he suffered permanent damage to his vocal cords. In 2000, he assaulted a former girlfriend and was ordered to pay $350,000, and that same year he was sentenced to sixty days in jail after admitting that he violated his probation by being drunk in public three times. In 2012 the lower half of Vincent's right leg was amputated due to an infection contracted through complications from peripheral artery disease, the result of another car accident. The actor was in *Sandcastles, Shadow of the Hawk, Damnation Alley* (based on the novel by Roger Zelazny), *The Return, Tarzan in Manhattan, Alienator, Deathstone, Xtro II: The Second Encounter, Haunting Fear, Raw Nerve, Abducted II: The Reunion, Ice Cream Man, Lethal Orbit* and *Jurassic Women*.

American character actor **Joe Sirola** (Joseph Anthony Sirola) died of complications from respiratory failure the same day, aged 89. Known as "The King of the Voice-Overs" for his 10,000+

commercials, he appeared in *Visions...*, *Seizure* and epsiodes of TV's *The Green Hornet*, *Get Smart*, *The Man from U.N.C.L.E.*, *Kolchak: The Night Stalker* ('Zombie') and *Wonder Woman* ('The Phantom of the Roller Coaster'). Sirola was also the voice of "Doctor Doom" in the 1967 *Fantastic Four* cartoon series. He later became a Tony Award-winning Broadway producer.

Italian-American character actor **Carmen** [Antimo] **Argenziano**, who portrayed "General Jacob Carter" in Showtime/The Sci-Fi Channel's *Stargate SG-1* (1998–2005), also died on February 10, aged 75. His other credits include *Night of the Cobra Woman*, *Grave of the Vampire*, *Search for the Gods*, *When a Stranger Calls* (1979), *Graduation Day*, *The Man Who Fell to Earth* (1987), *Remo Williams: The Prophecy*, *The First Power*, *Knight Rider 2000*, *Hellraiser: Inferno*, *Identity*, *Momentum*, *Angels with Angels*, *Death Interrupted*, *The Labyrinth*, *Singularity* and *Future World*. Argenziano also portrayed the Devil in the 2016 short film *Professor Phillips and the Devil*. On TV, he was in episodes of *The Bionic Woman*, *Mr. Merlin*, *Darkroom* (Curtis Harrington's 'A Quiet Funeral'), *The Greatest American Hero*, *The Phoenix*, *The Powers of Matthew Star*, *Viper*, *Babylon 5*, *NightMan*, *Level 9*, *Flashforward* and the 2009 mini-series *Meteor*.

1950s British actress **Isabel George** (Isabel Mary Snewin), who co-starred in the first season of Britain's first science fiction television series, *Stranger from Space* (1951–52), died the same day, aged 89. She also appeared in an episode of *Colonel March of Scotland Yard* (starring Boris Karloff) before retiring from the screen in 1955, after marrying American-born actor James Sharkey.

Swiss actor **Bruno Ganz** died of cancer on February 16, aged 77. His credits include *The Boys from Brazil*, *Nosferatu the Vampyre* (as "Jonathan Harker"), *Wings of Desire*, *The Manchurian Candidate* (2004), *The House That Jack Built* and the two-part TV movie of the eleven-hour stage-play *Johann Wolfgang von Goethe: Faust*.

Cuban-born Italian actress **Chelo Alonso** (Isabel Apolonia García Hernández) died on February 20, aged 85. A former exotic dancer at the Folies Bergères, the "*peplum* princess" appeared in such films as *Goliath and the Barbarians*, *Son of Samson* and *Atlas Against the Cyclops*.

American musician and actor **Peter Tork** (Peter Halsten Thorkelson), bass and keyborads player and a founding member of the seminal 1960s music group The Monkees, died of complications from adenoid cystic carcinoma (a slow-growing form of head and neck cancer) on February 21, aged 77. He starred with Davy Jones, Micky Dolenz and Michael Nesmith in NBC's often surreal TV series *The Monkees* (1966–68) and the spin-off movie, *Head* (1968). Tork also turned up (uncredited) in *Wild in the Streets*.

American actress **Beverley Owen** (Beverley Jane Ogg), who originated the role of "Marilyn Munster" in the first season of CBS-TV's *The Munsters* (1964), died of ovarian cancer the same day, aged 81. She left the show after just thirteen episodes to marry future *Sesame Street* producer and director Jon Stone. They divorced in 1974, and Stone died in 1997.

Cuban-American character actress [Maria] **Antonia Rey**, who portrayed "Assunta Bianchi" on Scyfy's *Happy!* (2017–19), also died on February 21, aged 92. She emigrated to the US in 1961 and was in *The Changeling* (1980), *Rappaccini's Daughter* (based on the story by Nathaniel Hawthorne), *The Clairvoyant* (1982), *Jacob's Ladder* (1990) and an episode of TV's *Life on Mars* (2009).

Canadian character actress and singer **Betty** [Muriel] **Phillips**, who portrayed "Granmama Addams" in TV's *The New Addams Family* (1998–99) died on February 22, aged 95. She was also in *The Haunting Passion*, *Runaway*, *The Boy Who Could Fly*, *I Was a Teenage Faust*, *2012* and *Cats & Dogs: The Revenge of Kitty Galore*. On TV, Phillips appeared in episodes of *The Odyssey* (1992), *Strange Luck*, *Millennium*, *Poltergeist: The Legacy*, *So Weird*, *The Outer Limits* (2000), *The Dead Zone*, *The Collector* and the two-part mini-series *Earthsea*.

Veteran American character actor [Thomas] **Morgan Woodward**, who appeared in two episodes of *Star Trek* ('Dagger of the Mind' and 'The Omega Glory'), died of cancer the same day, aged 93. His other credits include the movie *Battle Beyond the Stars* along with episodes of TV's *Tarzan* (1968), *Planet of the Apes*, *Logan's Run*, *Project U.F.O.*, *The Incredible Hulk*, *Salvage 1*, *Fantasy Island*, *Knight Rider*, *The Adventures of Brisco County Jr.*, *The X Files* and *Millennium*.

American character actress **Katherine** [Marie] **Helmond**, best known for starring in the 1977–81 TV sitcom *Soap*, died of complications from Alzheimer's disease on February 23, aged 89. Her other credits include *Locusts*, *The Legend of Lizzie Borden*, Alfred Hitchcock's *Family Plot*, Terry Gilliam's *Time Bandits* and *Brazil*, *Shadey*, Frank LaLoggia's *Lady in White*, *Ms. Scrooge* and *Mr. St. Nick*. On TV, Helmond was in episodes of *The Snoop Sisters* ('A Black Day for Bluebeard' with Vincent Price), *The Six Million Dollar Man*, *The Bionic Woman*, *Faerie Tale Theatre*, *Fantasy Island* and *Tru Blood*, along with the mini-series *World War III* and the 1993 pilot *The Elvira Show*. She was also the voice of "Lizzie" in the Disney/Pixar *Cars* movies and spin-offs.

American actress **Lisa Sheridan**, who starred in the TV series *FreakyLinks* (2000–01), *Invasion* (2005–06) and *Journeyman* (2007) died of chronic alcoholism on February 25, aged 44. She also appeared in *Strange Nature*, the TV movies *Healing Hands* and *Category 5*, and an episode of *The 4400*.

American actress **Kathleen O'Malley**, the daughter of silent screen actor Pat O'Malley, died the same day, aged 94. She made her screen debut as an infant in 1926, and she went on to appear in mostly small or uncredited roles in *Night in Paradise*, *Down to Earth*, *Brigadoon*, *The Toolbox Murders* (1978) and episodes of TV's *The Alfred Hitchcock Hour* (Richard Matheson's 'The Thirty-First of February'), *The Twilight Zone* (1964), *The Munsters*, *The Secrets of Isis* and *Misfits of Science*. O'Malley retired from the screen in the late 1990s.

American character actress **Mitzi Hoag** (Margaret Myrtle Hoag) died on February 26, aged 86. Her credits include Roger Corman's *The Trip*, *The Incredible Shrinking Woman* and episodes of TV's *Good Heavens*, *The Incredible Hulk*, *Time Express* (with Vincent Price) and *Highway to Heaven*.

Canadian supporting actor **Peter Dvorsky**, who was featured in David Cronenberg's *Videodrome* and *The Dead Zone*, died on March 2, aged 70. He was also in *Bridge to Terabithia* (1985), *Murder in Space*, *The Kiss* and *Millennium*, along with episodes of TV's *Seeing Things*, *Alfred Hitchcock Presents* (1987), *Beyond Reality* and *PSI Factor: Chronicles of the Paranormal*. Dvorsky retired from the screen in the early 2000s.

American leading man **Luke Perry** (Coy Luther Perry III), who starred in *Beverly Hills 9020* (1990–2000), *Jeremiah* (2002–04) and *Riverdale* (2017–19), died on March 4, aged 52. On February 27 he suffered a massive ischemic stroke in his home. Perry was hospitalised, but he had a second stroke days later, from which he never recovered. The former teen idol was in *Buffy the Vampire Slayer* (1992), *The Fifth Element, Storm, The Triangle, Descent, Supernova, Silent Venom, The Final Storm, Dragon Warriors* (aka *Dudes & Dragons*) and *It's Gawd!*. On TV, Perry appeared in episodes of *Voyagers!, Night Visions* and the mini-series *Invasion* and *The Storm*, and he did voice work for a number of cartoon shows, including *The Night of the Headless Horseman* (1999). The actor was posthumously honored with a star on the Hollywood Walk of Fame on March 11, 2019.

American actress **Susan Harrison** died on March 5, aged 80. She appeared in some films and TV shows during the late 1950s and early '60s, including episodes of *Alfred Hitchcock Presents* (Robert Bloch's 'The Gloating Place') and *The Twilight Zone*.

American character actress **Janell McLeod** (Janell Knight) died on March 11, aged 92. She only became an actress following her retirement, and she appeared in *The Handmaid's Tale* (1990), *Pet Sematary II, Target Earth* (1998), *The Gift* and an episode of TV's *The Young Indiana Jones Chronicles*.

American character actor **Richard Erdman** (John Richard Erdmann, aka "Dick Erman") died of complications from dementia on March 16, aged 93. His credits include *Aladdin and His Lamp* (1952), *Francis in the Navy, Face of Fire, The Brass Bottle, Visions...* and *Trancers*, along with episodes of TV's *Science Fiction Theatre, Mister Ed, The Twilight Zone, The Man from U.N.C.L.E., Mr. Terrific, I Dream of Jeannie, The Wild Wild West, The Six Million Dollar Man, The Bionic Woman, Time Express* (with Vincent Price), *The Amazing Spider-Man, Out of This World, Picket Fences* and *Joan of Arcadia*. Erdman also did voice work in *The Pagemaster* (1994) and for various cartoon series.

American character actor and TV host **Tom Hatten** died the same day, aged 92. His movie credits include William Castle's *I Saw What*

*You Did*, while on TV Hatten appeared in episodes of *The Man from U.N.C.L.E.*, *My Mother the Car*, Get Smart, *Lois & Clark: The Adventures of Superman* and *Beyond Belief: Fact or Fiction?*. He also contributed voice work to *The Secret of NIMH* (1982).

Welsh character actor **Clinton Greyn** (Clinton Stuart Greyn Thomas) died on March 19, aged 85. He appeared on TV in episodes of Algernon Blackwood's *Tales of Mystery*, *The Champions*, *UFO* and *Doctor Who* ('State of Decay' and 'The Two Doctors'). During the early 1970s, Greyn co-founded the "Save London's Theatres Campaign".

American actress **Denise DuBarry** died of complications from a deadly fungus on March 23, aged 63. Her credits include *The Darker Side of Terror*, Disney's *The Devil and Max Devlin*, *Monster in the Closet* (with John Carradine) and an episode of TV's *Magic Mongo*. The second of DuBarry's three husbands (1982–88) was actor Gary Lockwood.

American character actor **Noah Keen** (Isadore Keen) died on March 24, aged 98. He appeared in *Sole Survivor*, *Battle for the Planet of the Apes* and *She's Dressed to Kill*. On TV, Keen was in episodes of *The Twilight Zone*, *I Dream of Jeannie*, *The Girl from U.N.C.L.E.*, *Tarzan* (1967), *The Invaders*, *The Six Million Dollar Man*, *Project U.F.O.*, *Fantasy Island* and *The Next Step Beyond*.

British actress **Julia Lockwood** (Margaret Julia Leon), the daughter of Margaret Lockwood (1916–90), died of pneumonia the same day, aged 77. As a child she appeared in some of her mother's films, and her other credits include episodes of TV's *Alice in Wonderland* (1954), *The Invisible Man* (1959) and *Out of the Unknown*. On the stage she played "Peter Pan" four times (1959, 1960, 1963 and 1966) and appeared in a 1966 production of *Arsenic and Old Lace*. Lockwood was married to actor Ernest Clark from 1972 until his death in 1994.

American leading lady **Nancy [Jane] Gates** also died on March 24, aged 93. Best known for her Westerns, she co-starred with Hugh Marlowe in *World Without End* (1956) and appeared in episodes of TV's *Science Fiction Theater* and *Men Into Space*. Gates retired from the screen in 1969 to spend more time with her family.

American actor **Joe Pilato** (Josef Francis Anthony Pilato, Jr.), who appeared in George A. Romero's *Dawn of the Dead* and *Day of the Dead* (as "Captain Rhodes"), died the same day, aged 70. His other credits include *Effects*, *Alienator*, *Empire of the Dark*, *The Evil Inside Me*, *Portrait in Red* (aka *Fatal Passion*), *Wishmaster*, *Visions* (1998), *Bloodbath* (1999), *The Ghouls*, *Someone's Knocking at the Door*, *The Black Box*, *Shhhh*, the animated *Night of the Living Dead: Origins* (aka *Night of the Living Dead: Darkest Dawn*), *Ihailed*, *Parasites* (2016) and *The Chair*. On TV, Pilato was in an episode of *The Adventures of Brisco County Jr.* and was the voice of "Vexor" in *BeetleBorgs* (1996–97).

American character actor [James] **Kevin Scannell** died after a brief illness on March 25, aged 67. On TV he appeared in episodes of *The Twilight Zone* (1986), *Beauty and the Beast* (1989), *Picket Fences* and *3rd Rock from the Sun*.

Irish stuntman **Bronco McLoughlin** (Anthony Gerard McLoughlin) died on March 26, aged 80. He worked on *Jules Verne's Rocket to the Moon* (aka *Those Fantastic Flying Fools*), Hammer's *Creatures the World Forgot*, *The Wicker Man* (1973), *Star Wars*, *Superman* (1978), *Krull*, *Indiana Jones and the Temple of Doom*, *A View to a Kill*, *Willow*, *Hellbound: Hellraiser II*, *Indiana Jones and the Last Crusade*, Clive Barker's *Nightbreed*, *Total Recall* (1990), *The Tale of Sweeney Todd*, *Split Second* (1999) and episodes of TV's *The Young Indiana Jones Chronicles* and *Primeval*.

Canadian-born character actor **Shane Rimmer** died in London, England on March 29, aged 89. Best known as the voice of pilot "Scott Tracy" in Gerry Anderson's marionette TV series *Thunderbirds* (1965–66) and the spin-off films *Thunderbirds Are GO* (1966) and *Thunderbird 6* (1968), he also recreated the role in an episode of the show's 2015 revival. A former singer and radio DJ in his native Canada, Rimmer emigrated to the UK in the late 1950s. He appeared in Stanley Kubrick's *Dr. Strangelove or: How I Learned to Stop Worrying and Love the Bomb*, *The Bedford Incident*, the James Bond movies *You Only Live Twice*, *Diamonds Are Forever* and *The Spy Who Loved Me*, *Baffled!*, *Rollerball* (1975), *Twilight's Last Gleaming*, *Star Wars*, *The People That Time Forgot*, *Warlords of the Deep*, *Superman*

(1978), *Arabian Adventure* (with Christopher Lee and Peter Cushing), *Superman II*, *The Hunger*, *Superman III*, *Morons from Outer Space*, *Dreamchild*, *Whoops Apocalypse*, *The Return of Sherlock Holmes* (1987), *A Kid in King Arthur's Court*, *Space Truckers*, *Batman Begins*, *Mee-Shee: The Water Giant*, *Alien Autopsy* and *Dark Shadows* (2012). On TV Rimmer was in episodes of *Doctor Who*, *UFO*, *Orson Welles Great Mysteries*, *Space: 1999*, *Tales of the Unexpected*, *Hammer House of Mystery and Suspense*, *Space Police* and the mini-series *A Very British Coup*. He also wrote scripts for Gerry Anderson's *Captain Scarlet and the Mysterons* and *Joe 90*, while his two scripts for *Space: 1999* remain unproduced.

British model and actress **Tania Mallet**, who appeared as "Tilly Masterson" in the 1964 James Bond film *Goldfinger*, died on March 30, aged 77. A first cousin of Dame Helen Mirren, her only other screen appearance appears to be an uncredited role in a 1976 episode of TV's *The New Avengers*.

70-year-old American horror host **Ron Sweed** (Ronald D. Sweed), who appeared on various local Cleveland and Detroit TV stations as "The Ghoul" from 1971 through to the late 1990s, died on April 1 of complications following a heart attack the previous November.

American actor **David Manzy** (David Lamar Mooney), who portrayed the man-child "Baby" in the 1973 psychological horror movie *The Baby*, died the same day, aged 77. His few other credits include Disney's *Herbie Rides Again* and an episode of TV's *Bewitched*.

American actress **Roberta Haynes** (Roberta Arline Schack), who was often cast as exotic-looking women, died on April 4, aged 91. Best remembered for co-starring with Gary Cooper in the 1953 Western *The Nebraskan* and John Carradine and Peter Lorre in *Hell Ship Mutiny* (1957), her other credits include episodes of TV's *Starring Boris Karloff* (aka *The Boris Karloff Mystery Playhouse*), *Sherlock Holmes* (1955), *One Step Beyond* and *Knight Rider* (1986).

British character actor **John Quarmby** died on April 5, aged 89. He was in *A Christmas Carol* (1984) and *Arthur the King* (aka *Merlin and the Sword*). On TV, Quarmby appeared in the 1981 special *K-9 and Company: A Girl's Best Friend* and episodes of *Doomwatch*, *1990*, *The*

*Invisible Man* (1984) and *Prince Caspian and the Voyage of the Dawn Treader* (1989). He retired from the screen at the end of the 1990s.

Hawaiian character actor **Ernest Harada** died the same day, aged 81. He appeared in small roles in *Rosemary's Baby* (1968), *The Return of Charlie Chan* (as "Oliver Chan"), *Earthquake*, Disney's *The Devil and Max Devlin*, *Blue Thunder*, *Dreamscape*, *Wicked Stepmother*, *Hi Honey—I'm Dead* and *Death Becomes Her*. On TV, Harada turned up in episodes of *The Invaders*, *The Wild Wild West* and *The Girl with Something Extra*, and he was the voice of "Mr. Limp" in the animated *The Addams Family* series (1992–93).

Yugoslavian-born actress **Nadja Regin** (Nadezda Poderegin) died in London, England, on April 6, aged 87. She appeared (as different characters) in the James Bond movies *From Russia with Love* and *Goldfinger*, and her other movies include *The Magic Sword* (1950) and *The Man Without a Body*. Regin was also in an episode of TV's *The Invisible Man* (1959), and during the 1970s she worked as script reader/consultant for Hammer Films.

American character actor **Seymour** [Joseph] **Cassel** died of complications from Alzheimer's disease on April 7, aged 84. The Oscar-nominated actor appeared in *The Nutty Professor* (1963, uncredited), *Death Game* (1977), *Ravagers*, *Angel on My Shoulder* (1980), *Double Exposure*, Larry Cohen's *Wicked Stepmother*, *Dick Tracy* (1990) and Nicolas Roeg's *Cold Heaven*, along with episodes of TV's *The Twilight Zone* (1964), *Batman* (1967), *The Invaders*, *Voyage to the Bottom of the Sea*, *Tales from the Darkside* ('The Milkman Cometh', based on a story by Charles L. Grant) and *Star Trek: The Next Generation*.

British singer, dancer and actress **Mya-Lecia Naylor** committed suicide by hanging the same day, aged 16. She appeared in *Cloud Atlas*, *Code Red* and *Index Zero*.

Former professional boxer turned actor **Dominic Barto** died on April 10, aged 88. He appeared as "The Driver" in the 1980 horror movie *The Hearse* and also turned up on TV in episodes of *The Six Million Dollar Man*, *Voyagers!* and *Weird Science*. Barto retired from acting around the mid-1990s.

American character actor **Bruce M. Fischer** died on April 11, aged

82. On TV he appeared in episodes of *Electra Woman and Dyna Girl*, *Quark*, *Mork & Mindy*, *Fantasy Island*, *Buck Rogers in the 25th Century*, *Wizards and Warriors* and *Knight Rider*. Fischer's movie credits include *Earthquake*, *Something Wicked This Way Comes* (as "Mr. Cooger"), *Grim Prairie Tales* and the 1996 remake of *Humanoids from the Deep*.

British Shakespearan stage and screen actor **John** [Murray] **McEnery** died on April 12, aged 75. The younger brother of actor Peter McEnery, his films included Amicus' *The Land That Time Forgot* and *Schizo* (uncredited). On TV McEnery was in episodes of *The Storyteller: Greek Myths* ('Perseus & the Gorgon') and *Chiller*, along with the 1998 mini-series *Merlin*. He was married to actress Stephanie Beacham from 1973 to 1978.

American character actress **Georgia** [Bright] **Engel** died the same day, aged 70. She appeared on TV in episodes of *Mork & Mindy* and *Fantasy Island*. Engel was a Christian Scientist and didn't seek medical help.

Swedish leading lady **Bibi Andersson** (Berit Elisabeth Andersson), best known for her role in Ingmar Bergman's *The Seventh Seal* (1957), died of complications from a stroke on April 14, aged 83. Her other credits include Bergman's *The Devil's Eye*, *Vortex* and *Quintet*.

Former American character actor **Robert Lussier** died on April 19, aged 84. He was in *Pinocchio* (1965), *Jack and the Beanstalk* (1965), *Sandcastles*, *Welcome to Arrow Beach*, *The Night That Panicked America*, *Exorcist II: The Heretic* and *Salem's Lot* (1979). A regular on *The Kids from C.A.P.E.R.* (1976–77), Lussier's other TV credits include episodes of *Get Smart* ('The Wax Max'), *Bewitched*, *The Lost Saucer*, *Man from Atlantis*, *The Six Million Dollar Man*, *B.J. and the Bear* ('Coffin with a View', with John Carradine), *Buck Rogers in the 25th Century* and *Herbie the Love Bug*. He mostly retired from the screen in 1986 and was ordained into the priesthood in 1992.

British-born character actor **Victor** [Ernest] **Knight** died in Montreal, Canada, the same day, aged 96. His credits include *Terror Train*, David Cronenberg's *Scanners*, *Happy Birthday to Me*, *Visiting Hours*, *Scanners II: The New Order*, *Relative Fear*, *Dr. Jekyll and Ms. Hyde*, *The Legend of Sleepy Hollow* (1999) and two episodes of TV's

*Are You Afraid of the Dark?*. Knight was also the voice of the American version of *Danger Mouse* (1981–92).

American actor **Ken Kercheval** (Kenneth Marine Kercheval), who portrayed "Cliff Barnes" in both series of the TV soap opera *Dallas* (1978–91 and 2012–14) plus spin-off films, died on April 21, aged 83. He was also in the TV movies *The Disappearance of Flight 412*, *Devil Dog: The Hound of Hell*, *The Demon Murder Case* and *I Still Dream of Jeannie*, along with an episode of *Highway to Heaven*.

British character actor **Edward** [Harry] **Kelsey**, best known for playing "Joe Grundy" since 1985 on the long-running BBC Radio 4's *The Archers*, died on April 23, aged 88. His TV credits include episodes of *Doomwatch*, *Doctor Who* ('The Creature from the Pit'), *The Tripods* (1985, based on the novel by John Christopher) and *Uncle Jack and Operation Green*. Kelsey was also the voices of "Baron Silas Greenback" and "Colonel K" in the cartoon series *Danger Mouse* (1981–92), the voice of "The Thing" in Terry Pratchett's *Truckers* (1992) and the voice of "Mr. Growbag" in *Wallace and Gromit: Curse of the Were-Rabbit*. He also appeared in the 1987 movie *Crystalstone*.

66-year-old American actor and casting director **Brian Dragonuk** died while convalescing from foot surgery the same day. He appeared in *7 Sins of the Vampire* (2013) and made an uncredited appearance in *Book of Shadows: Blair Witch 2*.

British stuntman, stunt co-ordinator and actor **Frank Henson** died after a short illness on April 25, aged 83. A former Army paratrooper, his many credits include the James Bond films *Casino Royale* (1967), *You Only Live Twice*, *Octopussy*, *Never Say Never Again*, *A View to a Kill* and *The World is Not Enough*, along with *Star Wars*, *Dracula* (1979), *An American Werewolf in London*, *Return of the Jedi* (as a Stormtrooper, an Endor Rebel commando, a biker scout and a skiff guard), *Indiana Jones and the Temple of Doom*, *Brazil*, *Lifeforce*, *Enemy Mine*, *Rawhead Rex*, *Whoops Apocalypse*, *Amsterdamned*, *Willow*, *Who Framed Roger Rabbit*, *Without a Clue*, *Star Trap*, *Nightbreed*, *Shadowchaser*, *Death Machine*, *The Borrowers* (1997), *Sky Captain and the World of Tomorrow*, *Children of Men*, *The Golden Compass*, *Sherlock Holmes* (2009), *The Wolfman* (2010), *Sherlock Holmes: A Game of Shadows*, *Pokémon Detective Pikachu* and episodes of TV's *Space: 1999, Blakes 7, Tales of the Unexpected, Elidor, The Tomorrow People* (1995), *The Colour of Magic* and *Penny Dreadful*. Henson's 2018 autobiography was entitled *The Luck of Losing the Toss*.

American character actor **Larry "Flash" Jenkins** died of a heart attack the same day, aged 63. He appeared in *Fantasies* (1982), *Body Double, Prison* (1987) and *Elvira: Mistress of the Dark*.

American character actor **Jessie Lawrence Ferguson** died on April 26, aged 76. His credits include *Amazons* (1984), *The Adventures of Buckaroo Banzai Across the 8th Dimension, Neon Maniacs, The Supernaturals*, John Carpenter's *Prince of Darkness, The Spring*, Sam Raimi's *Darkman* and the short film *The Chosen One*, along with episodes of TV's *Buck Rogers in the 25th Century, Star Trek: The Next Generation, Beauty and the Beast* (1987) and *Swamp Thing* (1992).

Seven-foot, three-inch British-born actor **Peter [William] Mayhew** died of a heart attack in Texas on April 30, aged 74. In 1977 George Lucas cast the former hospital attendant as "Chewbacca", the 200-year-old Wookiee, in *Star Wars*. He went on to recreate the role in *The Empire Strikes Back, Return of the Jedi, Star Wars Episode III: Revenge of the Sith, Star Wars Episode VII: The Force Awakens* and the infamous *Star Wars Holiday Special* on TV. Having retired due to knee problems and declining health, Mayhew was replaced by Joonas Suotamo in *Star Wars Episode VIII: The Last Jedi*, but he stayed on as a consultant. His other credits include *Sinbad and the Eye of the Tiger* (as the "Minoton"), *Terror* (1978), *Shadows in the Woods, Killer Ink* and the 1981 TV series *Dark Towers*.

Italian-born actress **Alessandro Panaro** died in Geneva, Switzerland, on May 1, aged 79. In the early 1960s she appeared in the *peplums Ulysses Against Hercules* and *Conquest of Mycene*.

American stuntman and stunt co-ordinator **Kim Lovelett** died on May 2, aged 72. He was the stunt double for William Finley's "Winslow Leach" in Brian De Palma's *Phantom of the Paradise* (1974), and he also worked on *King Kong* (1976), *Eyes of Laura Mars, F/X, Jacob's Ladder, The Runestone, Freejack* and *Axcellerator*.

British character actress [Ethel] **Irene Sutcliffe**, who was a regular in the 1960 ITV series *Pathfinders in Space*, died on May 3, aged 94.

American character actress and dancer **Barbara** [Mae] **Perry** died on May 5, aged 97. In an acting career that spanned eighty-four years, the former child actress was in Universal's *Mystery of Edwin Drood* (1935) before going on to appear in *An Angel Comes to Brooklyn*, *Shock Corridor*, *Trancers* and episodes of TV's *The Twilight Zone*, *Shirley Temple's Storybook*, *Thriller* (1961), *My Favorite Martian*, *Bewitched*, *Quantum Leap* and *Beyond Belief: Fact or Fiction*. Perry was married to Walt Disney animator Art Babbitt from 1967 until his death in 1992.

American character actor **Kip Niven** (Clifford Wallace Niven), who played the masked killer in the 1980 "slasher" movie *New Year's Evil*, died of a heart attack on May 6, aged 73. His other credits include *Maneater* (1973), *Earthquake*, *Damnation Alley*, *A Fire in the Sky*, *Summer of Fear* (1996) and *A Deadly Vision*. On TV, Niven was in episodes of *The Sixth Sense*, *Rod Serling's Night Gallery* (Fritz Leiber's 'The Girl with the Hungry Eyes'), *The Bionic Woman*, *Project U.F.O.*, *Knight Rider* and the 1981 mini-series *Goliath Awaits* (with Christopher Lee and John Carradine).

American actress **Allene Roberts**, who co-starred opposite Johnny Sheffield's "Bomba, the Jungle Boy" in the Val Lewton-influenced *Bomba on Panther Island* (1949), died on May 9, aged 90. Roberts' other credits include *The Red House* and three episodes of TV's *Adventures of Superman* before she got married in 1955 and retired from the screen two years later. During her acting career, she donated 10% of her earnings to her Baptist church in Alabama.

British-born character actor **Clement von Franckenstein** (Clement George Freiherr von und zu Franckenstein, aka "Clement St. George"), died of hypoxia in Los Angeles the same day, aged 74. He had been in an induced coma for ten days. The son of Sir George Franckenstein, the former Austrian Ambassador to the Court of St. James before the Nazis took over, his credits include *Young Frankenstein*, *The Bermuda Triangle*, *Time After Time*, *The Man Who Wasn't There*, *The Lords of Magick*, *Transylvania Twist*, *The Haunting of Morella*, *The Invisible Maniac*, *Body Parts*, *Death Becomes Her*, *T-Force*, *The Landlady*, *The Future* and *Angels on Tap*. On TV Franckenstein appeared in episodes of TV's *Project U.F.O.*, *Misfits of*

*Science, Beauty and the Beast* (1989), *Star Trek: The Next Generation*, *The Adventures of Brisco County Jr.*, *Sabrina the Teenage Witch* and *Joan of Arcadia*. During the 1970s he turned up in a number of 1970s porno movies under the "St. George" name, and author Mary Shelley is said to have adapted his family's name for her 1818 novel.

American actress and singer **Peggy Lipton** (Margaret Ann Lipton), who co-starred as "Julie Barnes" in *Mod Squad* (1968–73) and the 1979 reunion TV movie, died of cancer on May 11, age 72. She also played "Norma Jennings" in *Twin Peaks* (1989–91 and 2017) and *Twin Peaks: Fire Walk with Me*, and her other credits include *Purple People Eater*, *The Postman* and episodes of *Bewitched*, *The Alfred Hitchcock Hour*, *The Invaders* and *The Hitchhiker*.

38-year-old Samoan-born actor **Pua Magasiva** was found dead from a suspected suicide in a New Zealand hotel room the same day. He portrayed "Shane Clarke"/"Red Wing Ranger" in the TV series *Power Rangers Ninja Storm* (2003) and *Power Ranger DinoThunder* (2004). Magasiva was also in *30 Days of Night* (based on the comic book by Steve Niles and Ben Templesmith) and *Panic at Rock Island*. It was later revealed that the actor had a history of domestic violence.

Japanese leading lady **Machiko Kyô** (Yano Motoko), who co-starred in Akira Kurosawa's *Rashomon* (1950), died of heart failure on May 12, aged 95. She was also in *Hana kurabe tanuki-goten* (as a witch), *The Face of Another* and *The Possessed* (1976).

Hollywood star and singer **Doris Day** (Doris Mary Ann Kappelhoff) died of pneumonia on May 13, aged 97. Although better known for her musicals and light comedies (such as *The Glass Bottom Boat*), she also appeared in *Midnight Lace* (1960).

42-year-old American actor and musician **Isaac Kappy**, who had small roles in *Thor* and *Terminator Salvation*, committed suicide the same day by jumping off a bridge in Arizona. A former lead singer with the band Monster Paws, in 2018 Kappy was investigated by police for allegedly attempting to choke actress Paris Jackson at a party and accused actor Seth Green, amongst others, of pedophilia as part of a QAnon conspiracy theory. Prior to his death he posted a lengthy note on social media detailing his drug and alcohol abuse. Kappy's other credits include *Klown Kamp Massacre*.

Five-time Emmy Award-winning American comedy actor and writer **Tim Conway** (Thomas Daniel Conway) died of complications from hydrocephalus on May 14, aged 85. He had been mute since undergoing brain surgery the previous year. Conway's movie credits include Disney's *The World's Greatest Athlete* and *The Shaggy D.A.*, *The Private Eyes* and *Dear God*. On TV, he co-starred in the sitcom *McHale's Navy* (1962–66) and appeared in episodes of *Faerie Tale Theatre*, *Touched by an Angel* and *Wizards of Waverly Place*. Conway also contributed voice work to numerous cartoons and video games, including *SpongeBob Square Pants*, *Scooby-Doo* and *Batman: The Brave and the Bold*. He was inducted into the Horror Host Hall of Fame in 2011 in the "Behind the Screams" category as "Original Writer for Ghoulardi" (for Cleveland's *Shock Theater* package in the 1960s).

British-born character actor and author **John Ronane** died in Eureka, Illinois, on May 15, aged 85. He appeared in *Doctor Blood's Coffin* (uncredited) and *The Spiral Staircase* (1975). On TV Ronane was in episodes of *Mystery and Imagination* ('The Beckoning Shadow'), Hammer's *Journey to the Unknown*, *The Avengers*, *Out of the Unknown*, *Survivors* and *1990*.

American former child actor **Bobby Diamond** (Robert LeRoy Diamond), who starred as "Joey Newton" in the 1955–60 TV series *Fury*, died of cancer the same day, aged 75. He also appeared in episodes of *The Twilight Zone* (1963) and *Mister Ed*, along with the low-budget 1981 horror movie *Scream* (aka *The Outing*). Diamond retired from the screen in 1990 to take up practicing law in Los Angeles.

Swiss-French leading man [Henri Louis] **Roland Carey** (aka "Rod Carter"), who starred as "Giasone"/"Jason" in Riccardo Freda's *The Giants of Thessaly* (1960), died on May 17, aged 86. In the late 1950s he attempted to break into Hollywood with bit-parts in such TV shows as *The Twilight Zone* and *Thriller*, and his other credits include 1969 Italian horror film, *The Doll of Satan*.

British actor **Andrew** [James] **Hall** died of cancer on May 20, aged 65. Best known as "The Gentleman" in the Syfy TV series *Blood Drive* (2017), his other credits include the 2011 horror film *Stormhouse*.

For the stage, Hall directed revivals of John Fowles' *The Collector* and Alan Ayckbourn's *Haunting Julia*.

American actress **Beverly** [Jane] **Lunsford**, who appeared in the 1964 horror movie *The Crawling Hand*, died on May 22, aged 74. She co-starred in Roger Corman's social drama *The Intruder* (1962), which featured performances by writers Charles Beaumont, George Clayton Johnson and William F. Nolan. Lunsford was also in a 1955 adaptation of Ray Bradbury's story 'The Veldt' on Street & Smith/NBC Radio's *X Minus One*. She retired from the screen in the late 1960s.

British actor **Stephen** [John] **Thorne** died on May 26, aged 84. He appeared in several episodes of the BBC's *Doctor Who* (including playing the horned beast "Azal" in 'The Dæmons') during the 1970s and was the voice of "Chemos" in the 1978 series *Sexton Blake and the Demon God*. Thorne also voiced "Aslan" in both the animated 1979 film and the 1988 BBC Radio 4 versions of *The Lion, the Witch & the Wardrobe*. On radio, he was also the voice of "Treebeard" in *The Lord of the Rings* (1981), "Fred Colon" and "Death" in Terry Pratchett's *Guards! Guards!* (1992), the "Dodo" in *Alice's Adventures in Wonderland* (1996) and "Inspector Lestrade" opposite Clive Merrison's "Sherlock Holmes" (1994–2009). Thorne's other credits include the TV series *Maria Marten or Murder in the Red Barn* (1980) and the 1984 SF movie *Runaway*. He also recorded more than 350 audio books, including the complete canon of Ellis Peters' "Brother Cadfael" stories.

85-year-old American character actor **Carmine Caridi** died on May 28 of complications following a fall. He appeared in *Kiss Meets the Phantom of the Park*, along with episodes of TV's *Tabitha*, *Fantasy Island*, *Darkroom* (Curtis Harrington's 'A Quiet Funeral', scripted by Robert Bloch, Brian Clemens and others) and *Tales from the Darkside*. Caridi became the first (of only three to date) members of The Academy of Motion Picture Arts and Sciences (AMPAS) to have their membership revoked, after he was implicated by the F.B.I. in a 2014 investigation into Academy screeners of recent movies appearing illegally on the Internet.

American actress **Peggy Stewart** (Peggy O'Rourke, aka "Peg

Stewart"), whose acting career spanned an incredible nine decades, died on May 29, aged 95. Best known as a leading lady in 1940s Westerns and serials for Republic Pictures, Stewart's other credits include *The Vampire's Ghost*, *The Ghost Goes Wild*, Herschell Gordon Lewis' *Something Weird*, *The Stranger*, *Terror in the Wax Museum*, *The Time Machine* (1978), *Beyond Death's Door*, *The Fall of the House of Usher* (1979), *Beyond Evil* and *The Boogens*, along with episodes of TV's *The Twilight Zone*, *Werewolf*, *Buffy the Vampire Slayer*, *Seven Days*, *Charmed* and *Flashforward*. Her first husband (1940–44) was actor Don "Red" Barry, and she was married to actor Buck Young from 1953 until his death in 2000.

**Leo**, one of four cats that played "Church" in the 2019 remake of Stephen King's *Pet Sematary*, died the same day. He was also the undead feline featured on the poster.

Cyprus-born American singer/songwriter **Leon Redbone** (Dickran Gobalian), who composed the theme music for TV's *Harry and the Hendersons* (1991–93) and voiced "Leon the Snowman" in *Elf* (2003), died in Pennsylvania of complications from dementia on May 30. He was 69.

American supporting actor **Jim McMullan** (James Patrick McMullan, Jr.) died of complications from ALS (aka "Lou Gehrig's disease") on May 31, aged 82. A familiar face on TV during the 1960s, '70s and '80s, he starred in CBS-TV's short-lived series *Beyond Westworld* (1980) and appeared in episodes of *The Alfred Hitchcock Hour*, *The Time Tunnel*, *The Sixth Sense*, *The Six Million Dollar Man*, *The Bionic Woman* and *The Hitchhiker*. McMullan was also in such movies as *Stowaway to the Moon* (with John Carradine), *The Incredible Shrinking Woman*, *Virus* (1995), *Austin Powers: International Man of Mystery*, *Batman & Robin* and *The Eighteenth Angel*. He retired from the screen in the late 1990s but went on to portray "Buffalo Bill" in a Wild West Show at a dinner theatre near Disneyland Paris from 1998–2002.

British actor **Graham Fletcher-Cook**, the older brother of actor Dexter Fletcher, died of the asbestos-related lung cancer mesothelioma in May, aged 55. A former child actor, he appeared in *Demonsoul* (1995), *Blood and Carpet* (which he also wrote and directed) and an episode of TV's *Survivors* (1975). Fletcher-Cook's widow subsequently sued the BBC for £800,000 compensation, claiming he was poisoned by asbestos dust while filming shows there as a child.

American character actor **Bingo O'Malley** died on June 2, aged 86. George A. Romero cast him in *Knightriders*, *Creepshow* (as the father of Stephen King's character) and *Two Evil Eyes* (as "Ernest Valdemar"). O'Malley's other credits include John A. Russo's *Heartstopper*, *Diabolique* (1996), *My Bloody Valentine* (2009), *Deadtime Stories: Volume 1*, *River of Darkness*, *Super 8*, *Death from Above*, *Twin Reflex*, *All Saint's Eve* and *Kantemir* (aka *Transylvanian Curse*, with Robert Englund).

British actor **Paul Darrow** (Paul Valentine Birkby), who played the sardonic second-in-command, "Kerr Avon", in the BBC-TV series *Blakes 7* (1978–81), died after a short illness on June 3, aged 78. In late 2014 he suffered an aortic aneurysm; due to complications he had to have both legs partially amputated, one above the knee and the other below it. Darrow's other credits include the James Bond movie *Die Another Day*, the Lovecraftian short film *Rough Magik*, and epsiodes of TV's *The Rivals of Sherlock Holmes*, *The Legend of Robin Hood* (1975, as the Sheriff of Nottingham), *Hammer House of Horror* ('Guardian of the Abyss'), *Doctor Who*, *Science Fiction* ('Sherlock Holmes and the Case of the Missing Link'), *The Strangerers* and *Twisted Tales*. He also contributed voice work to numerous video games. Darrow recreated the role of Avon in audio plays for BBC Radio (1998–99) and Big Finish (2012–19), and he played "Captain Samuel Vimes" in the 1998–99 touring production of the play based on Terry Pratchett's "Discworld" novel *Guards! Guards!*. He also wrote the tie-in novel *Avon: A Terrible Aspect* (1989), and his 2006 autobiography was entitled *You're Him, Aren't You?*.

American supporting actor **John O'Leary**, who was often cast as priests or doctors, died on June 5, aged 93. He appeared in *Demon Seed*, *The Girl the Gold Watch & Everything*, *The Last Starfighter*, *Stepfather II: Make Room for Daddy*, *The Haunting of Morella*, *The Haunted* (1991) and *Waxwork II: Lost in Time*, along with episodes of TV's *Wonder Woman*, *Highway to Heaven*, *Monsters* (Dan

Simmons' 'Shave and a Haircut, Two Bites'), *Xena: Warrior Princess*, *Beyond Belief: Fact or Fiction*, *Buffy the Vampire Slayer*, *Dexter* and the 1980 pilot *Ghost of a Chance*.

Canadian character actor **Sean** [Kenneth] **Hewitt** died on June 6, aged 83. He was in Hammer's *Vampire Circus*, *The Sender*, *Thinner*, *Battlefield Earth* and Guillermo del Toro's *Crimson Peak*. On TV, Hewitt appeared in episodes of *Seeing Things*, *The Ray Bradbury Theater* and the 1980s revival of *Alfred Hitchcock Presents*.

Austrian-born actor **Carl Schell**, the brother of Maximilian Schell, died in Switzerland the same day, aged 91. He co-starred in *Werewolf in a Girls' Dormitory* (1961) and was in the 'Mainly on the Plains' episode of TV's *I Spy*, which guest-starred Boris Karloff.

American actress **Julie Payne** died of chronic obstructive pulmonary disease (COPD) on June 7, aged 78. The daughter of actors John Payne and Anne Shirley, she was in episodes of TV's *One Step Beyond*, *Alfred Hitchcock Presents* and *The Wild Wild West*. Payne also turned up uncredited in *The Manchurian Candidate* (1962) before retiring in 1967. She was married to actor Skip Ward from 1964–65 and screenwriter Robert Towne from 1977 until the early 1980s.

Oscar-nominated American character actress **Sylvia Miles** (Sylvia Scheinwald) died of respiratory failure on June 12, aged 94. She appeared in *Violent Midnight*, *The Sentinel* (with John Carradine), Tobe Hooper's *The Funhouse*, *Sleeping Beauty* (1987) and an episode of TV's *Life on Mars* (2008).

Mexican actress **Edith González** [Fuentes] died of ovarian cancer on June 13, aged 54. She appeared in *Alucarda*, *Gorilla's King*, *Cyclone* (1978), *Guyana: Cult of the Damned*, *Hell's Trap*, *El motel de la muerte*, *El muerto*, *El descuartizador* and *Los cómplices del infierno*, but was better known as a star of TV *telenovelas*.

Canadian character actor **Sean McCann** died of heart disease the same day, aged 83. His credits include *The Uncanny* (1977), *Starship Invasions* (with Christopher Lee), *Ghost of a Chance*, David Cronenberg's *Naked Lunch*, *Roswell: The Aliens Attack* and *Possible Worlds*, along with episodes of TV's *Seeing Things*, *Friday the 13th: The Series*, *The Hidden Room* and *Haven*.

American cable TV host **Bob Dorian** (Robert Paul Vierengel), whose voice as "Professor Knowby" was heard in both *The Evil Dead* (1981) and the remake *Evil Dead* (2013), died on June 15, aged 85. He also introduced movies on AMC's *Matinee Classics* from 1984–2000 and appeared in Woody Allen's *The Curse of the Jade Scorpion*.

Prolific Filipino actor and director **Eddie Garcia** (Eduardo Verchez Garcia) died on June 20 after suffering a severe cervical fracture when he tripped over a cable while filming a TV drama twelve days earlier. The 90-year-old had remained comatose since the accident. Garcia appeared in *Creatures of Evil* (aka *Blood of the Vampires*), *Devil Woman*, *Beast of Blood*, *The Beast of the Yellow Night*, *Batuta ni Drakula* (as "Drakula"), *The Twilight People*, *Halik ng Vampira*, *Living Dead*, *The Woman Hunt*, *Beyond Atlantis*, *Black Mamba* and literally hundreds of action and exploitation movies, along with an episode of TV's *Conan* ('The Heart of the Elephant').

Welsh-born character actor **William Simons** (Clifford William Cumberbatch Simons), who was often cast as policemen or detectives, died of cancer on June 21, aged 78. A former child actor, he appeared in episodes of ITV's *Play of the Week* ('Frenzy'), *Tales of Hans Anderson*, *The Guardians*, *Doctor Who* ('The Sun Makers') and the 1989 version of *The Woman in Black*.

American actress **Sue Bernard** (Susan Bernard) died the same day, aged 71. The daughter of Hollywood glamour photographer Bruno Bernard, she became the first Jewish *Playboy* "Playmate of the Month" in December 1966. Bernard appeared in such exploitation movies as Russ Meyer's *Faster, Pussycat! Kill! Kill!*, *The Witchmaker*, Bert I. Gordon's *Necromancy* (with Orson Welles) and *The Killing Kind*. She was married to actor Jason Miller from 1974–78.

Yugoslavian-born actor and director **Steve Hawkes** (Stjepan Sipek), who starred as "Tarzan" in the Euro productions *Tarzan in the Golden Grotto* (aka *King of the Jungle*, 1969) and *Tarzan and the Brown Prince* (1972), died on June 23, aged 77. After being badly burned in an on-set accident, he retired from the screen in the mid-1970s to run a controversial animal sanctuary in Florida. Hawkes returned to acting in Gary Davis' low budget *2056: Escape from Zombie Island* (2012) and *2057: Return to Zombie Island* (2013). He also wrote, produced, directed and starred in the cult 1972 horror movie *Blood Freak*, in which he was transformed into a giant turkey monster.

American leading lady **Stephanie** [Lynne] **Niznik** died of chronic liver disease and chronic alcohol use the same day, aged 52. She appeared in *The Guardian* (1997), *Mr. Murder* (based on the novel by Dean R. Koontz), *Emma's Wish*, *Inferno* (1998), *Star Trek: Insurrection*, *Spiders II: Breeding Ground* and *Epoch*. On TV, Niznik was in episodes of *The Sentinel*, *Sliders*, *Viper*, *Star Trek: Enterprise*, *Eli Stone* and *Lost*.

American character actor **Billy Drago** (William Eugene Burrows, Jr.), who excelled at playing villians, died of complications from a stroke on June 24, aged 73. His credits include *Pale Rider*, *Invasion U.S.A.* (1985), *Vamp*, *Hunter's Blood*, *Hero and the Terror*, *Cyborg 2: Glass Shadow*, *Lunarcop*, *Phoenix* (1995), *Mirror Mirror 3: The Voyeur*, *Sci-Fighters*, *Convict 762*, *Mirror Mirror 4: Reflections*, *Tremors 4: The Legend Begins*, *Fort Doom*, *Demon Hunter* (2005), *Blood Relic*, *Seven Mummies*, *The Hills Have Eyes* (2006), *The Dead One* (2007), *Revamped*, *Zombie Hunters*, *Copperhead*, *Dark Moon Rising* (2009), *Ghost Town* (2009), *The Ritual* (2009), *World's End* (2010), *Children of the Corn: Genesis* and *Night of the Templar* (with Udo Kier and a long-dead David Carradine). On TV, Drago was a regular on such shows as *The Adventures of Brisco County, Jr.* (1993–94) and *Charmed* (1999–2004), and he appeared in episodes of *Automan*, *Friday the 13th: The Series*, *Monsters*, *The X Files*, *Masters of Horror* (Takashi Miike's 'Imprint') and *Supernatural*.

British-born leading man **Bryan Marshall** died in Australia on June 25, aged 81. He had an uncredited role in Hammer's *Rasputin the Mad Monk*, before going on to appear in *The Witches* (aka *The Devil's Own*) and *Quatermass and the Pit* (aka *Five Million Years to Earth*) for the same studio. His other credits include the James Bond film *The Spy Who Loved Me*, Marvel's *The Punisher* (1989), *Selkie* and episodes of TV's *The Avengers*, *The Frighteners*, *Thriller* (1973), *Late Night Theatre* (Gordon Honeycombe's 'Time and Time Again'), *The Boy Merlin*, *Tales of the Unexpected*, *Robin of Sherwood* and *Time Trax*.

American character actor **Max** [Edward] **Wright**, who starred as "Willie Tanner" in the NBC sitcom *ALF* (1986–90), died of cancer on June 26, aged 75. His other credits include *All That Jazz, Simon, The Boy Who Loved Trolls, The Shadow* (1994) and *Dead by Midnight.* On TV, he played "Dick Stetmeyer" on *Misfits of Science* (1985–86) and appeared in the pilot for *Tales from the Darkside* and episodes of *Faerie Tale Theatre, Ghostwriter, Quantum Leap*, the Stephen King mini-series *The Stand* (1994) and *Early Edition.*

French actress **Édith Scob** (Édith Scobeltzine), who starred in Georges Franju's influential *Eyes Without a Face* (*Les yeux sans visage*), died the same day, aged 81. Her other credits include *The Burning Court* (based on the novel by John Dickson Carr), Franju's *Judex, Fantasmagorie, Une aventure de Sherlock Holmes* and *Brotherhood of the Wolf.*

**Mark Montgomery**, who played "Daryl" in *The Curse of Dracula* (1979) TV serial, died on June 27, aged 66. He was also in an episode of *Shazam!* before retiring from acting in the late 1970s.

British supporting actor **Stephan Chase** died the same day, aged 74. He made his film debut in *Cry of the Banshee* (with Vincent Price), and his other credits include Roman Polanski's *Macbeth* and Disney's *Maleficent.* On TV, Chase appeared in episodes of *UFO, Arthur of the Britons, Orson Welles Great Mysteries* and *Hammer House of Mystery and Suspense.*

70-year-old American character actor **Charles Levin** died from an apparent accidental fall on June 28. He was reported missing on July 8 by his son, and four days later his car was found by the roadside with his deceased dog inside. His remains were eventually discovered on July 14. Levin appeared in *The Golden Child* and episodes of TV's *Tales from the Dark Side* (Harlan Ellison's 'Djinn, No Chaser') and *The Twilight Zone* (1985).

Welsh character actor **Glyn Houston** (Glyndwr Desmond Houston), the younger brother of actor Donald, died on June 30, aged 93. He appeared in *Circus of Horrors* (uncredited), *Invasion* (1965) and *The Mystery of Edwin Drood* (1993). On TV Houston was in episodes of *Colonel March of Scotland Yard* (starring Boris Karloff), *The Saint* ('The House on Dragon's Rock'), *Doomwatch, Beasts* and *Doctor Who.*

Diminutive American character actress **Pat Crawford Brown** died on July 2, three days after her 90th birthday. A former high school English teacher, she appeared in many movies from the mid-1980s onwards, including *18 Again!*, *Elvira: Mistress of the Dark*, *Cannibal Women in the Avocado Jungle of Death*, *Out of Sight Out of Mind*, *A Gnome Named Norm*, *The Rocketeer*, *Demonic Toys*, *Johnny Mysto: Boy Wizard*, *Jack Frost*, *Daredevil*, *Super Capers: The Origins of Ed and the Missing Bullion* and *Oliver's Ghost*. On TV, Brown turned up in episodes of *The Twilight Zone* (1986), *Beauty and the Beast* (1987), *Highway to Heaven*, *Quantam Leap*, *Murder She Wrote* ('Fire Burn, Cauldron Bubble'), *Time Trax*, *Lois & Clark: The New Adventures of Superman*, *Dark Skies*, *The Pretender*, *NightMan*, *Beyond Belief: Fact or Fiction*, *3rd Rock from the Sun*, *Buffy the Vampire Slayer*, *Ghost Whisperer* and the 2009 mini-series *Meteor*.

Very interesting...Emmy Award-winning American comedy actor **Arte Johnson** (Arthur Stanton Eric Johnson), who was a regular on *Rowan & Martin's Laugh-In* (1967–71), died of bladder and prostate cancer on July 3, aged 90. His other credits include *The President's Analyst*, *Once Upon a Brothers Grimm*, *Love at First Bite* (as "Renfield"), *Alice in Wonderland* (1985), *A Night at the Magic Castle* (as "Harry Houdini"), *Evil Spirits*, *Evil Toons*, *Munchie* and *Second Chance*. On TV, Johnson was in episodes of *The Twilight Zone* (1961), *Shirley Temple's Storybook*, *Alfred Hitchcock Presents*, *Bewitched*, *Lost in Space*, *I Dream of Jeannie*, *Rod Serling's Night Gallery*, *Fantasy Island* and *Bill & Ted's Excellent Adventures* (as "Albert Einstein"). He was also the voice of "Weerd" in the cartoon series *The 13 Ghosts of Scooby-Doo* (1985).

British character actor **William Hurndell** died on July 4, aged 85. He appeared in small roles (often uncredited) in *Goldfinger*, *City in the Sea* (aka *War-Gods of the Deep*, with Vincent Price) and episodes of TV's *Doctor Who* (as "Ike Clanton") and *Adam Adamant Lives!*. Hurndell retired from the screen in 1970.

Veteran Spanish-born supporting actor **Eduardo** [Martínez] **Fajardo** died in Mexico the same day, aged 94. He was in *La Llorona* (1960), *Los invisibles*, *Argoman the Fantastic Superman*, *Transplant of a Brain*, *The Murder Mansion*, Mario Bava's *Lisa and the Devil/The*

*House of Exorcism, Evil Eye* (1975), *Cross of the Devil, Espectro (Más allá del fin del mundo)*, Umberto Lenzi's *Nightmare City* (aka *City of the Walking Dead*), Jesús Franco's *Oasis of the Zombies, Hundra, The Exterminators of the Year 3000, Yellow Hair and the Fortress of Gold* and *The Brother from Space*. He mostly retired from the screen in the late 1990s.

Spanish leading man **Arturo Fernández** [Rodríguez] also died on July 4, aged 90. His credits include *Sound of Horror* (with Ingrid Pitt) and *Os 5 Avisos de Satanás*.

20-year-old American actor **Cameron** [Mica] **Boyce** died in his sleep from an epileptic seizure on July 6. He appeared in *Mirrors* and starred in Disney's *Descendants*, plus the two sequels and various animated spin-offs.

American character actor **Eddie Jones** (Arthur Edward Jones), who played "Jonathan Kent" in ABC's *Lois & Clark: The New Adventures of Superman* (1993–97), died the same day, aged 82. He was also in *The First Deadly Sin*, Larry Cohen's *Q* (aka *Q: The Winged Serpent*), *C.H.U.D., Invasion U.S.A.* (1985), *The Believers* and *The Rocketeer*. A regular in the revivals of TV's *Dark Shadows* (1991) and *The Invisible Man* (2000–02), he also appeared in the pilots for *Tales from the Darkside* and *Ghost Whisperer* and an episode of *Touched by an Angel*.

Busy British character actor **Freddie Jones** (Frederick Charles Jones) died after a short illness on July 9, aged 91. His many credits include *Marat/Sade* (he was in the original stage play), Hammer's *Frankenstein Must Be Destroyed* and *The Satanic Rites of Dracula* (both with Peter Cushing), *The Man Who Haunted Himself, Goodbye Gemini, Assault* (aka *In the Devil's Garden*), *Mr. Horatio Knibbles, Son of Dracula* (1973), *Alice Through the Looking Glass* (1973), *Old Dracula*, David Lynch's *The Elephant Man* and *Dune, Firefox, Krull*, the 1984 Stephen King adaptation *Firestarter, Young Sherlock Holmes, Erik the Viking, The Mystery of Edwin Drood* (1993) and *The NeverEnding Story III*. Jones also contributed the voice of "Dallben" in Disney's animated *The Black Cauldron*. On TV, he was a regular in *Children of the Stones* (1977) and *The Ghosts of Motley Hall* (1976–78), and he appeared in episodes of *The Avengers, Randall and*

*Hopkirk (Deceased)*, *Mystery and Imagination* (M.R. James' 'Lost Hearts', Edgar Allan Poe's 'The Telltale Heart' and as the title character in 'Sweeney Todd'), *Out of the Unknown*, *Thriller* (1975), *Space: 1999*, *The Return of Sherlock Holmes*, *The Case-Book of Sherlock Holmes* ('The Last Vampyre'), *The Young Indiana Jones Chronicles*, *Tales of Mystery and Imagination* (Poe's 'The Cask of Amontillado'), Neil Gaiman's *Neverwhere*, *The League of Gentlemen* and the 2001 revival of *Randall & Hopkirk [Deceased]*. One of Jones' sons is the actor Toby Jones.

American actor **Rip Torn** (Elmore Rual Torn, Jr.), best known for playing "Agent Zed" in *Men in Black* and *Men in Black II*, died of Alzheimer's disease the same day, aged 88. His other credits include *One Spy Too Many*, *The Man Who Fell to Earth*, *Coma* (1978), *A Stranger is Watching*, *The Beastmaster*, *Scarab*, *Dolly Dearest* and *RoboCop 3*. On TV Torn was in episodes of *Sunday Showcase* (Alfred Bester's 'Murder and the Android'), *Thriller* (1960), *The Man from U.N.C.L.E.* and *Circle of Fear*. He also narrated the 1997–98 TV series *Ghost Stories* and was the voice of "Zeus" in Disney's 1997 *Hercules* and spin-off video games.

Italian actress **Valentina Cortese** died on July 10, aged 96. She appeared in the films *Black Magic* (1949, with Orson Welles), Mario Bava's *The Evil Eye*, Federico Fellini's *Juliet of the Spirits*, Riccardo Freda's *The Iguana with the Tongue of Fire*, Lucio Fulci's *Dracula in the Provinces*, *Ring of Darkness* and *The Adventures of Baron Munchausen* (1988). Cortese was married to American actor Richard Basehart from 1951–60.

American actress **Denise** [Marie] **Nickerson**, who played the spoilt "Violet Beauregarde" in *Willy Wonka & the Chocolate Factory* (1971), died of a massive seizure the same day, aged 62. Her family took her off life-support in hospital, after she was found to have swallowed various medications the previous month. Nickerson had a recurring role as "Amy Collins" on the daytime Gothic soap opera *Dark Shadows* (1968–70), and she also auditioned for the role of "Princess Leia" in *Star Wars* and was reportedly considered for "Regan MacNeil" in *The Exorcist*.

Scottish actor **Rony Bridges** (Ronald Bridges), who appeared (uncredited) as a First Order Admiral in *Star Wars: Episode VII—The Force Awakens* (2015), died of cancer on July 14, aged 67.

84-year-old American actor **Barry Coe** (Barry Clark Heacock) died of the blood cancer myelodysplastic syndrome on July 16. He appeared in *The Wizard of Baghdad*, *Fantastic Voyage*, *One Minute Before Death*, *Doctor Death: Seeker of Souls*, *Jaws II* and an episode of TV's *Voyage to the Bottom of the Sea*.

American leading man **David Hedison** (Albert David Hedison, Jr., aka "Al Hedison"), who co-starred as "Captain Lee B. Crane" in ABC-TV's *Voyage to the Bottom of the Sea* (1964–68), died on July 18, aged 92. His other credits include *The Fly* (1958, with Vincent Price), *The Lost World* (1960), the James Bond movies *Live and Let Die* and *Licence to Kill* (as CIA agent "Felix Leiter" in both), Curtis Harrington's *The Cat Creature* (scripted by Robert Bloch), *The Power Within*, *Megiddo: The Omega Code 2*, *Spectres* (2004) and Ted Newsom's *Superman and the Secret Planet* (as "Jor El"). On TV he was also in episodes of Hammer's *Journey to the Unknown*, *Wonder Woman*, *Project U.F.O.*, *Fantasy Island* and *Knight Rider* (1985).

American actress **Darlene Tompkins** (Darlene Perfect) died the same day, aged 78. She co-starred, aged eighteen, as "Princess Trirene" in Edgar G. Ulmer's *Beyond the Time Barrier* (1958) and appeared in an episode of TV's *Alfred Hitchcock Presents*. Tompkins retired from the screen in 1967, but returned to TV in the 1970s as an uncredited stunt double and extra.

American actor **Robert Milli**, who co-starred as the ill-fated "Tom Gruneman" in *The Curse of the Living Corpse* (1964), also died on July 18, aged 86. Milli played "Horatio" in the 1964 Broadway production of *Hamlet*, starring Richard Burton.

Busy Dutch star **Rutger** [Oelsen] **Hauer**, best known for his iconic performance as outlaw replicant "Roy Batty" ("I've seen things you people wouldn't believe...") in Ridley Scott's *Blade Runner* (1982), died following a short illness on July 19, aged 75. In an eclectic acting career that veered between serious drama and direct-to-video trash, his credits include *Ladyhawke*, *Flesh + Blood*, *The Hitcher*, *Split Second* (1992), *Buffy the Vampire Slayer*, *Nostradamus* (1994), *Fatherland*, *Mr. Stitch*, *Precious Find*, *Crossworlds*, *Omega Doom*,

*Hemoglobin, Redline, The Ruby Ring, Bone Daddy, Simon Magus, Flying Virus, Scorcher, Dracula II: Ascension* and *Dracula III: Legacy* (as "Dracula III"), *Sin City, Batman Begins, Minotaur, Dead Tone, The Rite, The Reverend, Spoon,* Dario Argento's *Dracula 3D* (as "Van Helsing"), *2047: Sights of Death, The Scorpion King 4: Quest for Power, Valerian and the City of a Thousand Planets, The Broken Key* and *Corbin Nash.* On TV, Hauer appeared in the mini-series *Merlin, The 10th Kingdom* and *Salem's Lot* (2004, as vampire "Kurt Barlow"), along with episodes of *Lexx, Smallville, Metal Hurlant Chronicles, Wilfred, True Blood, Galavant* and *Channel Zero.*

Craggy-faced British character actor **Jeremy Kemp** (Edmund Jeremy James Walker) died after a long illness the same day, aged 84. He appeared in Amicus' *Dr. Terror's House of Horrors* (where he was strangled to death by a creeping vine), *The Seven-Per-Cent Solution* and *The Phantom of the Opera* (1983, with Maximilian Schell as the Phantom). On TV, Kemp was a regular as evil wizard king "Hissah Zul" in *Conan* (1997–98) and he also appeared in episodes of TV's *Space: 1999, The Greatest American Hero, Shades of Darkness* (L.P. Hartley's 'Feet Foremost'), *The Adventures of Sherlock Holmes* ('The Speckled Band') and *Star Trek: The Next Generation* (as Jean-Luc Picard's older brother Robert, although his voice was dubbed by Ian Abercrombie). He retired from the screen in 1998.

Russian-born American character actress **Ivy Bethune** (Ivy Vigder), who co-starred in the 1971 horror movie *Legacy of Blood* (with John Carradine), also died on July 19, aged 101. She also appeared in *This House Possessed, Dark Night of the Scarecrow, Back to the Future, Scissors* and *Get Smart* (2008). On TV, Bethune turned up in episodes of *The Outer Limits, The Alfred Hitchcock Hour* (John Wyndham's 'Consider Her Ways'), *Otherworld, Misfits of Science, Star Trek: The Next Generation* and *The Flash* (1991). She was also a regular on the *Superman* radio show and appeared on stage in *The World of Ray Bradbury* and such Bradbury adaptations as *The Martian Chronicles, Fahrenheit 451* and *Dandelion Wine.*

Italian actress **Ilaria Occhini** died on July 20, aged 85. Her film credits include *Sigfrido* and *The Man Who Laughs* (1966). On TV Occhini starred in the title role of *Jane Eyre* (1957).

Canadian voice and character actor **Gabe Khouth**, who played "Sneezy"/"Tom Clark" on ABC-TV's *Once Upon a Time* (2011–2018), died on July 23 after apparently suffering a heart attack while riding his motorcycle. He was 46. Khouth was born with a congenital heart defect (*tricuspid atresia*), and had heart surgery when he was ten years old. His other credits include *Terminal City Ricochet, IT* (1990), *Santa Baby, Christmas Town, Santa Baby 2: Christmas Maybe, Jim Henson's Turkey Hollow, Becoming Santa* and *Wish Upon a Christmas*, along with episodes of *Millennium, Ninja Turtles: The Next Mutation* (as "Leonardo"), *Andromeda, Fringe, Supernatural, iZombie, A Series of Unfortunate Events* and *The Crossing*.

American actor **Jim Malinda** (James Malinda, Jr.), who starred as the title caveman in ABC's *Korg: 70,000 B.C.* (1974–75), died the same day, aged 83. He also appeared in *The Beguiled* (1971) and *Once* (1973), along with episodes of TV's *The Snoop Sisters* ('The Devil Made Me Do It!', with Alice Cooper), *Kolchak: The Night Stalker* and *The Six million Dollar Man*. Melinda retired from acting at the end of the 1980s.

American actress **Russi Taylor** (Russell Taylor), who voiced Walt Disney's "Minnie Mouse" and "Huey, Dewey and Louie" from 1986 onwards, died of colon cancer on July 26, aged 75. She also worked on *Who Framed Roger Rabbit, Scooby-Doo and the Ghoul School, Runaway Brain, The Brave Little Toaster Goes to Mars, A Bug's Life, Fantasia 2000, Cinderella 2: Dreams Come True, Tales from Earthsea, Cinderella 3: A Twist in Time, WALL-E* and *Scooby-Doo and the Goblin King*. A regular on *The Simpsons* as the voice of "Martin Prince", Taylor's TV credits include being the voice of "Strawberry Shortcake" and such series as *The Flintstones Comedy Hour* (as "Pebbles"), *The 13 Ghosts of Scooby-Doo, Gravedale High* and *The Twisted Tales of Felix the Cat*, amongst numerous other shows. She was married to Wayne Allwine, the voice of Disney's "Mickey Mouse", from 1991 until his death in 2009.

Uruguayan-born Italian leading man **George Hilton** (Jorge Hill Acosta y Lara) died in Rome on July 28, aged 85. He appeared in *The Amazing Doctor G* (as "Agente 007"), *The Sweet Body of Deborah, The Strange Vice of Mrs. Wardh*, Sergio Martino's *All the Colors of the Dark, The Case of the Bloody Iris* and *Atlantis Interceptors*.

Brazilian actress **Ruth** [Pinto] **de Souza**, who co-starred as the voodoo queen "Mama Rata-loi" in *Macumba Love* (1960), died of complications from pneumonia the same day, aged 98. She was also in a 2001 episode of the TV series *The Clone*.

British actress **June Elvin** (June Elvin Gomersall), who appeared in the 1947 poltergeist comedy *Things Happen at Night*, died on July 31, aged 95.

British character actress **Freda** [Mary] **Dowie**, who was often cast as nuns, died on August 10, aged 91. She appeared in *Alice in Wonderland* (1966), *The Omen* (1976) and *The Monk* (1990). On TV, Dowie was in episodes of *Doctor Faustus* (1961), *Omnibus* (M.R. James' 'Whistle and I'll Come to You'), *Doomwatch*, *Jack the Ripper* (1973), *Alice in Wonderland* (1986), *The Return of Sherlock Holmes* ('The Devil's Foot') and the mini-series *Jason and the Argonauts* (2000). She was also in the 1968 BBC Radio 4 serial of John Wyndham's *The Day of the Triffids* with Barbara Shelley.

American stuntman-actor **Dango Nguyen**, who portrayed the Governor's bodyguard in episodes of AMC's *The Walking Dead*, died of cancer the same day, aged 48. The former Georgia firefighter also appeared in episodes of *The Originals* and *The Gifted*.

Canadian actress **Barbara March** (Barbara Jean Maczka), who portrayed the Klingon warrior "Lursa Duras" in episodes of *Star Trek: The Next Generation* and *Star Trek: Deep Space Nine*, as well as the movie *Star Trek: Generations*, died of cancer on August 11, aged 65. She also had a small role in the 1991 TV movie *Blood Ties*. March was married to British actor Alan Scarfe.

American stand-up comedian **Kip** [Francis] **Addotta** died on August 13, aged 75. He turned up in small roles in *Watchers II*, Tobe Hooper's *Crocodile* and an episode of TV's *Harry and the Hendersons*.

Hollywood actor and director **Peter** [Henry] **Fonda**, the son of actor Henry Fonda, brother of actress Jane Fonda and father of actress Bridget Fonda, died of lung cancer on August 16, aged 79. He appeared in *Lilith*, Roger Corman's *The Trip*, *Spirits of the Dead* (Roger Vadim's 'Metzengerstein' segment, with his sister), *Race with the Devil*, *Futureworld*, *Dance of the Dwarfs*, *Spasms*, *Nadja* (as both "Dracula" and "Dr. Van Helsing"), John Carpenter's *Escape from L.A.*,

*The Tempest* (1998), *Supernova*, *Ghost Rider* (as "Mephistopheles") and *Journey to the Center of the Earth* (2008). On TV, Fonda was in the 2007 mini-series *The Gathering*, and he also directed the 1973 SF movie *Idaho Transfer*.

British character actress **Anna Quayle** (Anne Veronica Maria Quayle) died of complications from Lewy body dementia the same day, aged 86. Perhaps her finest moment was in the 1967 *The Avengers* episode 'The Correct Way to Kill' (with Michael Gough), and her other credits include *Casino Royale* (1967), *Chitty Chitty Bang Bang*, *The Seven-Per-Cent Solution* and the 1976 TV movie *James and the Giant Peach*.

Cuban-born champion boxer **José Mantequilla Nápoles** (José Ángel Nápoles) died in Mexico City on September 16, aged 79. He co-starred with masked wrestler Santo in the 1974 movie *La venganza de la llorona*.

South African-born character actress **Sheila [Frances] Steafel** died in London on August 24, aged 84. Her film credits include *Daleks' Invasion Earth 2150 A.D.* (with Peter Cushing), Hammer's *Quatermass and the Pit*, *Digby: The Biggest Dog in the World*, *Bloodbath at the House of Death* (with Vincent Price) and *Back to the Secret Garden*. On TV, Steafal portrayed "The White Lady" in three series of the children's comedy *The Ghosts of Motley Hall* (1976–78) and appeared in episodes of *Woof!*, *Whizziwig* and *The 10th Kingdom*. She was married to actor Harry H. Corbett from 1958–64.

Emmy and Golden Globe Award-winning American actress **Valerie [Kathryn] Harper**, who starred in the 1974–78 TV sitcom *Rhoda* (a spin-off from *The Mary Tyler Moore Show*), died of brain cancer on August 30, aged 80. She appeared in *Don't Go to Sleep*, *The People Across the Lake*, *My Future Boyfriend*, *Shiver* and episodes of *Touched by an Angel* and *Drop Dead Diva*.

78-year-old Italian bodybuilder and actor **Franco Columbu** suffered a heart attack and drowned while swimming off the coast of Sardinia the same day. A former Mr. Europe, Mr. Universe, Mr. World and Mr. Olympia champion, he was a longtime friend of Arnold Schwarzenegger and turned up in small roles in *Conan the Barbarian*, *The Terminator*, *Predator* and *The Running Man*, along with an episode of TV's *Tales from the Crypt* directed by Schwarzenegger. Columbu also appeared in *Big Top Pee-wee*, but his own attempts to become an action star never really amounted to much.

American *anime* and video game voice actor **Michael J. Lindsay** (aka "Dylan Tully") died on August 31, aged 56. His credits include *Akira* (1988), *Vampire Princess Miyu*, *Transformers: Robots in Disguise* and *Digimon: Digital Monsters*, amongst many other titles.

American leading lady **Carol Lynley** (Carole Ann Jones) died of a heart attack on September 3, aged 77. A former child model, her movie credits include *Shock Treatment* (1964), *Bunny Lake is Missing*, *The Shuttered Room* (based on the story by August Derleth and H.P. Lovecraft), *The Helicopter Spies* (with John Carradine), *The Maltese Bippy*, *Weekend of Terror*, *The Night Stalker*, *Beware! The Blob*, *The Beasts Are on the Streets*, *The Cat and the Canary* (1978), *The Shape of Things to Come*, *Dark Tower* (1989), *Spirits* (with Robert Quarry), *Howling VI: The Freaks* and *A Light in the Forest*. On TV Lynley guest-starred in episodes of *Alfred Hitchcock Presents*, *Shirley Temple's Storybook* (in the title role of 'Rapunzel'), *The Alfred Hitchcock Hour*, *The Man from U.N.C.L.E.*, *The Invaders*, Hammer's *Journey to the Unknown*, *The Immortal*, *Rod Serling's Night Gallery*, *The Sixth Sense*, *Orson Welles Great Mystery*, *The Evil Touch*, *Thriller* (1975), *Future Cop*, *Fantasy Island* (eleven episodes!), *Tales of the Unexpected*, *Hammer House of Mystery and Suspense* and *Monsters*. She posed nude for *Playboy* magazine in March 1965.

American character and voice actor **Robert** [William] **Axelrod** (aka "Axel Roberts"), who voiced the evil "Lord Zedd" in the TV series *Mighty Morphin Power Rangers* (1993–96) and various spin-offs, died on September 7, aged 70. He appeared in *Alice in Wonderland* (1985), *Sorority House Massacre*, *Bates Motel*, *Terror on Alcatraz*, *The Blob* (1988), *The Lords of Magick*, *Midnight* (1989), *Alien Private Eye*, *Wishman*, *A Light in the Darkness*, *TheCampusHouse.com*, *Deep Freeze*, *Exorcism*, *A Light in the Forest*, *The Eden Formula*, *The Revenant* and Donald F. Glut's *Tales of Frankenstein*, along with episodes of TV's *Amazing Stories*, *Star Trek: Voyager* and *Bite Me*. Axelrod also voiced a number of characters (uncredited) in the English-language version of Michele Soavi's *The Church* (1989).

American character actor **John Wesley** [Houston], who starred as "Principal Pratchett" in the TV series *Superhuman Samurai Syber-Squad* (1994–95), died after a long battle with multiple myeloma on September 8, aged 72. He was also in *Timestalkers*, *Jack's Back*, *Raw Nerve*, Disney's *The Computer Wore Tennis Shoes* (1995), *13th Child*, *Believers*, *Cursed Angel* and *The Midnighters*, along with episodes of TV's *The Man from U.N.C.L.E.*, *Knight Rider*, *Highway to Heaven*, *Revelations*, *Night Stalker* (2005), *Medium* and *Cursed*.

American character actor **Jack Lindine**, who appeared as "Jack Ruby" in three episodes of NBC's *Dark Skies* (1996–97), died on September 9, aged 70. He was also in the 1997 movie *Jack Frost* and appeared on TV in *The Twilight Zone* (1986) and *3rd Rock from the Sun*.

British actress **Valerie Van Ost** died of liver cancer on September 10, aged 75. Best known for appearing in four "Carry On" films, the former teenage dancer was also in *Corruption*, *Incense for the Damned* (aka *Bloodsuckers*) and Hammer's *The Satanic Rites of Dracula*, all with Peter Cushing. On TV, Van Ost's credits include episodes of TV's *The Avengers*, *Ace of Wands* and *Space: 1999*. She was also the casting director on the 1984 ghost film, *Haunters of the Deep*.

American actor **Brian Turk**, who played strongman "Gabriel" in TV's *Carnivàle* (2003–05), died of brain cancer on September 13, aged 49. He appeared in small roles in the movies *The Lost World: Jurassic Park*, *A.I. Artificial Intelligence* and *Magus*. On TV, Turk was featured in episodes of *Weird Science*, *The Pretender*, *Buffy the Vampire Slayer* and *The Tick* (2001).

German actor **David Hurst** (Heinrich Theodore Hirsch) died of complications from a stroke and pneumonia on September 15, aged 93. His credits include *The Perfect Woman* (1949), *Mother Riley Meets the Vampire* (with Bela Lugosi), *Mad About Men*, *How to Steal the World*, *The Maltese Bippy* and *The Boys from Brazil*. Hurst also appeared in episodes of TV's *The Man from U.N.C.L.E.*, *The Girl from U.N.C.L.E.*, *Star Trek*, *The Flying Nun* and *Dark Shadows* (1971). He retired from the screen in the early 1980s.

**Jason** [David] **Lake**, the son of actors Alan Lake and Diana Dors, was found dead at his home in London the same day. The 50-year-old admitted to being an alcholic for most of his life. He appeared as a "Werewolf Child" in the 1980 *Hammer House of Horror* episode 'Children of the Full Moon', which co-starred his mother, and he also turned up in *Pink Floyd: The Wall* and an episode of TV's *Into the Labyrinth*.

American actress and Tony Award-winning singer **Phyllis Newman** died of complications from a lung disorder on September 15, aged 86. She was in episodes of TV's *The Man from U.N.C.L.E.* and *The Wild Wild West*, and the movies *The Naked Witch* and *Mannequin*. Newman was married to playwright and lyricist Adolph Green from 1960 until his death in 2002.

American adult movie actress **Jessica Jaymes** (Jessica Michael Redding) died of a seizure related to chronic alcohol abuse on September 17, aged 40. The buxom actress had a history of depression and suicide attempts, with her body showing multiple scars on the wrists and forearms. She had also been hospitalised three times on an involuntary basis after being deemed a danger to herself or others. Jaymes appeared in such X-rated movies as *Alien Love Fantasy*, *The New Devil in Miss Jones*, *The Twilight Zone: Porn Parody*, *Lust Bite*, *Demon Lust*, *Hot Chicks Big Fangs 2* and *Hills Have Thighs XXX*, along with the 2010 horror movie *Bloodstruck*. In 2004, Jaymes became the first contract model for *Hustler* magazine and was the "Pet of the Month" in the August 2008 issue of *Penthouse*.

British-born supporting actor **John Winston**, who portrayed Transporter Chief "Lt. Kyle" in eleven episodes of the original *Star Trek* TV series and the spin-off movie *Star Trek II: The Wrath of Khan*, died on September 19, aged 91. His other credits include the TV movie *Sole Survivor* (with William Shatner) and episodes of *The Man from U.N.C.L.E.*, *The Time Tunnel* and *Max Headroom*.

American character actor and Emmy Award-winning soap opera scriptwriter **Jan Merlin** (Jan Wasylewski), who co-starred as "Roger Manning" in the TV series *Tom Corbett, Space Cadet* (1950–55), died on September 20, aged 94. Often cast as villains, Merlin appeared in *Them!*, *The Twilight People*, *Covenant*, *Time Trackers* and *Buried Alive* (1990). On TV, he appeared in episodes of *The Man from U.N.C.L.E.*,

*Tarzan* (1966), *Voyage to the Bottom of the Sea*, *The Time Tunnel*, *The Invaders*, *Search* and *Tales of the Unexpected*. Perhaps Merlin's most famous work went uncredited, when he appeared under several of the star character make-ups in John Houston's *The List of Adrian Messenger* (1963). He retired from the screen in the early 1990s.

Distinctive American character actor **Sid Haig** (Sidney Eddie Mosesian) died of respiratory complications on September 21, aged 80. He had recently been hospitalised after a fall at his home and contracted a lung infection after vomiting in his sleep. Haig began his career in the early 1960s, appearing in such movies as *Blood Bath* (1966), *The Helicopter Spies*, *Spider Baby or the Maddest Story Ever Told* (with Lon Chaney, Jr.), George Lucas' *THX 1138*, the James Bond film *Diamonds Are Forever*, *Beware! The Blob*, *Beyond Atlantis*, *Wonder Women*, *Death Car on the Freeway*, *Galaxy of Terror*, *The Aftermath*, *Godess of Love*, *Warlords* and *Wizards of the Lost Kingdom II*. Frustrated with the type of roles he was being offered, the actor all but retired from the screen in the early 1990s, until director Rob Zombie cast him as "Captain Spalding" in *House of 1000 Corpses* (2003), a role he went on to recreate in Zombie's *The Devil's Rejects* and *3 from Hell*. Now considered a cult horror star, Haig's career underwent a revival, and he was cast in *House of the Dead 2*, *Night of the Living Dead 3D*, *A Dead Calling*, *Dead Man's Hand* (aka *The Haunted Casino*), *Halloween* (2007), *Brotherhood of Blood*, *Dark Moon Rising*, *Creature* (2011), *Mimesis*, *The Inflicted*, *The Lords of Salem*, *The Sacred*, *Hatchet III*, *Devil in My Ride*, *The Penny Dreadful Picture Show*, *Zombex*, *Bone Tomahawk*, *Death House* (2017), *Cynthia* and *Hanukkah*. On TV, he starred as the villain "Dragos" in *Jason of Star Command* (1978–79) and he turned up in episodes of *The Lucy Show* (as "The Mummy" in 'Lucy and the Monsters'), *Batman* (1966), *Star Trek*, *The Man from U.N.C.L.E.*, *The Flying Nun*, *Get Smart*, *The Six Million Dollar Man*, *Monster Squad*, *Electra Woman and Dyna Girl*, *Tarzan and the Super 7*, *Buck Rogers in the 25th Century*, *Fantasy Island*, *Automan*, *Misfits of Science*, *Amazing Stories*, *Werewolf*, *The People Next Door* and *Holliston*.

Diminutive American actor **Aron** [Scott] **Eisenberg**, who portrayed Ferengi "Nog" in TV's *Star Trek: Deep Space Nine* (1993–

99), died of heart failure the same day, aged 50. He was also in *Amityville Horror: The Evil Escapes, The Horror Show* (1989), *Playroom, Prayer of the Rollerboys, Puppet Master III: Toulon's Revenge, Pterodactyl Women from Beverly Hills* and *Brave New World* (1998), along with episodes of *TV's Tales from the Crypt, Star Trek: Voyager* and *Blade of Honor.*

Veteran American character actor **Jack Donner** (Jake Doner, aka "Jack Doner") also died on September 21, aged 90. He was in the 1958 "The Shadow" movie *Invisible Avenger, Hand of Death, The Night God Screamed, Johnny Mysto: Boy Wizard, Stigmata, Retro Puppet Master, Soulkeeper, Demon Under Glass, Exorcism, The Invisible, Brotherhood of Blood, Plot 7, Farm House, How to Be a Serial Killer, Guardian, All About Evil, Vampire* (2010), *Underground, Night of the Templar, The Wizard's Return: Alex vs. Alex* and *Unbelievable!!!!!,* along with episodes of TV's *The Man from U.N.C.L.E., My Favorite Martian, Get Smart, I Dream of Jeannie, Star Trek, The Flying Nun, Conan, Power Rangers in Space, Charmed* (1999), *Good vs Evil, Buffy the Vampire Slayer, Roswell, First Watch, Star Trek: Enterprise, Ghost Whisperer, Fear the Walking Dead* and *Starship Excelsior.* Donner was also cast as "Doctor Muñoz" in a 1999 short film adaptation of H.P. Lovecraft's story 'Cool Air'.

American character actor **Lee Paul** died on September 22, aged 80. He was in *Ben, Scream of the Wolf* (scripted by Richard Matheson and based on a story by David Case), Disney's *The Island at the Top of the World, The Golden Gate Murders* and Wes Craven's *Deadly Friend,* along with episodes of TV's *Wonder Woman, Fantasy Island, Herbie the Love Bug* and *Outlaws.* Paul retired from the screen in the late 1980s and became a writer.

Blonde and buxom American porn actress (both hardcore and softcore) **Candy Samples** (Mary Samples) died on September 23, aged 91. She appeared in *Flesh Gordon* (1974) under the name "Mary Gavin" and also worked as "Angie Parks", "Lydia Chase", Vivian Andresen" and "Ilona Lakes".

American character actress **Linda Porter** died of cancer on September 25, aged 86. She appeared in *The Mating Habits of the Earthbound Human, Mercy* (based on Stephen King's story

'Gramma') and *Pee-Wee's Big Holiday*, along with episodes of TV's *Beauty and the Beast* (1988), *Murder She Wrote* ('The Witch's Curse'), *The X Files*, *Good vs Evil*, *The Phantom Eye*, *Phil of the Future*, *American Horror Story* and the 2017 revival of *Twin Peaks*.

American character actor **Robert** [Scott] **Garrison**, best known for playing "Tommy" in the first two *The Karate Kid* movies, died of organ failure on September 27, aged 59. He had been ill for a long time. Garrison also appeared in *Starship Invasions*, *Prom Night* (1980), *Human Error* and an episode of TV's *The Munsters Today*.

French-born leading man **Alex Davion** (Alexander Davion) died in England on September 28, aged 90. He appeared in *The Two Mrs. Carrolls* (1961), Hammer's *Paranoiac* and *The Plague of the Zombies*, *Incense for the Damned* (aka *Bloodsuckers*, with Peter Cushing) and *Dark Echo*. On TV, Davion was in episodes of *Five Children and It* (1951), *One Step Beyond*, *Thriller* (with Boris Karloff), *The Avengers*, *Out of the Unknown*, *The Hunchback of Notre Dame* (1966), *Thirty-Minute Theatre* ('Come Death'), *UFO* and *Whoops Apocalypse*. He was also the voice of "Space Captain Greg Martin" in the 1966 spin-off movie *Thunderbirds Are GO*. Davion retired from the screen in the late 1980s.

[E.] **Richard Annis**, who played "Mr. Bloch" in the 1971 *Rod Serling's Night Gallery* episode 'Professor Peabody's Last Lecture', died on September 29, aged 78. After a few more acting roles he became an executive with Universal Studio Tours Hollywood.

American character actor and humorist **Marshall** [Harold] **Efron** died of cardiac arrest on September 30, aged 81. Although he appeared in George Lucas' *THX 1138* and other movies and TV shows, he was better known as a voice actor in such animated series as *Trollkins*, *The Smurfs* and *The 13 Ghosts of Scooby-Doo* and the movies *Twice Upon a Time*, *Ice Age: The Meltdown* and *Dr. Seuss' Horton Hears a Who!.*

American character actor **Lewis Dauber** died of liver cancer on October 3, aged 70. A former banker, he appeared in *The Island* (2005) and episodes of TV's *Misfits of Science*, *The Twilight Zone* (1986), *Max Headroom*, *Quantum Leap*, *Weird Science* and *Meego*.

British character actor **Stephen** [Vincent] **Moore** died on October 4, aged 81. Best remembered for his voicing of "Marvin, the Paranoid Android" in Douglas Adams' *The Hitchhiker's Guide to the Galaxy* radio and TV series, he was also in *A Christmas Carol* (1999) and episodes of TV's *The New Avengers*, *Polterguests*, *The Magical Legend of the Leprechauns*, *Starhunter* and *Doctor Who*.

American actress and singer **Diahann Carroll** (Carol Diahann Johnson) died of cancer the same day, aged 84. Her credits include *From the Dead of Night*, *Eve's Bayou*, *The Star Wars Holiday Special* and an episode of TV's *Touched by an Angel*. Carroll was also the voice of "Queen La" in the animated series *Disney's The Legend of Tarzan* (2001). Her fourth husband (1987–96) was singer Vic Damone.

Zany American stand-up comedian, cartoon voice actor and flamboyant personality **Rip Taylor** (Charles Elmer Taylor, Jr.) died of congestive heart failure on October 6, aged 88. He had suffered an epileptic seizure the week before. Taylor turned up in the movies *Chatterbox!*, *The Silence of the Hams*, *Virtual Combat* and *Silent But Deadly*. On TV he portrayed "Sheldon the Sea Genie" in *Sigmund and the Sea Monsters* (1973–74) and guest-starred in episodes of *The Monkees* and *Down to Earth*. Taylor was also the voice of "Uncle Fester" in the animated series *The Addams Family* (1992–93).

Dependable American leading man turned character actor **Robert Forster** (Robert Wallace Foster, Jr.) died of brain cancer on October 11, aged 78. He appeared in *The Darker Side of Terror*, Disney's *The Black Hole*, *Alligator*, *Goliath Awaits* (with Christopher Lee and John Carradine), Bert I. Gordon's *Satan's Princess*, *Peacemaker*, *In Between*, *Maniac Cop 3: Badge of Silence*, *Scanner Cop II*, *Uncle Sam*, *Night Vision*, *Psycho* (1998), David Lynch's *Mulholland Dr.*, *Supernova*, *Rise: Blood Hunter*, *Dragon Wars: D-War*, *Ghosts of Girlfriends Past*, *Automata*, *The Wolf of Snow Hollow* and the anthology movie *Grave Intentions* (Peter S. Beagle's 'The Bridge Partner'). Forster was also in episodes of TV's *Tales from the Dark Side* ('The Milkman Cometh' based on a story by Charles L. Grant), *Heroes*, *Intruders* (based on the novel by Michael Marshall Smith), *Twin Peaks* (2017) and *Amazing Stories* (2020).

Chinese-born actor **Jin Nakayama** (Jinpei Nakayama) died of lung cancer in Japan on October 12, aged 77. He portrayed "Kazuki Oyama", the Captain of Earth Defence Force in the TV series *Ultraman 80* (1980–81), and Nakayama's other credits include *Urutora Q za mûbi: Hoshi no densetsu* and *Ghost Shout*.

Italian character actor **Carlo Croccolo** died the same day, aged 92. He appeared in *Tototarzan* (1950), *My Friend Dr. Jekyll*, *Hercules in the Valley of Woe*, *The Twelve-Handed Men of Mars* and Mario Bava's *Danger: Diabolik*.

**Herbert Summer**, whose only movie credit is as a zombie in George A. Romero's *Night of the Living Dead* (1968), died on October 14, aged 91. He was also featured in Jeff Carney's 2009 documentary about the making of the film, *Autopsy of the Dead*.

American TV character actor **John** [Shelton] **Clarke**, who played "Mickey Horton" in the popular NBC soap opera *Days of Our Lives* (1965–2004), died of pneumonia on October 16, aged 88. He also turned up in episodes of *The Twilight Zone*, *Destination Space* and *My Living Doll*, while Clarke's few movie credits include *The Satan Bug* (1965).

American character actor **Bill Macy** (Wolf Martin Garber) died on October 17, aged 97. A former cab driver, he appeared in *Death at Love House* (with John Carradine) and episodes of TV's *Tales from the Darkside* (Michael Kube-McDowell's 'Lifebomb'), *Starman*, *Highway to Heaven*, *Millenium*, *Viper*, *Touched by an Angel* and *The Lone Gunmen*.

American character actor **Victor Mohica** (Victor Manuel Mojica) died the same day, aged 86. On TV he appeared in episodes of *The Six Million Dollar Man*, *The Fantastic Journey*, *The Incredible Hulk* and *Wonder Woman*, as well as turning up as an uncredited ghost in *Dark Shadows* (1969). Mohica was also in the movies *Don't Answer the Phone!*, *The Final Countdown* and *The Ghost Dance*.

Supporting actress **Wendy Williams** (Annette Wendy Rickman Williams) also died on October 17, aged 84. She appeared on British TV in episodes of *Tales of Mystery* (1963), *Jack the Ripper* (1973), *Thriller* (1975), *Doctor Who* ('The Ark of Space'), *Survivors* (1976) and *Leap in the Dark*.

American character actor **Jerry Fogel** (Jerome Samuel Fogel) died of non-Hodgkin's lymphoma on October 21, aged 83. A former radio disc jockey, he was in *Devil Dog: The Hound of Hell* and episodes of TV's *Good Heavens* and *Project U.F.O.*, before retiring at the end of the 1970s to work in local television news.

American character actor **Josip Elic**, who appeared in *Santa Claus Conquers the Martians* under the name "Joe Elic" died of complications from a fall the same day, aged 98. He was also in *The Halloween That Almost Wasn't* (as "Zabaar the Zombie") and two episodes of *The Twilight Zone*.

African-American supporting actor **John Witherspoon** (John Weatherspoon) died of a heart attack on October 29, aged 77. He appeared in *Ratboy*, *Killer Tomatoes Strike Back!*, *The Meteor Man*, *Cosmic Slop*, *Vampire in Brooklyn* and *Little Nicky*. On TV, Witherspoon was in an episode of *The Incredible Hulk*.

60-year-old American tough guy actor **Brian Tarantina**, a semi-regular on the TV show *The Marvelous Mrs. Maisel* (2017–19), died of heart problems on November 2. He had supporting roles in *Jacob's Ladder* and *Ghost Town* (2008) and was featured in episodes of *Now and Again*, *Heroes*, *New Amsterdam* and *Fringe*.

**Christopher Dennis**, who dressed in a Superman costume and posed with tourists along Hollywood Boulevard for more than two decades, was found dead the same day. The 52-year-old, who was the subject of the 2007 documentary *Confessions of a Superhero*, had battled addiction to crystal meth and homelessness in his later years, and his Superman costume had been stolen. He was found lying head-first in a metal bin used for clothing donations near his tent in Van Nuys.

American actress [Cora] **Virgina Leith**, who is best remembered as the disembodied head kept alive by Jason Evers' crazed scientist in *The Brain That Wouldn't Die* (1959/62), died on November 4, aged 94. The former hatcheck girl and model's other credits include episodes of TV's *One Step Beyond* and *The Next Step Beyond*. Her stepdaughter Mary Harron directed *American Psycho* (2000).

American character actor **William** [Richard] **Wintersole**, who played "Mitchell Sherman" on the soap opera *The Young and the*

*Restless* (1986–2011), died of cancer on November 5, aged 88. He was in *Seconds, Sole Survivor, Coma, Once Upon a Spy* (with Christopher Lee) and episodes of TV's *The Outer Limits, The Wild Wild West, The Invaders, Tarzan* (1967), *Star Trek, I Dream of Jeannie, The Immortal, The Sixth Sense, Search, The Next Step Beyond* and *Voyagers!*.

American character actor and dialogue coach **Steven Marlo** (Morris Miller, aka "Steve Marlo"), who portrayed "Karkov" in *Terror in the Wax Museum* (1973), died on November 7, aged 92. He also had small roles in *The Stranger* (1973), *Arnold* and *The Swarm*. On TV, Marlo was in episodes of *Star Trek* ('A Piece of the Action'), *Land of the Giants, Kolchak: The Night Stalker* (1974) and *Future Cop*. He retired from the screen in 1990.

British character actor [George] **Ian Cullen** died on November 12, aged 80. On TV he was in episodes of *The Haunted House* (1960), *Doctor Who* (1964), *Blakes 7* and *Strange But True?*. Cullen also appeared in the films *Children of the Damned, Cruel Passion* (aka *Marquis de Sade's Justine*, which he also scripted), *Hellbreeder, Paladin: Dawn of the Dragon Slayer* and *Shadows of a Stranger*. He voiced "Tollovar" in the two-part 'The Father of Time' story for *Doctor Who Online Adventures* (2013–14).

Italian supporting actor **Luciano Marin** died the same day, aged 87. He appeared in *The Giants of Thessaly, Hercules and the Captive Women, Colossus of the Stone Age, Samson and the Mighty Challenge*, and several other *peplums* of the 1960s.

Irish supporting actor **Niall Toibin** died on November 13, aged 89. He was in *The Sleep of Death* (based on the J. Sheridan Le Fanu story 'The Room in the "Dragon Volant"'), *Lovespell, Miss Morrison's Ghosts, Rawhead Rex* (scripted by Clive Barker) and *Rat*.

British character actor **Nicholas Amer** (Thomas Harold Amer) died on November 17, aged 96. His credits include *Disciple of Death* (with Mike Raven), *The Awakening* (2011, co-scripted by Stephen Volk), *ABCs of Death 2* and Tim Burton's *Miss Peregrine's Home for Peculiar Children*, along with episodes of TV's *Whoops Apocalypse* and *Jonathan Creek* ('Ghost's Forge'). Amer also appeared in the short films *Waiting for Gorgo* (2009) and *Lost Hearts* (2011/18), the latter based on the story by M.R. James.

Idiosyncratic American supporting character actor **Michael J. Pollard** (Michael John Pollack, Jr.), who was nominated for an Oscar for his role in *Bonnie and Clyde* (1967), died of cardiac arrest on November 20, aged 80. The baby-faced actor appeared in *The American Way*, *American Gothic* (1987), *Scrooged*, *Night Visitor* (1989), *Sleepaway Camp III: Teenage Wasteland*, *Heartstopper*, *Dark Angel*, *Dick Tracy* (1990), *The Arrival*, *Split Second* (1992), *Arizona Dream*, *Skeeter* and Rob Zombie's *House of 1,000 Corpses*. On TV Pollard was in episodes of *Alfred Hitchcock Presents*, *Lost in Space*, *Star Trek*, *The Girl from U.N.C.L.E.*, *Superboy* (as "Mr. Mxyzptlk"), *Eerie Indiana*, *The Ray Bradbury Theater*, *Tales from the Crypt* and the 1997 mini-series *The Odyssey* (with Christopher Lee).

American actress **Pamela Lincoln** (Pamela Gill), who co-starred with Vincent Price in William Castle's *The Tingler* (1959), died on November 21, aged 82. Amongst her few other credits was an episode of TV's *One Step Beyond*. Lincoln was married to actor Darryl Hickman from 1959–82.

American actress **Joan Staley** (Joan Lynette McConchie), a 1958 *Playboy* "Playmate of the Month", died of heart failure on November 24, aged 79. She appeared in *Midnight Lace* (1960, uncredited), *Valley of the Dragons* (aka *Prehistoric Valley*) and *The Ghost and Mr. Chicken*, along with episodes of TV's *The Munsters* and *Batman* (as sidekick "Okie Annie"). A horse-riding accident in the early 1970s mostly ended her screen career.

Australian-born polymath, writer, poet, critic, comedian, actor, presenter and raconteur **Clive James** (Vivian Leopold James) CBE, died in England of leukaemia and COPD the same day, aged 80. He had been diagnosed for many years with emphysema. James appeared in the comedy movies *The Adventures of Barry McKenzie* (1972) and *Barry McKenzie Holds His Own* (1974), the latter featuring Donald Pleasence as vampire "Erich Count von Plasma".

American character actor **Claude Earl Jones** (aka "Claude Smith"), who co-starred in Brian Yuzna's H.P. Lovecraft-inspired *Bride of Re-Animator* (1990), died of complications from dementia on November 25, aged 86. His other credits include *She Freak*, *Evilspeak*, *Dark Night of the Scarecrow*, *Impulse*, *Cherry 2000* and *Miracle Mile*. On TV,

Jones was featured in episodes of *Battlestar Galactica* (1978), *The Greatest American Hero*, *Max Headroom*, *Werewolf* and *Quantum Leap*. He retired from the screen in the late 1990s.

35-year-old Taiwanese-Canadian model and leading man **Godfrey Gao** (Tsao Chih-Hsiang) died on November 27 after suffering a heart attack on the set of a reality TV show in China. He appeared in *The Mortal Instruments: City of Bones*, *Legend of the Ancient Sword* and *Shanghai Fortress*.

Seven-foot-tall former professional basketball player turned actor **Tiny Ron** (Ronald Taylor) died of cancer on November 28, 2019. His movie credits include *The Rocketeer* (in make-up inspired by Rondo Hatton), *Camp Fear*, *Alien Nation: Body and Soul*, *Alien Nation: The Enemy Within*, *Six: The Mark Unleashed*, *Sasquatch Mountain* (as the Sasquatch) and *Revamped*. On TV he appeared in episodes of *Star Trek: Voyager* and *Star Trek: Deep Space Nine* (in the recurring role of "Maihar'du", the Hupyrian servant of Ferengi Grand Nagus Zek).

American model turned actress **Doris Merrick**, who co-starred in *The Neanderthal Man* (1953), died on November 30, aged 100. Her other movies include *Heaven Can Wait* (1943) and *Untamed Women*. She retired from the screen in 1955.

American character actress **Shelley Morrison** (Rachel Mitrani), best known for playing the sharp-tongued maid "Rosario Salazar" on the sitcom *Will & Grace* (1999–2006), died of heart failure on December 1, aged 83. She portrayed the sinister housekeeper "Lupe Tekal d'Esperanza" in *Castle of Evil* (1966) and was also in *Devil Times Five* (aka *Peopletoys*), *The Night That Panicked America* and *Conspiracy of Terror*. Morrison's other TV credits include episodes of *The Outer Limits*, *My Favorite Martian* and *Prey*, and she was a regular on *The Flying Nun* (1967–70).

Likeable American leading man **Robert** [Hudson] **Walker, Jr.**, the son of Hollywood actors Robert Walker and Jennifer Jones, died on December 5, aged 79. His career never really lived up to its promise, and his movie credits include such titles as *Eve* (with Christopher Lee), *Beware! The Blob*, *Hex*, *The Spectre of Edgar Allan Poe* (as Poe), *Death in Space*, *Evil Town*, *The Devonsville Terror* (with Donald Pleasence) and *Heaven's War* (aka *Beyond the Darkness*). On TV,

Walker appeared in episodes of *The Unforeseen*, *Golden Showcase* ('The Picture of Dorian Gray', 1961), *Star Trek* ('Charlie X'), *The Time Tunnel*, *The Invaders*, *The Next Step Beyond* and *The Six Million Dollar Man*.

American actress **Natalie Trundy** [Campana], who was married to *Planet of the Apes* producer Arthur P. Jacobs from 1968 until his premature death in 1973 and appeared in the sequels *Beneath the Planet of the Apes*, *Escape from the Planet of the Apes*, *Conquest of the Planet of the Apes* and *Battle for the Planet of the Apes*, died the same day, aged 79. Trundy's TV credits include episodes of *Thriller*, *The Twilight Zone* and *The Alfred Hitchcock Hour*. In later years she volunteered at Mother Theresa's hospice in Kolkata, India.

82-year-old American actor **Ron Leibman**, whose credits include *Slaughterhouse-Five* (1972), died of pneumonia on December 6.

Busy American character actor **René** [Murat] **Auberjonois**, who co-starred as "Odo" in *Star Trek: Deep Space Nine* (1993–99) and directed eight episodes of the TV show, died of metastatic lung cancer on December 8, aged 79. He appeared in *Lilith* (1964), *Images*, *King Kong* (1976), *Eyes of Laura Mars*, *The Wild Wild West Revisited* and *More Wild Wild West*, *My Best Friend Is a Vampire*, *A Connecticut Yankee in King Arthur's Court* (1989, as "Merlin"), *Star Trek VI: The Undiscovered Country*, *Batman Forever* and Disney's *Inspector Gadget*. On TV, Auberjonois appeared in the adaptation of Basil Copper's 'Camera Obscura' on *Night Gallery*, along with episodes of *The Bionic Woman*, *Man from Atlantis*, *Wonder Woman*, *Once Upon a Midnight Scary* (as "Ichabod Crane" in 'The Legend of Sleepy Hollow'), *Beyond Westworld*, *Faerie Tale Theatre*, *Blacke's Magic* ('Wax Poetic' with Vincent Price), *Eerie Indiana*, *The Burning Zone*, *The Outer Limits* (1998), *Poltergeist: The Legacy*, *Stargate SG-1*, *The Secret Adventures of Jules Verne*, *Star Trek: Enterprise*, *Warehouse 13*, *The Librarians* and the 1978 mini-series *The Dark Secret of Harvest Home*, based on the novel by Thomas Tryon. He also contributed voice work to animated TV shows and video games, and narrated numerous audio books.

American puppeteer-actor **Caroll** [Edwin] **Spinney**, who played "Big Bird" and "Oscar the Grouch" for half-a-century in *Sesame Street* and numerous spin-off movies and TV shows (including a 2015 episode of *Supernatural*), died the same day, aged 85. He had suffered from the muscle-contracting illness dystonia for many years.

American actor and producer **Philip** [Anthony] **McKeon**, a former child actor who co-starred in the TV sitcom *Alice* (1976–85), died after a long illness on December 10, aged 55. He appeared in *Return to Horror High*, *976-Evil II*, *Sandman* and *Ghoulies IV*, along with episodes of TV's *Fantasy Island* and *Amazing Stories*.

Italian-American supporting actor **Danny Aiello** (Daniel Louis Aiello, Jr.) died of an infection on December 12, aged 86. He began his acting career at the age of forty, and his credits include Woody Allen's *The Purple Rose of Cairo*, Larry Cohen's *The Stuff*, *Jacob's Ladder* (1990), *Hudson Hawk* and an episode of TV's *Tales of the Darkside*.

Hawaiian-born American character actor **John Fujioka** (aka "John Mamo") died on December 13, aged 93. Often typecast as Japanese or Chinese villains, he was in *Confessions of an Opium Eater* (with Vincent Price), *Tidal Wave* (1973), *Futureworld*, *Steel Dawn*, *Paint It Black*, *Mortal Kombat* (1995) and *Prehysteria! 3*, along with episodes of TV's *Voyage to the Bottom of the Sea*, *Kung Fu* ('The Devil's Champion', 1974*)*, *The Six Million Dollar Man*, *Wonder Woman*, *The Incredible Hulk*, *Buck Rogers in the 25th Century*, *The Greatest American Hero*, *Highway to Heaven*, *The Wizard*, *The Munsters Today*, *Freddy's Nightmares*, *Friday the 13th: The Series* and *The Invisible Man* (2001).

79-year-old Danish-born French actress, model and singer **Anna Karina** (Hanne Karin Bayer), who co-starred in her first husband Jean-Luc Goddard's *Alphaville* (1965), died in Paris on December 14 from complications following surgery for cancer. Her other credits include the 1968 film version of John Fowles' *The Magus*.

British actor **Nicky** [Victor Leslie] **Henson** died of cancer on December 15, aged 74. He appeared in *Witchfinder General* (aka *The Conqueror Worm*, with Vincent Price), *Psychomania* (aka *The Death Wheelers*), *Vampira* (aka *Old Dracula*), the James Bond spoof *No.1 of the Secret Service*, *A Midsummer Night's Dream* (1981), *Star Trap*, *Narcopolis* and *The Holly Kane Experiment*. On TV, Henson was in the 1990 mini-series of Kingsley Amis' *The Green Man* and an episode of *Whoops Apocalypse*. He was married to actress Una Stubbs from 1969–75.

French actress **Claudine Auger** (Claudine Oger), who co-starred as "Domino" alongside Sean Connery's 007 in the 1965 James Bond film *Thunderball*, died after a long illness on December 18, aged 78. The former model's other credits include Jean Cocteau's *Testament of Orpheus*, *Il mistero del tempio indiano*, *The Devil in Love*, *Black Belly of the Tarantula*, Mario Bava's *A Bay of Blood*, *Un papillon sur l'épaule*, *The Bermuda Triangle* (1978) and an episode of TV's *The Memoirs of Sherlock Holmes*. She retired from the screen in 1997.

British singer and entertainer **Kenny Lynch** (Kenneth Lynch) OBE died of prostate cancer the same day, aged 81. His acting roles include a role in the 'Voodoo' sequence of Amicus' *Dr. Terror's House of Horrors* (with Peter Cushing and Christopher Lee, 1965).

British supporting actor **Tony Britton** (Anthony Edward Lowry Britton) died on December 22, aged 95. He appeared in *Night Watch* (1973) and Amicus' *The People That Time Forgot*.

American actress **Sue Lyon** (Suellyn Lyon) died after a long illness on December 26, aged 73. Best known for starring in the title role in Stanley Kubrick's controversial *Lolita* (1962) when just fourteen years old, her other credits include *Arsenic and Old Lace* (1969), *To Love Perhaps to Die*, *Crash!*, *End of the World* (with Christopher Lee), *The Astral Factor* and *Alligator* (1980), which was her final screen credit. On TV Lyon was in episodes of *Rod Serling's Night Gallery* ('Miss Lovecraft Sent Me') and *Fantasy Island*. The second of her five husbands was a prison inmate convicted of murder.

British musician and comedian **Neil** [James] **Innes**, a member of the Bonzo Dog Doo-Dah Band and co-founder of The Rutles, died of a heart attack on December 29, aged 75. Described as the "Seventh Python" by Terry Gilliam, he appeared (uncredited) with The Beatles in *Magical Mystery Tour* (1968) and also turned up in *Monty Python and the Holy Grail*, *Jabberwocky*, *Monty Python's Life of Brian* and *Erik the Viking*. His song 'I'm the Urban Spaceman' was produced by Paul McCartney, and he contributed the whistling to Eric Idle's 'Always Look On the Bright Side of Life'.

Italian actress **Carla Calò** (aka "Carroll Brown"/"Cicely Clayton") died the same day, aged 93. She appeared in *Mystery of the Black Jungle* (aka *Black Devils of Kali*), *Goliath and the Dragon*, *Hercules the Invincible* and *Crypt of Horror* (aka *Terror in the Crypt*, with Christopher Lee).

Scottish-born actress **Elizabeth** [McDonald] **Sellars** died in France on December 30, aged 98. She made her screen debut in a 1947 TV production of *The Tragical History of Doctor Faustus* (with Hugh Griffith as "Mephistophilis"), and her other film credits include *Three Cases of Murder* and Hammer's *The Mummy's Shroud*. On TV, Sellars co-starred in the now-lost 1964–65 SF series *R3* and she was also in episodes of *One Step Beyond*, *The Avengers*, *Shadows of Fear* and *Beasts*. She retired from the screen in 1990.

British nude pin-up model and actress **Marie Devereux** (Patricia Sutcliffe) died the same day, aged 79. She had small roles in *The Woman Eater*, *Grip of the Strangler* (aka *The Haunted Strangler*, with Boris Karloff), Hammer's *The Stranglers of Bombay*, *The Brides of Dracula* (with Peter Cushing) and *The Pirates of Blood River* (with Christpher Lee), *Shock Corridor* and an episode of TV's *The Avengers* before retiring from the screen in 1964.

American character actor **Martin West** (Martin Weixelbaum), who was often cast as police detectives or deputies, died on December 31, aged 82. His credits include Alfred Hitchcock's *Family Plot*, *Hellhole* and *Mac and Me*, and he was in episodes of *The Invaders* and *Highway to Heaven* on TV before retiring from the screen in 1990.

American character actor **Jesse Bennett** died the same day, aged 90. He was in *Beyond Death's Door*, *Hanger 18*, *Earthbound*, *It Nearly Wasn't Christmas* and *Neon City*. On TV, Bennett appeared in episodes of *Teen Angel*, *Touched by an Angel* and the 1994 mini-series of Stephen King's *The Stand*.

## FILM/TV TECHNICIANS

Former professional football player **Wendell E.** (Edward) **Niles, Jr.**, who associate-produced the 1966 movies *Destination Inner Space* and

*Castle of Evil* (both directed by Francis D. Lyon), died of Parkinson's disease on January 2, aged 88.

American scriptwriter and producer **John** [Henry] **Falsey** [Jr.] died on January 3 of complications from a head injury sustained in a fall in his home. He was 67. Amongst the TV shows Falsey helped create was the 1985–87 NBC anthology series *Amazing Stories* (with his writing partner Joshua Brand and Steven Spielberg), inspired by the SF pulp magazine.

American artist **Tony Mendez** (Antonio Joseph Mendez) died of complications from Parkinson's disease on January 19, aged 78. In the mid-1960s he was recruited by the CIA as an "espionage artist". By 1977, Mendez was Chief of the CIA's Office of Technical Services (Disguise Section)—a position similar to "Q" in the James Bond movies. On November 4 that year militants invaded the US Embassy in Iran and took fifty-two American diplomats and citizens hostage. The resulting "Iran hostage crisis" lasted for 444 days, and Mendez was assigned to rescue six diplomats who had escaped to the Canadian embassy. He posed as an Irish film-maker scouting locations for a fictional science fiction movie called *Argo* and, supported by a bogus production office in Hollywood and fake ads and a poster, he successfully extracted the diplomats on January 27, 1980. Mendez was portrayed by Ben Affleck in *Argo*, the 2012 Oscar-winning movie based on the incident.

Hungarian film producer **Andrew G. Vajna** (Andras Gyorgy Vajna), who, with Mario Kassar, founded Carolco in 1975, died on January 20, aged 74. In 1989 he left Carolco and formed Cinergi Productions, Inc. and InterCom. Vajna executive produced such movies as *The Changeling, Superstition* (aka *The Witch*, 1982), *Angel Heart, DeepStar Six, Total Recall* (1990), *Jacob's Ladder, Judge Dredd* (1995), *The 13th Warrior, Terminator 3: Rise of the Machines* and *Terminator: Salvation*, along with the 2008–09 TV series *Terminator: The Sarah Connor Chronicles*. Since 2011, he was the Government Commissioner in charge of the Hungarian film industry.

American TV director **James** [Joseph] **Frawley** died of a heart attack following a fall on January 22, aged 82. He had suffered from a lung condition for many years. Frawley directed episodes of *The*

*Monkees* (including 'Monstrous Monkee Mash'), *Mr. Merlin*, *Wizards and Warriors*, *Wishman*, *Faerie Tale Theatre*, *Father Dowling Mysteries* (including 'The Mummy's Curse Mystery'), *Earth 2*, *American Gothic*, *Smallville* and *Ghost Whisperer*. As an actor, he turned up in episodes of *The Outer Limits*, *Voyage to the Bottom of the Sea*, *The Man from U.N.C.L.E.*, *My Favorite Martian*, *The Monkees*, *American Gothic* and *The Muppet Movie*, which he also directed.

Yugoslavian film-maker **Dušan Makavejev**, whose credits include the experimental *W.R.: Mysteries of the Organism* (1971), died on January 25, aged 86.

American special effects make-up artist and sculptor **Matt Rose** died the same day, aged 53. His credits include *Aliens*, *Invaders from Mars* (1986), *Star Slammer*, *Predator*, *Harry and the Hendersons*, *The Monster Squad*, *Hell Comes to Frogtown*, *Beetlejuice*, *Alien Nation*, *Fright Night Part 2*, *Gremlins 2: The New Batch*, *The Rocketeer*, *Wolf*, *Ed Wood*, *The Nutty Professor* (1996), *Men in Black*, *Batman & Robin*, *Psycho* (1998), *Batman Forever*, *Mighty Joe Young* (1998), *How the Grinch Stole Christmas*, *Planet of the Apes* (2001), *Hellboy* and *Hellboy II: The Golden Army*, *The Cabin in the Woods*, *Men in Black 3*, *The Ring*, *Star Trek Beyond*, *Bright*, *The Predator*, *Daniel Isn't Real*, the 1988 mini-series *Something is Out There* and the TV series *The Dark Crystal: Age of Resistance* (2019).

American movie sound archivist **Ron Hutchinson** died of colon cancer on February 2, aged 67. In 1991 he co-founded The Vitaphone Project to track down lost sixteen-inch synchronised soundtrack discs to silent films, match them to the moving pictures, and create digital copies of the restored motion pictures.

British special effects and animatronics designer **Richard** [James] **Gregory** died on February 7, aged 64. He worked on *Xtro*, *DeepStar Six*, *The NeverEnding Story III*, *Event Horizon*, *Lara Croft Tomb Raider: The Cradle of Life*, *The Dark Knight*, *John Carter* and three James Bond films. On TV, Gregory's credits include *The Lost World* (2001) and Gerry Anderson's *Terrahawks*, *Space Precinct* and the 2015 revival of *Thunderbirds*.

**Ron Miller** (Ronald William Miller), who was President and CEO of the Walt Disney Company in the early 1980s, died on February 9, aged 85. He married Diane Disney, the daughter of Walt, in 1954 and started working for the company in the late 1950s. Miller produced many Disney movies and TV shows, including *Son of Flubber, Escape to Witch Mountain, The Shaggy D.A., Freaky Friday* (1976), *Herbie Goes to Monte Carlo, Pete's Dragon, Return from Witch Mountain, The Cat from Outer Space, The Spaceman and King Arthur* (aka *Unidentified Flying Oddball*), *The Black Hole, The Watcher in the Woods* (1980), *Herbie Goes Bananas, The Devil and Max Devlin, Condorman, TRON, The Black Cauldron* and *Basil the Great Mouse Detective*. Miller was ousted by Roy E. Disney and other shareholders in the mid-1980s.

Sunglasses-wearing German fashion designer **Karl** [Otto] **Lagerfeld** died in France of pancreatic cancer on February 19, aged 85. His first work in the film industry was as star Janine Reynaud's costume designer for Jesús Franco's *Succubus* (1968).

American film director and producer **Stanley Donen**, best known for such classic musicals as *On the Town* and *Singin' in the Rain*, died of a heart attack on February 21, aged 94. The former choreographer's other credits include *Damn Yankees* (1958), *Bedazzled* (1967), *The Little Prince* and *Saturn 3*. The fourth of his five wives (1972–85) was actress Yvette Mimieux.

**Jay Douglas** who, as Senior Vice-President of Acquisition at Anchor Bay Entertainment in the 1990s turned the home video distributor into the "Criterion Collection for cult films", died on February 26, aged 65. Following his stint at Anchor Bay, Douglas worked with Blue Underground and headed up the film divison at Ryko Distribution.

American studio executive **Sid Sheinberg** (Sidney Jay Sheinberg), credited with turning Hollywood into a blockbuster-focused industry, died on March 7, aged 84. While studio chief at Universal Studios he discovered Steven Spielberg and helped get such movies as *Jaws* and *Back to the Future* off the ground. Under Sheinberg's watch, Universal turned out such hits as *E.T. the Extra-Terrestrial* and *Jurassic Park*, and the box-office flops like *Legend* and *Waterworld*. He also famously fought with Terry Gilliam over the final cut of *Brazil*. In later years Sheinberg produced *The Devil's Tomb* and

*Creature* (2011). He was married to actress Lorraine Gary, who starred as "Ellen Brody" in the *Jaws* series.

American production designer and art director **William C. Creber** died of complications from pneumonia the same day, aged 87. He worked on *Three in the Attic, Planet of the Apes, Beneath the Planet of the Apes, Escape from the Planet of the Apes, The Poseidon Adventure, The Towering Inferno, Mannequin: On the Move, Street Fighter* and episodes of TV's *Voyage to the Bottom of the Sea, Lost in Space* and *The Time Tunnel*. Creber was also production designer and second-unit director on *Flight of the Navigator* (1986).

American script supervisor **Edele Bakke** died on March 10, aged 91. Her credits include Disney's *Escape to Witch Mountain, TRON* and *Something Wicked This Way Comes*.

**George M.** (Milroy) **Lehr**, an associate producer on such TV series as *The Man from U.N.C.L.E.* (1966–68) and *The Girl from U.N.C.L.E.* (1966–67), died on March 14, aged 87. Lehr helped create the shows' "whip pan" transition effect between scenes, and it was also his silhouette seen firing a gun at Robert Vaughn's "Napoleon Solo" in the main title sequence for the first season of *The Man from U.N.C.L.E.*

1970s SF fan **Norm Hollyn** (Norman Hochberg) died of cardiac arrest in Japan on March 17, aged 66. As a film and music editor he worked on *Amityville II: The Possession, Dead of Winter, Meet the Applegates, Quicksilver Highway, Under Wraps, Jack in the Box* and the TV mini-series *Wild Palms*.

American low-budget special effects supervisor, make-up effects creator and film director **John Carl Buechler**, the Paul Blaisdell of his generation, died of prostate cancer on March 18, aged 66. Best known for his long association with Charles Band's Empire Pictures, Buechler was once described by Roger Corman as "the best in the business". He began his career as a make-up artist in the late 1970s, and his numerous (often direct-to-video) credits include *Dr. Heckyl and Mr. Hype, Sorceress, Android, Forbidden World, The Prey, Mausoleum, Deathstalker, Trancers, Ghoulies, Hard Rock Zombies, Re-Animator, Zone Troopers, Fright Show* ('The Thing in the Basement'), *Eliminators, TerrorVision, Crawlspace, From Beyond, Vicious Lips, Dolls, The Caller, Ghoulies II, Slave Girls from Beyond*

*Infinity, Prison, Demonwarp, Ghost Town, A Nightmare on Elm Street 4: The Dream Master, Halloween 4: The Return of Michael Myers, Spellcaster, Pulse Pounders, Arena, Robot Jox, Indiana Jones and the Last Crusade, The Phantom of the Opera* (1989), *Bride of Re-Animator, The Sleeping Car, Ghoulies Go to College, The Laughing Dead, Son of Darkness: To Die For II, Freddy's Dead: The Final Nightmare, Demonic Toys, Seedpeople, Carnosaur, Necronomicon: Book of the Dead, Scanner Cop, Dinosaur Island, Cyborg 3: The Recycler, Biohazard: The Alien Force, Tammy and the T-Rex, The Fear, Project: Metalbeast, Scanner Cop II, Halloween: The Curse of Michael Myers, Piranha* (1995), *Circuit Breaker, Carnosaur 3: Primal Species, Alien Escape, Casper Meets Wendy, The Fear: Resurrection* (aka *The Fear: Halloween Night), Krocodylus* (aka *Blood Surf), Dark Wolf, The Mummy's Kiss, Dr. Moreau's House of Pain, Tomb of the Werewolf, Countess Dracula's Orgy of Blood, Out for Blood, Mortuary* (2005), *The Gingerdead Man, Hatchet, Gingerdead Man 2: Passion of the Crust, Neowolf* (aka *The Band from Hell), Monsterpiece Theatre Volume 1* ('The Weed'), *Bunker of Blood Chapter 6: Zombie Lust: Night Flesh* and *Bunker of Blood: Chapter 8: Butcher's Bake Off: Hell's Kitchen.* Buechler directed (and sometimes also scripted) *The Dungeonmaster* ('Demons of the Dead' sequence), *Troll, Cellar Dweller, Friday the 13th Part VII: New Blood, Ghoulies Go to College, Watchers 4, Deep Freeze, Curse of the Forty-Niner, A Light in the Forest, Saurian, The Eden Formula, The Strange Case of Dr. Jekyll and Mr. Hyde* (2006), *Wizardream* and three episodes of the 1991 TV series *Land of the Lost.* He also acted in a number of the movies he worked on.

Maverick American screenwriter, producer and director **Larry Cohen** died of cancer on March 23, aged 82. His credits include *It's Alive, God Told Me To, It Lives Again, Full Moon High, Q* (aka *Q—The Winged Serpent), Special Effects, The Stuff, It's Alive III: Island of the Alive, A Return to Salem's Lot, Wicked Stepmother, The Ambulance* and an episode of TV's *Masters of Horror* ('Pick Me Up', based on a story by David J. Schow). Aditionally, Cohen scripted *Daddy's Gone A-Hunting, Scream Baby Scream* (as "Laurence Robert Cohen"), *Maniac Cop, Maniac Cop 2, Maniac Cop 3: Badge of Silence, Body*

*Snatchers, Uncle Sam* and *Captivity*, along with an episode of *Way Out* ('False Face' featuring Dick Smith's memorable "Quasimodo" make-up). Cohen also created the 1967–68 TV series *The Invaders* and co-wrote the 1995 mini-series.

**Michael Lynne**, a former entertainment attorney who co-ran New Line Cinema with Robert Shaye, died on March 24, aged 77. He executive produced Peter Jackson's *Lord of the Rings* trilogy, *The Golden Compass*, *A Nightmare on Elm Street* (2010), *The Mortal Instruments: City of Bones, Haunting on Fraternity Row, Ambition* and the 2016–19 TV series *Shadowhunters*, based on the book series by Cassandra Clare.

American real esatate developer, tennis professional and film producer **Ronald S.** (Sanders) **Dunas** died on March 29, aged 92. His small number of credits include *The Abominable Dr. Phibes* (1971, starring Vincent Price) and *Naked Fear*. Dunas also had a cameo in that film and (uncredited) in *Seconds* (1966). His first wife was actress Joyce Jameson.

Hollywood executive **David V.** (Victor) **Picker** died of colon cancer on April 20, aged 87. While head of marketing and production at United Artists, he helped secure a deal with Harry Saltzman and Albert Broccoli for the rights to the James Bond franchise. Picker subsequently worked in top jobs at Paramount, Columbia, Lorimar and Hallmark, and he produced or executive produced *The Man with Two Brains, Back to the Secret Garden, Hans Christian Andersen: My Life as a Fairy Tale* and the TV mini-series *Journey to the Center of the Earth* (1999) and *Aftershock: Earthquake in New York*.

American film producer **Steve Golin** (Steven Aaron Golin), the former co-founder and chairman of Propaganda Films, died of Ewing sarcoma on April 21, aged 64. The Oscar-winner's credits include *Hard Rock Zombies, Candyman* (1992), Clive Barker's *Lord of Illusions, Being John Malkovich, Eternal Sunshine of the Spotless Mind, Seeking a Friend for the End of the World, Comet* and the TV series *True Detective* and *The Alienist* (aka *The Alienist: Angel of Darkness*).

British-born actor, dancer, singer, choreographer, screenwriter, producer and director **David Winters** (David Weizer) died in Florida on April 23, aged 80. Best known for his role as "A-rab" in the musical

*West Side Story* (1961), he appeared in *The Last Horror Film* (which he also wrote and directed) and episodes of TV's *Atom Squad* and *Out of the Unknown*. Winters scripted (as "Maria Danté") and co-directed *Space Mutinity* (1988) and directed the 1973 musical version of *Dr. Jekyll and Mr. Hyde* (starring Kirk Douglas), *Alice Cooper: Welcome to My Nightmare* (with Vincent Price) and an episode of *The Monkees* ('A Coffin Too Frequent'). He also worked in various production capacities on *Pajama Party*, *The Island of Dr. Moreau* (1977), *Deadly Prey*, *Death Chase*, *Night Wars*, *Phoenix the Warrior*, *Deadly Reactor*, *Time Burst: The Final Alliance*, *Future Force*, *The Lost Platoon*, *Future Zone*, *The Final Sanction*, *Firehead*, *Raw Nerve*, *Night Trap*, *Devil's Harvest* and the infamous *Star Wars Holiday Special*.

British film editor **Terry Rawlings** (Terence Rawlings) died of heart failure the same day, aged 85. He worked on *Doctor Blood's Coffin*, *Licensed to Kill* (aka *The 2nd Best Secret Agent in the Whole Wide World*), *Where the Bullets Fly*, *Bedazzled* (1967), *The Devils*, *The Nightcomers*, *Lisztomania*, *The Sentinel*, *Watership Down* (1978), *Alien*, *The Awakening*, *Blade Runner*, *Legend*, *F/X*, *White of the Eye*, *Slipstream*, *Alien³*, *GoldenEye*, *The Core* and the 2004 version of *The Phantom of the Opera*.

Argentinean-born British director **John Llewellyn Moxey** died of complications from cancer in Washington State on April 29, aged 94. The prolific film and TV director's credits include *The City of the Dead* (aka *Horror Hotel*) and *Circus of Fear* (aka *Psycho-Circus*), both with Christopher Lee, along with the TV movies *The House That Would Not Die*, *Escape* (1971), *The Last Child*, *A Taste of Evil*, *The Night Stalker* (1971), *Home for the Holidays*, *Genesis II*, *The Strange and Deadly Occurrence*, *Where Have All the People Gone*, *Conspiracy of Terror*, *The Power Within*, *No Place to Hide*, *I Desire*, *The Cradle Will Fall* and *When Dreams Come True*, and episodes of *The Avengers*, *The Champions*, *Circle of Fear* and *Murder She Wrote* (including 'Fire Burn, Cauldron Bubble'). He retired in the early 1990s.

American talent agent and film producer **George Litto** died of complications from aortic stenosis the same day, aged 88. He co-produced client Brian De Palma's thrillers *Obsession*, *Dressed to Kill* and *Blow Out*. Litto also "packaged" such movies as *Planet of the Apes* (1968) and De Palma's *Sisters*.

American movie producer and music executive **Stephen I. Diener** died on April 30, aged 80. As Chairman/CEO of Heron Communications, he was an executive producer on *A Nightmare on Elm Street 2: Freddy's Revenge*, *A Nightmare on Elm Street 3: Dream Warriors*, *A Nightmare on Elm Street 4: The Dream Master* and *The Hidden*.

Tony Award-winning Broadway producer **Terry Allen Kramer**, whose 1981 theatrical presentation of *Frankenstein* (with John Carradine) opened and closed the same day, died of pneumonia on May 2, aged 85. Her other stage productions included *Gorey Stories*, *The Addams Family*, *Finding Neverland* and the troubled *Spider-Man: Turn off the Dark*.

Uruguay-born Spanish scriptwriter, producer, director and actor **Narciso [Estaban] Ibáñez Serrador** (aka "Luis Peñafiel") died on June 7, aged 83. Best known for the cult horror movies *The House That Screamed* and *Island of Death* (aka *Who Can Kill a Child?*), he also scripted Edgar Allan Poe's *Ligeia* (1959), *Berenice* and *Masterworks of Terror* (aka *Master of Horror*), while *Viaje directo al infierno* and *El hombre que volvió de la muerte* were based on his original stories. Serrador also created the TV horror anthology series *Historias para no dormir* (1966–68 and 1982) and wrote the 1961 mini-series *The Phantom of the Opera* (starring his father, actor Narciso Ibáñez Menta as "Eric") along with episodes of *Teatro de misterio*, *Mis terrores favoritos* and *La figura de cera*.

Italian stage and film director **Franco Zeffirelli** (Gian Franco Corsi Zeffirelli) died on June 15, aged 96. His credits include movie adaptations of *Hamlet* (1990) and *Jane Eyre* (1996).

American TV producer **Alan Cassidy** died on June 19, aged 76. He was an associate producer (1979–81) on CBS' *The Incredible Hulk*, and he also scripted one episode.

Polish-born producer **Ben Barenholtz** died in the Czech Republic on June 26, aged 83. He began producing films with George A. Romero's *Martin*, and also made cameo appearances in *Dawn of the Dead* and *Liquid Sky*. However, he is best rembered for running the

Elgin Theater, a repertory and art-film cinema in Manhattan's Chelsea neighborhood, in the late 1970s, where he pioneered a midnight screening of Alejandro Jodorowsky's *El Topo*. It was soon a huge hit with younger audiences, and other New York movie theatres quickly began holding their own midnight screenings—notably the Waverly in Greenwich Village, which revived Romero's *Night of the Living Dead* at midnight screenings in 1971 and opened *The Rocky Horror Picture Show* five years later. While running Libra Films in 1977, Barenholtz also agreed to release David Lynch's debut movie, *Eraserhead*.

Polish-born film producer **Artur Brauner** (Abraham Brauner) died in Germany after a short illness on July 7, aged 100. He founded the hugely successful CCC (Central Cinema Compagnie) in 1949, and his many titles as a producer and/or writer (as "Art Bernd") include *The Witch Beneath the Sea*, Fritz Lang's *Tiger of Bengal* and *The Indian Tomb*, *Mistress of the World*, Lang's *The 1,000 Eyes of Dr. Mabuse* (1960), *The Return of Dr. Mabuse*, *The Invisible Dr. Mabuse*, *The Terror of Dr. Mabuse*, *The Brain* (based on *Donovan's Brain* by Curt Siodmak), *Sherlock Holmes and the Deadly Necklace* (with Christopher Lee), *The Strangler of Blackmoor Castle*, *Dr, Mabuse vs. Scotland Yard*, *The Mad Executioners*, *The Phantom of Soho*, *The Death Ray of Dr. Mabuse*, *Frozen Alive*, *Die Nibelungen, Teil 1—Siegfried* and *Die Nibelungen 2. Teil—Kriemhilds Rache*, *The Unnaturals*, *De Sade* (1969), Dario Argento's *The Bird with the Crystal Plumage*, Jess Franco's *The Devil Came from Akasava*, *Las Vampiras*, *She Killed in Ecstasy* and *Dr. M schlägt zu*, *The Dead Are Alive!* and the depressing comedy re-mix of Lang's 1960 movie, *Die 1000 Glotzböbbel vom Dr. Mabuse* (2018). Brauner received Germany's National Medal of Honour and a Lifetime Achievement Award from the German Film Academy.

American evangelical Christian film producer, screenwriter and director **Donald W.** (Whitney) **Thompson** (aka "Jim Grant") died on July 17, aged 71. His credits include such low budget Rapture- or Second Coming-themed titles as *A Thief in the Night*, *The Enemy*, *A Distant Thunder*, *Image of the Beast* and *The Prodigal Planet*.

44-year-old special effects co-ordinator **Warren Appleby** was killed in Toronto, Canada, on July 18 when a stunt involving a car on the DC Universe series *Titans* went wrong and a piece of the vehicle unexpectedly broke off and struck him. Appleby's numerous credits include *Crash, Universal Soldier II: Brothers in Arms, Universal Soldier III: Unfinished Business, eXistenZ, Resurrection, Bless the Child, The Pretender 2001, Wrong Turn, Anonymous Rex, Dead Silence, Saw IV, Repo Men, Devil, The Thing* (2011), *Mama, Carrie* (2013), *Pay the Ghost, The Shape of Water, IT* (2017), *How It Ends* and *IT Chapter Two*, the Stephen King mini-series *Storm of the Century* and *11.22.63*, plus such TV series as *RoboCop, F/X: The Series, Odyssey 5, Hemlock Grove, Killjoys* and *The Strain*.

47-year-old Japanese *anime* director **Yasuhiro Takemoto** was killed, along with more than thirty of his friends and colleagues, in an arsonist attack on Kyoto Animation ("KyoAni") the same day. Shinji Aoba, aged 41, was indicted for the crime after he accused the studio of stealing his novels. Takemoto's credits include episodes of such TV series as *Gate Keepers, The Daichis: Earth's Defense Family, The SoulTaker, Tokyo Underground* and *Kobayashi-san Chi No Maid Dragon*.

Hollywood producer **Edward Lewis**, who helped break the Blacklist by hiring Dalton Trumbo on *Spartacus* (1960), died on July 27, aged 99. His other credits include *Seven Days in May, Seconds, Rhinoceros* and *The Blue Bird* (1976).

American TV production designer and set decorator **Sy** (Seymour) **Tomashoff** died on July 28, aged 96. He worked on 1,255 episodes of ABC's daytime Gothic soap opera *Dark Shadows* (1966–71) and was an associate producer for the show's final year.

American script and continuity supervisor **Cosmo Genovese**, who worked on TV's *Star Trek: The Next Generation, Star Trek: Deep Space Nine* and *Star Trek: Voyager*, died on July 30, aged 95. He was also a script supervisor on episodes of *Tales from the Crypt* and the spin-off movie *Tales from the Crypt: Demon Knight*.

Multiple Tony Award-winning American theatrical producer and director **Harold Prince** (Harold Smith) died in Iceland on July 31, aged 91. He staged the original theatrical productions of *Damn Yankees* (1955), *It's a Bird...It's a Plane...It's Superman* (1966),

*Sweeney Todd* (1979) and *The Phantom of the Opera* (1988). Prince also directed the 1982 TV version of *Sweeney Todd: The Demon Barber of Fleet Street* starring Angela Lansbury and George Hearn.

American voice director, actor and casting director **Stu Rosen** (Stuart Martin Rosen) died of cancer on August 4, aged 80. He worked on such cartoon TV shows as *MASK*, *Defenders of the Earth*, *Little Dracula*, *Attack of the Killer Tomatoes*, *The Legend of Prince Valiant* and *Phantom 2040*.

Italian costume designer **Piero Tosi** died on August 10, aged 92. His credits include *The Witches* (1967), *Matchless*, *Ghosts Italian Style* and Federico Fellini's "Tony Dammit" segment of *Spirits of the Dead*, which he also production-designed.

Canadian-born animation director **Richard** [Edmund] **Williams** died in Bristol, England, on August 16, aged 86. His credits include the Oscar-winning short *A Christmas Carol* (1971), *Who Framed Roger Rabbit* (for which he won two Academy Awards) and the long-delayed *The Thief and the Cobbler* (aka *Arabian Knight*, featuring the voice of Vincent Price). Williams also designed the animated title sequences for *Casino Royale* (1967), *Gawain and the Green Knight* and *The Pink Panther Strikes Again*.

Welsh TV producer and director **James Cellan Jones** (Alan James Gwyn Cellan Jones) died on August 30, aged 88. He worked on the 1966 BBC serial *The Hunchback of Notre Dame* (with Peter Woodthorpe as "Quasimodo"), *Dr. Watson and the Darkwater Hall Mystery*, *A Midsummer Night's Dream* (1971) and an episode of *Out of the Unknown* (Clifford D. Simak's 'Beach Head').

**Patricia Blau** [Price], who started as a receptionist in the late 1970s at Industrial Light & Magic and worked her way up to the newly-created position of ILM's vice-president of feature production in 1997, died of complications from Alzheimer's disease on September 17, aged 64. Amongst the many movies she worked on as a production co-ordinator, or in other capacities, were *Star Wars: The Empire Strikes Back*, *Raiders of the Lost Ark*, *Star Wars: Return of the Jedi*, *The NeverEnding Story*, *Indiana Jones and the Temple of Doom*, *Starman*, *Goonies*, *\*batteries not included*, *Willow*, *Indiana Jones and the Last Crusade*, *Back to the Future Part III*, *The Rocketeer*, *Death*

*Becomes Her, Jurassic Park, Meteor Man, The Nutcracker, Wolf, The Mask, Star Trek: Generations, In the Mouth of Madness, Congo, The Indian in the Cupboard, Jumanji, Star Trek: First Contact, 101 Dalmations* (1996), *The Lost World: Jurassic Park, Men in Black, Starship Troopers, Deep Rising, Planet of the Apes* (2001) and *Minority Report*. Blau retired in 2003 to concentrate on her career as a painter and sculptor.

British TV director **Diarmuid** [Seton] **Lawrence** died on September 20, aged 71. His credits include the six-part *The Witches and the Grinnygog, The Mystery of Edwin Drood* (2012) and *Peter and Wendy*, along with two episodes of *Sea of Souls*.

Emmy Award-winning American animation producer **J.** (Joel) **Michael Mendel** died on September 22, aged 54. After starting out as a production assistant in movies (including *Big*), he went on to produce TV's *The Simpsons, Solar Opposites* and *Rick and Morty*.

British TV producer and story editor **Irene Shubik**, who co-produced the first two series of the BBC SF anthology show *Out of the Unknown* (1965–67), died of dementia on September 26, aged 89. She was also the story editor on the 1962 series *Out of This World* (hosted by Boris Karloff) and worked on *BBC2 Playhouse* (1973–76), which included half-a-dozen dramas ('The Mind Beyond') about the paranormal.

American title sequence designer **Wayne** [Richard] **Fitzgerald** died after a long illness on September 30, aged 89. He worked on many movies, including *The Fly* (both 1958 and 1986 versions), *Midnight Lace* (1960), *Homicidal, The Unknown* (1964), *The Silencers, Incubus, Murderers' Row, Wait Until Dark, The Ambushers, Rosemary's Baby, The Wrecking Crew, Eye of the Cat* (aka *13*), *On a Clear Day You Can See Forever, Hauser's Memory, Lost Horizon* (1973), *The Return of Charlie Chan, The Six Million Dollar Man: Wine Women and War, The Six Million Dollar Man: The Solid Gold Kidnapping, The Day of the Dolphin, Escape to Witch Mountain, Murder by Death, The Seven-Per-Cent Solution, Heaven Can Wait* (1978), *Battlestar Galactica, The Lord of the Rings* (1978), *Buck Rogers in the 25th Century, Apocalypse Now, The Muppet Movie, The Nude Bomb, Wolfen, Blue Thunder, The Dead Zone, Splash, Firestarter, The*

*Adventures of Buckaroo Banzai Across the 8th Dimension, Cavegirl, Real Genius, Creator, Short Circuit, Perry Mason: The Case of the Sinister Spirit, Innerspace, Pulse, The Milagro Beanfield War, My Stepmother is an Alien, The Punisher* (1989), *Class of 1999, Total Recall* (1990), *Dick Tracy* (1990), *Ghost, Child's Play 2, Child's Play 3, Groundhog Day, Blankman, Tall Tale, Judge Dredd* (1995), *The Indian in the Cupboard, Waterworld, Dracula: Dead and Loving It, Diabolique* (1996) and *RocketMan*, along with such TV series as *The Invaders, Rod Serling's Night Gallery, The Snoop Sisters, Tucker's Witch, Automan* and *Sabrina the Teenage Witch*.

American animator **Alan** [Louis] **Zaslove** died on October 2, aged 91. His many credits include *The Incredible Mr. Limpet, A Charlie Brown Christmas, The Phantom Tollbooth, Gnomes, The Return of Jafar* and episodes of TV's *The 13 Ghosts of Scooby-Doo, The Jetsons, Challenge of the GoBots, Darkwing Duck* and *Aladdin*.

Oscar-nominated American art director and production designer **John W.** (William) **Corso** died on October 9, aged 89. He worked on *Exo-Man, Xanadu, Heartbeeps, Psycho II, Weird Science* and the 1981 TV series *Darkroom*.

Austrian-born American music editor and movie producer **Igo Kantor** died in Los Angeles on October 15, aged 89. He was a producer on *Kingdom of the Spiders, The Dark* (1979) and *Mutant* (1984). As head of post-production house Synchrofilm, Inc., Kantor was the music editor for *The Human Duplicators, Faster Pussycat Kill! Kill!, Women of the Prehistoric Planet, The Navy vs. the Night Monsters, Dimension 5, Cyborg 2087, The Bubble, Hillbillys in a Haunted House, Head, 2000 Years Later, Nightmare in Wax, The Monitors* and *Hammersmith is Out*. He was also the technical advisor on Edward D. Wood, Jr's infamous *Bride of the Monster* (starring Bela Lugosi), sound editor on *Serpent Island* (1954), music co-ordinator for NBC's *The Monkees* (1966–68), and music supervisor for the *Tarzan* (1967–68) and *Battle of the Planets* (1978–79) TV series.

Legendary American studio executive **Robert Evans** (Robert J. Shapera) died on October 26, aged 89. A self-confessed "half-assed actor" (he played studio head Irving Thalberg in the 1957 Lon Chaney biopic *Man of a Thousand Faces*), he became head of production at Paramount, where he was responsible for such movies as *Rosemary's Baby*, *Popeye*, *Sliver*, *The Phantom* and, most notably, Roman Polanski's *Chinatown*. His seven wives included actresses Camilla Sparv, Ali MacGraw and Catherine Oxenberg (which lasted ten days). Evans' autobiography, *The Kid Stays in the Picture*, was published in 1994.

British film producer **Nik Powell** OBE died of cancer on November 7, aged 69. His films include *The Company of Wolves*, *Dream Demon*, *High Spirits*, *Hardware*, *Dust Devil*, *Christmas Carol: The Movie* and *The Facility*. In the 1970s Powell was the co-founder, along with Richard Branson, of Virgin Records, before teaming up with Stephen Woolley in the early 1980s to create Palace Pictures, which distributed *The Evil Dead* (1981) in the UK. His second wife (1982–95) was singer Sandie Shaw.

American production designer and art director **Lawrence G. Paull**, who was nominated for an Oscar for his work on *Blade Runner* (1982), died of heart disease on November 10, aged 81. He also worked on *She Waits*, *Sherlock Holmes in New York*, *Back to the Future*, *Project X*, *Cocoon: The Return*, *Predator 2*, *Memoirs of an Invisible Man* and *Escape from L.A.*

American film and TV producer and director **Arthur** [Ronald] **Marks**, who ran exploitation distributor General Film Corp. in the 1970s, died on November 13, aged 92. A former child actor, he produced and directed the blaxploitation horror *J.D.'s Revenge* (1976), and he was an uncredited director on *Solar Crisis* (1990). Marks also worked as an assistant director on *Jungle Jim* (1948), *King of the Congo* and *Jungle Man-Eaters*, and he was executive in charge of production on *Wonder Women* (1973).

British polymath, writer, satirist, director, broadcaster and actor Sir **Jonathan** [Wolfe] **Miller**, died of Alzheimer's disease on November 27, aged 85. He is best known in our genre for writing, producing and directing revisionist TV versions of Lewis Carroll's *Alice in Wonderland* (1966), and M.R. James' 'Whistle and I'll Come to You' (1968) for the BBC's *Omnibus* series.

Veteran American special visual effects creator **Gene Warren, Jr.** died on November 28, aged 78. In 1992 he shared an Oscar for Best

Visual Effects for *Terminator 2: Judgment Day*, almost exactly thirty-one years after his father won the same award for his work on *The Time Machine* (1960). Warren, Jr.'s many other credits (often under the name of his company, "Fantasy II Film Effects") include *Spacehunter: Adventures in the Forbidden Zone*, *The Terminator*, *The Return of the Living Dead*, *The Fantasy Film Worlds of George Pal*, *Eliminators*, *Critters*, *Nightflyers*, *Bad Dreams*, *Lady in White*, *Killer Klowns from Outer Space*, *Fright Night Part 2*, *From the Dead of Night*, *Cyborg*, *Pet Sematary* (1989), *The Abyss*, *Tremors*, *Roger Corman's Frankenstein Unbound*, *It* (1990), *Captain America* (1990), *Danger Island* (aka *The Presence*), *Dr. Giggles*, *Bram Stoker's Dracula* (1992), *Nemesis*, *Freaked*, *Last Action Hero*, *My Boyfriend's Back*, *Attack of the 50 Ft. Woman* (1993), *The Shadow* (1994), *Roswell*, *Witch Hunt*, *Johnny Mnemonic*, *Magic in the Water*, *Lord of Illusions*, *Strange Days*, *The Beast*, *The Crow: City of Angels*, *The Cold Equations*, *Snow White: A Tale of Terror*, *House of Frankenstein* (1997), *Mr. Murder*, *Y2K*, *Scream 3*, *The 6th Day*, *The Mothman Prophecies*, *Vampires: Los Muertos*, *The Core*, *Underworld*, *The Punisher* (2004), *Underworld: Evolution*, *Underworld: Rise of the Lycans* and the TV series *Land of the Lost* (1974–76).

Scottish-born TV script and story editor **Donald** [Hugh] **Tosh** died on December 3, aged 84. He worked for the BBC on *Doctor Who* (1965–66) and the 1968 *Sherlock Holmes* series starring Peter Cushing.

Spanish director and screenwriter **Javier Aguirre** [Fernández] died after a long illness on December 4, aged 84. He directed Paul Naschy in *Hunchback of the Morgue* (1973) and *Count Dracula's Great Love* (1973), and Aguirre's other credits include *The Killer Is One of 13* (1973).

85-year-old American TV and movie executive **Leonard Goldberg** died the same day from injuries sustained in a fall. As Head of Programming for ABC he is credited for creating and developing the made-for-TV-movie, and he also served as President of Twentieth Century-Fox. Goldberg's credits include *Home for the Holidays*, *A Cold Night's Death*, *Satan's School for Girls* (1973), *Death Cruise*, *Death at Love House*, *This House Possessed*, *Fantasies*, *Deadly Lessons* (aka

*Highschool Killer*), *WarGames* and *SpaceCamp*. He also executive-produced (often in partnership with Aaron Spelling) such successful TV series as *S.W.A.T.*, *Starsky and Hutch*, *Charlie's Angels*, *Fantasy Island*, *Hart to Hart* and *T.J. Hooker*.

British academic, screenwriter and director **Peter Wollen** died of Alzheimer's Disease on December 17, aged 81. A film theorist, historian and former Professor of Film and Television at UCLA, he scripted and directed the political 1987 SF movie *Friendship's Death*, which starred Tilda Swinton as an alien android. Wollen also wrote the influential 1969 film-theory study *Signs and Meaning in the Cinema*, and in 2002 he collected some of his film essays in *Paris Hollywood: Writings on Film*.

Hollywood producer **David Foster**, who started out as Steve McQueen's publicist, died on December 23, aged 90. He produced or excutive produced *The Legacy*, *Caveman*, John Carpenter's *The Thing*, *Short Circuit* and *Short Circuit 2*, *The Core*, *The Fog* (2005) and the 2011 prequel *The Thing*.

Emmy Award-winning American scriptwriter, producer and director **Lee** [Maurice] **Mendelson**, best known for his many animated "Charlie Brown" and "Garfield" TV specials, died of lung cancer on Christmas Day, aged 86.

# USEFUL ADDRESSES

THE FOLLOWING LISTING of organisations, publications, dealers and individuals is designed to present readers and authors with further avenues to explore. Although I can personally recommend many of those listed on the following pages, neither the publisher nor myself can take any responsibility for the services they offer. Please also note that the information below is only a guide and is subject to change without notice.

—The Editor

## ORGANISATIONS

Australasian Horror Writers Association (*www.australasianhorror. wordpress.com*) is a non-profit organisation that was formed in 2005 and provides a community and unified voice for Australasian writers of dark fiction, fostering the evolution of the genre within Australia. AHWA is the first point of reference for writers and fans of the dark side of literature in Australia, New Zealand, and the Pacific Islands. It spreads the acceptance and understanding of horror literature to a wider audience, and in doing so gains a greater readership for established and new writers alike. They also publish the magazine

*Midnight Echo*, and offer opportunities to be published, mentor programmes, critique services, competitions and giveaways, opportunities to interact with other writers, publishers, artists and other key members of the community, genre news on the Australian scene, and links to horror-related and writing resources. E-mail: *australasianhorror@gmail.com*

**The British Fantasy Society** (*www.britishfantasysociety.org*) was founded in 1971 and publishes the *BFS Journal*, featuring articles and reviews, and *BFS Horizons*, which is devoted to fiction and poetry, along with occasional exclusive publications only available to members of the Society. Run by volunteers, the BFS offers an e-newsletter, free entry into the BFS Short Story Competition, free specialist writing workshops, discounted membership of FantasyCon and organised open nights and book launches. For yearly membership see the website for details.

**The Horror Writers Association** (*www.horror.org*) is a non-profit organisation of writers and publishing professionals around the world, dedicated to promoting dark literature and the interests of those who write it. HWA was formed in the late 1980s and today has more than 1,250 members—making it the oldest and most respected professional organisation for horror writers. One of HWA's missions is to encourage public interest in and foster an appreciation of good horror and dark Fantasy literature. To that end, they offer the public areas of their website, they sponsor or take part in occasional public readings and lectures, they publish a blog and produce other materials for book-sellers and librarians, they facilitate readings and signings by horror writers, and they are dedicated to recognising and promoting diversity in the horror genre. As part of the organisation's core mission, they also sponsor the annual Bram Stoker Awards® for superior achievement in horror literature at the annual StokerCon. E-mail: *hwa@horror.org*

## SELECTED SMALL PRESS PUBLISHERS

**The Alchemy Press** (*www.alchemypress.co.uk*).

**American Fantasy Press** (*www.americanfantasypress.com*), 919 Tappan Street, Woodstock, Illinois 60098, USA.

**BearManor Media** (*www.bearmanormedia.com*), PO Box 1129, Duncan, OK 73534-1129, USA.

**Black Dog Books** (*www.blacksdogs.net*), 1115 Pine Meadows Ct., Normal, IL 61761-5432, USA. E-mail: *info@blackdogbooks.net*

**Black Shuck Books** (*www.blackshuckbooks.co.uk*), "Hillbrow", Northbourne Road, Deal, Kent CT14 0LA, UK.

**Borderlands Press** (*www.borderlandspress.com*), POB 61, Benson, MD 21018, USA.

**Broken Eye Books** (*www.brokeneyebooks.com*).

**Cemetery Dance Publications** (*www.cemeterydance.com*), 132-B Industry Lane, Unit #7, Forest Hill, MD 21050, USA. E-mail: *info@cemeterydance.com*

**Chthonic Matter** (*www.chthonicmatter.wordpress.com*).

**The Clive Barker Archive** (*www.clivebarkerarchive.com*). E-mail: *philandsarah@clivebarker.info*

**Cōnfingō Publishing** (*www.confingopublishing.uk*), 249 Burton Road, Didsbury, Manchester M20 2WA, UK.

**Corona Books UK** (*www.coronabooks.com*), 76 North Road, Withernsea, East Riding of Yorkshire HU19 2AY, UK. E-mail: *lewis@coronabooks.com*

**Crystal Lake Publishing** (*www.crystallakepub.com*).

**Death's Head Press** (*www.deathsheadpress.com*).

**Earthling Publications** (*www.earthlingpub.com*), PO Box 413, Northborough, MA 01532, USA. E-mail: *earthlingpub@yahoo.com*

**Edgar Rice Burroughs, Inc.** (*www.erbbooks.com*).

**18th Wall** (*www.18thwall.com/*).

**Eraserhead Press** (*www.eraserheadpress.com*), PO Box 10065, Portland, OR 97296, USA.

**Flame Tree Publishing Ltd.** (*www.flametreepublishing.com*), 6 Melbray Mews, Fulham, London SW6 3NS, UK. E-mail: *info@flametreepublishing.com*

**Hersham Horror Books** (*www.silenthater.wix.com/hersham-horror-books#*).

**Hippocampus Press** (*www.hippocampuspress.com*), PO Box 641, New York, NY 10156, USA. E-mail: *info@hippocampuspress.com*

**IDW Publishing** (*idwpublishing.com*), 2765 Truxtun Road, San Diego, CA 92106, USA.

**Influx Press** (*www.influxpress.com*), 49 Green Lanes, London N16 9BU, UK.

**Independent Legions Publishing** (*www.independentlegions.com*), Via Castelbianco 8-00168, Roma, Italy. E-mail: *independent.legions@aol.com*

**Kurodahan Press** (*www.kurodahan.com*), 2305-9 Yunome Machi, Kuma-gun, Kumamoto 868-0600, Japan. E-mail: *mail@kurodahan.com*

**Len Maynard Publishing** (*www.lmp-lenmaynardpublishing.com*).

**Luna Press Publishing** (*www.lunapresspublishingcom*).

**McFarland & Company, Inc., Publishers** (*www.mcfarlandpub.com*), Box 611, Jefferson, NC 28640, USA.

**NewCon Press** (*www.newconpress.co.uk*), 41 Wheatsheaf Road, Alconbury Weston, Cambs. PE28 4LF, UK.

**Nightjar Press** (*www.nightjarpress.weebly.com*), 63 Ballbrook Court, Wilmslow Road, Manchester M20 3GT, UK.

**North Bristol Writers** (*www.northbristolwriters.wordpress.com*).

**Nunkie** (*www.nunkie.co.uk/theatre-shows/www.nunkie.co.uk/shop*).

**Omnium Gatherum** (*www.omniumgatherumediacom*).

**Parallel Universe Publications**
(*www.paralleluniversepublications.blogspot.co.uk/*), 130 Union Road, Oswaldtwistle, Lancashire BB5 3DR, UK.

**Pigeon Park Press** (*www.pigeonparkpress.com*).

**Plutonian Press** (*www.theplutonian.com*).

**P'rea Press** (*www.preapress.com*), c/-34 Osborne Road, Lane Cove, NSW, Australia 2066. E-mail: *dannyL58@hotmail.com*

**PS Publishing Ltd/Drugstore Indian Press/PS ArtBooks Ltd/ Stanza Press/PSi/The Pulps Library/Electric Dreamhouse/ Absinthe Books** (*www.pspublishing.co.uk*), Grosvenor House, 1 New Road, Hornsea HU18 1PG, UK. E-mail: *editor@pspublishing.co.uk*

**Raw Dog Screaming Press** (*www.rawdogscreaming.com*).

**Ritual Limited** (*www.adamlgnevill.com/ritual-limited-shop/*) is the primary outlet for UK author Adam L.G. Nevill's signed, limited edition books and bespoke merchandise (including T-shirts). Shipping rates are calculated at the checkout. If they do not currently ship to your country, e-mail them at: *rituallimitedshop@gmail.com*

**Sarob Press** (*www.sarobpress.blogspot.com*), La Blinière, 53250, Neuilly-le-Vendin, France.

**The Shadow Booth** (*www.theshadowbooth.com*).
E-mail: *dancoxon@gmail.com*

**Shadow Publishing** (*www.shadowpublishing.net*), Apt. #19 Awdry Court, 15 St. Nicholas Gardens, Birmingham, West Midlands B38 8BH, UK. E-mail: *david.sutton986@btinternet.com*

**Shadowridge Press** (*www.shadowridgepress.com*).

**Sinister Horror Company** (*www.sinisterhorrorcompany*).

**Subterranean Press** (*www.subterraneanpress.com*), PO Box 190106, Burton, MI 48519, USA. E-mail: *subpress@gmail.com*

**The Swan River Press** (*www.swanriverpress.ie*).
E-mail: *brian@swanriverpress.ie*

**Tartarus Press** (*www.tartaruspress.com*), Coverley House, Carlton-in-Coverdale, Leyburn, North Yorkshire DL8 4AY, UK.
E-mail: *tartarus@pavilion.co.uk*

**Telos Publishing** (*www.telos.co.uk*), 139 Whitstable Road, Canterbury, Kent, CT2 8EQ, UK.

**Traversing Z Press** (*www.traversingzpress.com*).

**TTA Press** (*www.ttapress.com*), 5 Martins Lane, Witcham, Ely, Cambs CB6 2LB, UK.

**Twisted Publishing/Haverhill House Publishing**
(*www.haverhillhouse.com*), 643 Broadway, Haverhill, MA 01830-
2420, USA.

**Undertow Publications** (*www.undertowpublications.com*) Michael
Kelly Editor, 1905 Faylee Crescent, Pickering, ON L1V 2T3, Canada.
E-mail: *undertowbooks@gmail.com*

**Valancourt Books** (*www.valancourtbooks.com*).

## SELECTED MAGAZINES

**Ansible** is a highly entertaining monthly SF and fantasy news-
letter/gossip column edited by David Langford. It is available free
electronically by sending an e-mail to: *ansible-request@dcs.gla.ac.uk*
with a subject line reading "subscribe", or you can receive the print
version by sending a stamped and addressed envelope to Ansible, 94
London Road, Reading, Berks RG1 5AU, UK. Back issues, links and
book lists are also available online.

**Bare•Bones** (*www.cimarronstreetbooks.com*), Peter Enfantino and
John Scoleri's little magazine—dedicated to unearthing vintage,
forgotten and overlooked horror/mystery/sci-fi/Western/weird film,
paperback, comics, pulp fiction and video—returns after an almost
twenty-year absence as an improved print-on-demand publication.
Cimarron Street Books, Santa Clara, CA 95050, USA.

**Black Static** (*www.ttapress.com*) is the UK's premier horror fiction
magazine, produced bi-monthly by the publishers of *Interzone*. Six- and
twelve-issue subscriptions are available, along with a lifetime subscription, from TTA Press, 5 Martins Lane, Witcham, Ely, Cambs CB6 2LB,
UK, or from the secure TTA website. E-mail: *andy@ttapress.com*

**Classic Images** (*www.classicimages.com*) edited by Bob King is a
monthly newsprint publication for those who love old movies. Most
issues contain material of interest to horror and SF fans, and

subscriptions are available. 301 E. 3rd Street, Muscatine, IA 52761, USA. E-mail: *classicimages@classicimages.com*

**Ghosts & Scholars** (*www.pardoes.info/roanddarroll/GS.html*), now published by Mark and Jo Valentine, is a scholarly journal published roughly twice a year. It is dedicated to the classic ghost story and to M.R. James in particular. Two-issue subscriptions are available from Mark and Jo Valentine, Stable Cottage, Priest Bank Road, Kildwick, Keighley, Yorkshire, BD20 9BH, UK.
E-mail: *lostclub@btopenworld.com*

**Illustrators** (*www.bookpalace.com*) is a beautifully designed and published full-colour periodical devoted to art and artists. The Book Palace, Jubilee House, Bedwardine Road, Crystal Palace, London SE19 3AP, UK. E-mail: *IQ@bookpalace.com*

**Locus** (*www.locusmag.com*) is the monthly newspaper of the SF/fantasy field (not so much horror these days). Contact Locus Publications, 655 13th St, Suite 100, Oakland, CA 94612, USA. Subscription information with other rates and order forms are also available on the website. E-mail: *locus@locusmag.com.*

**The Magazine of Fantasy & Science Fiction** (*www.fandsf.com*) has been publishing some of the best imaginative fiction for seven decades. Published bi-monthly by Gordon Van Gelder, single copies or an annual subscription are available by US cheques or credit card from: Fantasy & Science Fiction, PO Box 3447, Hoboken, NJ 07030, USA, or you can subscribe via the website.

**Night Land Quarterly** (*www.a-third.com/*), Atelier Third, Room 301, 1-21-24 Takadanobaba, Shinjuku-ku, Tokyo, 169-0075, Japan.
E-mail: *makihara@a-third.com*

**Occult Detective Magazine** (*www.greydogtales.com/blog/occult-detective-magazine/*). E-mail: *occultdetectivemagazine@gmail.com*

**Phantasmagoria Magazine** covers horror, fantasy and science fiction in all media. Copies can be purchased in print form on Amazon or from Forbidden Planet, London and Belfast, plus back issues are also available on Kindle. E-mail: *tkboss@hotmail.com*

**Pulp Horror/The Paperback Fanatic**
(*www.thepaperbackfanatic.com*). Justin Marriott's excellent, if irregular, publications for those who love old and new books. E-mail: *thepaperbackfanatic@sky.com*

**Space and Time** (*www.spaceandtime.net*) was founded in 1966 and is now under new management. It describes itself as "the oldest continuously published, speculative fiction semi-pro magazine in print". Luiz Peters joined the editorial team to curate submissions in original Spanish, Portuguese, French and Italian. Space and Time Publications, PO Box 214, Independence, MO 64050, USA.

**Supernatural Tales** (*www.suptales.blogspot.com*) is a fiction magazine edited by David Longhorn, with subscriptions available via PayPal, cheques or non-UK cash. Supernatural Tales, 291 Eastbourne Avenue, Gateshead NE8 4NN, UK.
E-mail: *davidlonghorn@hotmail.com*

**Synth: An Anthology of Dark SF** (*www.synthanthology.wordpress.com*).

**Weirdbook** (*www.wildsidepress.com*) is a PoD revival of the iconic fantasy and horror magazine, edited by Doug Draa and published by Wildside Press LCC, 9710 Traville Gateway Drive, #234, Rockville, MD 20850, USA.

## BOOK DEALERS

**All Data Lost Books** (*www.alldatalostbooks.co.uk*) is an online UK bookstore specialising in the esoteric and strange. They stock a wide selection of horror, occult, witchcraft and science fiction vintage paperbacks.

**All You Need is Books** (*www.allyouneedisbooks.co.uk*), in association with Zardoz Books, is a huge online resource for second-hand, vintage and collectable paperbacks, hardcovers and pulps, specialising in horror, science fiction, mystery and other genres. Catalogue available for a SAE to: 20 Whitecroft, Dilton Marsh, Westbury, Wiltshire BA13 4DJ, England. Tel: +44 (0)1373 865371. E-mail: *zardoz@blueyonder.co.uk*

**Cold Tonnage Books** (*www.coldtonnage.com*) offers excellent mail order new and used SF/fantasy/horror, art, reference, limited editions etc. Write to: Andy & Angela Richards, Cold Tonnage Books, Poundwater, Farway, Colyton, Devon EX24 6EG, UK. Credit cards accepted. Tel: +44 (0)1404-871001. E-mail: *andy@coldtonnage.com*

**DreamHaven Books & Comics** (*www.dreamhavenbooks.com*) is open Tuesday through Saturday and also has a mail-order outlet, offering new and used SF/fantasy/horror/art and illustrated etc. with regular catalogues (both print and E-mail). 2031 E. 38th Street, Minneapolis, MN 55406-3015, USA. Credit cards accepted. Tel: (612) 823-6070. E-mail: *dream@dreamhavenbooks.com*

**Fantastic Literature** (*www.fantasticliterature.com*) mail order offers the UK's biggest online out-of-print SF/fantasy/horror genre bookshop. Fanzines, pulps and vintage paperbacks as well. Write to: Simon and Laraine Gosden, Fantastic Literature, 35 The Ramparts, Rayleigh, Essex SS6 8PY, UK. Credit cards and Pay Pal accepted. Tel/Fax: +44 (0)1268-747564. E-mail: *simon@fantasticliterature.com*

**Hyraxia Books** (*www.hyraxia.com*), Toft Cottage, 1 Beverley Road, Hutton Cranswick, East Yorkshire YO25 9PQ, UK. Specialist sellers of rare and collectible modern first editions, including many genre titles. They also buy books. Tel: +44 (0)7557-652-609. E-mail: *shop@hyraxia.com*

**The Iliad Bookshop** (*www.iliadbooks.com*), 5400 Cahuenga Blvd., North Hollywood, CA 91601, USA. General bookstore that has a very fine selection of new, used and rare books, with an emphasis on literature and the arts. Tel: (818) 509-2665.

**Porcupine Books** aims to supply you with the rare, curious and unusual books you want at modest prices. Go to the website at *www.porcupinebooks.co.uk*, where you can view or download a list of available novels, collections, anthologies, magazines, young adult, non-fiction and pictorial titles, which are updated monthly. A crime and detective section is also available.

**Terence McVicker Rare Books** (*www.batsoverbooks.com*) is a mail-order business offering premium rare and collectible items—many H.P. Lovecraft, *Weird Tales* and Arkham House-related. 1745 W. Kenneth Road, Glendale, CA 91201, USA.
E-mail: *info@batsoverbooks.com*

**Ygor's Books** specialises in out of print science fiction, fantasy and horror titles, including British, signed, speciality press and limited editions. They also buy books, letters and original art in these fields.
E-mail: *ygorsbooks@gmail.com*

## ONLINE RESOURCES

**The Dark** (*www.thedarkmagazine.com*) edited by Sean Wallace and Silvia Moreno-Garcia is a free monthly online magazine that is also available for digital download.

**Fantastic Fiction** (*www.fantasticfiction.co.uk*) features more than 2,000 best-selling author biographies with all their latest books, covers and descriptions.

**File 770** (*www.file770.com*) is the Hugo Award-winning online version of Mike Glyer's science fiction fan newzine, reporting on

fanzines, SF clubs, conventions, fan funds and fanac.
E-mail: *MikeGlyer@cs.com*

**Hellnotes** (*www.hellnotes.com*) covers news and reviews of the horror genre—horror films, horror novels, horror reviews, writing horror, horror conventions and more.

**The Horror Zine** (*www.thehorrorzine.com*) is a monthly online magazine edited by Jeani Rector that features fiction, poetry, interviews and reviews. It is also available in a PoD edition and produces its own books.

**Locus Online** (*www.locusmag.com/news*) is an excellent online source for the latest news and reviews.

**The Marsden Archive** (*www.marsdenarchive.com*) sells rights to the works of famed photographer Sir Simon Marsden, or you can buy limited edition prints, books, calendars and cards from *www.simonmarsden.co.uk/shop.htm*

**Nightmare Magazine** (*www.nightmare-magazine.com*) edited by John Joseph Adams is an excellent monthly online site for fiction (both new and reprint), interviews and podcasts.

**Pseudopod** (*www.pseudopod.org*), the premiere horror fiction podcast, continues to offer a free-to-download, weekly reading of new or classic horror fiction by a variety of voices. The site remains dedicated to paying their authors while providing readings for free and offering the widest variety of audio horror fiction currently available on the net.

**Tor.com** (*www.tor.com*), publishes new fiction, articles, novel excerpts, artist galleries, reviews and a lot more.

**Vault of Evil** (*www.vaultofevil.wordpress.com*) is a site dedicated to celebrating the best in British horror with special emphasis on UK anthologies. There is also a lively forum devoted to many different themes at *www.vaultofevil.proboards.com*